THE WIDOW AND THE ORCS

A MONSTER FANTASY ROMANCE

FINLEY FENN

Edited by Eris Adderly
Cover artwork by Skadior Art
Cover design by Finley Fenn
Supported by the generous members of the Orc Sworn Patreon

ALSO BY FINLEY FENN

ORC SWORN

The Lady and the Orc

The Heiress and the Orc

The Librarian and the Orc

The Duchess and the Orc

The Midwife and the Orc

The Maid and the Orcs

The Governess and the Orc

The Beauty and the Orcs

The Widow and the Orcs

Offered by the Orc

Yuled by the Orcs

ORC FORGED

The Sins of the Orc

The Fall of the Orc

THE MAGES

The Mage's Maid

The Mage's Match

The Mage's Master

The Mage's Groom

To Amy,
the greatest Skaibrarian in the realm

1

I f Louisa wasn't careful, she was going to end up murdering her vile lord neighbour.

"Lord Rikard," she said to the surly, stumpy, dark-haired man now hovering before her. "To what do I owe this... call?"

She'd been out on her usual evening stroll over her lands, attempting to find a few moments' peace in the cool quiet air—so of course, Lord Rikard had apparently decided it was an excellent time for some trespassing. And Louisa's clammy hand was already gripping the knife at her belt, her heart thundering ominously through her chest, as her rational brain shouted distant, dire warnings, deep in her skull.

No. No. She needed to stay calm, and control her temper, and extract herself as quickly as possible. Rikard wasn't her odious departed husband, even if the resemblance became more pronounced with every passing day. Lord Scall was dead. *Dead.*

"Aren't you going to invite me to walk with you?" Rikard snapped, casting a brief, disdainful glance down toward Louisa's shabby riding dress. "So we can discuss this matter together, like civilized relations?"

Louisa clutched her knife tighter, and dragged down a deep, shaky breath. "No, I'm afraid not," she said, clipped. "You can tell me whatever you need to say right here."

Rikard's white face flushed with red, his broad chest puffing out against his beautifully tailored waistcoat. "Typical," he hissed. "Look, we need to discuss the orcs, Louisa. The orcs *you've* been allowing to illegally camp on your property. For *months!*"

The orcs. Louisa couldn't quite suppress her wince, and Rikard lurched closer, jabbing his thick finger toward her. "It's a disgrace," he continued sharply. "It's foolish, it's dangerous, and it's a *frightful* liability! To tolerate those thieving, bloodthirsty beasts on your lands? Squatting there with their feral little spawn? Only a few furlongs away from *my* property?"

Louisa drew down another deep, gulping breath, and fought the rising, overpowering urge to shout that if the realm's laws were fair, she would still be the rightful owner of said property, its beautiful house, and all its associated income. And Rikard would still be scuttling about in a cramped filthy townhouse in the city, just like the poisonous vermin he was.

"Remind me, Rikard," Louisa said instead, as smoothly as she could, "how you are even aware of what might be transpiring on my property, at any given moment? I certainly haven't been confiding in you, and surely my staff haven't been sending you reports?"

Rikard's wet mouth spasmed, because he knew—just as well as Louisa did—that her much-reduced staff complement would never betray her trust in such a way. Not even after the house had grown colder and colder these past months, and the meals smaller and smaller. Not even after—Louisa swallowed, lifted her chin—she'd had to tell them, just today, that their monthly wages would be late. Again.

"You think I don't notice what's happening in my own neighbourhood?" Rikard demanded. "Most of all when those dreadful squatting orcs are crossing *my* lands to get to yours?!"

The triumph rang through his voice, jangling deep and powerful into Louisa's churning gut, because—damn it. Damn it, were those orcs truly crossing Rikard's land to access hers? Surely they couldn't be that foolish? Surely they'd at least heard rumours of Rikard's pettiness, and his widely proclaimed public opposition to that tenuous peace-treaty between humans and orcs?

Even so, Louisa couldn't help an uneasy glance southward, toward the thick forest that covered the entire bottom half of her property. The group of orcs had been camping there for almost a year now, near a hidden cave opening that she strongly suspected was, in fact, a tunnel. A tunnel that undoubtedly led—her gaze shifted further south—to Orc Mountain.

As always, the orcs' huge home loomed grey and craggy on the horizon, pouring its steady streams of black smoke into the sky. It was a sight that had once struck fear into a young Louisa's breast, when her decades-older lord husband had first brought her here to his ancestral lands. But the more Lord Scall had raged about the foul orcs, and hurled his ill-gotten coin toward that endless war against them, the more Louisa had begun to doubt the entire damned proposition. Until finally, the year after Scall had passed, she'd become unwittingly entangled in an orc-related mess, and thereby had discovered...

"Do you have any proof of the orcs trespassing?" Louisa loudly asked, over that deeply disorienting thought. "Have you or your staff personally witnessed any orcs crossing your lands? Or have they left prints? Refuse? Remnants of fires?"

Rikard betrayed a brief but highly telling grimace, and Louisa's shoulders sagged, her sweaty grip loosening on her knife-hilt. Of course Rikard hadn't personally seen the orcs. Because in truth, Louisa had scarcely caught sight of them herself, either—and so far, they'd shown themselves to be surprisingly clean and conscientious, and even helpful. They'd cleared out an entire swath of invasive buckthorn, they'd installed a sturdy little bridge over the worst part of the swamp, and one day, Louisa had come home to find her latrines freshly dug out. A foul and expensive task she'd been putting off for months, and here it had been fully finished, in a single damned afternoon.

But most crucial of all, the orcs had begun to leave food, too. Choice cuts of fresh venison and boar meat in the kitchen, and mushrooms and vegetables in the root cellar. And given the appalling state of Louisa's ever-dwindling accounts—and the multiple mortgages her fool husband had piled onto his properties during his lifetime—it had felt like a gift from the gods. A handful of orcs on her land was a small price to pay, in order to keep her loyal staff housed and fed, and offer them a clean latrine to empty their bowels in. Right?

"I don't need to *witness* those trespassing orc bastards," Lord Rikard said now, his voice rising. "I've set up traps. Snares, that only I can decipher! And those great ugly beasts have betrayed themselves, again and again!"

Louisa's head was beginning to ache, the frustration crackling behind her tired eyes, and she couldn't bite back her harsh, high-pitched laugh. "Oh, you've set secret *snares*," she drawled at him. "Why, those must be utterly infallible! I can't *imagine* that a wandering deer or fox might have set one off! And"—she waved irritably toward the southwest—"didn't I hear that you just hosted a boar-hunting party a few days ago? Surely that alone would have lain utter waste to any top-secret snares you might have managed to cobble together?"

Rikard's eyes flashed with furious dislike, his little mouth opening and closing. "We didn't hunt anywhere *near* there," he shot back. "I know my own property, Louisa. And my poor lord uncle would be rolling in his grave to hear what you've done with his lands! Lands that by rights, ought to have been *mine!*"

Louisa barked another incredulous laugh, and gave a reflexive roll of her eyes. Because yes, Scall's death had granted her the ill-maintained, heavily mortgaged dowager house, and a few leagues of dense, swampy forest—but since she hadn't been able to bear Scall a son, his fool nephew Rikard had gotten all the rest. The big beautiful manor, the fields, the barns and livestock, and over a dozen leagues of prime forested hunting grounds. Rikard was now a very rich man, while Louisa grew poorer with every passing day, and had been reduced to relying on *orcs* for her suppers.

"Lord Scall's rotting corpse can do acrobatics in his grave, for all I care," Louisa snarled back. "These are *my* lands now, Rikard, so by law, what *you* think about them has no bearing on me whatsoever! And if you want to speak of trespassing"—she drew in a deep breath—"perhaps you can explain to me why the hell *you're* here, rudely interrupting what was supposed to be my peaceful evening walk!"

She waved a furious hand toward Rikard, and then toward the small creek that marked this part of the property line, a good thirty paces behind him. But predictably, Rikard's glower only deepened, his lip curling with distaste. "I felt it was only fair to attempt to address this matter with you directly," he replied. "But you'd best believe I'll be taking steps to defend my valuable property in future, Louisa. And I'm warning you, if you keep sheltering those trespassing orcs here"—he jabbed his finger toward her—"you *will* regret it!"

You will regret it. A cold ripple snaked up Louisa's back—was Rikard *threatening* her? But then she shook her head, tightened her grip on her knife. No. No. Rikard was just a foolish blustering boor, a petty minor lord who didn't even have a seat on the realm's ruling Council. He wasn't Lord Scall, she'd escaped Lord Scall, Lord Scall was dead...

"Look, I'll make sure the orcs respect the property lines, Rikard," Louisa bit out, through gritted teeth. "Now, I suggest you do the same!"

With that, she spun around, and strode off down the path, her eyes fixed straight ahead. Her breaths already coming steadier, she just needed some air, some space to think, some peace—

And then—something grasped her arm from behind. Someone. *Dangerous.*

It was pure instinct that whirled Louisa around again, her knife gripped in her fist. Its blade shoving straight back toward Rikard, toward that pale sweaty throat. Finding it, there, *here*, sharpened steel prodding cold and hungry into soft meaty skin—

And for a frozen, breathless instant, there was silence. Silence, as Rikard gaped at Louisa with appalled alarm blaring in his eyes, and a knife-blade jammed against his neck.

A shocked little mewl whimpered from his mouth, and then he released Louisa's arm and stumbled backwards, nearly tripping on a rock behind him. "What in damnation, woman!" he shouted. "What the hell is wrong with you?! I wasn't about to—I was only about to say—"

Louisa stared at him, waiting, breathing hard, as something dark and reckless curdled in her belly. No. Yes. No. She should know better, she shouldn't let this odious weaselly wastrel get to her. She'd escaped Lord Scall, she needed to forget Lord Scall, Lord Scall was *dead*...

"I was only about to *kindly* say," Rikard continued shrilly, as he staggered another step backwards, "that my previous generous offer still stands. Although perhaps"—he shot a dark look at the knife still in Louisa's hand—"I ought to rescind that offer, once and for all!"

His previous offer. Louisa might have laughed, had that darkness not still been screaming, surging bitter memories behind her eyes. Memories from the day after Scall's funeral, when she'd finally had a blessed moment alone—until Rikard had appeared in her sitting-room, and offered her a proposal of *marriage*.

A marriage of convenience, he'd called it. *A means of granting you security, now that you're past your marrying prime. A way to keep my dear uncle's lands undivided. A way to give you a child of your own to care for, perhaps.*

That last point had painfully pricked in Louisa's chest, because while Rikard didn't know it, she would never be able to bear children of her own—and even if she could, her sixteen years of marriage to Lord Scall had long ago shown her his nephew's true measure. Rikard had wanted her lands, as unprofitable as they were. He'd always been an avid sportsman, and he'd wanted the right to hunt in her forest unimpeded. And, of course, he'd also wanted the freedom to keep dallying with other women as he pleased, while gaining a convenient heir for his grand new fortune—without lifting a single finger to acquire a wife. Let alone needing to waste his time pretending to care for her, or her children.

Louisa's refusal had been furious and absolute, and she'd perhaps shouted at Rikard more than she ought, and betrayed far too much of her own grief, her own pain. She would never again be coerced into a marriage. She would never again share a bed with a man she didn't desire. And she would never, ever sell her freedom—her *life*—for a man's gain. Never. She was thirty-nine years old, and she was living out the rest of her days on her terms, on her own damned means.

"No, Rikard," she gritted out. "*No*. I have no interest in remarrying. *Ever*."

She'd kept her voice steady, her eyes desperately fixed on the twilight sky behind Rikard's head, but he lurched another step closer, blocking her view. "You let Lord Kaspar court you," he snarled back. "That fop was dangling after you for *months!*"

Louisa gripped her knife-hilt even tighter, and again fought down the surging darkness, thick with pain and grief. Kaspar had been her first and only attempt at a relationship after Scall's death, and he'd been a duke's son, and a handsome, clever scholar, who'd courted her with patience, kindness, and respect. So naturally, once Louisa had fallen head over arse for him, she'd been approached by one of his longtime mistresses—a sweet girl named Rosa—who not only had been sharing Kaspar's bed the entire time, but who also had been writing all his academic papers, while toiling for abysmal wages in his mouldering little library. And then Rosa had run away to Orc Mountain, and Louisa had even helped her, and met multiple orcs, and...

"No," Louisa managed again, though the word wavered this time. "Kaspar was an odious, deceitful cheat, who thoroughly misrepresented himself to me, and only wanted the grand inheritance he mistakenly assumed I had! Not only that, but he was taking advantage of his staff—and, he had fathered multiple children he refused to support! He was—a grave mistake."

But curse her, why was she telling Rikard any of this, because it only gave him more information, more ammunition to hurl back against her. And it had even sparked something in his beady little eyes, something bright and eager and sickening...

"Well, you can rest assured that *I* possess no illegitimate children," he pointed out, as if this was some grand achievement on his part. "And I pay my staff very fair wages, as well. More than *some* people in these parts, I might add."

Gods crush the smug little vermin, it was a jab at Louisa

again, even as he was offering her his hand in *marriage*. And the strangled sound from her mouth could have been a laugh, though her eyes were damnably prickling, and tightness spasmed in her throat. She was trying. She was trying so damned hard. And she'd just wanted a damned walk, a few moments of peace under the sky, and this horrid man was ruining everything, everything—

"No," she choked again, through her constricted throat. "No. Now get off my fucking land, you loathsome little rat. Unless you want me to call my orcs to heel, and send them over to *trample* you!"

Her voice rang through the cool air, echoing between them, flashing true fear across Rikard's eyes—because damn it, Louisa had just threatened him. She'd just implied that she not only knew about the orcs, but endorsed them, or even commanded them. And perhaps, perhaps even *wanted* them...

The shock on Rikard's face clashed with fury, with a horrible rising awareness. He knew. He knew, and Louisa should say something, do something, Lord Scall was *dead*—

But she was too slow, too late. And already Lord Rikard had whirled around, and scuttled away into the darkness.

2

When Louisa walked up her lane toward the kitchen's side door, her cheeks were dry, her back straight, her head high. Betraying no sign whatsoever of the unfortunate incident with Rikard.

Or so she thought.

"Lou-Lou!" Ame cried out, rushing over to greet Louisa with a wide smile on her little gap-toothed mouth—but then her smile faded, her blue eyes sobering. "What's wrong? You sad?"

Louisa swallowed and attempted a smile, rustling a hand against Ame's golden head. "Just a little overtired, sweetheart," she said, as lightly as she could. "Speaking of which"—she raised her brows at Ame—"isn't it almost your bedtime?"

The question had the desired effect, sending Ame sidling toward the door, while casting a wary look toward her mother Elise. Who was watching with distinct amusement from the kitchen counter, where she'd been kneading dough for the next day's bread.

"Soon, love," Elise told Ame, with an affectionate smile. "You and Stefan can play until I've finished this, all right?"

Ame nodded and rushed out the door, while Elise darted a too-knowing glance toward Louisa. "So what's wrong, then, ma'am?" she asked. "Something untoward happen out there? I told you, you oughtn't to be out in the dark alone, most of all with those orcs lurking about!"

Her voice was scolding, but her rounded pink face was as kind as always, the concern bright and genuine in her blue eyes. And while Louisa wanted to wave it away, she'd come to consider Elise a true friend these past few years. Perhaps because she'd been a strong recommendation from an old friend named Jule, who'd no longer been able to keep Elise on staff, because Jule had run away to none other than… Orc Mountain.

Truly, it was beginning to feel like a theme, or a curse, and Louisa sighed, rubbed at her aching temples. "I just ran into Rikard," she said heavily. "He's furious with me for allowing the orcs on the property. Told me I'll regret it, if I don't get rid of them."

Elise's mouth thinned, and she shook her head. "That scum," she snapped. "He's still just vexed because you won't marry him! Although"—she bit at her lip—"perhaps you *could* just send the orcs away? I mean, it really *is* quite… dangerous, having them so close. Don't you think?"

Her voice had dropped, her eyes uncertainly searching Louisa's face, and Louisa bit back another sigh. She knew Elise had been a firsthand witness to that entire situation between Jule and the orcs, which had begun with a deadly, terrifying orc raid on Jule's household—but it had also all happened well before the peace-treaty, when the orcs and humans had still been at war. And since then, Louisa hadn't heard a single reliable account of an orc raid anywhere in the realm—and instead, she'd heard multiple astonishing tales of orcs helping humans, just like they were helping her. Doing odd jobs, clearing roads and building bridges, giving food to people who needed it.

And without that food, how would Louisa keep feeding her household? Gods, what was she supposed to do?

"Look, Elise, of course I understand if you aren't comfortable with the orcs being nearby," Louisa finally replied, her voice wooden. "So if you'd rather start looking for other employment, please be assured that I will support you without qualification, and give you as many glowing references as you need. I'll do everything I can to ensure you and the children are—"

"No, ma'am!" Elise interrupted, her eyes a little wild, now. "That's not at all what I meant—I wouldn't like another post at all! You've been so generous, and I'm very, very happy here!"

Louisa's shoulders sagged, the relief studding through her chest, and she gave Elise a wan smile. "I'm glad to hear it," she replied, "but you don't owe me anything, Elise. Especially with your pay being late this month. Again."

But Elise rapidly shook her head, flapping her flour-covered hands. "We understand, ma'am!" she said. "We know times haven't been easy for anyone lately. And the children are so happy here, and you give them so much freedom—and me, too. We'd be so upset to leave here, *please*."

Louisa's shoulders sagged lower, her breath exhaling. "Then of course you'll stay as long as you like," she said, as firmly as she could. "And I'm going to just—head to bed early, and give this more thought. I'll see you in the morning, then?"

Elise warily nodded, and Louisa turned around, and trudged up the stairs toward her bedroom, high up in the attic garret. Where she'd always felt safest, alone in the peace and quiet, and as far away as possible from the likes of Rikard.

But damn it, maybe she would soon lose this, too. She'd already sold off so much—including her own heavily mortgaged house in the nearby town of Dusbury, and most of her horses, and all her fine clothes and jewels. She'd also cut costs wherever she could, and she'd pensioned off multiple staff. Leaving her only with Elise, her elderly housekeeper Gladys, and her capable, long-serving head groom Joan. And though Joan did her best to help out with the grounds and gardens, too, it was just too much for one person to handle— so Louisa had begun taking on much of the manual outdoor labour herself. Weeding, gardening, making repairs, feeding the chickens, fetching eggs, even hunting small game.

But it wasn't enough. Not nearly enough. The larder was bare. The root cellar was empty. The debts were still crushing, the payments never-ending. And what was Louisa supposed to do, she would not sell her freedom, she would not marry Rikard, not *ever*—

She strode into her dark bedroom without looking, yanking off her belt and riding dress, hurling them onto a chair. And then she lurched to the dressing table, feeling for the lamp in the dark, lighting it with a familiar flick of her fingers.

But in the lamp's sudden light, she caught sight of her own pale face, frowning back toward her in the large looking-glass. Showing in stark relief the heavy furrow between her brows, the dark shadows beneath her eyes, the deepening lines at the corners of her eyes and mouth. And even the silver hairs sprouting from her widow's peak seemed more plentiful than usual, silently shouting at her of being— Rikard's foul voice loomed in her thoughts—*past her marrying prime.*

Louisa shook her head, squeezed her eyes shut, gritted her teeth tight. No. No. She would never marry again. She was living her life on her own terms, and she was going to keep trying, find a way through this...

But how? Damn it, how? How the hell was she supposed to survive, for possibly another forty whole years? How could she take care of her staff, those children, herself? With no coin, no food, and Rikard breathing down her neck? And now she'd made it so much worse by threatening him with the orcs, and now she had to find a way to keep the orcs off his property, and—

A prickle. Something—wrong. Creeping up her spine, wrapping cold fingers around her chest. Something—*behind* her, oh hell, and Louisa whipped around so fast the room spun, her eyes searching, finding—finding—

The *orc*.

3

There was an orc. Here. In Louisa's *bedroom.*

He was sprawled sideways on the chair beside her writing desk, and his tall, scarred body was leaning back against the wall, his booted foot propped on the desk's edge. And he was—*half-dressed*, wearing only a ratty-looking pair of grey trousers, with a gleaming steel scimitar hanging from his belt. And his hair was bound up in a messy knot on his head, and there were two *daggers* stabbed through the knot, and...

And he'd been... *waiting* for Louisa. Waiting, and watching her, with cool, assessing black eyes. Eyes that gazed out of a lean, grey, sharp-looking face, framed with tall, pointed ears. And his supple quirking mouth was *smirking* at her, and what—what—

"What the hell," Louisa croaked, as she fumbled for her abandoned clothes, and somehow found the knife again, its hilt mercifully solid in her fingers. "This is—this is a private bedroom, orc!"

She brandished the knife toward him, and found—to her ever-increasing alarm—that he didn't seem even slightly disconcerted. Instead, his smirk only twitched higher, as his glittering eyes flicked down her form, and then back up again.

And wait, curse it, Louisa was now wearing only a thin, skimpy shift, and her chagrined glance downwards found it also stained, with multiple holes, as well. And it stretched far too tight across her hips and breasts, showing every lump and scar, every single imperfection, for this invading orc's perusal.

And the orc was perusing, damn him. His glinting eyes slowly, leisurely sweeping down Louisa's body, and back up again. Lingering on her groin, her hips, her breasts, her neck, before flicking down to—the knife, now visibly shaking in her outstretched hand.

"Ought not to hold your blade out thus, woman," he said, in a husky, accented voice, as his own hand—with its long black claws—rose to his hair, and snapped out one of the daggers from his topknot. "Ought to keep it tight and close. Better meets any attack from the side, ach? And guards your front, also."

He even demonstrated as he spoke, first holding out his own dagger just the way Louisa had, and then drawing it in closer to his bare chest. And she could easily see his point, curse him, and she instinctively drew back her own knife, matching his pose, which did feel better, and—

She whipped her head back and forth, and thrust the knife down to her side. What the hell. What the *hell*.

"I did not invite you here, orc," she snapped, as steadily as she could. "This is *my* bedroom!"

The orc gave a smooth, rolling shrug of his shoulder, and flipped his dagger in his fingers. "No, is it?" he said coolly. "I have become lost, then, for I thought this was a kitchen. Or mayhap a root cellar."

Louisa's disbelief surged, together with a sudden, sharp dislike. This trespassing orc was mocking her? Taunting her, here, in her own damned bedroom?

And—wait. Wait. If he was trespassing here, sneaking into her bedroom with such surprising ease, was it—was it possible that the orcs really had been trespassing on Rikard's land all this time, too? Had Rikard been... *right*?

"Then I suggest you start paying better attention where you wander off to, orc," Louisa shot back, too late. "Especially when it comes to my vile neighbour's property!"

But the orc just kept gazing at her, again with a faint smirk on his face. "We ken where your neighbour's property is, woman," he said blandly. "And we have no wish to tread upon it. What we wish for is here."

Here. It flashed more fear up Louisa's spine, and suddenly all those old, tired tales about orcs were jostling, screeching into her pounding skull. *Orcs want women. Orcs need women to bear their sons. They swive into their screaming victims with their huge orc-pricks, fill them with their spawn, and leave them bloody and broken afterwards...*

And wait, *wait*—what if this orc was here for—for Elise? She was so young and soft and sweet, already so terrified of orcs, this orc could not, he could *not*—

Louisa choked and lurched to stand before the door, gripping her knife close against her body, just as the smug bastard had said. "You will not even *look* at any of my staff," she hissed at him. "You will tell me what the hell you want, and then you'll get the fuck out of my house!"

But the orc didn't reply, let alone move. And as Louisa stared back at him, her breaths heaving, she felt her mouth crumpling, her throat choking on something much like a sob.

Gods, what the hell was she supposed to do? She had nothing to bribe the orc with, she had no food or coin to offer, and she would be no match for him physically whatsoever. And curse it, she'd been such a stupid, pathetic fool to allow these orcs on her property, to believe they wouldn't bring any harm, and...

"Ach, settle yourself, woman," the orc's drawling voice cut in, together with a dismissive wave of his clawed hand. "I have only come here to speak with you."

He wanted to—speak? Louisa blinked, and her trembling hand slightly lowered the knife, even as the visions of Rikard swarmed again, too. Because that rank little roach had also trespassed on her property tonight, invaded her own private space, for the exact same infuriating reason.

"Then get the hell on with it, orc," Louisa growled. "I've already dealt with enough unwarranted harassment today from rude, entitled, trespassing males who only want to take from me!"

There was an instant's stillness, something held, arrested, in the orc's eyes—but it vanished just as quickly, his expression back to smooth, careless nonchalance. And he lazily settled back against the wall, his hand still fidgeting with his sharp, gleaming dagger.

"I wish to make you an offer, woman," he finally said, very steady. "A fair offer. For both our gain."

Louisa's brows snapped up, but she held herself still, waiting. Watching as the orc kept fiddling with the dagger, his eyes dropping to study it, almost as if he were... nervous?

"I shall pay your debts," he said, even slower. "Grant you these lands, for all the rest of your days."

Wait. Louisa's breath caught, her eyes widening, because—no. He couldn't mean that. An orc couldn't pay her debts. Her mortgages. He couldn't possibly afford it. Could he?

But his eyes lifted again, meeting hers with calm, collected certainty, and Louisa gulped down air, fought to think. If he would pay that much, surely he wanted something major in exchange. Something monumental. Something utterly appalling, no doubt, something even worse than Rikard, something she'd never be able to countenance...

"And?" she asked, though her voice hitched. "What would you want from me in return?"

And at that, the orc... smiled. Smiled, swift and surprisingly stunning, showing her a mouthful of sharp, wolflike teeth. As if he truly was a stealthy, waiting, pacing predator, about to leap for the kill...

"First, you shall allow my kin to keep living on these lands," he said, still so smooth, so easy, so deadly. "For as long as we might wish. And second..."

Louisa waited, breath bated, her eyes fixed to his face. To where he was still smiling, or perhaps grimacing, as his dagger turned, and its sharp, shining tip pointed toward her...

"And for ten nights," he continued, a chilly whispered caress, "you shall welcome my fallen kin-brother into your bed, and your heart."

4

She would welcome his fallen kin-brother into her bed. For ten nights.

Louisa's mouth fell open, the shock roiling through her chest, flashing into her aching skull. He meant—another orc. He had to mean another orc. Right? In her bed? For *ten nights*?

And perhaps most alarming of all was that strange, unmistakable twitch, low and heated in Louisa's belly. An orc. In her bed. For *ten nights*.

The watching orc's smirk pulled even higher, as his too-aware eyes flicked down Louisa's front, and... lingered. As if—as if he suspected. He *knew*. He—

"Absolutely not," Louisa said, far too late, her hand clutching desperately to her knife-hilt. "I am not about to trade my body—my autonomy, and my *freedom*—for such a shocking and highly inappropriate proposal! At the behest of a rude, mocking, trespassing orc who broke into my *bedroom!*"

Her voice echoed shrilly through the too-small room, ringing with decision, with truth. It was the right response, of course it was, so why was Louisa's stomach plummeting, her throat convulsing. And why was the orc still smiling, cool and smug and dispassionate, as though he wasn't perturbed by this in the least.

"This has naught to do with your *autonomy*, or your freedom, woman," he replied, with a dismissive shrug. "I shall make no other demands upon you, beyond the camp on your lands, and these ten nights in your bed. And the camp is already there, you ken, whilst"—his black brows rose, his clawed hand waving toward Louisa's ancient four-poster bed—"your bed is now empty, is it not?"

Louisa shot a dark look over at her bed—which yes, had been devoid of guests for an excessively long time. Gods knew she'd tried with that cheat Lord Kaspar, but it had never gone further than kissing and touching, and even that had been fraught, tainted with dark, bitter memories of Lord Scall...

But—no. *No.* Lord Scall was dead. And Louisa glared ferociously back toward the orc, fighting to wade through his infuriating words, to find some coherent response. "Yes, and you think I don't know what happens to women who welcome orcs into their beds?" she finally demanded. "They soon end up welcoming orcs' *sons* into their bellies, too!"

It was an excellent argument, even if it didn't apply to Louisa herself—but she glared at the orc with ever-deepening suspicion, waiting for his answer. Was this all some devious ploy to get his kin-brother a son, without needing to bother with courting a woman, or caring for her? Just like Rikard wanted, too?

But the orc still looked entirely unconcerned, and gave a careless wave of his dagger. "Naught to fear, woman," he said. "My kin-brother cannot now beget sons, and I can prove this to you, should you wish. Your nights with him shall only be for pleasure, for you both."

Louisa's heart skipped, her breath frozen in her throat. His kin-brother couldn't have children, either? So it really would be... only for pleasure? Pleasure. With an *orc*. For *ten nights*.

"My kin-brother shall not harm nor mistreat you," the orc continued, spinning his dagger in his fingers. "He is also a big, strong, hearty warrior, and his face and form are pleasing to the eye. And"—another spin of the dagger, a higher arch of his black brows toward Louisa—"he bears one of the biggest pricks in our mountain, ach? This shall grant you great joy, I ken."

More strange, hurtling heat was simmering in Louisa's belly, and her affronted scoff back toward the orc felt too flat, too late. She didn't care about such things. She *didn't*. Many women considered Lord Rikard a strong, athletic, attractive man, when in truth he was the most odious little cretin in existence, and...

A big, strong, well-endowed orc warrior. In her bed. Touching her. Tasting her. Pleasing her...

No. *No*. Louisa squeezed her eyes shut and silently cursed herself, cursed this invading orc, this entire appalling situation. It made no sense, it had no point, it had to be some kind of nefarious orc trick, right? Right?

"If your kin-brother is such a stunning catch," Louisa finally said, glaring back at the orc again, "then why are you here, making his proposals for him? Why can't he come and ask me himself? And why isn't he already settled with some other happy woman instead?"

She fully expected the orc to answer with more dismissal, more flippant nonchalance—so she was surprised to see his gaze dropping, as something tightened on his mouth. "He has not been... himself, of late," he replied, slower than before. "He has faced and fostered deep darkness, some of it his own making, much of it not. He now seeks in earnest to make amends for his failings, and to regain his place in our clan, but..."

His voice trailed off, his eyes now fixed to his dagger, to

his claw scraping down the blade's sharp edge. "But amidst this," he continued, "He has... wilted. Faded. Become wounded and hollow and disgraced. In years past, he would oft laugh and command and play, and draw his kin to his side. But now"—he jerked a shrug—"he is quiet. Fearful. Alone. With no hope, and no peace."

Louisa's stomach dropped, her throat spasming with something damnably like sympathy, like... commiseration. But no, no, damn it, she didn't care about this downtrodden orc, about this ludicrous offer, or...

"Thus, he would not come to you himself," the orc continued, as his flinty gaze snapped back to Louisa's face. "But I ken having a woman in his bed again shall bring him deep joy. He was happiest, when he once had this—but it has been many, many summers now, and I wish to help him regain this. Not only for his sake, but for... our son's."

Wait. Their *son's*? They already had a son? But yes, yes, the orc's voice had slightly softened as he'd said it, and his eyes had softened, too. Looking almost... warm, or even affectionate. And it seemed to change his entire face, somehow, turning it from something hard and cold and forbidding into something... handsome. *Appealing.*

Too late, Louisa shook herself all over, and fought for air, for the next logical response. "What do you mean, you have a son?" she managed. "I thought you said you and this other orc were *brothers*?"

The orc huffed a short laugh, and shook his head. "Ach, we are kin-brothers," he said, clipped. "We are both from the Skai clan. But there is no blood shared between us, and our son is not our blood, either. You shall not even need to meet him, ach?"

Louisa blinked at the orc for another blank, bewildered moment, digesting all that. He wasn't related to his brother, to the co-parent of his son? And their son wasn't related to either of them?

But the orc's gaze on her sharpened again, as if daring her to challenge the validity of his chosen family. And no, no, Louisa wasn't going to question that, but...

"So are you two... a couple, then?" she tentatively asked. "You and your... kin-brother?"

A distant part of her whirling brain vaguely recalled hearing that relationships between males were common among orcs—but wait. If this orc was in a committed partnership with his kin-brother, surely he wouldn't be going around seeking out strange women to share his partner's bed?

But the orc's eyes flicked past hers, subtle but intentional, as his jaw tightened in his cheek. "Ach, he and I take pleasure together, when we wish," he said coolly, "but we have sworn no vows of matehood or fidelity to one another. I take as many others to my bed as I please, and he is free to do the same."

Oh. It seemed an unusual arrangement, and one that Louisa would personally struggle to bear—but then again, many humans of her acquaintance carried on with such arrangements too, didn't they? And at least this orc was openly telling her about it, as opposed to lying and sneaking about, the way her foul lord husband had. The way Lord Rikard certainly would, too.

"And you really think," Louisa croaked, and she wasn't saying this, she wasn't, "your kin-brother would want—*me*. I mean"—she waved an erratic hand at her torn, shabby night-dress—"I mean, I'm poor and widowed, I'm not that young anymore, I look like—"

She winced and belatedly clamped her cursed mouth shut, because she didn't care what this orc thought of her, she didn't... right? But the words just kept hanging there, betraying her, making her small and ashamed, and the orc—

The orc *scoffed*. Rolled his eyes. And then he again took his time looking at her, leisurely sweeping his glinting eyes down, and up, and down again. "You humans," he said, heavy with derision. "You ken I did not scent you, or look at you, before I came? You ken I would not seek out the best, comeliest woman I could find for my kin-brother? The one most suited to help him, and please him, and bring him joy?"

Wait. Really? This orc had intentionally sought Louisa out? On purpose? For this? And he thought she was—*comely*?

But Louisa was already frowning back at him, shaking her head, because there was no way. Absolutely none. Not when there was a lovely girl like Elise just downstairs. Not when there were countless other untouched, unencumbered, sweet-tempered women populating the realm, without scars and grey hair and holes in their dresses. And, more importantly, without raging, orc-hating lord neighbours.

But the orc just rolled his eyes again, even more impatient than before. "My kin-brother has now seen forty summers," he said flatly, "and as I have said, he has seen and sown much darkness, in all those days. You ken I wish to bring him some delicate, untested flower that he shall crush underfoot, before he has even followed what he has done? You ken I wish to grant him more regret and grief, more to fear and fret over? More weight to bear? Ach, and this is if"—his lip curled—"this woman should even speak to us, and agree to this, without running off and screeching in fear of him? Of *me*?"

Louisa's thoughts again darted toward Elise, toward how she would have reacted when faced with an orc in her bedroom—while the orc's mouth pulled into a grim little smile, his eyes chilly and triumphant. "But you," he said, with a careless wave of his dagger toward her. "You do not run in fear of me. You hear me. You speak to me. And you have done this in times past, also, when my kin came to you for help."

Louisa's unhelpful brain was now dredging up memories

of all the ways she'd helped that sweet girl Rosa, up to and including being locked in a library's tiny back room with an orc. He'd been huge and highly intimidating, frowning and towering over her—but when Louisa had gathered her courage and introduced herself, he'd given her a careful, kind smile in return. *I am Simon*, he'd told her, in a deep, rich voice that had rumbled in her belly. *Of Clan Skai.*

And wait, this new orc had said he was from the Skai clan too, hadn't he? And he was again circling his dagger toward her, his eyes speculative, his mouth pursed. "And now, for all these past moons," he continued, "you have allowed my kin to live on your land. You have seen the gain in this, in how it has helped you care for your own kin—and thus, you have made this trade. And you have made it without sulking or weeping, or casting demands or blame upon us."

Louisa attempted a dismissive shrug—she'd only done what any responsible person would have done in her place— but the orc was already speaking again, smooth and certain. "You have shown yourself to be a shrewd, strong, steady woman. You have borne much, but you have not buckled beneath its weight, nor abandoned those in your care. And this"—his circling dagger-blade jabbed a little toward her— "*this* is what I wish for. This is what any Skai should wish for. In his life, and in his bed."

What any Skai should wish for. It was a bizarre statement, an impossible claim, and it rang through Louisa's thoughts with strange, dizzying strength. Because—no. No. This orc didn't think this. No one thought this. *A shrewd, strong, steady woman. This is what I wish for...*

And as those words kept ringing, Louisa's gaze seemed caught, frozen, on the orc. On the quick glittering watchfulness of his eyes. On the way his long lashes slightly lowered as he looked back toward her. On how his throat bobbed, brief but unmistakable, and a sliver of a glistening black tongue brushed against his lips. As if inviting her to look at it, at him.

And yes, yes, Louisa was looking. Looking at the orc's tall, fluid, relaxed body, at his deft, long-fingered hand on his dagger. At the scarred silver skin of his arms and shoulders, at all the hard lean muscle beneath...

And then at his bare, exposed chest. The deep grey nipples, the ridges of his abdomen, the taut navel, the sharp cut of his hips above his shabby, low-slung trousers. And that distinctive line of black hair, leading down toward his groin, toward where those trousers now betrayed a... a *bulge*. A shocking, highly obvious bulge, one that seemed to swell even larger the longer Louisa looked at it...

He and I take pleasure together, as we wish. I take as many others to my bed as I please...

And for another startling, frozen instant, Louisa could almost see it, bright and alarmingly vivid behind her eyes. This orc coolly, carelessly taking his pleasure, tossing out easy commands, wielding his lean, supple body to gain whatever—or whoever—he pleased. And that was not—*not*—longing, or even jealousy, curling up deep in Louisa's belly, no, no, *no*—

When in a sudden movement, the orc's body stiffened all over, too. Its relaxed languidness snapping into cold sharp distance, as he again jabbed his dagger in Louisa's direction, far harsher than before.

"But you ken, woman," he hissed, "*I* have no wish for you. I only wish for you for *him*. And once this is done, I shall have naught more to do with it. Or with *you!*"

It was as though he'd hurled that dagger straight toward her, its sharpened end plunging deep into her gut—and Louisa had to drag for air, shaking her head, digging her palms painfully into her eyes. No. No. She didn't care. She *didn't*. This orc had broken into her house, he kept waving a weapon at her, making proposals that she did not want or need whatsoever...

"But would you keep taking pleasure with *him*?" her rasping, treacherous voice demanded, all on its own. "Your kinbrother? During his ten nights with me?"

She glared at the orc again, blinking back the damnable stinging behind her eyes—and she was viciously satisfied by how he betrayed a faint flinch, his eyes narrowing toward her. Because no, clearly he didn't want to be kept from his own enjoyments either, did he? *He is a big, strong, hearty warrior. His face and form are pleasing to the eye. He bears one of the biggest pricks in our mountain...*

"Then no," Louisa snapped, because maybe she just needed to strike back at him, to hit him where it hurt, just like he'd done to her. "If I'm sharing my bed with an orc, he's most certainly not sharing his bed with anyone else during that time, *especially* you. As if I have any desire to contract some sort of debilitating *orc-pox*, due to my bedmate being highly injudicious with his partners!"

Her voice scraped out between them, cold and contemptuous, and the orc's glower deepened, glittering with a dark, malicious dislike. While his long fingers hungrily caressed at his dagger, as if he indeed longed for nothing more than to hurl it into Louisa's belly, and watch her weep and scream upon it.

But Louisa kept frowning back toward him, unflinching, demanding. Until finally—finally—the orc looked away first, his mouth and jaw very tight.

"Ach, then," he replied, clipped. "He shall touch no other, whilst he shares your bed for these ten nights. Are we agreed, then? You wish to do this?"

Wait. *Wait.* No, they weren't agreed, hell no Louisa didn't want to do this—right? Right?

"Then here is a list of our terms for the camp, and our offer of payment," the orc flatly continued, as he produced a folded square of paper from his trousers, and tossed it onto her desk. "And mayhap I shall add my own terms to this, also. First, you shall not speak to him of his past, or ask him of this. You shall not bring him guilt or shame for what is done, and what cannot now be undone. Ach?"

Louisa might have nodded, even as she winced—was she really doing this?—and the orc rose to his feet, and reached into a little pouch she hadn't noticed before, hanging off his belt. "And second," he added, sharper than before, "you shall prove to me that you can please him. That you can bear *this*."

He thrust out something toward her, something long and thick and cylindrical. Something rather the size and shape of a—a *rolling pin*, perhaps, but with a wide flare at one end, and the other tapering to a blunt, rounded bulb. But unlike a rolling pin, it appeared to be carved entirely of grey stone, and it was polished to a smooth, glossy shine...

And even as Louisa reflexively reached to take it, gripping the cool heavy stone in her hand, her suspicion was rapidly rising. No. No, this couldn't be what she thought it was, he wouldn't dare...

"What the hell is this?" she demanded, but curse it, she already knew. And the devious bastard only smirked at her again, and even reached down to circle his fingers around the massive girth of it. His long claws scarcely touching on either side as he gave a slow, suggestive stroke up and down, easy and familiar, as if this was something he'd done a hundred times before.

"Ach, I wonder what it could be," he drawled at her, all smug slippery satisfaction. "A loaf of bread, mayhap. Or a shoe?"

Louisa glared at him, at his smoothly stroking hand, at his cruel vicious smile. "It is just the shape and size of his prick," he hissed. "And if you prove you can swallow this within you"—his brows arched up—"then we shall go forth with our vow. But *only* then, ach?"

Wait. *Wait.* They weren't—really making a *vow*, right? Louisa hadn't agreed to anything, had she? And this orc wasn't actually leaving this monstrosity here *with her*?!

But he was already spinning away from her, and striding toward the window. "It is newly made, so you need not fear any *orc-pox* upon it," he said over his shoulder, his voice flat and cold again. "And I shall come back tomorrow eve to gain your proof of this, and hear your answer."

What? Louisa gaped at him, and then down at the shockingly large stone still in her hand—but wait, the orc was thrusting up the window's sash, and casting a brief, surveying glance down beyond it. As if he was going to jump, gods curse it, and they were all the way up in the attic, and—

"Wait!" Louisa gasped, flailing her hands toward him. "*Wait*, orc!"

And to her surprise, the orc... hesitated. His body stilling, his shoulders hunching, as he glanced backwards over his shoulder. And for a brief, breathless moment, Louisa was again caught to stillness, held in the strange, glittering misery of his gaze.

Because maybe... maybe he hadn't wanted to do this. Maybe he regretted this. Maybe he wanted to keep his kin-brother—his son's other father—all to himself, in whatever unconventional relationship they already had. The relationship that he clearly felt wasn't... enough.

"And *you* really want this?" Louisa choked, and that wasn't at all what she'd meant to say, was it? "You really want to... give up your partner, like this?"

The orc's mouth betrayed a faint grimace, but suddenly the dislike was there again, snapping across his eyes. "Ach, no, woman," he said, his voice laced with snide, bitter sarcasm. "I only came here and made you this offer on a merry little lark, you ken. What deep joy it has been, to dangle the gift of my best, most steadfast Skai brother before a thankless human! Only to have her sneer at my gift, and claim he shall grant her *orc-pox!*"

Louisa winced, even as she shook her head, drew down a ragged, bracing breath. "Look, orc, you cannot possibly blame me for being wary of you!" she shot back. "I'm already in a—a highly precarious position, and you broke into my house, waved around your weapon, and made me this shocking offer, when I know absolutely nothing about you! I don't even know your name! Or the name of the orc you want me to go to *bed* with—though I suppose I at least know what he has down his trousers!"

She brandished her heavy stone—*replica*—out toward the orc, and she couldn't at all read his eyes as he gazed back, his mouth still very thin. But then his shoulders slumped, and his head tilted up and back, his eyes fluttering closed. Almost as if he were sending up a prayer, begging his gods for patience, for peace...

"I am Killik," he finally replied, without looking at her. "And my kin-brother is Ulfarr. The Wolf of the Skai."

The Wolf of the Skai. The words seemed to hang there, heavy with strange, unspoken meaning—but before Louisa could speak another word, the orc ducked out through the window, and disappeared into the night.

5

Louisa spent a long, sleepless night. A night full of ruminating, self-recrimination, and finally, rage.

How dare that mocking orc break into her house. How dare he essentially offer to pay her—to bribe her—for *bedroom services*. And how dare he not be now lying in a flattened bloody heap on her lawn, in the logical consequence of jumping out a garret window, rather than apparently walking away unharmed, and leaving her here to stew and seethe in his wake.

And how dare he leave her that list of terms, too. A list she'd rushed over and read the instant he'd left, searching for the hidden trap, the knife waiting to stab her in the back—but it had all seemed infuriatingly reasonable. Not only had it detailed the amounts and payment schedule—with twenty percent to be paid after the first night, and eighty percent at the end of the ten nights—but it had offered constraints and guarantees around the camp itself, too. No more than a dozen dwellings, and two dozen inhabitants, without written permission from the landholder. No unsustainable hunting. No tree-cutting beyond deadwood, no dumping or polluting or otherwise damaging the property. And perhaps most importantly, no trespassing on the neighbouring properties.

In truth, they were all terms Louisa should have thought of herself, and terms she would be relieved to have in place, too. Especially with Rikard blustering and raging about, making accusations and demands...

But—no. *No.* Of course Louisa still needed to refuse. Of course she needed to throw the orc out when he returned. She needed to shout at him that she didn't need him, or his coin, or his thoughtful terms, or his unhappy, infertile kin-brother. *The Wolf of the Skai.*

Those words still clutched unhelpfully in Louisa's belly, calling up highly alarming memories of that huge Simon orc she'd met in the library. How big and broad he'd been. How his massive body had been packed all over with powerful muscle. How he'd moved with such calm, easy assurance, and held such steadiness in his eyes. As if he could be relied upon. As if he would be... safe.

And curse it, how this new orc—this Killik—had somehow been even worse. His long, lean body so fluid, so relaxed, so... compelling. As if he would always know what to do. As if he could handle any unexpected incidents—like being accosted by a vile neighbour on one's evening walk—with smooth, careless ease. And he would surely take his pleasure the same way, flaunting his graceful body, cool and certain and...

Louisa's fingers gripped tighter against the stone still in her hand, and she flopped over onto her back in the bed, glaring at the ceiling. And how dare he give her this damned—*replica*, let alone demanding she use it. This thing was a travesty, an abomination, there was no way any man— any orc—could actually possess... well. No possible way.

And wait. Wait, that alone was reason enough to refuse this entire mess in the first place, wasn't it? Because there was no way it would actually... *work*, right? No way Louisa could... *swallow this inside her*, as Killik had said. And her inability to do so would be a simple, straightforward reason to refuse, wouldn't it?

It was with a strange, shaky desperation that Louisa thrust the stone down beneath the blanket, and yanked up her nightdress. Shivering all over at the feel of the cool, silken hardness already slipping up against her, finding its place...

She gritted her teeth, closed her eyes, drew down a wavering breath. Forcing herself to relax, to block all the truth of it away, just as she'd learned to do over so many miserable years of marriage to her horrid lord husband. And just focus on the sensation of it, the feel of it, nothing else, just this...

And to her vague surprise, it didn't feel... awful. Or even... aggressive, or invasive. In truth, it felt surprisingly smooth, gentle, its blunt rounded head just settling gently against her, fitting into the hollow of her, parting her sweetly around it.

Louisa took another breath, deeper this time, as the stone nudged a little closer. It already felt warmer than before, wetter, waiting for her to relax, to open wider upon it. To welcome its touch, its soft seeking against her slippery heat, delving just a little inside...

Louisa gasped as she began to feel the true girth of it, slowly but deliberately spreading her around it. Opening her wider, stretching her tighter, easing itself in breath by breath. While she clutched and spasmed back against it, not quite resisting, now, but perhaps even... welcoming it. Welcoming that strange, heady sensation of stretching tighter and tighter, fuller and fuller, until—

She hissed at the first twinge of pain, stinging and flaring behind her closed eyes—but oh, oh, it was in. It was in, it had stretched her wide open around it, and it was sinking still deeper, pain and pleasure sparking in its wake...

Louisa's hiss sounded more like a moan this time, and there was no thought of resisting, of stopping, as the stone sank even further. Occupying her, pushing her to the edge of her limit, filling her with hard solid strength. While her slick spasming body could only feel it, take it, welcome it, oh, *ohhh*—

The release flashed through her before she even saw it coming. Careening wild and rampant through her entire body, convulsing her hungry heat around the invading stone again and again and again. Wringing out burst after burst of fierce, fiery, painful ecstasy, as she gasped and arched and took it, her shaking hands clutching between her legs, her fingers trembling against the stone.

But then—then, it was over. Over, and Louisa was left lying there alone in bed, shivering all over. With an orc's absurd stone—*replica*—still jammed halfway up inside her.

She cursed aloud as she yanked at it, shoved it down, away. Where she could pretend she'd never, ever done such a shocking thing, never attempted such a shameful deed. Never felt the bizarre unthinkable—emptiness—it seemed to leave behind...

Louisa cursed again, whipping her head back and forth on the pillow, because damn her to hell, it had been... inside her. *Inside* her, just as Killik had demanded. *If you prove you can swallow this within you, then we shall go forth with our vow.*

And now, she'd not only gone and proven it, but she'd... obeyed Killik. She'd obliged him, given him exactly what he'd wanted. Her humiliation. Her mockery. Her *shame.*

Louisa fought the urge to scream, and to perhaps hurl the offending stone out the window where Killik had gone—but instead she squeezed her eyes shut, and shoved onto her side. She did not want an orc in her bed. She did not want Killik's payment, or his pity, or most of all his mockery. She *didn't.* She was refusing his preposterous proposal, and that was all.

But even once she somehow managed to fall asleep, her dreams were fitful and broken, swarmed with smug orc faces, with powerful orc bodies, with gigantic orc... well. And worst of all, with visions of sweet, painful pleasure, of raw rippling ecstasy, of solid strength filling her very core...

She finally dragged herself out of bed at dawn, frowning as she pulled on a shabby work dress, and then stomped downstairs to the kitchen. To where—her shaky hands gripped at the door—a fresh cut of venison was lying innocuously on the counter, together with a handful of mushrooms, and a few sprigs of fresh herbs.

Louisa's groan was almost a growl, and she whirled around, and stalked for the side door. Where she yanked on her sturdy, too-large boots—they'd once belonged to the now-retired gardener—and then snatched up her longbow and quiver. She'd made a point of teaching herself how to hunt these past years, and after multiple initial difficulties, she'd become somewhat passable at it, at least enough to bring in some small game each week. And along with providing a little extra for the household, hunting had proven to be a rewarding pastime, too. Acquainting Louisa with the earth and her land on a deep and intimate level, and allowing her time and space to be quiet, to breathe, to think through the constant stream of problems that kept plaguing her existence.

So of course, the morning's hunting efforts soon proved to be entirely futile. Not only did Louisa fail to catch sight of a single actual target, but she even foolishly shot at a misshapen stump, and therefore bent one of her costly arrows. And her cursed brain seemed even more full of orcs than before, now circling again and again around Killik's offer, his taunts, his promises.

I shall pay your debts. Grant you these lands, for all the rest of your days.

Louisa finally gave it up as a waste of a morning, and

trudged back to the house, where she was met by her baleful-looking head groom Joan, her thick black brows drawn together. "Sorry to tell you, Lou," she said flatly, "but the well's gone dry. Needs to be dug up again, I fear. We'll have to haul water from the creek until then."

Louisa stared at Joan's brown face with rapidly rising dismay, as the distant ache in her skull pounded closer. Hauling water was a tedious, time-consuming chore, and they didn't have time, they didn't have the bodies, gods curse it. And Joan knew it too, grimacing regretfully toward Louisa, and running both hands over her close-cropped black curls. "Hate to say this too," she added, "but we're out of oats for the horses, and they really should be reshoed, too. Do you want me to set it up, or...?"

Louisa dragged in a shaky breath, and again silently cursed her entire existence. She'd been desperately putting off selling her last two horses, because Max and May were the sweetest creatures, and didn't deserve to be parted after so many years. Not only that, but Joan had been born and raised on the property—she was the daughter of Lord Scall's now-deceased stable master, an Eziran equestrian prodigy—and she had made it clear that she had no interest whatsoever in leaving the horses, or the land she'd always considered her home.

I'll never get another post like this, Lou, she'd told Louisa in her usual blunt, matter-of-fact way. *No other rich landowner in the province is going to put me in charge of their stables, are they? I'm here until the end.*

But perhaps the end was closer than any of them wanted to admit, and Louisa rubbed at her aching temples, and fought fruitlessly for an answer. "Can this all wait until tomorrow?" she asked, her voice wooden. "I have a meeting with Bycroft in town this afternoon, and perhaps..."

Mr. Bycroft was Louisa's longtime banker, and perhaps he could find a way, somehow. Perhaps he could give her another loan. Perhaps she could lease out some of her land to someone who wouldn't instantly turn and lease it to Lord Rikard. Someone who wouldn't take offense to the orcs, and to them continuing to single-handedly feed Louisa's entire household...

But Louisa's trip to town soon proved to be just as frustrating as the rest of her day, and Mr. Bycroft's proposed solutions were even more enraging than Killik's had been. "Why don't you just rent to Lord Rikard?" Bycroft asked Louisa, with an air of puzzled bemusement. "Or even sell Rikard the old place entirely? He's already your only legal heir, and he's made multiple offers now, several of them very generous—more than enough to set you up on your own here in town, as long as you practice careful economy. I've even gotten the impression that Rikard would welcome your hand in *marriage*, Lady Scall, were you so inclined."

With great effort, Louisa refrained from shouting that she would rather starve to death than marry Lord Rikard, or even sell him her land, for that matter. It was her land, it was her house, she'd paid through the *teeth* to gain it from her vile lord husband, and Rikard was not taking it from her until she was cold in the ground. He was *not*.

Louisa was in a truly foul temper when she finally returned home, and Elise's tasty supper of roasted herbed venison and mushrooms tasted like ash in her mouth. Not even a round of playing ball in the yard with the children helped, and finally she put up her hands and pleaded exhaustion, before she could end up inadvertently hollering at them, and ruining their day, too.

Throughout it all, she'd been desperately fighting not to think of Killik, of his ludicrous offer. But as she finally dragged herself up to her bedroom, her steps heavy on the stairs, she couldn't seem to deny it anymore. Couldn't stop those tempting, taunting words from shouting and shuddering through her tired, aching head.

I shall pay your debts. Grant you these lands, for all the rest of your days.

And when Louisa banged open the door of her room, blinking into the lamplit darkness, Killik was there. Of course he was there. Sitting calmly in the same place as before, flipping his dagger in his fingers, and watching her. Waiting for her. Waiting for her answer...

"Fine," Louisa snapped, her voice a bitter croak. "Fine. I'll do it."

6

I*'ll do it. I'll do it.*

They were her own words, spoken by her own voice—but somehow, they still didn't seem real. They seemed like someone else's words, someone else's choices, someone else's life.

And perhaps Killik felt it too, because his dagger stilled in his hand, his eyes black and empty in the lamplight. "You... shall do it," he repeated, his voice as blank as his eyes. "You shall accept. With all my terms."

Louisa swallowed, and then belatedly shut the door behind her, fastening the latch for good measure, while distantly thanking the gods that all her staffers' bedrooms were on the first floor. "Yes," she said, as decisively as she could. "Your terms were fair, and you were right. The camp is already there, my bed is already empty, and I..."

Her voice cracked, her mouth crumpling, and she strode with shaky steps toward the bed, and sank her exhausted body down onto it. "I need the help," she said, rasping, toward her clammy hands in her lap. "I don't want to sell the property. I can't bear for Rikard to win, after everything my husband—well. And I can't bear the thought of being trapped indoors in a tiny town apartment for the rest of my days, mending clothes and counting every copper, and pretending not to notice my wealthy former friends when they pass me on the street. I'd rather *starve*."

Her voice broke again, and she swiped at her foolishly leaking eyes, and glared toward Killik with as much determination as she could muster. "So yes," she said, squaring her shoulders. "I accept."

But to her surprise—and her rapidly rising foreboding—Killik didn't look pleased. Or smug, or mocking, or triumphant, or any of the other responses Louisa had expected. Instead, he looked—uneasy. Uncomfortable. His lean body shifting on his chair, his long fingers rigid around his dagger-hilt.

"What?" Louisa demanded at him, because gods, she already couldn't bear it, she already wanted to weep beneath the shame. "Is something wrong? Have you changed your mind?"

She felt rigid all over now too, gripping her hands together, waiting in taut silence for Killik's answer. But he wasn't answering, and Louisa was struck by a sudden, over-powering urge to run over to that window, to jump straight out of it, just like he had...

"I only did not wish you to think," Killik finally replied, slow, as if he were weighing every word, "that we would leave you to... *starve*, should you not accept."

Oh. Louisa jerked a shrug, and again wiped an impatient hand at her eyes. "Well, I certainly wouldn't expect you to interfere," her shaky voice said. "My—circumstances—have nothing to do with you. You have no obligation whatsoever to me, so—"

She attempted another shrug, but then twitched at the sight of Killik's sudden, vicious glower. "Ach, we do," he snapped back. "And I—ought to have said this, last eve. You have granted us leave to stay on your lands. You have granted safety to Skai women and sons, and given them a home they do not fear, but which is yet near to the refuge of our mountain. This is a great gift to the Skai, and one we will not spurn. One we do not wish to lose."

His eyes had gone narrow, accusing, and he jabbed his dagger toward her. "Should you not accept my offer, but still allow our camp," he continued flatly, "we shall yet help you. We shall feed you, and care for your land. We shall even dig out your well, should you have need for this. Ach?"

He sounded angry, even offended, as if—almost as if Louisa had thought orcs incapable of gratitude, of paying their dues, or honouring their debts. Of coming to an agreement that benefited all sides. And Louisa winced at the realization of it—had she thought such things?—and again rubbed at her stinging eyes, shaking her head back and forth.

"I—thank you for that," she said thinly, without looking at him. "I didn't mean to offend, especially after—but wait. How did you know the well needed to be dug?"

She dropped her hands, frowning at where Killik was now looking past her, and giving a too-casual shrug. "So does this alter your choice?" he demanded. "If you ken you yet have all this—do you yet wish for my offer?"

Right. The ten nights. His unhappy kin-brother. Him paying off her debts. And Louisa dragged in a shaky breath as she looked at him, as she fought to work it through, fought not to think about the stone still shoved down beneath her blanket.

Even if the orcs kept helping her, feeding and supporting her, it still wouldn't be... enough. Would it? It wouldn't protect her land. It wouldn't pay her mortgages, or her expenses, or her staff. It wouldn't give her freedom to live her own damned life, and escape the scourge of Lord Scall, forever.

"Look, I appreciate the—clarification," she finally said,

toward Killik's flinty eyes. "But it's been almost five years since my husband died, and no matter what I do, I'm still—haunted by him. By his fool debts, and his fool nephew, and his—"

She winced, shook her head, drew in another unsteady breath. "I want to move past it," she croaked. "I want to forget it. I want to own my own land, and run my own life, and make my own choices, on my own terms. I want some fucking *peace*. And if you really can give me all that, in exchange for ten nights"—she lifted her chin, held his eyes—"then yes. I still want it."

Killik had listened to all this in blank, unblinking silence, his body rigid, his dagger still pointed toward her. And she couldn't at all read the look in his eyes now, whether it was anger, or comprehension, or... regret.

"But do *you* still want it?" Louisa asked him, sharper than before. "Or have you changed *your* mind?"

Killik's eyes shifted again, this time slipping into unmistakable coolness, or even contempt. "Ach, woman," he drawled. "I have come here to you again this eve, just as I swore I would, because I have *changed my mind*."

It was the mockery again, and Louisa glared back toward him, even as he barked a harsh laugh, and gave an angry roll of his eyes. "Ach, I oft *change my mind*, after I spend many moons making a plan," he spat. "After I have wasted the better part of a year seeking out a woman who will not play the fool with me, or ask me witless questions. A woman who I can *mayhap* bear in my wolf's bed!"

The viciousness scraped through his voice, through the room, raw and betraying—and as Louisa stared back at him, it occurred to her that he *was* angry. He hadn't expected her to accept. Or he'd at least held out hope that she wouldn't, and then he'd be able to rest assured that he'd tried. He'd made his best attempt, he'd sought to offer his kin-brother—

his *wolf?*—something he'd known he'd wanted. Something he'd thought might help.

But Killik hadn't actually wanted it, himself. He didn't *want* to share his partner—his wolf—with Louisa. He didn't want her in his bed, or in his life. And gods, he'd openly told her as much yesterday, hadn't he?

I have no wish for you. I only wish for you for him. And once this is done, I shall have naught more to do with you...

More miserable wretchedness churned in Louisa's gut, along with the familiar flash of her temper, because how—how—had she forgotten that? How had she somehow begun to think of this orc—of Killik—being part of it, too? Of him being tangled up in this, with his beautiful lean body, his long fingers, his crackling expressive eyes. And no, hell no, what the hell had come over her, she did not need him, she did not want him, she did *not*—

"Well, I'm afraid you won't have to trouble yourself any further," Louisa said, as coldly as she could. "Because as it turns out, *I've* changed my mind, after all. I have no desire to come between you and your precious... *wolf.* And most *certainly* no desire to tolerate your mockery and contempt, just because you're furious that I accepted an offer *you* made to me! An offer *you* supposedly spent all that time planning!"

Something flickered in Killik's hard eyes, but Louisa drew in breath, drew up more of her own fury and contempt. "Did it not *once* occur to such a clever orc as yourself that your carefully selected target might actually *accept* your offer?" she demanded. "That your brilliant plan might actually *work*? That you might actually *need* to share your wolf, though you clearly aren't willing to offer him any fidelity of your own?!"

Killik kept staring at her, his sharp claws flexing on his dagger-hilt, his body's tautness coiling into something new, something dangerous. And he was slowly rising to his feet, oh hell, and Louisa lurched up too, her head raised, her hands in fists, as the determination thundered dark and bitter in her belly. No. No.

"So we're finished here, orc," she hissed. "Now put that dagger away, and get the hell out."

Her voice rang through the room, loud and decisive, and for a silent, staring moment, Louisa was certain she'd finished this. She'd won, for good. Because that wasn't just danger, now, flickering across Killik's eyes. It was... gratefulness. *Relief.* And his lean body even angled toward the window again, as if he was about to run for it, and leap away to safety. To a world where he didn't need to share his wolf with an unwanted, unattractive, impoverished woman like her.

But then, Killik... stilled. Closed his eyes. And inhaled, slow and purposeful, his head turning toward Louisa's bed. Toward where it was still messy and rumpled, because she'd been too distracted to tidy it that morning, and—

Killik lurched toward it in a sharp movement, his dagger sweeping down, and flicking up against the blanket. Tossing it backwards, away, to reveal...

No. Oh, no, no, *no.* The damned stone *replica*, still lying there where Louisa had shoved it the night before. And curse her, why hadn't she thought to hide it, to hurl it down the latrine when she'd had the chance—and even as she belatedly lunged for it, Killik had already swiped it up, and brought it to his nose.

He was... *smelling* it.

The shame and alarm surged hot and miserable in Louisa's chest, in her face, and she again lunged for the stone—foolish, *foolish*, because Killik only snapped his long arm upwards, holding the stone fully out of her reach. And somehow it left Louisa touching him, clutching stupidly at his arm, while he gazed down at her with smug, disdainful mockery.

Damn it. *Damn* it. Louisa should have reeled backwards

again, shoved him away, accepted that she'd lost this round after all. So why was she just clutching at his arm again, still fighting him for this, jostling their bodies too tight together. Feeling that lean implacable hardness of his chest, the strength of his arm beneath her fingers, the heat of his skin against hers. The smell of him, musky and rich, curling up between them, filling her gasping breaths...

"You repugnant *rodent*," she choked, far too late, through her closed-off throat. "You have *no right*."

But Killik's eyes looked almost amused again, as if he was enjoying her humiliation, her pathetic attempts at salvaging this appalling situation. "Why do I have no right?" he asked, his voice damnably calm. "I only seek my own goods. And I only left this with you for one night, for this... *test*. Ach?"

Louisa cursed and lunged for his arm again, but he only looked even more amused than before—and in another flash of movement, something cool settled against her throat. Something long and slim, something—

His *dagger*.

Louisa froze all over, the furious heat in her body cracking into cold, staggering fear. Good gods, he'd had the dagger in his other hand that entire time. And what the hell had she been thinking, to try to fight with a powerful armed orc in her bedroom, over a ludicrous stone orc-cock.

And Killik was smiling again, the utter bastard, as he gazed down at Louisa's face, her frozen body. At where she'd begun to betray a slight but uncontrollable trembling, was he going to kill her, he could kill her so easily...

"Breathe, woman," came his low voice, cutting through the alarm still screaming in Louisa's ears. "You no wish to quake thus under threat, ach? You must breathe, and be wise. Be watchful."

Gods curse this odious condescending bastard, because Louisa was—doing it. Obeying it. Dragging in a long, desperate breath, and again, and again. And yes, the fear was even fading beneath it, her shoulders sagging, her awareness slowly returning. Pointing out that as infuriating as this orc was, he surely wasn't about to kill her. Killing her would only result in her land immediately going to Rikard, and his clan losing their camp for good. And Killik wanted that camp, didn't he? *This is a great gift to the Skai,* he'd said. *One we do not wish to lose...*

So Louisa kept standing there, breathing hard, only distantly noting that her trembling had stopped, too. But that dagger was still there, still resting cool and powerful against her skin, and Killik was still gazing down at her, something she couldn't at all read passing across his eyes.

"Better," he said, smooth and low. "Now speak truth to me, woman. You wielded my wolf's prick, last eve. Ach?"

The heat surged back into Louisa's face, into her belly, as her throat spasmed against the dagger's cold steel. And why wasn't she pulling back from this, from him, he wasn't even holding her here, she was the one still gripping at his arm...

"Ach?" he said again, deeper this time. "You wielded this, and tested this."

Louisa couldn't speak, wouldn't, and that dagger caressed a little against her throat, the movement almost gentle. "Did you swallow this within you?" Killik asked, his eyes glimmering, strangely alight. "Did you seek to prove this for me?"

To prove this, for him. Louisa's throat spasmed again, flexing against the cold steel, but she bit back her gasp, kept her breaths slow and deep. Inhaling that rich close scent of him, holding his glinting eyes...

"Did you swallow this whole, as I asked?" he murmured, raising a brow toward her. "Or did you whimper and tremble and retreat? Did you crumple beneath the strength of my wolf's prick?"

Louisa's defiance flared sharp and angry, and she might have scoffed at him, or shaken her head, if not for the cold steel still kissing gently at her throat. And perhaps Killik knew it, because he finally flipped the dagger around and away, letting its handle dangle down between two fingers, so he could pat his warm hand at her cheek.

"Speak truth to me, woman," he ordered, his harsh tone at strange, hurtling odds with the softness of his hand on her cheek. "Or I shall ask you to show me, instead."

Show him. And curse her, curse the entire damned realm, because Louisa—gasped. The sound loud and betraying, hurling out the shocking depths of her shame before him. Because no, she did not want such a thing, she would never want such a thing, she would never ever *ever*—

"Ach?" Killik asked, so smooth, so implacable, as a slow, satisfied smile curled at his lips. "You wish to show me, woman? Wish me to ask? Or mayhap"—something flashed, darker, in his eyes—"to command?"

Oh, hell. Oh hell no, no, she did not, this was ridiculous, unthinkable, utterly unconscionable. She wanted nothing from him, not that gentle touch of his hand, not this richness of his scent, not that look in his eyes. A look almost like approval, like... hunger.

"Good," he purred, all sharp, dangerous triumph. "Then show me, woman. Now."

how him. Now.

Louisa's breath betrayed another strangled, shameful gasp, even as her distant rational awareness finally flailed, shouting wild, desperate warnings. This was absurd, this was outrageous, this was an orc, she shouldn't, she couldn't...

"I said, *now*, woman," came Killik's voice, sharper than before. "Either you do this, or we stop this."

Louisa twitched, trembled, gaped at Killik's cold, implacable eyes. They couldn't stop this, he couldn't leave, not now, please—

"You choose," he continued, flat and decisive, as he dropped his hand from her face, flipping the dagger's handle back into his fingers. "I shall not force you, or bring you harm if you refuse. I only shall not waste my time any further here, ach? Yes, or no. Your *truth*."

Yes, or no. The truth. Her truth. The truth in Killik's glinting eyes, in his lean waiting body, in that brief brush of his tongue against his lips. In the strength of his arm, still clasped in Louisa's grip, and why hadn't he pulled it away, either. Why hadn't he left, why was he offering this, ordering this...

And why was it coiling like this, so hot and hungry in Louisa's belly. Why were her shameful eyes darting up toward his hand, still holding that stone—*replica*—above them. And why was he slowly bringing it back down, holding it here before her face, so she could...

Snatch for it. Clutch it tightly in her numb fingers. And lurch toward the bed, toward the familiar safety of its blanket, its hangings, her shaky body scrambling into it. She wasn't really doing this, and Killik wasn't... following her. Coming to stand close beside the bed, casting a brief, assessing glance down at the rumpled blanket, and then... grasping it. Yanking it down. Away.

Louisa might have protested, should have protested, but surely she'd already known he wouldn't allow her to hide this... right? And as she sank back onto the bare bed, there was the shouting realization that he likely wouldn't allow her to hide this under her skirts, either. And no, he didn't even need to say it, just raising his brows at her still-covered bottom half, waiting.

"Wish to stop already?" he asked, a chilly taunt in his throat. "Wish to *change your mind* again?"

This prick. This smug infuriating bastard, and he even stepped back a little, and gave a condescending flick of his dagger toward the door. As if he was ordering her to leave her own room, damn him, and Louisa was not letting him win this, she was *not*.

So with a jerky, shaky movement, she yanked up her skirts. Dragging them up to her hips, and revealing every-thing—*everything*—beneath them. Her shabby stockings, her muscled calves, her shaky thighs. And at the apex of her thighs, her bare exposed groin, with its thick thatch of dark hair. Hair that Louisa knew now betrayed traces of silver, too, and she fought back the urge to shove her skirts down again, to hide herself from Killik's watching, judging eyes...

Because yes, he was watching. Judging. His cool eyes sweeping up, and down, and up again. Assessing, lingering, while Louisa braced herself, her cheeks burning hot, her legs still trembling. What would he say, what was he thinking, would he walk away...

"Show me," came his voice, low and insistent, and Louisa shivered all over at the sight and the feel of his dagger, tapping gently at her quivering knees, at where they were still clamped together. "And breathe."

Breathe. Show him. *Breathe.* And Louisa gulped down air, gripped at the stone still in her hand—and in a jolting movement, she shoved it downwards. Down to... there. Parting her legs just enough to accommodate the stone's too-large width, its cool weight slipping between her thighs.

"I said, show me," Killik repeated, and oh, his hard steel was now nudging against the inside of her knee, guiding it sideways, apart. And Louisa didn't resist, oh hell, as her leg sprawled open—and then Killik did the same to the other knee, too. Opening her up wide and brazen for him, letting him see exactly what he wanted to see...

And perhaps—perhaps he did want to see it. Perhaps he wanted to see that cool stone nudging there, against Louisa's shamefully splayed heat. Because his eyes looked almost greedy on it now, triumphant, as a small, satisfied smile curled at his mouth.

"You truly ken you shall handle this, woman?" he asked, light and mocking. "You ken you are strong enough to swallow my wolf's prick inside you?"

Louisa shot him a dark, baleful look, but he only smiled wider, his gaze flicking up to her face. "Or shall he be too much for you?" he drawled. "Shall you tremble and cower beneath his great strength?"

Louisa kept glaring at him, the taunting enraging cretin,

but somehow that made it—easier. Easier for her tingling fingers to guide the stone a little closer, settling it deeper against her exposed open heat. Against where she already felt astonishingly slippery, swollen, maybe even eager...

And oh, Killik could surely see that too. Could see how Louisa's body kept spasming against the stone's rounded head, flexing and softening, as if again learning it, gauging it. Letting it meet her, find her, part her around it...

She gasped as it delved closer, finding its place, staking its claim—and then, oh gods, it began pressing. Pushing. Seeking. Harder and more insistent than the night before, and maybe that was because of Killik, still standing there, watching this with glinting, unblinking eyes. Watching as the stone's full girth slipped inside, stretching Louisa tightly around it, as she gasped and arched and shivered, pressed it a little deeper...

She had to hold it there for too many breaths, just fighting to accept it, to relax around it. Needed to sink into the sensation of it, just to feel it, like she had the night before. Try to forget about Killik's unblinking eyes, his mockery, his hand's strangely slack grip on his dagger.

"Ach, mayhap this shall fit, after all," came his smooth voice, as his gaze again flicked to Louisa's face. "How does my wolf feel, woman?"

Something dark and shameful heated in Louisa's belly, clasping her tighter against the stone. And amidst the dizzying smarting sensation of it, the sparkling wildness in her groin, she couldn't find a way to refuse the question, let alone speak false to it—

"It's—a lot," she gasped, as the stone's strength nudged a little deeper, opening her, occupying her, stretching her even tighter around it. "It's—so much."

Killik's eyes shifted as he glanced down again, to where the stone was now buried over halfway inside her. And gods, what must it look like, what did he see, her most shameful secret parts pulled taut and strained around this huge implacable invasion. An invasion that was plunging still deeper, because it was so strong, so good...

"But not too much, mayhap?" came Killik's low, rasping voice, and again the sheer sweeping sensation was swallowing everything, too strong to follow his intent, to question that look in his eyes. "I ken it pleases you thus, to be pierced so tight and full upon it?"

Louisa couldn't hide her nod, her choked moan, her surging swirling shame. But wait, what had she just betrayed, what had she just given him, and why was it flashing like that in his eyes, parting his lips, escaping his mouth in a slow, hitching exhale. And why was he flipping the dagger in his hand, gripping his fingers against the gleaming steel blade...

"More, then," he said, husky, as he eased closer to the bed, his eyes intent on the stone spreading her apart. "Deeper. Now."

Oh, hell. Louisa fervently nodded, gulped for air—and it almost felt like his touch, rather than her own tingling fingers, pressing the stone deeper inside. Pushing it harder, now, driving it against her body's resistance, battering through the stretch, the strain, the sweet shimmering agony. While Killik just stood there and watched, and maybe—maybe even approved...

She cried out as she gave one last desperate push, as deep as she could bear. So much further than the night before, so much bigger, jamming her thoroughly, utterly full. Packed and stretched to the brim, tighter than she'd ever felt in her life, her entire body arching and heaving and shuddering, trapped and impaled and pinioned for an orc's watching eyes.

She could scarcely focus on Killik's face, now, through her wildly fluttering lashes, but she didn't miss that flick of his tongue to his lips, or—or wait, the distinctive swell in his trousers. A swell that was even streaking a visible spot of wetness against the grey fabric, and oh, he didn't like this, he didn't want this, did he?

"This is as much of my wolf as you can swallow?" he asked, clipped, almost clinical. "No more?"

Louisa made a brief attempt, wincing as the stone shoved painfully against solid flesh, and shook her head. And then bit her lip, fighting to focus on Killik's face, because there was still plenty of stone left, at least several fingers' width, and would he be disappointed, disapproving, would this somehow ruin everything...

"Ach, I shall accept this, for now," came his murmur, hoarser than before, as his hand surreptitiously adjusted his straining trousers. "But you ken a worthy Skai woman does not just swallow a prick and sit pretty upon it, ach? She must welcome its rutting. Its good strong ploughing."

Oh gods, he didn't want that, but he did, he *did*, his intent eyes watching, waiting. And glittering with satisfaction, with hunger, with *victory*, as Louisa jerked a shaky nod, and her trembling fingers slowly drew the stone out, breath by breath. The loss of it almost as agonizing as the filling of it, oh, and she moaned again, or perhaps whimpered, as her stretched tender body finally pushed the invading hardness free, leaving her lax and empty in its wake.

But Killik was still waiting, wanting, and Louisa wanted it too, so much it ached. So much that it felt easier to guide the stone back inside this time, to feel it sliding into her slick, swollen, spasming sheath. Filling her again, bracing her again, opening her taut and wide and whole again—

She moaned as it reached its limit, maybe even a little further this time, oh—but Killik's dagger was now making an impatient little circle, its silent intent all too clear. "More," he hissed. "Faster. Show me my wolf's perfect prick ploughing you."

Oh, gods, yes. *Yes*. And Louisa was gasping, nodding, and... obeying. Guiding the stone out again, and then back in, over and over, faster and faster. Until it was plunging in and out with astonishing ease, conquering her slippery, swollen body again and again, making sloppy, shameful sounds that echoed through the room. But she felt almost feral with it, delirious with it, nothing had ever felt as good as this, as powerful as this, as wondrous and wild and all-consuming as this. Shoving away all her doubts, all her fears and griefs and regrets, burying them beneath the fierce ramming conquest of an orc's prick. And beneath the sharp gleaming approval of an orc's eyes, the shaky circle of an orc's sharp steel.

"Finish it," came Killik's voice, hot, commanding. "Find your release for me."

Oh, please, yes, *yes*—and it only took one hard, purposeful grind of Louisa's other hand, just there, to flare up the pure agonizing craving into—bliss. Into sheer, screaming, shattering bliss, thundering through her again and again and again. Unlike anything she'd ever known, like freedom, like *peace*—and she nearly sobbed as she gave herself to it, lost herself to it, surrounded, surrendered.

But when it finally began to fade, sinking into shivery little sparks and quivers, there was also a strange, sudden stillness. Something silent, and dark, and... wrong.

And even before Louisa's eyes focused on Killik's face, she knew. Knew what she would find there, with those vivid splotches on his hard cheeks, with the sudden bitter curl of his lip. And with his eyes, the eyes that had only moments ago been so hungry, so approving, now gone hard and flinty and... cold. Contemptuous. Mocking.

"That is enough," he snapped, as he spun away toward the door, swift enough that Louisa only briefly caught the growing dark stain across the front of his trousers. "I shall bring my wolf tomorrow."

And with that ominous promise thudding through the air, he stalked for the door, and slammed it shut behind him.

8

It should have been another endless, sleepless night. What with Louisa's shouting brain, her still-trembling body, the tenderness between her legs. And strongest of all, the sweeping, staggering shame.

What had she done. Good gods, what had she done. She'd given Killik exactly what he'd wanted. She'd impaled herself, pleasured herself, while he'd watched, and *judged*. He hadn't even spoken a single word of kindness, and then he'd just turned around, and left. Like the smug, infuriating bastard he was, and now Louisa had agreed not only to his proposal, but to his... wolf. To another orc. Possibly even a worse orc. In her bed. For ten nights.

It was without question the most shocking thing she'd ever done, the most foolhardy decision she'd ever made. So why was she sinking so heavily into her bed, and feeling almost... relaxed. Almost... *relieved*.

Maybe it was just that she'd done something. She'd accomplished something, and gained even some small, whispering promise of peace. Her debts paid, her staff safe and fed, her land and her life finally her own, free of Lord Scall, forever.

And maybe, her traitorous thoughts whispered, as she yawned and curled up beneath the blanket, it was also... having help. Having a confident, decisive orc like Killik standing by her side, lounging in her bedroom, watching her obey him. And even gaining his own pleasure from it, even if he hadn't wanted to admit it...

The vision of his wet-stained trousers followed Louisa into sleep, and into dark, heated dreams. Into visions of Killik's dagger, his claws, his smooth mocking voice, his wolf's massive solid prick. And maybe even his wolf himself, hovering huge and leashed and obedient in the darkest shadows, until Killik gave the command, and...

"Missus!" came a shrill, scraping voice. "The *orcs*!"

Louisa jerked and flailed up in bed, blinking blearily at the bright morning light, and toward—Gladys. Her small, silver-haired housekeeper, who was hovering in the doorway, her lined, usually genial face gone drawn and white. "Beg pardon, missus," she gasped, "but the orcs have finally come to the house! In the yard! Poor Elise has gone and locked herself and the children in the cellar!"

Louisa's heart kicked and galloped in her chest, and she dragged her shaking hands at her face. "Just—give me a moment," she managed, as she shoved out of bed, and stumbled over to the wardrobe. "How many orcs are there? What are they doing?"

"I don't know!" Gladys wailed. "But they've got shovels and pickaxes, and they're all by the well! As if they're going to dig a tunnel into the *house*!"

Wait. Louisa halted in place, gazing blankly at the threadbare work dress in her hands. The well. The *well*.

She lurched over to the window, and yanked the drapes open with numb fingers. Because—yes. There. All the way across the yard, standing around the well. Three tall, grey-skinned orcs, gesturing and speaking to each other, and tying a rope around the sturdy support beams of the well's small shelter. And yes, yes, that nearest orc had to be Killik, the daggers in his hair flashing in the sunlight as he waved another one of the orcs—a huge, hulking fellow with a gigantic shovel—toward the well's black opening.

"They're going inside!" exclaimed a horrified Gladys, who'd rushed over to join Louisa at the window. "They're going to dig into the cellar! They're going to get Elise and the children!"

Louisa bit back a strange, overpowering urge to laugh— good gods, if the orcs had wanted to get into the cellar, they could have simply walked into the house—and dragged down a thick, bracing breath. "There's nothing to worry about, Gladys," she said, as firmly as she could. "They're not here for Elise or the children. They're here to dig out the well for us."

Gladys' shocked face jerked to stare at Louisa, her mouth fallen open. "They're here to dig out the well?" she echoed. "But—*why*?!"

Louisa swallowed, fought to ignore the heat now prickling in her cheeks. "Because I asked them to," she replied. "Because we need the help."

Gladys kept gaping at her, slack-jawed, and Louisa took the opportunity to yank on the dress, pulling it down over the shift she'd slept in, before lurching to the washbasin, and splashing cold water on her face. Killik had come to dig out the well, just as he'd promised. And he'd also promised to... to...

"I'm going out to meet them," Louisa said, her voice not quite her own. "I assure you, there's no cause for concern. But if you'd like to join Elise in the cellar, or ask Joan to drive you all to town for the day, of course you're more than welcome—"

"We're not leaving you here alone with them, missus!" Gladys hissed. "Though what you were thinking, to ask orcs for help, I can't fathom! It's already on the outside of enough for them to be camping on your property, and hunting your game, and..."

She kept going on, louder and more frantic with every breath, but Louisa was already turning toward the door, and waving Gladys after her. Knowing full well that despite Gladys' protestations—which always came from a place of genuine care—she would be loath to miss an opportunity to investigate, or be involved in an exciting new development. And Gladys indeed trotted eagerly along behind Louisa down the stairs, even as she kept up a steady stream of fearful warnings, conjectures, and accusations.

Louisa strode out into the yard with as much poise as she could muster, her head held high, her eyes sweeping over her property. Not finding any other obvious signs of orcs, though Joan was frowning from the stable door, and over by the well, Killik had already turned to face Louisa and Gladys, his arms folded over his chest.

He was standing alone now—the other orcs must have both gone down into the well—and his eyes had sharply narrowed, glaring down his nose toward Louisa. As if he disdained the very sight of her, or disapproved of her coming to speak to him—or, perhaps he was thinking of the night before. Of how she'd moaned and writhed beneath his cool commands, how he'd made that stain in his trousers...

And curse Louisa, she had not been looking for some kind of welcome from him, or even some kind of reassurance, had she? No. No. Absolutely not. And with effort, she raised her chin to frown back at him, and crossed her arms over her shabby dress, too.

"You didn't say you were coming this morning," she said, betraying only a faint waver in her voice. "You gave my staff a nasty shock, showing up unannounced like this."

Killik's lip curled, and his long claws drummed impatiently against his bare arm. "I did speak to you of this, woman," he snapped back. "It is not my doing if you did not pay heed. If you were too... *full* of other matters."

Too... full. He was talking about *that*, the utter prick, and Louisa gaped at him with sudden jolting fury, her hands snapped to fists at her sides. "That *was* your doing," she retorted. "Every last bit of it!"

Killik's laugh was sharp and mocking, his lip curling higher. "You ken it was not my doing," he hissed back. "For if it had been, *every last bit* would have gone where I wished it to be!"

Wait. Was he—was he judging her? Was he saying—he was... *disappointed* with the night before? He was disappointed with her failure to... to *take every last bit* of that giant stone, as he'd asked?

A sudden, stark bitterness shot through Louisa's chest, flaring hot and shameful in her cheeks, and she gritted her teeth, and fought to drag in breath. She didn't care. She did not. She wanted her well dug out, wanted to save her property, to escape Lord Scall, and that was all.

"Look here, orc," cut in a shaky voice, Gladys' voice. "Whoever you are. I'll thank you not to walk onto my missus' property without her leave like this, and start speaking such hogwash to her in such a disrespectful manner! As if she hasn't already borne enough from brutish bounders like you!"

Louisa winced, and shot an alarmed glance toward Gladys—who was looking truly terrified, now, her lined face gone almost white, even as she kept glaring up at Killik's now-unreadable eyes. And damn it, Louisa just wanted to get her well dug, and Gladys didn't at all deserve Killik's rubbish—and if this was ever going to work, Louisa's staff needed to be fully in support, not running about anxious and terrified of orcs.

"Thank you, Gladys," Louisa made herself say, with an attempt at a reassuring smile. "But there's nothing to be alarmed about, I promise. Killik and I are just teasing one another, aren't we, Killik?"

She aimed her smile up toward him, holding it with brittle, painful effort, and she didn't miss the faint bob of his throat, the slight incline of his head. "Ach," he said thinly. "Only jesting."

Louisa exhaled, and twitched a nod back that felt almost grateful—but Killik only glanced away again, toward the well. And then he swiped for the rope dangling down into the darkness, and gave it a sharp, purposeful yank, as he called down something into the well. Speaking in what must have been the orcs' tongue, the unfamiliar words harsh and strange, and ringing with cool, unmistakable command.

And in response, the rope tautened. Quivered. As if— someone was climbing it. Surely the two other orcs who had been with him, the ones who were now digging the well.

Louisa couldn't seem to look away from that taut, trembling rope, her heart suddenly thudding in her chest. *I shall bring my wolf tomorrow*, Killik had said, and was this what he'd meant? Had he brought his depressed kin-brother here, today, to dig out her well?

And maybe he had, maybe—because that was unmistakable stiffness in Killik's shoulders, his jaw, as he glared down at the well's opening. At where an orc was already climbing up the rope, and swinging out to stand beside them. He was a tall, lean, bare-chested fellow, built much like Killik himself—but Killik hadn't spared this orc a glance. Instead, he was still frowning down into the well, toward...

Another orc. A much, much bigger orc, his body a huge dark mass in the shadows, slowly brightening as he heaved himself up, higher, closer. Climbing the rope with visible effort, hand over hand, while his broad back shoved against one side of the well's stone wall, his booted feet pushing against the other.

It was an astonishing show of strength, and Louisa

couldn't stop watching, waiting, caught on the sight. On how the orc's huge hands kept steadily grasping up the rope, pulling him higher and higher, until Killik reached out one arm toward him, bracing his other arm around the nearest support beam. And with a deep grunt, the climbing orc's big hand clasped Killik's, and he pushed off and leapt out of the well entirely, landing before Louisa in a low, surprisingly graceful crouch.

Louisa's heart was galloping now, hollering in her ears, as her eyes ran up and down the orc's huge, slowly rising form. Good gods, he was big. He was quite possibly the largest living creature she'd ever seen in her life—except, perhaps, for that Simon orc in the library. His shoulders were wide and packed with muscle, his hair-dusted bare chest broad and firm, his belly sturdy and thick. And his dripping-wet skin might have been a rich shade of grey, if not for the vicious-looking scars cut liberally into it, in varying shades of light and dark. Scars that worsened as they reached his face, and suddenly Louisa was looking at his face, caught in his dark blinking eyes.

He was—handsome, a distant chattering voice whispered. Handsome in a hard, rugged kind of way, with his thick black brows, his heavy square jaw, his strong nose that had clearly been broken multiple times. And even with his ears, not nearly as tall or elegant as Killik's, but which instead bore the puffy distortion of frequent close combat. But they suited him, somehow, along with that messy braid unravelling over his shoulder, and even—even those pale streaks of silver, threading through his otherwise black hair.

Louisa swallowed as she blinked at it, as her shaky hand smoothed her own silver-streaked hair back from her sweaty forehead. A movement that seemed to catch the orc's dark eyes, and for an instant, Louisa felt frozen beneath his gaze, beneath his own silent, steady perusal of her in return. Looking at her straggly hair—gods, why hadn't she thought to fix it before coming out here?—and then down at her tattered, threadbare dress, and her muddy, overlarge boots. And damn it, she truly looked a frightful mess, she hadn't made even the slightest effort, and what must he think, was he judging her, was he repulsed or revolted or—

"Er, I'm Louisa," she blurted out, as she thrust her clammy, tingling hand out toward him. "And believe it or not, I do bathe."

She'd attempted a wry, twisting smile, but oh gods, her face was already burning, her eyes dropping to where her hand was still outstretched, wavering, *foolish*. Gods curse her, why had she said such a damned stupid thing? No rational person announced to absolute strangers that they bathed, it was the most obvious giveaway that in fact the opposite was true, right? And Louisa winced, shaking her head, about to drop her hand, when—

When something caught it. Something warm and wet and solid, clasping carefully against her palm, and giving it a gentle, careful shake.

It was—his hand. The orc's hand. And Louisa stared at it, at the sheer size of it, almost entirely covering her own—and then her gaze snapped up. Up to the orc's scarred face, and his watching, unreadable eyes.

"Ach, I am sure you do, Lady Louisa," he said, in a deep, rumbling voice. "And mayhap I ought to say the same."

He'd nodded down toward his own bulky body, and it took Louisa far too long to realize that he was talking about—the bathing. Because yes, he was wet all over, and his trousers were smeared to the thighs in dense dripping muck. And gods, how hadn't Louisa noticed, how much worse did this make her fool bathing comment, and why was she now staring at his trousers? At his wet, clinging trousers, and at...

The *ridge*, inside them. The thick, ever-growing ridge, visibly swelling against the fabric, tenting it out around it. A ridge that looked remarkably like a certain shameful replica, a replica that was still hidden beneath her blanket, and that had been buried deep inside her, *twice*. And why couldn't Louisa stop staring, why was she just watching it swell fuller and fuller, oh gods above, it was—he was—

"You're—Killik's kin-brother, right?" Louisa's cursed mouth demanded, and the shocked shame of it was enough to snap her eyes back to his face. To where he was looking decidedly flushed, his nostrils flaring, his chest filling with his breath. And his huge hand over hers had spread a little, covering more, his finger brushing soft and tentative against the rapid pulse in her wrist...

"Ach, Lady Louisa," he said, his voice a low, devastating caress. "I am Ulfarr, of Clan Skai. And I am ever at your service."

9

Louisa was losing her mind.

There was no other explanation, a distant part of her shouted, as she stood there staring at this Ulfarr orc, breathing hard, clasping her hand tighter against his. She was almost forty years old, and she was supposed to be reasonable. Rational. She most certainly was not supposed to be fighting the urge to gawk at an orc's trousers, or perhaps even to reach out and...

No, no, hell no, and Louisa painfully bit the inside of her cheek, and clamped her free hand to a fist. Which had the unfortunate effect of reflexively clamping her other hand tighter against the orc's, and oh, he was still holding it, he was still looking at her, too.

And wait, wait, now he was raising her hand, and bringing it to—his *mouth*. He was kissing Louisa's hand, oh sweet gods, his lips hot and soft and astonishingly gentle against her skin. And was that his tongue, slipping out between his warm lips, licking her, *licking* her—

Louisa's gasp was far too loud, too clear, too betraying. Earning her a brief, upwards glance from beneath the orc's thick black lashes, and good gods, now his kiss was...

deepening. Hardening. Even sucking a little, as if to leave a mark, before trailing sideways. His warm hand slowly turning her own hand over as he went, until he was kissing at the hollow of her palm, and her trembling fingers were brushing up against the harsh stubble of his chin...

And had anyone ever kissed her like this before? Had anything ever felt so vivid, so intimate, so... powerful? Maybe only last night, when his huge stone cock had plunged in and out of her while Killik had watched—and Louisa couldn't bite back another gasp, even as she darted a brief, betraying look toward Killik. Toward where yes, he was watching this, too, his mouth pressed thin, as a strange, bitter satisfaction flared in his narrowed eyes.

"Ach, enough," Killik snapped, as he caught Ulfarr's arm, and yanked it away. Knocking Louisa's hand away in the process, and she clutched it back against her torso, her palm still tingling with the strange, surreal truth of that kiss. And her eyes were still frozen on this Ulfarr's face, on where he was gazing back at her, holding her eyes for an instant too long, before angling a searching glance toward Killik beside him.

"Ach, so now that you have remembered the rest of us," Killik drawled, as he flipped his dagger out of his hair and waved it between them, "this is our Skai brother Halthorr. And this is Louisa, the lady of these lands, and her kin-sister, Gladys."

Louisa blinked at that odd word *kin-sister*, but her sluggish brain was somehow working again, thinking again. And she belatedly attempted a polite smile toward this Halthorr orc, who smiled and nodded back. "We thank you for sharing these lands with us, Lady Louisa," he said, with a low, flourishing bow toward her. "And you also, Lady Gladys."

Gladys looked both startled and deeply gratified by this, and she gave an imperious little nod toward Halthorr in return. "Well, it's certainly not *my* doing," she said primly. "And you're not to come near the house, you understand."

This Halthorr solemnly nodded and bowed again, to which—wait, was Gladys *blushing*?! But yes, yes, she was, and without at all meaning to, Louisa shot an amused, appreciative glance toward Killik. Who was already looking back toward her, and giving a brief but telling roll of his eyes.

It was enough that Louisa almost, *almost* smiled—at least, until Killik's mouth clamped into a thin line, and his gaze flicked toward Ulfarr. And wait, Ulfarr was now glancing between Killik and Louisa, his eyes darkening with something like... suspicion. Or maybe—maybe even *jealousy*?

Louisa twitched and grimaced, and drew in a shallow breath. Ulfarr couldn't possibly think something was going on between her and Killik, right? Surely he wouldn't, especially when Killik clearly wanted no such thing from her...

"Er, could I offer you anything, perhaps?" Louisa said into the stilted silence—and too late, she heard the too-suggestive implication in that question. "I mean, something to eat or drink, maybe? Or some fresh towels?"

She tried for another smile, angling a traitorous glance down toward Ulfarr's muddy trousers, which had—oh. Lessened. Flattened. That too-visible ridge almost entirely vanished. And why was Louisa's belly twisting at the sight, the heat draining from her face, what was happening to her, why wasn't he answering her, and—

"No, there is naught we need," came Killik's clipped reply. "We shall return to work at once, and send word when we are done."

Right. There didn't seem to be an answer to that, and Halthorr was already nodding and turning toward the well again, swinging his lean body onto the rope. While Ulfarr hesitated for another instant, his unreadable eyes holding Louisa's—but then he lurched away too, reaching for the rope, and then sliding back down into the well with surprising ease.

It left Louisa standing there with Gladys and Killik, who, despite his previous announcement about returning to work, showed no inclination whatsoever to enter the well himself. Instead, he eyed Louisa with his lips pursed, before jerking his head toward the nearby copse of trees.

"Wish to speak to you, woman," he said flatly. "Alone."

Alone. Louisa blinked, first at Killik, and then sideways, to where Gladys was looking predictably shocked by this request. But before Gladys could give voice to her outrage— which she was clearly winding up to do at once—Louisa cleared her throat, and pasted on another smile. "Yes, of course," she replied. "If you'll excuse me a moment, Gladys, I'll be back shortly. And please don't worry, he's perfectly safe."

Gladys didn't look slightly convinced by this blatant lie, and no wonder—but Louisa's patience was already far too frayed for one morning, and she spun toward the trees, without waiting for Killik to follow. But he was beside her in an instant, his steps falling together with hers, his shoulders square and stiff.

"Wolf pleased you, ach, woman?" he asked curtly, once they were a fair distance into the trees. "You shall welcome him into your bed, when I bring him tonight?"

Louisa's steps faltered, enough that she nearly tripped over a root, while Killik shot her a disdainful glance, and drew to a halt. "Ach?" he demanded, with an impatient spin of the dagger still in his hand. "Or have you now *changed your mind* again?"

Gods, he was so infuriating, and Louisa glared back toward him, and folded her arms over her chest. "I haven't changed my mind," she snapped. "He was..."

Killik's brows rose, waiting, and Louisa let out a slow

breath, squeezing her eyes shut. "I liked him," she made herself say. "You were right. He's... handsome. Pleasing."

Her face was burning, now, but she'd said it, she'd gotten it over with, given Killik his damned victory. But when she opened her eyes again, he didn't look victorious, or even smug. He just looked... grim. Resigned.

"Ach," he said, voice flat. "I shall bring him this eve, then. After nightfall. And you shall honour our terms, ach? You shall not ask upon his past, or his sins, or his griefs. You shall seek to show him kindness, and *peace.*"

Louisa didn't at all recall that being part of it, but she swallowed and nodded—to which Killik just kept frowning, spinning that dagger in his hand. "And," he added, "when I bring him to you this eve, you shall seek to court him, and woo him. To... persuade him, to this."

Wait. Wait wait wait. Killik wanted her to... *woo* Ulfarr? To persuade him to do this? As if—

"What the hell do you mean, *I* need to persuade him?" Louisa demanded, her voice sharp. "Haven't you already discussed this with him yourself? And worked out the terms between you?"

But damn it, Killik's jaw was set, his gaze intent on the dagger still spinning in his hand. As if he indeed hadn't spoken to Ulfarr about this yet, not in the slightest—and Louisa's disbelief escaped in a choked laugh, a furious shake of her head.

"You devious snake," she snarled at him. "You can't honestly mean to tell me you haven't actually talked to Ulfarr about *any* of this? You haven't told him about the agreement? About—*me*?"

Her voice cracked, because wait, the way she'd behaved when Ulfarr had kissed her hand, the way she'd so shamefully ogled his trousers—it had all been with some vague under-standing that he'd already known who she was. That Killik had already discussed it with him, and made... arrangements. While in truth, Ulfarr hadn't had the faintest idea who Louisa was? She'd just been some addled, messy, tarty stranger, blatantly taking one look, and trying to get into his trousers?

"Ach, I spoke to him of you, woman," Killik snapped back, a little too late. "I told him I knew he should find you pleasing, and that he ought to meet you."

But he'd clearly said nothing beyond that, especially about the deal, the debts, the ten nights together—and Louisa gaped at him, as fury screeched higher in her chest. "So what was your plan for tonight, then?" she demanded. "To dump him into my bedroom, and hope for the best? And hope I didn't betray how it was *your* plan the entire time? Or how you're paying my debts in exchange?!"

Killik's face looked pinched, now, his gaze still fixed on his spinning dagger, and Louisa barked another furious growl, and jerked a step toward him. "That is a *horrible* plan, you menace," she hissed. "What if Ulfarr doesn't *want* that? What if he doesn't actually want a woman as part of a plan, or a *deal*? What if he doesn't want—*me*?!"

Her voice rang out between them, far too carrying, and Killik darted a brief, hunted look back toward the well, before lurching deeper into the trees, and waving Louisa after him. And maybe she should have refused, but she was already rounding on him again, and desperately fighting the urge to spit in his face. "You said you were trying to *help* him, you prick," she growled. "How the hell is it helping him if you trick him into a transactional liaison with a stranger, based on nothing but coin and false pretenses and *lies*?!"

She was too close to Killik now, close enough that she could see his eyelid twitching, could hear the shaky sound of his breath. And with a sharp snap of movement, he caught his still-spinning dagger-blade in his hand, and lurched a step toward her, almost near enough to touch.

"Your *liaison* is not based on lies," he hissed back, low in his throat. "I scented you, over there. I scented him. He wishes for you, and you for him, as I knew you would. So ach, I grant you both a gift, and make this truth!"

Louisa scoffed, and jerked a furious shake of her head. "Stop dodging my point," she snarled. "And stop pretending that you're justified in this rubbish. You lied to him, and you lied to me, and therefore put your entire grand plan at risk! Did you really think I'd be foolish enough to just drag him into my bed tonight, without discussing any of this first?!"

The disdain curled on Killik's lip, and he huffed a contemptuous laugh—suggesting that yes, indeed, he did think Louisa that foolish... or that desperate. And for an instant, she could only blink back at him, as something crumpled dangerously in her belly, and her thoughts churned with irrelevant, highly unhelpful memories of the night before. Of how she'd so easily capitulated to every one of his commands, greedily impaling herself on a stone orc-prick for him again and again, lost in the heat in his voice, the look in his eyes...

No. *No.* Louisa yanked backwards, away from him, and dragged her hands through her frayed, frizzy hair, now half-fallen from its bent hairpins. No. He was awful. She didn't care about him, she didn't need him, or his help, or his lies. She could find another way, *something...*

"Look, I don't need this," she choked out. "I'm finished with this, again. Just like I should have been the first time you—"

Her voice wrenched into a high-pitched yelp, because Killik—snapped. His taut, tall body streaking forward, far too close, as his strong hand gripped Louisa's straggly hair, and hauled her backwards. Shoving her into something rough and hard—a tree-trunk, solid and immobile behind her. And with another swift movement, he yanked up both Louisa's wrists by her dress' loose sleeves, thrust them against the rough wood above her head, and...

And stabbed his dagger through the fabric. Holding her there. *Trapping* her there.

Louisa choked and kicked and glared, but she was firmly pinned to the tree by her sleeves, while a furious, growling Killik loomed tall and menacing before her. "No, woman," he spat, his teeth bared. "You wish for my answer, then you stay, and you hear it! You no keep shouting and raging at me, calling me *menace* and *snake* and *prick*, and no even grant me breath to speak!"

His voice was rough and rasping, his accent thicker than before, and Louisa's retort faltered in her throat, her gaze caught on his face. On where his rapidly blinking eyes looked strangely bright, exposed, and... miserable.

"I fear for my wolf's *life*," he breathed, through his twisting, quivering mouth. "I fear that one day, he shall awaken, and find he can no more bear the shame—or he shall decide its taint upon our son is too great. And then he shall slit his throat, or fall on his sword, or walk into a river with a boulderstone."

The sudden, sickening vision of it flashed behind Louisa's eyes, that huge handsome body lying bloated and wasted on a riverbank, and she winced as she dragged down a ragged breath, and uselessly yanked at her pinned sleeves. "Then it sounds like he needs real and meaningful help," she managed. "Far beyond you bribing a woman into his bed, and lying to him about it!"

Killik's growl sounded more like a bark, his head whipping back and forth. "You ken I no try to help him?!" he demanded, his accent even thicker. "I try all else I can dream of. I seek help from clan, from elders. I draw out old vows and secrets, throw them into light. I adopt son with my wolf, even when I *never* wish to be father—for I see how much *he* long for this, and our clan no allow him this, without keeper like me. I grant him my ploughing and pleasure, whenever he wish for this, even when I *know* he true want woman!"

Louisa blinked, drew in breath, but Killik jabbed a claw toward her, its tip almost touching her exposed, straining neck. "And ach, *naught* of what I do heal him," he hissed, "so now I seek woman for him, even if she think me *snake* and *prick*! I seek to help her, to make good fair deal for her, with good pay and clear end, so she give my wolf chance! For why else she do this? And how else he ever find this, without me?!"

Oh. Louisa's rage skidded, faltered, caught on the true misery in Killik's eyes, the desperation on his broken voice. "And I only ask you here to speak," he continued, almost a gulp, "so you now know this! So I mayhap gain your help in this, and come to terms before this eve, and no grant him yet more pain or grief or shame! I wish to grant him *peace*!"

His voice scraped into Louisa's pounding ears, plunged deep into her heaving chest, her twisting belly. And though a contrary part of her wanted to keep arguing, she couldn't find the words. And instead she just swallowed and stared up at him, and then sagged backwards, heavy and resigned, against the tree. The tree he'd *pinned* her to, with a sharp deadly dagger. And she should be remembering that, and refusing this, and running. He was unpredictable, dangerous, he couldn't be trusted...

"And you really still think," she croaked at him, "a woman might make that much difference? After everything else you've tried?"

Killik's growl was exasperated, but not quite as harsh as before. "No, I only do all this for *fun*," he drawled, even as he grimaced, and rubbed at his eyes. "I already tell you, again and again, ach? He was happiest with a woman. He has always longed for a woman. He *reek* of envy when he see our

Skai kin-brothers with their mates. Did you no see how he greet you today? How he look at you? How he kiss your hand, and taste you? Make clear what he wish from you, even with me there beside him?"

Right. The strength of that moment was already here, coiling hot and hard in Louisa's groin, and Killik huffed a low, bitter laugh as he sank closer into the tree, his elbow now resting against the trunk, his hand again rubbing at his eyes. "This hope is all I have left," he said, a low choke in his throat. "Must needs *try*, ach?"

Must needs try. Louisa's own throat spasmed, her blinking eyes caught on his drawn face, now far too close to her own. Close enough that she could see the black stubble on his chin, could feel his harsh breaths on her cheek. And it would only take a tiny tilt up of her head to brush their noses, to make their mouths meet...

And oh, his lean body was already shifting closer, his lips parted, his black tongue brushing brief against them. But he wouldn't, surely he wouldn't, he didn't want her... right?

"Then we'll try," Louisa rasped, dragging her gaze back up to his hooded, long-lashed eyes. "But to start, we're telling Ulfarr the truth. All of it. Tonight."

Killik's face was still so close, his wince so strong it felt like a touch, his lashes fluttering heavy against his hard cheek. And the strange, palpable temptation was lurching higher, nearer, a hot whispered promise, and all Louisa had to do was—

But then Killik stumbled backwards, away. The movements jerky and stiff, his eyes wide and disbelieving on Louisa's face, on her own parted lips. And what the hell had she been thinking, he didn't want her, and she didn't want him. She wanted to escape Lord Scall, live her life on her own terms, find her own peace, and that was all.

And suddenly Louisa couldn't bear to stay here, to look at him for another moment. And with a hard, wrenching yank, she tore her sleeves free of the dagger, and spun toward the house.

"Tonight," she hissed, over her shoulder, blinking back the prickling behind her eyes. "We tell him everything, or I'm done."

10

Louisa's grim determination lasted only as long as it took to reach the house. Where Gladys slammed the kitchen door shut, and rounded on her with narrow, incredulous eyes.

"With all due respect, missus," she hissed, "what in the gods' names are you doing, allowing those orcs on the property! Digging *tunnels* in the well!"

Louisa's head was already beginning to ache, and she drew in breath—but now here was Joan, stalking up out of the cellar, her face hard. "Don't like to whinge, Lou," she said. "But Gladys is right. It's not safe. Most of all with the little ones. Elise is overwrought, and won't come up. Won't let the little ones out, either."

Louisa winced toward the cellar door, and then shot a helpless glance around at the kitchen's empty shelves. "Look, I have full sympathy for your concerns," she replied woodenly, "but it's either this, or I sell. The orcs have committed to helping us, and—"

"*Helping* us," Gladys interrupted, her voice rising. "Helping themselves *to* us, you mean! Did you not notice that huge orc pawing at you earlier? Or what he was growing in his trousers as he did it?"

Louisa's face flooded with heat, and she fought to shove away the vivid vision of Ulfarr's tented trousers. "He was very polite and respectful," she said firmly. "Much more than many humans I could name. Surely you can admit that tolerating a few orcs is still preferable to handing over the property to someone like Rikard?"

Her voice sounded pleading, and she didn't miss Gladys and Joan's brief exchanged glance, or the sudden tightness on Joan's mouth. "Look, yeah, anything's better than Rikard," Joan finally replied, with a sigh. "It's just—"

She broke off at the sound of a knock at the nearby door, and strode over to open it—and then startled to stillness, because standing in the door was—*Halthorr*. The lean, friendly orc from the well, and he was carefully smiling at Joan's shocked face, and thrusting out a paper-wrapped package toward her.

"I ken you did not wish us at the house," he said, with a regretful glance toward Gladys, "but we wished you to know that the well is now fixed, and safe to drink again. Also"—his gaze dropped back to the package—"Killik wished me to bring you this cake. It is fresh from our own cook today, with fruit grown from our mountain's garden."

There was an instant's awkward silence, and Louisa belatedly drew in breath, and made to go collect the cake—when Joan nodded, and grasped the cake from Halthorr's outstretched hands. "Uh, thanks," she said stiffly. "For this, and fixing the well."

Halthorr waved it away, though he'd shot a wry glance downwards, to where he was dripping wet, his bare torso gleaming, his trousers drenched tight to his lean, muscled form. "Ach, it was no trouble," he said, with a dismissive wave of his hand. "It is only fair, after all the great kindness you have granted us. If there is aught else you might ever need, only come and speak this to any of us, and we shall do our best to help, ach?"

It was another very pretty speech, though Louisa was still vaguely surprised to see Joan's curt nod. "Er, thanks," she said again. "We'll—keep that in mind."

Halthorr flashed Joan a broad, toothy smile, and gave another flourishing bow before turning and striding out again, quietly shutting the door behind him. Leaving Joan standing there warily eyeing the door, while Gladys loudly harrumphed into the silence. "Well," she said. "I suppose that one knows his manners, at least."

Joan didn't reply, so Louisa took a breath, and went to collect the cake from her unmoving hands. "Well, I could certainly use some cake," she said, into the stilted silence. "Joan, do you think Elise and the children would like some as well?"

This proved to be a productive distraction, thank the gods, and soon the frightened children were exclaiming delightedly over cake, a treat the household's limited budget had long ago prohibited. And though Elise kept leaning heavily against Joan, her colour slowly returned as she ate several slices of cake, and soon she was even wanly smiling at Gladys and Joan's banter. Including—once the children had run off—Gladys' florid tale of the huge orc who'd licked Louisa's hand, and grown a tree-trunk in his trousers.

Louisa laughed along with them, but her face was burning, and she was deeply relieved when they all dispersed to their tasks for the day, their concerns about orcs apparently forgotten beneath the comforts of clean water and fruitcake. It was one challenge dealt with, for the moment, and Louisa couldn't deny a grudging gratitude toward Killik for so deftly arranging it.

But that brought to mind the entire mess with Killik from earlier, and how they'd fought, and how he'd pinned her to that damned tree. And even as Louisa fought to shove it aside, to focus on her own day's work, the questions wouldn't stop scraping through her aching head. What had Killik been playing at, with all that? Was he truly that concerned about Ulfarr's wellbeing, about his *life*? And gods above, how much power did he have over Ulfarr, if he could promise to deliver him to a strange woman's bedroom at a specific date and time, without even bothering to inform him in advance?

And, even more disconcerting, if Ulfarr hadn't known about the plan, why had he still kissed Louisa's hand like that? Perhaps—perhaps that was something he did with every woman he met? Perhaps he often walked around growing tree-trunks in his trousers? Did he really want her? Would he really want her, when he came tonight? *Tonight*?

It was all so wretchedly unnerving, and it all kept shouting louder and louder as the day plodded on. And even a large list of tedious, time-consuming chores offered no relief, and by the time she finished for the day, Louisa was filthy, exhausted, and deeply, desperately anxious.

She was doing this, really doing this, for the first time since Lord Scall. She was welcoming a new partner—an orc—into her room, and her bed. Tonight. Soon.

She scarcely tasted Elise's supper—served with more fruitcake on the side—and then she stomped about hauling hot water for a much-needed bath, which somehow turned tepid the instant she sank into it. And as she scrubbed herself all over, her heartbeat kept pounding faster, her hands trembling in the water.

Why had she ever agreed to this? What the hell was she supposed to say to Ulfarr? What was she supposed to wear? And why was she was so completely, utterly terrified?

She ended up fully dressing again, in the most presentable clothes left in her wardrobe, before combing out her knotted hair as thoroughly as she could. And then she straightened the drapes, tidied her room, and neatened her bed—where she found that incriminating stone still hidden beneath her blanket, damn it. And once she'd hurriedly cleaned it at the washbasin, she shoved it deep into the wardrobe, and began pacing back and forth, as the sky beyond the window slowly sank into blackness. Killik had said he would come at nightfall, what if he'd changed his mind, what if Ulfarr had refused after all, what if—

A rap, quiet but brisk. At the door.

Louisa rushed toward the door, flinging it open so hard it bounced off the wall beside her. And yes, no, no, revealing the pair of silent, staring orcs, hovering like two wraiths of doom in the dark hallway.

They were here.

11

For a breath, there was silence. Horrible, hanging, dangling silence, during which Louisa stared at Killik and Ulfarr, and they stared at her.

They were both far better dressed than earlier that day, Louisa's distant thoughts pointed out, and Ulfarr was wearing a flattering, close-fitting tunic and trousers, along with a thick, polished, heavy-looking chain around his waist. His long dark hair was neatly braided, his face looked freshly shaven, and his shadowed eyes on Louisa looked—wary. Uncertain. Afraid.

"Is this not now a good time?" came Killik's voice, cuttingly polite. "Ought we to come back later?"

Louisa darted a guilty glance toward him—he also looked irritatingly compelling in his slim-fitting, low-slung trousers—and flapped her hand toward the room behind her. "N-no, this is perfect, thank you so much for coming," she said. "Won't you come in, and make yourselves comfortable?"

Killik rolled his eyes and stalked inside, while behind him, Ulfarr hesitated in the doorway, glancing uncertainly around the room. And as Louisa followed his gaze, she could admit that her garret room probably still looked relatively opulent in the lamplight, what with the impressive size of it, the old built-in furnishings, the gigantic bed with its tall corner posts and hanging heavy curtains.

"It's not nearly as grand as it looks," Louisa said, too quickly. "The rugs are almost bare, the drapes are a bit moth-eaten, and we've sold everything that isn't bolted down. And the bed is ancient, and liable to break under the slightest weight or duress."

It had been a bad attempt at a joke, but wait, had she just told a gigantic heavy orc that her bed was likely to break under weight or duress? An orc who she'd invited here for the sole purpose of *sharing* said bed?!

Her face flooded with heat, her fingers rubbing painfully at her eyes, and she twitched at the sound of Killik's heavy sigh, and then the scrape of chair legs on the floor. "I am sure we care naught for this," he said flatly, and when Louisa glanced up, he was already sprawled onto the chair by the writing desk, his dagger already in hand. "Now come in, Wolf, and sit."

He imperiously jabbed the dagger toward the bed Louisa had just warned them against, and she was vaguely surprised when Ulfarr jerked a nod, and... obeyed. Shutting the door quietly behind him before lumbering over to the bed, and sinking down heavily upon it.

It did creak under his weight, but otherwise held, and Louisa again found herself staring at him, at his set face, at the strange hunted wariness in his eyes. It seemed fully at odds with his demeanour earlier that day, when he'd seemed so... confident. Capable. Hungry.

Louisa's traitorous, searching eyes had even darted down to his trousers—but if there was anything happening there, it was fully concealed by how he was sitting, his huge shoulders hunched, his big hands tightly folded in his lap. As if he was waiting, bracing himself, for some sort of—blow. Or even a punishment.

"Uh, thank you for coming," Louisa said, and then winced, because she'd said that already, hadn't she? "So, Ulfarr, has Killik... I presume he's told you we wanted to meet with you? To... discuss something?"

She was already forcing the words out, too rushed and flat. And she was disconcerted to see Ulfarr's answering flinch, his brief glance toward Killik that looked almost wounded.

"Ach, but Killik would not say what," he replied, his deep voice heavy, even weary. "But I ken it—it has aught to do with how I... met you today, ach? How I... tasted you, without your leave."

Louisa blinked at Ulfarr, not following, and she could hear his swallow, spasming hard in his throat. "I had no wish to cause you distress, or alarm," he said thickly. "I—I ken I lost my bearings, upon the sight and scent of you, and I can only ask your—your pardon, and your mercy. I vow before Skai-kesh that I shall not again touch you without your leave, and I hope—I pray—I beg—"

His voice broke as he dragged in breath, and his eyes on Louisa's face were far too bright, too pleading. "I beg you, please do not punish my kin for this," he whispered. "Please do not send them from these lands, or take them from this hope of a new home. The fault in this was fully mine, and I shall seek—to atone—"

His breaths kept shuddering through his chest, as if every word was agony. And it *was* agony, plummeting deep in Louisa's belly, constricting painfully around her chest. Ulfarr truly thought she'd called him here to gain a personal apology? To earn his atonement, and his misery, for his grave sin of kissing her hand? When him kissing her hand might have been the loveliest thing a male had ever done in her *life*?

"Oh, no, please—please don't," Louisa stammered, and without even catching it, she lurched toward him, and snatched up his hot, heavy hand in hers. "Please don't apologize, that wasn't at all what I meant. I'd have told you if I wanted you to stop, and in truth, I wanted you to come here so I could—"

She dragged for air, for rational thought, and curse her, she was drawing his hand up to her mouth, and—kissing it. Kissing it, just like he'd kissed her own hand that morning. Her lips brushing against warm skin, her tongue even darting out, tasting the salty sweetness of him...

"I wanted to ask if you'd like—more," she whispered, hot, shameful, into his skin. "If you might like to—to stay. The night."

Stay, the night. Gods, she hadn't just said that, had she? But yes, yes, she had. And this wasn't the plan, they were supposed to explain everything first, what the hell was she *doing*—

But she couldn't seem to take it back, either. Not even with Ulfarr gaping at her like that, his eyes wide and shocked, his mouth slack, his big body utterly unmoving. Except, perhaps, for the faint tremor in his hand, now frozen in Louisa's grip.

And wait, no, he'd apologized for kissing her own hand earlier, perhaps he still disapproved of such behaviour—and with a jolt, Louisa dropped his hand, and stumbled backwards, away. "But of course there's no—no obligation whatsoever," she stammered. "And if I've been too forward, I—I offer my apologies in return. I just thought perhaps—Killik said you might—we should—"

She darted a desperate glance over her shoulder, toward where Killik was still sitting there, watching. His eyes now blank, unreadable, though he'd apparently gone and gouged his dagger into Louisa's desk, his hand gripped tight to its hilt.

"Ach, I thought you two would well suit," his clipped

voice said, into the heavy silence. "And this woman has shown herself brave, hearty, and wise, with good lands, and great power to help us, and our kin. Thus"—he smiled, brittle and cold, as he yanked the dagger out of the desk, and jabbed it toward Ulfarr—"I offered her *you*, Wolf, for her pleasure. Along with our payment of her debts, if she shall come alongside us, and help care for our kin."

Wait. Wait, that wasn't right. Killik was making it sound as though him offering up Ulfarr to Louisa—offering her those ten nights—had been him sweetening the pot for her, rather than him paying her to tolerate an orc in her bed. But that hadn't at all been how it had gone, damn him, and Louisa could see the uncertainty glimmering in Ulfarr's suspicious eyes. In how he glanced between her and Killik, as one of his hands absently caressed the other—the one she'd kissed, oh gods.

"Ach, I follow now, Killik," he said, his voice resigned. "I ken you more likely offered her this coin so she would agree to bed me, ach?"

Louisa twitched, her gaze darting back to where Killik shrugged, and flipped his dagger in his fingers. "I cannot foretell how fickle humans shall hear my words," he said flatly. "But I can scent how eager they are, when I make this offer. And beyond this, I can scent"—he fluidly rose out of his chair, and strode toward the wardrobe—"how deeply they long for a good, strong Skai prick."

Wait. Wait, he was opening the wardrobe, and reaching inside—and though Louisa jerked toward him, it was too late, too late. Because gods *fuck* Killik, he'd already plucked out that huge incriminating stone—that *replica*—and tossed it toward Ulfarr.

Ulfarr caught it with an easy snap of his fingers, his forehead furrowing—and then he startled, his eyes widening, as he stared down at the stone. The stone he surely recognized, no, no, *no*—and now he was bringing it to his *nose*. His eyes fluttering as he inhaled against it, slow and careful and deep.

He was *smelling* it. Smelling *Louisa* on it. Smelling what she'd done with it.

The humiliation felt like a sharp, staggering slap to Louisa's face, and her shaky body rounded on Killik, her hands in fists at her sides. "You odious cheating *swine*," she hissed at him. "You have no right whatsoever to—to—"

She couldn't even finish, the words tangled in her throat, and her rage fused even higher at the sight of Killik laughing, the sound icy and mocking. "Thankless woman," he drawled. "I bring you this good Skai gift, and when I see how eagerly you spurt and squeal upon this, I bring you this even better one. You ought to be kneeling, and praising me!"

Louisa glared and sputtered at him, while from the bed, there was a deep, choked sound from Ulfarr's throat. "You... witnessed this, Killik," came his voice, low and disbelieving. "Her... joy, upon this."

Killik's smug eyes slid to Ulfarr, his smile drawing up tight and thin. "Ach, I did," he said smoothly. "I wished to be sure of her, before I brought you here. Wished to be sure she would welcome your prick deep, and caress and cherish it, as she should."

There was another choked sound from Ulfarr, and for an instant, his glance toward Louisa looked almost... longing. A look Killik surely saw too, something unpleasant curling on his mouth, and he strode over toward Ulfarr, and plucked the stone out of his hands.

"But this was not all good," he coolly continued, as he traced his claw against the stone's thick shaft, stopping perhaps two-thirds of the way up its length. "Mayhap you cannot scent this, but she could only take you to here, ach? I should wish for better for the Wolf of the Skai, and thus, I promised her only ten nights with you."

Louisa gaped at Killik again, her humiliation screaming

against the furious disbelief, while he just kept smiling at her, with scorn flashing in his eyes. "If she can show herself strong enough to bear this much. Or shall she run away screeching at her first true sight of a Skai prick?"

He'd spoken with shameless relish, even licking his tongue at his teeth, the vile deceitful *snake*. And Louisa was one breath away from shouting at him, launching herself at him, punching his smug infuriating face, when—something grasped her hand. Something big and warm and solid, something—

Him. Ulfarr.

"Do not allow Killik to vex you, Lady Louisa," he said, his eyes searching hers, his voice very low. "And should you truly wish to grant me any nights with you—even one night—I should be—most honoured."

Oh. It was like he'd deflated all Louisa's rage at once, her shoulders sagging, her breath exhaling. Her blinking eyes again caught on his scarred, handsome face, his tentative, searching gaze. On that undeniable flicker of hope in his eyes, there for just a moment, and gone again.

"But mayhap Killik has not... told you," he added, quieter, "all I have done. All my past... sins. The deep... shame I have brought, upon my clan, and my kin, and my—ach. And you ought—you ought to know—"

He was breathing heavily again, his face contorting with effort, with grief, with regret. Just like when he'd made her that miserable apology, and Louisa frantically flapped her hand at him, and shook her head.

"Look, you don't need to get into it," she said, in a rush. "Just like you don't need to hear any of my own awful—well. If it's just ten nights, we can just—not. Can't we?"

She'd spoken too quickly, perhaps betraying too much— but that was relief in Ulfarr's eyes, in the sudden drop of his shoulders. And in the way his hand found hers again, closing warm and gentle around it, and Louisa's own breath shuddered out, shaky and relieved. Her eyes holding, blinking, as Ulfarr again brought her hand to his mouth, and pressed a brief, careful kiss against it.

Louisa shivered as heat streaked to her groin—and Ulfarr's eyes fluttered, his breath hitching against her skin. Against where he was kissing again, lingering longer this time, and oh, it felt so good, it had been so long, did he really, really want to...

But then—Ulfarr hesitated. Drew back. His eyes darting sideways, toward where Killik was still standing there watching this, his hand gripped to his dagger. And Ulfarr's head tilted as he studied Killik's face, his thick brows drawing together.

"But you are sure of this, Killik?" Ulfarr asked, quiet. "You do not... mind this?"

Killik's expression instantly hardened into something incredulous, furious, and his answering scoff rang through the room. "Ach, why should I *mind*?" he demanded. "You are long past due for a woman in your bed again, and *my* bed shall not be empty this eve. I shall be happily ploughing tight Skai arses long after this weak woman is bloody and spent upon you!"

He was glaring at Louisa again, and she glowered straight back, a low growl burning in her throat. "You arrogant, ignorant scum," she snarled at him. "You are such a—"

But Killik flailed his dagger in midair toward her, and then spun toward the door, yanking it open. Because he was going to leave them here together, alone, were they really going to do this...

"I shall see you come morn, Wolf," Killik hissed over his shoulder, with a cold, deadly smile. "I hope you make her *scream*."

12

Louisa glared at the closed door for a moment too long, her breaths heaving hard, her hand clamping tightly to the warm strength within it. To... Ulfarr's hand.

Right. This. Louisa twitched and blinked back toward him, toward this huge, handsome, highly alarming orc. Just sitting here on her bed, holding her hand, and watching her with wary, uneasy eyes. As if he still wasn't at all sure of her, either.

But they could do this. Right? Louisa had to do this, she wanted to do this, to gain her freedom, to escape Lord Scall...

So she attempted a smile down toward Ulfarr, though it still felt shaky, not quite her own. "Gods, Killik is enraging, isn't he?" she said, her voice strained. "I'd love nothing more than to steal those daggers of his, and throw them down the nearest latrine. Or a muddy flooded well, maybe."

She winced even as she said it—gods, what if complaining about Killik was crossing a line somehow—but oh, that was a faint, fleeting warmth in Ulfarr's eyes, a brief curve of his mouth. "Ach, this would hurt him more than aught else, I ken," he replied, in his low, rumbling voice.

"Though I ought to warn you against this, for he might next throw *you* into the latrine also."

Louisa's relieved laugh bubbled up on its own, her shoulders slightly relaxing. "Of course he would, the utter bastard," she said, with a wry grin toward Ulfarr's face. "I can't imagine what it must be like co-parenting with him. You must have the patience of a saint."

She'd again meant it as a joke, perhaps just wanting to see Ulfarr smile again, to hear his lovely deep voice. But instead, his big body stiffened on the bed, his eyes wary again, his fingers spasming against hers.

"Killik... spoke to you of this?" he asked, in a tone she couldn't quite read. "Of... our son?"

Louisa swallowed, and gave what she hoped was a dismissive shrug. "Not in detail," she said quickly. "But he did mention that you weren't able to have sons of your own, so you ended up adopting together instead."

She was watching Ulfarr too carefully now—would he argue any of that, or had he perhaps not wanted her to know about his son? And yes, something dark had indeed passed across his eyes—but then he nodded, his breath slowly exhaling.

"Ach, we have had our son for two summers now," he replied. "His name is Sune, and he is now fourteen summers old. He is a quick, clever Skai, but just as stubborn and headstrong as his strike-father—as Killik, you ken."

As he'd spoken, his voice had softened again, his eyes glimmering with unmistakable affection, with pride. Enough that something convulsed in Louisa's throat, twinged low in her belly. "Well, I'm sure he's lucky to have you," she said. "And you're lucky to have him, too."

She couldn't quite hide the wistfulness in her voice, and Ulfarr's head tilted as he looked at her, not unlike the way he'd looked at Killik earlier. "You have no young of your own, then?" he asked. "I cannot smell this upon you, but my scenting—"

He grimaced and rubbed at his nose, but his eyes were intent on Louisa, waiting for her answer. And the air suddenly felt too hot, too thin, and Louisa jerked a shrug, a shaky wave of her hand. "No, no children," she said thickly. "Though in truth, it was for the best, because my late husband was a cruel, vicious old degenerate who only cared about himself. And any child cursed with him as a father would have ended up—"

Gods, she couldn't even say it, but there was a grim, surprising comprehension in Ulfarr's eyes as he nodded. "Ach, I follow," he said, quiet. "I ken this was the hand of our father Skai-kesh upon you. His blessing."

Oh. That name sounded familiar—he'd mentioned it before, and it had to be some kind of deity, right? And though the idea of an unknown orc deity blessing Louisa with childlessness was utterly laughable, she found her breath exhaling, her hand squeezing against Ulfarr's still-clasping fingers. As if in... solidarity. In gratitude.

And perhaps he felt it too, his warm hand drawing hers a little closer, as if he wanted her closer, too. And it was too easy to follow it, to lean into his strength, into that widening space between his spread knees. Into the rich, sweet scent that hung and whispered all around him, inviting her to draw in long, deep lungfuls of it. Gods, he smelled good, he looked good, and his thighs bracketing hers were so solid, warm, safe...

He was still studying her with intent, watchful wariness, and his hand slowly guided hers back to his mouth. So he could press a soft, careful kiss against her skin, even as his eyes kept searching hers. Seeking, perhaps, for any sign of hesitation, or reluctance, or fear.

But there was only a deep, convulsive shiver, rippling up Louisa's spine, escaping in a ragged gasp from her mouth.

And she could see Ulfarr's shoulders settling, could feel his own unsteady exhale, as he kissed her hand again. Lingering longer this time, his lips warm, his tongue brushing light and soft. As if he truly wanted to taste her, to treasure her, to savour every slow, shaky breath.

It was Louisa who turned her hand over this time, wanting to feel that warm tongue seeking into her palm, trailing up the inside of her wrist. And yes, yes, it was there, gentle and eager and bizarrely, impossibly intimate. An orc, sitting here in her bedroom, lavishing her with his lips and tongue, his nose brushing up against her dress' sleeve. Feeling so, so good, fluttering Louisa's eyes closed, tilting her head back, sinking her into...

A hand. A strong, unfamiliar male hand. Touching her, gripping powerfully at her hip, as if—

Louisa yelped and staggered backwards across the room, her own hands flailing, clutching at her hip, at where there was—nothing. Nothing, no hand, no pain, no creeping sickening lord husband.

Only—she gulped for air, briefly squeezed her eyes shut—the orc. The orc she'd invited into her bedroom. The orc she'd wanted to kiss her, to touch her. And the orc who had already raised both hands between them, palms out, his face hunted and pale.

"F-forgive me," he rasped, a sharp scrape in his throat. "I ought not—I did not wish to—I am—sorry, I—"

Oh gods, no no no, and Louisa flapped her hands, whipped her head back and forth. "P-please, it's nothing," she gasped back. "I'm only—nervous, that's all. It's been a long time, and I'm just not used to—"

She winced, shook her head again, and made a desperate attempt at a smile toward Ulfarr's face. But his mouth was wavering, twisting, and his eyes looked even more hunted than before, almost... afraid.

"Killik," he said, low and bitter. "He... did he truly bribe you to this, after all? Or trick you, mayhap? Threaten you?"

A cold, helpless misery flashed up Louisa's spine, and she lurched a step back toward him, still shaking her head. "No! No, I mean, yes, he did offer to help me with the debts, but"—she drew down more air—"I've been wanting something like... this. Like you. For a long time. And when we met today, you were so lovely, and kind, and—and handsome—"

Good gods, she wasn't truly saying this, spouting all this to an orc she'd just met? But yes, yes, damn it, she'd said it, she'd made it into stark, shameful truth between them. She wanted this. Gods, she wanted this. She wanted to drown all the horrible memories of Lord Scall in this, she wanted to find even a few moments' peace in this, with this handsome gentle orc in her bed. And she'd have wanted it even without the coin, without the agreement, or the ten nights. And for an instant, she silently cursed Killik for not just asking, for making it into this horrid awkward mess...

But before her, Ulfarr was staring at her again, his eyes wide with disbelief. "You—you have this all wrong," he replied, his voice cracking. "I am not any of these, Lady Louisa, I am—"

But Louisa couldn't bear it, not for another instant, and before she could stop it, she hurled herself the rest of the way toward him. Toward his lap, oh gods, she was straddling an orc's lap, throwing her shaky arms around his neck—

"Just—call me Louisa," she choked. "And just—touch me. *Please.*"

But wait. Wait, no, what was she doing, what if Ulfarr didn't want this from her, either—and curse it, he'd again frozen to stillness beneath her, his eyes shocked on her face. And far too late, Louisa winced and made to scramble backwards again, what the hell was wrong with her, what must he think of her...

"Wait," Ulfarr breathed, and in a swift movement, his hand swiped for hers, caught it in his grip. "Wait, Louisa."

Louisa instantly obeyed, now hovering rigid and awkward over his thighs. And watching, her breath catching, as Ulfarr again raised her hand, and brought it to his mouth. His lips brushing against her skin, kissing soft and gentle, but eager, too. Still wanting her. Still wanting this.

Oh. The relief dipped and swirled, shuddering Louisa closer against him. Her hand slipping back over his shoulder, feeling the solid strength of him beneath his tunic, while her other hand shivered and tingled beneath his slow, sweet kisses. Kisses that were now trailing up her wrist, up to her sleeve—

Louisa shuddered again, her eyes fluttering—and in another wild flash of desperate compulsion, she yanked at the sleeve, at the dress. Undoing the buttons, jerking the dress up and off over her head, and tossing it away. Leaving her clad in only her flimsy shift, straddling an orc's lap, an *orc*—

But the orc was staring again, and—groaning. Groaning, inhaling deep, as his hungry kisses found Louisa's bare shoulder, scattering out furious flares of sensation and heat. But his hands still weren't touching her, they were clamped to tight fists at his sides, as if trying to keep away from her—

And Louisa was losing her mind, she was, as she gripped his heavy hand, and yanked it to her hip. To exactly the same place he'd touched her earlier—yes—and this time, she moaned as his fingers settled soft and possessive, and his other hand carefully came to her other hip, too. Slowly spreading wider, and then drawing her closer. Wanting more.

It was too easy to comply, to hitch forward on his lap, deeper into his warm solid strength. Into where his hot mouth was now kissing further up her shoulder, and she ducked her face into his neck, inhaling deep. Gods, he smelled so good, sweet and musky and masculine, and his hands felt so good too, now tentatively stroking up her back. While something large and rigid swelled against the front of his trousers, against Louisa's own too-close groin, and she gasped at the feel of it, the truth of it. And then quivered all over as his hot mouth settled into the crook of her shoulder, his kisses deepening, until—

Something sharp. *Teeth.* Scraping against her skin. And Louisa again couldn't control the startled jerk of shock, the roll of churning panic in her belly. The silent shouting screeching of no, danger, run, *Lord Scall*—

But wait, no, it was just him, just Ulfarr—but he'd already yanked backwards too. That hunted look flashing back through his eyes, his hands snapping away from her. And no, no, no, Louisa's own hands were fluttering at his face, needing him to stay, to stop looking like that, please—

"It's fine," she gasped. "Really, it is. I liked it."

But Ulfarr still looked uneasy, afraid, his eyes shifting miserably on her face. And damn it, Louisa couldn't keep making this worse, and she hauled in a shallow breath, and attempted another smile toward him. Holding the smile as brightly as she could, though she knew it didn't reach her eyes.

"Perhaps I could just—touch you, then?" she ventured, desperately working to keep her voice light. "If you'd... be comfortable with that?"

Ulfarr's nod was jerky, instant, and that was surely relief in his eyes—so Louisa let out a shaky breath, and just began... touching. Sliding her hands over his broad shoulders, and then down his arms, smoothing over the coarse fabric of his tunic.

He didn't betray even a twitch, his eyes fixed on Louisa's face, so she kept stroking, kept her movements slow and careful. Learning the size and strength of his powerful arms, his solid shoulders, his firm upper chest. And then the smooth skin of his neck, the rasp of stubble on his taut jaw, even the puffy mangled mess of his ear.

"This looks—painful," she murmured, as she gently traced a finger up to the ear's pointed tip. "Does it hurt?"

Ulfarr shook his head, wincing as the movement poked his ear at her finger. "No," he said, rough. "Not now."

Not now. Suggesting that it had hurt, at one point, and Louisa compulsively bent closer to his ear, so she could... kiss it. The touch of lips brief, only for a breath, but Ulfarr still shuddered beneath it, his lashes fluttering. As if... as if he liked it.

And that was something, something to help them find their way again, please—so Louisa kissed his ear again, as her hands slowly, tentatively traced back down his front. Over where she could feel the rigid jut of his nipples, hard beneath his tunic, and the relative softness of his thick belly. And then down, down, toward his trousers, toward...

Her trembling hand brushed over his groin, so light as to almost not be a touch at all—but then her fingers spasmed, her eyes snapping downwards, as a sharp, sudden misery fired deep into her chest.

Because he was... soft. Slack. Uninterested. Uninterested in the half-dressed woman touching him, kissing him, welcoming him into her bed.

Oh. Oh, gods. The heat was already swarming Louisa's face, as the bitter memories of Lord Scall kicked and surged, sweeping dark and devastating behind her eyes. *It's not my fault, is it?* he would demand at her, his sharp voice breaking. *If you'd dressed nicer, if you took more time on your looks, this wouldn't be a problem—*

But back then, Louisa *had* taken the time. She'd followed fashions and dressmakers, she'd outfitted herself as well as she could, she'd curled her hair, buffed her fingernails, worn costly cosmetics and jewels—and she'd been a dozen years younger, too. Whereas now, she was here in a shabby old shift, with her scarred body and silver-streaked hair, foolishly trying to seduce an orc who was—

Grasping her hand. Squeezing it tight, and roughly yanking it back to his mouth. Kissing it again, oh, with just as much frantic urgency as she felt. "Forgive me, Louisa," he croaked. "I only—cannot always control this, ach? It is not—"

His breath heaved powerfully through his chest, his eyes glimmering with shame, with misery. As if he truly regretted this, as if he wanted to stay, to keep trying. And he wasn't Lord Scall, he wasn't, she needed to forget Lord Scall, Lord Scall was *dead*—

Louisa desperately fought for breath, for clarity, please, please. And she managed a jerky nod, and even another empty pasted smile on her mouth, as she gave a dismissive wave of her hand.

"It's absolutely fine," she said, too quickly. "No trouble whatsoever at all. And hey"—her voice rose as her blinking eyes suddenly caught sight of a familiar item on the bed—"we can always use that if we need it, can't we?"

It was that huge, obscene stone replica, still lying there innocuously on the blanket, just where Ulfarr must have left it, after Killik had given it to him. And Louisa had only meant it as a reassurance, or perhaps a joke, anything to make this disaster better, please—

But it had been stupid, so stupid, because the instant Ulfarr glanced toward the stone, his big body—flinched. Froze. The colour fully fading from his face, the light draining from his eyes. Making him look haggard, almost ill, as his throat convulsed, his mouth painfully contorting, as if—

As if he was about to be sick. As if Louisa had gone and kicked him in the groin, too, and then stood back, and pointed, and laughed.

"I'm—sorry," she gulped, whipping her head back and forth. "I didn't mean—it was only a—"

But it was too late, because Ulfarr's hand clapped against his mouth, his body lurching sideways, up, away. Off the bed entirely, oh gods, he was—he couldn't—

"Forgive me," he rasped, without looking at her, his voice muffled from his hand still over his mouth. "I—cannot. I am... sorry."

And with those awful words echoing through the air, he staggered toward the door, and left.

13

I t had been years since Louisa had wept like this. Sobbing into the darkness with ugly, choking gasps, her body slumped, her face hot and sticky in her trembling hands.

Gods, she'd been so stupid. So, so stupid, to think she could attempt such things, have such things. She should have known better, after Lord Scall, after Kaspar, after godsdamned Rikard. After her last hope had been an *orc*, and she'd managed to ruin that, too.

And worst of all, she *had* liked Ulfarr. She'd wanted him so damned much. He'd felt so good, tasted so good, smelled so good, and he'd clearly intended to be considerate, to follow her lead. And in return, she'd been jumpy and erratic and unpredictable, and she'd told him—to his face!—that she'd be just as happy with his stone... *replica*.

Gods, no wonder he'd left. In truth, it was a miracle he'd stayed as long as he had. And curse Louisa, what would happen now? What would happen to all Killik's plans and promises? Surely he would withdraw his offer to pay the debts, right? Would he stop the food, too? The help with the property, the terms around caring for her land? Would

Louisa finally need to sell the horses, pension off her staff, give up her home?

There were no answers, only dread and misery and regret, and those harsh, wracking sobs into her pillow. And by the time the sobs finally faded, late into the night, Louisa was exhausted and aching all over, with a vicious headache, and scratchy, swollen eyes.

Her state wasn't at all improved by the bright morning sunlight, streaking through the drapes far too early, and pounding even more pain behind her aching eyes. Gods, how was she going to face this. What the hell was she going to do.

She groaned as she rolled over, shoved herself up on shaky arms—and then started, her heart leaping into her throat. Because there, against the wall, was—

A shadow. Moving. *Alive.* And making a repetitive shirring sound, over and over, like that of someone sharpening a blade...

Wait. It was—Killik?

Louisa's charging panic collapsed into a flat, frustrated disappointment, and she rubbed painfully at her swollen eyes. Of course it was Killik. Come to tell her she'd ruined this beyond imagining, and it was all over, forever.

"Well, get it over with, then," her scratchy voice said, as she blinked blearily at his shadowy form in the faint light. "How bad is it?"

There was an instant's silence—and then Killik's scoff rang out between them, as he leapt to his feet, and stalked toward her. His lean body coiled, his gleaming dagger clutched in his fist, his eyes flashing with rage.

"You told me you *wished* for this," he snarled at her. "You wished for my wolf, and you *knew* of his pain—and you meant to bring him joy, and *peace.* So why did you then spurn him! Why did you bring him yet more darkness, and more pain and grief!"

He jabbed his dagger toward her, the blade glinting sharp and deadly, and Louisa cringed backwards on the bed, dragged her trembling hands over her face. "I didn't mean to," she gulped. "I tried, Killik. I really did!"

Killik's answering laugh was cold and brittle, and he spun sideways, pacing back and forth across the room. "You did *not*," he spat. "I have not seen Wolf so lost in many, many moons. Ach, I had to throw out my own bedmate for the eve, and instead spent all this night soothing him, and ploughing him out of his wits. Until he could finally forget his great grief and pain, and sleep! And"—he whirled around and jabbed his dagger toward her again—"you cannot say I have broken my word upon not touching him, for *you* have failed in your side of this, also!"

It felt like he'd slapped Louisa across the face, again and again, because he—Killik really had taken another lover, last night. And then he—he'd *ploughed* Ulfarr, to comfort him. And Ulfarr had been lost, miserable, in pain, because of *her*—and oh, she could even see it, the darkness in Ulfarr's expressive eyes, the bitterness on his mouth. *We can always use that if we need it, can't we—*

Louisa couldn't look at Killik anymore, and she blinked miserably down at her knees, her hands clutching tightly together. "I didn't mean to hurt him," she whispered. "I should never have brought up using your stone, I—"

"You brought up *what*?!" Killik roared, his eyes wild in his hard face. "You told him you should rather have his *rassja*? Instead of he *himself*?!"

Louisa's prickling, pleading eyes blinked at him, her head shaking. "Not—not like that!" she gulped. "I was just trying to comfort him, to make a joke, to help him relax. And I know it was stupid, I was so stupid, and he didn't—"

Her breaths were dragging in and out now, her eyes burning with shame and misery, and there was an alarming lump quivering high and close in her throat. "He didn't even—want me," she said, wretched, toward her knees. "And—and no wonder. I was such a frightful mess, I can't do it, I can't get over it, I can't get fucking Lord Scall out of my head! And now I've ruined everything. I've lost—*everything.*"

The last word was a choked, agonizing sob, wrenching from her throat—but now more sobs were pouring from her again, tearing out of her gasping, trembling mouth. And her clammy hands shaking over her face were doing nothing, because Killik could still see it, and hear it, and now he would mock her, and abandon her to drown in her weakness, her shame.

But then—something shoved against her hand. Something soft, something—

Oh. A handkerchief. One of Louisa's own handkerchiefs, threadbare but clean. And it was Killik's clawed hand holding it, wanting her to take it—and Louisa's bewildered glance upwards found his eyes distant, his mouth grim. But he wasn't shouting, wasn't condemning her, so she took the handkerchief with tentative fingers, and wiped at her leaking eyes, her nose. Her body was still curled in on itself on the bed, and she only belatedly realized she was still wearing her skimpy, threadbare shift, no doubt giving Killik a clear first-hand view of why Ulfarr had walked away.

"Look, I'm sorry," she said, in something more like her usual voice, once her face felt somewhat dry again. "I really—I really did want it. He was lovely, and patient, and very attractive, and I could tell he was trying to—to make it work. It's just—"

She gave a shaky, furious wave down toward her clothes, her face, her fear, her foolishness, *herself.* And oh, gods, the water behind her eyes was welling up again—at least, until Killik thrust something else into her hand. A fresh handkerchief, one that didn't look at all familiar this time.

"Ach, enough, woman," he snapped, though there was no real heat in his voice. "I now follow how this went. Neither of you knew how to face this, so you both faltered, and fell to your fears. Ach?"

It was an unnervingly succinct representation of the night's events—at least, from Louisa's point of view—but then she shook her head, mopping at her eyes with the fresh handkerchief. "*He* didn't," she gulped. "He had every right to leave, and I don't blame him in the slightest. Especially when—"

She again waved angrily down at herself, at her flushed leaking face—when Killik snatched at her hand in midair, his claws sharp against her skin. "I said, enough of this, woman!" he snarled. "There is naught amiss with you, or how you look, or how you scent, or speak, or behave. You ken I should have sought out some weak, stupid, unsightly wretch for my wolf to touch, and cover with his scent?!"

Louisa blinked her wet eyes at Killik's face, and attempted to protest—but he clamped his claws tighter against her hand, the pain a distant reassuring whine beneath her skin. "No more," he said flatly. "Ach, you speak and scent just as he did last eve! I am weary of this, and I have no wish to tend to *you* all day also—and ach, *my* prick should not grow hard for you after all this, either! You are a strong, capable, comely woman, so you shall stop this whining and pitying, and *listen!*"

For an instant, Louisa could only stare blankly toward him—wait, was he implying that he might have considered *tending* to her, if he hadn't already done so to Ulfarr all night?—and she didn't miss the wince on his mouth, his purposeful glance toward the wall beyond her.

"There is naught amiss with you," he repeated, flatter and slower this time, as if he were speaking to a child. "Wolf longed for this. He longed for you. And he only left because he thought *you* had no wish for *him!*"

Louisa grimaced, swallowed, wiped at her wet eyes. Because gods, she'd wanted Ulfarr so damned much. In that moment, she'd wanted him even more than the coin, or the land. She wanted so desperately to escape Lord Scall, forget Lord Scall, forever. And if anything could shove Lord Scall's loathsome ghost out of her life, surely it would be Ulfarr. With his gentle hands, his sweet scent, his sad wounded eyes...

But even the thought made Louisa's eyes well up again, her head shaking. "Of course I wanted him," she croaked. "And I'd be happy to tell him so, but—he surely won't even *speak* to me again, after all this."

But Killik only scoffed, and rolled his eyes. "Ach, why do you ken I am here?" he drawled. "To laze about and pass the time with you? To kick up a merry lark with you? Or mayhap to make you squeal upon my wolf's *rassja* again?"

Louisa's relief instantly plummeted, into something damnably like hurt, like shame. Of course Killik wouldn't do such things with her, and she already knew that, didn't she? And gods, she would not weep again, not over him, and it took all her willpower to hold her head high, to ignore the painful heat again burning in her cheeks, behind her eyes. She had to try.

"Are you saying you'll take word back to Ulfarr for me?" she managed, through her constricted throat. "A letter, perhaps?"

Something shifted in Killik's eyes, but then he shrugged, glanced away. "Ach, if you truly wish for this," he said. "If you choose to write to him, of your own will. It shall have naught to do with me."

And maybe Killik still didn't want it, maybe he'd still rather have Ulfarr all to himself—or maybe he still thought Louisa didn't mean it. Maybe he thought she hadn't really wanted it, either.

"I understand," Louisa said, the determination firm in her voice, in her belly. "Of course I'll be happy to write him. At once."

She didn't wait for Killik's reply, but instead lurched past him for the writing desk. Where she yanked over her quill, and a fresh sheet of paper—and then stared blankly down at it, her hand hovering over the page. Gods, what was she supposed to write? *I was afraid of you? You reminded me of my vile dead husband?* Or even more shameful, *I don't know how to do this anymore?*

"Write him the truth, woman," came Killik's low voice behind her. "He shall not condemn you for this, and I ken it would do you both good."

Right. Louisa nodded, swallowing hard, and then put her quill to the page, and began writing. Making her letter as clear and heartfelt as she could, despite the way her hand kept trembling on the quill.

I had a lovely evening with you, and shall never forget it, she wrote. *And I deeply regret if I hurt you or insulted you during our time together. I would be honoured if you might be inclined to see me again, but of course I understand and accept whatever decision you might choose to make.*

As she wrote, Killik kept hovering behind her, blatantly reading every word over her shoulder, and after a baleful glance up toward him, Louisa drew in breath, and wrote out a little more. Explaining how her past experiences in such matters had not always occurred in a positive light, and how she perhaps hadn't realized—she had to pause and rub at her prickling face, as the memories burned through her thoughts—how that might carry forward in unexpected or unwelcome ways.

I am most sorry to have visited my own fears upon you, she wrote, her breaths now heavy enough to flutter the page beneath her. *You showed me unwarranted patience and generosity, and you deserved far better. No matter your decision upon this, I wish you only the deepest happiness and peace.*

In gratitude, Louisa.

She was still blinking hard as she blew the ink dry, and

thrust the letter up toward Killik. Toward where he was now eyeing it—and her—with distinct, uneasy suspicion. "A very pretty letter," he said, clipped. "Ach, are you some sort of *scholar*, in secret? One who hides indoors and studies *books* for fun, and then chatters about them to all you meet?"

He sounded almost offended, his nose wrinkling with distaste, and Louisa blinked at him, and shook her head. "Gods, no, of course not," she snapped back. "But it was forced onto me as a child, for writing pretty letters is a major portion of a lord's wife's miserable existence."

An unmistakable relief passed through Killik's eyes, and his gaze lingered on Louisa, for an instant too long. And with a flick of movement, he produced yet another handkerchief, which he raised to her face, wiping at her hot cheek.

"Ink," he said, the curtness of his voice at strange odds with his gentle, still-wiping fingers. "Should not wish to leave you walking about *looking* like a scholar, then."

Louisa blinked again, her skin tingling beneath the bizarre, quiet carefulness of his touch. And she wasn't moving, or even trying to get away, and Killik wasn't stopping, either. His expression shifting as his breath slowly exhaled, shuddering against her skin.

"This letter shall help, I ken," he finally said, as he dropped his hand. "I shall bring you word of Wolf's answer. And also, as I vowed"—he plucked a jingling bag out of his pocket, and dropped it onto her desk—"your first payment."

Her first payment? Louisa stared at it for a moment, uncomprehending—but right, right, the contract had promised twenty percent after the first night, and eighty percent at the end of all ten. And had Killik still counted that as the first night, after all?

But when Louisa opened her mouth to ask, Killik had already spun around, and stalked for the door. Closing it behind him with a decisive thud, and leaving her sitting there staring after him, still breathing too hard, her heart kicking unevenly in her chest.

Maybe there was still hope. Maybe they could still make this work. And if nothing else—her shoulders sagged, her breath exhaling—Killik had given her this. The payment.

She opened the bag with trembling hands, and counted it all out once, and then again. And yes, yes, it turned out to be exactly as much as Killik had promised. A truly shocking amount of coin, more than she'd seen at once in many, many years.

It was enough to prod her back to her feet again, and she washed at the basin, and put on her best day dress. And then, after a quick bite of breakfast with her staff and the children, she saddled May, and headed back into town. First to her banker Bycroft, who took Killik's coin with palpable confusion, but then informed her it would be enough to cover her staff's monthly salaries, her debts' current interest owing, and even a little of the principal, too. And next Louisa went to her usual lawyer Matts, and asked him to review a copy of Killik's contract—with a few key points removed—and to ensure there were no possible loopholes, or looming legal quagmires.

But it all seemed sound enough—Killik had clearly done his research—and Louisa headed home with a grim, resigned gratefulness. Her staff were paid. Her property was safe, for now. And if Ulfarr agreed to come back—and if she could manage to spend the next nine nights with him without panicking—she could still do this. Right?

But once Louisa returned home, and then threw herself into what should have been an enjoyable afternoon of hunting, she still couldn't find the hope, or the peace. And instead, her cursed thoughts kept wheeling back to Killik, to Ulfarr, to that damned letter.

Had Ulfarr received the letter by now? What would he think of it? Would he actually consider returning? Or, more likely, would he think the letter embarrassingly forward, for a woman who had already so thoroughly embarrassed herself? Would he laugh at it, or throw it away? Swear never to see her again?

By the time the sun was setting, still with no sign of Killik—or any viable game for supper, other than a highly alarming skunk—Louisa was fully convinced the letter had been a total waste, just like her afternoon spent hunting. And with a heavy sigh, she finally turned back toward the house, trudging through the trees, rubbing at her prickling eyes. Of course it had been useless, what else had she—

When suddenly, something dropped down before her. Something tall and grey and far too close, sending Louisa reeling backwards, her heart screeching in her chest. It was—Killik?

But yes, yes, it was Killik, rising gracefully from his crouch, and giving a longsuffering roll of his eyes. "What did you ken I was, a porcupine?" he said dryly. "A wandering chicken?"

Louisa's heart was still pounding too loud, her breaths quick and shallow—but her mouth twitched, and she attempted a halfhearted glower toward him. "Well, then?" she demanded. "What did Ulfarr say to the letter?"

A small smile curled across Killik's mouth, smug and satisfied. "Ach, this helped, as I knew it would," he replied. "He did not believe you had written it, at first, but it was luck that you wept upon it, and thus, he could scent this."

Luck, that Louisa had wept on the letter, and she kept glaring at Killik, waiting. But he was enjoying this, damn him, plucking one of his daggers out of his hair, and giving it a leisurely whirl. "He has never before had a letter from a woman, ach?" he continued, with relish. "He read this again and again, and then demanded I tell him all you said and did. For once"—his smile was a full-on smirk, now—"all this weeping and wailing served to my gain, ach?"

Louisa rolled her eyes back toward him, but her alarm and irritation had entirely faded, in place of a strange, lurching eagerness. "And then? What did he say?"

Killik kept smirking at her, and gave another lazy whirl of his dagger. "He said it was a pretty letter," he replied blandly. "And that you write"—he betrayed a faint wince—"just as sweetly as a Ka-esh."

As a Ka-esh. That was another one of the five orc clans, Louisa vaguely recalled, and—she cast her thoughts backwards—it had been the clan that sweet scholarly girl Rosa had been affiliated with, right? A clan Killik didn't want involved with his precious wolf, perhaps.

"Very well, but what then?" Louisa demanded, now playing straight into the smug bastard's hands, but Killik's expression shifted again, back to triumph, or even relief. As if—as if he really did want this to work, too. As if he'd genuinely welcomed Louisa's letter, and her concerted attempt at making amends.

"Then," Killik drawled, his eyes almost warm on Louisa's face, "he bathed, and dressed, and braided his hair. And he now sits in your bedroom, and awaits your return."

Wait. Ulfarr was in Louisa's bedroom? Waiting for her? *Now*?

Louisa could only stare at Killik, her heart now galloping against her ribs, as his smile curled even higher, into something dark, something dangerous, full of menace and glee.

"So you shall ready yourself, and come to us," he said. "And this time"—his voice dropped, into a soft, vicious threat—"this time, I shall make *sure* you scream."

14

By the time Louisa climbed the stairs to her bedroom, she was trembling with nervousness, her hands tingly and clammy, her thoughts screaming unhelpfully through her pounding skull.

What if she messed this up again? What if it was even more of a disaster than last time? Or what if Ulfarr had already changed his mind, and left?

But no, no, Killik had gone on ahead to Louisa's bedroom, while she'd washed up and eaten a quick supper. And if something had changed, surely he would have let her know. Right?

So Louisa squared her shoulders as she clutched for her door, and shoved it open. Revealing her familiar room, lit by her familiar flickering lamp, and...

The orcs. Two orcs. Killik, sprawled in his usual chair by the desk, and... Ulfarr. Once again seated in that same place on the bed, fully dressed, his hands tightly folded in his lap.

Ulfarr's eyes instantly darted up toward Louisa, his big body stiffening—and then he lurched to his feet, and lumbered over toward her. His steps heavy and unsteady, his gaze uneasy on her face.

"Ach, Louisa," he said thickly, and his hand twitched forward, almost as if to grasp hers—but then it dropped just as quickly, snapping to a fist at his side. "I hope you do not mind—ach. Killik said—your letter—"

His face was flushed, the sweat beading on his brow, and Louisa took an instinctive step toward him, before jerking belatedly to a halt. "No, I'm—so glad you came back," she said, in a rush. "You—got the letter, then?"

Even as she said it, she shot a chagrined grimace toward Killik, who predictably scoffed, and rolled his eyes. But Ulfarr's eyes stayed solemn and intent on hers, his head giving a curt nod.

"Ach," he said. "This letter was... very kind. Most of all after I... left you, last eve, as I did."

His voice and eyes dropped, his mouth bitterly twisting, and Louisa shook her head, flapped her hand between them. "It's fine," she replied, too quickly. "Completely fine! I absolutely understood, of course."

But Ulfarr's eyes darkened, gone even more morose than before. The sight of it clutching miserably in Louisa's gut, strong enough that she jolted toward him, almost as if to touch him—

But then, Ulfarr—flinched. Flinched, as if he couldn't bear her touch—or perhaps couldn't bear to be here at all. And Louisa froze in place just in time, as ice cracked up her spine, and heat burned behind her eyes. Gods, he still didn't want it, there was no way this was ever going to—

"Ach, enough," cut in Killik's flat, impatient voice. "Enough, both of you!"

Louisa startled, and Ulfarr did too, both their heads snapping sideways. Toward where Killik had leapt out of his chair, and was now stalking irritably toward them, and jabbing his dagger at the bed.

"Sit," he snapped. "Both of you. *Now.* And we shall have a lesson, ach?"

There wasn't even a thought of disobeying, amidst the frantic mess swarming Louisa's thoughts, and she twitched a nod, stumbling toward the bed. And Ulfarr obeyed too, his big body sagging heavily down beside her, while Killik began pacing back and forth before them, his dagger now aiming erratically between their faces.

"First, woman," he said, with a frown toward Louisa, "if you wish to gain an orc's trust, you cannot speak false to him upon your fear, or your grief, or your shame. He shall never welcome this, or believe this as truth. For he can scent the truth of these feelings upon you!"

What? Louisa blinked blankly up at Killik, who was looking alarmingly sincere, and jabbing his dagger toward her. "Almost all orcs can scent these," he continued flatly. "Even an orc with such weakened scenting as Wolf's. And this is even worse when the speaker's scent shouts their truth as loud and clear as yours! You were *not* glad when Wolf left you last eve, this was not *fine*, and you yet *reek* of grief and shame upon this!"

Oh. Oh, *no*, Ulfarr couldn't possibly have smelled all that—but beside Louisa, he was rubbing at his nose, and not meeting her eyes. While Killik whirled back toward Ulfarr, and poked his dagger into his chest, hard enough that the tip pricked through the neatly tied laces of his tunic.

"And you, Wolf," he snapped. "You left this woman alone in her bed last eve, without a word of kindness or farewell. And after this, she yet wrote you this pretty letter, and told you her truth, and welcomed you back here again! Why do you not thank her, and seek to speak pretty words in return? Or if not this, at least offer her your own truth, before she decides you are not worth her time or forgiveness?!"

He sounded genuinely irate, his eyes flashing on Ulfarr's drawn face, and something swooped in Louisa's chest, catching in her throat. Killik was—defending her? Supporting her? Taking her side?

But yes, yes, he wasn't backing down, his glinting eyes fixed to Ulfarr. And to Louisa's ongoing astonishment, Ulfarr—nodded. Nodded, even as his mouth contorted, his breaths heaving, his eyes angling dark and miserable toward Louisa's face.

"I—thank you, for welcoming me here again, Louisa," he said, with a quiet, stilted formality. "And for writing me this kind letter, also. I deeply regret how I left you, this past eve, and I shall seek to—make amends to you, upon this."

But gods, his voice, his eyes, the misery and the resignation coiling in Louisa's gut, and she was already shaking her head, waving it away—when Killik's dagger swivelled back toward her, dangerously close to her throat. "Truth, woman," he hissed. "Not the pretty words you ken he wishes to hear. He should far rather hear *you*, ach?"

You. Truth. Louisa winced, searched Ulfarr's wan face—but yes, yes, he was nodding again. He wanted to hear... *her.* Her truth.

Louisa's heart pattered faster, her hands gripping clammy to her knees, but she drew in a shaky breath, let it out. "W-well," she finally managed, into the choking silence. "I... I suppose I *was* quite upset when you left last night. It brought to mind a lot of things I thought—I hoped—I'd forgotten. Things I thought I should be—over, by now."

She cringed as she said it, her eyes fearful on Ulfarr's face, but he only nodded again, his swallow convulsing in his throat. "Ach, Louisa," he said, hoarse. "Me—also, I ken."

It settled something in Louisa's chest, because yes, yes, Ulfarr had his own dark past, too. And did his have to do with... women? With... this?

But Louisa shoved that question aside, and hauled in another shaky breath. Searched for her own words, her own truth. "But I still—wanted you, Ulfarr," she whispered. "I still—do. I just—I just like you very much, and find you very attractive, and"—she dragged in more air, forced out the words—"I really still want to try to make this work, for the rest of our ten nights. If you still do. And not just because of Killik helping me, but also because of—you."

Her voice sounded rushed, pleading, her eyes still frozen on Ulfarr's face. Because what if he still balked at the ten nights? At the still-lingering truth that this was just a deal Killik had made? With a time limit, and a very significant payment at the end?

And yes, Ulfarr's eyes briefly flicked to Killik, too—but then he exhaled, and met her eyes. "Ach, Louisa," he said, softer than before. "I yet long for you, also. You are so lovely, and you have shown me such kindness, and your hunger scented so... so sweet. It should grant me deep joy, to yet spend the rest of these ten nights with you."

Well. Louisa couldn't stop her sudden, weepy smile toward him, and oh, he was smiling back, too. Slow, shy, tentative, but gods, it looked good on him, warming his rugged face, flickering like that in his eyes. And when he glanced downwards, and carefully moved his hand toward hers, she willingly met it, clasping her clammy palm against his warm skin, squeezing tight.

His hand squeezed back, his shoulders sagging even lower. And Louisa couldn't seem to speak, or look away, and she was distantly grateful when Killik huffed a satisfied grunt from where he was still standing before them. And when she glanced up, he twitched an approving nod toward her—and then brought up his hand, and gave a brief, approving pat to her cheek.

And wait, his other hand was patting Ulfarr's cheek, too, his still-clutched dagger-blade swaying dangerously close to Ulfarr's eyes—but if Ulfarr noticed, he didn't seem at all concerned. If anything, he'd even tilted his head a little into Killik's touch, his eyes fluttering, his breath exhaling harsh.

"Good, both of you," Killik said firmly. "Now, how did you begin this, last eve? What eased you into this, to start?"

Louisa fought to consider that, casting her thoughts backwards, to when it had felt most... easy, the night before. Before the awkwardness, and the embarrassment, and the mess.

"Well, we... talked," she said, with a sidelong glance toward Ulfarr. "About... other things."

She didn't miss the shift of gratefulness in Ulfarr's eyes on hers, the heavy exhale as he twitched a nod. While before them, Killik gave an exasperated sigh, and again waved his dagger back and forth between them. "Then speak," he snapped. "Of more... *other things*. For the love of Skai-kesh."

Right. Louisa drew down another breath, let it out shaky and slow. "Well," she said, too quickly. "Um. What... what kinds of things do you enjoy, Ulfarr? How do you like to spend your spare time?"

It came out sounding high-pitched, wholly artificial, and she belatedly winced up toward Killik, who might not approve of her asking such personal questions, especially if they might risk touching upon the forbidden topic of Ulfarr's past. But thankfully, Killik didn't seem disconcerted, and he'd swung his imperious dagger back toward Ulfarr, waiting for his answer.

But for an instant, Ulfarr looked—blank. Confused. As if the concept of enjoying something, liking something, was almost too foreign to grasp. But Louisa could see him dragging in breath too, filling his huge chest, as he rubbed his free hand at his sweaty forehead.

"Ach, I—I ken I work to serve and help my kin, and my—my son," he replied, his voice stilted. "With much—sparring. Scouting. Teaching. Hunting. Fighting."

It all sounded heavy in his voice, weighing down his big shoulders, and Louisa sought her way through it, fought to find some kind of answer. "Um, well, I've been learning to hunt lately, too," she said, as steadily as she could. "But it certainly isn't easy, even with small game. Just this afternoon,

I almost managed to get sprayed by a skunk! I bet you *really* would have enjoyed coming back here again, after that."

She attempted a rueful smile at Ulfarr's face, and was rewarded by a twitch of amusement—or maybe even interest—in his dark eyes. "What do you hunt with?" he asked, and that might have been genuine interest in his voice, too. "A bow? Or blades?"

Louisa let out another breath, her smile coming easier this time. "I make attempts with both," she replied, "but I'm sure they're probably quite ramshackle, compared to what you likely use."

She aimed a wry glance toward Killik's bright, gleaming dagger, which was now pointed toward her face—but wait, Killik himself had leaned down over her, and plucked something off her belt. Something—oh. Her knife, which she'd entirely forgotten she was still wearing, until this moment.

"This is not bad, woman," Killik said, assessing the knife with a critical eye, before silently holding it out toward Ulfarr. Who carefully released Louisa's hand, and then proceeded to inspect the knife with surprising care. Balancing it on his palm, spinning it in his fingers, and even taking his time smelling it, before dragging a black claw down the sharp edge.

"Ach, it has a good heft and balance," Ulfarr said, with a nod toward Louisa. "And it scents of many kills, which speaks to your skill. I ken it only needs sharpening, to better serve you."

Really? Louisa's smile back toward him felt genuine, even grateful—and her hand found his again, giving it an impulsive squeeze. But Ulfarr's warm fingers willingly curled around hers, his eyes soft on her face. Looking almost appreciative, almost... hungry, and above them Killik snorted, and snatched Louisa's knife back out of Ulfarr's slack hand.

"Ach, this does need sharpening," he said coolly, as he went and picked up his chair, and brought it back to set beside the bed. "And thus, I shall sit and play with your weapon, woman, if"—he flashed her a smug smile as he dropped onto the chair—"you now play with *his*."

Wait. Wait, he meant *Ulfarr*, he wanted Louisa to play with Ulfarr's *weapon*—and curse her, but Louisa's mouth twitched, her eyes darting amused to Ulfarr's face. To where he almost, *almost* smiled back, even as that familiar unease simmered through his eyes. Instantly calling up the bitter memories of the night before, of all that painful awkwardness, of how he'd jumped up and left...

But he was still here with her, still clasping her hand, and Killik was still here, too. His presence still strangely reassuring, even as he leaned back in his chair, and began tossing what appeared to be a small whetstone in his hand.

"Did you not hear me, woman?" he demanded at Louisa, his brows imperiously raised. "Lie him down, and take out his prick. With *care*."

The hunger bloomed sharp and sudden in Louisa's belly, tinged with rising alarm—but Killik kept gazing at her like that, waiting. Wanting her to turn toward Ulfarr, to nudge his shoulder with a trembling hand...

And yes, yes, Ulfarr exhaled, nodded, and... obliged. Sinking down heavy to lie on his back on the bed, even as his eyes stayed dark and uneasy on Louisa's face.

The memories of the night before again felt too close, too strong—and Louisa couldn't help an anxious look downwards, toward where there wasn't even the slightest bulge in Ulfarr's trousers. But Killik cleared his throat, loud and meaningful, and when Louisa glanced up, he was glowering at her, and jabbing her own knife toward her face.

"With *care*," he snapped again, harder this time. "You must be tender with his prick, and patient. You must treat it as the sweet Skai prize it is."

Louisa twitched a nod, and darted a brief, searching glance toward Ulfarr's face—toward where his cheeks were flushed, his mouth tight, his eyes flicking nervously between her and Killik. As if he still expected her to refuse, or reject him, or maybe... maybe even mock him.

So Louisa squared her shoulders, and attempted another smile as she dropped her shaky hand to Ulfarr's trousers. "I—I'll try," she said, as she tugged at the thick chain of his belt with tingling, twitching fingers. "But please do tell me if I—"

She'd loosened the chain, and gently drew it aside, pulling the front of Ulfarr's trousers open. Revealing the sight of his scarred grey lower belly, the thickening spread of black hair, and then... his bare, exposed cock.

It was surprisingly small and stubby, lying soft and slack against his hip. But it wasn't the size that caught Louisa's breath, or set her hands spasming against his trousers.

It was... the scars.

15

Louisa had never seen scars like this in her life. Masses of white and black and green, mottled and latticed, spread all over that soft swell of skin.

But deepest of all, cut straight across Ulfarr's base, was a thick, gouging line, with multiple more lines and breaks fraying off from it. As though...

As though someone had tried to *cut it off*. As though he had almost been... *skinned*.

"W-what happened?!" Louisa's breathless voice choked, before she could possibly stop it. "This wasn't done—on *purpose*?!"

Ulfarr flinched, jolted, as if about to lurch upwards, away, out of the bed entirely—but wait, Killik jerked forward, too. His eyes narrowing sharply on Louisa's face, as his hand snapped out, and clutched at Ulfarr's *neck*. Circling it with astonishing ease, as if to hold him there on the bed, to trap him in place. To make him stay.

And Ulfarr... didn't fight it. Didn't resist. And instead, he seemed to relax beneath it, his eyes squeezing shut, his big body sagging back into the bed.

"These are old wounds," Killik said to Louisa, his eyes

flashing, his voice curt. "And there is naught you need to ask about them, beyond how best to handle him, and avoid bringing him pain. Ach?"

The questions kept swirling through Louisa's frantic thoughts—what the hell had happened to Ulfarr? Who the hell had done such a thing? And surely it was related to his mysterious past, too?

But she was already wincing and nodding, silently pleading her apology to Killik's narrow eyes. To which Killik jerked a nod back, and then released Ulfarr's neck. "Now, try this again, woman," he snapped. "*Gently.*"

Right. Louisa shot Ulfarr an apologetic look he couldn't see—his eyes were still tightly closed—and lowered her shaky hand back toward that slack, scarred cock. Looking somehow even smaller than before, more wounded, more defenseless—and it was only Killik's flinty, waiting glare that finally brought Louisa's fingers closer, closer. Until they finally, briefly touched, brushing light and tentative against that soft, marred skin.

Nothing happened, not even a twitch, and Louisa shot another helpless glance toward Killik's face—but he was still waiting, watching, his hand now stroking against Ulfarr's stiff, corded neck. "Ach, thus," he said, clipped. "It is sweet to the touch, is it not?"

The warning flashed again in his eyes, and Louisa fervently nodded, shot another chagrined look toward Ulfarr's still-closed eyes. "Y-yes," she stammered, as she brushed that soft skin again. "Very smooth. Warm. Like touching—silk. Or velvet."

Killik's eyes shifted, his glower slightly softening, as he kept stroking Ulfarr's taut throat. "Ach, just thus," he said, steady. "It is even sweeter when you pet it, or hold it in your hand."

It was a hint—an order—and Louisa carefully obeyed, as slowly and gently as she could. Circling her trembling fingers around that soft nub, lifting it up, enclosing it fully inside. Fighting not to marvel at the difference in it, compared to that huge stone she'd taken inside her, and instead just focusing on the sensation of it, the truth of it. Of this huge, handsome, powerful orc, lying silent and exposed in her bed, allowing her this touch, this vulnerability. This... gift.

And it was a gift, her swirling thoughts pointed out, as she softly stroked her thumb against the warm, velvety flesh in her hand. It was a sign of Ulfarr's trust in her. His willingness to face this with her, to show her his own truth, amidst his own fears and darkness. Allowing her to caress him, to care for him, to hold and handle him, do whatever she wished with him...

"Good, ach?" came Killik's voice, and when Louisa glanced toward him, his disapproval had fully faded, his eyes sliding lazy and half-lidded between Louisa's hand, and her hot-feeling face. "He pleases you, does he not?"

Louisa rapidly nodded, licking her tongue at her dry-feeling lips. "Y-yes," she choked again. "Very much."

Killik's mouth curled up, and his eyes flared with satisfaction, or even triumph. And only then did Louisa realize that Ulfarr's eyes had opened again, too, staring at her with blank, dazed disbelief, while Killik's hand kept caressing at his throat.

"Good," Killik said, his voice low and liquid in the taut, heated silence. "Both of you. Now, woman, mayhap you should wish to bare the rest of him, and learn it, also?"

Louisa's breath shuddered from her lungs, so thick that she almost didn't catch Ulfarr's breath shuddering out, too. But his wide, expressive eyes were bright and searching on hers, as if longing, begging for her answer.

"Yes," she whispered to him, truth, truth. "I'd be so honoured. If you'd like it too, sweetheart."

And oh, the way Ulfarr shivered all over as he nodded, his sharp tooth biting his lip, the longing flashing in his eyes.

The sight of it spearing yet more craving into Louisa's belly, her breath, and her fingers shook as she reached for the hem of his tunic, and tentatively slid it upwards.

But Ulfarr was helping her now, his warm hands skittering against hers, guiding the tunic up and off over his head, and into Killik's waiting hand. And when Killik waved Louisa toward Ulfarr's boots and trousers, Ulfarr helped her with those too, first bending up to kick his soft black boots off his huge feet, and then lying back, lifting his hips, so Louisa could pull off the trousers, too. Leaving him lying there fully naked on the bed, his huge, powerful body utterly exposed to her hungry, searching eyes.

Gods, he was gorgeous. Despite all the vicious scars, he was so broad, so well-built, his skin so smooth, the muscles so taut and ready beneath it. Even the hair all over him was lovely too, its thick black threaded with silver, most of all across his chest. And oh, the way he was looking at her, both fearful and hopeful, as if he wanted her to approve, wanted her to want him...

"Even better, ach, woman?" came Killik's cool voice, even as he leaned back in his chair again, propping his booted foot on the bed, and then began casually sharpening Louisa's knife against the whetstone. "You like?"

Louisa twitched a fervent nod, her greedy eyes still running up and down Ulfarr's bared body, as heat pooled low in her belly. And Killik laughed, husky and only a little mocking, as he nudged her with his own soft black boot, and waved her knife back at Ulfarr.

"Then keep touching him," he ordered. "Show him."

It suddenly seemed deeply bizarre, or even profoundly unfair, what with Killik and Louisa both still dressed, and Ulfarr fully naked on the bed. But Ulfarr's eyes on hers were still so hungry, so pleading—and Louisa could only nod, yes, please, as she shifted closer, and spread her hands against the warm, smooth skin of his chest. Feeling it twitch and shiver as his breath exhaled, his eyes fluttering closed, his head tilting back with unmistakable pleasure. Wanting more. Wanting *her*.

And with every tentative touch, Louisa's own hunger hitched higher, too. He was so beautiful, so warm, so responsive. So lovely to touch, to caress, to learn. And it felt so good, so damned good, to stroke over that smooth skin of his broad shoulders, his bulky arms, his solid chest and softer belly. And then back to that scarred, soft bulge at his groin, still just the perfect size to fit in Louisa's hungry fingers.

"Is this—all right?" she croaked at him, as she circled her shaky fingers around his heavy bollocks, even as her other hand kept gently caressing his warm, velvety cock. "It isn't—painful?"

Her voice sounded far too loud in the hushed, heated silence, as if she'd broken a spell—and beneath her, Ulfarr's big body spasmed, his eyes snapping open. And for a breath, he looked disoriented, alarmed, almost panicked. His gaze darting between her and Killik, and then widening on the sight of Louisa's hands, fully enclosing his cock and bollocks in her careful caressing fingers.

"N-no new pain, thus," he gulped, between heavy breaths. "B-but ach, woman, you ought—I ought—ought to touch *you*. Taste *you*. Grant you a strong Skai—"

His chagrined eyes held to his groin again, as misery spasmed across his rapidly reddening face. His mouth contorting, his head shaking, no, no—but Louisa couldn't find words, her body frozen, her eyes darting toward—

Killik. Killik, already snapping forward in his chair, his eyes intent on Ulfarr's flushed face. "Not now, Wolf," he said, low. "I can scent how deeply it pleases her, to touch you and see you thus. You should not wish to cease offering her this, or bringing her such joy, ach?"

Ulfarr's uneasy gaze flicked to Louisa's hot face, to where she was desperately drawing down air, and still fighting to find her voice. And now Killik was looking at her too, his eyes flinty and assessing, his mouth curling into a chilly smile. "And for her next lesson," he drawled, "I ken she wishes to taste you, ach?"

To taste him. Louisa gasped, just as Ulfarr groaned, his eyes again wide and uncertain on hers—while beside them, Killik just kept smiling, placid and satisfied. "Ach, woman?" he asked coolly. "You wish to kiss my wolf's sweet prick, and taste his good Skai seed?"

Louisa's heart skipped a beat, but she was already nodding, yes, *yes*. And with a jolting movement, she bent lower over Ulfarr, curling her fingers closer around that soft bulging warmth, breathing in the hot scent of sweetness, her watering mouth hovering over his scarred skin—

And then she pressed a quiet, careful kiss to the tip of it.

And oh, oh, she was tasting him. Tasting an *orc*. And fuck, he tasted just as sweet as he smelled, and his low, rumbling moan was even more staggering sweetness, pooling more hungry heat to her groin...

And maybe—maybe—also... to his. Because in Louisa's careful fingers, he... shuddered. Spasmed. Almost as if... responding to this. Wanting this.

Oh, hell. Louisa's groan choked from her mouth, and she bent lower again, pressed another soft kiss against him. Lingering longer this time, while he again shuddered and swelled—and this time, that was a brief spurt of sweetness, spreading warm and liquid against her kissing lips. And when Louisa's tentative tongue sought a little deeper, sought the source of it, there was another spurt, and another. Squeezing out with every swelling shudder, wanting to give this to her, oh gods—

"Good, Wolf," Killik murmured, hot and husky. "Feel this woman kissing you, as she should. Scent how hungry she is. See how she longs to suck out your strong Skai seed."

Ulfarr moaned again, his hips slightly bucking, as he

shuddered even fuller between Louisa's lips, and spurted out more hot sweetness into her mouth. And then more, and more, because she was just sucking him now, caressing him with her lips and tongue...

And in return, he kept growing longer, thicker, harder. As if kissing her back, oh gods, swiping his slick sweetness against her lips, while also expanding within her hand's grip, stretching her fingers apart. Until they weren't even touching around the width of him, and Louisa drew back to look at it, licking at her sweet-tasting lips, as the soft scarred skin at its head slowly, smoothly peeled back. Exposing the fullness of his glossy grey crown, with its deep-cut slit, and yet more visible scars scattered across it.

Damn. It still wasn't quite as large or rigid as that huge stone she'd used, but it was warm, quivering, alive. And its scarred skin was still so soft, sliding so smooth beneath her tentative stroking fingers, and now she could see that thick white sweetness, oozing out from within that cleft. Growing into a shining bead of white, larger and larger, until it slipped downwards, drawing a streak of smooth liquid over all those messy scars. And Louisa's exhale sounded more like a groan, her tongue again brushing at her lips.

"Do not waste it, woman," came Killik's low hiss. "Drink what my wolf grants you."

Yes, please, and Louisa's glance toward Killik was almost grateful as she again bent low, and began... licking. Tasting. Messier and hungrier than before, trying to catch that sweetness, to lick that scarred shuddering shaft clean all over—but more just kept coming, streaking down all sides of him, coating him in slippery white. Until finally Louisa just swerved back up to the source of it, sucking in that huge pulsing head as deep as she could, but there was no way she could take him any further, it was too much, please...

"Use your hand to pump the rest of him, and milk out more to drink," Killik's voice ordered. "*Gently.*"

Louisa groaned and nodded as she obeyed, pumping him up and down, darting a furtive look upwards. Finding Killik still watching this with glittering eyes, while Ulfarr openly gaped at her, his eyes blown wide with awestruck disbelief. His groan now a low steady rumble, vibrating through his huge chest, and Louisa might have even smiled—or tried to smile—as she gave him another slow, soft, messy kiss, her tongue twining and twisting against him.

His groan broke, his eyes furiously fluttering, so Louisa kept kissing, kept lavishing him, adoring him. Scarcely noticing as Killik's hand shifted downwards, reaching toward Ulfarr's knee, guiding it lower, sideways—until that knee slipped up between Louisa's own trembling thighs. Grinding up broad and powerful against her, oh, just where she most craved it, and she couldn't bite back her gasp, or her shocked, chagrined glare at Killik's smug face.

"Better," Killik said coolly. "Ach, Wolf?"

Ulfarr only groaned again, his body arching as his thigh ground up harder, and Louisa met it, pressed shaky against it, as her watering mouth again found that hard, scarred, leaking head, and sucked it. Revelling in its rich spurting sweetness, its hungry shudders against her tongue, and the truth of Ulfarr writhing and bucking beneath her, his groans harsh and deep. All of it flooding Louisa's senses at once, pouring her full of need, grinding her shamelessly against that big solid thigh. But she couldn't stop, please, and her pleading glance toward Killik found him still intently watching, his brows raised, his knife making a slow circle that meant, *more.*

Yes, Louisa wanted more, needed more, sucking that sweet leaking crown further into her mouth, slipping her tongue even deeper against its slit. While Ulfarr's moans wrenched higher, his head tipping back, his huge fists straining against the bed—and Killik's eyes swept up and down the full length of him, his own hand surreptitiously adjusting his trousers, as he again circled his knife at Louisa. Meaning, *Do it again. More.*

Louisa obeyed, making Ulfarr cry out this time, and it was so much, too much, swaying and weaving through her wheeling thoughts, flooding her mouth and her breath. She was sucking an orc, she had an orc in her mouth, he was huge and powerful and beautiful and he was here, hers, in her bed, in her mouth, in her hands, in her thrall.

And there was nothing, *nothing* like this, nothing she'd ever imagined in all her years, the pleasure and the power coiling, coalescing, his thigh grinding and his cock swelling and his moans rising and rising, flooding even the air with his sweet, stunning surrender. While Killik just kept watching, kept circling that knife, his eyes glinting with command, with satisfaction, with bright, feral glee—

"Swallow all my wolf gives you," he ordered, low. "Do not waste a drop, woman."

And wait, did he mean—but yes, Ulfarr's groans sharpened into a deep, dizzying shout, his bollocks tightening, his huge body rigid all over. And with one last, jolting jerk, he bucked up, and—broke. Thrashing and howling as spurts of hot, succulent sweetness poured into Louisa's mouth, surging and swarming her in a fierce flooding rush. And how could there possibly be so much, so full—and she had to slurp and gulp to keep it in, to swallow, to drag it down, while her helpless, desperate moans choked out around it.

Oh, he was so good. So sweet. Giving her all of this, offering it up to her so freely, and there was nothing like this, no pleasure like this, so strong she was trembling all over, hitching hard against his thigh, his warmth, his—

Her own release smashed through her like a hammer, hurling out blasts of battering bliss again and again. So stunning that Louisa didn't care if she was shouting, or brazenly rutting on Ulfarr's thigh, or if her dress had somehow slipped up, so he could surely feel her slick, starving body clutching and spasming against him. And she didn't even care if Killik was still watching, his eyes dark and blazing, his fingers tight and pale against the knife...

But then Killik lurched to his feet. Moved—toward Ulfarr. And there was a flash of his hand, shoving down his own trousers, showing a brief glimpse of a long, scarred grey shaft—and then he grasped a handful of Ulfarr's hair, yanked his head up and sideways, and...

And plunged himself deep into Ulfarr's *throat*.

Louisa froze, staring, her heart kicking in her chest, her mouth slackening around—around where Ulfarr was still in her mouth, oh gods. He was still in her mouth, his spurting spasms finally slowing, even as Killik gouged into his own throat—and oh, Ulfarr was visibly sucking Killik, working him with his lips and tongue, his eyes fluttering closed, as another low moan rumbled through his huge, trembling body. As if... as if he liked this. He wanted this. He wanted... *Killik.*

And oh, Killik let out a low hiss as his head tilted back, his claws scraping red marks against Ulfarr's sweaty neck— and Louisa could feel Ulfarr's cock swelling again, squeezing out more hot fluid between her lips, as his own throat audibly, rhythmically gulped, swallowing all Killik was giving him. And it was so much, it was still happening, what was Killik doing, what the hell was this—

And gods, what the hell had Louisa just done? She'd sucked off an orc and gotten herself off on his damned *thigh*, and now he wanted—this?

Too late, she squeezed her eyes shut, and lurched backwards, off, away. Wiping her shaky hand at her swollen lips, her stupidly leaking eyes, fighting to ignore the bitter, miserable plunge in her gut. Ulfarr wanted Killik, not her, and now—now—

Now something—grasped her arm. Something that made her flinch and flare up, her heart screeching, until—

Oh. Ulfarr. But he was already wincing, drawing backwards, dropping his hand. And the dazed, hungry look in his eyes had entirely vanished, snapped back to—fear. To alarm. To sheer, searching panic.

"For-forgive me, Louisa," he gulped, hoarse. "I did not wish to—displease you, or disappoint you. This was—such a great, great gift to me, and if there is aught I could do to—to return this, or show you the depth of my—my—"

Oh, gods, oh no, he was struggling for air, he was breathing hard, as if he was about to weep. "P-please," he gasped. "Please do not—send me away, or my kin, for my failing. I have no intent, I had no intent, cannot bear to bring more shame, more harm, more blood and wrath and death, I am—"

No, no, it didn't even make sense, it was as though he wasn't even seeing her, his eyes wild and glazed, the whites of them visible all around. "Please," he gulped. "Please, I am sorry, I—"

But Louisa couldn't bear another moment of it, no—and she shook her head as she lurched back toward him, and grasped his hand tightly in hers.

"N-no need, sweetheart," she rasped, before she could stop it. "Nothing to worry about at all. I was just a little—overwhelmed. Not used to having such a lovely, handsome orc in my bed, is all."

Ulfarr blinked back at her, as vivid disbelief flared through his wide panicked eyes—and fuck, maybe Louisa was still lying, maybe he could scent it, and she squeezed his big hand tighter, brought it to her lips. "This was wonderful," she choked, and she meant it. "You were wonderful. The sweetest, most stunning lover I've ever had in my life."

The disbelief kept shifting in Ulfarr's staring eyes, but with it was something new, something with less panic in it, so Louisa kissed his hand again, and fought to draw up a true, genuine smile. "You're beautiful, sweetheart," she whispered.

"Absolutely beautiful. I'm so glad you came back here tonight."

Ulfarr kept blinking at her, unmoving, now looking almost stunned, or confused—and Louisa smiled again, kissed his hand again. "Now, how do you like to relax afterwards," she managed. "Are you one of those men—er, orcs—who needs a pipe? A snack? A raid in the kitchen?"

But Ulfarr just kept blinking at her, churning up more frantic, anxious unease in her belly—was he overwhelmed, unhappy, unwell? And Louisa couldn't stop her half-pleading, half-accusing glance up at Killik—fucking Killik—who was now just standing there like a useless slug, and staring at her, too. With his trousers still sagging around his arse, and his own slack, scarred grey cock hanging brazenly out the front, still wet from Ulfarr's mouth.

But then he twitched all over, and yanked up his trousers with a jerky hand. And he shot Louisa a look she couldn't at all read as he sank down to sit on the bed beside Ulfarr, and his hand—now with its claws somehow drawn in—reached to spread against Ulfarr's heaving bare chest, and gently stroked down it.

"He likes best to be petted, ach, Wolf?" Killik said, his voice clipped. "To be cared for, and tended to, with sweet words and touches."

Louisa blinked, her eyes darting back to Ulfarr's face, to where he still looked stunned, dazed, and maybe—maybe even ashamed. As if an orc wasn't supposed to want to be petted, or to need care or comforting, even as his big body—which was still sitting up—visibly tilted into Killik's touch.

"How fortunate, sweetheart," Louisa managed, with another smile toward him. "Because that's just what I'd love to do to you next. If you're willing, that is."

But oh, Ulfarr was already nodding, jerking his head with surprising intensity, even as his eyes stayed dazed and disbelieving on hers. And Killik's other hand slid to his shoulder, guiding him downward, until he was lying on his back on the bed between them, his eyes darting from Louisa, to Killik, and back again.

"Good, sweetheart," Louisa murmured, and her hand joined Killik's on his heaving, sweaty chest, caressing him with as much steadiness as she could muster. "Does this feel all right?"

Ulfarr's nod was again rapid and fervent, his gaze flicking faster between them, and Killik made a low shushing sound, and slipped up his hand to pat Ulfarr's cheek. "Good, Wolf," he said. "This was all so good, ach? You have brought this woman much joy, this night."

Louisa nodded, smiling, still stroking Ulfarr's hot chest, feeling the thud of his heartbeat beneath it. "So much joy," she breathed. "So good. So sweet."

Ulfarr's eyes looked so dazed now, like he was lost in a dream, but the tension in his mouth had softened, his expression gone almost reverent, or even worshipful. And Louisa could have wept with her relief, and she swallowed, and bent down to press a brief, careful kiss to his hard cheek. "So lovely, sweetheart," she whispered. "And you'll come back again soon, won't you?"

Ulfarr's nod was slower this time, his eyes shining on hers, and Killik's hand slid up into his silver-streaked hair, his fingers threading slowly through it. Doing it again and again, gentle and deliberate, until Ulfarr's eyes had begun to flutter closed, and his hand groped up to grasp to Killik's other wrist. And Killik grasped back, his other hand still caressing, as Louisa kept stroking his broad chest, feeling his breaths steadily deepening, his heartbeat thudding slower, slower.

Ulfarr's eyes finally fluttered closed, his breath drawing in—and then exhaling in a faint, telltale snore. And Louisa could almost feel Killik's sudden, sinking relief, his shoulders sagging, his hand dropping from Ulfarr's hair.

"He shall be himself again when he awakens," he said, quiet and curt. "I should be grateful if you could then seek to set him at ease, and send him home."

He didn't wait for Louisa's answer, and instead lurched to his feet, and stalked toward the window. As if—as if he was going to leave, just like that. And too late, Louisa leapt up after him, scrambling over Ulfarr, who still—thank the gods—seemed to be fast asleep.

"Wait!" she hissed at Killik. "You can't just—leave! Not without—"

She broke off there, clamping her mouth shut, because what the hell did she even want from him? But curse it, Killik had already spun around to face her, his lip curling, his hand still clutching her knife. "What, must I now pet *you* to sleep also?" he snarled. "Must I offer you both my wolf, *and* my pride?"

Louisa recoiled, blinking wide-eyed toward him—and then she whipped her head back and forth, her hands tightening at her sides. "*You* were the one who wanted this, you prick!" she shot back. "And you could have damn well told me about—"

Her voice caught, her eyes darting toward Ulfarr's sleeping body in the bed, and before her, Killik gave a low, dangerous growl. "I told you all you needed to know, woman," he hissed. "I told you he is oft not himself. I told you he has faced deep darkness, and is oft empty and fearful and alone. And I told you, *just yesterday*"—his lip curled higher—"that I feared for him. And that women hold much power for him! What more do you wish from me!"

Louisa's mouth opened and closed, her heart kicking erratically in her chest, tangling with a strange, hurtling misery. "Well," she gulped, "maybe you could have told me that you had no intention whatsoever of keeping your promise not to touch him! And that you'd be sure to jump in at the most pivotal moment, and remind us all who's really in charge! And who your wolf *really* wants!"

Her voice shamefully hitched, catching on something much like a sob, and for an instant, Killik stared at her, his eyes blazing—and then he barked a dark, furious laugh, jabbing her sharpened knife toward her. "If you ken," he hissed, low and deadly, "he did not want you, you are far greater a fool than I thought! I have never scented him thus, in all my days, and I ken this has mayhap *ruined* him for all I might offer him!"

Louisa stared at him, and then jerked a wild shake of her head. "Oh fuck off, you snake," she snarled. "He sure as hell wanted you, too. He wanted you sitting there watching him, and touching him, and telling him what to do! He was *nothing* like this yesterday, without you!"

And wait, why was she even giving Killik this, giving him this damned power over her, that flash of bitter satisfaction in his eyes. "Ach, you speak this, woman," he drawled, "but here you yet seek to forbid me from touching him! You wish to deny him this!"

And to deny *Killik* this, was his clear meaning, and Louisa scoffed, too loud and mocking. "I'm not denying him anything," she shot back. "*You're* the one who's still running around welcoming all and sundry into your bed! And whether you like it or not, *I'm* allowed to have a boundary that I don't want them all in *mine*! And I told you that from the beginning, and yet *you* still wanted to proceed, so how the hell is that *my* fault?"

Killik's growl had kept rising as she'd spoken, his lean body almost vibrating with rage. "Eight—more—nights, woman," he rasped, punctuating each word with a jab of the knife, dangerously close to Louisa's face. "For eight more nights, I shall honour this, and deny Wolf my touch and my comfort and my seed. But after this"—he bared his teeth—"I shall be gladly free of you for the rest of my days, and shall never set eyes upon you *again!*"

Oh. It felt like he'd hurled that knife straight into her heart, like he'd taken all that dizzying warmth and pleasure and smashed it before her eyes. And why couldn't she breathe, why was her chest crumpling like this, she couldn't weep before him, she couldn't...

"I'm sure that will be lovely for us both," she somehow managed, through her too-thin breaths. "Now get the fuck out of my house."

There was an instant's dangling stillness, a spasm in Killik's throat—and then a laugh, low and vicious, as he spun on his heel, and strode to the window.

"With joy," he snarled, without looking at her. "And if you dare touch my wolf again this night"—a low, vicious hiss in the darkness—"it shall be to your doom."

16

It was another night of broken, miserable sleep. With Louisa lying stiff and fully clothed on the edge of her bed, as far away from Ulfarr's unconscious body as she could possibly get.

Killik had... threatened her. He'd hissed and growled at her. He'd jabbed at her with her own damned knife.

And while part of Louisa wanted to rage and weep, another part of her just felt cold, and resigned, and empty. This had been... foolish. So foolish. Another foolish, selfish decision from a lonely, desperate widow. Seeking a way to escape Lord Scall, and thereby locking herself into a bargain with another devil instead. A devil who wasn't only cold and mocking, but genuinely, viciously dangerous.

If you dare touch my wolf again this night, it shall be to your doom.

Louisa's heart skipped at even the thought of it, and she edged further away from Ulfarr, her eyes blinking on his shadowed, sleeping face. His face that somehow looked even more handsome, more vulnerable, in the guttering light of the lamp. His grey skin so scarred, his black lashes thick against his hard cheeks, his mouth drawn downwards, hinting at sadness even in rest.

And for a breath, Louisa desperately wanted to reach out, to touch him, to curl up close and quiet against him. To again taste even a whisper of how she'd felt, in the midst of all that. So... safe. So right. So... at peace.

But no. No. That would risk all of Killik's wrath, and ruin all that hope for her future. And gods, should she even be hoping for her future anymore? Because Killik had shown her tonight how deep his promises went, right? And should she back out now? Should she take the loss and run, and never see them again?

She didn't know how long she stayed there, breathing too hard, blinking at Ulfarr's sad face in the darkness. But she must have fallen asleep at some point, because when next she jolted awake, it was to the shift of Ulfarr's big body twitching up in the bed, his breath audibly catching in his throat.

Louisa's eyes snapped open, blinking in the faint morning light from the window, and for an instant, she could only seem to stare at Ulfarr, as he stared back. His eyes shifting first with confusion, and then disbelief—and then a rapidly rising alarm, as he glanced around the room. "Where am—" he croaked, and then he squeezed his eyes shut, shook his head. "Where—where is Killik?"

Right. Of course. He still wanted Killik too, just as Killik wanted him, and Louisa had to fight for air, shove back the memory of Killik snarling at her, pointing her own knife in her face. "He—left last night," she replied, as steadily as she could. "He wanted to let you sleep, I think. But he asked me to send you along after him, once you awoke."

There was another instant's silence, and then Ulfarr nodded, and heaved to his feet. Giving Louisa a sudden, shocking view of his broad scarred back, his firm rounded arse—and then just a shadow of bulky, hanging bollocks between his hairy thighs as he bent to swipe for his trousers. Yanking them on with sharp, shaky movements, and then doing the same with his tunic, before kneeling and pulling on those soft black boots.

Only then did he glance back at Louisa in the bed, something again shifting in his eyes—and she couldn't tell if it was unease, or urgency, or maybe even regret. Or maybe he was waiting for her to say something, to ask him to stay, or come back again—but Louisa couldn't find a single word to speak. And now he was looking away, looking at the door. As if he wanted to leave, of course he wanted to leave, he couldn't just *leave*—

"I can—walk you out, if you like," Louisa managed, her voice a rasp. "Just in case you—run into someone."

And gods, why hadn't she thought of that sooner? Ulfarr should have gone while it was still dark, while there was no risk of him being seen. And she could see that same awareness passing across his eyes, his mouth thinning to a grim line as he nodded.

So Louisa clambered out of bed too, smoothing down her rumpled dress with shaky hands, and then staggering for the door. Waving Ulfarr out ahead of her, and he instantly went, his shoulders stiff, his gaze held straight ahead. And though his steps were almost silent, the narrow stairs still loudly creaked under his weight, making Louisa wince with every step—but thank the gods, there was no sign of movement downstairs, no trace of her staff or the children. And once they stepped outside, Ulfarr gave a heavy exhale, his body sagging in the orange light of the rising sun.

"I... thank you, Louisa," he said, quiet, with a brief, searching glance toward her. "It was a true honour to spend this night with you."

Oh. Some of the tension untwisted from Louisa's belly, and she nodded, and twitched a wan smile toward him. "You too, sweetheart," she replied, choked. "I had such a lovely time."

She meant it, meant it so much it ached, and there was a sudden, foolish compulsion to lurch toward him, to embrace him, or clasp his hand, or press a kiss to his cheek. But Killik had said no touching, and he'd maybe even threatened to kill her. And she should be telling Ulfarr she couldn't see him again, it was too dangerous, that would be the safe, logical thing to do...

But she could only seem to stand there blinking at him, her hands now tightly clasped together. Waiting, not breathing, not weeping, as Ulfarr finally nodded, and turned and strode away. His steps still lurching, his shoulders hunching, as if he didn't want to leave, either.

Louisa watched him go in stiff, miserable silence, her nose slightly sniffling with her breaths—and only once Ulfarr was halfway down the lane did she notice the unmistakable silhouette of Joan, standing in the stable door. Watching Ulfarr leave the house, gods damn it, while Louisa—she shot a mortified glance downwards—was horribly rumpled, and still wearing yesterday's dress, her hair surely a frizzy, highly betraying mess.

Louisa cursed under her breath, and she knew she should go straight over to Joan, and attempt some explanation, some excuse. But there was only more cold, tired resignation, a dull ache behind her eyes. She didn't want to lie to Joan. She didn't want to pretend they weren't all in danger. She didn't want to acknowledge how foolish she'd been. She couldn't bear to even think of how she'd touched Ulfarr, praised him, how desperately she'd wanted him, rutting wild and shameless upon him.

So instead of speaking to Joan, like any decent employer should, Louisa covered her eyes with a shaky hand, and ducked back inside, toward where she kept her bow. She could go hunting, she could get some air, some space, try to think, to work through this mess. And then she would come back, and talk to Joan, and make some kind of decision...

But even that plan instantly proved fraught, because once Louisa had slung the bow over her shoulder, and gripped at her belt for her knife, she discovered—her knife was gone. Her knife, that Killik had sharpened last night, and waved around, and used to threaten her... and then he'd left. He'd left, and he'd taken her damned knife with him.

Louisa could have screamed with frustration, but instead she gritted her teeth, and swiped for a far inferior, rust-streaked old blade the gardener had used for pruning. And then she stomped out into the forest, her eyes still stinging, her head pounding louder with every step.

What had she done. What was she supposed to do.

Even the fresh air didn't help, or the morning quiet, or the usually soothing sight of thick greenery all around. And if there was any game to hunt, Louisa couldn't find it through her blinking eyes, her choked gasps, her racing heartbeat. And her screaming thoughts only swirled faster, harsher, because there was no good answer, there was never a good answer, why was nothing ever easy...

"Louisa!" cut in a voice, a sharp, scraping, horribly familiar voice. "I need to speak with you!"

Louisa spun around so fast she staggered, her rusty knife wavering in midair before her. Her bleary eyes fighting to see, to focus on—

Lord Rikard. Here. Standing here in Louisa's woods, on her property, and glowering triumphantly toward her.

Louisa's stomach plunged, and for an instant she could only stare at him, her mouth opening and closing, as her heart blared even louder in her chest. What the hell. What the fuck was this creeping cretin doing here, again?

"What the hell, Rikard," she croaked. "I told you to stay off my property!"

Rikard's smile didn't falter, his beady eyes glinting with

vicious, satisfied glee. "It won't be your property much longer, Louisa," he shot back. "I went to see Bycroft the other day, and he told me you're deep in arrears, and if you don't sell soon, you're bound to be foreclosed!"

What? Louisa's sluggish brain skipped backwards, back to her own recent meetings with her banker. But yes, she'd only given him Killik's coin yesterday—and at that first meeting a few days ago, Bycroft *had* told her to sell, or to accept Rikard's generous offer of marriage. And damn it, he'd probably thought he was doing Louisa a favour by telling Rikard of her struggles, and gods spare her from vile meddling males, who couldn't leave her the hell alone for a single damned morning.

"Bycroft has no right to speak to you about my personal affairs," Louisa belatedly replied, her voice clipped. "Especially when I very clearly told him I wasn't going anywhere, or selling anything. This is *my* land, and I fully intend to keep it!"

But Rikard shook his head, his beady eyes narrowing. "You won't," he snarled. "You can't concoct funds out of nowhere, Louisa. It's about time for you to accept your situation—and if you were wise, you'd now be begging me to re-extend my very generous offer to you!"

To re-extend his offer. His offer of marriage, he meant. The very thought striking like a sickening punch to Louisa's gut, and for a brief, dizzying breath, there was only—Ulfarr. Ulfarr, gasping and straining on her bed, grinding his thigh between Louisa's legs, watching her with such raw, reverent awe in his eyes. And after that, even the thought of Rikard touching her, kissing her with that wet little mouth, it was— it was—

"No," Louisa choked, over the bile surging in her throat. "No, Rikard. I won't."

Even saying it was a relief, a staggering certainty in her pounding chest, but Rikard's eyes flashed with rage, and he lurched a step closer. "You're a damned fool, Louisa," he hissed. "And you can begin preparing to move out at once. Because if I'm not getting the land through marriage, I'll be getting it by buying up the mortgages, and throwing you and your little lackeys out, once and for all!"

Louisa's breaths heaved, her heartbeat painfully pummelling behind her eyes. He wouldn't, she wouldn't. No. And Killik had promised to pay her at the end of this, and then he'd stolen her knife and threatened to *kill* her, and—

"You won't," Louisa managed, through her gasping breaths. "I've arranged—a new source of income. And if you were up-to-date on your ill-gotten gossip, you'd know I gave Bycroft a significant installment just yesterday! So"—another dragging desperate breath—"you can kindly get off my property, and leave me the hell alone!"

Her voice rang through the air, too thin and shrill— because what if she'd still failed at this, what if she'd only bought herself a little more time? And Rikard only came closer, his mouth twisting, his eyes narrowing to slits. "A new source of income," he repeated, low and dangerous. "What kind of income? How? From where? Wait. Wait"—he jerked even closer, jabbing a thick finger toward Louisa's chest—"is it from the *orcs*?"

Louisa stumbled backwards, her hand spasming on her wrong-feeling knife-hilt, as her heartbeat flared louder, thudding into her aching skull. "That's none of your concern, Rikard," she gulped, as steadily as she could. "This is my land, and my business, and I'll thank you not to—"

But without warning, Rikard's hand flashed out—and *grabbed* her. Clutching painfully at Louisa's arm, and holding her here, trapping her knife down at her side, no, no, *no*. "It is from the orcs?" he demanded. "Are those orcs paying you, Louisa?!"

He was so close that his spittle was flying into Louisa's face, and too late, she fought to shove at him, to wrench backwards, away. But he was so damned strong, and she was so damned tired, after almost no sleep, and not even a bite of breakfast. And Rikard's other hand clutched to her other arm, holding her powerfully in place, and giving her a jagged little shake.

"What are you doing with the orcs, Louisa?" he growled, his voice grating through her pounding head, flashing up pure, pummelling panic. "Are you allowing them to compromise you, and defile the integrity of these lands?"

The darkness screeched behind Louisa's eyes, coiling in her belly, cold and bitter and terrifying. Rikard wasn't Lord Scall, Lord Scall was *dead*, so why wasn't she shouting, why wasn't she stabbing him and running, why couldn't she ever escape him, why did she just want to curl up on the ground and weep—

"Are you?!" Rikard shouted again, giving Louisa another jerky, painful shake. "Are you in bed with those awful orcs, Louisa?!"

And then, something—dropped. Dropped straight from the tree above. Landing lightly on its feet beside them, a dagger flashing in each clawed grey hand.

It was—it was Killik?

"Ach, fool man," Killik said to Rikard, with dark, deadly certainty. "She is."

17

Killik was here. Here. With his certainty, his sharpened daggers, his lean, powerful body, looming over Louisa and Rikard both.

Rikard flinched and fumbled backwards, his eyes wide and horrified on Killik's face. And when Louisa followed his eyes, she startled too, shocked to silent, staring stillness.

Because yes, she'd seen Killik angry before—or so she'd thought. But this was something else. Something new. His narrow eyes blazing with danger, his sharp white teeth fully bared in a cold smile, the bones of his face standing out stark and unnerving beneath his scarred grey skin. And the daggers in his clawed hands were spinning, moving so fast Louisa could scarcely see them, scattering flashes of light as they whirled.

"I ken you are trespassing, fool man," Killik said, his cool voice at strange odds with the seething fury in his eyes. "And threatening this woman, also. Attacking her, with your grubby hands, and your reeking ugly scent."

Rikard's face had drained of all colour, and he staggered further backwards, nearly careening into a tree behind him. "You have—no right, orc," he snarled, though his mouth was trembling. "No—*right*, to be on this land. It's my uncle's land, my family's land, and I'm still Louisa's heir! When she dies, it will be *mine!*"

The thought of it seized in Louisa's chest, but beside her, Killik only kept smiling, as a soft growl purred through his teeth. "Ach, you ken?" he drawled. "But what makes you believe she shall die before *you?*"

Rikard's beady eyes dropped to Killik's spinning daggers, and his throat convulsed, the sweat trickling down his brow. "This is *unpardonable*, Louisa," he choked toward her. "You'll rue the day you ever allowed these vile monsters to—"

Killik cut him off with another step closer, his daggers still spinning as he kept smiling, sharp and deadly. "Last warning, fool man," he hissed. You shall leave this land, *now*. And you shall never, *ever* touch this woman again."

Rikard's mouth opened and closed, his eyes now intent on Killik's spinning daggers—and then Killik snapped one to stillness, and lunged forward. Not touching Rikard, not even close—but it still drew a high-pitched yelp from Rikard's mouth, his hands flapping over his head. And then he finally staggered around and ran, slipping and stumbling as he went, while Killik's scornful laughter rang through the air.

"Faster, fool man," he called. "Lest a *vile monster* catch you!"

Rikard's reply over his shoulder sounded much like a wail, while Killik laughed again. The sound light, almost merry, as if he'd never seen such an amusing sight in all his days.

But when he spun back toward Louisa, his face had gone stark again. His eyes flashing black and deadly, his dagger still spinning in his hand. "Are you hurt?" he demanded, in a voice that scraped up her spine. "Did he harm you?"

Louisa twitched backwards, her heart still thundering in her chest, her hands reflexively rubbing at where Rikard had gripped her arms. "N-no," she managed. "I'm... fine."

The unnerving darkness in Killik's eyes didn't falter, and he swept a slow, fluid step toward her. "You are not," he snarled. "You yet *reek* of fear and hunger and weariness, woman. Why have you not eaten, or rested? Did you not even sleep, last eve?"

Good gods, this orc, and Louisa's mouth made a sound like a groan, or a sob. "No," she choked. "No, actually, I didn't sleep last night. Because you raged at me, and stole my knife, and threatened to *kill* me! And now Rikard's come here and done exactly the same thing, and now you've gone and just made it worse, and I—"

No, no, she was about to start weeping again, she was so damned tired, so sick of all of this. Sick of Killik, of Rikard, of Lord Scall, of poverty and failure and fear. And she wasn't going to let Killik see her blubbering again, she was going to leave, and try to find another way. Because now that Rikard had seen Killik, had seen Louisa with an orc, gods only knew what he would do next...

"Ach, wait, woman," came Killik's flat voice, and when Louisa blinked up again, he was standing before her, his body too tall, too close. And the darkness in his eyes had shifted into something else, something she couldn't at all read.

"I did not—threaten to kill you," he said, clipped. "I would not, woman."

What? Louisa gaped at him, shaking her head, while Killik stepped closer, his eyes glinting on hers. "I would not harm you," he insisted. "I have made this vow with you, to the gain of all my kin. And thus, I must keep you safe."

Louisa's laugh escaped on its own, too loud and shrill, and no, no, now the water was spilling from her eyes, streaking down her cheeks. "Safe?" she echoed. "You told me you would bring me *doom*, if I dared to so much as touch your precious wolf! And now this, and—"

She shook her head, dragged her shaky arm over her

cursed leaking eyes, almost scraping her cheek with the rusty knife. While before her, Killik twitched, and then snatched the knife from her hand. And after a brief, disapproving scowl down toward it, he hurled it away over his shoulder.

"I would not harm you," he repeated, harder than before. "Last eve, I was only..."

But then he grimaced, frowning beyond her, his breath exhaling harsh. "You... did well, last eve," he said curtly. "You handled Wolf with care and kindness, and brought him pleasure, and joy, and peace. This was all what I asked of you, and you honoured your word in this, and I ken I..."

His voice faded again, and he rubbed at his mouth, shook his head. "I ken I have only ever witnessed him finding such joy thus," he said thinly, "with *me*."

He winced, his gaze briefly catching Louisa's, and looking almost... regretful. Almost apologetic, even. Though this damn well wasn't an actual apology, and Louisa had no right to feel even the slightest sympathy, none whatsoever.

"Well, in case you've forgotten," she snapped back, "he *was* with you! It *was* you in charge, and you telling him what to do. You setting it all up, and sorting it out, and guiding us both, and giving him that. *None* of that would have happened, without you!"

Her voice was too sharp again, too tenuous in her heaving chest, and she half-expected Killik to snarl and snap back, but instead, he... sighed. Nodded. And for an instant, his eyes on hers looked almost... grateful.

"Wolf... thanked me, when we met this morn," he said, hoarse. "Said I had given him a great, great gift. And then he offered to kneel for me, and grant me whatever I wished."

Oh. And that wasn't, *wasn't* jealousy, surging in Louisa's chest, coiling with the longing and relief—and before her, Killik rolled his eyes, and sighed again. "But no, I did not," he said flatly. "I made up some fool excuse, and sent him away. And I shall keep spurning him, and fending him off, for these next eight nights. But when they are done"—his eyes flashed—"I shall have him weeping and screaming for me, beneath a ploughing he shall never forget."

Right. Of course. And even amidst the still-whispering jealousy, Louisa exhaled, her shoulders sagging. And she even rolled her eyes back toward him, earning what might—might—have been a twitch of a smile in return.

"So naught to fear, woman," Killik said smoothly. "And I shall speak to my kin upon this Rikard. You ken they are aware of all this, for we are well used to these fool lords raging against us, ach? But we shall take further care, and be sure to stay well away from his lands. Ach?"

Well. Louisa's body sagged a little more, her hand rubbing at her mouth. "And what about you *threatening* Rikard?" she asked, though her voice was more tired than accusing. "You taunting him, and running him off like that?"

Killik's gaze cut toward where Rikard had gone, and he gave a careless shrug. "What about this?" he asked. "He was on your land, and he touched you without your leave, and sought to harm you. He ought to be thanking me for not throwing my dagger into his eyeball instead."

Louisa should not, *not*, have betrayed a smile at that, let alone the low lurch of warmth in her belly. Killik had... defended her. Helped her. And he was still here, studying her with something shifting, shimmering, in his dark eyes.

"Now, you ought to eat," he said, in a tone she couldn't read. "Come with me, and hunt for a spell."

Wait. Really? Killik wanted Louisa to come with him? Hunting? *Now*? And she could only blink at him, blank and disbelieving, while he grimaced, and then pulled something out of the rear of his trousers. Something... wait. Louisa's knife?

And yes, yes, it was her knife, but it was also... different. Slimmer. Brighter. Sharper. Looking more powerful, more deadly, than before.

"Our smith Argarr was at the camp, so I had him alter this for you," Killik said, flipping the knife in his fingers, and passing it into Louisa's hand. "This shall now better serve you, and keep you safe."

Louisa blinked down at the knife—it even had new soft leather wrapped around the hilt—as more warmth simmered in her belly. Killik had taken her knife, and then he'd... fixed it. Improved it. To help her.

And when Louisa glanced up at him again, he was intently looking away—but that might have been a faint flush, creeping up his neck. He'd helped her. He'd done it on purpose. Maybe even... as an apology.

"Now come, woman," he said, deep and decisive, coiling more heat, more hope, into Louisa's belly. "And learn to hunt like a Skai."

18

Hunting with Killik was... delightful.

It made no sense, because he still wasn't kind or considerate, not in the slightest. He had no qualms with hissing orders at Louisa, curtly waving her this way or that, or glowering at her whenever she stepped on an errant cracking twig.

But damn it, he knew so much. He saw so much. He pointed out prints and burrows, he followed paths she'd never before noticed, and he could track scents with astonishing ease. And before they'd even walked half a furlong, he dodged sideways, into a small thicket, and came back bearing a dead rabbit in his bloody clawed fingers.

"Breakfast," he said, with satisfaction. "You ken how to make a fire, woman?"

Louisa did, and soon she had a small blaze crackling between them, while Killik skinned the rabbit with rapid, astonishing efficiency. His dagger flashing swift and silver, his clawed fingers tossing multiple bloody bits into his mouth as he went. A sight that should have set Louisa's stomach churning, but instead her mouth felt dry, her eyes oddly caught on his deft hands, his sweaty bare chest, the blood trickling down his chin.

"This is a good one," he said, with satisfaction, as he put the meat onto a makeshift spit, and set it up over the fire. "I ken I ought to gain you herbs or mushrooms, or some such, but I am not much for fancy cooking, ach?"

Louisa waved it away, and shot him a wry, grateful smile. "Me, neither," she replied. "This is perfect. Thank you."

Killik shrugged, and turned his focus to cleaning and sharpening his daggers, pausing only to occasionally sniff at the air around them. But it felt almost... companionable, somehow, sitting here across from him over the crackling fire, as the late morning sun streamed through the trees around them.

The meat indeed proved to be delicious, too, and once Louisa had eaten her fill, Killik polished off the rest, and stomped out the fire. And then he stretched, straightening his long arms over his head, as he turned to the south, and drew in a slow, deep inhale.

"Next, your supper," he said firmly. "I scent a buck to the south, just beyond that bog."

For an instant, Louisa stared at him—he wasn't really going to hunt her supper, too?—but then she made a face, and shook her head. "You can't get through that bog. You'll have to go around, and by then the buck will be long gone."

But Killik's brows only snapped up, his mouth curving into a smug smile. "Try me, woman," he said. "Now come."

It seemed impossible to resist the draw of his wicked eyes, his quirking, satisfied smile. And soon Louisa was indeed following him on a narrow, convoluted, often muddy, but perfectly viable path through the bog—a path Killik had again apparently determined by scent alone.

"There is naught to it, for most orcs," he said over his shoulder, in answer to Louisa's question. "Even if I could not scent the earth, I could yet scent which way the buck went, before us."

Louisa's smile toward him was awestruck, maybe even envious. "That's incredible," she said, her voice thick. "You're so lucky to be an orc, and have skills like this."

But Killik's laugh was low and hard, his head twitching back and forth. "I would not call being an orc luck, woman," he replied, clipped. "In truth, I ken it is more of a curse. A plague of blood and darkness and *death*. Most of all for the Skai."

Louisa blinked toward him, and suddenly her thoughts swarmed with visions of the night before, of all those vicious scars, marked all over Ulfarr's huge, powerful body, cut straight across his most vulnerable place. And how he'd looked at her, how panicked his eyes had been, as he'd said, *I had no intent, cannot bear to bring more shame, more harm, more blood and wrath and death...*

It had all spoken so strongly of... hurt. Of suffering and pain. And why hadn't Louisa been more focused on that, rather than her own mess? How much darkness had Ulfarr—and Killik—faced, in that endless war between orcs and humans? How much death and agony had they borne, at the hands of men like Lord Scall?

"I'm so sorry to hear it," she said, quiet, toward Killik's stiff back before her. "Is it... getting better for you, at least? Now that the war is over?"

Killik kept walking in silence for a few breaths, his shoulder shrugging. "It is... better, I ken," he said finally. "But the war yet left many wounds, both from within and without. And many of these have not yet healed, ach? And mayhap"—he sighed—"mayhap they never shall."

A stab of sympathy shot through Louisa's chest, while those visions of Ulfarr's scars, Ulfarr's sadness, again swarmed behind her eyes. And though she couldn't relate to wounds from a battlefield, she still knew too much of hidden darkness, of scars. Gods, even these past few days had shown how deep her own scars went, how those griefs and fears still whispered, long after their source was gone. Lord Scall was dead, dead...

"I'm so sorry, Killik," she said again, and gods, it sounded so paltry, punctuated with a sucking *splooch* as her boot slipped into a puddle. "Has the camp... helped, at all? You said"—she cast her thoughts backwards—"it's given safety to your clan's families. And a home they didn't... *fear*."

And perhaps she was pushing too much, now, but the camp was still on her land, she had a right to know, didn't she? And though Killik's glance back was narrower this time, he sighed, and nodded. "Ach, it has," he replied. "After all these wounds, many Skai do not yet wish to return to our mountain—but they yet long for a safe place nearby for their mates and sons. So with this camp, we can offer them help, and a quiet place to rest. Mayhap even room for this... healing. This peace."

Healing. Peace. It clutched deep in Louisa's belly, and she nodded, let out a slow breath. "I'm glad, Killik," she said. "I really hope it helps."

She meant it, her voice low and earnest, her eyes sober on where he was glancing over his shoulder toward her, and twitching another nod. And for a breath, Louisa was caught on the sight of him, on the truth of him telling her all this, trusting her with this, even taking her hunting like this, it was...

"Ack!" she yelped, as her too-big boot slipped on a rock beneath her, nearly hurling her sideways into the surrounding bog—but Killik had already whirled around, and lunged back toward her. His strong hands gripping her shoulders, hauling her upright again. Holding her still, solid, safe.

Louisa gulped for air, fought to calm her racing heartbeat, to attempt an apologetic smile toward him—but to her vague surprise, Killik didn't release her, or step back. Instead, he just kept standing here, holding her in place on the uneven rock, which was still doing its damnedest to tip her into the marshy muck all around them.

"Breathe, woman," Killik told her, steady and firm. "Breathe into your foot, and the rock. Draw deep into the earth, feel it draw up into you."

And somehow, Louisa obeyed. Hauling in more deep, dragging breaths, drawing them up from the earth, through the sharpness of the rock beneath her. And it did feel steadier, easier, her weight sinking onto the rock, finding the strength of it, the solid ground beneath.

"Thank you," she said, with another grateful smile at Killik's unreadable face. At where he was still standing here holding her, his hands gripping tightly onto her arms. The touch not calling up even a twinge of that familiar old alarm—and he'd never touched her at length like this before, had he? Beyond those brief pats to her cheek?

And perhaps Killik had realized that too, his gaze darting down toward his hands—but he still didn't release her. Just took a slow step backwards, without even looking, and thereby revealing another pointy, slippery rock between them.

"Now again," he ordered. "With the earth."

Louisa nodded, a foolish action that almost staggered her sideways—but Killik still held her steady, safe. So she drew in a long, fortifying breath, envisioned the earth drawing her down, as she drew it up into her foot. And though her step forward was slow, shaky, she didn't slip on the stone, or the next. And Killik kept guiding her backwards, step by careful step, until he drew her to solid earth again, on the opposite side of the bog.

"Oh, thank the gods," Louisa said, with genuine relief. "And thank you. Again."

Killik's eyes shifted, flickered on hers—but then he

shrugged and glanced away, angling his head toward the south. "Ought to keep going," he said curtly. "The buck is yet there, but mayhap not for long."

Right. Hunting. The thought flipped in Louisa's belly, twisting her mouth, because of course this wasn't—anything. This wasn't Killik taking her into his confidence, or wanting to spend time with her. This was all just some bizarre manifestation of his guilt from the night before, or maybe even his well-placed fear that she would decide this wasn't worth it, and abandon him—and his camp—for good.

She fought to keep repeating that truth as they quietly tracked the buck through the forest, heading steadily southwest. Until Killik signed for her to be still, and Louisa could just catch a glimpse of antlers, jutting up from the brush ahead...

And then Killik kicked off, and ran. Sprinting with sudden, shocking speed across the clearing, his body a graceful grey blur of movement. His hand drawing back, a flash of silvery steel flying through the air—

Killik whooped even before the buck fell, his laugh joyous and bright. And then he launched into one last flying leap, another blade flashing in his hand—and it was over in an instant, the buck's body twitching to stillness beneath him, the scent of fresh blood flaring through the air.

"That was—a very impressive kill," Louisa managed, once she'd caught up to where Killik was already cleaning his daggers beside the fallen buck. "Congratulations."

Killik shrugged, but then he waved her forward, and—to her surprise—launched into another lesson. This one about how to tie and hang the buck, and then carry it safely back toward her house. And then, once they'd reached the yard, he even showed her how to dress the buck, and ready its pelt for drying.

It was all new to Louisa—deer-hunting was well beyond what she could manage alone—and while it was a grisly, messy business, Killik worked quickly and cleanly, offering clear explanations as he went, and answering Louisa's questions without complaint. It also turned out that her knife had been noticeably improved by his alterations, making the work far easier than it surely would have been otherwise.

"Good," he finally said, with satisfaction, as he helped her heap fresh venison onto a large pallet she'd fetched. "Now help me carry this to your house."

Louisa gratefully nodded, mopping the sweat off her brow with her sticky, bloody sleeve before helping Killik lift the heavy pallet between them. And it was only then that she caught sight of Joan, standing stock-still beside the stable, and gaping at Louisa and Killik with abject disbelief in her eyes.

Damn it. Louisa still hadn't talked to Joan since the incident with Ulfarr leaving that morning, and she shot her an apologetic half-smile. "Afternoon, Joan," she called out, as steadily as she could. "Killik's hunted us a deer. Could you go collect Elise and Gladys, and start the fire, and ready the kitchen? We'll need to cook some of the venison, and then salt the rest."

Thankfully, Joan didn't argue, and she curtly nodded before dashing off ahead toward the house. And when Louisa and Killik reached the side door, the kitchen was already bustling with activity—Elise clearing the counter, Gladys stoking the fire, and Joan hauling up a heavy bag of salt from the cellar. And wait, the children were here, too, both of them casting shocked, wide-eyed glances toward Killik, and then rushing toward Elise.

"Orc here!" Stefan yelped, clinging to Elise's skirts, while Elise staggered backwards, her face ashen. And curse it, Louisa didn't need another dramatic scene right now, and suddenly she couldn't bear the thought of it, not after today. Not after all Killik had done.

"Yes, this is an orc," Louisa said to Stefan, as she and

Killik settled the heavy pallet onto the counter. "His name is Killik of Clan Skai, and he hunted us this entire buck today, all by himself! You want to know how he killed it?"

Elise cringed, shaking her head and drawing the children closer, but Stefan's eyes were bright with eagerness, and Ame looked cautiously curious, too. "How?" she asked, her small voice carrying through the room. "He scare it to death?"

Louisa winced, and shot a rueful glance toward Killik beside her. "No, even he couldn't do that," she replied, fighting to keep her voice light. "But instead, he pulled out his hairpin, and threw it! Killed the buck with a single hit to its head!"

Both Stefan and Ame gasped, and between them, Elise looked truly horrified—but when Louisa darted another glance at Killik, he was... nodding. Nodding, his expression almost tolerant, as he reached up, and plucked one of the daggers out of his hair.

"This one," he said, holding it out so the children could see it. "It is good for throwing, ach? The end is sharp, and the blade thin, so it flies fast and true. Like a deadly little bird."

He accompanied this with a light, bobbing sweep of his hand, indeed making the dagger look remarkably like a bird, and now it was Louisa's mouth falling open, while both children watched with delighted awe in their eyes. "You keep it in your *hair*?" Stefan squeaked. "Does it hurt?"

"Or cut your hair?" Ame interjected, frowning up at where Killik's topknot had begun falling around his pointed ears. "How's it still so long?"

Louisa's breath had strangely caught, her eyes fixed on Killik's face, on that tumble of shiny black hair now slipping to his shoulders. On where he still didn't look annoyed, or contemptuous, and instead was again holding out the dagger, and making a show of dragging his finger—with its black claw drawn fully in—down the blade's gleaming edge.

"Not sharp here, ach?" he said. "Only at the end. This way

it does not shear off my hair, so I can always keep it close, and throw it whenever I need."

More awe flashed across both children's faces, and beside Elise, even Joan was looking reluctantly impressed. While Elise still looked shaky and pale, and Gladys was frowning suspiciously toward Killik, and giving Elise a reassuring pat to her shoulder.

"That's very useful, I'm sure," Gladys said to Killik, her voice frosty. "Now, missus, where do you want us to start with this?"

Right. Louisa took a deep breath, forced her attention back to the venison. And though she managed some basic instructions, she still couldn't shake the awareness of Killik still here, still standing in her kitchen. Not moving, not leaving, until she finally mumbled an excuse, and ducked for the door. And yes, yes, Killik was here, following her back out into the cool air, into the fading light of the setting sun.

And wait, it meant they'd somehow spent an entire *day* together, and as Louisa turned and blinked up at his face, again framed by that fall of shining black hair, it occurred to her that it had quite possibly been the best day of her entire adult life. A day she would never, ever forget, and it felt hard to breathe, suddenly, the swallow thick in her throat.

"Thank you," she said, her voice hitching. "That was— lovely. All of it."

Her hand flapped around on its own, flailing at the woods, the house, the dagger still in his hand. And Killik twitched a faint smile as he shook his head, and absently began winding his hair around the dagger again. "Ach, it was naught," he said. "Part of our vow. Wish you to eat."

Louisa exhaled and nodded, even as her eyes held to his face, his deft hands binding up his hair. "Well—it was still well beyond what you needed to do," she replied. "Especially with all the lessons, and setting the children at ease just now, like you did. You're—a good teacher."

Killik shrugged, though his gaze had flicked beyond her, toward the distant sight of his mountain to the south. "Ach, I have practice," he said dismissively. "Oft teach orclings Skai ways, at the mountain."

Wait. Really? Killik was a teacher? Of *orclings...* of *orc children?*

But yes, yes, his eyes were flinty, now, and he jerked a curt nod. "Wolf does this, also," he added, clipped. "It is also part of why we seek to help this camp, for we have seen many Skai orclings who do not have this schooling or safety."

Louisa's stomach flipped, her breath juddering in her chest, because *Ulfarr* taught children too? But of course he did, he'd even mentioned teaching, hadn't he? And of course he'd be wonderful at it, too, and how was Louisa ever supposed to forget this, only eight nights—

"Well, you should—take the rest of the venison, and the pelt," she croaked, waving a shaky hand across the yard toward the rest of the meat. "For them. At your camp."

There was an instant's silence, in which Killik blinked at her, and then back at the meat. "I hunted this for *you,*" he said. "And you... helped. More than I... would have thought."

It certainly wasn't high praise, but it still caught in Louisa's chest, shimmering sharp and strange. "You did most of it," she replied. "And you gave us so much. Of course we'd be happy to share."

She meant it, meant it so much it hurt. And finally Killik sighed, nodding, shifting on his feet. "Ach, then. They shall be glad of this, I ken."

Louisa's grin was swift and grateful, her shoulders sagging with her exhale. "I'm glad too," she said. "Thank you, Killik. Again. I really... enjoyed this, today."

Her voice came out sounding fervent, strained, quivering into the silence. Into where Killik was just staring at her again, and she winced, looked away, bracing for his mockery, his contempt. This was still only a deal, only eight nights, he'd just told her last night he never wanted to see her again after it was done, and...

"Ach, well," Killik finally said. "I ken you shall enjoy tonight even more, woman."

Wait. Wait, what did he mean? And when Louisa darted a glance back toward him, his eyes were glinting on hers, his mouth quirking—and then his clawed hand rose up between them, and gave a brief pat to her cheek.

"For tonight, you shall again meet my wolf," he said coolly. "And for your next lesson, he shall learn to please *you*."

19

Bedtime found Louisa pacing back and forth across her bedroom, her hands in fists, as that promise of Killik's echoed again and again through her skull.

He shall learn to please you.

It brought up stunning visions of Ulfarr, of his beautiful body, his deep voice, his gentle hands—but just as strong were the visions of Killik. Killik's lessons, Killik's hands on her shoulders, Killik's hair falling around his face...

But—no. Damn it, no. Louisa wasn't supposed to be thinking about Killik. Killik wasn't even supposed to be part of this. This was supposed to be about helping Ulfarr, and securing her future, and escaping Lord Scall. Forgetting Lord Scall, forever. Finding *peace.*

And Killik didn't even want her, right? He didn't care about her. He'd been truly horrid last night, and he hadn't even actually apologized, had he? No. *No.* Eight nights. That was all.

But an evening had never passed so slowly, and Louisa nearly tripped at the sudden sound of a tap at the window behind her. And when she whipped around toward it, she found—Killik. Killik hovering his head in the window, and—predictably—rolling his eyes toward her.

"What is it?" Louisa hissed at him, once she'd thrust the sash open. "Is something wrong?"

More alarm flared in her chest, because what if Ulfarr couldn't come after all—but Killik rolled his eyes again, and shook his head. "Naught is amiss," he said. "Wolf awaits you in the stable, this time."

In the stable? Louisa wrinkled her nose, while visions of cramped stalls and scratchy hay swarmed behind her eyes. "Really?" she said doubtfully. "And what about Joan?"

Joan often worked late, Louisa well knew, but again Killik shook his head, his eyes wryly amused this time. "She is busy with your other sister," he replied. "Offering her comfort, I ken, after I brought such terror upon her today."

Oh. Louisa blinked at him, because he didn't mean—or wait, surely, he did. And though she'd occasionally wondered about such a connection between Joan and Elise, it was also none of her business, especially when she was here setting up clandestine meetings with an orc. With two orcs. In a *stable*.

"So none shall witness this," Killik said firmly, "and we have readied it for you, also. Now come."

With that, he spun around, and dropped from the window entirely. And when Louisa blinked downwards in the faint moonlight, he was already on the ground, striding off toward the stable with smooth, rolling steps.

So Louisa took a deep breath, and then grasped her lamp before heading downstairs. Stepping as quietly as she could on the stairs, and pausing on the ground level, straining to hear toward Elise's room—and yes, that was the sound of a murmur, and then a bright, breathless laugh.

It was good to hear Elise happy, at least, and Louisa headed out into the night's cool darkness with genuine relief, and a rising, hitching eagerness. Ulfarr was here. Waiting for her. And now Killik was going to teach him to please her...

Her heart thundered as she stepped into the stable, and found Killik waiting by the ladder to the hayloft. "Up," he said, as he stalked over, and snatched the lamp from her hand. "Carefully."

Louisa nodded and began climbing, her face already burning, her feet foolishly tripping on her skirts. She'd ended up wearing her cleanest, neatest day dress, after far too much consideration earlier in the evening—but it suddenly felt woefully inadequate, and now all her doubts from the night before were rushing back, too. Did Ulfarr still really want this, what if he decided to leave again after all—

But then Louisa halted, blinking over the top of the ladder into the hayloft, because yes, Ulfarr was here. Here, sitting stiffly on a small carpet of soft-looking furs, with several square haybales scattered about. While behind her, Killik leapt up into the hayloft, and then went to sprawl on one of the haybales, his dagger already in his hand.

"Sit," he told Louisa, jabbing his dagger toward Ulfarr. "Settle yourselves together, and speak."

Louisa swallowed, but nodded and obeyed, aiming a shaky smile at Ulfarr as she sat down across from him on the fur. "Hello," she said, her voice thick. "How—how are you?"

Ulfarr's mouth twisted, and his big shoulder shrugged, his eyes shifting with obvious unease. While Louisa's heartbeat pounded louder, her breaths already coming fast and shallow. What was she supposed to say next, what did she do now, this had been a bad idea, the worst idea...

"Skai-kesh save us," Killik muttered, snapping both Louisa and Ulfarr's heads toward him—and he loudly sighed, and irritably circled his dagger between them. "Undress. Both of you."

What? Louisa jolted all over, and Ulfarr might have

flinched, too. But Killik only raised his brows, and again circled the dagger between them. "You had your chance," he snapped. "Now you shall do as I say, or you shall leave. And I said, *undress*."

Across from Louisa, Ulfarr grimaced and nodded, and after an apologetic glance toward her, he bent forward, and began pulling off his boots. While Louisa's heart just kept pounding faster, because this meant... she was going to be fully naked with an orc. With two orcs. And they hadn't come anywhere close to that the night before, and...

"What is amiss, woman?" Killik said, frowning toward her, as Ulfarr pulled off his tunic, and began shuffling out of his trousers beside her. "You cannot now be longing to leave?"

His voice sounded incredulous, his eyes increasingly impatient—and maybe confused, too. Because he had to know how much Louisa wanted this, and she hauled in more breath, and searched for her courage, for an answer. *Truth, woman*, he'd told her the night before. *He should far rather hear you.*

And Louisa wanted to keep trying. To be honest. To move past Lord Scall, to forget Lord Scall. Lord Scall was dead...

"No, I—I want to stay," she managed, attempting a wavering smile toward Ulfarr's face. "I'm just—a little nervous. It's been a long time since I've been fully— undressed with anyone."

The words hovered there between them, bare and appallingly shameful, while Ulfarr's head tilted, his brows drawing together—and then Louisa flinched at the feel of Killik's soft boot, nudging at her knee. "There is naught to be *nervous* about," he said firmly, as he jabbed his dagger toward Ulfarr beside her. "Look at Wolf. Ought he to feel *nervous* thus, when he is bared here with you?"

Louisa exhaled and glanced back toward Ulfarr, who was

now indeed fully undressed, his head still tilted, his eyes searching hers. Watching her, waiting for her answer, and Louisa fought to consider the question, glancing up and down his seated body on the fur. Catching on his rugged, lined, handsome face, his neat silver-streaked braid, his broad powerful shoulders, his scarred chest, his softer belly. And even his slack, scarred cock, bulging out small and chubby beneath the wholly inadequate concealment of his veined, muscled forearm.

"Ach?" Killik demanded. "Is there shame in this? Speak this."

Louisa took a breath, choked a hoarse little laugh. "Of— of course not," she gulped. "He's—stunning. Gorgeous. But it's—different, with him, and—"

"No, woman," Killik broke in, with an aggravated wave of his dagger. "How is this different? This is just the same! The only difference is that you long for Wolf, and he longs for *you*! And I ken he has been dreaming of you undressed since the first moment he saw you, so why should you deny us this!"

He sounded truly irate, his eyes flashing, as his impossible words twisted and tangled in Louisa's chest. *Why should you deny us this.*

Us, he'd said. *Us.*

Killik's eyes flicked away, and surely he hadn't meant that, surely it had just been a slip of the tongue. But it kept pulsing there, swirling and simmering between them, and finally Louisa jerked a nod, and fumbled her shaky hands at her dress. Yanking at the buttons, pulling it up and off over her head. And then kicking off her boots, her stockings, before tugging at her stained shift, and hauling that off, too.

It left her fully naked and shivering on the fur, with every single scar, bulge, and imperfection on display for the eyes of two watching, judging orcs. And Louisa couldn't even look at them, couldn't bear to see their faces. What were they thinking, please...

"Now you speak, Wolf," came Killik's voice. "Tell her what you think upon this."

There was an instant's horrible silence, the misery scraping up Louisa's spine—and she could feel Ulfarr's slow exhale, prickling against her bare, quivering skin. Against her breasts, her belly, he was looking at her, he was going to say...

"You are—lovely, Louisa," said his low, hitching voice. "Mayhap the loveliest sight I have ever set eyes upon."

What? No. He was taunting her, this was some kind of trick—but when Louisa's eyes darted up, searching Ulfarr's face, his expression was earnest, almost painfully so. "So lovely," he repeated, quieter. "I am honoured to witness such a gift."

Louisa couldn't seem to breathe, or look away from his sober, intent eyes. And when his hand slipped toward hers, his fingers curling warm and safe around her palm, she didn't even twitch. Just watched, her heartbeat stuttering, as he brought her hand to his mouth, and gave it a slow, careful kiss.

"See?" came Killik's clipped voice, from where he was now stretching on his haybale, and smirking with distinct satisfaction. "And I can scent this as Wolf's truth, woman. So you shall now accept this, and settle yourself. Mayhap now"—his smirk drew higher—"in Wolf's lap."

Louisa's alarm skittered again, her hand spasming in Ulfarr's, her eyes snapping to his face. To where his cheeks looked oddly flushed, his black tongue brushing his parted lips...

"Only—should you wish, Louisa," he rasped, as he gave her hand a gentle, reassuring squeeze. "You ken you must not always obey Killik, ach? This is always your choice, and—"

But Louisa had already flailed forward, lurching shaky and awkward toward Ulfarr, crashing into his solid bare body with shameful, pathetic urgency. And for an instant, there was only more shrieking alarm, because what the hell was she doing, what would Ulfarr do, his muscles stiffening against her, his wide eyes darting toward Killik, who—

Nodded. And even smiled, brief and approving, as he reached out his dagger, and tapped its blade against Ulfarr's cheek. "Good," he said firmly. "Now breathe, and *settle*, both of you."

Right. Ulfarr twitched and nodded, his body slowly relaxing beneath Louisa, while Killik's eyes flicked back and forth between them. "Sink into him, woman," he ordered, "and feel him draw up into you. Feel how warm and strong he is. Ach?"

It was just the same way he'd spoken that afternoon in the forest, when Louisa had nearly fallen into the bog. And to her vague surprise, it felt almost instinctive to obey, to curl up sideways in Ulfarr's lap, to sink into the solid steadiness of him. So warm and strong, just as Killik had said...

Ulfarr's big arms slowly circled around her, drawing her closer against him, tucking her into his chest. And oh, it felt so good, his warm bare skin so smooth and alive against hers, his breaths steady and slow. His hands gently spreading, stroking against Louisa's back and shoulder, and her breath shuddered out in a sigh, her eyes fluttering closed. Gods, how long had it been since someone had just touched her, held her like this, breathed in against her hair...

"Good," Killik said again, and when Louisa blinked toward him, he did look pleased, spinning his dagger in his fingers. "Now, again, we speak. Mayhap"—his lips pursed, his brows raising toward Louisa—"you tell him of how you spent this day."

Louisa managed a nod, and drew in a deep, fortifying

breath. "Well," she began, "Killik took me hunting today. And he got a buck for us!"

Her voice sounded far too shrill, and it belatedly occurred to her that Killik had probably already told Ulfarr this, right? And beneath her, Ulfarr's body indeed didn't betray any surprise, and his hands kept stroking, tentative and slow. "And how... was this?" he asked, his voice just as careful as his touch. "Did Killik shout at you, or swear to bind you to a tree if you spoke to him?"

Wait, he was making a *joke*—and Louisa's laugh was wry and genuine, her head shaking. "He was actually—very patient," she said, with a glance toward Killik's face. "He's an excellent teacher, and I learned a lot."

She could almost feel Ulfarr's surprise beneath her, while Killik shrugged, and looked away. "Ach, I ken this was only because you did not babble at me all day," he replied, with a careless wave of his hand. "Or stomp about making noise at the worst moments. This was almost... restful."

Louisa blinked, while beneath her, Ulfarr's chest faintly shook, in what might have been a laugh. "This is true praise, Louisa," he murmured, "for Killik never finds humans restful, ach?"

His voice sounded warm, almost easy, and Louisa sank closer into him, flashing a brief, grateful smile up at his face. But he was looking at Killik, who again rolled his eyes, and huffed a loud snort. "You humans speak too much," he said archly. "Always speaking, prattling on and on and on, whilst never taking time to watch, and listen, and *learn*. Never asking the right questions, or"—he jabbed his dagger toward her—"allowing the truth of the answers. Never seeking the other side of the tale!"

There was surprising vehemence in his voice, enough that Louisa stiffened in Ulfarr's arms—but Ulfarr only cleared his throat, and drew her a little closer. "Ignore him,

Louisa," he said. "You ken if he is forced to be kind all day, this is oft what comes next."

He sounded almost indulgent, his eyes soft on Killik's face. And to Louisa's vague surprise, Killik's eyes softened, too, and he barked a laugh, and kicked his foot at Ulfarr's knee. "Traitor," he snapped. "Ought to bind *you* to a tree, instead."

Behind Louisa, Ulfarr's breath drew in, short and sharp—and when Louisa glanced up again, his eyes were glinting on Killik's face. As if he would very much enjoy being bound to a tree by Killik... and wait, that was new, wasn't it? And curse it, that was not jealousy, plummeting low in Louisa's belly—and maybe Killik had caught that, glancing narrow toward her, and away again.

"Now keep speaking, both of you," he snapped, waving his dagger between them. "And keep touching her, Wolf. Cover her all over with your hands, so she shall scent fully of you."

Beneath Louisa, Ulfarr betrayed a curious shiver, his hands stilling on her skin—but he was still so warm, so damnably comfortable, that Louisa sank closer into him, and twitched him a hopeful little smile. As if... as if she did want him to keep touching her, and yes, yes, she did. And what was she supposed to do, speak about something, anything, so he would keep going...

"Um, well, Killik also told me more about your camp," she said, a little rushed. "And how you're trying to help your clan, and give them a safe place close to your mountain."

Something flared in Ulfarr's eyes, warm and surprised— and yes, his big hands were touching again, one slipping tentative toward Louisa's hip, the other skimming up her shoulder. "Ach, this is truth," he replied. "In days past, our clan oft had camps like these. Women oft prefer them to the mountain, and it is good for our young brothers to run free under the sky, and learn our Skai ways. These camps bring gain to our mountain also—they serve as outposts, and as a refuge for any passing orcs. Skai travel the most out of all the clans, so we ought to bolster this, and offer our brothers safety."

It was perhaps the most Louisa had ever heard him speak at once, and the enthusiasm was almost palpable in his voice, in his touch. And it was easy to keep smiling back up toward him, to sink deeper into the caress of his warm hands. "Do you still have other Skai camps as well?" she asked. "Or were they all... taken, during the war?"

She belatedly grimaced, recalling how Lord Scall had raged against the province's hidden orc camps. How he would seek to hunt them out like fox-holes, and then come home covered in fresh blood. But no, no, Lord Scall was dead, dead...

"Ach, many camps were taken," Ulfarr replied, his voice rough, his exhale fluttering at her hair. "But three now yet remain, all to the west and south of the mountain. We have long wished for one to the north, and now"—his hand spasmed, just below her collarbone—"you have granted us this, Louisa. This is... a great kindness."

Oh. Louisa's skin was prickling, her body sinking deeper into his touch. "I'm—glad to help," she said, and then gasped as his warm hand stroked lower. Skimming over her soft breast, the rough skin of his thumb brushing her nipple, sending out sparks of heat and hunger all around it...

"Ach, she likes that," Killik's voice cut in, his eyes glittering. "More, Wolf. Both hands. *Gently.*"

Ulfarr nodded, darting a grateful glance toward Killik, and then he slipped his other hand up, too. Both hands cupping and cradling Louisa's breasts at once, now, and oh, it felt so good, arching her against his solid strength...

"Good," Killik murmured, his dagger circling, saying, *keep going.* "I ken she wishes for more, Wolf. One of your hands down her front, mayhap."

Yes, please, and Louisa couldn't stop her full-body shudder, her pleading look up at Ulfarr's eyes. And that was a low, heated groan in his throat as he nodded, and slipped a hand downwards. His fingers spreading over her belly, gently smoothing lower. Easing slow but certain toward where Louisa most wanted it, craved it...

"Ought to make her more comfortable, I ken," Killik purred, his smug smile quirking at his lips. "Turn her to face me, mayhap, so she can lie back against you."

There was no thought of refusing, no resisting. Just following the purposeful movement of Killik's dagger, the careful guidance of Ulfarr's strong hands. Turning Louisa so she was facing Killik, her back flat against Ulfarr's chest, her bare arse jutted against his groin, which—she shivered all over—felt distinctly more prominent than before. While Killik appeared entirely unaffected, looking them both up and down, and then leaning forward, and tapping Louisa's knee with his dagger.

"Open wider," he ordered. "So my wolf can touch you, and learn you."

And oh, this wasn't happening, Louisa wasn't doing this, nodding, shifting, obeying. And Ulfarr was even helping, lifting her lower body with astonishing ease, so she could settle lower between his big crossed legs, and... spread her knees wide over his.

It was a shocking, thoroughly compromising position, with Louisa's body now fully, blatantly on display—not for Ulfarr, but for *Killik*. For where Killik was still sitting over them both, his eyes cool and assessing, lingering for far too long on the sight he'd exposed between Louisa's spread legs, oh hell.

"Good," he said, husky. "Now touch her there, Wolf. Claws in. *Gentle.*"

Louisa could feel Ulfarr's nod, his shaky exhale, the

tremble of his fingers against her thigh. But yes, yes, he was doing it, his warm hand slipping down further, closer...

Louisa gasped as it skimmed between her spread thighs, just brushing against her—but Killik's dagger was still circling, his eyes alight. Watching as Ulfarr's hand lingered, skating over where Louisa already felt swollen and hot, quivering against his gently stroking fingers. But he just kept touching, slipping up and down against her clutching wetness, flaring out bright spikes of sensation with every juddering breath...

"How is she," came Killik's voice, as his eyes flicked between Ulfarr's face, and Ulfarr's hand between her legs. "Is she wet and hungry for you? Enough to touch inside?"

Ulfarr's shudder wrenched through them both, his fingers skittering against Louisa's slick, pulsing heat. "A-ach," he croaked. "Very much."

Louisa's face burned, her leg reflexively drawing in—but Ulfarr's gentle hand held it there, making her obey, showing her off for Killik, oh gods. Showing how his finger could slide up and down, lingering against where she was brazenly grasping at him, welcoming this, wanting this...

"Good," Killik said, husky. "One finger, then, to start."

To start. Louisa's groan escaped on its own, her body desperately trembling against where that thick gentle finger was again... obeying. Nudging closer, firmer, carefully seeking its way... and then pressing, slow. Sinking its way inside her, filling her breath by breath, while Killik watched, judged, with such cool, approving eyes...

"Deeper," he ordered. "All the way."

Oh gods, oh please, Ulfarr was doing it, sinking further and further, that one finger feeling far too large, too powerful, please. And Louisa choked as she felt the last of it, his warm hand pressing close against the curve of her, his finger buried fully inside.

"Good, woman?" Killik asked her, brows raised, and

somehow Louisa nodded, shivering against Ulfarr's strength behind her. To which Killik smiled, dark and dangerous, as he kicked his foot at Ulfarr's other hand, still gripped against Louisa's thigh. "Now use this hand upon her, too. Mayhap she can show you how it could best bring her pleasure."

Louisa was scarcely following, barely breathing, but that big hand skittered toward hers, again seeking to oblige, to obey. Wanting her to show him what felt best, and it was just this, just his warm fingers gently grinding against the top of her opened crease, while his other hand kept pressing below, that finger still buried inside.

"Only thus?" Ulfarr murmured, soft in her ear, and Louisa fervently nodded, her breaths heavy and gasping as her body trembled and circled, pressing into his safety, his touch, his everything...

"So good," she choked, tight in her throat. "You feel so *good*, sweetheart."

Ulfarr's breath caught, in something that felt like disbelief, or maybe a shocked little laugh—while before them, Killik smiled, his eyes gleaming with approval. "Good," he said. "Now give her more, Wolf. Wish to see her full of you. Writhing and whimpering upon you."

His voice lowered as he spoke, his eyes hooded and hot, and both Louisa and Ulfarr shivered as Ulfarr drew in a deep breath, and again... obeyed. Gently drawing his first finger out, and then nudging a second one in alongside it. Easing it in slow and careful, stretching Louisa wider and wider upon it, filling her full of him, please...

"Good," Killik said again, his voice hitching. "More."

More? Oh, it was already so much, so full, everywhere, inside and outside, and Ulfarr hesitated again, too—but Killik's laugh was low and scornful, his tongue dragging against his lips. "I watched you swallow his *rassja* whole, woman," he drawled. "I ken you can bear three fingers for us, ach? Breathe, and *open*."

Fuck, fuck, and yes, Louisa was nodding, gasping, opening wider—and oh, that was the third finger, obediently nudging up beside the first two, and slowly, gently pressing. Stretching her wide open around him, tight and strained and spasming, but she dragged in deep breaths, fought to relax, to welcome it. While those fingers kept sinking deeper, filling her to her limit, just to the edge of pain—

But then they stilled, buried deep inside, because yes, yes, they'd done it. And Louisa was gasping and shivering all over, impaled deep on an orc's strong jutting fingers, while Killik just sat there and watched. His throat bobbing, his black tongue brushing his lips, as he reached down beside the haybale, and drew up—

The—the replica itself. The huge stone—*rassja*, he'd called it. Here. Now.

Louisa's heart skipped, her body jolting to stillness—and behind her Ulfarr flinched too, his breath hissing out harsh against her shoulder. While Killik smiled again, a little softer this time, and held the—*rassja*—out toward them. Toward Ulfarr.

"Now, I ken you ought to welcome this, Wolf," he said. "Ought to see how she shivers and squeals upon it. Upon *you.*"

Ulfarr hesitated, his breath still heavy against Louisa's neck, and her own face was burning, her eyes darting wildly between them. But Killik just kept waiting, holding it out, holding his gaze on Ulfarr's face.

"For it is yet *you*, Wolf," Killik added, husky. "Even if this *rassja* was not made after you, it is yet you, granting her this. It is you, offering her this pleasure. Ach, even if this was another Skai ploughing her, here in the flesh, it is yet you— for she is *yours*, for these next nights. Yours to open and plough and please as you wish. Ach?"

Louisa should have countered that, somehow, but instead she just kept waiting, searching Ulfarr's face. At where he looked just as stunned as she felt, his face flushed, his mouth tight, his eyes intent on Killik's. As if he were truly considering this, facing this...

He swiped for the stone with a sharp jerk of his hand, but oh, now he had it, he was holding it, turning it around with easy familiarity, guiding it down between Louisa's splayed thighs. And then—Louisa spasmed, choked—he slowly, gently drew his slick fingers out of her, and instead nudged that smooth round hardness against her opened, clutching heat.

"You are sure?" he whispered, close in her ear, and Louisa gasped and nodded, already craving it, consumed by it, shaking all over at the feel of it. Its huge strength already slipping deeper, spreading her open around it, oh...

"Ach, thus," Killik murmured, his eyes held on the sight, his dagger making slow circles in midair. "Open her wide for you, Wolf. Fill her with you. Make her feel you."

Fuck, yes, Ulfarr was doing it, guiding it in deeper, and his other hand had resumed its stroking, circling gently above the huge stone stretching her open. And it was so much, too much, most of all with Killik watching like that, his eyes still brazenly fixed on the sight, on Ulfarr's hand guiding the stone deeper, deeper, deeper...

"More," Killik purred, as Louisa shuddered and moaned. "Fill her with as much Skai as she can bear, Wolf. Can you scent how she longs for this? For you?"

Ulfarr groaned, and that was a nod against her shoulder, as the stone pressed in even deeper. So much more intense than his fingers, invading and conquering her breath by breath, until Louisa was impossibly, unthinkably full, her entire body writhing against him, her moans high-pitched and helpless, please...

"Good, ach?" Killik's cool voice asked, and in the spinning shouting chaos, Louisa couldn't tell if he was asking her, or Ulfarr—but they were both nodding, shivering together, and

Killik's smile drew wider, hungrier. "Now more, Wolf. Wish to see you ploughing your hungry woman. Making her spurt and squeal upon you."

Oh, hell. Louisa gasped, as Ulfarr growled behind her, his face ducking into her neck. His own cock's hardness now straining behind her, streaking wetness against her back, while the one in his hand began slowly moving, gently slipping in and out of her, as his other hand kept grinding exactly where she wanted it. The hunger hitching and swelling, wheeling higher with every touch, every slick slide of his thick strong stone...

Louisa couldn't stop trembling, now, her thighs quaking hard, her body helplessly spasming against his slow, steady thrusts. The sounds wet and lurid, now, slurping out shamefully between them—but Killik didn't seem to care, his eyes fluttering as he watched, his dagger still circling, saying, *More, more, more.* And yes, Louisa needed more, needed all of it, arching and writhing for it, so close, so close, please—

The ecstasy charged through her with a shout, a desperate careening crush, crumpling her against Ulfarr's stone again and again and again. So good, so right, so *glorious*, the release and the relief flying and flailing and finding—safety. Safety in Ulfarr's huge body all around her, beneath her, inside her, and safety, somehow, in Killik's hooded watching eyes, too. In the immutable truth of his presence, his dagger, watching and guarding over them, guiding them to this pleasure, this peace.

And it was peace, now, only peace, as Louisa's eyes fluttered closed, her shaky, boneless body collapsing back into Ulfarr's solid warmth. Her awareness floating, whispering away, only vaguely noticing as Ulfarr drew out the stone and then sank sideways, settling them both down onto the fur. It was so soft, he was so warm, and Killik's voice was so far away...

"Good, Wolf," it was saying, flickering low into Louisa's ears. "Now rest, ach?"

Louisa could feel Ulfarr nodding, his fingers spreading against her skin, his breath exhaling heavy into her hair. And it was so easy, so right, to curl closer into him, into that warm thud of his heartbeat, into those strong arms circling around her, her thoughts twining away into darkness...

When something—nudged her. From behind. Snapping Louisa's heavy eyes open, whipping her around to where— oh. Killik. Jabbing at her with his boot, as his eyes angled brief but purposeful toward—her house.

"Do you wish to sleep here, woman?" he asked, his voice carefully light. "I have elsewhere to go after this, so I shall not be here to awaken you before sunrise."

Right. Louisa's stomach dropped, and she squeezed her eyes shut, shaking her head. No, no, she couldn't risk sleeping here, and having her staff wake up to find her missing—or worse, curled up in the hayloft with an orc. But— wait, was this just a tactic to get her away from Ulfarr? And— was this why Killik had wanted to meet out here? Because unlike in Louisa's bedroom, now he could send her away, and keep Ulfarr all to himself, and as soon as she left, he would break his word to her, and—

But beside Louisa, Ulfarr had stiffened and shoved up too, his brow furrowed, his eyes clouded with confusion. "You are—leaving, Killik?" he asked thickly. "Why? Where? What must needs now be done?"

Killik shrugged and glanced away, his mouth thin. "Naught of import," he said, a little too casually. "And I yet wish you to sleep here for a spell, Wolf, and heal."

And heal. Louisa blinked at Killik, and then at Ulfarr, who was grimacing, and shifting his forearm downwards. As if seeking to cover his groin, where he was now fully soft again, but—wait. Wait, was that *blood*? But yes, yes, it was blood, seeping out dark red from inside him, dribbling down his thigh toward the fur.

"Oh, hell, sweetheart," Louisa gulped, her eyes wide on Ulfarr's face. "Was—was that—something I did? Or didn't do? Damn it, I didn't even—"

She winced and shook her head, because curse her, she hadn't even touched him, or attempted to return his generosity in the slightest, had she? And now he was lying here wounded, *bleeding*, and looking at her like this, with such mortified misery in his eyes.

But then—another nudge of Killik's boot, jabbing light but purposeful into Louisa's bare side. "I told you, woman, these are old wounds, and have naught to do with you," he said, clipped. "Or what you have done, or not done. This only comes upon him now and then, and I ken he would not have wished it touched tonight at all. Ach, Wolf?"

Ulfarr's mouth contorted, his eyes dropping, clearly betraying the truth in Killik's words—and wait, was this why Killik had directed them the way he had, too? Ordering Louisa into Ulfarr's lap, wanting her to face him, giving them all those commands. Not because Killik had actually wanted to see her, or please her, but because... because he hadn't wanted her trying to touch Ulfarr. He hadn't wanted her to bring Ulfarr pain.

"Oh," Louisa managed, over the sudden lump in her throat. "Well. I—hope you heal quickly, Ulfarr, and I'm sorry I—didn't realize. I still had—such a lovely time. Thank you."

There was only silence from Ulfarr, another twisting grimace on his mouth, and finally Louisa jerked away, groping for her clothes, yanking them on with shaking hands. Because suddenly she just needed to leave, needed to be away from him, from this, from them. Seven nights, only seven more nights, now, and how did she keep forgetting that? And even if Killik wasn't yelling and raging this time, he'd still made his point just as loudly, made Louisa's place just as clear. No matter how many hunting trips he took her on, no matter how much pleasure he gave her, he still only cared about Ulfarr. This was only a deal, only about gaining her land, her freedom, her future. And that was all.

But even as Louisa lurched up, her eyes fixed on the hayloft's ladder, something—grasped her. Something hot and powerful and—familiar, curling around her wrist.

Louisa flinched, whipped around toward it—but she was already relaxing again, because it was only Ulfarr. And when he blanched, and hurriedly released her wrist, she even clutched for his hand again, squeezing it tightly in hers. Because she—she liked Ulfarr touching her. She wanted Ulfarr touching her. Ulfarr was... safe.

"What is it, sweetheart?" she asked him, searching his eyes. "Is there anything else you need?"

Ulfarr's big shoulders heaved, his pained eyes rapidly blinking on hers. "I only—" he rasped, wincing, shaking his head. "I wished to say—if you should ever wish to—to visit our camp, I should be most honoured to—take you there. Show you."

Really? Louisa's eyes widened, as a slow, genuine smile pulled at her mouth. "That's—very thoughtful of you," she said. "I would—love that. Of course. Anytime."

Ulfarr's breath exhaled, his stiff shoulders sagging, and he smiled back toward her, small but true, the warmth shimmering in his eyes. And then he brought Louisa's hand to his mouth, pressing a soft, sweet kiss against it. And for a breath, she only wanted to throw herself at him, curl back up in his strong safe arms, forget Killik, forget everything...

But she could still feel Killik behind her, could almost taste his rapidly rising anger, scraping against her skin. Because she surely wasn't supposed to have agreed to such a thing with Ulfarr, this was only supposed to be seven more nights, right?

But she couldn't seem to take it back, couldn't bear to

break that hopeful smile on Ulfarr's face. And finally she twitched backwards, away, drawing her hand out of Ulfarr's warm grip, away from his soft sweet mouth. Away, past Killik, past his frowning, disapproving eyes, scramble down the ladder, away...

And though Louisa kept her head bowed as she went, she could still feel Killik's eyes, burning into her, dragging down her back with seething, unsettling certainty.

He's mine, they said, without speaking a word at all. *Seven more nights, and then I shall never set eyes upon you again.*

20

Louisa woke the next morning to the sight of a frantic, flush-faced Gladys, bursting into her bedroom.

"Missus!" she yelped, her voice grating through Louisa's sluggish thoughts. "There's an orc at the kitchen door!"

There was an orc at the door. Louisa's heart skipped, and she shoved up in bed, rubbing at her eyes. "Which one?" she demanded, too sharp. "And what does he want?"

"He asked for *you!*" Gladys wailed, jabbing a finger toward Louisa in the bed. "And it's the one who grew the tree-trunk in his trousers!"

Oh. Ulfarr. Ulfarr was here? Asking for her? And wait, maybe it was an emergency, maybe something had happened, and Louisa scrambled out of bed, and threw on the first dress she could reach, before haphazardly pinning up her messy hair, and splashing her face with cold water. She'd again slept terribly, taunted by dreams of blood and mockery and furious orcs, and now Ulfarr was here—

She nearly tripped as she raced down the stairs, sprinting past a blinking Joan in the corridor, and a terrified-looking Elise in the kitchen. And when she threw the door open, her chest heaving, there was indeed—Ulfarr. His huge, fully clothed body nearly filling the entire doorframe, his hand rubbing awkwardly at his neck.

"Ach, Louisa," he said, with a brief, uneasy glance toward the kitchen beyond her. "I—wished to ask—if you might yet wish to—come to the camp. With me."

He wanted to go visit the camp—now? And for an instant, Louisa could only stare at him, still dragging for breath, her heart clanging wildly in her chest. While before her, Ulfarr's already-flushed face seemed to go even redder, and he winced, and lurched a step backwards.

"But I ken—I mayhap—misunderstood," he said, rushed and hoarse. "I ought to have first—sent word. I am—sorry, I—"

But wait, no, no, and Louisa jolted forward, clutched his stiff hand in hers. "No, of course," she replied, too quickly. "I'd be delighted to. Please. Just give me a moment, while I—"

Tell my staff, she'd been about to say, but when she glanced over her shoulder, she found all three of them standing assembled behind her, and staring at her. "Not to intrude, missus," said Gladys, curling her lip, "but I don't think it's particularly... wise, to be going out alone and unchaperoned with an orc, is it?"

Unchaperoned? Good gods, as if Louisa was a blushing debutante, and she shot an incredulous look at Gladys, even as Ulfarr cleared his throat from the doorway. "I had... thought of this," he said. "So I asked Halthorr to come, also."

Wait. He'd invited Halthorr? As a *chaperone*? And yes, yes, Louisa's darting glance into the yard beyond Ulfarr found Halthorr poking his head out from behind a nearby tree, and giving her a cheerful wave. And as she blinked back toward him, there was the strangest urge to laugh, and to hurl herself into Ulfarr's arms, and squeeze him as tightly as she could, while fondly informing him that an orc was truly the worst possible chaperone, but he was so sweet to think of her comfort, and…

"I'll go," cut in a grim voice, and when Louisa glanced over, it was Joan, a look of weary resignation in her dark eyes. While beside her, Elise gasped, her hand clapping over her mouth—and at the sight of it, Louisa's muddled brain jolted into clarity again. She still didn't want to upset or frighten her staff, no—but she'd also somehow decided, without deciding at all, that she wanted to be honest about this. Maybe just because of Ulfarr, coming straight up to her door like this, just as he'd promised, without demand or complaint.

"If you're really willing to come, that would be lovely, Joan," Louisa said, as steadily as she could. "And I know Ulfarr will take very good care of us. Right, sweetheart?"

Ulfarr's eyes widened, while behind Louisa, there were several affronted gasps—but oh, it had been worth it, because Ulfarr's mouth softened, his eyes shimmering into something warm, almost reverent. "Ach, always, Louisa," he murmured, as he gently clasped her hand, and brought it to his mouth. "It should be a great honour."

Oh. Well. Louisa's face heated as she smiled back, and she said a shaky goodbye to Elise and Gladys, before following Ulfarr out into the bright morning sunlight. It was another lovely day, the air crisp and clear, and Louisa drew in a deep breath as they began walking, with Joan trailing behind—and now Halthorr was jogging over too, and looking decidedly delighted by Joan's presence.

"Good morning, sisters," he said, with a sweeping bow toward them both, though his eyes lingered on Joan. "Are you ready for your tour of our camp, with two strong, stalwart Skai as your guide?"

Joan rolled her eyes, but didn't protest when Halthorr fell into step beside her, a satisfied smile curling at his mouth. And as Louisa glanced at Halthorr over her shoulder, she was suddenly, starkly reminded of Killik, strong enough that her own smile faded, her eyes darting sideways toward Ulfarr's face.

"So where's Killik today?" she asked, as lightly as she could. "Still—away? On whatever project he had to go off to work on last night?"

Ulfarr's shrug was quick and jerky, his gaze held straight ahead. "Or mayhap now sleeping," he said. "When I found him early this morning, he was yet... *busy.*"

The word sounded flat and bitter, hinting at some deeper meaning—and Louisa blinked at him, as a blank, shocked incredulity flashed behind her eyes. "Wait," she said. "You don't mean Killik was busy—in *bed*?! With—someone *else*? After he left you in the—"

She broke off there, darting a chagrined glance back at Joan and Halthorr, but they'd fallen a little behind, and now seemed intently occupied with looking through the trees. And beside her, Ulfarr heavily exhaled, and gave another sharp shrug of his shoulder.

"Ach, why should he not?" he replied, his voice steady. "Killik is a strong and lusty bedmate, and pleasure always calms him, and grants him peace and ease. And his other bedmates are always very pretty and hale, also, and they can always fulfill what a Skai ought to—"

But perhaps he'd seen the way Louisa was staring at him, because he audibly swallowed, and looked away. But his face was flushed, his shoulders slumped, and Louisa could almost feel the ache, the misery, the shame. Far too close, too tight and familiar in her chest.

"Well, I'd say you're just as handsome and hale as any of them," she said firmly, as her hand found his, and gave it a squeeze. "And just as able to fulfill whatever you think a Skai ought to, either. I mean, last night was—"

Ulfarr shot a brief, searching glance toward her, and

Louisa drew in a breath, squared her shoulders. He wanted her truth, right? Wanted her to do this with him...

"It was probably the most pleasure I've ever had in bed," she said, quieter. "Ever. Maybe only rivalled by the other night with you. You felt—you were *incredible*, sweetheart."

Her voice cracked, her face heating, but she held his eyes, let him see—or smell—that truth. And yes, he was inhaling, as something like shock, and then relief, filtered across his eyes. "Ach, you also, Louisa," he replied, low. "I... I thank you."

It curled quiet and contented in Louisa's belly, settling her shoulders, and it felt easy, suddenly, to squeeze his hand again, and smile up at his face. "And as for Killik," she said, as bracingly as she could, "I know he cares deeply about you, too. He's made it very, *very* clear to me how highly he thinks of you. How much you—mean to him."

But wait, why was she bringing Killik back into this, or defending him? Or even seeking to reassure Ulfarr on his behalf? After Killik had run off and left Ulfarr alone like that last night, so he could take his pleasure with someone else...

But maybe this was why she'd said it, that stark gratefulness in Ulfarr's eyes, his breath hitching out. "Ach, Killik is a good friend," he replied. "Better than I ever deserved. I shall never forget all he has done for me, even if he no more wishes for me in his—"

He winced and shook his head, squeezing his eyes shut. "Ach, forgive me, Louisa," he said, faster than before. "I ought not to be speaking of—ach. I should never wish you to think—I have no need of other—I deeply long for what we—"

His voice choked, his eyes searching panicked on hers, and Louisa desperately shook her head, clutched back at his hand, and gave him a too-wide, frantic-feeling smile. "Not to worry, sweetheart," she said quickly. "I know we're not—exclusive. And I certainly understand that you and Killik already have a long-term relationship, and that's not something you can just..."

But now it was her voice trailing off, because curse it, she'd been the one to demand that Killik stay out of Ulfarr's bed. She'd been the one to require Ulfarr's fidelity toward her, even after Killik had told her how unhappy Ulfarr was about it. How Killik had needed to *deny* him, and had made excuses to him, and taken away his touch and his comfort...

And—wait, was *that* why Killik had left Ulfarr last night? Was that why Ulfarr was now so miserable about this? And damn it, had Louisa even discussed any of this with Ulfarr? She hadn't, had she?

"Wolf!" interrupted a small, squealing voice, startling Louisa all over—but when her swirling thoughts refocused again, there was... a *child*. A small, grey-skinned orc child, bursting out of the trees up ahead, and racing toward them. His slim body was dressed only in a knee-length kilt, his hair a wild black mess about his head, but his gap-toothed grin was broad and delighted, his eager eyes fixed on Ulfarr's face. "We found you, Wolf!" he crowed. "We hunted you, and caught you!"

Beside Louisa, Ulfarr was smiling, too, slow but genuine, and he released her hand so he could catch the little orc up into his arms. "Ach, this was good hunting, brother," he said, as his eyes angled toward the trees—toward where another small orc appeared, and then another. All three of them rushing over to pile onto Ulfarr at once, and then proudly regaling him with the details of their hunt, and how they'd so carefully tracked his scent. And glancing backwards, Louisa realized Halthorr had fallen quite far behind with Joan—but he was now fondly grinning toward the little orcs, suggesting that perhaps he'd been partly to blame.

"*She* scent of you too, Wolf," one of the small orcs announced now, pointing his tiny black claw toward Louisa. "Make this extra easy for us, ach?"

Ulfarr chuckled, a low, warm rumble in his throat, even as he shot Louisa a distinctly apologetic look. "This is Louisa," he told them. "She is... a friend, and the owner of these lands. And it is polite"—he raised his heavy brows between them—"to bow and say a greeting when you meet someone new. And to speak your name, mayhap."

The three little orcs nodded, and to Louisa's ever-rising surprise, they took turns introducing themselves, giving careful little bows toward her. The first one with the wild hair was named Leikr, and the other two were Oski and Sindri. And apparently, they all lived at the camp with their guardians, though—Leikr solemnly informed her—Sindri's father was gone, and Oski lived with his grandparents.

"But we are all brothers and sisters," Ulfarr said firmly, with a gentle rustle of his hand to Sindri's hair. "And we all help care for one another. Now, mayhap you three can help us hunt our way to the camp?"

Leikr excitedly nodded and squirmed out of Ulfarr's arms, and soon he was racing back through the trees, with the other two close behind him. And Louisa smiled as she watched them go, and when she met Ulfarr's eyes, he was still smiling, too, and looking more relaxed than he'd seemed today yet.

"They're adorable," Louisa told him, as they followed the little orcs deeper into the forest. "Is your son here today, too?"

She couldn't quite hide the curiosity in her voice, but Ulfarr regretfully shook his head. "Not this time," he said. "But next time, mayhap."

His voice was a little too careful, and it belatedly occurred to Louisa that perhaps it wasn't an accident that his son was away. Perhaps Ulfarr hadn't wanted to introduce her to his son yet. And while she might have once been insulted by that, she now felt only appreciation, simmering warm in her chest. Because of course a good father wouldn't introduce his son to a casual bedpartner after only a few nights—and in truth, she'd likely have thought less of Ulfarr if he'd done otherwise.

"So is the camp close?" she asked. "I thought I remembered seeing a tunnel around here?"

Her gaze settled on the small clearing up ahead, where there was an obvious firepit, surrounded by a stand of tall oaks and pines and hemlocks. And beside her, Ulfarr nodded, twitched a small smile, and looked... up.

Louisa followed his eyes, blinking up at the heavy cover of leaves and branches above them—but wait. Dotted high amidst the trees, interwoven with the thick branches, there were... platforms. Bridges. And were those... *tree houses*?!

Louisa's mouth dropped open, her eyes snapping to Ulfarr—who was still smiling, warm and rueful. "Many Skai like to live in trees, for it is safer, and more secret. Shall you come up, and see?"

Louisa numbly nodded, and then shot a searching look back at Joan. Who was looking just as stunned as Louisa felt, but then she sighed, and nodded too. While Ulfarr signalled up toward the huge pine tree beside them, to where a lean, grey-skinned face poked over the edge of the nearest platform.

"Need the ladder, Wolf?" called a voice, and with it was another new face, joining the first. "Bringing woman up?"

Ulfarr nodded toward the faces, and then his big hand began... making movements. Pointed, purposeful movements, his fingers fluently shifting in midair, and above them, the new face rolled its eyes, and huffed a loud sigh. "Ach, ach," the voice said. "Watch your head, lady."

With that, something hurtled down over the edge of the platform, something big and wooden and coiled. And Louisa ducked just in time as a large rope ladder rapidly unfurled and swung over them, swaying back and forth from the platform.

Behind Louisa, Joan let out a low, muttered curse—and

no wonder, because while the ladder did look relatively sturdy, with solid wooden rungs, the platform above was still at an alarming height. And though Louisa personally wasn't bothered by heights, she'd still never climbed a tree that high in her life, and she couldn't imagine Joan had, either.

"Ach, naught to fear," came Ulfarr's steady voice, as he reached toward the ladder, and pulled it taut. "This is strong, and safe. Halthorr, you go first, to show them."

Halthorr nodded and winked toward Joan before leaping lightly onto the ladder, and climbing up with swift, impossible ease. And within a matter of breaths, he bounded onto the platform above, and his grinning face joined the other two—no, three—now watching them from above.

"Show-off," Joan muttered, frowning up toward him—but then, to Louisa's ever-rising astonishment, Joan sighed, and lurched for the ladder, too. Climbing it far more slowly than Halthorr had, but Ulfarr held the ladder firm as she went, and soon Halthorr was reaching down a hand, and helping Joan over the top, too.

"Now you, Louisa?" Ulfarr asked. "I shall be sure to catch you, should you fall."

Well. Louisa drew in a breath and nodded, and accordingly reached for the ladder. And while it was indeed awkward going—especially with her damned swinging skirts—the ladder did seem sturdy enough, and Louisa's feet moved faster and easier as she went. And soon Joan was hauling her up over the platform, too—and then Louisa froze, her breath catching, her eyes sweeping over the sight before her.

It was—a whole treetop *village*. A cozy, clever collection of platforms and small wooden structures, embedded into the trees, and connected by those long, dangling rope bridges and ladders. Spreading as far as Louisa could see into the treetops all around them, and how—how was this even possible? And how had she not once noticed it, when she'd come here before?

But the longer she blinked at it, the deeper the comprehension sank into her thoughts. It all seemed to have been intentionally built to blend in as much as possible, each platform shaped to mimic the branches above and below, and all of them camouflaged with leaves and canvas and furs. And the huts were small, and sometimes open on the sides and tops, and now Louisa could make out a smattering of hammocks, swaying within and beside them, the brown and green ropes and furs blending with the rich foliage all around. Just the same as the bridges and ladders, and it occurred to Louisa that they would all be easy to hide and remove, should the necessity ever arise.

It was truly a marvel of engineering, of sheer damned cleverness, and Louisa couldn't stop staring at it, as the awe caught and convulsed in her throat. And she gave a shaky exhale at the feel of Ulfarr stepping beside her, his hand again clasping hers—and when she turned toward him, he was watching her closely, his eyes warm and maybe even hopeful.

"Is it... what you expected?" he asked, quiet. "Do you... mind it, being here, thus?"

Louisa shot another glance at the sunlit, shimmering greenery all around them, and all the cozy, camouflaged little shelters. All tucked in with such obvious care and respect for the surrounding environment, just as Killik's contract had promised—and suddenly there was only longing, or perhaps even envy, clutching in her chest. She'd spent most of her life living in cold, drafty houses, full of heavy furnishings and empty rooms, and surrounded by large, manicured lawns no one ever used. And what must it be like, to live in a place like this? To have this closeness with nature and the trees and the sky? To feel such freedom? Such... peace?

"Of course I don't mind," she said, blinking toward Ulfarr's watching eyes. "It's—it's beautiful."

Her voice was low and fervent, her hand squeezing Ulfarr's, and oh, the way he was looking at her, his swallow bobbing in his throat. "I am glad," he murmured, with a gentle squeeze back to her hand. "It is a good, safe home for our kin, ach, my brothers?"

He glanced backwards as he spoke, toward—right. Joan and Halthorr, and the three new orcs. All of them younger, perhaps in their early twenties, and all eyeing Louisa and Joan with open, incredulous curiosity.

"Uh, this is the landlady, ain't it, Wolf?" one of them finally asked, high-pitched. "How'd you get in bed with *her*?!"

There was an instant's awkward stillness, during which Louisa's face heated, and redness crept up Ulfarr's neck, too—but then he raised his hand, and began making more of those swift, purposeful movements. Movements that clearly meant something to the three young orcs, because the one who'd spoken grimaced, and then bowed low toward Louisa, his long braid falling over his shoulder.

"Sorry, woman," he said. "An' welcome to the camp. I'm Ragni, and these are my Skai brothers, Kori and Fasti. We three live here, and oft serve as the camp's scouts and guards, when Killik and Wolf ain't around."

His chest puffed out, a proud smile drawing at his mouth, and Louisa couldn't help a warm smile back toward him. "That sounds very important," she replied. "Thank you so much for welcoming us to your lovely home."

The orc's chest puffed out even further, and after a glance toward Ulfarr, he waved Louisa toward the rope bridge at the platform's edge. "Well, come and see it, then," he said. "Watch your step on the bridges!"

Louisa shot a rueful grin at Ulfarr—hopefully he didn't mind?—but he was smiling fondly toward Ragni, and his hand had slipped to her back. Guiding her gently forward, toward where Ragni and his brothers were already breezing across the bridge.

It certainly wasn't as easy as they made it look, but as Louisa carefully followed, she could almost hear Killik's voice, firm and decisive in her thoughts. *Breathe, feel the earth, draw it up into your foot.* And Ulfarr's steady hand on her back helped too, and thankfully, they reached the next platform without incident. Where an eager-looking Ragni had already begun talking, and waving at the attached little cabin, which apparently served as both a defensive structure, and where they kept all their tools and weapons.

"There's only one easy way up for humans, see," he said, pointing back toward the ladder, "and you gotta get past this to get to the living quarters. Keep our kin safer this way, ach?"

Louisa tried to ignore the fact that he was referring to possible invasions by humans like her—or perhaps Lord Rikard—and smiled back toward him. "That sounds very wise," she replied. "And what is that one for?"

She waved at the next open-walled structure up ahead, with what appeared to be a variety of chests and shelves— and Ragni rapidly led their little group across the next bridge toward it, explaining how it was used to store food and goods. And finally, across another bridge, were the houses. The half-dozen small, cozy little houses, tucked into trunks and leaves and branches... and all of them occupied by people. Not just orcs, but women, and children, too. *Families.*

And while that shouldn't have been a surprise, Louisa's astonishment kept rising higher as Ulfarr and Ragni made multiple rounds of introductions. A small, dark-haired woman named Polly was mated to a tall orc named Igull, and not only were they Leikr's parents, but Polly had a small, wide-eyed orcling on her hip, too. Another woman named Annie was plump and blonde, and she laughed as she chased her equally plump orc toddler over the rope bridges. And a smiling, white-haired woman named Flora was curled up in a clever rope swing with a bald, one-armed orc named Galmr—who also turned out to be Oski's grandfather.

And then, in the last tree-house, they met a *human man*. A slim, smiling, sandy-haired man named Thomas, who'd been bustling about on his little platform, laying out strips of seasoned meat to dry in the sun. And once he'd whistled a tune across the clearing, he was soon joined by the rest of his family—a small, sandy-haired human boy named Angus, and a burly, stern-faced orc named Elgr.

"It is good of you to share your lands with us thus, woman," Elgr told Louisa, in a deep, slow voice, as he settled his big arm around Angus' shoulder. "It means much to us, to have such a safe home for our mates and sons."

On either side of him, Thomas and Angus aimed matching, stunning smiles toward Louisa, and something skipped in her chest as she smiled back. "I'm so glad it helps," she said. "You've all built a lovely camp here."

Thomas and Angus both beamed even brighter, and then plied Louisa and Joan with snacks of dried berries, and strips of delicious, honey-flavoured meat. And once they'd finished and said farewell, and climbed back down to the ground again, Louisa still felt slightly stunned, staring up at the circle of tree-houses high above. These orcs had truly built a life here. A community. A home.

"Now, our tunnel toward the mountain is over there, but it's not much to look at," Ragni cheerfully cut in. "But I ken you'd like to see our underground common-room? It still needs work, but it's an important part of the camp, too."

Louisa took a deep, bracing breath, and nodded—but then caught sight of Joan, whose mouth was hanging open. "Really?" she asked, high-pitched. "Underground? Into a place that's likely to fall on our heads at any moment?"

But beside her, Halthorr gave a broad, reassuring smile, and swept into a graceful bow. "I swear to you, woman," he said, his hand over his heart, "naught shall fall upon your pretty head whilst I am with you, ach?"

Joan rolled her eyes, but then sighed, and threw up her hands. "Fine, let's go," she snapped. "You realize it might kill you too, though."

But Halthorr just kept grinning, and waved Joan ahead of him with a flourish. Past the edge of the clearing, and toward a tall, jagged wall of stone. And when Halthorr and Ragni pulled on a jut of rock, a large, square section of the stone drew out, as if it was an actual *door*.

Louisa gasped, her eyes meeting Joan's equally shocked face, while Ragni ducked through the door, and waved them into the darkness. And Ulfarr's hand was still on Louisa's back, gently guiding her forward, though his eyes had flicked backwards, toward Ragni's companions Kori and Fasti.

"You two stay here and stand guard, ach?" he told them. "And call if aught is amiss."

Both Kori and Fasti nodded, their expressions solemn but pleased. And as Ulfarr guided Louisa toward the cave's dark opening, it occurred to her that while Ulfarr hadn't often spoken during the tour, instead allowing Ragni to take the lead, he still seemed very much in charge, somehow. And even now, as they stepped into the cave, Ulfarr was again signing something to Ragni—and Ragni accordingly nodded and spun around, snatched something from the wall, and blazed it into light.

It was a torch, Louisa realized, squinting in the sudden light—and then she stilled all over, blinking around at... the room. The large, stone-walled underground room, with a smooth polished stone floor, a huge stone fireplace, and a variety of furniture scattered about. Long wooden tables and benches, shelves and chairs, and even what appeared to be a few fur-covered beds, partially obscured behind a large, hanging red curtain.

"This is our common-room," Ragni proudly announced,

with a sweeping wave of his hand. "It is where we oft come to rest and play, and also our safe place to stay whenever we are under threat. And when the rest of the tunnels are finally dug"—he waved at the bare stone walls around them—"they shall lead into other rooms, also."

Louisa was struck truly speechless by this point, gaping at this impossible room, and then at Ulfarr's face. At where he was twitching another small smile toward her, his hand squeezing against hers.

"Mayhap now this is too much, ach?" he asked, quiet. "I ken you did not expect to find all this here."

But Louisa flapped her hand toward him, and shook her head, blinking back the prickling behind her eyes. Because suddenly it just felt—right. Right, somehow, that this camp should be here, on this land.

Because—how many orcs had Lord Scall killed, in that endless war? How much grief and pain had he caused, when Louisa had been powerless to do anything about it? And now—now Lord Scall was dead, and the orcs were still here. Louisa was still here, using Lord Scall's land to help the people he'd harmed. Giving them... peace.

"No, I'm glad it's here," she told Ulfarr, and she meant it. "I mean, yes, it is definitely more than I expected, but none of it is beyond what Killik's contract said, either. And it's—so lovely. I appreciate how it's camouflaged, and how it respects the natural surroundings so well. And I'm so glad you have such a lovely place to call home. You"—she drew in a deep breath—"you deserve it, sweetheart."

Ulfarr's hand spasmed against hers, and his eyes flicked past her, toward where Halthorr and Joan were now standing with Ragni by the fireplace. "This is so kind of you, Louisa," he said, hoarse. "But I—I do not make my own home here. I must needs yet live back at the mountain, for I am not—"

He broke off, grimacing, his eyes darting back toward the fireplace. "But ach, it is a good home for them," he added, faster than before. "And it shall be even better and safer once the tunnels are dug, most of all for our orclings."

It was a clear bid to change the subject, and despite the sudden surging question—why wasn't Ulfarr able to live here?—Louisa attempted to nod, to follow. "Er, so why haven't you dug the tunnels yet, then?" she asked. "Is it a matter of not having the workers to manage the job?"

Ulfarr shook his head, his shoulders sagging. "It is not the workers we lack, but the guidance, and the safety," he replied. "The Ka-esh are the only orcs amongst us who can guide this, but they shall not even grant us a date to visit. Helping the Skai is not their—"

He broke off again, huffing a heavy sigh, his eyes squeezing shut. Suggesting that this was something deeply important to him—indeed, something that again had him speaking with confidence and purpose and ease. So Louisa forced her scattered thoughts to keep following, to draw together everything she remembered about the Ka-esh clan. Killik's obvious derision toward them, and that sweet clever girl Rosa she'd helped...

"What about Rosa?" Louisa asked, searching Ulfarr's face. "Is she still living at your mountain? Maybe she would be able to help, somehow?"

Ulfarr's glance toward Louisa was surprised, but he nodded. "Ach, she yet lives there," he said, "and we did seek help from her and her mate, but they were not able to sway their kin upon this, either."

Oh. Louisa grimaced, and squeezed Ulfarr's hand. "I'm so sorry to hear that, sweetheart," she told him. "If I knew a geologist, I would march them off to you at once."

Ulfarr squeezed her hand back, and then slowly brought it to his mouth, as his warm eyes held to hers. "You are again too kind, Louisa," he murmured, with a soft kiss to her skin. "But we already should not have any of this without you, ach? We are most glad for what you have yet given us."

His voice rumbled into her belly, firing low and hot, and Louisa's brief glance toward the fireplace now found Halthorr, Joan, and Ragni all caught in what appeared to be... a dagger-throwing game? But yes, Joan was even reluctantly smiling as her dagger sank into the wooden panel above the fireplace, while Halthorr loudly whooped beside her.

It meant they weren't paying the slightest attention to Ulfarr and Louisa, to how Ulfarr's warm mouth had begun gently kissing up Louisa's hand, to the sensitive skin of her wrist. And oh, Louisa knew how this went, and her breath caught, her eyes snapped wide on Ulfarr's face—but yes, he was still doing it, still kissing higher, his breath inhaling as he skated his lips over her sleeve, up her arm, over the curve of her shoulder...

Louisa gasped as his mouth met her bare neck, his lips so warm, so sweet, so alive. And somehow she'd already clutched him closer, her hands spreading against his solid back—and then she even drew him a little sideways, behind that nearby red curtain. Where she could still hear Halthorr and Joan and Ragni, but they could no longer see this, Ulfarr's hungry face buried in Louisa's throat, kissing her, tasting her, his teeth gently scraping her skin, as her tingling hands stroked up and down his back. Feeling the impossible breadth and strength of him, feeling him shudder as he eased closer, his body so big, so strong, quivering with need and longing...

Louisa's own longing was hitching, surging, so strong she scarcely heard Halthorr cheerfully calling toward them, saying something about waiting outside. But it meant they were alone down here, oh gods, it meant Ulfarr's big hand could skim down over her arse, and she could arch back into his touch, his solid, steady certainty. And even skitter her hand over his own arse, too, feel the firm muscle of it, feel how it pressed his hips forward, grinding him into her belly.

And not just grinding him, but... that. That bulge in his trousers, which wasn't soft in the slightest, and seemed to be growing, thickening, hardening, with every gasping breath. Expanding into something impossibly, unthinkably large, something very akin to that stone *rassja* he'd plunged inside her the night before, and oh, there was only more wild, desperate craving, firing Louisa from the inside out. She needed more, more, please...

"Ach, how *sweet*," drawled a voice, thick with scorn and fury. "*Now* you learn to do this, now that you are well rid of me?"

Louisa's heart kicked, her body flailing back, away, as Ulfarr staggered back, too. But it was too much, too little, too late...

It was Killik. Standing there watching them, with his dagger in his hand, and murder in his eyes.

21

Louisa stared at Killik for a jangling, frozen moment, her hand clutched over her wildly pounding heart.

Killik was here. He'd seen that. And he was even smiling, rigid and cold, as his eyes snapped and blazed with fury.

"Killik," Ulfarr croaked, and his eyes squeezed shut, his hand rubbing at his nose. "Did not—scent you."

"Ach, I saw," Killik said, and his voice might have almost been pleasant, if not for the rage still glittering in his eyes. "If you had scented me, what should you instead have done? Leapt apart before I saw you? Play-acted as though you should never do this, whilst your scents betrayed your falsehood?"

His voice scraped up Louisa's spine, cold and bitter, while Ulfarr flinched, his hand rubbing at his face. "I should not have—done it thus—without you, at all," he said, hoarse, "had I known it would—vex you, thus."

Louisa's stomach twisted, not just at Ulfarr's words, his clearly stated regret at kissing her like that—but also at the horrible, palpable misery in his eyes, sagging down his shoulders. Looking hurt, sad, wounded, and curse Killik, he was lurching closer to Ulfarr, staring him in the eyes, as his dagger viciously whirled in his fingers.

"Ach, would you?" he drawled. "Just the same as you would have told me you were fetching this woman today? Bringing her *here*? Without even granting me a *warning* of this?"

Ulfarr's eyes closed, the pain spasming on his mouth, and Killik laughed, his dagger spinning even faster in his hand. "Ach, it *so* pleases me when my dearest brother speaks false to me," he crooned, and he even raised his hand to Ulfarr's face, stroking sweetly down his cheek. "It brings me *such* joy when he takes my help, and my gifts, and my pleasure—and then turns about and offers me secrets and sneaking and *lies!*"

He was almost shouting by the end, spitting in Ulfarr's face, even as he kept caressing his cheek. While Ulfarr betrayed a jerky, visceral flinch, as sharp as if Killik had slapped him across the face.

And gods damn Killik, it was like he was kicking a cowering dog—and before she'd even caught it, Louisa lurched forward, and knocked Killik's stroking hand away from Ulfarr's face.

"Leave him the hell alone, you prick," she snarled. "He's an adult, and he's damned well allowed to decide how he wants to spend a day, and who he wants to spend it with! Especially when"—she hauled in a deep breath—"he *did* come to you first this morning! And he found you busy in bed fucking someone else!"

Her voice echoed through the stone-walled room, and for an instant, Killik's taut body stilled, his eyes angling narrow toward Ulfarr's face. But then he spun toward Louisa, his teeth bared, his eyes shimmering with something like glee, or mockery, or... or hatred.

"Ach, and have you yet told him why he found me thus, woman?" he purred, his eyes glinting dangerously on hers.

"Have you told him whose rule this was? Whose selfish demand this was? Who will no longer allow me to even *touch* him, let alone share his bed, so I must now seek relief elsewhere?"

No. No. Damn it, damn Killik, he hadn't just thrown that out between them, not now, not like this. But yes, yes, he had, his eyes blazing with triumph, with that same seething hatred.

And even as Louisa recoiled, the misery plummeting in her belly, her gaze snapped back to—to Ulfarr. To where he again looked as though he'd been struck, his eyes wide and disbelieving on Louisa's face.

"You... demanded this?" he asked her, the bewilderment scraping through his voice. "You did not wish Killik to touch me? But only today, you said—you told me you did not mind this. You said you knew Killik was my—we had a—"

His dismayed eyes darted toward Killik, whose mouth was now pressed into a thin, spiteful smile. "Ach, but she is a human," Killik spat. "And we ken how humans hoard their secrets, do we not? How they speak their falsehoods so smoothly, whilst seeking to gain our trust, and bend us to their will!"

What? Louisa's mouth fell open, her head rapidly shaking, her hand clutching for Ulfarr's cold, sweaty fingers—but no, no, he yanked his hand away, he was backing away from her, from Killik, slightly stumbling over a fur rug behind him. And he looked so pale, so horrified, his eyes almost fearful on Louisa's face, no, no, no—

"No, sweetheart," she gulped, on a lurching, staggering step forward. "I wasn't—I didn't mean to—I just didn't want to—"

But her thoughts were scattering, scrambling, and her helpless eyes darted toward—Killik. Who just kept smiling at her like that, cruel and malicious, as if he would gladly use that dagger, and slit her throat wide open, and laugh.

"What, woman?" Killik drawled at her. "Why can you not speak this to him? It could not be that you do not wish him to hear it?"

Oh, fuck this lying vicious snake, and Louisa half-laughed, half-roared as she whirled back toward him. "Fuck—you," she spat. "*Fuck you*, you absolute scum. If you felt so damned distressed about this, you could have damn well told him yourself! Rather than letting him think you didn't even *want* him, and then leaving him alone last night, and running off and fucking someone else! And when you got caught, blaming all your guilt on *me!*"

Her voice was fully shouting, now, ringing out between them, but she couldn't stop, she couldn't. "And you *should* feel guilty," she snarled. "If you really care about him so much, maybe you could keep your cock in your trousers for a week or two! We only have seven more nights, for fuck's sakes!"

But Killik only laughed, and growled, and spun that dagger toward her, pointing its sharp, gleaming tip at her chest. "Six," he hissed. "You now only have six nights, woman, for you have come here and near ploughed my wolf today, without my leave. And if you test me further, mayhap I shall grant you no more nights at all!"

Louisa's breath froze in her chest, her eyes caught on that gleaming dagger-tip pointing toward her. But he wouldn't, surely he wouldn't, what about her property, her staff, her *home*—

And curse it, Ulfarr. Ulfarr, who was still staring at them like that, backing away from them, shaking his head. And in a sudden, jerky movement, he wrenched around, and strode for the door. His head down, his shoulders hunched, his big hands in tight fists at his sides.

Damn it. *Damn* it. Louisa choked an unintelligible noise, reached a shaky hand after him—but foolish, he was gone, already gone. And beside Louisa, Killik was staring after him too, his own hand outstretched, his dagger shivering in midair—but then he dropped the hand and frowned darkly at Louisa, cursing under his breath.

Louisa cursed too, and dragged both hands against her sweaty hair. Should she follow Ulfarr? Try to apologize? Tell him she hadn't meant to lie to him, she hadn't meant any of this, it was Killik, always fucking Killik—

"Are you happy now?" she belatedly demanded, spinning around to glare at him. "Was that just as satisfying as you've been dreaming it would be?"

Killik gave a low hiss, baring his teeth toward her, but Louisa hissed straight back. "You did *not* say I couldn't ever touch Ulfarr without you," she growled. "I thought you *wanted* this for him. And of course he thought so too! Especially since you *left* him last night, and then he walked in on you fucking someone else this morning! What the fuck else did you expect?!"

She was shouting again, flailing her arm between them, and Killik's sharp growl vibrated in her chest, deep in her belly. "I expected *you* to know better, woman!" he shot back. "Our pledge was for ten nights. It was for pleasure. It was to teach him to find joy with a woman again, and this is *all*. It was not for you to spend a whole day larking about with him, here at our camp, whilst I was away working, with no knowledge of this! It was *not* for him to bring you here alone to our *home*, to meet all our *kin*, with his scent—and *only* his scent—reeking all over you, so they shall now see you as his *mate*!"

What? Louisa gaped at him, as a sudden, striking comprehension flashed through the sheer sweeping rage. Ulfarr bringing her here had been... a statement, to all these people? Or... or even an announcement of their relationship, somehow? And had Ulfarr... known that? Had Ulfarr *wanted* to make that statement? He didn't like Louisa enough to want her as a mate... right? Because—wasn't a mate more like... a *wife*?

Louisa blinked, swallowed, gave a bracing shake of her head. "There's no way that's what he was trying to do," she said, though her voice wavered. "He was lonely, and hurt, and wanted company! And he even brought Halthorr along as a *chaperone*, probably because"—the awareness belatedly jolted through her brain—"he didn't want to upset you! And besides, he told me he doesn't even live here, this *isn't* his home, and that's probably because of you, too!"

Killik stared back at her, his eyes glittering with furious disbelief. "That has *naught* to do with me," he snarled back. "That is a sentence from our kin upon him, to keep him trapped in that curst mountain, where he shall never again find joy! But I swear upon Skai-kesh"—another sharp jab of his dagger toward her—"he longs for this camp as his home! And now he has marched *you* straight into it! He would have ploughed you here today, and flooded this room with his claim upon you, had I not walked in, and broken this!"

Louisa's thoughts were spinning, her heartbeat pounding in her ears, her head whipping back and forth. Killik was so wrong, he was so enraging, and he was just jealous, and he really thought... he thought...

"Gods damn it, Killik," Louisa managed, tight in her throat. "I'm not trying to—to take Ulfarr from you. To *steal* him from you."

But Killik's laugh had a strange, brittle edge to it, far too loud in the silence. "Ach, no," he drawled. "You will not. For we both know you shall never do what you must to be a true orc's mate. Shall you?"

Louisa's mouth opened and closed, her brow furrowing— and Killik laughed again, gave a wild whirl of his dagger. "Shall you abandon your home, and your lands?" he asked. "Shall you come to live at Orc Mountain, and stand tall with the shamed

Wolf of the Skai? Shall you learn of all his grief and his sins, and yet wish for his touch and his scent and his name? Ach, shall you flaunt your form for him, walk bare for him, allow him to rut you—to plough you, again and again—before all our kin?"

Oh. Louisa swallowed hard, as more shock and disbelief swirled through her chest, choked at her throat. Because if that was what was expected of a *true orc's mate,* then—no. She couldn't. She couldn't leave her lands. She couldn't abandon her staff and the children. And gods, she'd barely been able to handle being naked with Killik and Ulfarr in an otherwise empty hayloft, let alone in front of other people, and...

Killik laughed again, so sharp and bitter, and he brought up his gleaming dagger, and gently tapped it at Louisa's cheek. "No," he said, cold. "No, you shall not. And thus"— another bitter laugh, another tap of the dagger to her cheek—"as I told you from the start, this is only ten nights. This is only pleasure. This is not you coming to Wolf's home, and play-acting as his mate, and then *leaving* him! This is not you bringing the shamed Wolf of the Skai yet more pain, and more grief, before all his kin! Before his *son!*"

Gods damn it. Louisa rubbed hard at her eyes, shaking her head, but Killik's words kept ringing, swinging into a distant, miserable kind of sense. He didn't want to hurt Ulfarr. He didn't want to add to Ulfarr's pain and grief. So he'd created these boundaries, set this time limit, to protect not only Ulfarr's heart, but his name. His reputation. Maybe even his relationship with their son.

"So why did you even bother?" Louisa demanded, her voice a rasp. "If this was so damned risky for you—that a day's visit to the camp on my own fucking land ruins all your grand plans—why did you even come to me with your deal! Why even start this mess in the first place!"

Killik's growl bellowed through her chest, thudded through her aching skull. "I told you this again and again, woman!" he hissed. "Because he longs for this! Because this helps him! Because it seems he is now himself enough to fetch you alone, and show you our camp, and seek to plough you in our common-room! And ach, I wish to help him learn this, I wish to grant him pleasure and strength and peace! I wish to see him happy, and *alive!*"

He was gasping by the end of it, his eyes frenzied, his breath hot and sweet in Louisa's face. And his dagger had somehow slid down to her throat, and when had that happened, and why hadn't she even noticed. Why was she still looking at him, raising her chin, daring him to do it...

"And you really think this made him happy, just now?" she bit out. "With you yelling at him, and mocking him, and threatening him like this? Threatening *me* like this?"

Her voice hitched, her throat convulsing against the cold steel of that dagger. And there was a moment's frozen, halting stillness, Killik's eyes flashing again, his lip curling, as if...

"Gods, Killik, you obviously adore him," she said. "So why can't you just show him? Why can't you just be honest with him? Why do you need to play these games, and fuck around on him and hurt him like this? It seems to me"—she swallowed, drew in more breath—"like maybe *you* don't want to stand tall with the shamed Wolf of the Skai. Maybe *you* aren't willing to make that kind of sacrifice for him, either."

Killik had gone still by the end of it, his eyes boring into hers, and she drew up straighter, drew in a deep breath. "And until you sort out your mess, and your ghastly temper," she hissed, "I'm staying the hell out of this. I'm staying the hell away from *you.*"

And did she mean it, gods, yes, she meant it, the certainty sharp in her voice, striking strong and deep through her body. "Please tell Ulfarr I'm sorry," she said. "And that I had a lovely time today. And if you can ever stop threatening to *murder* the people *you* invited into his bed, I'll be very happy to see him again!"

Killik betrayed a faint flinch, his eyes flicking down to the dagger he was still holding at Louisa's throat—and he abruptly lowered it, curling it into his fist. But it was too late, too late, and Louisa even laughed as she shook her head, and spat on the floor at his feet.

"But we both know you won't change either, you prick," she snarled. "So goodbye. For good."

22

Louisa ended up stalking back to the house with Joan and Halthorr, her hands in fists, her fury and frustration still seething through her chest.

How dare Killik threaten her like that again. How dare he throw all his mess onto her again. How dare he blame her for his own damned inability to keep his own damned cock in his own damned trousers.

And worst of all, how dare he hurt Ulfarr like that. How dare he take such a lovely, wonderful day, and stomp all over it, because he'd been jealous. Because Ulfarr had touched her and kissed her, which was exactly what Killik had wanted him to do.

But as Louisa stalked along, keeping her eyes straight ahead, there was a new, bitter twinge of something almost like... guilt. Because curse it, maybe she *had* overstepped the bounds of their agreement. Maybe she *had* led Ulfarr to believe this was something... more, beyond just the ten nights. Maybe she was setting him up to be more hurt, more wounded than before.

And curse it, maybe she could even admit that despite all Killik's rubbish, he'd still made it excessively clear that he wanted to... supervise. He'd wanted to watch, to approve, to control. He'd wanted to be there with Ulfarr, maybe just to guard him, or direct him, but maybe also because he... he cared.

Louisa groaned, shook her head, rubbed at her eyes—and belatedly found Joan watching her as they walked, her eyes uneasy and searching. While on Joan's other side, Halthorr was glancing toward Louisa too, with something not unlike sympathy in his eyes.

"Are you... all right, Lou?" Joan asked, with a wince. "Did something... happen... down there, with those orcs?"

Right. Louisa let out a shaky exhale, sought to dig through her scrambled thoughts for an answer. No matter how she felt about Killik, she still didn't want to create animosity between her staff and the orcs, to create doubts about that beautiful little camp...

"No, I'm fine," she said. "Killik and I just had a... small disagreement."

But her voice came out flat and bitter, and she was vaguely surprised by Halthorr's brief, cheerful chuckle. "Killik never has *small disagreements*," he told her. "He shall either be calm and smiling as he mocks you, or else flying at you with his dagger in hand, seeking to slit your throat."

Louisa blinked, and that was a hoarse, bitter laugh, barking from her throat. "Yes, I've noticed," she replied flatly. "Many times."

And wait, she wasn't supposed to be betraying that to Joan, sparking more of that unease in her eyes—but beside Joan, Halthorr looked sympathetic again, giving a wincing little smile. "Ach, well, you ken Killik would not fight you thus, if he did not think you worthy of it," he said. "And he has always been a touch... *zealous*, when it comes to Wolf."

Wolf again. Louisa's head tilted, her thoughts hitching backwards, catching on Killik's accusations, his rage. *Shall you stand tall with the shamed Wolf of the Skai. Shall you learn of all his grief and his sins. That is a sentence from our kin, to keep him trapped in that curst mountain, where he shall never again find joy...*

But damn it, Killik had also forbidden Louisa to ask questions, to try to learn of Ulfarr's past—and she didn't still care about Killik's rules, did she? *You humans speak too much. Never asking the right questions, or allowing the truth of the answers...*

"Why... do you all call Ulfarr *Wolf*?" she tentatively asked toward Halthorr, searching his genial eyes. "I know Killik also calls him the *Wolf of the Skai*?"

She was vaguely surprised to see Halthorr's easy nod, his smile that looked almost approving. "Ach, this is a name that has long been borne by Wolf's fathers," he replied. "And *Wolf* is even there in his own name, for Ulfarr means *Wolf-Spear*, in our tongue."

Louisa considered that for a moment, frowning at Halthorr's face. "And what... what does it mean?" she asked, her voice careful. "What does a Wolf actually... do?"

But Halthorr's smile was again warm and genial, his shoulder shrugging. "In days past, the Skai oft ran in packs," he said. "Each pack would hunt and travel together, and fight together in battle, and offer care and safety to its warriors' kin. Wolf's fathers before him all led packs, oft the strongest packs amongst us—and his fathers oft also served as our clan's Enforcers, a role of great power amidst our kin."

Louisa kept studying Halthorr, following that, searching carefully for the next question. "And did Ulfarr ever have a... pack? Or serve as this Enforcer?"

Halthorr's eyes flicked away, and his smile had gone rather fixed. "No, Wolf was never Enforcer," he replied, "But he did have a pack, for many, many summers. I was part of this, and Killik, and Elgr and Igull, and Ragni and Kori and Fasti, also. Mayhap a dozen of us."

Really? Louisa blinked at Halthorr, as her thoughts flicked back to the orcs at the camp, to how Ulfarr had seemed in charge of them all, somehow. But Halthorr had been speaking about what *had* been, in days past... right? And Louisa wasn't supposed to ask—was she?—but perhaps Halthorr had followed the next question anyway, his breath exhaling in a heavy sigh.

"But when our brother Simon became Enforcer, after Wolf's father," he added, a little stilted now, "he disbanded all the packs. So I ken Wolf is now only a name, ach?"

Wait. Simon. *Simon* had taken Ulfarr's father's title, and disbanded Ulfarr's pack? Simon had been the orc Louisa had met in the library that time, right? The huge, hulking orc who'd shaken her hand, and smiled at her?

"And this change had to be permanent?" she cautiously asked. "It wouldn't be possible for Ulfarr to... rebuild his pack, somehow? To be... the Wolf again, beyond just the name?"

There was an instant's silence, and then a curt laugh from Halthorr. "Ach, no," he said, short. "It would not."

Well. That wasn't helpful, and if anything it only raised even more damned questions. Had Simon's decision to disband the packs been targeted toward Ulfarr? Had it been some kind of punishment for Ulfarr's sins?

And gods, what *had* Ulfarr done? And if his actions had been that serious, why did he still have the support—and obviously the respect—of orcs like Halthorr, like Killik? Even if—Louisa winced—Killik still clearly kept that distance, too?

But Halthorr wasn't talking, now, still staring straight ahead, toward where Louisa's grounds were now visible through the trees. And as she blinked at the overgrown lawn, the shabby outbuildings, the big square house with its peeling paint, her thoughts hitched, stuttered, with sudden, too-sharp visions of that camp. The cozy little shelters, the cover of leaves and branches, even that firelit underground room, dark and snug and safe...

"I shall leave you here, then, sisters," Halthorr said, with a flourishing bow toward them, though his eyes lingered on Joan's face. "It was a true joy to spend this day with you."

Joan looked surprisingly flustered, suddenly, but she jerked a nod, and mumbled something under her breath. And as she and Louisa watched Halthorr walk away, Joan looked just as unsettled as Louisa felt, and finally she veered off toward the stable without a single word of farewell.

Louisa's own mood only darkened as she strode into the house, first facing Gladys and Elise's waiting litany of questions, and then all the looming chores she'd put off by going to the camp. But even as she plodded through the day, doggedly working through into the evening, the misery kept catching, circling, seething with guilt, and with something like grief.

Gods, she shouldn't have let Ulfarr kiss her like that. She shouldn't have gone off alone with him like that. And she certainly should have been honest with him about her own boundaries around his other bedpartners, and his fidelity toward her during their ten nights. She shouldn't have left it to Killik to communicate—or not communicate—those boundaries to Ulfarr. Because Killik couldn't be trusted, she *knew* that, and how did she keep forgetting that? Why did she keep trusting him, giving him more chances, after all his rages? His threats?

And even as Louisa finally stalked into her dark bedroom, and slammed the door shut behind her, why did she keep looking over her shoulder for him? Why did she keep jumping at the faintest sounds, the slightest prickle on her back? She didn't want Killik to come back, did she?

Until you sort out your mess, she'd snarled at him, *and your ghastly temper, I'm staying the hell out of this. I'm staying the hell away from you.*

And she'd meant that. She had. Even if it meant the end

of their ten nights, she could try to find another way. She could try to get over this. She could. Right?

She repeated that thought to herself again and again as she hurled off her clothes, and threw her naked body into bed. Lying there stiff and furious, glaring up into the darkness, and blinking back the cursed prickling behind her eyes. But not sleeping, not even close, because it was almost like she was still waiting, listening, as if... as if...

"Will you just talk to me," she snapped into the darkness, her voice cracking. "Please."

And what was she saying, what was she doing, and...

A sigh. Slow, heavy, resigned, trailing up her spine like a hot, shivery touch.

"Ach, then," Killik said, his voice hoarse in the darkness. "I wish you to come back."

23

Killik was here. And Killik wanted her to... come back.

Louisa's laugh grated into the silence, thick and incredulous and almost—relieved. "You do *not* mean that," she shot back. "You threatened to kill me today! Again! Good gods"—she drew in a shaky breath—"it's like some sort of horrendous pantomime I keep walking into, over and over and over again. The Killik-Killing Extravaganza! A miserable musical entertainment where you *die* at the end!"

There was an instant's startled-feeling silence, and then—curse Killik—a low, reluctant laugh. "You should not *die* at the end," came his voice, huskier than usual. "You should only limp away from this entertainment bloody and raging, mayhap. For how else would I keep you buying entry for next time?"

Louisa glared viciously up into the darkness, pressing her mouth into a tight line that was not—not—anything like a smile. "I'm finished attending your terrible show, Killik," she snapped back. "I want a refund."

There was another silence, longer this time. "You do not," he said, his voice steady. "You only wish for a better seat."

Louisa's scoff was too loud, and certainly not even close to a laugh. "There are no good seats to this hellshow," she replied. "Only ones where you get spat on, and shouted at, and blamed for the host's mess!"

But Killik's silence felt taut and watchful this time, quivering into the darkness. "Ach, but woman," he drawled, and was he moving, why was he moving? "You forget the best seat in the theatre. The seat you have been seeking all this time. The seat where"—she could almost feel his smirk—"you sit stuck and screeching upon my wolf's prick."

Gods curse him, and Louisa's breath caught, her head shaking. "That seat doesn't actually exist," she shot back. "It's only a taunt from you! A dangled temptation in the advertisement!"

But that was his laugh, low and mocking and far too close, and then—Louisa froze—a touch. Something hard, smooth, cool, trailing suggestively at her neck...

Louisa's hand snapped up, clutching tightly against it—and found—that. The stone *rassja*, damn it. And Killik's fingers, warm and steady against it, and trailing it... downwards. Down Louisa's front, to her collarbone, nudging down the blanket with it...

"What the hell are you doing," she hissed, but she wasn't even stopping it, her hand even releasing Killik's as he kept purposefully sliding that cool stone down. Tracing it between her bared breasts, over her belly, toward her navel...

"I am granting you a better advertisement," came his infuriating voice, as he slipped it down further, further, over the coarse hair at her groin, nudging it against the crease of her tightly closed thighs. "Reminding you what you have to gain, from visiting my show."

Louisa should have stopped it, should have ignored that imperious little tap of the cold stone to her thigh. And she should not, *not*, have let her thighs fall a little apart, let that firm head prod in between...

"More false advertisements," she belatedly snapped, frowning up toward the sound of Killik's voice above her, even as that cool blunt tip kept nudging, stroking, seeking. "You might as well stop acting, Killik. You don't want to share your precious wolf. You want to keep him all to yourself. But"—she gasped as the stone found its place, pressed a little deeper—"you're not willing to—admit that—to him! Or—yourself!"

Oh gods, it was pushing into her, it was breaching her, stretching her wide around it, oh. Feeling so strong, so damned good, and a choked moan escaped Louisa's mouth as she fought to relax, to open her thighs wider. This wasn't happening, Killik wasn't doing this, this was just—just—

"Wrong, woman," came Killik's clipped voice, as the stone hovered, halted, jutted just up inside her... and then slowly slipped out again, and tapped firmly against her knee. Wanting her to open more, oh hell, waiting for her to oblige, before easing itself back against her slick, convulsing heat.

"I have shared my wolf with you again and again, woman," Killik's flat voice continued. "Ach, I have taught you how to touch him. Commanded you to suck him. Taught you to be bared for his touch and his pleasure. And now"—another gentle little push of the stone inside her—"I ready you for his prick, also."

Wait, that wasn't what he was doing—was it? Surely it wasn't, and Louisa had told him she was finished with this, with him, for good. And she couldn't think, not through the fullness and the ache, the thrilling stretching tautness of that stone now driving inside her...

"You still," she gasped, even as it pressed deeper, "don't—want me. Taking him. From you."

There was another instant's silence, punctuated by the abrupt, visceral sensation of the stone slipping out, releasing from her body's slick grip with a mortifying sound. "No," Killik said coolly, as that slippery head trailed up and down her crease, teasing, taunting. "I do not. I am Wolf's oldest, most faithful friend. I am the one who stayed with him, amidst all his darkness. And no matter what you might think, woman, I am the one who *saved* him. I am the only one who has stood beside the shamed Wolf of the Skai, for all these years!"

His voice had deepened, gone hard and vicious—and Louisa's swirling, scattering thoughts flashed with memories of that afternoon, of everything Halthorr had told her. How Ulfarr had lost his pack, and he would never get it back. And what had he done to deserve that? How bad had it been? Why had he needed Killik's saving...

But then the thought twisted, splintered, as Killik's stone pushed back in, stretched her around it again, harder this time. "And thus," he added flatly, as it kept shoving deeper, deeper, "I do not wish for you to prance onto my stage, and start playing the part of my wolf's mate, before all our watching kin! Most of all when I *know*—better than any other—that this is only play-acting, for our ten nights! For my *coin!*"

Play-acting. For his coin. For the ten nights, for the deal. And Louisa still couldn't think, couldn't wield her wheeling thoughts toward it, could only gasp and choke as that huge driving stone kept pressing. Plunging itself deeper, deeper, it was everywhere, everything, stretching her, baring her, stripping her down into raw, shivering shame...

"But what if it—isn't play-acting," she gasped, helpless, quivering, as the stone kept pressing, demanding, flooding her from the inside out. "What if I just—*like* Ulfarr. And your camp. And y—"

And you, she was about to say, damn her to hell and back—but it broke it off just in time, as the stone rammed even deeper. Deep enough that she could suddenly feel Killik's hand, curving warm and alive against her, his sharp claws gently prodding into her taut, too-sensitive skin.

Holding there, silently shouting of command and power and control, because he'd buried the stone all the way inside her. He'd done that, he'd done this, he'd wanted to do this, he'd wanted her fucked and opened and shaking upon his wolf's prick while he watched...

"Then show me," came his voice, harsh and hot above her. "Prove this to me, woman."

It fired through Louisa like a blast from a furnace, because it was—a command. A promise. Show him. Prove this.

Her awareness was flickering, her breaths dragging, her entire body rigid and shaking and needing, needing, needing. So strong, screaming with such single-minded fervour, that she could only nod, and arch, and flail her trembling, tingling hands downwards. Down to press over Killik's fingers, to grind him harder, closer, digging those claws in, burying the stone even deeper. Plunging her full of orc, of him, taking him all the way, just as he'd asked, just like he wanted, please, oh, *please*—

The flash and the maelstrom burned through her in a bright trammelling charge, crushing and consuming her in its wake. Convulsing her upon Killik, around Killik, her inflamed open body spasming against his firm pressing hand. And no, no, that even felt like liquid, streaking and streaming out onto him, this wasn't happening, not while he watched, not while he witnessed her utter undoing in such cool collected silence...

When it finally finished, Louisa felt raw and trembly all over, her face burning with shock and shame. Gods, what had she just done, just betrayed, and what must he think of her, what if he laughed, what if he left...

Her shaking fingers were still clutched over his hand, still holding him there, damn it—and when she snatched her hand away, his stayed for a moment, slick and warm and far too powerful against her. And then—oh—it gave a light, gentle slap against her before easing away. Allowing the stone to push out after it, Louisa's still-convulsing body pressing it into his hand, as if they were still doing this, as if...

She gasped as the stone finally slipped free, out into Killik's fingers. And then, it began trailing its way back up over her again. Its wet blunt tip dragging against her belly, her heaving chest, up to her neck, her chin...

"Better," came Killik's low, taunting voice, as that still-slick tip brushed against—her lips. As if yes, they were still doing this, and she was still proving this. Showing him.

So Louisa's mouth... opened. Welcomed the soft kissing press of the stone, its demand, its hard threat against her teeth. And its tangy taste against her tongue, the taste of *her*, because Killik had buried it all the way inside her, and now he wanted this. This statement, again, of his power, his command, his control.

And as bizarre as it was, as exposed and bared and humiliating, Louisa suddenly again—understood. Killik needed that command. That control. Over Ulfarr, and maybe—over her. And maybe that was what the other bedpartners were about, too, or maybe—maybe even the ten nights in the first place. Not just a means of gaining pleasure, but a way to wield that control. A way of maybe finding his own peace, amidst all this.

Pleasure always calms him, Ulfarr had said, *and grants him peace and ease...*

She could feel Killik's exhale, the stone slightly trembling as he finally drew it away—but then Louisa clutched for it. For his hand. Felt it stop, taut beneath her fingers, warm against her cheek. Waiting, obliging, as she turned her face, and...

She kissed *him*. Kissed that smooth, rich-scented skin of his fingers, his knuckles. Letting her tongue slip out, shuddering an exhale at the taste of him...

But Killik didn't resist. Didn't pull away. Just let her do it, let her prostrate herself like this, licking him, tasting herself upon him. Offering up that power, that control.

And Killik didn't even need to speak, or ask, as his long finger slipped smoothly between her lips. Allowing her to suck him, to clean him of her juices, to risk her tongue against his viciously sharp claw. And then the next finger, and the next, she was sucking an orc's fingers and he wanted it, she wanted it, the longing again pooling in her belly, oh please...

"Enough," came Killik's voice, firm but surprisingly mild, as his hand slipped away, and gave a brief pat to her cheek. "Now, shall you come speak your truth to my wolf, woman? And face your next lesson?"

Louisa's breath shuddered out, shivering into yet more longing, and maybe even a nod. Yes, she wanted to see Ulfarr again. Yes, she wanted another lesson from Killik. And she wanted that warmth in Killik's voice, suggesting that maybe—maybe he truly wanted it, too. Wanted the power, the pleasure, the... peace. With his wolf, and maybe... maybe... with her?

"Good," Killik said, the single word flaring more hunger, more warmth, deep into Louisa's belly. "Now rise, and dress, and come."

24

They found Ulfarr still at the camp, in the underground common-room.

The room felt even cozier this time, with a large fire now crackling in the grate, and multiple now-familiar faces turning toward Louisa at the entrance. There was Halthorr, sharpening a knife by the fire, and raising his hand in an easy wave. There was Galmr and a smiling Flora, sitting together at a table, playing what appeared to be a dice game. And there, not even slightly hidden by the half-closed curtain, the dark-haired woman named Polly was sprawled on one of the beds with her orc mate Igull, and giggling as he palmed her breast, and nibbled his sharp teeth at her throat.

But Louisa scarcely spared them a glance, because her eyes had caught on the bed beside them, half-hidden by the curtain. On the bed with—the orc. The orc curled up on his side, his huge body huddled into something strangely small, his dark head bent low into his chest.

Oh. Oh, gods. And as Louisa stared at Ulfarr, suddenly there was only sympathy, shot through with grief and misery and stark, sweeping regret. She'd done this. She'd kept her truth from Ulfarr, and she'd hurt him, and brought him sadness and pain. And he hadn't at all deserved it, especially after he'd given her such a lovely day, after he'd so kindly shown her the beautiful place he longed for as his home. And now this, she'd left him with this, alone, all damned day.

Killik had scarcely said a word to Louisa during the entire walk here, but now he clasped her arm, his jaw set. "I have already spoken to him," he told her, his voice low. "And he said he has forgiven me, for how I kept our truth from him. But I ken"—his eyes angled narrow toward her—"it is also yet your truth to speak, woman."

Her truth to speak. Louisa swallowed and nodded, and then lurched forward without thinking, without waiting for Killik behind her. Just needing to speak with Ulfarr, to touch him, to help him...

She hurled herself onto the bed beside him, snatching up his heavy hand into hers. And in return, he shifted and started, jerking around to look—and now Louisa could see his face. His pale, haggard-looking face, with his bleary, blinking eyes, his grim twisting mouth.

"Oh, sweetheart," Louisa gulped, and though she tried to smile, she was miserably failing, almost about to weep. "I'm so, so sorry. Forgive me."

Her voice scraped through the air, too loud, too presumptuous, too—ridiculous. And no wonder Ulfarr was staring back at her like that, with such blank disbelief in his eyes— and Louisa abruptly released his hand, shaking her head. Oh, gods, what was she doing, what if she'd already ruined this beyond repair, what if he hadn't wanted to see her and now—now—

Killik. Killik, swinging himself onto the bed on Ulfarr's other side, and grasping firmly at Louisa's shoulder. Holding her there, letting his claws dig in, as his eyes briefly caught, flared, on hers. As if he was saying—*stay.*

"Ach, you ought to beg my wolf's forgiveness, woman," he said coolly, as his hand dropped from her shoulder, and patted at Ulfarr's pale cheek. "And after this, mayhap you shall offer to suck his prick, also."

What? Louisa gaped at him, her heart skipping—while between them, Ulfarr shoved onto his back, so he could blink blearily at Killik, too. "*Killik*," he said, sharp, almost a reprimand. "Did you compel her to come here? You cannot ask her to—"

But Killik cut in with a growl, and a cool smile toward Louisa. "Ach, I can ask her whatever I wish," he said coldly, "for she has brought me naught but trouble all this day! Now speak, woman. Tell him your *truth*, as you promised you would."

Louisa betrayed a faint flinch, and shot a baleful glare at Killik's smug, infuriating face. At where—for the briefest of instants—something again caught, glimmered, in those eyes. As if... as if... he was giving her a challenge. An opening.

Show me. Prove this to me.

So Louisa dropped her gaze back to Ulfarr's wary face, and drew in a slow, shaky breath. "Right," she began, hoarse. "I—I really am sorry about today, sweetheart. I never, never meant to hurt you, or keep the truth from you. But yes"—she swallowed hard—"I did ask Killik to abstain from— er—*bedding* you. During our time together."

She couldn't read that look in Ulfarr's eyes, but it might have been hurt, or resignation—and she drew in another breath, made herself keep talking. "Not because I had a problem with it! Or with you two enjoying one another. But only because"—she shot another dark look at Killik—"Killik won't stay out of everyone *else's* bed! And I don't *want* everyone else in my bed! I just want you and him, and not—"

But wait. Wait, damn it, what had she just said, and Killik's eyes widened on hers, his nostrils flaring. As if he was scenting it, scenting the truth of it, oh gods, and Louisa snapped her eyes back to Ulfarr, dragged up more words, the rest of the shameful miserable truth. She would be honest, just for a moment, and then she would forget it again, forever...

"It's just—my husband," she croaked, too fast, no, no, no. "Lord Scall. He was never faithful, he was always bedding other women, from the earliest days of our marriage. But he still expected me to—pushed me to—well. And I was too young and afraid to refuse, and twice, I caught—infections from him, and the second time, it was so serious I almost—I couldn't—after that I—"

She clamped her mouth shut, whipping her head back and forth, her eyes blinking hard. No. No. She had to escape it, forget it, Lord Scall was dead. Dead, *dead*...

"So that's why I asked Killik—not to touch you, during our nights together," she gritted out. "I truly wasn't trying to hide it from you, sweetheart, or hurt you, or deny you something you longed for. It was just me being—scared. Selfish."

Her voice cracked, her mouth contorting into a wobbly, pathetic attempt at a smile. But beneath her, Ulfarr wasn't speaking, or smiling back. Instead, his face looked even harder than before, his dark eyes dangerously flashing—and Louisa braced herself, awaiting his censure, his judgement, his...

His hand. His big, warm, safe hand, slipping up to curve against her cheek, wiping the foolish streaking wetness away. "Ach, this was not selfish, Louisa," he said, low and rough. "I am sorry you needed to bear this."

What? He—meant that? But yes, yes, he just kept looking at her like that, touching her like that, and oh, it was so kind, and so generous—and it felt almost painful, cracking and swaying in Louisa's chest. So strong she couldn't stop the sniff from her nose, the streak of new water from her eyes.

"Oh, don't say that, sweetheart," she gulped. "Not when I'm the one who should be apologizing to you. I truly didn't want to hurt you."

But Ulfarr didn't stop stroking her face, his eyes still

glimmering with such palpable sympathy. While beside him, Killik huffed a loud, impatient sigh, and gave a longsuffering roll of his eyes. "There is no need to weep over this, woman," he said flatly. "Though I cannot fathom why you did not just tell us this from the start! And then I may not have raged at you so much, or thought you such a jealous harpy! And also"—he jabbed a finger toward her—"our mountain's healer was at the camp today, and he said orcs cannot even carry this *pox*! And I am a *perfect specimen of health!*"

Louisa twitched and frowned back at Killik, but suddenly it somehow felt easier to breathe, easier to choke down the lump in her throat. "Well, then why didn't you look into that from the start!" she snapped back. "And as if you weren't a jealous ogre yourself! And *you* could have been clearer with *me* that Ulfarr actually *wanted* you in his bed! How the hell was I supposed to know you were a good enough lover that he would actually miss you?"

Killik's scoff was loud and affronted this time, but his eyes were dancing on hers, his clawed hand blatantly sliding, spreading, against Ulfarr's broad bare chest. "How could he not miss me?" he demanded. "Skai know pleasure better than any others in our mountain, and I"—he waggled his black brows as he glanced between Ulfarr and Louisa—"am a *magnificent* Skai. Ach, Wolf?"

Louisa couldn't stop her snort of laughter, or her disbelieving glance down at Ulfarr's face. At where his bleary eyes were now darting back and forth between her and Killik, looking both chagrined and surprised, and maybe even... curious.

"Magnificent, my arse," Louisa shot back at Killik, even as she gave Ulfarr her sweetest smile. "Has he always been this full of codswallop, sweetheart? I'm sure you only missed him a *very* little, between all his whining and posturing and raging—"

Killik cut her off with another loud scoff, and a

purposeful jerk of his head toward Ulfarr's front. Down to where—oh, hell—he'd somehow already taken Ulfarr's cock out of his trousers, and was brazenly... fondling him. His hand sliding and caressing over that soft scarred bulge, moving with surprising gentleness. And beneath his careful strokes, Ulfarr was... shuddering. Swelling.

Louisa's breath caught, her heartbeat skipping, her eyes darting wide and panicked at the room around them. At the half-closed curtain, mostly blocking off the bed from view, but anyone could still walk around at any moment, and see this. Although, they could already see—Louisa's breath caught—the situation in the next bed over, where Polly's skirts were now rucked up around her waist, while her bare-arsed orc rapidly pumped his hips over her.

Louisa watched them for an instant too long, her eyes frozen on Polly's flushed face, on her hand scraping against her orc's sweaty back. As if she truly didn't care, as if none of them cared—and oh, Killik certainly didn't care, smirking like that at Louisa as he kept blatantly stroking Ulfarr's growing, shuddering cock.

"What were you speaking now, woman?" he drawled, as his deft fingers slipped up to catch the bead of slick white pooling in Ulfarr's cleft, and then stroked it back down his spasming length. "Yet more *codswallop*, I ken?"

The air seemed too thin, Louisa's brain far too sluggish, and she hauled in a gulping, shaky breath. "Ulfarr and I were *discussing*," she managed, her eyes darting back to the relative safety of Ulfarr's face, "how irritating you are, Killik, and how enraging you are, and how you always need to be..."

But oh, Ulfarr's expression was not helping, his black lashes heavy and hooded, his scarred cheeks flushed, his lips parting with his gasp. But his eyes were still fixed to Louisa's face, shimmering with something between awe and unease. As if he needed to see her, needed to be sure she didn't mind this, needed her to want this as much as he clearly did...

"How Killik—he always needs to be in charge," Louisa somehow said toward Ulfarr, between her heaving breaths. "Always bossing other people around, trying to get his own way, to run their damned show—"

And oh, Ulfarr was nodding, nodding, even as he gasped and moaned, his eyes flashing on hers. But then he stiffened, winced, with what must have been pain, damn it—and when Louisa shot an alarmed glance downwards, she found Killik's hand tightly squeezing Ulfarr's shuddering shaft, his black claws digging into the slick scarred skin.

"You do *not* agree with the jealous harpy, Wolf," Killik drawled, with a lazy snap of his sharp teeth toward her. "You tell her you *like* my show. You *like* when I make you dance and sing and *weep* upon my stage."

Ulfarr didn't reply, but he certainly wasn't denying it, either. And gods, that look on his face, the pleasure blazing in his eyes, the way his breaths were heaving, his black tongue sweeping at his lips...

"And I ken," Killik crooned, shifting downwards so he could kiss and nibble at Ulfarr's scarred ear, "for all her bleating, this woman also longs to watch you in my show. She longs to see how pretty you are, when you are undone thus. She even longs, I ken"—his glinting eyes angled back to Louisa—"to help me make you dance for us. Ach, woman?"

Gods, this arrogant presumptuous prick, Louisa did not, she so very much did not, the craving coiling so hard she couldn't breathe, her wide eyes desperately darting between Killik and Ulfarr. Killik smirking, leisurely rolling his hips up into Ulfarr's side, nipping at his ear, stroking his straining massive cock, while Ulfarr gasped and arched and bucked beneath Killik's ministrations, his fluttering eyes still hot and intent on Louisa's face. Seeking, questioning, wanting, and it was ringing in Louisa's ears, sparking behind her eyes...

"Ach, we can scent you, woman," came Killik's low,

insolent voice. "Now, as I told you—suck him. Kiss him. Help me ready him to plough you."

Ulfarr's groan was hoarse and unfeigned, his eyes shocked on Killik's face—and oh, hell, Killik just kept smiling at him, warm and even affectionate. "Ach, you should welcome this for tonight's lesson, Wolf, should you not?" he murmured. "You should wish to finally fill this woman this night? Make her shout and squeal upon you? Pump her empty womb full of your strong Skai seed?"

Ulfarr groaned again, and damn it, Louisa gasped, too—and Ulfarr's eyes darting between her and Killik looked just as hungry, just as helpless, as she felt. "But you did not—wish for me and Louisa to do this, together," Ulfarr gasped at Killik, between straining breaths. "Today, you—you—"

There was a shift in Killik's eyes, shuttering him, hiding him away—and somehow, Louisa cleared her throat, found her voice. "No, he just—needed to be here," she said, with a foolish little smile at Killik's face. "Just needed to be—in charge of the show, like the overbearing obnoxious tyrant he is. Should have—realized."

A hushed stillness seemed to echo after her words—until it was broken by a shrill shout from Polly in the next bed. And Ulfarr's throat bobbed, his head nodding, his gaze flicking from Killik, to Louisa, to Killik again. "Ach, I follow," he said, hoarse. "Ought to have—"

But Killik shook his head, sudden and fierce, his eyes oddly bright—and then he bent down, and pressed a sharp, biting kiss to Ulfarr's mouth. "You ought only to lie back, Wolf," he breathed. "And welcome this sweet woman's mouth tending to your perfect prick, ach?"

And rather than a command this time, an order, it felt almost like a question. A plea. Killik's still-bright eyes darting toward Louisa's face, holding with a sharp simmering intensity, and why was she nodding, smiling, shifting downwards...

"Just so, sweetheart," she murmured, and was it to Killik, or Ulfarr, or both. "Now you just relax, and let me take care of you."

And gods, had she truly just said that, offered that—and was she really still doing this, she was. Sliding down an orc's taut, trembling body in a wide-open room, next to a loudly cavorting couple. And offering to *take care of* his scarred, swollen cock, while his arrogant, infuriating lover watched with hungry, approving eyes.

And while his lover now shifted his grip on that huge, leaking cock, and... guided it upwards. Guided it toward Louisa's mouth, oh gods, and nestled it against her parted lips.

"Better," Killik said smugly, with a light pat to her hot cheek. "Now, *gentle*. No teeth."

It was utterly laughable, given how not-gentle Killik had been with Ulfarr's goods just now, but Louisa was still... obliging. Obeying. Kissing at that silken sputtering crown, tasting its stunning sweetness on her tongue. While beneath her, Ulfarr bucked and moaned, his hands clutched to fists on the bed, his eyes wild on Louisa's face.

Louisa couldn't stop her own moan, vibrating through her mouth, as she kept touching, tasting, kissing at his shuddering, still-swelling cock. While Killik's audacious hand slipped further downwards, curving and caressing against Ulfarr's big heavy bollocks. Both of them tending to him at once, lavishing him, seeking to care for him, to comfort him...

"Mark this, Wolf," Killik murmured now, his hooded eyes flickering on Louisa's face. "Look at how lusty and comely you are, with this woman's mouth on your perfect prick. Look how much good Skai seed you are granting her."

Ulfarr's groan was hoarse, desperate, but he was nodding, watching, obeying. His wide eyes still shocked, dazed, on Louisa's face, as his spasming heft spurted out more slick white, sputtering it down his length, pooling it over Louisa's fingers. While Killik's own hand slipped back up into it, too, his warm fingers brushing against Louisa's kissing lips as he stroked up and down, coating Ulfarr with it, oh...

"I ken you are now almost ready for her womb, ach, Wolf?" Killik purred, so soft, so tantalizing, into Ulfarr's ear. "And I have already opened her up wide for you, before we came here—so I ken she is ready for you, also."

But at that, Ulfarr's body stilled, his hazy eyes snapping to Killik's face. "You—you did?" he breathed, hoarse, and oh, he was even swelling fuller against Louisa's tongue, sputtering out more slick sweetness. "But I cannot—scent you thus, upon her?"

He sounded uncertain, uneasy, and almost—*hopeful*. As if—as if he might have actually wanted that. *Welcomed* that.

Louisa's alarmed glance up at Killik found him snapped to stillness, looking just as unsettled as she felt. "Ach, no, Wolf," he told Ulfarr. "I only used your *rassja* upon her again, ach? She is for you."

But curse it, that was still hope, or even longing, shimmering in Ulfarr's eyes. "But why would you not welcome this, Killik?" he murmured back. "I can scent your hunger for her, and you have never been one to refuse pleasure thus. And our scents together upon her, this would be..."

He shuddered even fuller against Louisa's mouth, oh gods, but she'd somehow gone still and slack against him. Because Ulfarr wasn't truly proposing this, Killik would never countenance this—and that was not, *not*, even more dizzying yearning, shuddering Louisa all over, holding her wide eyes on Killik's face. He wouldn't. He *wouldn't*.

"She does not wish for this from me," Killik said, a little too quickly, though his narrow eyes were glinting oddly on Louisa's face. "Ach, woman?"

But oh, Louisa couldn't speak, couldn't breathe, couldn't find even a semblance of a reply. Her gaze just caught, frozen, on Killik's watching face, on the brief brush of his black tongue against his parted lips...

And now—now that was Ulfarr's hand, his big warm hand, finally touching Louisa, skittering against her hair, snapping her eyes toward him. Toward where he suddenly looked... calm, somehow. Collected. In control. And his hand felt steady as it slipped down to Louisa's chin, lifted it up so he could better look at her, so he could give her a small, crooked, too-knowing smile.

"No, you said you wished for *us*, ach, Louisa?" he murmured. "Killik and me both. You only wished to be wise and careful upon this, so you did not find yourself sickened from Killik's other bedmates."

Oh, hell. He'd caught that, he'd heard that, he'd somehow just plucked up all of Louisa's most shameful scattering thoughts, and spoken them all aloud. And what— what was this?! *Who* was this? What was this cool certainty, glimmering in Ulfarr's watching eyes, making him into something almost—almost—

It was too much, too overpowering, churning Louisa's belly with shock and disbelief and a strange staggering longing—and her helpless glance at Killik found him looking shocked, too. Shocked, and then even shy, and was that a flush, creeping up his neck?

"And you had your seed blocked from bearing sons, ach, Killik?" continued Ulfarr's low, inexorable voice, and oh, his hand slipped away from Louisa's chin, so he could cradle Killik's cheek, and tilt his face toward him. "So there is naught to this, but for your vow that you will henceforth only share your bed with us, until these ten nights are done. Ach, pup?"

Pup? Louisa's mouth dropped open, because Ulfarr— nervous, sweet, uncertain Ulfarr—was saying this. Commanding this. Looking at Killik like this, holding him utterly in his thrall like this. And for an instant, Killik again looked—shy. Small. Uncertain. As if Ulfarr was indeed the wolf, and Killik the prey…

But then Louisa could see Killik collecting himself, drawing in a slow, gulping breath, perhaps feeling the strength of the solid bed beneath them. "Ach, for the love of Skai-kesh," he grumbled, with an exaggerated roll of his eyes. "Ach, well enough. I shall vow this to you, but only—*only*—for the rest of these nights. This is *all*."

He'd even plucked his dagger out of his hair, his hand slightly wavering as he jabbed its gleaming blade back and forth between Ulfarr and Louisa. "And then, no more demands, from either of you!" he snapped, in far more his usual tone. "And I shall plough as many tight Skai rumps as I wish, whenever I wish!"

Louisa nodded, though her heart was thundering in her chest, now, her eyes still darting between Killik and Ulfarr. This wasn't happening, they hadn't just agreed to this, and fuck, that smile on Ulfarr's mouth, swift and certain and impossibly stunning, as his big thumb gently stroked at Killik's flushed cheek.

"Ach, I follow," he told Killik, husky, almost fond. "I… I thank you, pup."

And with that, it was almost as though the roles had switched again, the jaunty certainty flashing across Killik's eyes. "Ach, you shall regret thanking me, I ken," he replied, as he shoved up onto his knees beside Ulfarr on the bed, and began unfastening his trousers. "For I shall have this woman so stretched and sloppy, even your pole of a prick shall no longer feel this."

What? No. He wasn't—he wouldn't—the utter raging menace—and Louisa's clamouring shock and disbelief finally caught, coiled on his words, and escaped her mouth in a loud, furious scoff. "You are such an arrogant, insolent, condescending *shrew!*" she managed. "You don't even want—you don't even *like*—"

But her voice scraped back into silence, because Killik's long, scarred grey cock was now jutting hard and ruddy from above his trousers. And he was even stroking his hand up and down it, pumping out an opaque, shiny strand of white, oh *hell*.

"Ach, but I *like* spilling my seed," he drawled back at her. "And if you are both so set upon binding me to your bed, then you shall both need to offer me good cause to stay in it!"

Louisa's thoughts whirled faster, her mouth opening and closing, her traitorous eyes frozen on Killik's steady stroking hand. He meant this. He really, really meant this. He wanted to do this. With her. Now. *Now*?!

Until something—touched her. Ulfarr touched her, his warm hand gently clasping hers, bringing it to his mouth. "Ach, but Louisa shall only do as she wishes, Killik," he said, gently kissing at Louisa's knuckles, and oh, that was the certainty again, flickering through his eyes. "If ever you do not wish for him, Louisa—or for me—you *shall* speak this. And"—his gaze slid to Killik—"you also, pup. Ach?"

Killik rolled his eyes again, but more redness was creeping up his neck, his gaze holding for an instant too long to Ulfarr's face. "Ach, ach," he said irritably. "But I ken she shall not speak this, shall she?"

His voice was a taunt, a challenge, and his eyes were cold as they flicked back to Louisa, holding, glittering. And suddenly, flashing through her shrieking thoughts, were his hushed words from earlier that night.

Show me. Prove this to me.

The challenge kept glinting in Killik's eyes, even as he shot a brief, meaningful glance back toward Ulfarr. Flaring yet more awareness, more certainty, deep in Louisa's chest, because—Ulfarr wanted this. Ulfarr was showing them how much he wanted this. And that meant Killik wanted it, too. Because Killik would do anything for Ulfarr, anything, even more than Louisa had imagined. Even if it meant... this.

And maybe, maybe Louisa would do anything, too. And what would it be, really, anyway? It didn't have to be anything, didn't have to mean anything. It was just for Ulfarr, just for the deal, just a few more nights...

"Ach, woman?" came Killik's taunting voice, backed by Killik's taunting eyes, Killik's taunting hand stroking his jutting, leaking cock. "Even you shall not refuse the great gift of two strong Skai pricks in one night, shall you? You wish for us? For *this*?"

For this. For what he was showing her, flaunting to her, just like the arrogant menace he was. And oh, he'd even reached down to grab at Ulfarr's still-swollen length, stroking it together with his own, showing Louisa what was on offer. While Ulfarr gasped, arched, his hooded hungry eyes darting between Killik's hand, and Louisa's face...

And—fuck. Fuck, Louisa wanted this, she couldn't refuse this, not with the raw reeling craving charging through her, heating in her belly. It didn't mean anything, just a deal, that was all...

"Fine, you raging prick," she snapped. "Fuck me."

uck me.

They were shocking words, a shocking demand, ringing out bare between them, into this damned open room. Into where anyone could see it, still, and how had Louisa forgotten that, oh gods—

But beneath her, Ulfarr was smiling again, watching her with warm steady eyes, as his big hands gently drew her a little upwards. So she was kneeling straddled over his lap, oh hell—and Killik gave her one last cold, mocking look before shifting around... behind her. Behind her, so he could settle himself between Ulfarr's knees, and begin sliding up her skirts.

Louisa was already shivering, her heart pounding, her gaze darting sideways—toward where Polly and her orc had apparently finished their own activities, and were now curled up together, and casting curious glances toward them. Enough that Louisa froze again, the heat burning through her cheeks—but wait, oh, that was a gentle clamp of claws on her thigh, a silent but certain reprimand behind her.

"Eyes on Wolf, woman," Killik's low voice snapped. "You shall pay heed to naught else but us, whilst we plough you."

It sent a furious shudder up Louisa's trembling body, as a low moan escaped her mouth—but somehow, she obeyed. Her gaze back on the safety of Ulfarr's face, the softness of his smile, the raw, shimmering hunger of his eyes. He wanted this, wanted her, his hand again rising, gently stroking at her hair...

"Good, Wolf," came Killik's voice, as his hands kept sliding up Louisa's skirts, his knees nudging hers wider apart. Exposing her, opening her, baring her for all this room to see...

And Louisa was just... letting him. Just gasping and shivering and waiting for him, he still wouldn't, he wasn't, he—

There. A touch. Warm, firm, alive. Jutting just *there*, straight into Louisa's slick, swollen-feeling heat. And not holding, not waiting, just—sinking. Pressing. Taking. Fucking. The feel of it so hard, so hot, carving into her with such smooth, steady certainty, until—

"Fuck," Louisa gasped, as Killik's hips gently slapped hers, his cock already plunged fully inside, buried all the way into her slick clamping heat. "Oh, *gods*."

It sounded like a whimper, a prayer, and behind her, Killik actually laughed, and gave her bare arse a light little slap. "Ach, you ought to pray, woman," he drawled, as he eased back again, drawing himself out, oh hell, oh please. "Ought to beg for your strong Skai ploughing."

Gods, the audacity of this utter prick, and Louisa somehow growled over her shoulder, her eyes narrowing at Killik's smug watching face. At where he just kept smirking back at her, mocking her, as he raised his brows, and snapped his hips forward. Again seating himself deep in one sharp, devastating stroke, while Louisa shuddered and moaned, and nearly collapsed onto Ulfarr beneath her.

Killik's laugh rang into the air, hard and bright and gleeful, and this time he ground himself deep, made her feel it, made her clutch and spasm and writhe beneath it. And fuck,

fuck, she wanted him, she hated him, he was mocking her and using her and—and *punishing* her, and—

"Look at me, Louisa," came a voice, Ulfarr's voice, so low and certain beneath her—and yes, yes, he was still here, he was still just calmly lying there and watching this, his big hand still caught in her hair. While Louisa could scarcely breathe, or move, or even focus her eyes on his face. "You must breathe, ach? Draw down deep from the air, from this strong bed beneath you."

Wait, what? It—it sounded like Killik, exactly like Killik, but if Killik was paying attention, he wasn't letting on. Just sliding himself out of Louisa again, almost all the way—and then slamming back inside, in another jolting, dizzying stroke. While Ulfarr just kept watching, his eyes so steady, so patient, his other hand now stroking at Louisa's hot cheek. "Breathe with me, Louisa," he said, as his own breath slowly drew in, swelling his chest beneath her. "In, and out."

Right, right, and Louisa somehow, somehow, obeyed. Hauling in a gulping, shaky breath, heaving it out, as Ulfarr did the same beneath her, and kept stroking his steady hand at her face. "Good," he said. "Again. Breathe, and settle. Seek to be soft and steady, so you can welcome Killik's strong Skai ploughing."

Again, it was too close to Killik's own words, too strange and surreal on Ulfarr's mouth—but Louisa was still obeying, nodding, as she fought to hold his eyes, to follow his breaths. While Killik's thrusts just kept picking up speed, that rigid strength driving into her again and again and again. Hurling her full of sharp, staggering sensation, flaring it out from the deepest core of her, so intense and utterly overwhelming that it took every shred of her awareness to keep watching Ulfarr, keep finding that breath...

"Good," Ulfarr said, though his eyes on Louisa's were glittering now, and it looked like his breaths were taking more effort, too. "Ach, this is very good. It is not every woman who can bear such a strong Skai ploughing, ach? Most of all from a Skai"—his gaze flicked beyond Louisa's shoulder—"as fierce and lusty as Killik, bearing a prick just as sharp and true as his blades."

Oh, hell, Ulfarr was not saying such things, talking about Killik's vicious slamming prick with such astonishing eloquence, with such warm, genuine approval in his eyes. While he just kept breathing with Louisa, holding her through this, guiding her through this, please...

"You show us great honour, Louisa," he continued, through his own still-heaving breaths, "when you welcome this. When you open so sweetly for us, and allow us to fill you, and fuck you."

It was so much, too much, his soft filthy words, his gentle touching hands, his warm hungry eyes. Still in such shocking, stunning contrast to Killik's sharp, squelching plunges inside her, and—Louisa flinched all over—another firm slap of his clawed hand to her arse.

"So good," came Ulfarr's crooning voice, between his still-steady breaths. "And this shall be even better if you beg him, ach? If you ask for the great gift of his scent, and his strong Skai seed. I ken you shall both welcome this, ach?"

Oh, it was everything, they were everything, and Louisa was nodding, babbling, breaking apart, please. "P-please, Killik," she choked, her voice cracking, her eyes rolling back. "Please. Grant me. Your—your scent. Your—strong Skai seed."

And what the hell was she saying, why was she doing this—but yes, yes, that was Killik's hiss, harsh and hot behind her, as his slamming hips drove deep one last time, and—and stayed. Stayed, held, as Louisa's slick, helpless heat clutched and convulsed at him, stroking his stabbing length in some obscene mockery of intimacy—

Until oh, fuck, there it was. The raw, visceral sensation of that rigid cock swelling, locking, and—spraying. Blasting out into her, flooding Louisa with spurt after spurt of his hot slick seed. Pouring it inside her, Killik was emptying himself inside her, and he—he was even groaning as he did it, the sound low but unmistakable behind her. And with it, now, the lurid sounds of wetness, of slick slippery squelching, as he gave a few more brief, experimental little plunges, his shaft slowly softening inside her.

"Now you, Wolf," came his voice, mild and astonishingly even. "Quickly, to keep the seed within."

The words seemed to scrape past Louisa's reeling thoughts, her still-scrabbling craving, because how could Killik even speak like this, think like this, let alone guide her shaky body downwards like this, toward where—yes— Ulfarr's hard, leaking head was already nudging, guided by both his and Killik's hands. Shifting closer, pressing up easy and hungry against Killik's softening bulk, so they could—

So they could *switch*. So Killik could slip out of her, just as Ulfarr's hot, fat, pulsing head could push in. Releasing only a small spurt of Killik's slick seed around it, and fuck, Louisa was again arching, shouting, shaking all over, as that huge jut of flesh stretched her wide open around its slick silken crown, and then began gently pressing its way up inside.

It was so much, so powerful, just as devastating as Killik had been, despite the comparative gentleness of its thrust. No slamming, no shoving, just that massive dizzying slide, that steady inexorable occupation. Ulfarr was going to fill her, he was going to stretch her to her absolute limit, and she was going to take it, to welcome it, just as she'd welcomed it with Killik, oh *please*—

"Good, Wolf?" came Killik's low voice behind Louisa, as his hard, sweaty body hitched closer behind her, his hands spreading on her hips beneath her skirts. Guiding her downwards, too, wanting her to do this, to take this, yes, oh gods, yes—

"A-ach," came Ulfarr's gasping moan, and when Louisa's hazy eyes focused on him again, she found his eyes squeezed shut, his head arching back, the cords tight and exposed in his scarred throat. "So—sweet. So—so *tight*."

Even the words had Louisa clamping harder against him, making his entire upper body curl up, his head whipping back and forth. "Ach," he gasped again. "Like a—a sweet perfect mouth, but with—no end. Like—naught—*naught* else. You are—*wondrous*, Louisa."

Oh, gods, oh please, Louisa was shivering all over again, her upper body skittering down heavy onto him, onto his frantic heaving chest. His previous steady breaths now lost in his own chaos, his own need, his own body still driving, pressing, deeper and deeper. And wait, Killik was touching him, touching *them*, his warm hand stroking between their legs, exploring against their taut locking bodies...

"Ach, I am glad I readied her as much as I did for you, then," came Killik's reply, his voice still impossibly smooth, even clinical. "Is my seed helping also, you ken?"

Ulfarr's nod was fervent, desperate, his hand now powerfully shaking against where it was still caught in Louisa's hair, and Killik huffed an amused laugh as he leaned forward, and carefully plucked the hand away. Settling it on Louisa's bare arse instead, oh gods, and Ulfarr moaned as he grasped her, as he sank deeper, tighter, fuller, just on that perfect quivering edge of pain. And oh, that was again Killik's hand, brazenly stroking against their joined bodies, caressing them, and then drawing back, and giving them a light, taunting slap.

"All the way," Killik said coolly. "She bore my ploughing, Wolf, and your *rassja*, so she can surely bear this, ach? Now breathe, woman, and welcome my wolf inside you."

Gods, Louisa loathed him, she loved him, she needed all of this, more of this, these deep dragging breaths, that firm stroking hand, this huge unyielding strength filling her, opening her, anchoring her upon it. Pressing just a little harder, a little deeper, she needed more, please, breathe, more. And Ulfarr did too, his eyes wild and frantic and shot with craving, with frenzied urgent need, more, breathe, more—

"Ach, sweet Louisa," he choked, between his dragging breaths. "You are—you feel—so good, so *perfect*, you cannot wish for—for—"

"More," Louisa finished for him, quivering and convulsing all over, drinking up his face, his longing, his beauty, the memory of his sweet filthy instructions from only moments ago. "Please, Ulfarr. Please, grant me—your strength. Your—scent. Your—your strong Skai seed. I—I need it, I need to have it, please—"

And fuck, yes, the way his eyes rolled back, as his hips jolted up, finally burying himself all the way. Slamming her full of sharp, shattering sensation, pleasure and pain and more power than she'd ever held in her life. As this huge orc relented, released, obeyed. Spraying into her with a raw, disbelieving shout, his entire body arching and thrashing beneath her as he poured, flooding her full of him, swarming her with his strength and his seed—

But somehow, it was Killik's strong body holding her there, holding her safe—and that was Killik's hand, slipping swift and certain against her front, grinding just above where Ulfarr's spasming cock was jammed inside her, oh *fuck*. And now it was Louisa thrashing and screaming, her face buried into Ulfarr's hot throat, while the blasting barrelling bliss shot through her again and again, blacking out her sight and her breath, ravaging her whole beneath it.

She didn't know how long they rode it together, gasping and trembling and clutching one another—but when her awareness flickered back again, she was utterly slack, utterly spent. Collapsed heavy and sweaty on Ulfarr's hard heaving body, as streams of hot sticky wetness oozed out from between them, and pooled down toward the bed.

But if either Killik or Ulfarr noticed, they didn't seem to care, and Ulfarr's huge shaking arms had tentatively curled around Louisa's back, cradling her closer against him. Wanting this, truly wanting her here like this, folding her so warm and safe into his embrace, into his rapidly beating heart.

And oh, it was too much, too strong, escaping in a strange choking gasp from Louisa's mouth, as wetness squeezed hot and shameful from her eyes. As if—wait, she wasn't *weeping*, was she? Oh gods, oh gods, she was weeping over this, where they both could see it, and what was happening to her, she—

"Hush, woman," came Killik's drawling voice, too close beside her—and when Louisa blinked her leaking eyes open, he was here again, lying casually on the bed beside them, his head propped in his hand. "There is no shame in a Skai's bed. And I ken"—he smirked at her—"any worthy woman *ought* to weep with joy, after gaining two strong Skai pricks in one night."

It was enough to slightly settle Louisa's shaky breaths, and she blinked her eyes, and made a halfhearted attempt at a snort. "You," she breathed, her voice a thick rasp. "You are such a—such a—"

But there were no words, nothing but bright swaying warmth, and something damnably like gratitude—and Killik barked a low, rolling laugh, and patted his hand at her sticky cheek. "Such a magnificent Skai bedmate, I ken," he crooned. "You ought to have witnessed how you quaked and squealed beneath my good strong ploughing."

Even the thought set Louisa shivering again, blatantly betraying her to Killik's keen watching eyes, and he laughed again, shook his head. "Or mayhap I ought to say," he continued lightly, "how you danced and wept beneath my command, until you collapsed upon my stage. And upon the sweet stabbing seat of my wolf's perfect prick."

Louisa's shaky, helpless laugh escaped before she could stop it, even as Ulfarr's huge sticky body gave a curious little shudder beneath her. And when she shifted up to look, he was blinking back and forth between them, as flares of awe and longing and disbelief flashed across his eyes. As if he couldn't possibly fathom what this was, or how it had happened, and as Louisa blinked her prickling eyes back down at him, there was only more of that strange, stilted gratitude, quivering so strong it felt like it might break. Gods, he'd been so kind, so sweet, so—so wonderful, and—

"Fine, Killik, I'll give you that," she heard herself say, hoarse, though her eyes were still on Ulfarr's dazed face. "Your wolf does have a perfect prick, doesn't he? And he's such a perfect gentleman, too, and so damned handsome. With a perfect body, and a perfect smile, and"—she hauled in breath, gave a wobbly half-smile at Ulfarr's incredulous face—"and just... everything, sweetheart, *everything*."

Her voice cracked, her head shaking, and oh, that was the water again, pooling behind her eyes. "This was so good," she whispered, and she meant it, meant it so much it ached. "So fucking *good*, sweetheart."

And it—it was. It had been quite possibly the most meaningful, most powerful thing Louisa had ever, ever known. Strong enough that for a blessed, beautiful moment, Lord Scall finally felt like a vague, distant memory, overlaid with Ulfarr's kindness, his patience, his praise. His... peace.

But—wait. The way Ulfarr was looking back at her, blinking back at her, his mouth twisting, his head suddenly lurching back and forth. "N-no," he croaked, the word harsh in his throat. "No. N-not thus. *Not*."

Something cold streaked up Louisa's spine, recoiled her a little backwards—oh, gods, had this not been good for him, after all?—and Ulfarr blanched, betrayed a full-body flinch beneath her. Hard enough that his softened strength finally slipped out of her, releasing a surge of thick fluid between them, even as his hand frantically groped for hers, clasped it tight.

"Y-you do not," he gasped at her, "know the full truth of me. Of my—failings. Ought never—never—to bed you thus, bind you to me, for I will fail you. I will fail all of you, as I have always done—"

Oh no, no, it was this again, Louisa's thoughts flashing back to the other night in her room, when he'd been just like this. With this exact same wildness shimmering in his eyes, this visceral terrible fear. As if that calm, collected, commanding Ulfarr she'd glimpsed amidst all that pleasure was just a figment, a memory, a ghost...

And what was Louisa supposed to do, what was she supposed to say, her wide eyes darting panicked toward Killik beside her. Toward where, for a breath, he looked just as startled as she felt—but Louisa could see him drawing in that breath, grounding himself into the bed, as his hand came up, and patted against Ulfarr's cheek.

"No, Wolf," he said, his voice impressively steady. "You can bleat upon failing everyone else if you wish, but you cannot ever say you failed me. Never. Not *once*."

Ulfarr blinked blearily at him, shaking his head, but Killik gripped his stubbled chin, snapped it to stillness. "Mark me, Ulfarr of Clan Skai," he hissed. "You have stood beside me for the better part of my thirty-odd summers. You saw me. You guarded me. You destroyed my enemies. You heard my words, and honoured my truth. You tended me whenever I needed this, again and again. And not once did you ask for aught in return! For me, or all the other fatherless Skai you watched over, as the good Wolf's son you were! As the good Wolf you *are*!"

His words struck into Louisa's chest, ringing through her skull, because—Ulfarr had done all that, for Killik? For years? For the better part of his thirty-odd summers, he'd said—and wait, Halthorr had said Killik had been part of Ulfarr's pack, right? And had this been part of that, too? Ulfarr had watched over fatherless Skai, as their Wolf?

"*Not* Wolf," Ulfarr rasped back at Killik, his eyes flaring with urgency, with grief. "Wolf is dead. Simon *kill* him, break him, shame him before all the clan. *Dead.*"

Wait, Simon had—what? Louisa couldn't suppress her flinch, the shocked gasp in her throat—but Killik growled and shook his head, his expression fierce, uncompromising. "No," he hissed, digging his claws into Ulfarr's cheek. "Not dead. Here. Helping kin. Building this camp. Caring for the fatherless. Making this pretty, hungry woman scream and beg and *weep* upon your perfect Skai prick."

His glance at Louisa was sharp, purposeful, and far too late, she drew in breath, dragged a smile to her mouth. "So perfect, sweetheart," she said, with only a faint hitch in her voice. "I've never had such a kind, generous lover in all my life. Gods, you even helped me so sweetly through that bludgeoning I just bore from Killik! Though why you think he's a good lover is still entirely beyond fathoming!"

There was an instant's stillness, in which Ulfarr blinked at her, his heavy brow furrowing—but beside him, Killik's eyes shifted, softened, into something almost... relieved. "Ungrateful harpy," he sneered at Louisa, though there was no real heat in his voice. "I should have liked to see you try to swallow my wolf's prick without my ploughing first! I was only readying you for him, as any good Skai should, when he knows his clanmate bears such a prick as his! What kind of bedmate should I be, to offer him only half a dry, tight womb to fuck? Rather than one that is soft and ready and open, and eager to suck him whole?"

Something caught in Louisa's belly at even the thought— had that really been Killik's intent with all that?—and she had to fight for air, for conscious thought. "Well, you could have been a little gentler about it!" she shot back. "Or a little slower! Why did you need to resort to—to *immediate stabbing!*"

Killik's snort was incredulous, his glimmering eyes darting down to Ulfarr, as if seeking confirmation of Louisa's utter folly. "You would ken this woman has never *met* me, Wolf," he groused. "When have I ever shown the least wish for aught but *immediate stabbing*? Skai-kesh above, did she think I should cuddle her, or call her pretty names? Mayhap write her a fancy Ka-esh letter whilst I wait?"

The derision on his voice was so sharp, so absolute, that Louisa's cursed mouth barked a short, helpless laugh—and oh, Ulfarr's mouth was quivering, too. His eyes a little clearer, a little calmer, and Louisa didn't even care when Killik poked her in the shoulder, his sharp claw digging into her skin. "And also, woman," he went on, as if warming to his theme, "what kind of bedmate should I be, to dawdle and fritter about with you, whilst my hungry wolf was watching, and waiting! I wished you for a gift for *him*, and not *once* did I dream you would be fool enough to bind *me* into this, also!"

And curse it, Louisa was still smiling at him, warm and damnably genuine, because he'd gone and brought that *binding* up again—and in truth, he didn't even look that angry about it. Especially when he glanced back down at Ulfarr, at where Ulfarr's face looked clearer, more focused than before, his eyes glimmering with something almost like... hope.

"But you are—sure you do not—mind, Killik," Ulfarr said, between his heaving breaths. "You shall not—miss your other—bedmates—too much."

But Killik only scoffed, and waved it away. "Ach, I shall endure," he replied, with a too-casual shrug. "And it is only for five more nights, is it not?"

Right. Five more nights, now. Already halfway. And Louisa had to fight to hide her disappointment, to swallow down the sudden rising lump in her throat, the prickling behind her eyes. Gods, she was already going to miss Ulfarr so much, and maybe even Killik, too. Especially after what they'd just done, even if it hadn't meant anything, especially on Killik's part—right? And there was the sudden, sinking realization that of course Killik hadn't wanted to be kind about it, or intimate about it, because this had only ever been for Ulfarr in the first place...

But damn it, now Ulfarr was slightly wilting beneath her too, that darkness weighing down his eyes, thinning his mouth. And Killik caught it too, his body lurching closer, his hand again patting Ulfarr's cheek. "And now, Wolf," he added, "for these next five nights, I shall take great joy in further stabbing this woman, and watching her squirm and squawk and squeal upon me. You shall need to offer her much comfort, I ken. And much sweet relief with your fat Skai prick."

And yes, that seemed to ease away the darkness, Ulfarr's mouth softening again, his eyes shining on Louisa's face. And she twitched a smile back, and even reached her hand up to mimic Killik's, patting against Ulfarr's other cheek. Almost as if cradling his face between them, both of them coming together to care for him, to comfort him.

"I can't wait, sweetheart," she told him, as she kept stroking his cheek, matching Killik's movements on the other side. "And maybe you can keep me from stealing Killik's daggers, and stabbing him straight back. Because it would be so damned satisfying to watch *him* squirm and squeal too, don't you think? Maybe even"—she raised her brows at Killik—"upon a perfect Skai prick?"

Killik instantly balked, sputtering, while Ulfarr's eyes warmed even more as they flicked toward Killik's face. As if he wouldn't at all mind the idea, oh gods—but Killik certainly did, and in a flash of motion, he whipped his dagger out from his hair, and waved it dangerously close to

Ulfarr and Louisa's noses. "No, you spiteful harpy," he hissed at Louisa. "This is *my* show. You dance for *me!*"

But Ulfarr was still almost smiling, and Louisa was grinning too. And maybe—maybe that was even a dimple, quivering in Killik's cheek, undermining his thunderous glare between them. "Out, meddlesome woman," he snapped, pointing his dagger toward the curtain. "Off with you. Before you provoke me to stab you again!"

Louisa made a face at him, but that shimmering warmth was still there, because he—he was again suggesting he might do that again. He would. And somehow it smoothed over that quiet, aching awareness that he was sending her away again, getting rid of her again, even after all that...

But then Ulfarr's big hand snapped up, circled tight around Killik's wrist. "But you shall yet walk Louisa back to her home," he said, "and be sure she is safe. Ach?"

The command glinted in his eyes, rumbled deep in his voice, and for an instant, Killik again seemed caught in it, disconcerted. "Ach, ach," he replied, with a roll of his eyes, a too-dismissive wave of his hand. "But only if you rest, and *stay.*"

He'd again flipped the dagger in his fingers, pointing it imperiously down toward Ulfarr's nose. But Ulfarr's smile back was slow, grateful, his heavy gaze flicking to Louisa's face. "I thank you for such a great gift, Louisa," he murmured. "You have brought us both much joy, this night."

Louisa's throat convulsed, and she gave a short, shaky nod, and a small, true smile. "You too, sweetheart," she said. "It's been such a pleasure."

Ulfarr nodded back, again with such reverent gratefulness in his eyes—until he flinched, and hissed through his teeth. Because—because Killik had produced a large, clean-looking rag, and had lightly settled it over Ulfarr's exposed groin. And wait, the rag was already spreading with red, oh gods, and Ulfarr was—

Was Ulfarr... *injured*? From... from that? From what they'd just done?

But curse it, Ulfarr was studiously looking away now, his jaw tight, and Killik's claws clamped at Louisa's arm, as his other hand shoved another clean rag toward her. And his glittering eyes on hers seemed to say, *No. Don't you dare.*

"Now come, woman, and clean up your own mess," Killik snapped. "Before I lose my patience, and lock you out in the dark alone."

It was probably more empty threats, or even more teasing, but suddenly Louisa couldn't seem to hold his eyes, couldn't even begin to find a reply. Could only nod, and try to obey, blocking off the seeping liquid as surreptitiously as she could. While fighting to ignore Ulfarr's ongoing stilted silence, his turned-away face, the ever-spreading redness pooling across that rag...

"Bye, then," she whispered at him, foolish, foolish. "Feel better soon, sweetheart."

And without waiting for an answer, she spun toward the door, and fled.

26

Escaping that underground room, it turned out, wasn't as easy as Louisa might have hoped.

It first required walking past a still-watching Polly and Igull, while Igull grinned and waved. And next had been the large, open room beyond the curtain, where a half-dozen heads instantly swivelled toward Louisa and Killik, as if they all knew exactly what had just gone on—but of course they would know, wouldn't they? If nothing else, they would have heard it, right? Would have heard Louisa whimpering and shouting as two orcs had taken turns with her? In *public*?

Louisa kept her head down as she walked past, her face furiously burning—and making matters even worse was the situation between her legs, which was rapidly overwhelming Killik's useless rag. And once they finally stepped out into the moonlit night, she had to run for the nearest bush, clawing up her skirts, as hot streams of thick, sweet-scented fluid gushed out onto the ground at her feet.

Of course, Killik didn't even have the decency to give her some privacy, and instead silently stalked over, plucked up her sodden rag, and handed over a new one. And Louisa couldn't seem to look at him, let alone speak, not even to tell him to leave her the hell alone, because—because he'd done this. He'd done it, on purpose, he and Ulfarr had bedded her, filled her with their orc pricks, flooded her with their combined orc mess, and it meant nothing, nothing, *nothing*. Five nights.

And Killik didn't even need to say it, didn't need to remind her, because this already said it all, didn't it? The way he was just standing here in silence, coolly observing her ongoing humiliation, silently reminding her who was in charge. *This is my show. You dance for me.*

Louisa still couldn't look at Killik once they finally began walking again, heading due north, back toward her house. But despite the moonlight above, and her attempts at breathing into her steps, the path was still almost impossible to see—and she soon tripped over a root, and almost sprawled face-first into the earth.

But then—Killik. Killik, here, catching her with strong hands, holding her steady. And gods, what the hell was wrong with her, because even the feel of him touching her again, holding her again, was making something clench and churn in her belly, as heat prickled behind her eyes. No. He didn't care. It meant nothing, not even if he'd just bedded her. Five nights.

"Slower steps, then, woman," Killik said now, as he settled his hand to her elbow, and guided her forward again. "Feel the earth beneath you."

Louisa gave a weary sigh, but nodded, fought to redouble her efforts, to focus on her feet. Just one step, and then another, and another, he didn't care, five nights...

"I ken this... went well, this night," Killik abruptly said, into the silence. "Ach?"

Louisa couldn't hide her flinch, her sharp glance toward his face. But it was too dark to see any of it, too dark to tell if he was mocking her, or baiting her, or...

"Oh?" she replied, as steadily as she could. "How so?"

There was an instant's silence, a faint twitch of Killik's claws on her elbow. "This—pleased Wolf," he said, clipped. "You saw how he was amidst this, ach? How he was"—he hesitated—"more... *himself.*"

Right. And while Louisa couldn't lay claim to having known how Ulfarr had once been, she also couldn't deny that he'd felt almost... *right*, somehow, in the midst of all that. He'd felt calm, and confident, and commanding, even as he'd willingly let Killik take the lead. But even that had almost felt like a... a conscious choice, on Ulfarr's part, rather than a necessity. He'd wanted Killik in charge, he'd liked it, so he'd supported it. Encouraged it.

"He did seem... better," Louisa finally said, into the silence. "He seemed to enjoy your... dynamic... a lot."

And gods, why was she even giving Killik this, offering him anything whatsoever—but that might have been a chuckle beside her, low and indulgent. "Ach, he did," Killik replied. "Even I did not guess how much he should welcome having a fine lady to defend and care for. How this should speak to him, and draw him out, thus."

Oh. Louisa shot another narrow look toward him—had he therefore been insulting her on *purpose?*—but she still couldn't make out Killik's face, couldn't weigh the meaning behind his heavy sigh. "Our son sometimes draws this from him, also," he continued. "Wolf was oft thus, before, with any of us who needed his help, or his guarding, or his comfort."

Louisa's sideways glance was startled this time, because—was Killik offering up information about Ulfarr's past? In the face of all his demands, all his orders?

But he'd said it, on purpose, and now he was even letting it hang there, hovering like this between them. As if—as if he wanted her to ask. To try. *You never ask the right questions...*

"You said, back there, that Ulfarr cared for fatherless Skai," Louisa ventured, tentative, into the darkness. "Was that... his job, somehow? Maybe as part of... his pack?"

She fully expected Killik to refuse to answer, or maybe demand where she'd heard about the pack—but he only sighed again, heavier this time. "Ach, it was," he replied. "At first, Wolf's pack was only meant to be a punishment from his father, a curse—but Wolf faced this, and did this. He helped our clan's orclings, and tended them, and guarded them, for many, many summers."

Oh. Louisa's breath caught, because that did sound like Ulfarr, that was exactly what he would do—and *Killik* had told her this. Killik had told her this, about Ulfarr's past, despite his own rule against it, and he was even drawing in another slow, deep breath. "But Wolf was only a youngling himself, at first," Killik added. "Mayhap a few summers older than our own son now. And I ken"—he barked a hoarse laugh—"if we dumped a pack of wild orclings upon Sune, he should gladly let them all die within a fortnight."

There was something warm and wistful in his voice, or maybe even proud, and Louisa twitched a smile toward him, despite the odd clench in her chest, in her throat. "And you were part of Ulfarr's pack?" she asked, carefully. "From the start?"

She again expected Killik to refuse, but she could just make out the slow shake of his head. "Not at first," he replied. "I was older than the rest of them. But Wolf saw me, saw how I needed help, and he... he offered this."

It was another question, hanging there between them, and Louisa took a breath, let it out. "What... what happened, then? Why did you need help?"

There was another long moment's silence, broken only by the crackling leaves beneath Louisa's heavy boots. "My father was killed in battle before I saw five summers," Killik replied, very steadily. "And my mother never wished to know me. So I lived by following Alfver's pack, hunting and eating scraps, and offering... *favours* to his warriors. Doing aught I could to stay alive, in the midst of this war."

Oh. Oh, gods. He made it sound almost simple, almost normal, and not like the sickening horrifying experience it must have been, and Louisa couldn't keep her breath steady, or keep the shock out of her voice. "I'm so sorry, Killik," she gasped. "That must have been—*awful.*"

Killik shrugged, but Louisa could hear his exhale, juddering from his throat. "Ach, it was war," he said, his voice still unnaturally calm. "But Wolf was a gift of Skai-kesh toward me. He called me one of his pups, ach, but he always treated me as his equal. His—friend. And together, we tended our little wolf-pack, and trained them up, and taught them to stay safe. And even when Wolf was called more and more to fight, and to lead Skai bands in battle beside his father, he did not forget me, or his pack. He never, ever stopped guarding us, or caring for us. Not until—"

But there his voice broke, and Louisa could finally feel his barrier snapping back into place, surging tall and impenetrable between them. He still didn't want to talk about that. About, surely, whatever darkness Ulfarr had hinted at back there, with such grief and shame in his eyes. *Wolf is dead. Simon kill him, break him, shame him before all the clan.*

So Louisa took a deep breath, searched for another question, another way. "So how long," she began, "have you and Ulfarr been... intimate, then? For... quite some time?"

She grimaced even as she said it, because maybe it sounded like an assumption, an accusation—but she was deeply relieved to catch that shake of Killik's head. "Only mayhap five summers, now," he said. "Wolf always refused to touch me, for he saw it as a stain upon all those years of his care for me, or some such foolery. But he is not my blood, he is *not* my father. And he never *was* this, not for me—so once I was of age, there was no good cause for him to spurn me!"

Killik's voice had risen, suggesting this was something important to him, and—oh. Something he'd been hurt by. He'd wanted Ulfarr, he'd made that clear to Ulfarr, and

Ulfarr had refused him. Maybe for years. And now—now Killik had the upper hand, Killik was the one with all the bedmates, while Ulfarr longed for... him.

And damn it, Louisa could understand it, could understand *him*—and she sighed and nodded, her elbow twitching against the still-sharp grip of his hand. "So how did you convince him, then?" she asked, as lightly as she could. "You must have done a damned good job of it, because he's certainly not spurning you now."

She could feel Killik's surprise, his glance toward her—and then a catch of an exhale, maybe a laugh. "Ach, no, he would not dare," he replied, and his voice was smooth again, satisfied. "But ach, I had seen how he was not—himself. How he was less and less himself with each passing day. He would not heed my counsel, nor speak his truth to me, but I knew he needed help, needed relief, needed *peace*. So I—pushed him into my bed. I wielded my daggers and steel against him, until he gave it. Until he was weeping and *begging* me for it."

There was a fierce, vindictive satisfaction in his voice, and an unmistakable relief—and Louisa's exhale felt relieved too, coming out heavy and hushed. "I'm glad," she said, quiet. "That was—very generous of you, Killik."

She could feel his shrug, shifting the grip of his hand still on her elbow, but then a brief squeeze of that hand, too. "Ach, it was to my own gain also," he said dismissively. "After all his denial toward me, I took great joy in witnessing the powerful Wolf of the Skai bound in my thrall, whimpering upon my daggers, spraying his seed upon my command. Praising me, and begging for yet more of his helpless little pup's strong Skai ploughing."

Louisa's breath caught, too loud and betraying, because gods, that would have been a sight. And what would they look like together, would Killik have done it the same way he'd just done with Louisa? The way he'd promised to again...

But no. No, she was not thinking about that. It didn't mean anything. Killik was very clearly in this for Ulfarr, and that was all. And she needed to remember that, and...

"And... it helped, after?" she asked, too quickly. "At least a little?"

Killik sighed, but nodded. "Ach, it did," he replied. "More than aught else until then. And once Wolf... let me in, you ken, I could follow what else he longed for, also, and then help to gain this. I helped him care for his former packmates and their kin. I helped him face old vows and burdens, and make amends to those he has wronged. I guided him to help younglings again, to keep them safe, to even adopt Sune as his own. And whilst it has all helped, he is not yet healed. Not yet himself. So now"—he sighed again, heavier—"I help him gain a woman, also."

Right. Back to this again. But suddenly Louisa couldn't bear to think of it, couldn't stand the thought that she was just another ploy, another sacrifice in Killik's ever-lengthening list of sacrifices. Another attempt at gaining the loyalty of the orc he longed for, or maybe—maybe even repaying the orc he felt he owed. To the point where he would even go to bed with the woman, too, and make sure he couldn't have sons...

She flinched at the thought, at that sudden memory of Ulfarr saying Killik had somehow blocked off his seed—because gods, she'd barely even bothered to question that back there, had she? And curse it, she could feel Killik's eyes studying her, his claws pricking into her elbow, almost as if saying, *What? Speak this.*

"So is that why you're supposedly not able to father sons now, too?" she asked, too high-pitched. "Because you wanted to be able to—*help* Ulfarr in bed like this? Without risking children from it?"

There was an instant's stillness between them, a spasm of Killik's hand on her elbow. "Ach, no," he snapped, his voice hard. "I found a healer to stopper my seed as soon as I was old enough to do this. You ken I have *any* wish to raise sons of my own blood, after helping Wolf raise a dozen of them?"

He sounded incredulous, almost irate, and he'd even snapped a dagger from his hair, its blade gleaming in the faint moonlight. "And I now have Sune," he added flatly, "*and* our teaching at the mountain—and even beyond this, I am yet beset by orclings on all sides! They flock to Wolf like needy little fleas, who shall never again unlatch from their hapless host!"

Louisa blinked, as something knocked against her ribs—Killik really didn't want to father sons, either?—and then her breath escaped in a laugh, choked and relieved from her throat. "I can see that," she said lightly. "I met Leikr and his friends today, and they definitely seemed very fond of Ulfarr."

Killik's scoff was loud and instant, but it sounded a little warmer, too. "No, you ken?" he drawled, with obvious derision. "And you ken there are five more just like him, lurking behind every bush! And some days, our grown brothers are just as bad as the orclings! Ach, just last week"—he wildly waved his dagger back toward the camp—"Wolf spent half an afternoon tending Fasti's broken claw! Fasti is more than *twenty summers old!*"

Louisa's laugh rippled out between them, shaking her shoulders, quivering on her mouth. And suddenly the darkness around them felt warm, almost safe, especially with Killik's hand still on her elbow, his claws gently prodding into her skin.

"But it must be good for Ulfarr, right?" she asked, with only a little hesitation in her voice. "I mean, Halthorr told me he's not allowed to rebuild his pack, not like it was before— but surely having this camp still helps, too?"

She could just make out Killik's nod, and then his long, slow exhale. "Ach, it does help," he said. "Many of the orcs now here are our old packmates, and they yet care for Wolf, and he for them. And he is always—better, when he is here. Where his help and his strength is seen, and honoured, and needed."

Louisa nodded, because that had been very evident, throughout the entire day today. Ulfarr had been valued at the camp, and respected, and needed, and... and...

"And he really can't just... stay, then?" she asked, before she could stop it—and oh, even the thought of it was too powerful, drawing too deep at her own foolish, selfish longing. Gods, if Ulfarr could just stay, that would solve so many problems, and even do away with the most painful part of Killik's accusations toward her earlier, right? *Shall you abandon your home, and your lands? Shall you come to live at Orc Mountain...*

The hope thumped higher in Louisa's chest as she waited, her eyes uselessly searching Killik's profile in the dark. *Prove this to me,* he'd demanded, and without that damned leaving-her-lands requirement, Louisa could keep trying to prove it, couldn't she? Gods, hadn't she just fucked them both in a public room? Hadn't she given both Killik and Ulfarr exactly what they'd wanted from her?

But Killik's silence was too long, too heavy, and finally he gave another slow, resigned sigh. "No, woman," he said, his voice far flatter than before. "Staying at the mountain is a term of Wolf's punishment, and he cannot break this, if he wishes to keep his life. Even now, we have spent too much time here, and must return home to the mountain tomorrow."

Right. But Louisa's longing was still clutching, coiling hard and miserable in her belly. "And Ulfarr couldn't just live at the mountain, and—have a woman friend who lived here?" she asked, but no, no, what was she saying, *no.* "Just like—his old packmates are here? And he could—visit? Or she could... visit there? Even after the ten nights?"

Too late, she winced and clamped her mouth shut, but it was out there, she'd said it. And surely Killik could see her burning face, her eyes dropping to the ground, and why wasn't he answering, what was he thinking, please...

"No, woman," he said finally, his voice wooden. "Not with how this now stands. He cannot. And *you* cannot."

His voice was so hard, so certain, so utterly decisive—and so brutally painful, like a sharp kick in the chest. And Louisa couldn't look up, couldn't stop blinking her suddenly wet eyes, and it was so foolish, so ludicrous. She knew what this was, Killik had made it so clear, and what difference did it make if he'd touched her, stabbed his sharp hungry body into her, poured out his seed inside her...

"I—understand," she said, her voice wavering. "I'll just—go, then."

She jerked her head sideways, toward where she could make out the edge of her yard up ahead—and when Killik didn't answer, she wrenched away from him, and lurched forward. Just needed to escape him, to forget him, to clear out the mess in her brain from him...

"Louisa," Killik said behind her—he'd said her *name*—and oh, that was his hand, curling against her elbow again. "Wait."

Louisa froze, her heart hammering, her breaths panting too rapid from her lungs. And she could hear Killik's sigh, could feel his body shifting closer...

"I—I thank you, for tonight," he said, his voice a rasp. "This was... good. This... pleased me."

What? Louisa blinked up at him, at where he was so close, so close she could feel his breaths, could almost taste the echoes of his words. *This was good. This pleased me.* As if... as if maybe she'd proven something, after all.

"Now go, and rest," he murmured. "I shall come for you when next we are here, ach? We shall be out working for the clan these next few days, so next week, mayhap."

Next week. Louisa's stomach plummeted again, but it was still something, something, a small flickering hope. And then—the touch of something that might have been Killik's lips, brief but warm against her forehead.

He'd... *kissed* her.

Louisa froze in place, and for an instant, she wanted to shout at him, to claw at him, to beg. To say, *Please stay, how can you just say no, how can you just walk away...*

But Killik didn't care, he didn't. This was only a deal, only five more nights. He was leaving. Leaving...

And suddenly Louisa couldn't bear it, couldn't stand to watch him go. And after a brief clutch against him, a foolish stroke to his hard forbidding chest, she twisted away, and staggered off into the darkness.

27

ouisa spent yet another restless night. Kicking and twisting in her bed, frowning tiredly at the ceiling, shoving at the thoughts of Killik and Ulfarr that just wouldn't go away.

This is very good. You show us great honour. So sweet. You are wondrous, Louisa.

No. He cannot. You cannot.

It wasn't at all helped by the silken wetness still seeping from inside her, or the rising dull ache deeper within. Or the cursed hunger that kept swirling at the memories of it, of Killik groaning as he'd pulsed out into her, of Ulfarr's too-large strength opening her, pushing its way inside...

Louisa finally had to use her hand to wring out her own pleasure—twice—before she could fall asleep. But even that was fraught, because her dreams were full of it, of them, of a longing so strong it felt like it was crushing her, wringing her empty beneath its weight.

By morning, she was exhausted and irritable, but there was also a grim, resigned awareness as she washed and dressed. As wondrous as last night had been—and as tempting as Killik's challenge of proving it had been—she needed to remember the actual truth of it. This was a deal. It was only five more nights. And maybe she should even tell Killik she was done with it again, try to abandon it, forget it for good, just like Lord Scall...

But—no. No. She wouldn't. Last night had been unlike anything she'd ever known. It had given her so much pleasure, so much wonder—and even those fleeting, beautiful moments of... peace. Just like the peace she'd felt seeing the camp the day before, and knowing that she was using Lord Scall's land for good. Not forgetting what he'd done, but instead perhaps... facing it. Helping the people he'd harmed. Making amends.

It was almost enough to drown out the lingering longing, and the ache of Killik leaving, and not coming back for a week. Because yes, it still hurt, it still clutched deep in her belly—but Louisa could face it. She still had five more nights with them, and then her land would be hers, forever. She could focus on the hope, and the healing, and the peace.

So she threw herself into the day with as much determination as she could, laughing and chattering with her staff and the children over breakfast, and then tackling the task of cleaning the kitchen's oven and chimney, a daunting project she'd been putting off for months. And while it was filthy, exhausting work—especially without the help of Elise and Gladys, who were still dealing with the venison in the cellar—it at least shoved away the memories from the night before, until they were only nattering away in a tired corner of her brain. Next week, an entire damned week, and then—

A bang. At the door behind her.

Louisa whipped around, her heart pounding—just as more bangs pounded, sharp and staccato against the door. As if someone needed in. Urgently.

It had to be Joan, some kind of emergency—and Louisa leapt up, rushed over to yank the door open. And found—

An orc. A... young orc. A young, slim, grey-skinned orc,

maybe fourteen or fifteen years old, with pulled-up hair, and a flushed, wet, wide-eyed face. Looking frantic, and in pain, because—Louisa's eyes rapidly swept down over his tunic and trousers—he was *bleeding*. His trousers were badly torn at the knee, and his calf was a horrifying mass of deep, vicious-looking cuts, pooling bright streams of red down onto his soft leather boots.

Louisa's eyes held on the boots for an instant too long, and then she yanked the door open wider, and fervently waved the orc inside. "Good gods, sweetheart," she croaked, "what the hell happened to you? Did you—get attacked? By an animal, maybe?"

The orc grimaced and shook his head, but willingly limped inside, pain flashing across his eyes with every step. And he kept glancing backwards, too, toward the still-open door behind him, toward—Louisa groaned aloud—toward *Rikard*. Gods *damn* it.

"Stop that orc!" Rikard hollered, huffing and gasping as he staggered up toward her door, with two of his armed stooges jogging along behind him. "Get that trespasser, Louisa!"

Louisa shot a look back at the young orc now hovering behind her—at his pale face, his quivering mouth, the genuine terror glimmering in his eyes. And without thinking, she shoved him further behind her, and firmly planted herself between him and the open door.

"What the hell is this about, Rikard?" she demanded. "You can't honestly be accusing this—this juvenile—of trespassing, while you're about to shove your way into my house?!"

Rikard shot Louisa a dark, baleful glare, but reeled slightly back from her open doorway, so he could loom menacingly just outside it. "I'm only seeking to uphold the law, Louisa," he snarled. "And that orc"—he jabbed his thick finger toward the orc behind her—"was caught openly trespassing, on my property! As you *swore* to me those odious orcs wouldn't do!"

Louisa darted another look back at the orc, at his drawn face and pleading terrified eyes, and she drew in a shaky breath, fought to follow this, to think. "I know the orcs have been very careful about the property lines, Rikard," she countered. "And do you even have proof that he was on your land?"

"Yes, I do have proof!" Rikard roared, waving a furious hand toward the orc. "He was caught in one of my traps!"

The horror surged in Louisa's chest, her eyes snapping back down to the orc's injured leg. To where those sharp, deep cuts suddenly did look a lot like the marks from a trap, from a strong steel wire, perhaps. And those smaller cuts all around it, those would be—Louisa closed her eyes—from the orc's own claws, scratching at the wire, desperately trying to break himself free.

"That is vile, Rikard," Louisa hissed, and suddenly she was so furious she was shaking with it. "You said your traps were snares, not steel! That is disgustingly inhumane, and a shockingly disproportionate punishment for a minor petty crime! And for the three of you to chase him all the way here, with weapons?! He's badly injured, and he's not even of age! What the *fuck*!"

But Rikard only bristled and glowered at her, his lip viciously curling. "Your language is unbefitting for a lady, Louisa. And he's not *human*, he looks full-grown to me, *and* he was trespassing! How is it *my* doing if he learned the consequences of his own illegal actions! And we *did* even kindly untangle him, but"—he shot another vicious glare toward the orc—"then he *assaulted* us, and *ran*!"

Louisa's glance backwards found the young orc even paler than before, his head slightly shaking. And damn it, Louisa could easily envision how this had gone, and she squared her shoulders, glared back at Rikard's red face. "He assaulted you, or he fought you off so he could escape?" she demanded. "What were you going to do, extort a fine for his return?"

But even as she said it, she knew it was far too rational, especially with that familiar petulant look in Rikard's beady eyes. "Or," she continued, clipped, "you were going to keep him confined? Trap him in a dark cellar or a shed somewhere, until he told you every incriminating thing you wanted to hear, so you could use it against me, and try to force the orcs off my land? Or"—more comprehension flashed across her thoughts—"to try to force *me* off my land?"

There was a horrible moment's silence, in which Rikard's pouting face betrayed all of that as truth, damn him. "I told you, the orcs need to go, Louisa," he replied, his voice hard. "They have no right to be here!"

Louisa gritted her teeth and glared back, her hands clenched tight at her sides. "They have every right to be here," she retorted. "This is still *my* land, Rikard, and I'm allowed to share it with whoever I please! And orcs are people under the law, just like you, so legally, there is *nothing* you can do about them!"

Rikard's snarl was more like a roar, and he furiously waved toward the young orc again. "There is," he drawled, "when they're trespassing on my property! When they're breaking the *law*! At that point, I can do whatever the hell I want!"

A cold chill flared up Louisa's back, but she drew herself up taller, drew up strength from the solid floor beneath her feet. "Rikard, he's not of age," she shot back. "It was a mistake, and it won't happen again. And besides"—she shot a glance back at the pale, still-bleeding orc—"he now needs urgent medical care, because of you! You ought to be grateful he escaped you and came here, because if he'd died in your custody, due to *your* inhumane treatment, his kin would have every right to accuse you of murder! So I suggest you leave this at once, and get the hell off *my* property!"

Rikard huffed and sneered, puffing out his chest. "At this rate, it won't be your property for long, Louisa," he hissed. "You'll be hearing from me again very soon!"

It fired another sharp chill up Louisa's back, but she gave a cold, furious smile as she reached for the door. "How unfortunate for us both," she said, her voice hard. "Now have a good day, gentlemen. Goodbye!"

With that, she slammed the door in their faces, and snapped the locking bar down into place. And then she spun and sagged back against the closed door, her heart still pounding too fast, her breaths still thin and shallow. Waiting for more shouting, more demands, maybe for Rikard to try to break down the door—but wait, thank the gods, they were leaving. Crunching loudly down the lane, grumbling and clattering as they went.

It left Louisa finally alone with the young orc, who was now clutching at her counter, gazing warily toward her, and drawing in slow, gulping breaths. Breathing all the way to his uninjured foot, feeling the earth through it, letting it out...

Something hitched in Louisa's chest, and for an instant, she could only seem to stare back at him. At his breaths. His soft leather boots. And his bound-up hair, which—she swallowed—had a slim, gleaming dagger stuck through it. Just the same way Killik always wore his hair, and the sight of it jolted Louisa's suspicion higher, into something much like certainty...

"I—I'm Louisa," she said, into the stilted silence. "And you are...?"

The orc didn't reply, only drew in another slow, deep breath, and stared at her with flinty, defiant eyes. But he didn't even need to say it, because the truth of it was shouting between them, like a shuddering drumbeat in Louisa's chest.

It was Sune. Killik and Ulfarr's *son*.

28

Killik and Ulfarr's son was here. Here, in Louisa's kitchen.

It was taking Louisa's stuttering brain far too long to follow it, especially with the way he kept looking at her, with that open defiance still flashing in his dark eyes. And for an instant, Louisa was starkly reminded of Killik, strong enough that her mouth twitched—but damn it, Killik and Ulfarr's son was here, he was injured, he was bleeding all over her kitchen. And she needed to think, needed to focus, to help.

"Can I—can I look at your leg, then, sweetheart?" she said, still a little shaky. "Perhaps we can try to stop the bleeding?"

The orc—Sune—twitched a nod, and with a grimace and a shove of his hands, he hopped up backwards to sit on Louisa's counter. And once Louisa had fetched a clean cloth and a bowl of water, she knelt to inspect his wounded leg, still dripping blood onto her floor.

Gods, it was ghastly. Those thick wire-cuts had gone viciously deep, to the point where she could even catch a glimpse of white bone beneath—and Louisa's first, tentative touch of the wet cloth at one of the smaller scratches sent a sharp, visceral shudder through Sune's leg, his breaths panting, his eyes bright with unshed tears. And when Louisa gritted her teeth, tried again, he choked a thin yelping sound, and leapt off the counter, staggering toward the door.

"Wait!" Louisa gasped, throwing the cloth aside, and raising both hands. "Wait, don't go. You can't walk like this, what if—what if you—"

What if you collapse and die, she wanted to say, *what if Rikard finds you again*—but she bit her lip just in time, and shook her head. "It's not safe for you to go out alone and wounded like this," she said, as firmly as she could. "Your fathers would have my head, all right?"

Sune's eyes snapped up at that mention of his fathers, something twisting on his mouth. And for the first time in this mess, Louisa's jolting brain wondered—where the hell *were* Killik and Ulfarr, anyway? They couldn't know Sune was here, right? Especially since Ulfarr had made it clear he hadn't wanted Sune to meet Louisa yet?

But maybe—maybe they might follow him here, somehow, and a sudden hopefulness lurched in Louisa's chest. "Is there any chance Killik and Ulfarr might be following you, or searching for you? Or that they might be—nearby? Maybe still at the camp?"

Sune's mouth twisted again, his eyes now fixed blankly beyond Louisa's head, and he jerked a firm shake of his head. Because no, wait, of course, Killik had said last night that they were returning to Orc Mountain today, right? And that they would be away working for the next week?

"Is there any chance Killik and Ulfarr might still be at your mountain, then?" Louisa ventured. "Perhaps we could—send for them?"

But Sune twitched another shake of his head, and then made a walking motion with his fingers that first went south, and then east. Clearly suggesting the direction Killik and

Ulfarr had gone, and damn it, if Sune knew that, why was he here? Had he waited for them to be away, on purpose? Had he come here to spy on her? To speak to her?

But he still wasn't meeting her eyes, and Louisa's gaze darted again to his wounded leg, to where the blood was pooling dark and unnerving over his boot. "Then would you be willing to allow me to call a physician?" she asked, tentative. "Confidentially, of course?"

Sune wildly shook his head, his eyes again flashing with panic, and he again lurched toward the door. And curse it, he'd already escaped three full-grown men, he was nearly as tall as Louisa was, and she would be no match for him, would she? There was no chance of forcing him to stay, but he still needed help, she needed to think, think...

"Is there anyone else you know who could help you?" she asked. "Anyone at—at the camp? Or at your mountain, even?"

Sune's throat bobbed, his eyes darting back to Louisa's face—but then, thank the gods, he nodded. Nodded, and very clearly waved his hand up and south to indicate the mountain, even as he edged toward the door again. Trying to leave again, to go home again. To where he knew he could find help.

But—no. No. He couldn't travel all that way alone. Not like this. Louisa couldn't dare risk it. And she lurched back toward the door, holding his eyes, drawing herself as tall as she could.

"Right, then, sweetheart," she said, as firmly as she could. "I'm taking you home. Now."

She didn't miss the unmistakable relief in Sune's eyes, even as he shot a wary glance toward the cellar door— toward where Elise and Gladys were now walking in, gods damn it. And upon catching sight of Sune, Elise gasped, her hands clasping over her mouth, while Gladys put her hands to her hips, and looked Sune up and down with incredulous disbelief.

"What now, missus?" she demanded. "Where'd this one come from? And why's he bleeding on the floor?"

So Louisa made a quick round of introductions, and then explained the situation as succinctly as she could, as well as her plans to take Sune to Orc Mountain. Which, predictably, led to an impassioned round of protests and arguments, but Louisa stood firm throughout it all, truthfully informing them that there was nothing else to be done, and she would return home as soon as she could.

"It's perfectly safe," she told them, while desperately hoping that was true. "I already know a few women living there, and the orcs wouldn't hurt me, or trap me there. They'll just be glad to have Sune back again."

Sune had stood through all this in blank silence, his face looking more drawn with every passing moment—but at that, he jerked a nod, and made a sharp motion with his hand. Speaking in similar-looking signs to what Ulfarr and the other orcs had used at the camp, and Louisa silently cursed herself for not having attempted to learn even a little of it. But she gave a grateful smile toward Sune anyway, and a decisive nod toward her staff.

"See?" she said, as lightly as she could. "Now let's hurry this along, so we can get there before nightfall."

Thankfully, they gave up arguing after that, and Elise even packed a lunch for them, while Joan helped Louisa get the horses ready, and then guided a shaky-looking Sune up onto May's back. And though it was clear Sune had never ridden a horse before, he also looked reluctantly intrigued, and didn't protest as May jolted into motion beneath him.

"So I've never been to Orc Mountain before," Louisa told him, once they'd ridden out of the paddock. "I'm hoping you can help direct our route? Something as easy as possible for the horses would be ideal."

To her vague surprise, Sune nodded, and pointed purposefully off to the southeast. Even as May kept plodding on down the lane, so Louisa showed him how to use the reins, and explained how to be clear but gentle with May's mouth. A lesson he seemed to follow easily enough, carefully guiding May toward where he'd pointed, and then looking both surprised and pleased when she obliged.

It was without question the most promising expression Louisa had seen on him yet, so she drew in breath, and just kept on talking. Explaining how best to hold his seat, how to use his thighs and his heels to communicate with May, how to walk and trot and canter. All of which Sune again seemed to follow with impressive ease, and when Louisa finally showed him how to gallop, across a large patch of open clearing, he even smiled as he crouched lower over May, his black hair streaming out of its topknot, whipping around his still-pale face.

It was something, at least, and it meant they could travel faster than Louisa had expected—especially when it turned out that Sune's directions led to first a wide path, and then, further along, to an honest-to-gods road. A road Louisa certainly couldn't recall being there before—but then again, she hadn't travelled in this direction in years, either. And when she said this aloud to Sune—perhaps just in hopes of distracting him from his still-bloody leg—he signed something back toward her, something again utterly incomprehensible to her eyes.

"I'm so sorry, but I don't know any of your sign language at all," she told him, with a grimace. "But if you'd be willing to teach me a few words, I'd love to try to learn."

Sune shot her a wary, narrow-eyed look, as if he didn't at all believe her—but then he exhaled, and gave a very Killik-like whirl of his fingers. One that clearly said, *Go on, then.*

So Louisa drew in breath, and glanced forward at the still-distant bulk of Orc Mountain, looming over the trees up ahead. "How about—the sign for your home, then," she said. "Orc Mountain."

Sune's response was immediate, a swift upwards slice of his flat hand. But when Louisa attempted to repeat it, he shook his head, and did it again. And again, and again, until Louisa seemed to catch the way of it, speeding up the motion a little toward the top, and holding there for an instant, before dropping again.

"How about... your name, then?" Louisa asked next. "Sune?"

He nodded, and this time there were two parts to the sign, one for each syllable of his name, which he mouthed along as he signed. *Soo* was a brush of his fist to his navel, and *neh* was a tap of his fingers to his mouth.

"Soo-neh," Louisa repeated, mimicking the sign until he seemed satisfied. "It's a lovely name."

Sune's glance toward her was suddenly narrow, suspicious, so Louisa drew in breath, searched for something else. "How about Killik and Ulfarr's names, then?"

That earned her another narrow look, but then he pursed his lips, and again obliged. *Killik*, aptly enough, was a sideways punch of Sune's fist that looked much like a dagger-strike, while *Ulfarr* was an odd rising flare of his hand from his mouth. One Louisa had to attempt a few times, before realizing it was mimicking a howl. Like... a wolf.

The thought fluttered low and strange in her belly, and it occurred to her that Sune was looking wistful too, or maybe even sad. His eyes now fixed on May's head, his swallow visibly bobbing in his throat.

"So—what's it like, having Killik and Ulfarr as fathers?" Louisa asked, too quickly, into the silence. "I hope Killik is more careful with his daggers around you than he is with me? Though I'm sure Ulfarr would keep him in check, at least."

She half-regretted it even as she spoke—gods, what if

Sune thought she was criticizing them—but his expression softened again, and he nodded. And his fist slowly rose to his heart, thumping twice against it, before again making that howl sign, that wolf. *Ulfarr. Wolf.*

And though Louisa hadn't known what the heart-fist sign meant, its meaning was still far too clear, skipping her own heartbeat in her chest. Sune—loved Ulfarr. Very much.

"I can understand that," Louisa said now, and gods, maybe that wasn't appropriate, either. "Ulfarr is lovely, isn't he? So kind, and patient, and—and *safe.*"

Sune shot her another narrow sidelong look, but then sighed, and nodded. And then, after an instant's stillness, he squared his shoulders, and rapidly gestured something else. Something that looked like—him mimicking putting a ring on his finger, and then... then rocking a *baby*. And then, oh gods, he jabbed his slim clawed finger at Louisa, and made the *Ulfarr* sign again. As if Sune meant—he thought—he thought Louisa and Ulfarr were going to... get married? Have a baby?!

"Oh, gods, no!" Louisa exclaimed, too shrill, rapidly shaking her head. "No, nothing like that! Ulfarr and I are only friends, only for a short period of time, nothing more, and..."

Her voice trailed off into silence, because Sune was viciously glaring toward her, and shaking his head. And then, very slowly and deliberately, he pointed toward her, rapped his nose, and made the *Ulfarr* sign again. She— nose—Ulfarr—

Louisa couldn't bite back her groan, and squeezed her eyes shut. Damn it. She *smelled* like Ulfarr, he meant. And orcs could smell such things, yes, and even *Sune* could smell such things? And Louisa was not thinking about this, she was not, what the hell was she supposed to say, what if she lied and he could smell that, too...

"Look, it really isn't—serious," she finally said, with a

grimace. "I have my own home, with people I'm responsible for, and Ulfarr has a home with you and Killik, with his own people to care for, too. So marriage is truly out of the question, for both of us. And—and children, too."

Sune shot her another narrow, skeptical look, but his shoulders sagged a little, and that might have been relief, exhaling from his mouth. As if... as if he didn't *want* Ulfarr to marry Louisa, or have children with her.

And maybe Louisa should have felt insulted by that, but as she studied Sune's face, there was only sympathy, or maybe even sadness. And maybe she should just tell him the truth, that it wasn't something he would ever need to worry about—but it felt too tight, suddenly, too shaky in her throat. She needed to forget Lord Scall, Lord Scall was dead...

"And besides, Ulfarr already has a son," she said instead, attempting a smile toward Sune. "And I know he cares for you very much. And so does Killik."

Sune's mouth spasmed at Killik's name, and his glance toward her looked searching this time, uncertain. And then he jerked a shrug, one that might have meant something like, *Maybe. I'm not sure.*

And blinking at him, at that uncertainty on this wounded boy's face, Louisa suddenly wanted to curse Killik, to grab his own damned daggers, and start waving them in his eyes. Because she knew, with a deep, unshakeable certainty, that Killik loved Sune—but it would be just like him to not even say it, or make sure Sune knew it, right? Just like him to take a woman to bed, and then tell her maybe he'd come back in a week.

"Killik loves you, Sune," Louisa said, sharper now. "He would do *anything* to help you, and keep you safe. And if he hasn't made that *excessively* clear to you, you can be sure it's no fault whatsoever of your own, and is only due to Killik having the emotional sensitivity of a *slug!*"

Sune blinked at her, looking genuinely taken aback—but

then a brief smile twitched across his mouth. Looking almost grateful, for an instant, and Louisa couldn't help her own quick grin back, or the roll of her eyes. "An ancient, crispy, dried-out husk of a slug," she continued flatly. "Like the kind I often find mouldering in my compost pile."

Sune's mouth twitched again—and then he broke into silent laughter, his slim shoulders shaking, his mouth pulled into a broad, adorable grin. And Louisa laughed too, suddenly feeling light, easy, almost hopeful. Sune was alive, and she was going to get him safely home. And she was damn well going to have a word with Killik about this, too.

The rest of the trip passed with surprising speed, between their ongoing sign language practice, and then a brief break to eat and rest the horses. And while getting Sune off May's back still presented a challenge, his wounds' bleeding had noticeably lessened, and he seemed in less pain than before. And when he saw the lunch Elise had packed for them, his eyes lit up, and he gobbled it down as though he hadn't eaten in a week. And afterwards, he waved for Louisa to guide May under a tree-branch, so he could climb the tree with his hands and his one good leg, and then drop down onto May's back.

Louisa whistled as she watched, genuinely impressed, and earned a shy but pleased little grin in return. And as they headed back down the road, Sune's expression looked almost eager, his eyes bright and intent on the sight of the mountain up ahead.

Louisa had been trying to ignore that slowly rising spectre of Orc Mountain, looming ever closer and larger before them, but her heart was now racing in her chest, her breaths short and shallow. She was going to Orc Mountain, willingly, *now*. And she couldn't just turn around and leave again, either, because it was already late afternoon—and even if there'd been enough time to get home again before nightfall, Max and May still needed to rest. And Louisa still needed to make sure Sune was taken care of, and safe.

"Do you know when Killik and Ulfarr will be back here?" she tentatively asked Sune. "Soon, maybe?"

Sune bit his lip with a sharp tooth, and shook his head. *No*, he signed. *Killik and Ulfarr——nightfall.*

Nightfall was one of the many signs Louisa had learned that afternoon, mimicking the sun setting over the horizon. And though she nodded back, her heart thudded louder in her chest, her hands tight and clammy on Max's reins. So she would need to try to sort this out herself, then, and find a place to camp for the night. And maybe she could try asking at the mountain for Jule or Rosa, hope they remembered her, hope they were even still here...

But then the horses rounded a bend in the road, and suddenly—there it was. Orc Mountain.

And oh, good gods, it was huge. Soaring grey and craggy above them, its white peak nudging into the clouds above, its multiple smoke-streams wafting gently toward the west. And around it was a large rocky clearing, a smattering of wooden outbuildings, and a lane that went straight toward what appeared to be its front gate.

Louisa swallowed, her eyes darting uneasily up and around—was she just supposed to walk in?—when suddenly, sprinting out of the mountain, there were—people. Two people, two young people, both around Sune's age. One was another orc, with neatly braided black hair and greenish skin, while the other person was—a *girl*. A slim, blonde human girl, dressed in a frothy white dress, and a pair of sturdy-looking black boots.

"Sune!" the girl yelped, her hand clapping over her mouth, her eyes gaping at the sight of his mangled leg. "What in the gods' names did you *do*?!"

The green orc looked deeply alarmed too, his nostrils flaring, his clawed hand gripping the girl's arm, holding her still. While beside Louisa, Sune rolled his eyes, and began rapidly signing back toward them, so swift Louisa couldn't follow.

"It doesn't look like nothing, Sune!" the girl retorted, wringing her hands. "It looks like your leg is about to fall off! And what will Killik say, what if he makes you stay here for another whole fortnight again? Oh, I *told* you not to go, and now—"

She broke off there, her eyes darting warily toward Louisa—while the green orc rushed forward, his eyes fixed on Sune's bloody leg. "Ach, Sune," he croaked. "This looks and scents—*dreadful*. Ach, what did this to you, you must be in such pain, you must come to the sickroom at *once*."

He was speaking very quickly, his voice cracking, and he snatched for Sune's hand, dragging him toward the mountain—a futile effort, since Sune was still on an immobile May's back. But with a lurch, Sune awkwardly dismounted, sliding down into his friend's waiting grip, and he only slightly grimaced as he balanced on his good leg, and signed back something that might have meant, *I'm fine.*

But the green orc shook his head, and circled his arm around Sune's back, holding him upright. "You are not fine," he countered. "I can scent you, you stubborn Skai fool, you have *never* scented thus before, we must send for your fathers at *once*."

Sune heavily sighed, but he didn't argue this time, and gave a reassuring pat to his friend's shoulder. But his friend didn't look at all comforted, giving him another anguished, wet-eyed look, while the girl let out an irritated huff, and rushed over to grip at Sune's other arm. "Oh, he'll be all right, Timo," she said firmly, though she shot a worried look down at Sune's leg, too. "You should be telling him he deserves it for running off alone like that, and doing something so *stupid*, and making you worry all day like this!"

But the green orc—Timo, apparently—only shook his

head, guiding Sune along faster. Leaving Louisa alone with the horses, outside Orc Mountain, and she blinked helplessly up at its smoking bulk, and then back to Max and May. What the hell was she supposed to do? Should she follow Sune, leave the horses out here, go ask for help, or...?

But then Sune twisted around to look at her, and rapidly waved for his friends to stop. Followed by more signs, his hands flying fluid and purposeful, still too fast to follow—until Sune elbowed Timo, and then nodded purposefully back toward Louisa. As if saying, *Tell her.*

Timo jerked a nod, and then shot a distracted glance toward Louisa. "Sune says to put the horses in the stable for the night," he said hoarsely, as he pointed toward one of the nearest outbuildings. "They shall be safe there. And whilst you do this, we shall send someone to meet you, and welcome you for your stay."

Her stay? Louisa blinked at him, at Sune, and then grimaced, shook her head. "Look, I don't want to—impose, or stay any longer than necessary," she replied. "But I need to make sure you're safe, Sune, and that you get proper care, and—"

But Sune gave a rather Killik-like roll of his eyes, and again waved toward his friend, who drew in a breath, met Louisa's eyes. "Ach, Sune is safe now," he told her. "Our healer is the best in the realm, and shall do all he can for him. We shall take good care of him, also."

Louisa's heart was still thumping, her eyes darting warily between them—but Sune again caught her eyes, and gave an irritated wave toward the stable. And then signed something else, sharp and decisive, while Timo winced, and drew in a breath.

"Sune says you shall stay," he said. "You shall settle yourself, and wait for Killik and Ulfarr to come for you. You shall"—he twitched a faint smile toward her—"make our mountain your *home.*"

29

*Y*ou *shall make our mountain your home.*

Those words banged and echoed through Louisa's head as she guided Max and May into the stable, and settled them into an empty stall. The stable was clean and dry, with several other horses in it, and it felt bizarrely unreal to be taking off Max and May's tack, brushing them down, preparing for a visit to Orc Mountain. A place Sune had told her to make... her *home.*

But no. No. He surely hadn't meant it like that. Louisa was only reading into it, and feeling unsettled, nervous, unprepared. She hadn't at all intended to stay here, Killik had only wanted to see her in a week, and Ulfarr hadn't even wanted her to meet Sune... but what the hell else was she supposed to do? She was trapped here now, and her only choice was to keep going, right?

But gods, she hadn't properly anticipated it whatsoever, and she frowned down at her clothes as she stepped out of the stable. Along with the ash and dust from her morning stove-cleaning project, her shabby work dress was now covered with dirt and straw, and she looked abominably filthy, not at all ready to meet—

And then she stumbled straight into someone new, standing just outside the stable. Someone tall and dark-haired and capable-looking, wearing a men's tunic and trousers, and looking—familiar?

"Louisa!" the newcomer exclaimed, grinning broadly toward her. And Louisa startled and stared, her heart skipping, as recognition flashed through her thoughts.

It was *Jule*. Her old dear friend from years ago. They'd both been lords' daughters, and while Louisa had been a good five years older than Jule, they'd often spent time together, even after they'd both married their horrid lord husbands. Until Jule had abandoned her life as Lady Norr, and had run off to Orc Mountain.

Since then, Louisa had heard multiple sordid tales of Jule's demise—everything from death in childbirth to being eaten alive by the orcs' cruel captain. But they'd also exchanged a few letters over the years, and Jule had been the one to recommend Elise to her—so Louisa had known Jule was alive and well, at least. But now, blinking at her long-lost friend's smiling, pink-cheeked face, Louisa felt struck through with the truth of it, and the staggering, gods-damned relief.

"Jule!" she gasped, lurching forward, and suddenly she was caught in a tight hug, while water prickled behind her eyes. "Gods, it's so good to see you! I hope you've been well?"

She could feel Jule's fervent nod, and when they pulled apart Jule was grinning, her eyes bright. "Better than ever," she said. "And you too, I hope?"

Louisa swallowed, searched for an answer—but then was spared by the sudden appearance of another woman, racing out from the mountain. This one was small and slim and beaming, her blonde hair flying out straight behind her.

"You're finally here!" the new woman exclaimed, as she too hurled herself into Louisa's arms. "Oh, this is so exciting! I've been asking Killik when he'll bring you, and he just keeps giving me the runaround! Leave it to him to snag *you* as his new mate, and then swan around pretending it's some grand secret! How you've been able to bear him, I can't fathom! Are you here to stay?"

Louisa's thoughts were spinning again—what was this about Killik's new *mate*?—but she choked a laugh, and drew back to grin at the woman's eager face. It was Rosa, the clever, talkative, scholarly girl she'd helped escape Lord Kaspar's clutches several years before—and Rosa looked happy and content, the warmth shining in her blue eyes. And she was also dressed in an unusual ensemble, featuring a long, belted men's tunic, and a bright gold choker around her throat.

"It's so good to see you too, Rosa," Louisa said over the lump in her throat, even as she smiled so broadly it hurt. "Though I—I'm only here for a short visit. Perhaps"—she glanced uncertainly toward the mountain—"perhaps just until morning?"

But Rosa's blonde brows snapped together, her head shaking. "But why can't you stay longer?" she demanded. "You've just gotten here! Although wait"—she shot a brief, searching glance around the clearing—"is Killik not with you, too?"

Right. Of course they wouldn't have heard the entire tale—Sune's friends would have been rightfully focused on getting him to the sickroom—so Louisa drew in a breath, and then quickly told them the day's events. Starting with Sune's injury, and then how she'd defended him against Rikard, and brought him here to get medical help.

"You did the right thing, of course," Jule said firmly, once Louisa had finished. "Our healer is a marvel, and he'll have Sune back to normal in no time. But"—her brows furrowed—"did you say *Lord Rikard* did this to Sune? That horrid nephew who inherited your lands after Scall died?"

Louisa grimaced and nodded, and then explained that

entire situation, too. Telling Jule about the so-called trespassing, the traps, and Rikard's threats and ultimatums. While Jule's eyes went darker and darker, her mouth tight and thin.

"I'm so sorry you've gotten dragged into this," she said, once Louisa had finished. "Those lords have given us nothing but trouble, and the last thing we need is them targeting the camps. While you're here, I'd love to sit down together and have a proper discussion about all this—so surely you'll stay longer than just overnight, at least?"

But at that, Louisa hesitated, and shot another uneasy glance up at the looming mountain. Gods, even staying for one night would be pushing it, right? Killik was already going to be furious, and surely he wouldn't welcome her involvement in any political meetings, either...

But before she could reply, another small group of people emerged from the mountain up ahead. Another grown orc, together with two orc children, and another woman. The adult orc was huge and bare-chested, propping the smaller child on his hip, while the woman was tall and striking, with dark hair and golden skin. And like Rosa, she was also dressed only in what appeared to be a large belted tunic, though hers also had a gleaming steel dagger hooked onto the belt.

"Oh, good!" Rosa exclaimed, excitedly waving them over. "You'll want to see your fellow Skai, Louisa. You remember Simon, I'm sure! And this is Simon's mate Maria, and their sons Bjorn and Arnthorr!"

Her fellow Skai? And... Simon? Louisa twitched all over at the shock of recognition, because yes, yes, this was the same Simon orc she'd met back in the library when she'd first helped Rosa, wasn't it? The same Simon who'd smiled at her, and greeted her with such surprising politeness.

But... wait. That meant this was the same Simon Halthorr had spoken of, too. The Simon who was the *Enforcer*, he'd said. The Simon who had made that rule, and broken apart Ulfarr's pack, permanently.

And also—Louisa's stomach clenched—this was the Simon Ulfarr had brought up, just the night before. *Wolf is dead*, he'd said, with such grief in his wild eyes. *Simon kill him, break him, shame him before all the clan.*

And blinking at this Simon, it occurred to Louisa that he was the only orc she'd met so far who was even bigger than Ulfarr. He was impossibly tall, his chest and shoulders broad and powerful, and covered all over with vicious-looking scars. He also had several shining weapons hanging from his belt, and that might have been one glinting in his neat black braid, too. And had he used one of those weapons to... *kill Ulfarr's wolf?* To shame him before all the clan?

"Er, hello," Louisa made herself say, far too late, pasting a smile to her mouth. "It's, er, good to see you again, Simon. And nice to meet you all, too."

She'd managed a nod toward Maria, and then the two children. Earning a curious smile from the smaller orc in Simon's arms, and a suspicious nod from the older one, who might have been twelve years old. While this Maria flashed Louisa a swift, stunning grin, and even reached forward to shake her hand.

"It's so good to see you again, Louisa," she said warmly. "I'm not sure if you remember me, but we've met a few times. Back when I was the Duchess of Warmisham."

What? Louisa's mouth dropped open, her eyes gaping at this Maria's face. Because yes, the Duchess of Warmisham had been a young, beautifully dressed woman with golden skin and dark hair, and she'd always seemed deeply unhappy—and no wonder, because Duke Warmisham was yet another horrid warmongering lord, and also the father of Lord Kaspar, that vile cretin Louisa had gotten entangled with after Lord Scall. And yes, she had heard rumours of something gone wrong with Warmisham's wife, hadn't she?

And something about her running off a few years ago, never to be seen again...

Louisa's overwhelmed brain was still taking far too long to digest this, to make sense of it. How the hell had the *Duchess of Warmisham* ended up at Orc Mountain? And mated to this huge Simon? With two sons?

"Well," Louisa finally said toward the duchess—Maria—with an attempt at a smile. "I offer you my deepest congratulations on escaping your ghastly toad of a husband. And gaining such a lovely family, too."

Maria grinned back, and squeezed her older son a little closer. "It was a much-needed improvement," she said wryly. "And we're all so glad Killik has finally found a mate too, aren't we, Simon?"

The *mate* thing again. Louisa couldn't hide her wince, and opened her mouth to counter that point—but then froze at the look on this Simon's face. Because he hadn't answered Maria's question, and instead, he was frowning at Louisa, his heavy brows furrowing as his glinting eyes flicked up and down her form. As if... as if he was *judging* her.

Louisa shot a chagrined glance downwards, following his eyes—and again found the alarming sight of her shabby, filthy ensemble. "Er, I hope you'll forgive my appearance, this all happened quite suddenly today," she said. "And I was just telling Jule and Rosa, I won't be staying long, either."

Simon's eyes shifted as she spoke, but he kept looking at her like that, almost as if he was angry with her. While beside him, Maria looked confused, and a little alarmed, too—until finally Jule cleared her throat, and stepped forward between them.

"If you haven't already, Simon, we ought to send for Killik at once," Jule said. "He and Ulfarr will want to hear about their son's injury, and I'm sure Killik will want to welcome Louisa here, and show her around the mountain, too."

Louisa couldn't help a grateful look at Jule, but then her

eyes caught on Simon again, on his grim, forbidding face. "Er, but that's certainly not necessary," she said quickly. "I'd originally meant to camp elsewhere anyway, or I could even just sleep out here with the horses…"

Jule and Rosa both instantly balked at this, Jule waving her hands, and Rosa loudly protesting that she could do no such thing. But Louisa's eyes stayed fixed on Simon, because he clearly didn't want her here, and she didn't want to cause trouble, either. Especially if it might involve Killik and Ulfarr, or Sune, and…

"No, woman," Simon cut in now, in a deep, accented voice. "You ought to stay until Killik comes home. We shall speak with you again then."

Oh. There was another instant's awkward silence, in which Maria cast another confused look at Simon's face, and Jule and Rosa exchanged uneasy glances. Until beside Louisa, Rosa pulled herself taller, and cleared her throat. "Well, the Enforcer has spoken!" she said, a little too brightly. "So you'll stay the night, at least, right?"

There didn't seem to be any point in arguing, and finally Louisa twitched a nod, and said a strangled thank-you. And soon she found herself being herded off between Jule and Rosa toward Orc Mountain, leaving the others behind. And when Louisa shot a furtive glance backwards, Maria still looked just as confused as she felt, while Simon kept frowning beside her.

"What's with Simon?" Rosa demanded, once they were hopefully out of his earshot. "It's not at all like him to be so rude! You'd think he'd be pleased to have his kin-brother's new woman come to visit!"

She'd shot Louisa an affronted look, dragging her a little faster toward the rising stone wall of the mountain before them, while on Louisa's other side, Jule gave a too-casual wave of her hand. "I'm sure it's nothing," she said, though she didn't quite meet Louisa's eyes. "Now, Louisa, what would you like to do first? Would you like to rest? Or have a meal, or a hot bath? Or check in on Sune, or take a tour of the mountain?"

But as she'd spoken, she'd led Louisa toward what appeared to be a corner, or maybe a crack, in the mountain's sheer stone wall before them. And suddenly they were... inside.

Inside *Orc Mountain*.

Louisa gasped, blinking at the sight around her, as genuine shock flashed through her chest. Because it wasn't— small, or dark, or cramped, or musty, or any of the things she'd expected. And instead, she was standing in a broad, beautifully carved stone corridor, with a series of flickering lamps lining the stone walls, and large, brightly coloured rugs covering the flat stone floor.

"Uh," she said, still gaping around at it, and then at Jule and Rosa, and then up at the corridor ahead. Which seemed to break off into more rooms, and more corridors, as if it truly was a home. A home, here, under a mountain. Killik and Ulfarr's home. The home that had apparently brought Ulfarr such pain and grief—and clearly at least one enemy—even as he was still bound here, held here for his sins.

And Louisa was here now too, fully trapped in this, whether Killik approved of it or not. And suddenly, there was Killik's own voice, jostling up into Louisa's whirling, whipping thoughts.

Shall you stand tall with the shamed Wolf of the Skai. Show me. Prove this to me...

And then Sune's words, too. *Stay. Settle yourself, and wait for Killik and Ulfarr to come for you. Make our mountain your home...*

So Louisa swallowed hard, drew in breath, squared her shoulders. "Well, since I'm here, I might as well do—all of it," she said. "And see and learn as much as I can. If you don't mind?"

But both Jule and Rosa grinned at her, as if this was exactly what they'd been hoping for. "Oh, we don't mind at all," Rosa replied, with a devious-sounding cackle. "Now come along, sister, and enjoy the all-new, all-empowering Orc Mountain New Mate Experience!"

30

The Orc Mountain New Mate Experience was, Louisa soon discovered, an actual plan. An introductory guided tour which had been personally developed by Rosa herself, and served as a complement to her related written publication, which was apparently titled *The Orc Mountain Manual for Modern Mates.*

"As soon as I heard Killik was seeing you, I gave him a copy, too," Rosa informed Louisa, as they walked through the lamplit corridor. "I hope he passed it on to you for review, and answered any questions you had?"

Louisa twitched, because the thought of Killik passing on an informative publication for her review—let alone answering her questions from it—seemed utterly laughable, and she couldn't quite hide the quiver on her mouth, or her brief glance at an equally amused-looking Jule. "Er, no, I'm afraid Killik didn't mention it," she replied, as steadily as she could. "Perhaps he just—forgot?"

But Rosa huffed an irritated growl, and threw both her hands in the air. "That stubborn Skai," she snapped. "His perpetual blatant contempt toward the written word is foolish, and short-sighted, and utterly unconscionable! I still can't tell whether he really is that ignorant, or whether he just enjoys provoking me, and obstructing any Ka-esh attempts at our mountain's betterment!"

She'd been speaking very quickly, her voice high-pitched, and Louisa belatedly recalled that Rosa's orc mate—and therefore her clan—was Ka-esh. The same clan Killik had complained about several times, right? And also, the clan who hadn't been able to send anyone to guide the camp's tunnel-digging efforts.

"Er, well, I wonder if it might just be that they need help digging some tunnels?" Louisa carefully replied. "I know they were very eager to have that done, out at their camp."

"Oh, *that*," Rosa said, with a sigh, and a wrinkle of her nose. "I do agree that the delays are deeply unfortunate, but our engineers do have a process, and an extensive waiting list full of urgent matters! And even John-Ka—my mate, I'm sure you remember—isn't able to sway that list. Which I *tried* telling Killik, but he only sneered at me, and told me the list was a Skai-shafting scam, and ought to be shoved up the engineers' tight Ka-esh arses! Which was a highly unnecessary comment, and which still"—she drew in breath, and frowned at Louisa—"has no bearing whatsoever on why he didn't give you my *Manual for Modern Mates!*"

Right. Louisa's mouth was twitching again, and she fought to suppress it, to say what she should have said from the start of all this. "Uh, well, it's probably also because I'm not actually anyone's—*mate*," she replied. "We're just— friends, that's all. So perhaps Killik thought giving it to me might imply that—"

But Rosa loudly scoffed again, and on Louisa's other side, Jule snorted, too. "So damned typical," Rosa said, with a roll of her eyes. "They never learn! And those Skai are perpetually the worst! Let me guess, Killik offered you some sort of agreement? Some kind of limited-time deal, so he could enjoy the benefits and pleasures of your company, without actually having to offer up any commitment or vulnerability or emotional investment of his own?"

Louisa's steps faltered, her eyes snapped wide on Rosa's face—how did she *know*?—and Rosa gave her a sympathetic glance, and a reassuring pat to her arm. "Just ignore them," she said crisply. "If Killik's not your mate already, he will be soon—if you really can bear him, that is. And in the meantime, if you'd like to give him a taste of his own foolishness, or move things along"—her eyes glinted—"feel free to try to leave him, or go spend some quality time with another orc instead. Now, why don't we make some introductions? And properly start our New Mate Experience here?"

Louisa was still fighting through her clamouring thoughts—Rosa was certainly mistaken on this, there was absolutely no way Killik would ever become her *mate*, right?—but she gave a belated nod back, and allowed herself to be drawn into Rosa's grand tour of Orc Mountain.

And just like the camp, Orc Mountain wasn't at all what Louisa had expected. It was impossibly large, extending both above ground and below, and it was made up of multiple corridors and rooms, each one more astonishing than the next. There were bedrooms, meeting-rooms, common-rooms, sparring-rooms, forges, shrines, and spring-fed baths. And even a large, clean central kitchen, where three lovely women of varying ages offered Louisa a delicious meal of tender meat and fresh-baked bread.

It also turned out that Orc Mountain was divided into five sections, one for each of the five clans of orcs—Ash-Kai, Bautul, Skai, Ka-esh, and Grisk. And not only was each section unique, with distinctly different lighting and layouts, but each clan's orcs seemed to share common characteristics, too. The Ash-Kai and Bautul orcs tended to be big and bulky and carefully courteous, while the Grisk—the clan Sune's friend Timo belonged to, apparently—were generally both smaller and kinder. And Rosa's Ka-esh clan, who lived deepest beneath the mountain, indeed seemed to be comprised mostly of scholars—some polite, some uninterested, and several just as cheerfully chatty as Rosa.

But most intriguing of all—and perhaps most confusing—were the other Skai orcs. The Skai clan's wing was situated nearer to the top of the mountain, and it was darker than many of the other sections, with narrower, twistier corridors. And as Rosa and Jule led Louisa through the corridors, making introductions to various Skai orcs they met along the way, Louisa found herself faced with a bizarre array of greetings in return. Some Skai were friendly and welcoming, while others responded far more like Simon had—frowning at her, and looking alarmed, or surprised, or even troubled. Again, almost as if... Louisa wasn't welcome. As if she wasn't supposed to be here.

But if Rosa and Jule noticed, they didn't mention it, and they merrily kept on with their tour. Next showing Louisa the admittedly impressive Skai bath, made of a thundering waterfall pouring from the ceiling, and then the huge, echoing Skai arena, and then the Skai forge. Where they met a burly, bearded, silver-haired smith by the vaguely familiar-sounding name of Argarr, who greeted Louisa with genuine-seeming kindness—even as he pulled over what appeared to be a waiting orc client, and yanked down his trousers.

"Argarr!" Rosa yelped, wrinkling her nose toward him. "Not in public, remember?! And Louisa's our *guest!*"

But this Argarr only shrugged, flashed Rosa a devious smile, and then proceeded to bend his quarry over his workbench, before pulling down his own trousers to reveal his scarred, dripping prick. "Ach, and this woman is a Skai, with my brothers' scent fresh upon her, so I ken she is not easily frightened," he said with a wink toward Louisa, as he began casually feeding himself into the orc's upraised backside, while the orc shuddered and moaned. "And we are not *public,* for you are in *my* forge, ach? How are you to question how I do my work? And if Voggr here"—he slapped the bent-over orc's arse—"wishes for his blade today, then he is free to move himself to the top of my list, ach?"

Rosa scoffed and muttered something about highly unethical list management, but Jule only rolled her eyes, and looked wryly resigned. And Louisa—while still rather shocked by this development—had finally remembered where she'd heard the name *Argarr* before, and couldn't help a flustered-feeling smile toward him as she yanked her knife from her belt.

"You're the one who fixed my knife, right?" she said, holding it out between them. "It really was impressive work. Thank you."

She meant it—the knife really had been much improved—and Argarr looked distinctly pleased as he inclined his head, and kept grinding into the orc's upraised rump. "Ach, I am glad this was of worth to you, woman. I wish my brothers' mates to be kept safe with good Skai steel."

The *mate* thing again. That somehow seemed more disconcerting than his steady circles into his moaning client's backside, and Louisa still felt hot and unsettled as they traipsed back into the corridor again. Surely Killik and Ulfarr—especially Killik—didn't see her that way, right? It was only a deal, she wasn't even supposed to be here...

No, woman. Five more nights. Prove this to me...

"Now, I'm sure you'd like to see our new communications office next!" Rosa announced, with an excited grin toward Louisa. "I'm sure you remember the informational campaigns I launched when we first met, right? And you must have noticed our ongoing outreach efforts, too."

She had? Louisa fought to cast her overwhelmed brain backwards, dredging up the memories of how Rosa—during the time Louisa had helped her—had begun creating and distributing informative pamphlets throughout the province, seeking to correct human misconceptions about orcs. To the point where Louisa had introduced Rosa to several printers and distributors she'd known from her life as Lady Scall, and she'd even offered them initial payments from her rapidly dwindling coffers, too.

"Yes, of course I remember," Louisa replied, though it sounded slightly forced. "And wait"—more awareness was slowly dawning—"all that community service the orcs have been doing around the province... is that *your* outreach? The road clearing, and the like?"

Rosa's eyes lit up, her head rapidly nodding, and she eagerly commenced a detailed explanation of all the orcs' ongoing outreach activities. Which apparently not only included the road clearing, bridge building, and various odd jobs upon request, but also regular orc participation in markets and fairs, and attendance at community meetings. All of it supported by a constant rotation of flyers and pamphlets, which were all now printed here in Rosa's new communications office, by several steel contraptions called *hand-presses.*

It truly was an impressive endeavour, and Louisa praised it as enthusiastically as she could, even as her head began to ache from the smell of the ink permeating the room. And her unhelpful thoughts kept wandering to Killik, who would long ago have rolled his eyes at all this, and left. But no, she shouldn't think of Killik, he didn't want her here, and...

"So, how about the school next?" Rosa said brightly, once she'd finally guided Louisa back out into the corridor. "You can see where Killik teaches! And he's part of our advisory committee too—I'm sure he's told you about it? The *Orc Mountain Educational Congress?*"

The what? Louisa's scrambled thoughts were struggling to catch up again, because yes, Killik had told her about his teaching, right? But he'd never actually mentioned an actual school... had he? Let alone the *Orc Mountain Educational Congress?*

But despite Louisa's ever-rising consternation, she again allowed herself to be guided along, up toward what indeed turned out to be a schoolroom. A busy, full-on schoolroom, outfitted with bright artwork, toys, and books, and occupied by several dozen young orcs of all ages. They were currently in the midst of what appeared to be a loud, enthusiastic drumming lesson, led by two drummers—a bulky, smiling orc, and a beautifully dressed Eziran woman with multiple gold beads in her tightly braided hair.

"Oh, you're *Louisa!*" the woman said, once Jule had waved her over, and introduced her as Geva, the school's director. "We've been dodging impertinent questions about you for what feels like an age now! I'm sure you've heard all about Killik's work here, have you? He's such a wonderful teacher—and Ulfarr, too. The orclings absolutely adore them both."

Louisa was again stunned into blank silence, because no, no, she hadn't known there was an actual school here, because they weren't together, they weren't... mates. This was only for the deal, only for five more nights, and Killik had only wanted to see her in a week. And gods, she wasn't even supposed to be here, and what was Killik going to say—and something spasmed in her throat, even as she attempted a jerky, too-late nod.

"It—I'm so glad to hear it," she managed. "It looks like such a lovely little school. What kinds of subjects do you teach?"

Thankfully, this led to an in-depth discussion of the school's curriculum, including a list of all the subjects Killik and Ulfarr apparently taught, which included sparring, climbing, agility training, and hunting. And even as Louisa kept the smile on her face, kept asking what she hoped were appropriate questions, that tightness kept worsening in her throat, clenching in her belly, too. She shouldn't be here. She shouldn't be giving these lovely, friendly women the wrong impression. After this, she would probably never see them again...

She was deeply grateful when they finally said farewell, and Rosa waved her and Jule out of the room. "Next on the New Mate Experience is the nursery!" Rosa said brightly. "And our sons are staying there this afternoon, so you can meet them, too!"

Their sons? Louisa's belly clenched again, but she nodded, and soon found herself in a cozy, well-appointed nursery. It was apparently run by a group of caretakers from the Bautul clan, orcs and women both—and they were caring for perhaps a dozen young orcs, including Rosa and Jule's tiny, adorable sons. And yes, Jule and Rosa apparently both had two orc sons—*each*—and Louisa felt almost dizzy as she watched their small grey bodies eagerly clinging to their mothers. Her friends had... orc sons. Two *each*.

"This is Tengil, and Tykkr," Jule told Louisa, as she hoisted them on each hip. "Can you say hello to Louisa, Tengil?"

Jule smiled toward the older of her two sons—he might have been around three years old—and he solemnly nodded toward Louisa, and even put his little clawed hand over his heart. "Hewwo, Woo-isa," he said solemnly. "We we-come you to our home."

Oh, gods, he was so adorable it hurt, and Louisa put her own hand to her heart, and bowed back toward him. "Thank you, Tengil," she said thickly. "It's so good to meet you. And you, Tykkr."

Tykkr just gazed at her with his huge baby eyes, so impossibly bright in his plump baby face, and Louisa had to force herself to breathe, and to turn toward Rosa's sons, too. They were named Thorin and Samuel, and they were just as painfully adorable, clinging to their mother with their tiny orc claws.

"They're just the absolute sweetest," Louisa said to Rosa

and Jule, her voice only slightly cracking. "My heartfelt congratulations. To both of you."

Both Jule and Rosa smiled and waved it away, but even as Louisa smiled too, her throat felt even tighter, and a distant ache had begun pulsing behind her eyes. Because she'd never told either Rosa or Jule about her inability to have children, and while neither of them said it, she could still feel the silent inevitable questions, dangling too powerfully between them. *Do you want children? When will you have them? Will you have them with Killik...*

"Could we go see Sune next?" Louisa asked, through her constricted throat. "I'd love to see how he's faring."

Both Jule and Rosa willingly agreed, and soon they were back in the corridors again, and heading downwards. While Louisa fought to find her breath, to settle her whirling, shouting thoughts. She needed to just get through this, and leave first thing in the morning. Five more nights, that was all...

It was a relief to finally reach the sickroom, which was situated in what seemed to be the middle area of the mountain. It was large, clean, and well-appointed, with beds separated by tall dividers, and multiple orcs resting in the beds. And Louisa's eyes instantly caught on Sune, lying on a nearby bed with his leg outstretched, and his two friends sitting on either side of him, their heads bent together.

They all glanced up as Louisa approached, and then the green orc—Timo, his name had been—leapt to his feet, and gave a bow toward Louisa. "Please forgive my rudeness when first we met, woman," he said. "I am Timo of Clan Grisk, and we thank you for keeping Sune safe, and bringing him back to us. He is already much healed, ach?"

Louisa's shoulders sagged, the tightness loosening in her chest, and she smiled toward Timo, and toward Sune in the bed, too. "I'm so glad to hear it," she said, glancing down toward where Sune's leg did look much improved, the trap's awful cuts now almost—*fully healed?!* "You're looking—so much better?"

She couldn't quite hide the disbelief in her voice, and in return Sune angled a brief glance across the room, toward where another new orc—a big, heavily scarred fellow—was striding over toward them, and nodding curtly toward Louisa. "It was a good thing you brought him, Skai, and kept him off his leg," he said, in a clipped, matter-of-fact voice. "It would have eventually healed on its own, but he'd never have walked properly again. But now that I've fixed the bone fracture, and healed together all the torn tissues around it, he should be as good as new within a few days."

Oh. Well. Louisa's confusion studded through with a sharp, sinking gratefulness, and she let out a shaky, relieved exhale. "Thank you so much," she told him. "That is—truly miraculous work, sir. Is there some kind of—bill I ought to pay for your services?"

She fought down her wince at the thought—she'd have to dig into Killik's final payment to cover it—but the orc scoffed and waved it away. "Call me Efterar," he replied. "And we don't take payments here. But"—he darted a wry look at Sune—"I do expect you to stay put, Sune, so no running off on that leg, unless you want to be knocked out for the day."

With that, this Efterar turned and strode off again, leaving Sune frowning resentfully after him. But Timo and the girl exchanged a decisive, meaningful look, and Timo clasped Sune's slack hand, as the girl gripped at his shoulder. While Sune gave a Killik-like roll of his eyes, followed by a brief, incomprehensible sign of his hand, and a jerk of his head at—Louisa?

"Oh, of course," the girl said quickly, as she leapt to her feet and lurched toward Louisa. "I haven't introduced myself either, have I? I'm Cecily, and it was so lovely of you to help Sune, and defend him like you did. If there's anything you need during your visit, just let me know, though I'm sure Jule and Rosa have been taking good care of you, and..."

Her voice trailed off, her eyes darting uneasily between Jule and Rosa, and then narrowing as they settled back on Louisa. Or wait, damn it, on Louisa's still-filthy *clothes*. Which she'd entirely forgotten about, and which she'd just worn while traipsing around on a full tour of Orc Mountain, meeting gods knew how many people, and making them think this ratty, grimy woman was Killik's *mate*.

"Look, no judgement, because you're obviously a helpless fashion disaster of a Skai, just like him," this Cecily said now, with an irritated wave of her hand toward where Sune was glowering at her from the bed. "But—you two! Why haven't you offered her a bath? Or taken her to the shop for a new outfit?"

She was glaring between Jule and Rosa, both of whom had blinked at each other, and then glanced down at Louisa's ensemble, as if they'd just noticed it, too. "Damn it, I completely forgot," Jule said, with a wry, apologetic grimace. "So sorry, sister."

Rosa nodded too, looking deeply chagrined, while before them, Cecily gave a smug smile, and pulled herself up straighter. "Well, fortunately, you've now found the right Ash-Kai," she said firmly. "Now let's get you a proper Orc Mountain makeover!"

31

The Orc Mountain Makeover, it turned out, was just as overwhelming as the Orc Mountain New Mate Experience.

It began with an admittedly much-needed bath in a huge heated pool, while Jule, Rosa, and Cecily stood guard outside the door. And once Louisa had dried off, wrapping herself in the huge towel Cecily had fetched, Cecily began what felt like an attack on her wet, messy hair, plying it with a light oil, and then detangling it with a wide-toothed comb. And then, explaining her process as she went, she twisted it up with two long, pointed crossed hairpins, not unlike how Killik wore his daggers.

"There, that's better," Cecily said, stepping back to admire her handiwork. "It keeps it up out of your face, but still shows off this silver in front, too. Which is such a good Skai colour, and so lovely on you, don't you think?"

Even a few weeks ago, Louisa might have protested this statement, but now she felt her overwhelmed thoughts bizarrely catching, and twining toward... Ulfarr. *You are lovely, Louisa. Mayhap the loveliest sight I have ever set eyes upon...*

"Er, thank you, Cecily," she said, over the catch in her throat. "This is—very kind of you."

But Cecily only smiled, and gave a dismissive wave of her hand. "You Skai really do just need good Ash-Kai guidance in these matters," she said airily. "Now, let's go get you some new clothes!"

Louisa smiled and nodded back, and allowed herself to be chivvied toward the door, even as a new, uneasy question surged in her thoughts. "Uh, but what about payment?" she asked. "I didn't think to bring any coin with me, so—"

"Oh, don't worry about *that*," Cecily interrupted, with another wave of her hand. "Of course Sune's fathers will be happy to help out their new—*friend*."

Louisa shot Cecily a careful look—she was quite possibly the first person who hadn't made that *mate* assumption, and who had included Ulfarr in this, too—and also, surely Killik and Ulfarr wouldn't want to pay for something so frivolous as clothes? But Cecily was already tugging Louisa up the corridor again, while Jule and Rosa followed closely behind. And if anyone noticed Louisa was dressed only in a large towel, they didn't seem to care, and several new orcs even nodded and smiled as they passed.

"Here we are!" Cecily announced, as she ushered Louisa toward yet another door. "The Grisk Shop. The most wondrous place in all the mountain!"

It was a grand claim, given all the admittedly impressive rooms Louisa had seen so far—but once she'd stepped inside the shop, her feet faltered, her breath catching in her throat. It was—huge. Without question the biggest shop she'd seen in her life, with its rows and rows of fully stocked shelves, extending backwards behind a long front counter. And on the shelves, Louisa could see crates, tools, weapons, and furs, and bags of flour, and barrels of salted meat, and cooking-pots, and—

"Welcome to the Great Grisk Showroom-Shop!" said a

bright voice, and Louisa blinked toward where a pretty, dark-haired woman was standing behind the counter, and beaming toward them. "Are you new to the mountain, sister? I'm Kitty, and I'd be happy to help you find whatever you need."

Louisa was feeling decidedly stunned again—not least because this woman was dressed in a highly orc-inspired ensemble that flaunted her pregnant bare belly—and thankfully, Jule made another round of quick introductions. This Kitty turned out to be from the Grisk clan, and she was apparently mated to two Grisk orcs—one of them a tall, messy-haired orc named Thrain, who worked in the Grisk forge just up the corridor, and had just come down to introduce himself, too.

"Killik, ach?" he said to Louisa, with a too-knowing wink. "I hope you like weapons then, woman. And chains."

Chains? Louisa was again nonplussed, but comprehension slowly filtered in as she stared at the orc's impish grin. He meant... he meant Killik liked chains in the *bedroom*. Right? And—she hadn't known that either, had she? This was something else they'd kept from her?

But perhaps Kitty had caught Louisa's unease, because she cheerfully swatted at Thrain, and shot Louisa an apologetic smile. "Enough of that," she said firmly. "Now, let's get started!"

She excitedly waved toward one of the aisles behind the counter, so Louisa drew in another deep, fortifying breath, and obliged. Following along with Jule, Rosa, and Cecily down the long, lamplit aisle, which indeed seemed to be bursting with clothes—dresses, trousers, tunics, shifts, underclothes, shoes, boots, and even jewelry. More clothes than Louisa had ever seen in any shop in her life, and she swallowed as she stared around at them, shaking her head.

"Uh, I'm afraid I—I don't even know where to start with this," she said. "I haven't followed fashions in years, and back when I needed to dress a certain way, I used to just rely on dressmakers to tell me what to buy, and..."

Her voice trailed off, her stomach twisting, because again, what was she even doing here? Killik didn't care what she looked like. He didn't want her here, in their lives, or their business, or their shops. This was ridiculous, this was only five more nights, Louisa should have stayed out with the horses after all...

"But that's what we're for!" Kitty's voice cut in, and she was beaming again, looking unnervingly sincere. "I love clothes, and I love helping our clients dress however best suits them. And that allows you to focus on doing what *you* do best, right?"

Beside Louisa, Cecily nodded too, and gave a reassuring pat of her hand to Louisa's arm. "And of course you're terrible with clothes, you're Skai," she said comfortingly. "Now, tell us, do you spend your days doing typical Skai things, too? Tromping around in the mud and forest? Doing dirty jobs no one else wants to do? Killing things, maybe?"

Louisa opened her mouth to protest, but then winced and closed it again, because she did do all that, damn it. And around her, all the women laughed, and Cecily gave another encouraging pat to her arm. "Believe us, we know," she said. "So something close and comfortable you can move in, then. Dark colours, since they're easier to keep clean. And a pair of decent Skai boots, not like those clodhoppers you came in with."

Kitty gave a decisive nod, and had turned to start tugging items from the nearest shelf. And soon Louisa was caught up in a dizzying whirl of dresses, trousers, underclothes, and boots, trying on outfit after outfit over the slim black shift Kitty had given her, while answering an astonishing array of enthusiastic questions. *Is this one itchy, do you prefer trousers over dresses, do you mind this hemline, can you reach your dagger beneath that tunic?*

Throughout it all, the women also gave Louisa an overview of orcish clothing customs, and how they differed from humans'—and how, in particular, the orcs cared very little about modesty. And apparently ensembles like Kitty's were standard among her Grisk clan, and in the Skai clan, orcs and women often wore just a *loincloth*—a thin leather waistband, with more leather hanging down in front and in back, just enough to cover the essential parts.

"They really are quite comfortable," Kitty said brightly, as she thrust out several loincloth options toward Louisa. "Why don't you try on a few, just to see what you think?"

Louisa was far too dazed to argue at this point, so she obligingly tried on the loincloths beneath her shift, and kept the one that seemed the most comfortable. While Kitty and Cecily continued sifting through their piles of dresses, trousers, tunics, and boots, now instructing Louisa to try on her favourites again, and then to move around as much as she could. Until she was twisting and jumping and even jogging up and down the aisles, while the women chattered and laughed.

By the end of it, Louisa found herself clad in a knee-length, close-fitting black dress—more like a long tunic—together with a pair of tall slim boots, made of soft black leather. Beneath the dress, she was also wearing the loincloth she'd chosen, and around the waist of the dress, Kitty had fastened a chain belt—apparently forged by Thrain himself—for Louisa's knife, along with a new, perfectly sized leather scabbard.

It was unlike anything Louisa had ever worn before, but it was all surprisingly comfortable, and easy to move in, too—the boots were almost like walking barefoot, and none of it itched or pinched or poked, or dug into the softness of her breasts or her waist. And once Kitty and Cecily had given her one last look-over—and gained Jule and Rosa's praises, too—they finally marched Louisa down the aisle, to where a tall, silvery looking-glass stood at the very back of the shop.

"What do you think?" Kitty eagerly asked, waving toward the looking-glass. And for an instant, Louisa could only seem to stand there and stare at her reflection, as her heartbeat skipped in her chest.

She looked... different. So different. So simple and straightforward and... *right*, somehow. Like a woman who knew who she was, a woman who got things done, a woman whose clothes served her life, and not the other way around. And maybe Cecily had even been right about the silver in her pinned-up hair, because against all the black it looked almost striking, almost like it was meant to be there.

And as Louisa kept numbly standing there, staring at herself, there was again that jolting, incongruous feeling of... peace. That peace she'd felt at the camp, and in that bed with Killik and Ulfarr, too, stroked into truth by their hands, their voices, their hunger.

You are wondrous, Louisa. You are so good. So perfect.

"I—thank you," Louisa stammered, glancing between Kitty and Cecily, and waving a shaky hand at her hot-feeling face. "You are definitely much better at this than I am, and it was so kind of you, but you shouldn't have—you didn't need to—"

And oh, gods, she wasn't going to start weeping, not over some new clothes—but she was already sniffling, blinking hard, shaking her head. But beside her, Kitty looked a little weepy too, and she frantically waved it away, and yanked Louisa into a tight hug. "Oh, I'm just *so* glad," she said. "You deserve to feel comfortable in your own skin. And you look fabulous, too."

Louisa gave another weepy, grateful smile, and then willingly joined all the cheerfully chattering women as they headed back toward the front of the shop. And for a brief, wonderful moment, that whispering peace shimmered with something almost like... hope. She could face this. Prove this. And maybe she could someday even belong here, with these lovely women, in Killik and Ulfarr's home...

At least, until they reached the front of the shop. Where a tall, lean orc was stalking swiftly into the room—and then, in a jolting movement, he stopped. Stilled. And stared at Louisa, with shock and menace and fury flashing in his eyes.

It was Killik.

32

Killik was here. He'd returned.

Louisa's heart kicked and surged, her mouth dry, her gaze fixed to Killik's face. To his pale, taut, grim-looking face, with its furious flashing eyes. And for a hanging, frozen moment, those eyes only stared at her, and then flicked down her body, and up, and down again.

"Ach, woman," Killik finally said, his voice very smooth, as he reached out a hand toward her. "You shall now come with me, shall you not?"

Louisa's head was already nodding, her hand reaching to clasp his, feeling the rigid tension in his clammy fingers against hers. "Good," he said, with a cold, empty smile. "And thank you, sisters"—his eyes flicked toward the assembled women—"for your kind welcome toward her."

None of the women seemed to notice anything alarming about this—Jule and Cecily both smiled and waved it away, and Kitty was even beaming toward Killik with unabashed approval. And while Rosa wasn't smiling, she still looked mildly gratified, raising her blonde brows at Killik's tight, rigidly smiling face.

"Aren't you going to say anything nice about Louisa's new

outfit?" she asked, with an unmistakable challenge on her voice. "She looks fabulous, doesn't she?"

Killik's glittering eyes briefly flicked down Louisa's body again, sweeping a strange shiver over her skin. "Ach, she always does," he said coolly, without sparing another glance toward Rosa. "Now come, woman."

Louisa swallowed and nodded, allowing him to draw her toward the door, even as she shot a helpless glance backwards. "Er, thank you all, again," she told them. "It's been so lovely."

Again, the women seemed to easily accept this, smiling and waving goodbye, while Killik yanked Louisa harder, dragging her out into the lamplit corridor. But he wasn't looking at her now, only staring straight ahead, his jaw flexing in his cheek.

"So you—got Simon's message, then?" Louisa asked him, through her too-tight throat. "Did you see Sune already?"

Killik nodded, but still didn't look at her, just pulling her along faster down the corridor. His fury almost radiating from him, leaching into Louisa's churning gut, and she drew in a breath. "Has anything else—happened? Or are you just—angry with me?"

Killik huffed a low, sudden laugh, or perhaps a growl, his eyes cutting sharp to hers. "I told you, woman," he breathed. "*No. No*, to all of this. You were not to come here, and parade yourself all over this mountain, and play-act as our *mate!*"

Louisa flinched all over, and shook her head. "That wasn't at all my intention, Killik," she said, fighting to keep her voice low. "I didn't tell *anyone* I was your mate. And I didn't even want to come here, let alone stay here, but—"

Killik cut her off with another growl, louder and harder this time. And after a baleful look at the corridor around them—and the handful of unfamiliar orcs up ahead—he pulled Louisa sideways, into one of the dark rooms lining the corridor. An empty meeting room, perhaps, with only a large low table set in the middle of it.

"Then why are you yet here," Killik hissed, as he flipped one of his daggers out of his hair, and pointed it toward her. "You wished to make some ploy against me? Some vengeance against me for not falling at your feet last eve, or handing over my wolf to serve your whims?"

Louisa stared back at him for an instant too long, as her exhausted, overwhelmed brain fought to catch up. Killik thought—he really thought this was a ploy? He thought Louisa was trying to gain—*vengeance*? By helping Sune?

"It—it wasn't," she snapped back at him, though her voice wavered. "Look, Killik, it wasn't anything of the sort. I was only—"

But Killik sharply sliced his dagger toward her face, close enough that she staggered backwards into the solid wood table behind her. "You only came to my home, to all my kin, this *very next day* after I told you no," he snarled. "Just as you did with the camp! I have told you the truth of this again and again, and again and again you ignore this, and do only as you wish!"

Louisa's breaths were coming too fast, her gaze fixed on that dagger before her eyes, and she desperately fought for something, anything, please. "In what realm have you given me your truth, Killik?" she shot back. "You've hidden your truth from the moment we first met! Good gods, just today, I learned you and Ulfarr are apparently both regular teachers at an actual *school*, and apparently you like to use *chains* in your bed!"

But Killik only gave a furious roll of his eyes, a wild jab of his dagger toward her. "I told you we taught orclings, did I not?" he hissed back. "And ach, how else do you ken I break through Wolf's grief, and bring him to his knees for me? With honey and kisses and pretty ribbons? This is not at all the same"—his voice deepened—"as you saying last eve you understood this, and then coming *here* this very next day!"

Louisa grimaced, dragged in a shaky breath. "Look, I told you, I didn't plan to come here," she managed. "Sune needed help, so—"

"So why did you not take him to the camp?" Killik's harsh voice cut in. "Why did you not take him to the closest place, to where you knew he had kin? You ken you needed to bring him all the way here? When you *knew* we were away?"

Louisa's breaths heaved harder, her stomach now churning in her belly. "Sune said—it was best to come here," she countered. "I just wanted to help, I offered to stay outside, or go camp somewhere else, but—"

"But then why did you not!" Killik shouted at her, his voice ringing through her ears, scraping into her skull. "Why did you defy me, and betray me, and destroy all I have done!"

Louisa stared at him, at his enraged flashing eyes, at his dagger still pointing at her face. Its sharpened tip so damned close, curdling genuine fear in her belly, drawing bitter misery behind her eyes. Would Killik truly punish her over this? Would he call the deal off, or would he—would he hurt her? And why was she shaking, why was she on the verge of weeping, why did she keep tolerating this, again and again and again—

"I—wasn't," she choked. "I wasn't, Killik, I swear, I—"

But just then, there were—voices. A rising swarm of voices and footsteps, and now—a person, lurching into the room. It was—Sune?

But yes, that was Sune, but his lean body was on crutches, and he looked—furious. Hopping with astonishing speed straight toward them, toward Killik, and—Louisa bit back her yelp—he swung up one of his crutches, and hurled it straight toward Killik's head.

Killik leapt sideways, easily avoiding the flying crutch, but Sune kept hopping toward him, signing toward him, his hand's movements far too swift for Louisa to follow. But clearly Killik understood, his eyes shifting as he watched, as his hand flipped his dagger upwards, tightly gripping its blade in his palm.

And then—then more voices, more people, surging into the room. Cecily, and Timo, and—and *Ulfarr*. And both Cecily and Timo lunged for Sune, both of them loudly pleading with him at once, while Ulfarr froze in the doorway, his big body utterly still, his eyes fixed blankly on Louisa's face.

Louisa was still breathing hard, her heart pummelling against her ribs, the cursed wetness now streaking down her cheeks. And damn it, Ulfarr looked shocked, and then aghast, the colour draining from his face—and then he came toward her with jerky, erratic steps, and...

And dragged her into his arms.

"Ach, Louisa," his voice rumbled, as he folded her trembling body into his, curved his warm safe arms around her back. "Ach, do not look thus. Do not scent thus. You are safe here. *Safe.*"

Oh, gods. It was like he'd cracked something, broken something deep inside, and Louisa clung to him, buried her face in his chest. Sank into the stark, stunning strength of him, the steady solidness of him, the sound of his thudding heartbeat beneath his warm chest. Safe here. Safe. At peace.

But then—Ulfarr stilled. Stiffened. His breaths caught, his hands clenched on Louisa's back. And then he slowly, carefully drew himself away from her, and turned toward the door. Toward—oh. Maria, and Simon.

They were standing immobile inside the doorway, both of them staring at Louisa, and at Ulfarr. And while Simon's face was again grim, disapproving, Maria looked pale, and shaky, and... afraid.

"Louisa?" she said, though her voice wavered. "Could we... speak to you for a moment? Alone?"

There was an instant's empty, dangling silence, hanging over the room. And Louisa's rapid sweeping glance found Cecily and Timo looking uneasy, Sune darkly frowning, while Killik looked downright murderous. And beside Louisa, Ulfarr's face looked suddenly haggard, almost bleak—but he twitched a nod, and then strode with jerky steps toward the door. Keeping his head down, and giving Maria and Simon a wide berth as he slipped out the door, even as his head ducked lower toward them, his hand clenching over his heart.

Louisa's belly twisted as she watched him go, her heartbeat thundering louder in her ears—and then Timo and Cecily silently tugged Sune along, too. Leaving Louisa alone with Simon and Maria, and—Killik. Who hadn't moved in the slightest, and was still tightly gripping his dagger's blade in his fingers, even the sharpened tip, enough that blood was dripping toward the floor.

"I shall not stop you, or refute you," Killik said toward Simon, his voice emptier than Louisa had ever heard it. "But much of this was my doing, so I wish to stay."

Simon angled a searching glance toward Maria, who sighed, and nodded. And then she clutched a hand to her own dagger at her side, and turned toward Louisa.

"I'm sorry to tell you this, but you deserve to know," she said, her eyes glinting with pain, with regret. "Ulfarr can't be your mate. Ulfarr's not—safe. He's—a *monster*."

33

Ulfarr's not safe. He's a monster.

Louisa's heart skipped a beat, and she suddenly felt curiously frozen in place, as a distant buzzing swarmed in her ears. Not safe. A monster.

A monster.

But wait, no, *Killik*. Killik was here, Killik knew that couldn't be possible... right? But Louisa's desperate darting glance toward him found his face rigid, immobile, his eyes slowly sliding shut. As if he was... resigned. Defeated.

As if it was... true.

He has faced and fostered deep darkness. Shall you stand tall with the shamed Wolf of the Skai...

Louisa's breaths were coming rapid and shallow, and she forced her gaze back to Maria's pained, regretful face. "Would you be willing," she began, "to tell me why?"

And even as she said it, there was a strange jolting hopefulness, because—because it didn't make sense, did it? No, no, it didn't, and perhaps it was all some kind of awful misunderstanding, something that could easily be corrected...

But Maria's expression didn't change, and she drew in a

deep, shaky breath. "Ulfarr—wanted me, when I first came here to the mountain," she said. "So he—trapped me. He threatened me. He tried to seduce me. He tried to force Simon to—share me. He tried to *kill* Simon so he could steal me, and our son. And when none of that worked, he—he finally *kidnapped* me. He dragged me away, deep underground, alone. And if Simon hadn't found us, Ulfarr would have—he would have—"

Her voice broke, her head shaking, and Louisa couldn't look away, couldn't think through the wild wailing of her heartbeat. Ulfarr had—done that? Ulfarr? Kind, sweet, considerate Ulfarr? Trapping? Seducing? *Kidnapping?*

Something was jamming in Louisa's brain, crumpling in on itself, and she shot another helpless, pleading glance at Killik. Killik, who still had his eyes closed, the blood still steadily dripping from his fingers on the dagger.

And curse Killik, curse him to hell and back, because... because maybe this was why he'd been so furious with Louisa for coming here. Because once again, he hadn't wanted her to know. He hadn't wanted her to hear...

"And," Maria's choked voice continued, was there more, there was more, "throughout all that, Ulfarr did everything he could to undermine Simon, and his judgement as the clan's Enforcer. Even when that judgement was desperately needed. Even when"—she took another shaky breath—"the orcs in question had been involved in horrible things. Against other orcs, and women, and *children.*"

Oh. Oh, gods. And that couldn't be true, it couldn't, it was impossible, Ulfarr adored children, Ulfarr had built and tended that pack of his, he would do anything to protect them... right? But Louisa's frantic glance at Killik found only more blankness, more resignation, more grief. As if... as if Ulfarr truly had done that.

As if Ulfarr was truly... a monster.

Bile surged in Louisa's throat, sharp and bitter, and she

fought to drag down air, to grasp at her churning, shouting thoughts. But there was nothing, nothing, only shock and darkness and grief. Ulfarr was a monster. Killik had lied to her. Killik had manipulated her into bed with Ulfarr, he'd fought to keep her away from here, to prevent her from learning the truth. And then he'd raged at her, again and again, when he'd been the one hiding all this? Orchestrating this?

And curse Killik, he still hadn't even looked at her. He just kept standing there with his eyes closed, with such empty grief on his face. And as Louisa stared at him, waiting, needing him to look at her, to explain himself—he slowly opened his eyes again. But they were empty too, cold black hollows in his stark shadowed face, and it looked so wrong, it felt so wrong, this was all so wrong and they were all looking at her and what the hell was she supposed to say—

"I'm sorry for putting this onto you so suddenly," cut in a low voice, Maria's voice, and when Louisa blinked back toward her, her face was still troubled, even sad. "You're still welcome to stay the night, of course. And if you have any questions..."

Her voice trailed off, her mouth twisting, and gods, Louisa suddenly couldn't bear the thought of asking this poor woman to relive even more of what had clearly been a deeply traumatizing experience. And too late, she shook her head, twitched a shaky wave of her tingling hand.

"No, and I—" she began, and then shook her head again. "I—thank you. I'm—so sorry you had to bear all that. And so sorry you were obliged to revisit it by—by telling me, like this."

She couldn't help another narrow, searching glance toward Killik, but he still wasn't moving, wasn't showing any signs of having heard this—not even when both Maria and Simon looked at him, too. And for the first time, it occurred to Louisa that they would have also expected Killik to tell her all this, and Killik had—he had wanted to hide Louisa from them, too. He hadn't wanted them to know about her.

Because maybe—maybe a monster wasn't supposed to have pleasure. He wasn't supposed to have a woman in his bed, let alone a mate...

Killik still wasn't looking at her, or looking at them, but his shoulders were rising and falling now, his chin tilting toward Simon. "But I ken you ought to know, brother," he finally said, "I was the one who brought this woman to Ulfarr's bed. I was the one who gained both their silence upon this. I swore to Ulfarr I had told her all she needed to know. And"—his mouth pulled into a shape much like a smile—"I led you all to believe I meant her for *me*, rather than him."

Simon's heavy brow furrowed as he stared at Killik, his mouth hard and grim. "Why, brother," he said. "Why would you do this, and speak false to us?"

Killik's not-smile slightly faltered, and he jerked a short shrug. "I care for Ulfarr," he said, without inflection. "I wished to grant him this."

His voice seemed to hang there, dangling empty and unfinished between them. And Simon's brow furrowed even deeper, his jaw flexing in his cheek—but before he could speak again, Killik squared his shoulders, and fully turned toward him, his eyes holding blank and unseeing on Simon's face.

"I shall not refute your judgement upon this, brother," Killik said, his voice just as blank as his eyes. "But I should be grateful if you could grant me the night to settle some matters first."

There was an instant's horrible silence, and Louisa's heart skipped a beat, her eyes frozen on Killik's empty face. What did he mean about Simon's *judgement*? And about asking for a night to settle matters, as if... as if...

But Simon twitched a curt nod, his mouth gone even

grimmer, his big hand curling into a fist at his side. And Killik nodded back, and then turned his empty eyes toward Louisa, and held out his hand. Not the bloody one—which was still gripping his dagger—but even so, this one was still slightly shaking, his claws extended sharp from his fingertips.

"Come, then, woman," he said, a hollow hoarse rasp. "I shall take you home."

34

Louisa followed Killik down the corridor in stark, stinging silence. Her steps short and jerky, her clammy hands clasped together, her eyes held to Killik's rigid back before her.

He was taking her home. He was going to be punished. He'd hidden something truly vile from her. Ulfarr was a monster. Ulfarr had attacked Maria, and *kidnapped* her. He'd defended orcs who'd done horrible things.

It was unconscionable, utterly unimaginable, and Louisa's stuttering thoughts still couldn't seem to grasp at it. It didn't make sense, it didn't, Ulfarr had a son, he was a teacher, he'd made that pack—but wasn't that what they always said? Wasn't that what she'd always heard about Lord Scall, too? *Such an upstanding, well-respected man, there must be some mistake...*

But the longer they walked, the longer Louisa stared at Killik's stiff back, the louder the questions started jostling. She'd witnessed Lord Scall's cruelty firsthand. She'd caught hints of it very early, even if she hadn't known what it had meant at the time. And Scall's friends and lackeys had always either ignored or justified his behaviour, they certainly hadn't agreed to be hauled up and judged over it, without so much as a protest. Had they?

And maybe—maybe that was what was catching Louisa the most on this. Killik always protested. Killik always fought and shouted and raged, especially when it came to his precious wolf. So for him to just stand there, and accept those accusations, accept this defeat, it was...

You never ask the right questions, or allow the truth of the answers...

But wait. Wait, that was the mountain's exit up ahead—and was Killik truly taking her home, already? Now?

Louisa's steps stuttered, her head shaking—and it was enough that Killik glanced back at her, with those dark, empty eyes. Eyes that again spoke of such defeat, and such... grief.

You never ask the right questions...

"Could I—could I go see Ulfarr first?" her choked voice asked. "Please?"

Killik's expression didn't change, but his shoulder shrugged, and without a word, he turned sideways, into another corridor. One that tilted back upwards again, maybe toward the Skai wing.

And yes, it soon proved to be the Skai wing, the corridors growing narrower and twistier, the orcs all nodding at Killik as they passed. Though some of them looked troubled, too, and a few looked almost afraid.

"Here," Killik said, with a curt wave of his hand toward a nearby door, cut into the corridor's stone. And when Louisa nodded and ventured through, the room was silent and dark, the light so dim that it took far too long to see him. Or rather, to see *them*. Ulfarr and Sune, sitting together on the floor against the large bed. Ulfarr with his knees pulled up, his head bowed over them, while Sune's injured leg was stretched out on the fur rug, his crutches lying haphazardly on the floor beside him.

Louisa froze in place, and she could feel Killik stilling, too—but then he drew in a deep, shaky breath, grounding himself into the earth. "Ach, what is this?" he said, with passable lightness. "Sune, you ought to be yet in the sickroom, should you not?"

Sune's head snapped up, his eyes narrowing toward Killik, and in a surprisingly fluid movement, he snatched for his crutches, and leapt up onto his one good leg. While one of his hands began furiously signing at Killik, again moving far too fast for Louisa to understand, but Killik was again grounding himself into the floor, and even attempting a not-quite-genuine smile.

"Ach, I could not be a *slug*," he told Sune, raising his brows. "They are far too slow, you ken. Mayhap a centipede, if you must. Or better yet, a serpent."

Sune answered this with an aggrieved roll of his eyes at Killik, and then shoved his way past him, hopping on his crutches toward the door. But then he halted and spun back toward them, signing something else. But as he did it, he wasn't looking at Killik, or even Ulfarr, but at—Louisa?

But yes, he was looking at her, and his hand was repeating the signs, again and again. *You —— this. You —— this.*

Louisa blinked at him, and shot a searching look at Killik—who sighed, and shook his head. "He says he wishes you to fix this," he said, under his breath, before shifting his gaze back to Sune again. "But you ken is not so easy to fix, ach? And after this, this woman shall not—"

Sune cut Killik off with a flailing wave of his hand, and then he again made those signs—that plea—toward Louisa. *You fix this. You fix Wolf.*

Louisa swallowed, but before she could reply, Sune again spun around, and hopped off into the darkness. Leaving her staring after him, her stomach twisting, while Killik groaned, and rubbed both hands at his face. And when Louisa glanced toward him, she found he'd streaked blood all down his cheek, and wait, that wasn't just blood, was it? Was he—was he *weeping*?

He angrily dashed a hand at his eye, turning his face away, but Louisa had seen it, she had. And what was happening, what was this, why did Sune think she could fix it, what the hell was she supposed to do next...

Her eyes darted back toward Ulfarr on the floor, his big body curled up like that, gone strangely small and quiet. Gone so... wrong. And as Louisa gazed down toward him, her thoughts jolted back to the night before—had it only been the night before?—at the camp, when he'd been so commanding, so easy, so confident. So unlike this empty, silent shell on the floor, lost in grief and defeat.

You fix this. You never ask the right questions. Prove this. Shall you stand tall with the shamed Wolf of the Skai...

And then, from longer ago, Ulfarr himself gripping her hand in her bedroom, pleading at her with wide, miserable eyes. *I had no intent, cannot bear to bring more shame, more harm, more blood and wrath and death...*

And finally Louisa... moved. Stepped on shaky legs toward him, toward the wolf, the kidnapper, the monster...

And then she sank to her knees beside him, and carefully reached to take his hand in hers.

"Sweetheart," she whispered, into the wavering silence. "If you'd like to talk, I'd be honoured to listen."

35

For a moment, nothing happened. No sound, no movement, not even a twitch from Ulfarr beside her.

But Louisa drew in a breath, and drew Ulfarr's hand closer. And then slowly threaded her fingers through his, feeling how he quivered at her touch, but didn't resist. Didn't protest.

So Louisa just... kept kneeling there, and waiting. Kept holding Ulfarr's hand, and breathing. Because somehow, in the midst of all that, she'd made a decision. She wasn't going to offer Ulfarr easy excuses, or easy forgiveness. But before she cast her own judgement, she wanted to hear his truth. His side of the tale.

She didn't want to ignore this, or forget it. She wanted to... face it. To learn the truth.

Another moment passed, with only their breaths breaking the silence, and finally there was—movement, above them. Beside them. Killik, sinking down to sit on Ulfarr's other side, and clasping his other hand close.

"Might as well tell her, Wolf," he said, his gaze fixed on where he was threading his own fingers between Ulfarr's, too. "Naught to lose now, ach?"

A hard shudder wrenched up Ulfarr's body between them, and he twitched a nod of his bowed head. And though he drew in breath, opened his mouth, no sound came out, only more empty, aching silence.

"Mayhap I can begin this, then," came Killik's low voice. "Should you allow this, Wolf."

Ulfarr shuddered again, but then, another nod. And Louisa waited, her heartbeat thudding in her ears, as Killik breathed deep too, sank himself into the earth.

"I told you of Wolf's pack, woman," Killik finally said, into the silence. "I told you how this pack was at first a punishment from his father Alfver, ach?"

Louisa nodded, studied where Killik was staring straight ahead, the blood still streaked down his cheek. "Alfver was the strongest, most feared warrior amongst the Skai," he continued. "He built and led our most powerful pack, renowned for its great power in battle. Not only this, but he also served as our clan's Enforcer—our keeper of our ways, and our judge and punisher. Alfver was... a king, amongst us."

Louisa nodded again, and Killik drew in another deep breath, let it out. "But Alfver was also oft a cruel, selfish orc," he said. "He punished his rivals. He hoarded all our clan's wealth. He served the mountain's fool captain Kaugir, and drove us to fight to our deaths upon Kaugir's command. He only appointed other pack leaders who would obey him. And he granted his own pack freedom to do all that they wished, no matter the harm this caused. Whether within our clan, or well beyond it."

Louisa swallowed, her thoughts flipping back to Lord Scall. To the kinds of choices it took to gain that much power, to all the darkness that followed and festered in its wake. "And there was no way to... weaken Alfver?" she asked, quiet. "Or undermine him?"

Killik's laugh was curt and bitter, his head shaking back

and forth. "Not lest you wished to be cast out of the pack, or sent to the front of the next battle," he replied. "And Alfver would oft seek to fetter any strong Skai before they could become a threat. As he did with his own son, by granting him this pack. A dozen weak, helpless, fatherless orclings, who needed constant feeding and guarding and care. Orclings who no one else would miss, if they were to face some... mishap."

The sudden horror of that heaved deep in Louisa's belly, and she shot a searching look at Ulfarr's bowed head. "That's why your father gave you that pack?" she asked, too sharp. "So he could control you? By using *children* against you?"

Ulfarr's body betrayed another shudder, and Louisa squeezed his hand tighter, shook her head. Gods, it was such a perfect and vicious trap, because even without that looming threat of their deaths, the amount of time and energy it would have required to care for that many children would have been utterly debilitating, especially in the midst of a war.

"But Wolf yet faced his fate, and did his best," Killik added, fiercer now. "He cared for his pack, and guarded us, even against his father. He oft took our blame and our sins and our grievances upon himself, so naught fell back upon us. And amidst all this, he yet sought to weaken his father from within, and raise up those who might someday defeat him."

Louisa exhaled and nodded, because yes, that all sounded true. That sounded like the Ulfarr she knew, the Ulfarr she'd seen with her own eyes. The Ulfarr who cared so deeply for his son, and his kin.

"But few Skai beyond our little pack saw this," Killik said, his mouth thinning. "They did not see all the ways Wolf fought his father to help us, and uphold our clan. They did not see how he stood back—how he gave up his own *birthright*—so that our brother Simon could gain the strength to defeat Alfver, and then take his place as Enforcer. And ach, even when Simon then chose to break apart the packs"—Killik sighed—"Wolf did not once fight this, even as he grieved his pack's loss. He swore his vow to honour Simon as our new Enforcer, and urged us all to swear this, also."

Louisa drew in a deep breath, and searched Killik's hard profile in the darkness. "And what... what did *you* think of all this?" she asked, careful. "Did you support Simon's decision to disband the packs?"

Killik's jaw flexed in his cheek, but he twitched a shrug. "No, I did not," he replied, slower. "But I yet saw this wisdom in this. The packs wielded far too much power and freedom, and brought much grief upon us. Simon needed to show his strength before our kin, and bring them change, and hope. And even if Wolf's pack was not a threat, Simon could not only leave this one pack, and disband all the others, ach? Most of all with Wolf yet being Alfver's son, and yet bearing much power and honour amongst his kin."

Right. That made sense, but Louisa's eyes were again caught on Ulfarr's bowed head, on all the weight he'd borne in this. Trapped by his father, burdened with a pack he hadn't asked for—and then offering up his birthright to another, and losing the pack he'd given so much to build.

"And has Simon been a good leader, at least?" she asked, squeezing Ulfarr's hand tighter. "Has he been an improvement for your clan, over Alfver?"

"Ach, yes," came Killik's reply, without hesitation this time. "Simon has been a far better and wiser Enforcer than Alfver. And from the start, we all sought to honour him, but"—another sigh, another shrug—"many of us yet trusted Wolf, and turned to him when we needed help. And after Alfver, none of us wished to live beneath one orc's judgement—so if ever we doubted Simon's judgement, we came to Wolf for this, too. And Wolf would then defend us, and oft draw upon the old ways of the clan to do this—for even Simon could not argue or refute these."

Louisa considered that for a long moment, pulling it together, envisioning where it led. "So did the clan become... divided over this?" she asked, tentative. "With Ulfarr rivalling Simon for the leadership, after all?"

Killik shrugged again, and pursed his lips. "Not at first, I ken," he said slowly. "The role of Enforcer yet carries much weight, and is also upheld by the role of our Right Hand, Drafli—a strong Skai who stands for us beside our mountain's captain. So I ken most Skai only saw Wolf as a strong brother who freely spoke his kin's truth, and sought to defend us and our ways. But then"—another heavy sigh—"then came Maria."

Maria. Ulfarr's hand spasmed in Louisa's, but he otherwise didn't move, and Louisa's eyes darted between his head, and Killik's sharp, grim profile. His mouth tight, his jaw clenched, the blood still streaked down his cheek.

"You ken who Maria was, ach?" Killik asked, with a brief glance toward her. "The Duchess of Warmisham?"

Louisa nodded, and Killik flipped a dagger out of his hair, and frowned down toward it. "Three summers past, Maria came to our mountain alone," Killik said. "But she did not tell us she was a duchess. Instead, she play-acted as though she was only a common woman, seeking refuge with us. But"—his mouth tightened—"but once she set eyes upon Simon, she at once offered to bed him, and bear him a son. For *coin*."

Louisa blinked at him, tilting her head. The *Duchess of Warmisham* had come to Orc Mountain, and pretended she wasn't a duchess at all? And then she'd instantly offered to bear one of their most powerful orcs a son? For *payment*?

"So... was it some kind of attack, then?" Louisa cautiously asked. "I assume Duke Warmisham sent her? Perhaps he blackmailed her, or paid her off, so he could claim his helpless young wife had been abducted by orcs, and then use that to drive his war efforts against you? And maybe blackmail you with her son afterwards, too?"

Ulfarr's body against her betrayed a flinch, and on his other side, Killik's glance toward her looked almost surprised. "Ach, this is all just as we thought," he said flatly. "But Simon longed for Maria, and he believed she wished to betray her duke husband with us. And thus, he pushed us all to take the risk. And our mountain's other leaders—and even our own Right Hand—were swayed into this, in hopes that we might twist it to our own ends. So"—he barked a bitter laugh—"a lying duchess came to live amongst the Skai. Walking our halls, and eating at our tables, and sharing our Enforcer's bed. Whilst we all played along with her fool little game."

Damn. Louisa winced, shaking her head, biting back the first words that came to her mouth. "That is... unfortunate," she said. "And not to judge, but... why didn't you just tell Maria you knew the truth from the start? Or perhaps give her an isolated waiting period, until you could be sure what Warmisham was planning? Or at least keep her housed well away from here, so you could add some degree of plausible deniability about your involvement with her, and help protect your mountain against him?"

Beside her, Ulfarr flinched again, and Killik's sideways glance looked almost grateful this time. "Again, this is what we wished for, also," he replied, clipped. "But Simon would not hear of it. We all thought"—another cold, bitter laugh— "he was fuck-drunk beyond saving, ach? For Maria is a lusty, needy woman, who was well able to bear his hard ploughing, and eagerly begged him for his gifts. Just as Skai like best."

Something dropped in Louisa's belly, but she fought to shove it away, to keep following this where it went. "So that left only... Ulfarr to defend you," she said slowly. "To stand up against Simon, on your behalf."

Killik's grim eyes held to hers as he nodded, and then he glanced at Ulfarr, and gave a gentle bump of their clasped hands against Ulfarr's knee. "Ach, it was only Wolf left," he said, quiet. "For again, the rest of us had all spoken vows to honour our Enforcer, ach? But though Wolf had also sworn this, he had long before sworn to honour *us*. To protect his pack against our enemies. And against the sins and the greed of even our closest and strongest brothers."

Right. Right, of course, it was exactly what Ulfarr would do, after having lived through everything with his father—and Louisa let out a shaky breath, and squeezed his big hand in hers, too. "So you challenged Simon about keeping Maria here, and putting you all at risk?" she carefully asked toward him. "And as part of that"—her thoughts twisted, floundered back to what Maria had said—"you... tried to seduce her? And... *share* her?"

Ulfarr flinched again, but still didn't reply, and beside him Killik barked another low laugh. "Mark me, woman, none of us wished for Maria in our beds," he said dryly. "She was fickle and flighty and fearful, and was only bearable when she was stuck screeching upon Simon's pole of a prick. But ach, the easiest charge against her was that Simon broke our clan's ways of taking mates with her, so"—he shrugged against Ulfarr's shoulder—"this was what Wolf first called upon."

Louisa wasn't following again, and searched Killik's hard profile, how he was intentionally looking away, now. "So what were your usual *ways* around taking mates, then?" she asked. "Not paying one for a child, I would hope?"

But Killik still wasn't looking at her, and he was again drawing in breath, drawing up strength from the earth. "No," he replied. "In days past, true Skai mates were only gained through a hunt, or a rut. In a hunt, a Skai seeks out the mate he wishes, and makes her an offer. In the rut, a Skai shares a woman with his closest clanmates. And whichever orc fathers her son then gains her, and keeps her as his mate."

Wait—what? Louisa's mouth dropped open, as shock roiled through her gut. "You can't—mean that?" she demanded. "Good gods, you would actually *do* that to a woman?!"

Killik's lip curled, and he shot a narrow glance toward her. "If you ken this was always—or even oft—forced upon the woman, you are a fool," he said, his voice curt. "I did not see *you* whining about us sharing you last eve, ach? Was this something you loathed, and would wish never to repeat?"

Right. Louisa couldn't hide her shaky exhale, or the sudden low pull in her belly, and Killik huffed a sharp laugh, and jabbed his dagger toward her. "Ach, I thought not," he said. "Now, only think if there had been a few more of us in our bed last eve, ach? If you had a whole band of hungry Skai who all wished to touch you, and taste you, and grant you joy with us?"

Curse it, Louisa was not thinking about that, she was *not*, and Killik rolled his eyes, and gave an exasperated sigh. "Ach, we can scent you, woman," he snapped. "But even beyond pleasure, this rut had other gains, ach? It brought the woman into the clan. It offered her many Skai scents, and thus, the clan was well able to track her and keep her safe. And no matter which orc fathered her son, the son would yet bear the scents of the others, most of all if they kept finding joy together after this first rut. So in this, the son gained many fathers, who would all help to feed him, and raise him, and guard him against their foes."

Oh. Louisa's belly was still unhelpfully clenching, enough that it only belatedly occurred to her that Killik sounded... wistful. That maybe... maybe he'd *wanted* that. He'd wanted a group of devoted Skai fathers watching over him, caring for him. Rather than his own miserable-sounding upbringing, orphaned and abused and forgotten, relying on the kindness of a teenager to keep him safe.

But then, between them, Ulfarr finally... shifted. Raised his head. And though his face looked haggard and pale, his mouth was set as he turned to look at Killik, his head twitching back and forth.

"No, Killik," he said, his voice a scraping rasp. "I ken this was the good side of these ruts, but you ken there was not a good side, also. You ken many women feared this, or became bound to orcs they did not wish for. You ken orcs like my father wielded this as a weapon, and used the bonds built by these ruts to their own cruel gain. My father wielded his women as commands, and as *rewards*."

Louisa's stomach plummeted, as the horrifying possible visions of that flashed behind her eyes—and Ulfarr glanced toward her, his hand tightening against hers. "There is naught now to fear upon this, Louisa," he said, his voice still hoarse. "Simon altered this practice amongst us, and he was right to do this. Just as he was right to break apart the packs. Just as he was right"—Louisa could hear his swallow— "about Maria."

Wait, he was? Louisa blinked at Ulfarr, at the bleak regret etched into his sad, shadowed face. "Simon was right, and I was wrong," he said thickly. "For Maria had no scheme with her duke husband. She only wished to spurn this man, and escape his cruelty toward her. And in my fear and my fury, I only heaped more cruelty upon her, and sowed more strife and darkness amidst our clan."

Louisa couldn't move, couldn't speak, could only stare at that grief glimmering in Ulfarr's eyes. "I sought to drive Maria away from us, and from Simon," he continued. "I sought to mock her, to frighten her, to lure her into my bed. And when none of this swayed her"—he drew in a slow, shaky breath—"I turned my rage toward Simon, and his rightful role as Enforcer. I challenged him for his place, and fought his judgement, and scorned his wisdom, and mocked his closest brothers. And amidst this, I upheld the orcs who stood for me in this battle, even when they had done great wrongs. I believed my defenders when they spoke their falsehoods to me, and thus I allowed deep darkness to fester within our clan. And I yet did not repent, and…"

He heaved another harsh breath, his mouth contorting, his head shaking back and forth. "And then I stole Maria away, against her will," he whispered. "I meant to take her away from Simon and our kin forever, far across the sea. I thought this was the only way to save us. I thought I was guarding my kin from this cruel duke, from mayhap the greatest threat we had ever faced. But—I was *wrong*."

Wrong. His voice was flat and cold on the word, and he again shook his head. "I was wrong," he repeated. "I was wrong, and I was short-sighted, and I was cruel. Maria did not deserve my judgement, or all the fear and pain I brought her. And my kin did not deserve my rage, and my foolishness, and my failure to see the evil amongst us. The evil"—his voice dropped—"within *me*."

Louisa couldn't look away from his face, couldn't think through the whirling mess in her thoughts, the pain in Ulfarr's eyes on hers. "And since all this," he continued, slower, as if he was forcing the words out, "Maria has proven me wrong, again and again. She has shown herself a good, strong, lusty Skai mate to Simon. She wears our garb, she fights in our arena, she flaunts her form and her hunger for all our clan to see. She has even wedded Simon in the way of her own kin, and has borne him a strong Skai son, also."

Louisa's thoughts whirled faster, louder, flashing back and forth, even as her eyes stayed frozen on Ulfarr's face. Because yes, that was sadness, and grief, and regret—but strongest of all, perhaps, was the… wistfulness, low and heavy in his voice. The… longing.

Ulfarr… *wanted* all that. He wanted a good, strong, lusty

Skai mate. He wanted a woman who wore his garb, fought in his arena, flaunted her body, bore him a son...

Louisa's eyes squeezed shut, but it all kept parading on, too sharp and painful behind her eyes. Because no matter what Killik said, maybe—maybe Ulfarr had also truly wanted... *Maria*. Maybe he *had* wanted Simon to share Maria with him. Maybe he had wanted to seduce Maria, to lure her to his bed, and maybe even the kidnapping had been part of that, too. He'd wanted to run away with her, across the sea, alone...

"So what... what if your efforts had worked, then?" Louisa made herself say, into the silence. "If Maria had... agreed to run away with you? Or if Simon had agreed to share her? Would you have... *proceeded*?"

Gods, why was she even asking this, she didn't want to know this, it wasn't the important question... was it? But as she opened her eyes again, found Ulfarr's haggard, stricken face, she found she—needed to know. She needed to hear what he was capable of, needed to find a way through the desperate wheeling jealousy clamping at her throat. Was Ulfarr still a monster, or was he not, were his awful actions justified, or were they not, and did he still want Maria, or did he not, and...

And Ulfarr just kept looking at her like that, with such aching, bitter sadness in his eyes. But then he sighed, and closed his eyes, and... and *nodded*.

"Ach," he said, almost a whisper. "I ken I should have... welcomed this."

Oh. It was like all the air had sucked away, like he'd kicked Louisa in the belly, or clawed her in the throat. Of course Ulfarr had wanted Maria. Of course he would have shared his affections and his stunning, powerful body with her, and surely he would never struggle to be aroused for her, either. She was so young, so beautiful, flaunting her form, wearing their garb, bearing their sons...

And gods curse Louisa, why did it hurt so much, why was she so painfully jealous? And how selfish was this, how short-sighted was this, how could she possibly justify any of this, what the hell was she supposed to do with this, what the hell was she supposed to say? She had to leave, of course she had to leave, and escape this, and forget any of this had ever happened. She couldn't share her bed with a kidnapper, an enabler, with someone who truly wanted another woman, who wanted a son, who maybe always would—

And maybe—maybe Ulfarr knew it, too. Maybe he saw it, or scented it, because his clammy hand spasmed in Louisa's, and he slowly drew her hand to his mouth, and—kissed it. Kissed it with such soft furtiveness that it felt like his lips had barely touched her at all.

"I am sorry, Louisa," he said, his eyes shimmering in the darkness. "I am so sorry I touched you, and shared your bed, without first telling you these dark truths, and the depths of my great sins. This was—selfish, and greedy, and—wrong. I ought to have known—that even ten nights with a woman such as you—would be—should be—"

Oh gods, oh gods, was he weeping, the words choking in his throat, the wetness streaking from his eyes. And was he smiling, trying to smile, a travesty of a smile, something broken and defeated and sickening on his mouth.

"I wish you only happiness, and wealth, and Skai-kesh's greatest peace, Louisa," he whispered. "Farewell."

36

Farewell.

As if... as if Louisa was leaving.

But—yes. Yes. That was what she was supposed to do. That was all she could do in this moment, with all this horrible miserable chaos screaming in her skull. Escaping. Forgetting. Leaving.

So when Ulfarr carefully released Louisa's hand, extracted his fingers from hers, she... didn't argue. Didn't look at him, or at Killik. Just nodded, swallowed, shoved up to her shaky, staggering feet. Forgetting. Leaving.

She turned toward the door without looking, without thinking, leaving, leaving—

When suddenly—Killik. Killik, whirling in front of her, blocking the doorway, his dagger gleaming in his clawed hand.

"No, woman," he snarled. "*No.* You shall not leave thus!"

Louisa halted, gazed at him, her heart clamouring in her chest, as he wildly waved his dagger toward her. "You agreed to this," he spat. "You *swore* you cared not for Wolf's past. You swore you would not ask. And here you are, breaking your word to me, *again*! And hurling yet more guilt and shame upon him!"

Louisa's breath hitched, her head shaking, but Killik was still here, still furious, still waving that flashing dagger. "You humans never ask the right questions, or seek the other side of the tale! You ken Wolf did all this upon a merry little lark? You ken he took joy in any of this? You ken he did not pray and weep over this, night after night? You ken when he stole Maria away, he thought he would ever return home, or see any of us again? Or, if Simon caught him, that he should even *live* to see the next morn?"

Louisa swallowed, shot an uncertain glance back to where Ulfarr's head was bowed again, his big body curled even smaller than before. As if he didn't want to hear this, maybe couldn't bear to hear this, had she really hurled yet more guilt and shame upon him...

"I watched him wrestle and weigh this," Killik's hard voice continued. "I watched him weep as he spoke his farewells to his pack, and to me. He knew this was the end of all he cared for, of mayhap his *life*, and yet he did this, for he thought we were at great risk of death, from one of the most powerful lords in the realm! So he chose to draw this upon himself, instead! As he has *always* done!"

His voice rang through the small room, his fury flashing through his eyes, thudding into Louisa's frantic heartbeat. And she was just listening now, just needing to hear the rest of it, please...

"And for his judgement," Killik hissed, lower now, "Maria near cut off his prick—and then Simon near *killed* him. Simon defeated him in combat before all the clan, all his pack. Simon broke eight of his bones, weakened his scenting beyond repair, and refused to allow our healer to touch him. He left the Wolf of the Skai to *rot* in his blood and his agony and his *shame*."

What? No. Simon had done that? That Simon? The

Simon who was supposed to be a good leader in their clan? The Simon they'd all sworn to uphold and respect?

Louisa's sheer horror must have shown on her face, because Killik slowly smiled at her, his eyes glinting with mockery and pain. "It was near half a year before Wolf healed," he said coldly. "And you ken what he did amidst this? He swore yet more vows to Simon. He gave Maria gifts, and begged for her forgiveness. He swore to stay here at the mountain. He swore he would not seek to gain a mate or bear a son of his blood, until he had gained the fealty and forgiveness of Skai-kesh and the clan. Until he was restored to the clan as a true Skai son."

Oh. Oh, gods. Ulfarr had publicly sworn not to take a mate. A *mate*. And here Louisa had come to his home, and let all these people believe that he'd done it anyway. That Ulfarr had broken his word to Simon, and to all his kin.

"And we can't just—tell them I'm only a friend?" Louisa asked, high-pitched. "Or that you're only—paying me, just the way Simon did with Maria? Because it's true!"

She winced even as she said it, and Killik laughed, low and weary. "Ach, I meant to only call you Wolf's bedmate, once they caught your scent upon him," he said. "But now you have come here, with our son, and paraded yourself all over this mountain, reeking of Wolf's seed, before mayhap every orc in our clan! And if we now claim this is naught, and we are only *paying* you"—he laughed again—"you ken how this looks, coming from Wolf, ach? After all he has done?"

Damn it. Louisa stared at Killik, her mouth slack, as waves of hot and cold flashed up her spine. Because it would look—like mockery. Like a challenge. Like Ulfarr was mimicking what Simon had done with Maria, and flaunting it before all his clan, in order to break his own vow toward Simon. In order to escape his own punishment.

It would look like Ulfarr was standing against Simon, again. And no, of course they couldn't risk that now, surely that would be even worse than Ulfarr only breaking his vow, seeking to take a mate...

"Gods *damn* it," Louisa croaked, whipping around to stare at Ulfarr's curled-up body. "Fuck. I'm so, so sorry."

Her voice cracked, her head whipping back and forth, her hands clamping to her mouth. And she could almost feel the effort it took for Ulfarr to raise his head, to hold his shimmering eyes to hers. "Naught—for you—to regret," he said, his voice halting. "I ought—to have—told you."

And without waiting for her answer, he slowly dropped his head again, his powerful body gone so small and sad and alone. And as Louisa stared at him, she felt a sudden, stuttering fear. Maybe—maybe the same kind of fear Killik had felt when he'd first come to her, seeking those ten nights...

I fear for my wolf's life. I fear that one day, he shall awaken, and find he can no more bear the shame. And then he shall slit his throat, or fall on his sword, or walk into a river with a boulderstone...

"And you ken Wolf should have chosen to do all he did, if he had found another way?" came Killik's cold, implacable voice, now close behind her. "If Simon had heard his truth, and offered to bring him alongside, or to seek joy together with his willing woman—you ken Wolf should have refused this? You ken he should have wished for all this pain and grief instead?"

No, damn it, of course not, and it was like Killik was just twisting the dagger at this point, his voice scraping in Louisa's ear. "And I told you," he hissed, "how deeply Wolf longs for a woman. He longs for a strong, hungry Skai woman to tend and plough and enjoy, and mayhap even share with those he cares for most! So ach, woman, this is why I hunted *you*!"

You. Something sharp and cold prodded into Louisa's back as Killik spoke—the tip of his dagger, curse him—but there wasn't even a twinge of fear or alarm. No, no, because his unthinkable, impossible words were still ringing, raging, roaring through her skull. *This is why I hunted you. You. You.*

In a hunt, a Skai seeks out the mate he wishes, and makes her an offer...

But no. No. Absolutely not. There was no way that was what Killik had done, right? No.

"For after all this," Killik continued, that dagger still nudging softly against her spine, "Wolf deserves a Skai woman even better than Maria. He deserves a woman with power and knowledge amongst her kin. He deserves a woman who does not faint or falter. He deserves a woman who knows work and fealty and sacrifice, a woman who knows what it is to have kin to care for. A woman who welcomes not only his own good Skai prick, but the strong Skai ploughing of his closest bedmate, also. And a woman"— his voice lowered—"who sees not his shame, but his strength. A woman worthy of the Wolf of the Skai."

Louisa's throat convulsed, her heart skipping in her chest. And when her eyes darted sideways, Killik was behind her, almost, *almost* touching her, his mouth so close his breath tickled her ear.

"So show me," he breathed. "Prove this to me."

His words stuttered harsh and fierce into Louisa's belly, into her groin, into the cool teasing tip of that dagger against her back.

Show him. Prove this.

And she should have been questioning it, should have been calling Killik out on his constant rubbish, on this absolute mess. Or on what they should do now, what this all meant, what they had left...

But instead, Louisa was looking at Ulfarr. Grieving for Ulfarr. Aching at the sight of him, the sadness crushing him beneath its weight. Maybe he was still a monster, maybe he still didn't deserve forgiveness, but maybe...

Maybe for now it didn't matter. Maybe Louisa could

just... take a breath, and grope for Killik's hand, and tug him back across the room. She could face this. Prove this...

And as they went, she could tug at her new chain belt. Let it fall open around her waist. Let her dress fall open, too, let it show her loincloth, let it show her breasts and her belly and her scars...

"Thank you for telling me all this, sweetheart," she whispered, toward Ulfarr's bowed head. "And now, will you come to bed with us?"

37

W*ill you come to bed with us.*

It was without question the most brazen, most ridiculous thing Louisa had ever said—or done—in her life. Undressing like this, showing her body like this, and propositioning an orc. An orc who was grieving, weeping, lost in his past and his sins, and surely not thinking about her in the slightest.

But she was facing it, and she was doing it. Standing here and shaking and doing it, half naked, and clinging tightly to Killik's hand. Dragging him into this too, but he'd damn well wanted it, he'd all but told her to do it, and...

And then Ulfarr... raised his head. Opened his sad wet eyes. And then he startled, and stared, his mouth slack, his gaze darting up and down Louisa's front.

Louisa couldn't hide her grimace as she followed his eyes—gods, why hadn't she chosen a more full-coverage loin-cloth, and had she really needed the knee-high boots? She looked like some kind of... *seductress*, especially with that chain and knife still hanging off her dress—and why was Ulfarr still staring? What was he thinking, was he going to refuse, or laugh...

And curse it, now Killik had stepped around to look at her properly, too. And if Louisa hadn't been so mortified, she might have been gratified by the way his brows snapped up, his lips quirking with something like... approval?

"Ach, mark this, Wolf," Killik said, his voice light, conversational, as his hand gently tugged at the dangling front of Louisa's loincloth. "She has gone and dressed for you. Looks just as a Skai woman should, you ken."

Ulfarr's throat convulsed, his arm wiping at his wet face, but now it was just confusion, flickering across his shadowed eyes. "But she—you wished—to leave, Louisa," he said, between hitching breaths. "You learnt—my deep sins—my shame—so why—"

Louisa's own breath shuddered, her eyes blinking hard, because gods, had Ulfarr not even heard everything Killik had just told her? Had he not followed how little she'd known, how she hadn't even asked for his side of the tale? But no, maybe not, because beside her Killik shrugged, and reached to stroke his clawed fingers against Ulfarr's hair, still pulled back in his ever-present braid.

"No, for she has come to her senses, I ken," he said smoothly. "She knows what a fool she should be, to walk away from the Wolf of the Skai, and the promise of sharing his bed."

Louisa should have countered that, somehow, but Ulfarr's wide wet eyes snapped up to hers, looking skeptical, but almost painfully hopeful, too. So she swallowed down the lump in her throat, and smiled, and twitched her own hand toward him, caressed it at his pale, scarred cheek.

"Just so, sweetheart," she murmured. "And also, today I learned you like chains in bed, too."

She flinched even as she said it, because gods, why would she say something like that? And even if she had slowly been realizing how thoroughly Kitty had set her up with this outfit—down to the chain still hanging from her open dress—Louisa hadn't needed to say it, to throw that out there too, had she? Even if some fool part of her had hoped it might help, might draw Ulfarr's attention, might prove something to Killik, just like he'd asked...

Ulfarr was still staring at her, his mouth fallen open, but beside her, Killik chuckled, and reached an easy hand to tug at her new belt. "If you ken this flimsy trinket shall hold our wolf, woman, you are yet lacking your senses," he said lightly. "Although"—he frowned, and yanked the chain up to his nose, inhaling deep—"did *Thrain* forge this?"

Louisa felt nonplussed again, and far too hot and exposed—but yes, Kitty had said something to that effect, hadn't she? And when Louisa nodded at Killik, that was a slow, devious smile, drawing at his lips—and he casually began tugging the rest of the chain away from her dress, until it swung long and shimmering between them.

"Ach, then, woman, we might as well test this, and have another lesson," he said. "Bind Wolf's wrists with it, shall you?"

What? Here? *Now?* But the glint in Killik's eyes was far too meaningful, especially when he glanced down at Ulfarr's face. At where Ulfarr still looked stunned, blank, not at all sure of himself, and then he twitched, shook his head. "You cannot—" he began, then took a heavy breath. "Cannot yet wish for—for—"

But Louisa was already nodding, taking the chain from Killik's hand with shaky fingers, as comprehension kept jostling through her thoughts. Dragging up the memories of the other times they'd done this, all the other times Killik had taken control. Perhaps... perhaps not because Ulfarr was fundamentally oriented toward submission, but perhaps because he didn't think he deserved to be desired, or cared for. And maybe this was a way of showing him otherwise. Of proving it.

It ached deep in Louisa's belly, resonated in her chest, and she dropped to kneel beside Ulfarr on the fur, clasping one of his big hands in hers. "If you don't mind it, sweetheart," she murmured, "We'd really like to have our way with you. Make sure you can't escape us."

Ulfarr's eyes widened, but his tongue brushed his lips—and then he twitched a curt, rapid nod. And when Louisa drew out his hand, he willingly raised it higher, and watched with strange, shifting intensity as she carefully wrapped the chain around his wrist.

"Ach, not thus," came Killik's clipped voice, as he knelt on Ulfarr's other side, grasping for his other hand. "Place his wrists thus together, and then wrap around, and lock the chain. Not too tight."

Louisa followed his directions as well as she could, and after a moment Killik even caught her hand in his, guiding her movements, his claws gently scraping against her skin. "Ach, thus," he said. "Now lock—thus. Good. And let us hope it may hold him for a spell, at least."

He'd actually grinned at her, and at Ulfarr too, and for a breath, Louisa almost forgot the bizarre convoluted mess of this, and the ridiculous fact that she was wearing a loincloth, and chaining up a grieving, guilty monster of an orc so she could have her way with him. And instead, she found herself smiling back at Killik, caught in the strange crackling warmth, the glint in his eyes.

"Now on your knees, Wolf," Killik ordered, with a gentle slap to Ulfarr's hip. "Toward your pretty Skai woman, in her pretty Skai garb."

Oh. Killik didn't mean that, surely he didn't, he was just saying it for Ulfarr... right? But yes, Ulfarr was already nodding, obeying, shifting his big body around to kneel on the fur. And then leaning forward onto his hands, while the chain kept his powerful wrists held tight together.

"Now check the chain again, woman," came Killik's clipped command. "You must look each time he moves, for stubborn Skai that he is, he will never speak of pain. And we should never wish to truly harm him."

Louisa could readily agree with that, and she carefully slipped a finger inside the chain against Ulfarr's wrists, testing the tightness while Killik watched. And when she nodded, he nodded back, and gave her a smug smile.

"Good," he said. "Now, woman, for our next lesson—I ken you have not yet learnt the joys of a Skai's tongue, ach?"

What? Louisa jolted all over, darted a shocked glance between Killik and Ulfarr—but Killik's eyes were already flinty, and Ulfarr's looked glazed, and hungry, too. His black tongue sweeping to his lips, and his gaze dropped to Louisa's loincloth, oh gods...

"Closer, woman," Killik ordered. "Knees apart. Let your wolf scent you."

Oh, they were doing this, they were really doing this, now, and Louisa obeyed, hitching closer on the fur, toward Ulfarr's... face. Toward where his face had lowered, lining up with that front leather of her loincloth, his breath inhaling slow and deep...

"I wonder what you shall find beneath that pretty loincloth, Wolf?" came Killik's cool question, and Louisa only distantly noticed his hand stroking Ulfarr's bare back, moving downwards in slow, easy circles. "I wonder how your woman might taste?"

Ulfarr's kneeling body betrayed a hard, sustained shudder, and Killik's eyes flicked up to meet Louisa's, a sly smile on his mouth. "I said, taste her, Wolf," he purred. "Teach her the great power of a Skai's hungry tongue."

And yes, yes, Ulfarr's face shifted closer, lower, his nose nudging at the hanging leather of the loincloth. Guiding it aside, oh hell, so he could slip his head beneath it, and...

Lick her.

Louisa gasped at the slick startling sensation, flashing hot and shivery through her skin, firing deep into her belly—and oh, fuck, Ulfarr did it again. Just touching her with his tongue, light and gentle at the top of her crease, but she again spasmed all over, and clutched a hand to his hair. Drawing out a hoarse moan from Ulfarr's mouth, while Killik smugly smiled, and stroked his hand further toward Ulfarr's still-clothed arse.

"Good, ach?" he asked, maybe to both of them, and Louisa frantically nodded, and Ulfarr nodded, too. Even as his tongue kept touching, tasting, seeking a little lower, oh...

"Then tell him how this feels, woman," Killik said, curt. "When he is using his tongue, you ought to use yours, also."

Right, right, and Louisa rapidly nodded, drew in breath. "Feels—so good, sweetheart," she choked, and oh, he was already licking harder, deeper. "Feels like nothing—nothing else—oh gods—"

It was too hard to think, too hard to find words in the sweeping swirling chaos, but Ulfarr moaned again, and Killik circled his finger, saying, *Keep going*. And suddenly there was the vivid memory of Ulfarr speaking to her in that bed at the camp, praising her, offering her such reassurance, such... peace.

"You're—incredible, sweetheart," Louisa gasped, between her heavy breaths. "You're the most incredible lover I've had in my life. You're so—kind, and so generous, and so patient, and you feel so—so—"

Her voice broke into a moan, because Ulfarr's kisses had deepened, hotter, closer, oh. And her tingling hands were frantically clinging to his head now, her body shivering, fighting to stay upright, as his slick seeking tongue slipped... *inside* her.

Louisa yelped and swayed on her knees, strong enough

that she almost tumbled sideways, and Killik rolled his eyes, huffed a low laugh. "I ken you are already too much for her, Wolf," he drawled. "Mayhap she ought to lie back and open wide, so you can fully feast upon her, ach? Just as a good wolf should."

Louisa and Ulfarr moaned in unison this time, but Louisa accordingly shunted herself backwards, so she was half-lying on the fur. But then she stilled, hovering shaky and awkward with her knees clamped together, was she really supposed to open wide, could they really want that—

But oh, wait, now it was Ulfarr's bound hands guiding her thighs apart, his body shifting forward and down with astonishing ease, settling on his elbows. So he could again seek his face beneath her loincloth, between her legs, and...

Louisa couldn't stop her shout, her wildly shaking thighs, because fuck, how that felt. Like a furious flood of sensation, of impossible jangling pleasure, whirling out from Ulfarr's warm lips, his swirling seeking tongue. His tongue that was still sinking deeper, oh gods, filling her with slick sinuous strength, oh please, please—

"Please," she gasped, as her fluttering eyes again caught Killik's glinting gaze, his raised brows, his still-circling finger. "Oh, gods, yes, please—"

Ulfarr's groan rumbled into her, juddering and vibrating from the inside out. While Killik just kept watching, looking darkly pleased, and now—now shifting around further behind Ulfarr, and yanking down Ulfarr's trousers. Exposing his bare hips and arse, still raised up in the air, and Killik's eyes were looking, glimmering, his hand coolly caressing downwards...

"You keep feasting upon her, Wolf," he purred, "and mayhap I shall feast upon you."

Louisa's eyes widened, her body shuddering at the next dizzying plunge of Ulfarr's tongue—but yes, Killik meant that, he was doing that. Licking his own lips as he bent downwards, his eyes hooded and hungry, his hands drawing Ulfarr apart, so he could...

Ulfarr's moan rumbled through his mouth, rang deep into Louisa's core, and that was a low, satisfied laugh from Killik as he settled closer, deeper. Offering to Ulfarr what Ulfarr was offering to her, oh gods, and Louisa had never once imagined prickly, angry Killik doing such a thing, freely giving something so intimate, so... so obscene. Something that again shifted the power of all this, the weight of this, because Ulfarr was the bound kneeling monster, and yet— and yet Killik was kneeling, too. Kneeling, and worshipping his wolf in the most flagrant way possible, eagerly kissing and licking and lavishing his—well.

"So good," Louisa gasped, maybe at Ulfarr, or at Killik, or at both of them. "Oh gods, yes, so good, please, fuck, *please.*"

And yes, yes, it was working, both Killik and Ulfarr moaning now, rumbling over the slick sounds of their slurping mouths. So Louisa kept babbling, kept gasping helpless incoherent praises at them, her hands skittering in Ulfarr's hair, her impaled body clamping desperately at Ulfarr's plunging tongue. She needed more, needed him to keep going, so close, please, *please—*

And then, gods curse it, Ulfarr—drew back. Drew his glorious slippery tongue out, away. And gave her one last hot, wet, lingering kiss before shifting around, and—and reaching his hand down to spread against Killik's head. As if—wait. He'd broken out. He'd gotten free? Of that solid steel chain?

But when Killik lifted his head, he didn't look even slightly surprised, and that was a rueful smile on his mouth, at such striking odds with the dazed hunger in his eyes, the flush creeping up his cheeks. And Louisa couldn't look away from him, and shuddered again as he slowly licked his lips, leaned his head into the touch of Ulfarr's hand.

"Ach, Wolf," he murmured. "What do you wish?"

And in this instant, it was again as though—as though the power had shifted, and spun upside down. As if maybe Ulfarr had been in charge all along, as if even the slightest nudge of his hand could make Killik halt and obey...

"I ken our woman is now soft and open," came Ulfarr's deep, rumbling voice. "And ready for your strong Skai ploughing, pup. Should you—both wish."

His eyes darted up to Louisa's face, searching, questioning—but not flinching or hesitating, either. No, no, this was *that* Ulfarr again, the easy confident Ulfarr, and the truth of it caught Louisa's breath, clutched tight between her legs. And when her blinking eyes glanced at Killik, he was—he was looking there, looking at where Ulfarr had opened her for him, oh gods...

And they weren't doing this, Killik didn't really want this... right? But he was still looking, and then—then glancing at Ulfarr's face, as that flush crept higher up his cheeks, and his tongue again brushed his lips. As if—as if he—wanted to.

And maybe it was just to oblige Ulfarr, just to keep this version of Ulfarr here, looking at him like this, touching him like this. Maybe it wasn't about Louisa at all. But when Killik's glittering eyes glanced at Louisa's face, asking her the silent question, she swallowed against her dry throat, and then—brought up her hands. Signed at him, shaky but fervent, because maybe that was easier, easier than saying it to those stunning asking eyes.

Yes, Killik. Yes.

And oh, the way his eyes widened, his lips parting, as the flush spread higher up his cheeks. "Curst woman," he muttered, but yes, yes, he was shifting upwards, following the gentle pull of Ulfarr's guiding hand toward her. "I shall not be gentle, you ken."

But Louisa betrayed a gasp, a nod, and Ulfarr was smiling at Killik, looking fondly indulgent as he drew him closer.

Settling Killik's knees between Louisa's spread legs, and then reaching his big hand down, slipping it with proprietary ease into Killik's trousers. And then drawing him out, exposing that hard grey jabbing length, already leaking white at the tip...

"Good, pup," Ulfarr said, low, as his hand stroked Killik up and down, and then guided him closer. Closer toward Louisa, toward where his other hand was spreading her thighs wider apart, and then slipping down in between. Gently drawing her swollen heat open, so he could bring Killik's hard jabbing cock even closer, and... touch it there. Settle it there, easing it inside her, oh hell.

"She is so soft, ach?" Ulfarr murmured. "Well able to bear you, pup, and welcome your strong Skai ploughing for me."

Both Louisa and Killik gasped at once, because oh, Killik was pushing into her now, slower than last time, maybe because of Ulfarr's warm hand still between them. But gods, the feel of it, that hard jutting length sinking smooth and deep into her, carving into the slick path left by Ulfarr's tongue...

Killik hissed as he sank all the way, his hard cock fully plunged inside, his groin grinding against hers. And against that still-present press of Ulfarr's hand, warm and safe between them, because he'd opened Louisa for Killik, and now he was giving them this, please...

But Killik was—waiting. Waiting, the flush staining his cheeks, the hunger flaring in his eyes as he glanced between Louisa and Ulfarr...

"Plough her, pup," Ulfarr breathed. "Find your pleasure with her. Show us what a strong and lusty Skai you are."

Killik's moan was shaky, trembling into Louisa's belly— but then he nodded, and swept himself out again. Held himself there, just at the edge of Louisa's slick clutching heat, as his eyes found hers, glinted bright and greedy on her face—

She shouted as he slammed inside, hard enough to shake her all over—and then he held there, firm and deep, watching her writhe and choke upon him. "Already too much, woman?" he asked, his smooth voice at dizzying odds with the craving flashing in his eyes. "Too much Skai for you?"

Louisa shivered, gulped for air, clamped helplessly at the hard flesh jabbed so deep inside her—but wait, that was Ulfarr again, settling his body long and close beside her on the fur, as his hand shifted a little, too. Spreading warm and safe down over the curve of her, with Killik's cock jutted between his fingers, oh gods...

"Remember to breathe, Louisa," Ulfarr murmured, his eyes shimmering on hers. "Draw deep from the air, from the earth beneath you."

Right, this, and Louisa held his eyes, desperately pulled in air, as Killik slowly drew out, took himself away—and then slammed back in. Making Louisa convulse and quake, clamping hard against it, but she was still watching Ulfarr, holding his eyes, following his breaths...

"Good," he said. "In, and out. And if my hungry pup ever brings you pain, or you wish him to stop, you shall only speak thus to me, ach?"

Yes, yes, she would, and Louisa nodded, hauling in more air, keeping time with Ulfarr's slow, steady breaths. While Killik drew out again, swifter this time, and slammed back in—and then again, and again. Until he was driving himself in and out of her, his hips pumping, his bollocks slapping with every staggering thrust. Jolting Louisa again and again, until her gasps were more like shouts, and it was taking all her effort, all her shattering focus, to hold her eyes to Ulfarr's, to draw up his strength, his breath...

"Good, Louisa," he purred, as his free hand slipped beneath her head, cradling against the base of her skull, so he could tilt her face a little more toward him. "Ach, this is so good. You are so lovely, and so sweet, with such a strong Skai prick ploughing you thus, and drawing up your joy."

Oh, gods, yes, and Louisa's glance at Killik's flushed face found him looking at Ulfarr too, wanting to hear this, wanting more of this, please. And yes, maybe Ulfarr knew that too, giving a gentle approving caress of his hand between them, even as his head leaned forward, his mouth pressing a soft kiss to Louisa's sweaty temple.

"Ach, just thus," he murmured. "You breathe, and welcome this good gift my fierce pup grants you. And should you wish, you could even grant him your own gifts in return, ach? You could touch him, or praise him, or beg for his strong Skai seed."

Oh, yes, Louisa could do that, if Killik didn't mind that, if he really wanted that—but maybe he did want it, he did, his wild eyes now darting between Ulfarr and Louisa, his breath hitching as his hips plunged in harder. So Louisa somehow nodded, found more air, breathed into the earth, as she skittered up her shaky hands, and spread them against Killik's hard, sweaty chest. Felt the warmth of him, the strength of him, the furious rapid pulse of his racing heartbeat.

"So good, Killik," she choked. "You feel—so good. Look so good. And you're so—fierce, and clever, and—and—devoted, and I want—I want—"

She couldn't even say it, couldn't speak it into the light and the power and the maelstrom, the sheer disbelieving need of Killik's glittering eyes on hers. And oh, hell, that was Ulfarr's hand shifting, slipping out from between their slamming bodies, so he could raise it between them, and... sign.

"This is *fuck me*," he murmured, so soft, as two of his fingers gently jabbed downwards toward her, until they nudged at Louisa's gasping throat. "And this"—all those fingers spreading, easy and proprietary—"is *fill me*. And—*please*."

Please was his hand flattening, resting just below Louisa's collarbone, above her jiggling breast. And yes, please, please, and she clutched his hand there, held it there, making it speak for her, making them speak together, as her other shaky hand snapped up, and signed the rest of it. *Fuck me, Killik. Fill me, Killik. Please, Killik.*

And gods, the way Killik's lashes fluttered, his mouth groaning, his hips plunging fierce and furious. So much, too much, and now Ulfarr's hand was slipping down Louisa's front again, sliding so easy back between them, and... touching. Touching her, stroking her just there, the way she'd taught him in the hayloft, whipping it harder and higher and hotter, her hands begging *please Killik please Ulfarr please*—

Louisa screamed as the bliss crashed and thundered, charged through her in great sweeping torrents—and Killik shouted too, all hissing rasping words she didn't recognize. But then he bore down, holding hard, so hard it hurt, mashing them together, so his swelling stabbing cock could spasm, and spray. Surging into Louisa, spewing out in sharp seizing bursts, filling her again and again with his hot slick seed, while she writhed and clutched it, milked at it, needing more, more, more.

But then—then, it was done. Done, because Killik had already yanked himself out, away. Not even looking at her now, just holding his gaze downwards as he swiped for his sagging trousers, and jerked them up. Hiding himself, even as his slick liquid mess bubbled out from inside Louisa, sputtering all over the fur beneath them.

And, oh gods, what was she supposed to do with this, with how Killik's eyes were now carefully fixed across the room. And damn it, she was even still touching him, and...

And wait. Wait, Ulfarr's warm hand had followed hers, found hers, spread over hers against Killik's chest. Wanting her hand to stay there, held tight against the uneasy truth of Killik's still-pounding heartbeat.

"Good, Louisa," Ulfarr murmured, soft in her ear. "This

was all so good. And unless Killik tells you to stop, you may yet touch him, ach? It pleases him, when you show him how much you wish for him. And when you show him how thankful you are"—his voice dropped, as his big hand eased sideways, stroked slow and possessive up Killik's heaving side—"for his hunger, and his wisdom, and his fealty. For his great, great kindness."

Killik's rigid body betrayed a faint but distinct twitch, his eyes darting back to Ulfarr's face. To where a twinge of that darkness had passed across Ulfarr's eyes, fading that hint of a smile on his mouth.

"Such great kindness, Killik," Ulfarr said, quieter. "I have not thanked you enough."

Killik's mouth spasmed, and his gaze again flicked away as he shook his head, jerky and dismissive. But the look on his face, the too-bright glint in his eyes, said something else, shouted something else, and oh gods, Louisa wasn't going to weep, she wasn't.

"Really?" her fool voice demanded, into the pulsing silence. "Kindness? *Him*? Not to question your judgement, sweetheart, but do you know how many times this stubborn Skai has shouted and sulked and raged at me, and waved his daggers in my face?"

And curse her, what was she doing, what was she saying, snapping Ulfarr's surprised eyes to hers like that—but wait, yes, that was relief on Killik's face, maybe even gratefulness, as he bared his teeth toward her, and reached up to yank one of his daggers out of his topknot.

"Ach, for you are the most provoking woman to ever walk this earth!" he snapped, flipping the dagger in his fingers, pointing its tip at her nose. "And you never cease with your trouble and your meddling! You ken I wished to have my peaceful life upended by such a spiteful ungrateful harpy?"

Louisa blinked up at him, fought to shove down the instant's low hurt in her belly—damn it, she'd started this, hadn't she? And what did it matter if he'd just fucked her like that, and then called her a *spiteful ungrateful harpy*…

But beside her, Ulfarr had tilted his head, and oh, that was his warm gentle mouth, kissing again at her temple. As his hand kept stroking Killik, smoothing up and down his side, as if settling a wild frightened beast…

"Ach, my unruly pup is only barking at you, woman," Ulfarr murmured. "And only now seeking to play. But even when he falls into a temper, you ken this always passes as quick as it comes, ach? There is naught of true weight or danger in this. When he is truly enraged, he shall smile and speak sweetly to you, even as he plots your doom, ach?"

Oh. Ulfarr's voice sounded—fond, even affectionate, his hand still stroking at Killik's side, his eyes warmer again, softer again, as they held to Killik's unreadable watching face. "And it is the same with his daggers, you ken," Ulfarr's low voice continued. "They are part of him, just as much as his claws or his teeth or his temper. But"—his stroking hand paused, gave a light pat to Killik's flank—"he should never unwittingly cut you or catch you with them, no matter how close they come. For he is mayhap our finest weapons wielder, and if he truly wished to harm you, you should be screaming before you saw him move."

Louisa swallowed, blinking between them, while her thoughts lurched backwards to that day with Rikard in the forest. When Killik had indeed given Rikard that terrifying smile, and laughed as Rikard had staggered away.

"Well, he's still an arrogant, infuriating tyrant," Louisa finally managed. "Who can't even be bothered to *hint* at his bedmates that he might have enjoyed himself!"

But Killik rolled his eyes at her, and again waved his dagger in her face, maybe just to prove Ulfarr's point. "If I did not *enjoy* myself, woman," he drawled, "do you ken I should yet be here? Do you ken I should have put my strong Skai prick anywhere near your grasping human womb again, let alone answered your pleas for my good Skai seed?"

Louisa sputtered and glared at him, and then shot Ulfarr a wry, disbelieving look. "How do I sign *fuck you*?" she demanded at him. "Or maybe, *I hope our wolf makes* you *scream on his strong Skai prick?*"

Killik instantly snarled, giving another furious flail of his dagger, but oh, Ulfarr half-smiled back at her, and then signed it, just as she'd asked. Gently jabbing two fingers at Killik's bobbing throat—*fuck you*—and then a touch at his own chest, his hands pressing together as if in a prayer. And then one hand brushing Killik's bare chest, and then reaching up to tug at Killik's mouth, while his other hand dropped to his own trousers, and made a very clear, very obscene stroking motion. As if he was caressing a huge prick, and then aiming it toward... Killik.

There wasn't even an actual bulge in Ulfarr's trousers— and maybe there hadn't been, that entire time. But as Louisa watched him sign it, watched Killik's eyes sharply widen at the sight of it, it was still too much, too stark and strong, all helpless desperate yearning shouting in her chest. And without at all meaning to, she turned toward Ulfarr's too-close face, drew in a deep breath against his sweet-scented skin.

"Don't think I fully got that, sweetheart," she whispered. "Could you show me again?"

Killik visibly twitched this time, even bared his teeth toward her, but he was still watching, too. Watching with almost as much raw, quivering longing as Louisa felt, as Ulfarr's warm, steady eyes looked back at him, and his hands easily signed those too-powerful words. His fingers touching Killik's throat, then his own chest, then the prayer, then Killik's mouth—and then that obscene stroking toward Killik, as if aiming at him, longing to be inside him...

Fuck you. I pray you scream upon my strong prick in you.

Killik's mouth opened and closed, his face now flushed deeper than Louisa had ever seen it, and she could see the effort in his slow shaky breath, in how he drew the strength from the floor—and then darted his wide eyes toward Louisa's face.

"*You*," he said, hoarse. "You are a scourge upon the realm, woman. Before you, my days were peaceful! Full of friendly spying and killing and fucking! And now you swan in and shower us with this! Rules, and loincloths, and weak flimsy chains! And now seeking to make sure I shall never walk *again!*"

But he was—barking at her, Ulfarr had said, wanting to play, and Louisa drew up her coolest, sweetest smile, and aimed it toward his disgruntled face. "Oh, rubbish," she said, as lightly as she could. "Unlike *some* people, Ulfarr actually knows how to be gentle in bed, don't you, sweetheart? So I'm sure you'd walk again, Killik. Eventually."

Killik snarled and gave another furious whirl of his dagger, this time between her and Ulfarr both. "How great a fool do you ken I am?" he snapped back. "Ach, before I should risk putting that cudgel of his anywhere near my rump, I should like to see *you* try it first, woman. We shall see how you walk after, and then, *mayhap*, I shall ponder this."

Louisa hadn't missed that sharp catch of Ulfarr's breath beside her, his gaze rapidly darting between them. And Killik shot him a brief searching look, holding an instant too long, and then rolling his eyes.

"Gird your loincloth, then, woman," he said, jabbing his dagger toward her. "You now have four more nights."

Four more nights. It should have been a lowering reminder of that time limit, of how this was still only a deal—or how with everything that had happened today, maybe they wouldn't have four more nights at all. Maybe there were only more punishments after this, more retaliations and regrets, maybe Louisa would never see them again, maybe she wouldn't want to see them again, either...

But in this moment, this breath, blinking at Killik's cool, glittering eyes, it felt almost like... a promise. A challenge. *Prove this to me...*

"Fine, then, you smug raging snake," Louisa hissed, low and hot in her throat. "Four more nights."

38

Louisa spent the night with Killik and Ulfarr in the bed, curled up close against Ulfarr's solid, snoring body.

It shouldn't have been easy to sleep like that, after all the confusing chaos of that endless day—but once she'd gone and cleaned up in a nearby latrine, she'd found herself utterly exhausted, rubbing at her aching eyes as she'd staggered back into the room. And Killik had taken one look at her, and sharply ordered her into the bed.

"You really—don't mind?" Louisa had asked, blinking her bleary eyes at him. "Is it—your bed?"

She'd cast a searching look around the room, which she'd scarcely noticed until now—but it was a small, sparse room, furnished only with the large bed and several sturdy wooden chests. But Killik had irritably waved her toward the bed, and then nudged Ulfarr toward it, too.

"No, it is Wolf's bed," he'd said. "But he does not mind if we share it, ach, Wolf?"

Ulfarr had shaken his head, and he'd even reached for Louisa's hand, drawing her closer. And once they'd settled down together on the soft fur, Ulfarr had tucked Louisa close into his side, and then settled Killik down into his other side, too, before pulling another large, heavy fur over them.

And even amidst Ulfarr's low, steady snoring, all the night through, Louisa had perhaps never slept so long, or so deep. What with the soft fur above and below her, and the warm solid safety of Ulfarr's strong body against her. And there was even something about the truth of Killik lying there too, sprawled easy and familiar over Ulfarr, his arm brushing hers.

When Louisa's full awareness returned, what felt like a long time later, the room was still dark, and Ulfarr was still lightly snoring beneath her. But there was just enough light from the lamplit corridor to illuminate the sight of Killik, still sprawled across from Louisa on Ulfarr's other side. His face looked so different in sleep, almost peaceful, though his black lashes occasionally fluttered against his cheek. And he even still had one of his daggers out, his clawed fingers loosely wrapped around it, its blade resting casually against the fur, dangerously close to Ulfarr's throat.

But if either of them were concerned by this, they certainly weren't showing it. And as Louisa blinked toward them in the shadows, it occurred to her hazy brain that this was surely familiar to them both. Something they'd done many, many times before.

That thought seemed to catch, circling, and Louisa kept letting it spin, holding her gaze on Killik's sleeping face. Killik and Ulfarr... cared for each other. And they clearly had for a very long time, to the point where they'd adopted a son together.

But even so, it felt like much of last night had still been... new, for them both. The way they'd looked, when Ulfarr had signed those heated words at Killik. When Ulfarr had thanked Killik for his kindness. When he'd spoken so fondly of Killik's temper, and his daggers, and his fierceness, and his loyalty.

It had obviously meant something to Killik, more than he'd wanted to admit. It had meant enough that he'd looked shocked, and maybe even afraid, even as his desire for it had been far, far too clear.

And as Louisa kept watching Killik's sleeping face, she wondered if maybe—maybe that distance between them was related to Ulfarr's past, too. Or even to those vows Ulfarr had apparently made, as part of his punishment. *He swore he would not seek to gain a mate.*

Which meant... Ulfarr couldn't take *Killik* as a mate, either.

And had Killik... wanted that? Had that been something he'd hoped to gain, by helping Ulfarr? By supporting him the way he had, helping him earn the forgiveness of the clan...

But could Ulfarr ever gain forgiveness? Should he? Even if he had fully believed he'd been making the right choices, even if he'd agonized over those choices, his actions had still been abominable, his oversights maybe insurmountable. His failings had led to true and lasting harm for others, and Louisa couldn't suppress her cold shudder at the thought of how terrified Maria must have been, to be kidnapped by a huge, powerful orc from her mate's own clan.

Louisa swallowed, and shot an uneasy look up at Ulfarr's still-sleeping face. He looked peaceful now too, his hard features distinctly softened—but the scars were still just as stark, cut deep and plentiful into his skin. And he had so many scars, he'd suffered so much, he hadn't healed for a half a *year*, Killik had said...

Louisa winced and dropped her gaze again, back to Killik—and then startled as one of his eyes squinted open. "If you ken I cannot feel you watching me, woman," he said, his voice hoarse with sleep, "you are again an even greater fool than I thought you."

Louisa rolled her eyes at him, but her exhale felt almost relieved. "I didn't want to wake him," she replied, quiet, darting another glance up at where Ulfarr still seemed to be sleeping—for now, at least. "Is it morning?"

Killik nodded and yawned, stretching his lean body long against Ulfarr's. "Do not fret about waking Wolf, for he could sleep through a pitched battle. It is the one gain of ruined scenting and unhealed wounds, I ken."

His voice was rueful, but his glance up at Ulfarr was sympathetic, almost sad. And again Louisa was caught in all this, trapped in the miserable mess of it, all that pain and darkness and grief.

"So speak, then, woman," cut in Killik's voice, as his foot kicked at hers beneath the fur. "What is it."

Louisa shot a wary look toward him, but that wasn't mockery in his watching eyes. If anything, he still just looked tired, and resigned. As if—as if maybe he still expected her to condemn Ulfarr, reject Ulfarr, and leave.

But Louisa drew in a slow breath, drew up the strength of the bed beneath her, just as Killik had taught her. "Do you think," she began, breathed again. "Do you think some sins are unforgivable? Do you think wrongdoers can never be—redeemed?"

It wasn't at all what she'd meant to ask, or was it, and Killik's head raised to look at her, even as his shoulder twitched a shrug. "Some, mayhap," he said slowly. "But I ken it hinges upon the acts, and what drove them. And then, after, the repentance, and the amends."

The acts, and what drove them. The repentance. The amends. Louisa let out her breath, fought through her twisting, tangled thoughts. While Killik kept watching her like that, a crease deepening between his brows. As if he might have caught something in that, as if he might even ask...

But no. No. This was about Ulfarr, it had nothing to do with Louisa, she was forgetting that, escaping that, Lord Scall was dead...

"And do you think," Louisa added, too quickly, "Ulfarr

should be forgiven? Do you think"—another breath—"he's done enough to repent? To make amends?"

Killik's mouth thinned, his eyes flicking beyond her. "I ken he has done more than enough," he said flatly. "More than he ever ought to have borne. But my wishes"—a hard little laugh—"are not the clan's."

Louisa studied him for another breath, fought to follow that glimmer of anger in his eyes and his voice. "And what is the current... perspective toward Ulfarr, then, within the clan?" she asked carefully. "Does he still have any support?"

"Ach, some," Killik replied, low. "All of his old pack yet stands behind him, and yet many more yet remember his care toward them. But"—he jerked another shrug—"they all watched Simon destroy him, ach? They saw his pain and his weakness and his shame, lain bare before all the clan. And none of them would wish to draw this upon themselves, or those they care for."

Right. Louisa drew in more breath, kept searching through the muddle of her thoughts. "And what about Simon himself, then?" she asked. "You said you still think he's a good leader—so is there any way of making amends with him? I mean, he must have made a few concessions toward Ulfarr after all that, right? If nothing else, he would have allowed you to adopt Sune, right?"

The question of Sune had been increasingly nagging at the back of Louisa's thoughts, because if Simon really saw Ulfarr as an ongoing danger, he wouldn't have allowed Ulfarr to adopt Sune, right? He wouldn't have trusted him to raise a child?

But Killik barked another brittle laugh, and shook his head. "Ach, Simon is a good leader, but I ken he has not yet forgiven Wolf's sins, and mayhap never will," he replied, clipped. "And thus—no. Simon would not have allowed Wolf to adopt Sune, but for me, and but for Sune himself."

Louisa blinked, not following again, and Killik sighed,

glanced up toward Ulfarr's sleeping face. "Before all this came about, Wolf had kept watch over Sune for many, many summers," he said. "Sune's blood-father was not well, and they did not live at the mountain. So Wolf oft went and fed Sune, and gave him clothes and goods, and taught him to sign and track and hunt. And once Wolf was wounded"—Killik's voice dipped—"and could no longer go see Sune, Sune came here, raging and half-starved, and refused to leave his side."

Louisa winced, squeezed her eyes shut against the vision of that, but Killik was still talking, his voice curt. "Even then, Simon wished to part them, and place Sune elsewhere. But Sune's blood-father could no more care for him, and I knew Sune was all that drew Wolf's mind from the pain, and kept him from slitting his own throat. So ach, I adopted Sune for him, instead."

Louisa kept following that, fighting to think it through, maybe to see the other side of the tale. "But perhaps Simon truly did fear," she began, tentative, "that Ulfarr still would harm Sune, somehow? Simon's first concern would have been Sune's safety... right?"

But Killik exhaled a heavy sigh, maybe a growl. "Our Right Hand Drafli is mated to mayhap the realm's best scenter," he countered. "They knew there was not a single scent wrong upon Wolf, nor upon Sune, nor any of Wolf's pack, *ever*. So no, this was not about Sune's safety. This was about Wolf, and his sins, and his suffering. It was about his payment, and his penance. It was meant to be more of his *justice*."

His voice caught on that last bit, dark and angry. And Louisa fought the inexplicable urge to reach over and touch him, maybe even caress him—but she held herself still, watching, waiting, as Killik drew in another deep, shaky breath.

"And not once has Wolf defied this *justice*," Killik

continued, even harder. "He has borne his wounds, and shouldered his shame. He has said not a word about his broken pack, or his ruined scenting, or his maimed bloody prick that brings him always more pain with his pleasure, or oft denies him its pleasure at all. He has done all within his power for the clan, for the school, for any Skai who needed this. And those orcs who spoke false to Wolf, and harmed our kin, and sought to escape Simon's judgement"—Killik's voice cracked—"it was Wolf who went and killed them, and wept as he burned their bodies before Skai-kesh. It was Wolf who suffered for this, again, and again, and *again!*"

Killik was almost shouting by the end, his voice scraping loud and harsh through the room, surely enough to startle Ulfarr awake—but when Louisa shot a furtive glance up toward him, he was still sleeping, his low snores a strange steady counter to Killik's gasping breaths.

"And not *once* has he sought to forget this," Killik went on, his voice a sharp hiss. "Not once has he sought to escape it, or play-act as though it was not his burden to bear. He has faced it with all his strength, and done all within his power to fix this. To make these amends."

Those words rang through Louisa's chest with sudden, vivid power, swallowing her breath. Ulfarr hadn't tried to escape his past. He hadn't tried to forget it. He'd faced it, with all his strength...

"But how much suffering is enough?" Killik demanded. "How much suffering is just? How much pain and work and shame must be borne before the taint is lifted? Or must it be borne for a full life? Must the wrongs of one moon be repaid a hundredfold? Must the suffering be only ended with death? Is this justice? Is this kinder than a swift clean death, from the start? Because but for Sune, I ken Wolf would have gladly welcomed this, over a lifetime of loss and weakness and pain!"

His voice dragged raw and harrowing through Louisa's

belly, clawing at her spinning thoughts. And as she looked at him, at that sheer helpless misery in his eyes, there was the thought, sudden and unbidden, that perhaps Killik had never spoken of this to anyone else. Perhaps he couldn't speak of it, to a clan he didn't agree with, to an otherwise good leader he resented, to people he couldn't trust.

And without at all meaning to, Louisa finally reached over to him, and ran her hand down his warm bare arm. "But he's also had you," she said, through her too-tight throat. "And all the help you've given him. Right?"

Killik's eyes angled away, but he didn't flinch from her hand. "Ach, mayhap," he replied, his voice thick. "With Sune, and the camp, and with pleasure, and all his hidden vows and secrets. And there is yet much more I should wish to do, many more battles I should wish to wage, but..."

His voice trailed off, that helpless misery again flashing in his eyes, and Louisa kept waiting, kept stroking, as he drew in another shaky breath. "But Wolf wishes to *earn* this forgiveness, from Skai-kesh, and Simon, and the clan," he continued. "He longs to keep his vows, and make his amends, and pay for his sins. He longs, more than aught else, to truly regain his place as a true Skai son. And if he sees me as driving this on his behalf, testing or defying our Enforcer, or pushing the clan, or taking his own burdens upon myself..."

His voice faded again, his mouth twisting, and this time Louisa drew in breath, and said the rest of it. "He'll sacrifice you, too, won't he," she whispered. "He'll fight you, or shut you out, or push you away. So you won't be able to help him anymore at all."

Killik's throat bobbed, and he pulled up his hand still holding the dagger, and halfheartedly jabbed it at Louisa's face. "But Wolf *needs* this help, woman," he rasped back. "He needs *me*."

It was like he was daring her to challenge him on this, to argue or refute it. But there wasn't even a thought of it, not even when Louisa shot another glance up at Ulfarr's scarred, sleeping face. Ulfarr did need Killik. He needed pleasure, he needed purpose, he needed strength and comfort by his side. He needed someone who could see beyond his past and his sins.

And more than that, it was clear that Ulfarr needed Sune, too. He needed his son, and his old pack. And maybe he even needed that camp, that distance from this mountain, that purpose. That... peace.

And maybe—maybe Ulfarr even needed that title again, too. The Wolf of the Skai.

"I know," Louisa finally said to Killik's glinting eyes. "Of course he needs you, Killik. But"—her thoughts flipped backwards, toward something else that had been simmering, nagging, louder and louder—"but now *you're* going to face Simon's judgement. Aren't you? *You* tried to take all the blame for all this. For setting me up with Ulfarr, and lying to him, and bringing me here. So now—now Simon's going to punish *you* for that?"

Her voice was rising, sharpening, her eyes searching Killik's face. His face that just looked tired again, resigned, all the spark faded from his eyes. And what had he told Simon about this, just yesterday? *I shall not refute your judgement upon this. But I should be grateful if you could grant me the night to settle some matters first...*

"How—how will Simon punish you, then?" Louisa demanded, clasping her hand tighter at Killik's arm. "Will he—separate you from Ulfarr? Will he still blame Ulfarr? Will he separate either of you from Sune? Will he *hurt* you, Killik?"

Her voice had gone even louder, grating between them, and in return something shifted in Killik's eyes, convulsed in his throat. "I cannot see Simon wounding me for this," he replied, hoarse. "And he would not part Sune from us now, either. He is not a *brute*, you ken. He yet seeks to do his best for his kin."

Louisa couldn't bite back her hard, disbelieving snort—this Simon had apparently ignored Ulfarr's contributions and concerns, broken apart his pack, and then he'd almost beaten him to death, and let him suffer for months, and tried to part him from his *son*. And Killik didn't think that same orc was capable of hurting Ulfarr? Of hurting *them*?

Killik had surely followed that thought, and his mouth gave a brief, rueful twitch. "I ken Simon might rather bar us from the camp, mayhap," he said. "And bar us from *you*, also."

Oh. *Oh.* He said it so lightly, so easily, as though it wouldn't bother him in the slightest. And of course he wouldn't care, it didn't mean anything—but it still plunged in Louisa's belly, prickled sudden and dangerous behind her eyes. And she didn't want to ask, didn't want to know, but...

"And you would—obey?" she asked, or maybe challenged. "You wouldn't fight Simon's so-called *justice* on that, either?"

The corners of Killik's mouth tightened, but he glanced away again, toward the wall beyond her. "If it was only me, mayhap I would," he replied, very quiet. "But I cannot risk Wolf or Sune in this. You ken I cannot."

Right. That was that, then, that was his answer. No, yet again. And Louisa couldn't even fault him for it, especially with that admission, that confession, hovering too strong between them. *If it was only me, mayhap I would.*

But it still curdled and churned in her belly, stung hotter behind her eyes. So she didn't have those four nights, after all. She didn't have Killik. She didn't have Ulfarr. It didn't even matter what she thought about all this, what she'd decided...

And gods curse it, maybe she *had* decided, without even meaning to. Because maybe—she wanted to face this. She wanted to believe in forgiveness, and redemption, and amends. But none of it mattered now, it was already over, already too late, and she was—she was—

A trickle of hot liquid squeezed from Louisa's eye, streaking down onto Ulfarr's big shoulder beneath her. And though she winced, dashed it away, another escaped after it, and another. And Killik could see this, and mock this, oh gods she needed to leave, she wasn't even supposed to be here, and...

"Come, woman," cut in Killik's voice, and when Louisa blinked up, he was shifting up off the bed, and holding out his hand. "There is—one you ought to meet, I ken."

Louisa blinked again, shot an uncertain look down at Ulfarr beneath her—but he still appeared to be sound asleep, so she nodded, and reached her shaky hand to Killik's. Letting him guide her up and out of the bed, and once she was on her feet, he silently held out her new dress, too. And it was only then that Louisa realized she was only wearing that damned loincloth, and giving Killik a full-on view of everything else.

And curse him, he was taking a good eyeful, leisurely glancing up and down, and even giving a light little slap against the loincloth's leather band over her hip. "This new garb was good, you ken," he said, a little too casually. "Wish you had scented Wolf, when he first saw it. The strength of his hunger near knocked me over, ach?"

It was a kind thing for him to say—too kind, still too much like a goodbye. And though Louisa attempted a smile back, it felt wan and thin, and she couldn't seem to hold it as she tied the dress over the loincloth with her fumbling hands. And next were the boots, those tall lovely expensive leather boots, and she hesitated as she pulled them on, and grimaced toward Killik's watching face.

"I didn't even—pay for these," she said. "Or any of this. Rosa said you wouldn't mind, but—"

Killik betrayed a brief sneer at Rosa's name, but then he shrugged, and gave a dismissive wave of his dagger. "No, keep them," he replied. "Your old boots should have one day killed you, and now I shall not be at fault for this."

Well. Louisa's smile felt more genuine this time, though it faltered again when Killik next handed over her knife, and the chain. The chain that—wait, didn't even seem broken, did it?

"It was only the latch that failed," Killik supplied, without her even asking. "Next time, we ought to—"

But he broke off there, looking away, because there wouldn't be a next time, would there? He knew it, and Louisa knew it, and she couldn't meet his eyes as she fastened on the belt, and then her knife. And then let Killik draw her from the room, leaving Ulfarr still alone and asleep in the bed behind them.

It felt wrong, lonely and miserable and wretched, and Louisa kept her head down as Killik led her through the dim, narrow corridors. Around this corner, and that, deeper and deeper into the Skai wing, until he drew her into a room.

It wasn't one Louisa had seen during Rosa's tour, and it was large and round, and scented of sweet incense. And in the middle of the room, surrounded by fur-covered benches, there stood a cluster of life-sized, beautifully carved grey stone orcs. All of them fully bared, flaunting their strong, impressively endowed bodies—but Louisa's eyes were drawn to the largest figure of all, standing tall and proud in the midst of the others. He was big and broad, with messy cropped hair, and he seemed to look straight toward her, *into* her, with his intent, black-painted eyes.

"This is our father Skai-kesh, and his faithful pack," came Killik's low voice beside her. "If ever you seek guidance, or comfort, or strength, he will always freely offer this. And no matter the sin"—Louisa could feel Killik studying her, almost as strong as this Skai-kesh—"he shall always welcome our repentance. He shall always offer his strength and forgiveness, and guide us to amends, and peace."

Forgiveness. Amends. *Peace.* The words swaying too deep, too powerful, and Louisa couldn't even look at Killik as she nodded, and lurched toward the nearest bench. Sinking down onto it, holding her gaze to Skai-kesh's watching, piercing eyes.

And then, somehow, she prayed. Prayed to a god she didn't know, to an ancestor that wasn't hers. And it didn't even make sense, she'd never been a pious person, but as Killik sank down to sit beside her, his elbow lightly brushing hers, it still felt like—a relief. A relief to silently pour out all this darkness and doubt, all her own guilt and sins, the things she'd never told another living soul. And to know that maybe, maybe even just here, in this room, beneath this Skai-kesh and his too-knowing eyes, there was strength. Forgiveness. A guide to amends. A way to peace.

And when Louisa opened her eyes again, what felt like a long time later, it did feel like peace. Like certainty. Like a direction given, a decision made, deep and certain in her bones.

She'd faced this trial here, and she'd survived. She was alive. She was whole. And Killik and Ulfarr had helped her, had granted her so much kindness—and now, she was going to grant the same to them. She was going to stand tall with them, and their pack, and their camp. And with their son, who'd looked at her last night, and begged for her help.

Fix this, Sune had said. *Fix this.*

And Louisa was damned well going to try. She was going to fix this mess.

39

Louisa began her fixing with none other than Killik himself.

"What's something you and Sune like to do here together?" she asked him, without preamble, once he'd looked up from his own prayers beside her. "Some kind of interest you share, something you won't argue about?"

Killik eyed her with distinct wariness, but then shot a brief glance up at Skai-kesh, and shrugged. "Sparring, or throwing knives, mayhap," he said. "In the arena."

Louisa gave a decisive nod, and then waved him toward the corridor. "Then you need to go find Sune, and if he's well enough, you ask him to do that," she said flatly. "He went through a horrible ordeal with Rikard yesterday, and he seemed very upset about Ulfarr last night, too. So you need to go stand beside him, and reassure him, and remind him that you care about him. Remind him that you'll always be here for him, no matter what."

Killik blinked at her, clearly nonplussed—and Louisa gripped at the odd comfort of her knife-hilt at her side, and then yanked it out, pointed it at him for good measure. "You will do this now, Killik," she hissed. "And also, for the foreseeable future, you need to make it repeatedly, excessively clear to Sune that you didn't just adopt him for Ulfarr. You need to make it clear to him that you fully consider him your son, too. And if that's not actually the case, then you should damn well seek the forgiveness on offer"—she jabbed her knife at Skai-kesh—"and then take that secret to your *grave.*"

Killik kept blinking at her, his head tilting, his hand fidgeting with his own dagger, too. "Ach, ach, well enough, woman," he said, and though his tone was exasperated, that might have been guilt in his eyes. "And whilst I am off sparring with Sune, what shall *you* do?"

There was an unmistakable challenge on his voice, and Louisa didn't balk from it, just kept gazing back toward him, her eyes steady. "I have a few confidential matters to address here, alone," she said firmly. "Without you, and without Ulfarr. And then, I'm going home."

Killik blinked again, once, but otherwise stayed still for a long, silent moment, his eyes locked on hers. But when he finally exhaled, glanced away, she could almost feel his comprehension, and then his capitulation, passing silent but certain between them. Maybe even his permission.

Because if Louisa didn't try to fight this, to fix this, it would be over anyway. Wouldn't it? And as an outsider, as an expendable and unwanted interloper, she had freedoms that Killik and Ulfarr didn't have. She could take their burdens on herself, and do her best to help them, even if she never saw them again. She could face this, and seek forgiveness. Amends. Peace. Maybe not even for them, or for Ulfarr, but... for herself.

"I would be grateful if you could say goodbye to Sune for me, and give him my best wishes for a quick recovery," she said, as she jerked to her feet beside the bench. "And please tell Ulfarr I had a wonderful time, too. And that I—I'll write him a letter, maybe. And leave it with Halthorr at the camp."

Killik's eyes flicked back to hers, and his throat bobbed, his breath inhaling. But then he rose to his feet, spun away from her, turning toward the door—

And then—he hesitated. Turned back. And before Louisa had caught it, seen it, he grasped for her chin, drew her forward, and... kissed her.

It was light, brief, barely a brush of breath, but he'd done it, he'd done it. And oh, Louisa could still taste him, could feel the roughness of his lips, the sweetness of his breath, the soft scrape of his claws on her chin.

"I..." he said, husky, as he drew back again, and briefly met her eyes. "Thank you, Louisa."

Thank you, Louisa. It seemed to hang there, shimmering and tangling with that still-lingering taste of him, deep and dizzying on her lips. And Louisa couldn't speak into it, couldn't break it, could only twitch a shaky nod toward him. And when he nodded back, it was curt, decisive, almost like... almost like a farewell.

He didn't speak again as he left, just striding from the room with his back very straight, his dagger gripped in his fist. And as Louisa watched him go, she couldn't deny the stinging behind her eyes, the quiver on her mouth. Maybe this was still over. Maybe it was still farewell. Maybe she would never see him again.

But she could—try. She could square her shoulders, grip her knife, take one last look at Skai-kesh's watching, knowing eyes. And then she could take a breath, draw up strength from the earth, and walk out the door.

"Could you help me find Jule?" she asked the first orc she saw in the corridor, a Skai she vaguely recalled meeting the day before. "I'm supposed to meet with her today."

Thankfully, the orc didn't seem at all disconcerted by this request, and waved Louisa after him up the corridor. Toward the Ash-Kai wing, perhaps, the floor tilting higher, the corridors broadening and brightening. And when the orc stopped outside a room, and nodded toward it, she profusely thanked him, and strode inside without looking. Into—a meeting?

But yes, it seemed to be a meeting in progress, with a handful of attendees all seated on the floor around a low table. There was Jule, leaning into a large, heavily scarred orc—her mate, surely—and flanking them were two unfamiliar orcs, one lean and grey and severe, one broad and green and genial-looking. And there was a smiling Rosa, too, with a large stack of papers in front of her, and her handsome mate John-Ka by her side.

But nearest to the door, on this side of the table, there was—Simon, and *Maria*. Both of them glancing back toward Louisa, Maria with palpable unease, Simon with dark, settled solemnity.

"Louisa!" Jule exclaimed, into the sudden silence, as she leapt to her feet. "I'm so glad you're up. You'll come join us, won't you?"

Louisa blinked, as a distant whirling part of her brain pointed out that she'd perhaps walked straight into them discussing this situation, discussing *her*—but then there was the vision of Skai-kesh again, the echo of Killik's words. *He shall guide us to amends, and peace.*

So Louisa nodded, and thanked Jule, and smiled as Jule introduced her to the orcs she hadn't yet met. First was the big scarred orc, who indeed turned out to be Jule's mate Grimarr, the captain of the entire mountain. Next was the genial green orc, who was named Baldr, from Clan Grisk, and the severe grey orc—Louisa's attention sharpened on his face—was Drafli, of Clan Skai. Surely the same Drafli who Killik had mentioned, the Drafli who served as the Skai's Right Hand. One of those traditional Skai leadership positions, together with the Enforcer.

Drafli didn't speak to Louisa when Jule introduced them, but instead briefly touched his fist to his bare chest. It was the sign Louisa now knew to be the standard Skai greeting, so she signed it back to him, and then flattened her hand to say *thank you.* Earning in return a brief rise of Drafli's eyebrows, as if he was surprised, or maybe even impressed.

It was something, something Louisa needed to cling to in this, because if she was going to make any headway here, she needed to convince this Drafli—as well as Simon and Maria, and likely the rest of them, as well. And she needed to stay focused, to make a clear case, to show them she wasn't an enemy, but a friend. So she signed another *thank you,* and then sat down beside Maria, and drew in a deep breath.

"If you're all willing, I'd like to discuss the Skai camp on my lands," she said, before anyone else could speak. "I understand the camp is a tactical advantage for you, isn't it? And a support for your women and sons, and a shelter and safe stopping place for travellers, as well."

There were a few exchanged glances around the table, and then Jule cleared her throat, and nodded. "Yes, of course," she replied. "Many Skai prefer the camps, and it's to all our benefit to have reliable outposts that can pass on information, guard our own lands around the mountain, and support our strategic priorities as needed."

Louisa shot Jule a grateful smile, and drew in another breath. "I'm glad to hear it," she said, "because the camp is a benefit to me, too. The financial support has been very helpful, and the Skai there have kept us fed, and made multiple improvements to my property. However, as we discussed yesterday"—another smile toward Jule, more wavering this time—"the orcs' presence has also led to some... conflicts, especially with my neighbour, Lord Rikard. He's trespassed on my property, made multiple threats, and put up dangerous traps on his borders—one of which severely hurt an orc *child* yesterday."

No one at the table seemed surprised by any of this, suggesting that Jule had shared it all already—so Louisa kept at it, speaking faster now. "I want to support the camp," she said firmly. "I want to face and address these risks, and ensure the camp's security and long-term viability on my property. However"—another deep breath—"I need support. I need to have people I can trust close at hand. And respectfully, I would like to have Killik and Ulfarr. Permanently."

And yes, that was it, Simon's brow deeply furrowing, Drafli's mouth pursing, Rosa's eyes widening, and Jule darting an uneasy look toward Simon and Maria. "Of course we understand that, Louisa," Jule finally said, with a wincing half-smile. "Especially since you've recently become, er, *close* with Killik and Ulfarr both. But there are a few challenges there, you understand, and..."

"Yes, I understand perfectly," Louisa said, maybe louder than was warranted. "I understand that Ulfarr has been convicted of several serious crimes, and is still serving his sentence. However, I'd still like to make this request, based on his good behaviour, and his good work at the camp. His good work with *me*."

There was more silence, more raised brows and exchanged looks around the table, and Louisa drew in more breath. "Along with all Ulfarr's work at the camp, and on my property," she continued, "he has been a great help to me, personally. I'm not sure how much you've heard of my deceased husband, or my dealings with Lord Kaspar afterwards, but I have"—she drew in another breath, more shaky this time—"I have struggled. And I've been—very lonely, and very uncomfortable with men, and with my past, for a long time. And Ulfarr—"

Oh gods, was she really going to say this, was she going to announce this to all these orcs she'd just met, to the leaders of Killik and Ulfarr's clan—but yes, yes, she was. She was alive. She was whole. She was speaking her truth.

"Ulfarr has been—wonderful," she said, her voice hitching. "He's been so respectful toward me. So patient, and so careful, and so kind. He's made me feel so—safe. At—peace. In a way I haven't felt in a long, long time."

Her thoughts flashed back to Skai-kesh again, to that promise of peace, and it was enough that she could draw in a breath, keep speaking to all those watching, judging eyes. "Ulfarr and I both entered this—relationship—on the understanding that it was only for a limited time. It wasn't meant to be a permanent agreement, and I certainly wasn't ever planning to become his—mate. So"—another deep breath—"if you feel it's best that our personal relationship doesn't continue, under the terms of his sentencing, I will honour that. However, I still would prefer to have Ulfarr and Killik at the camp, over any others. I would still feel—safer. More prepared to defend the camp, and face Rikard, and whatever else might come."

There was another moment's silence, Jule briefly meeting the eyes of her mate beside her. "We certainly realize that Rikard needs careful handling," she said, "and we're very grateful to you for all your support. So we'd be happy to provide you with ongoing support and intelligence in return, and protection, as well. Perhaps from a dedicated team of scouts and warriors?"

Louisa's smile felt genuine, truly grateful, even as she shook her head. "I do appreciate that," she replied, "but with all due respect, I still would prefer Killik and Ulfarr. Killik is extremely observant, an excellent scenter and hunter, and hyper-aware of his surroundings. And"—she drew in a breath—"Ulfarr is well able to manage difficult situations and circumstances, and he commands the loyalty of multiple Skai who are already at the camp. Skai who will work to support him and his goals."

She was glancing around the table now, her eyes pleading on her listeners' faces—but most of the orcs' expressions were inscrutable, impossible to assess. While

Jule was looking thoughtful, Rosa sympathetic, and Maria perhaps... suspicious.

"Look, it's understandable that you'd feel... partial, toward Ulfarr," Maria said now, her voice decisive in the silence. "But his crimes against the clan were still very severe. And you can't discount the undeniable truth that he stands to gain significantly from a permanent move to the camp—*and* from behaving kindly toward you, and earning your trust. And having you advocate for him like this."

She was accusing Ulfarr of having ulterior motives, of using Louisa to escape his punishment—and while Louisa couldn't fathom Ulfarr consciously doing that, she still made herself follow it, consider the premise of it. "That's a fair point," she said slowly. "But to my understanding, earning the trust and forgiveness of the clan is an integral part of Ulfarr's punishment. So if he's serious about his rehabilitation, wouldn't he therefore seek to treat women well, and serve the clan where he knows he can make the most positive impact, with people he knows and trusts?"

Maria didn't immediately counter that, so Louisa drew in another breath, pushed on again. "And given Ulfarr's history here"—she gave a vague wave toward Maria and Simon—"it makes sense that he would prefer to live elsewhere, doesn't it? I deeply respect your decision to offer him a chance at rehabilitation, rather than more permanent punishments, but I can't imagine it's been easy for any of you to keep living together as part of it, has it? For either him, or you."

Maria and Simon exchanged a brief, speaking look, and maybe they were considering it, maybe. And maybe Louisa was going to ruin it now, but she had to keep going, keep trying, please. "And I don't mean any disrespect by this," she added, "but if you truly are still committed to rehabilitation, I personally don't see how the pain requirement of Ulfarr's sentence is—helpful. I can't see how it encourages him to move forward, or keep pursuing positive change, if he's constantly hurting. Especially with something that's tied so deeply to pleasure, and seemingly to your culture as well, and—"

But Jule had suddenly waved a hand toward Louisa, her brows drawn sharply together. "What do you mean, the *pain requirement*?" she demanded. "Is that an ongoing part of Ulfarr's judgement?"

Her eyes darted toward Simon, who was also frowning, his gaze flicking back to Louisa. "I ken it was, at the start of this," he said, in his deep steady voice. "We did not wish to grant Ulfarr swift and easy healing, and thus lessen the weight of his wrongs. But he has long ago healed now, for this was mayhap three summers past, ach?"

But beside him, Maria's face had paled, and she gripped at Simon's arm. "But Simon," she said, low. "*Did* you ever grant Ulfarr permission to go to Efterar, after that? I mean, I know orc healing is usually much better than humans', but..."

She winced, and her other hand dropped to her own knife, belted to her side. And Simon's eyes followed the movement, his head tilting. "No, I ken not," he said slowly. "But Ulfarr has not once asked, nor spoken of this."

Right. Louisa's smile felt more like a grimace, and she twitched a shrug. "But of course you can see why he wouldn't, right?" she asked. "He wants to earn this from you, and fairly win back his place in the clan. He would never want to be seen as needy, or weak, or unable to bear the punishment you deemed suitable for him. The punishment he's required to bear, in order to regain his place among you."

Simon looked genuinely unsettled, glancing sideways toward Maria's uneasy eyes, so Louisa kept going, faster now. "But I can assure you, he *is* in pain," she said flatly. "And it seems to affect him in multiple deeply unpleasant ways. I personally think it's very commendable that he's done as much as he has, and been such a good father to Sune, while dealing with apparently unnecessary *agony* for years on end."

The disapproval was too sharp-edged in her voice now, veering toward anger, or even contempt. And damn it, she couldn't risk ruining this, not now, not when they were maybe, maybe considering it—so she shoved up to her feet, and attempted a smile toward them.

"Of course it's your decision," she said, "and I'll respect whatever you decide. But"—her voice was hardening again, all on its own—"I hope you'll also acknowledge and respect the fact that the camp is still on *my* land. And my feelings about it being there long-term may very well change, depending on my assessment of the safety of me and my household!"

The words swung out strong and certain between them, very much like—a threat. Because it was a threat, Louisa had just threatened all these people—including her generous friends—with shutting down the camp if she didn't get her way on this. And damn it, she wasn't even going to take it back, she was just going to stand there and glare at them, with her hand on her knife—and she scarcely managed to sign a curt *thank you* before spinning around, and stalking toward the door.

But then she halted, gripped her knife, drew in breath from the earth. And then she slowly turned around, and faced this, one more time.

"If nothing else," she said, "you should come see the camp. You should see for yourselves the good work Ulfarr has done there. I would be happy to do my utmost to make your stay comfortable. It would be—an honour."

With that, she signed another swift thank-you, and then spun around, and left. Walking down the corridor with unsteady steps, her hands twitching, her heartbeat thundering in her ears. Because damn it, even despite that invitation at the end, she'd threatened them. She'd done so well, she'd kept so calm, and then she'd gone and *threatened* them.

But she couldn't seem to turn around again, either, and she kept striding forward, gripping her sweaty hand at her knife. No, she hadn't been kind, but she'd still been—honest. She'd spoken truth. She'd done her best to make amends, and to repay the kindness—and the peace—Ulfarr and Killik had shown her. To gain them peace in return.

And even if that was the wrong decision, even if she never saw them again, it still felt—right. Right in the same way her clothes had, the same way the camp had, the same way her pleasure with Killik and Ulfarr had. Right the way it had even felt praying to Skai-kesh. Repentance. Amends. Peace.

So she focused on moving, escaping, aiming in what she hoped was the general direction of the front entrance—but yes, that corridor looked familiar, and so did that one. And a short time later, Louisa was striding out of the mountain into the bright mid-morning sun, and dragging in deep breaths of the cool clear air.

She'd survived Orc Mountain. She'd faced it, and done her best. And now—another deep breath, into the earth at her feet—she was going home.

40

Louisa's trip home was thankfully, blessedly uneventful. No orcs, no Rikard, only sun and fresh air and her reliable beloved horses.

But the further she travelled from Orc Mountain, the more she kept glancing back toward it, fighting to ignore the tightening knot in her belly. She might never return there again. Might never see Sune or Jule or Rosa again. Might never learn if she'd gained anything today, or whether they'd listened to her at all.

And worst of all, she might never see Killik and Ulfarr again. *I'll respect whatever you decide,* she'd said at the meeting, and she'd meant it—but it suddenly felt deeply unfair, like a punishment that had been thrown upon her, too. A penance for the grievous sin of falling for a sweet, generous bedpartner, and then not even saying goodbye...

But—no. No. She wasn't supposed to be falling for Ulfarr, and this wasn't—anything. Only a deal. She'd only ever had four more nights, and maybe not even that.

It was too much misery, too much curdling mess in her thoughts, and Louisa was deeply grateful when she finally returned home late that afternoon, back to her familiar land, her familiar house. And best of all, to Joan and Elise and Gladys and the children, who'd all rushed outside to meet her, their faces bright with excitement and relief.

"We were so worried about you!" Elise gulped into Louisa's shoulder, squeezing her tight. "We thought the orcs *murdered* you!"

Louisa winced and awkwardly patted Elise's back, but beside them Joan was wryly smiling, and shaking her head. "Yeah, and then that Halthorr showed up last night," she said, with a roll of her eyes. "And said he'd gotten word from Killik that you'd be staying overnight, so he was going to guard us in your absence. And then he slept right outside the damned front door, all the night through!"

Louisa blinked—had Killik really taken the time to send word back, amidst all that?—but then chuckled, and asked whether they'd offered Halthorr breakfast, at least. Which apparently they had, much to the children's delight, because it turned out Halthorr had forgone utensils in favour of only eating with his dagger, and had then made a show of using it to toss bits of egg into the children's mouths, with only partial success.

By the end of the tale, even Elise was reluctantly smiling, and Gladys urged Louisa to come in for supper, and tell them everything she'd seen at Orc Mountain. "And also," she said, looking Louisa up and down, "you need to tell us how you got all this dashing new finery!"

Louisa laughed and allowed herself to be hauled inside, and soon she was regaling them with a slightly edited version of her visit to Orc Mountain, focusing particularly on all the different rooms, and the school, and the gigantic shop, and the healer she'd met who might have been magic.

It made for a lovely, cozy evening together, enough that Louisa could almost forget the tightness in her belly, the quiet nagging at the back of her thoughts. But once they'd all finally said a cheerful goodnight, and she headed up to the attic alone, it all seemed to creep back again, bitter and lonely and sad.

It might be—over. Finished. Forever. Not even four more nights. No more sweet Ulfarr, no more snarling Killik. And why did the thought of losing Killik hurt nearly as much as the thought of losing Ulfarr, and why the hell did she even care? And why the hell had Killik gone and kissed her like that today, when he damn well knew it was probably over, knew he'd never see her again...

Louisa drew in a shaky breath, rubbed at her stinging eyes—and then caught sight of her writing desk, with its ink and paper and quill. And wait, she'd promised Killik she would write Ulfarr a letter, and that was something, some tiny tenuous thread to cling to. A way to at least say goodbye.

She sat down at the desk with genuine relief, and lit her lamp, drew over the quill and a fresh sheet of paper. *Dear sweet Wolf*, she wrote, her hand only slightly unsteady. *I wanted to express my deepest regrets for not saying a proper farewell to you—*

When something—thudded. Behind her. And when Louisa whipped around, her heartbeat surging in her chest, it was—Killik. Killik, leaping through the now-open window, and landing on the floor in a smooth, graceful crouch.

Louisa's breath choked, her eyes locked on his familiar rising form, the daggers glinting in his hair. And that glint of his eyes in the shadows, too, the flash of his sharp white teeth, because he was—smiling. Smiling. At her?

"Ach, do not look at me so shocked and blameless thus, woman," he said. "For we both know what a shrewd vicious harpy you are, ach?"

What? Louisa sputtered and attempted a frown at him, while her heartbeat kept kicking, her eyes roving over his lean muscled body, the gleam of his bare chest in the lamplight. He was here. He'd come back. *Hers.*

But no, no, that was ridiculous, and she hauled in a breath. "I have no idea what you're talking about," she snapped back. "And have you never heard of a door? Or of waiting to be invited inside?"

But Killik was still smiling, even warmer than before, and he shrugged as he sauntered over toward her. "Ach, no," he said, as he peered over her shoulder, his eyes blatantly sweeping down her letter. "And Wolf shall be glad to see this, I ken. Finish it, and I shall take it to him this eve."

Take it to him this eve. Louisa twisted to better frown up at Killik's face, at that still-twitching smile on his mouth. That... that *happiness.* As if...

"What do you mean, this eve?" she demanded. "Where is he? Shouldn't he be all the way back at the mountain? Even you and all your unnatural sneaking couldn't get back there that quickly, and..."

And oh, the way that warmth sparkled in Killik's eyes, quivered on his mouth. "Ach, but he is no more at the mountain," he said, his voice far too light. "He is now at the camp, with Sune. Where he shall stay for the next fortnight, until Simon and Maria come to visit, and review his work here."

At the camp. A fortnight. Until Simon and Maria came to visit. Louisa's gasp sounded much like a yelp, her eyes searching Killik's smug, happy face. "You mean it? It actually *worked*?!"

Her voice came out far too loud, but Killik was still smiling, and even rolling his eyes. "Ach, no, it was a rank failure, woman," he replied. "Wolf is only here in spirit, mayhap. Or mayhap he has forever abandoned the clan, and resolved to instead become a Ka-esh."

But even the sarcasm sounded warm, almost soft on his voice, and without at all meaning to, Louisa leapt to her feet, and hurled her arms around him. "Oh, I'm *so* glad, Killik," she said, muffled, into his chest. "How did it happen? Why?"

Killik's body briefly stiffened against hers, but even as Louisa made to back away, his hands belatedly clamped closer, stroked up and down her back. "Ach, I wonder why," he drawled, his voice vibrating through his chest against her, feeling almost like a chuckle. "There was this vicious harpy, you ken, who stood before those with the most power amongst our kin, and threatened them with ousting our camp, if Wolf could not be there."

Louisa choked a laugh, even as she yanked back from Killik again, and attempted a glare up at his face. "I didn't threaten them!" she protested, as primly as she could. "I only—informed them of my position. And—reminded them of my rights, as the owner of these lands."

But Killik laughed too, low and easy and approving. "Ach, only thus, woman," he replied. "All these pretty words, even speaking them with your hands, Drafli said, whilst also gripping your knife, and reeking of rage. And drawing upon your kinship with the captain's mate, and calling upon Simon's failings as Enforcer, and reminding Maria that she should be far gladder not to see Wolf each day. Whilst also"—Killik's voice lowered—"speaking so fiercely of how Wolf has helped you, and gained your trust. Not—pushing or gaining this for him, but only speaking of what he has already done. Showing him as strong and able and faithful, and willing to make amends."

Louisa's breath shuddered from her throat, her body sagging back into Killik's warm steady strength. "It was all true," she managed, with a shrug. "It wasn't—anything I did."

She could feel the huff of Killik's chuckle on her hair, the spasm of his fingers on her shoulder. "No, naught you did at all," he said lightly. "And after this meeting, when Jule stomped off to fetch Efterar, and took him to heal Wolf at once, this was naught of your doing, either."

Louisa jerked back again, clutched at his arms, searched

his warm shimmering eyes. "Really?!" she demanded. "And did it help? Is he better?"

Killik's throat convulsed, and he twitched a short nod. "Ach, much," he replied, without even a trace of sarcasm in his voice. "I—I near forgot how he scents when he is not in pain, or how easy he laughs. Even Sune scented it at once, and has scarce left his side since. And before we left"— Killik's laugh sounded thick this time—"Sune and his little packmates dragged us to the shop, so we might buy you more gifts. Those crafty Grisk and Ash-Kai had a stack of costly garb just waiting for us."

He'd jerked his head toward the window, toward where there was an overstuffed canvas pack Louisa hadn't noticed before, with a generous quantity of black fabric spilling out the top. "Oh," she said numbly. "You—you didn't need to do that, Killik."

Killik scoffed, but it was halfhearted, almost rueful. "Ach, I did," he replied, "lest I wished my own son to fly into another rage at me, and again call me a *slug*. Which I now ken"—he jabbed his claw at Louisa's face—"was *your* doing also, you meddling witch! A *slug*?"

Louisa's laugh felt shaky but genuine, her eyes dancing on Killik's face. "What, would you have preferred something worse?" she asked lightly. "How about a maggot? Or a tapeworm? Or maybe a limp little leech?"

Killik's eyes flashed, and he barked a low, incredulous laugh, shivering deep into Louisa's belly. "A limp little *leech*?" he demanded, though his voice was husky. "You wish to test me on this, woman? Wish to meet my leech?"

Louisa couldn't seem to stop grinning at him, her heartbeat skipping—and in a flash of movement, Killik *grabbed* her. Grabbed her by the hips, and then spun her around toward the desk, facing away from him. Shoving her upper body down, and—yanking up her *dress*.

"Killik!" Louisa yelped, at the sudden, shocking sensation

of cool open air on her legs, her arse, her—well. "What the hell are you *doing*?"

Killik's laugh was low and triumphant behind her, and his booted foot kicked between her ankles, shoving them apart. "Ach, it is a great mystery, I ken," he drawled, and oh, that was the sound of shifting fabric, of his own trousers, oh gods. "Having a nap, mayhap. Or eating a picnic?"

Louisa choked and twisted around to glower at him, at where his eyes were gleefully glinting, and then dropping down to the sight he'd exposed between her legs. "Or sharpening my dagger, mayhap," he murmured, lower, as he shifted forward, and nudged himself just—there, into Louisa's opened, quivering heat. "Or digging tunnels."

He raised his brows at her, the challenge glimmering in his eyes—and oh, oh, Louisa wasn't challenging it. Hell no, she wanted him, she needed him so much she felt dizzy with it. And he damn well knew it, just watching her like that as he slowly pushed in, opening her breath by breath, oh *fuck*.

But there was still something, something important, curse it, and Louisa fought to grasp it, even as she shuddered and moaned, felt her body clamp at his hard flesh steadily sinking inside her. "But—*Ulfarr*," she managed, her voice breaking as Killik's hips gently slapped against her skin. "Won't he—mind, if you—if we—"

But Killik huffed a chuckle as he began drawing out again, his eyes hooded on the sight. "Ach, no," he replied, husky, as he slipped free of her with a soft squelch. "I asked his leave, before I came."

Wait, what? He'd—*planned* to do this? And Louisa couldn't think, couldn't follow it, not with him already easing back inside, faster this time. "You—did?" she gasped, as her traitorous body gripped him tighter, maybe even shoved back deeper upon him. "And what—what did he say?"

Killik's half-lidded eyes flicked to hers, as his skin again slapped tight, his hard spasming cock plunged deep inside.

"He said, *Ach, pup, you ought to plough her, and grant her your joy*," he replied, in a creditable imitation of Ulfarr's voice. "*But seek to be gentler with her, this time.*"

Louisa's breath was heaving too hard, her body helplessly clutching against him, because—was Killik *obeying*? Was he obliging Ulfarr with this, being slower, gentler, Ulfarr had given him permission, Ulfarr had wanted this...

"I ken it pleased him, to be asked," Killik added, with a rolling shrug of his shoulder, as he slowly drew out again. "To have the right and the power to grant a woman as he pleases. To know he has offered up this womb for my ploughing, and for my good Skai seed."

Louisa attempted a snort back toward him, because of course Killik would be giving Ulfarr the credit for this, rather than the actual woman he was currently fucking—but then he drove back in, so hard she shook all over, a harsh gasp choking from her mouth. "You—absolute—fucking—prick," she gasped, as he dragged out again. "You—slimy—slug—"

But Killik again broke it off with a swift, stunning slam in, swirling her full of sensation, of sweeping shattering strength. "And after I have finished with you, my foul-mouthed little harpy," he crooned, with another draw out, another sharp slam in, "and flooded you with my scent and my good Skai seed, I shall go back and tell Wolf the full tale of this, ach? I shall tell him"—his voice deepened as he drove in again, again—"how you shivered and shouted and squealed for me. How you begged me for my touch and my seed."

Gods curse this infuriating bastard, and his infuriating incredible cock, now plunging in and out of her, sparking more jarring jolting ecstasy with every driving thrust. "You— leech," Louisa managed, between gasps. "I will not beg you for anything, you—you—"

But oh, hell, he'd abruptly stopped thrusting, and his warm sweaty body shifted closer over her, his hand slipping down her front. Rubbing at where she most desperately wanted it, moving in hard, perfect little circles, and she moaned and shivered against it, against the sudden shocking scrape of his sharp teeth against her throat.

"You shall beg," he murmured, a hot whispered promise. "You shall beg, woman, or I shall stop."

What? No. He wouldn't stop, he couldn't—but wait, he was already slackening his hand's touch, drawing himself out from inside her, damn it. "I shall stop, and leave," he breathed, even as he scraped his teeth harder against her neck. "I shall deny you all relief, lest you beg me."

Gods, Louisa loathed him, and she needed him, and he had no right to feel so good, to sound so good, to be everywhere, everything, trampling all her awareness at once. And she should be fighting it, she needed to fight it, to fight all this power he wielded over her, all the ways she craved him and longed for him, four more nights...

"Beg me, Louisa," Killik whispered, his fingers only a flutter now, his cock finally falling free of her. "Only say, *please, Killik*, and I shall grant you all you long for."

Oh. No, he didn't mean it, it was only four nights, he still wanted to walk away—but Louisa couldn't bear it. Couldn't bear to stop it, couldn't bear to lose any more of it, oh gods...

"Please, Killik," she choked. "Please, give it to me, all of it, please, *please*."

His growl in her ear was low and triumphant, almost a laugh—and then it all swarmed her at once. His fingers grinding, his mouth scraping, his cock again finding its place, and rooting itself slow and deep inside. While Louisa quaked against it, against him, quivering all over with the staggering strength of him, the ecstasy swirling out from him, pooling harder and deeper with every touch, with every grinding thrust. Until he was plunging into her again, both of them gasping with every sharp slam of hips, raw and reckless and rutting, closer and closer and closer—

Killik broke before she did, his gasp choking as he shoved in even harder, plunged so deep it was pain—and then he shook, and surged out deep inside. Filling her with him, with his seed and his certainty and his peace, giving her all she longed for, in this perfect overpowering moment—

And then Louisa was the one shattering, shouting, breaking apart beneath him, shuddering into his beauty and his relief. He was so good, he was so fucking good, and she wanted to beg him, to melt into him, to drown in him.

But somehow, somehow, she kept it all clamped down inside, but for her shaking body, and her deep dragging gasps. And Killik wasn't saying anything either, just breathing hard against her ear, his softening strength still faintly spasming as it ground deep inside.

"Ought to write Wolf's letter," he finally said, into her ear. "He shall welcome hearing from you thus, I ken."

What? Louisa twitched all over, but the shock and disbelief she should have felt were muted somehow, along with all her resistance. And she could only seem to nod, groping for the letter with one shaky hand, dipping the quill with the other.

Killik came to see me while I was in the midst of this letter, she wrote. *He told me that you sent him, and that you wished to grant me joy. I want to reassure you that he has diligently followed your instructions, and—*

She paused there, breathing hard, because her hand was still trembly, and Killik was still faintly pulsing inside her, holding there, waiting. Watching. Wanting her to do this.

And even as I write this, he is wielding his considerable Skai attributes against me, and taunting me. He is excessively enraging, and impossibly infuriating, and I can only hope—

Killik's growl was low in her ear, not even close to a laugh this time, and Louisa shuddered, and made herself keep writing. *I can only hope he will continue granting me such gifts, and offering me his strength and his scent.*

Killik's body had slightly relaxed over her again, his cock gently swelling again inside her, and oh, he'd even begun pumping again, just small circling movements. "Write this to him also, woman," he murmured. "In your pretty words. As you feel this."

Gods damn him and his overwhelming, overpowering body, his tempting voice, and the way Louisa wanted to oblige him, wanted him to be pleased, wanted him to want her. *He is even now growing restive again*, she wrote, *and making certain I feel the same. I cannot help but long for more of him, for the way he stirs within me seems to set me aflame with yearning, and a growing need for...*

Killik's thrusts were hardening again, lengthening, the sounds now slick and sloppy between them, the hot fluid streaking down her thighs. *For his deepening labours, and the promise of his further enrichment. For though he has already emptied his loins once, and poured out his blessings upon me, he is brimming with abundance yet again, and flourishing yet fuller, teeming and thronging within me—*

Her quill scrawled sideways as Killik yanked her tight, and again sprayed out deep within her. Pulsing again and again as his hips convulsed, and his growl rasped deep into her ear. And Louisa was moaning too, scrabbling helplessly at the desk, lost in the flashing floundering truth of it, of him, pouring her full of him, yet again.

And when he slowly drew out again, releasing yet more hot fluid around him, and then sank back inside, she knew this was part of it, too. His slow, taunting thrusts, pumping brazen into his own slick mess, spreading it, leaking it, pooling it down her thighs, down his own groin, onto the floor...

And now I am again bursting with him, she wrote, with her shaky, tingling hand. *He has borne so much fruit for me, I am utterly overcome. I cannot fathom a more—*

She hesitated again, wincing, because gods, what had she

been about to write, to betray—but here was Killik's plunge in again, a gentle scrape of his teeth on her tender-feeling neck. And she hauled in more breath, strength from the desk beneath her, as she scrawled out the rest of it, as quickly as she could.

A more wondrous and generous gift. I only wish you were here to join us, sweetheart, and to praise your fierce lusty pup, and make him blush and smile at you. Much love, Louisa.

She exhaled as she shoved aside the quill, and squeezed her eyes shut. As if she could somehow pretend she just hadn't written that, that it was all just sitting there for Killik to read. For him to lord over her, or mock her, or...

Or to thrust something into her trembling hand. A clean-looking rag. And then he gave a firm pat to her hip, and slowly began drawing himself out again. Giving her enough time to shove the rag into place before he stepped backwards, and then swiped his clawed hand over her for the letter.

"Very pretty scribbling, woman," he said, his voice far too smooth, as he deftly rolled the letter into a scroll. "He shall enjoy this."

Well. Louisa attempted a nod as she awkwardly turned to face him, to where his trousers were already tied up again, his eyes not quite meeting hers. "And does—does this count as one of our four nights?" she asked, before she could stop it. "Or—or is Ulfarr still even able to see me? Did they—did they have an answer on that, too?"

Killik's eyes flicked to hers, and away again. "Ach, you yet have your four nights with him, woman," he said. "Ought to use them wisely."

Louisa should have been pleased by that—she was pleased by that—wasn't she? And that wasn't disappointment coiling in her belly, because she hadn't still been hoping that maybe—if Simon allowed it—maybe Killik would extend the four nights, once their deal was finished.

Maybe he would just let them keep having this, enjoying this, especially if Ulfarr was here at the camp...

"So you're only here for a fortnight, you said?" Louisa asked, her voice thin. "Until Simon and Maria come to visit?"

Killik's eyes met hers again, and he nodded. "But just as you asked, I ken this visit is to... judge Wolf," he replied. "To witness his camp and his work. And if he can prove himself, show himself worthy and faithful and true, then mayhap"—his throat convulsed—"mayhap they shall allow him to stay."

The hopefulness flared back into Louisa's chest, so strong it was almost painful. "And what about the rest of it?" she asked, high-pitched. "His place in the clan? His title? His right to take a mate?"

Killik's mouth twisted, his breath exhaling slow. "Mayhap that also," he said, lower. "We must put on a good show, I ken."

A good show. The warmth flared up with the hope, because if anyone could put on a good show, it was Killik, right? But the longer Louisa searched his eyes, the more she realized he was—nervous. Uncertain. Maybe even afraid. He'd worked for so long, for so many years, and now the prize was so close, just within his reach—

Or perhaps about to be lost forever. Because Simon had already judged Ulfarr harshly once, hadn't he? He'd taken away Ulfarr's pack, his title, his happiness, his hope, even his health. And did he have the power to take more? To make it even worse?

Louisa swallowed hard, took a shaky breath. "But I hope Ulfarr's healing is permanent, at least?" she finally asked, hollow, into the silence. "He won't need to bear the pain anymore?"

Killik shook his head, and something shifted in his eyes as he huffed a slow exhale. "No, thank Skai-kesh," he said. "I ken he may never be the same as before, and his prick yet may never obey him as it once did. And his scenting was too broken to heal, also. But that is naught compared to the pain, and Efterar even said—"

Killik hesitated, his eyes again flickering, his shoulders squaring. "Efterar even said with more time, Wolf may yet be able to beget—sons," he continued, quieter. "Of his own blood and seed."

Oh. Something flashed up Louisa's back, flared behind her eyes, and her body snapped to stark, peculiar stillness. "Really?" she demanded. "Is that—something he actually wants? Something *you* want? I thought you said you didn't want more children!"

Her voice sounded too sharp, almost accusing, and Killik's eyes looked strange, distant, as he jerked a dismissive shrug. "*I* have no longing for this," he said, a little flat. "But should Wolf wish for this, ach, I should welcome this for him."

Louisa's mouth felt suddenly dry, her throat tight. And she somehow managed a nod, blinking hard at the sudden wetness pooling behind her eyes. Because that—that would change things. Wouldn't it? And maybe—maybe that put the limit, the four more nights, in an entirely new light. Because of course Ulfarr should have more sons if he wanted them, he was clearly a devoted and attentive father, and why were Louisa's churning thoughts suddenly trapped on Sune, running alone and bloody across her lands, looking so uncertain when she'd told him Killik cared for him. *Maybe. I'm not sure.*

"Right," she finally said, into the stilted, empty-feeling silence. "I'm—very happy for Ulfarr. And for you."

But when she glanced at Killik's face, he didn't look particularly happy, and he'd even snapped up a hand to pluck out one of his daggers from his topknot. "Ach, well," he said, as he watched the dagger spinning in his fingers. "We shall not need to think of it for some time yet, I ken."

Oh. Well. And that was something, some small hope to

cling to—and maybe it still wouldn't happen at all, right? Maybe it still wasn't even possible?

So Louisa inhaled and nodded, and held her eyes on Killik's spinning dagger, too. "So will I—see you again soon, then?" she asked him, hoarse, and though it was giving him too much, she just needed to say something, anything. "You'll be staying at the camp too, right?"

Again, it was too much, too damned betraying, and she didn't miss Killik's twitch, and then the clutch of his fingers snapping the dagger to stillness again. "Ach, I shall," he replied, with an arch of his brow. "And so shall you, woman. Every day."

What? Louisa blinked at him, at that familiar glint in his eyes, the curve on his mouth. "We now only have a fortnight to put on this show," he said flatly. "To ready the camp for Simon's judgement, and seek to regain Wolf's name, his hope, his *life*. And this"—he jabbed the dagger toward her—"was all *your* doing, woman! So ach, you shall come to the camp each morn, and help us, until this is done!"

Help them. Killik wanted Louisa's help. For an entire fortnight. And she couldn't hide the lurch of eagerness, the sudden delighted grin on her mouth—and before she could catch it, she lurched toward him, and reached up for his cheek. Felt him go sharp and still all over, but not protesting, not resisting, as she bent his face down, and brushed his lips with hers.

And gods, she shouldn't be doing this. Shouldn't be letting herself feel this again. The roughness of his lips, the sweet heat of his breath. That slick, thrilling touch of his tongue, slipping brief but certain between her parted lips...

But then he drew back again, his eyes intently fixed away from her. As if it was still too much, too presumptuous, too betraying. But curse it, he already knew, didn't he? Louisa had written it all out for him in plain damned ink, called him *a wondrous and generous gift*...

But it still didn't mean anything, it was still only four more nights... or was it? *Show me. Prove this to me...*

So Louisa ignored Killik's distant eyes, his tight mouth, and instead drew herself straight, drew in breath from the earth. She would face this. Fix this.

"I'll see you first thing in the morning, then," she told him, with only a faint waver on her voice. "And we'll put on a damned good show."

41

As she'd promised, Louisa headed for the camp first thing the next morning.

She was dressed in more of her new clothes, courtesy of the overstuffed pack Killik had brought the night before. Which had turned out to contain multiple items, many of them dresses Louisa had tried on in the shop—all of them in similar styles and dark colours. And at the bottom of the pack there had been several new loincloths, too, and Louisa had huffed a rueful laugh at the sight of them, and then pulled one on beneath her new navy dress.

She would prove this. She would help Killik put on a show, and save Ulfarr's life.

But once she'd said farewell to her staff, and headed down the path toward the camp, the doubts again began to whisper, nagging at the back of her thoughts. It could still fail. It was still only four nights. And after that, maybe Ulfarr would go and have a new son, even if Killik and Sune didn't want it, and...

She was frowning to herself, stalking around a large tree without looking—and then she yelped, and staggered backwards. Because there, in the middle of the path, stood—

Ulfarr. *Ulfarr.* Huge and broad and bare-chested, and here. *Here.*

"Forgive me, Louisa," he said with a tentative smile, his voice rumbling low in her belly. "I held no wish to startle you."

Louisa was still desperately dragging for air, but her shoulders were already sagging, her smile flashing back toward him. "Think nothing of it, sweetheart," she said, with a dismissive wave of her hand. "It's—good to see you."

Her eyes ran up and down his big body, catching, lingering—because he looked... different, somehow. Almost—easier. His stance more fluid, his shoulders low, his hands relaxed at his sides, with their claws drawn in. And his face looked easier, too, the lines less etched, perhaps, despite the crinkles deepening at the corners of his eyes.

"And you also, Louisa," he murmured, as he came a slow step toward her, reaching to gently clasp her hand in his. "I wished to come and meet you, and say—thank you."

Louisa blinked, attempted to wave it away—but now Ulfarr grasped for her other hand, too, and brought it to his mouth. "Thank you, Louisa," he said again, as he softly kissed her skin. "I ken not what possessed you to go to my kin yesterday, and defend me as you did, and speak such kindness upon me. And then to invite our Enforcer here, to witness our camp, and mayhap..."

His voice trailed off, the hope and the fear mingling bright in his eyes, as he pressed another kiss to her hand. "Was it... Killik who sent you to this?" he continued, even quieter. "He swore to me he did not, but..."

His voice faded again, his eyes searching hers, clearly wanting her to corroborate Killik's claim. And thank the gods, Louisa could shake her head and mean it, and give a wavering smile back toward him. "No, Killik didn't have anything to do with it. But he did take me to meet your Skai-kesh yesterday, and I prayed, and..."

And now it was her own voice fading, and she drew in breath, squeezed Ulfarr's hands tight. "I want to believe in forgiveness," she said thickly. "I want to believe in redemption, and amends. And I didn't think your punishment was—fair. Especially if they went and *forgot* about it."

But it was perhaps too pointed, too sharp, because Ulfarr winced, shook his head. "It was Simon's right to Enforce me as he felt best," he replied. "I threatened him and his mate, and sought to steal her away from him. And amidst this, I divided and weakened and failed my clan, also."

Louisa exhaled and nodded, holding his eyes. "But you've also been working so hard to make amends," she said. "You've faced the pain and punishment. You've helped your clan, and built this beautiful camp. You helped Sune. You helped Killik. You helped *me*."

Ulfarr's hands clenched back on hers, and he shook his head, made a sound much like a laugh. "But I yet—I cannot fathom how I have helped you, Louisa," he said, hoarse. "I have not been a—a good or clever or lusty bedmate. I have done naught on my own to bring you joy. Ach, that first night I *ran* from you, as only a true coward would. I know not why you keep welcoming this from me, and I was sure..."

His voice faded again, but Louisa kept waiting, kept holding both his hands, watching as he drew in another breath. "I was sure you only bore this for—Killik's payment," he continued, with a grimace. "For his—his coin, after these ten nights are done."

For the coin. Louisa's stomach pitched, and she squeezed her eyes shut, fought to drag in breath. Ulfarr hadn't mentioned the coin since the beginning of all this, and she certainly hadn't wanted to think about it, either, had she? But of course it had still been hovering over them, whispering its dark, unhappy truth. This still had a time limit, with a payment, and a very clear end. Four more nights.

And gods, it just felt so damned wrong, all of it. And again Louisa just wanted to curse Killik, to demand he forget the deal altogether, or at least continue on after it was done—but she'd already tried asking, hadn't she? And Killik had said—*No. No.*

And yes, then he'd told her to show him, to prove it to him—but that still didn't mean anything, did it? He'd still made no commitments to Louisa whatsoever, beyond these four nights. And while she could perhaps try to undermine him, or try to make her own arrangements with Ulfarr afterwards, she still had no interest in trying to steal Ulfarr away from him, either. Ulfarr did need Killik. He needed Killik's help, Killik's strength at his side. He needed his family, and his son. And Louisa would not risk taking that from him. She would not.

And worst of all, she still needed Killik's payment. She needed to protect her property and her people. She needed to forget her past, forget Lord Scall...

But right now—she swallowed, blinked back at Ulfarr's face—she needed to face this. She needed to tell Ulfarr the truth.

"Look, I do still need Killik's help," she said, holding Ulfarr's eyes, squeezing his hands. "But I still meant it when I told you I wanted this, sweetheart. I wanted—you. You've been so patient, and so kind, and I—I've liked that you haven't always had all the answers, either. I've liked how we've been learning—together. It's not—not something I've ever had the chance to do before, and it really has... helped. It's been... affirming, for me. Empowering. Healing."

Gods, it sounded so ridiculous, and if Killik were here, Louisa would have fully expected some mocking comment in return—but Ulfarr just kept looking at her, holding her hands, as warmth and gratefulness shimmered in his eyes. "I am honoured, Louisa," he replied, quiet. "You have been such a great help to me also, and brought me this same... healing. And if there is ever aught else I might be able to offer you, or if you might ever wish to speak, or have an ear to listen..."

He didn't finish, but his eyes kept studying hers, and Louisa fought back her wince, the barbed twist in her belly. He meant her past, he meant Lord Scall, he was giving her an opportunity to face this—but no. No. She couldn't bear to speak of it, she couldn't risk it, not even with him. She needed to forget it, to escape it, forever...

And surely Ulfarr had caught her hesitation, her refusal—but there was no hurt or judgement in his eyes. Only more warmth, and maybe even sympathy, as he brought her hand back to his mouth, and gave another soft kiss against her skin. "And also, Louisa," he murmured, "I thank you for this letter you sent me, last eve. This was very... lovely."

Right. That damned letter. Louisa's face heated at even the thought of it, and she huffed a choked, relieved laugh. "Well, you *can* blame that letter on Killik," she said, with a wincing little smile. "He said you would like it, and you were fine with it, but..."

She winced again, searching Ulfarr's eyes, but they were still so warm, so approving. "Ach, how could I not welcome this? It brings me great joy to know my fierce pup has found such a good woman to welcome his strong Skai ploughing. A woman who now scents so sweet, with his fresh scent yet upon her."

Oh. As if Ulfarr really thought that, really welcomed that. And Louisa gave a bemused smile back toward him, even as she kept gripping his hands, holding him here. Wanting him to keep looking at her, to keep saying such kind things, to stay...

When suddenly, above them, something—rustled.

Something in the tree, curse it, and Louisa yelped and leapt backwards, craning her head up toward it. And yes, that was someone leaping down out of the tree, his dagger flashing in his hand—

It was Killik. And he was furious.

42

Killik rounded on Ulfarr and Louisa with his eyes flashing, the growl burning from his throat.

"What is this?" he demanded at them. "And what did I tell you"—he pointed his dagger toward Ulfarr's face—"about running off alone thus!"

Louisa balked and stiffened all over, her heart pounding—gods, not this again, already—but then she blinked. Stared. Because was Ulfarr... smiling? Smiling, at *Killik*, and then reaching his big arm to circle around Killik's waist, and drawing him close.

"There you are, pup," he murmured, as he bent his head and pressed a kiss to Killik's hair, dangerously close to the blade of the dagger still in his topknot. "Knew not where you went, this morn."

For an instant, Killik looked nearly as astonished as Louisa felt—but then he jabbed his dagger toward Ulfarr again, waving it before his eyes. "Hunting!" he retorted, though his voice was less sharp than before. "You ken it is always hunting, you great witless mongrel!"

Louisa blinked again—had she ever heard Killik insult Ulfarr before?—but Ulfarr was still smiling, and even snapping his teeth at Killik's tall pointed ear. "Ach, and now you have caught your prey, pup," he said, as he glanced over Killik's head, and quirked his smile toward Louisa. "What shall you do with it next?"

Louisa's heart skipped a beat, because, oh, gods, it was again *that* Ulfarr. The easy, commanding Ulfarr, and he was even teasing Killik, and—and teasing *her*. And he *liked* it when Killik twitched and spluttered like that, and waved his dagger back at him, nearly close enough to nick the tip of his nose.

"Oh, you ken what I shall do next," Killik shot back, and he'd even settled his dagger against Ulfarr's mouth, kissing its sharpened tip at his lips, before trailing it down toward his throat. "I shall truss it up, and drain it, and make it *scream*."

Oh, hell. They didn't mean this, they weren't doing this, not here, not now, not in the middle of the woods like this—but Killik was already pulling at the chain of Ulfarr's belt, drawing it out slow and brazen from around his waist. And beneath Ulfarr's trousers, Louisa could see him... twitching. Swelling. Even as Killik's other hand kept nudging the dagger at Ulfarr's throat, as if it was a taunt, or a caress.

"Back to that tree, Wolf," Killik hissed, nodding toward a large nearby pine, as he tugged the chain free from Ulfarr's waist, and gave it an experimental little snap toward the earth. "Arms up."

Louisa's heart was still thundering, her breaths heaving, the disbelief still echoing through her skull—they were really, really doing this?—and Killik darted a look toward her, his brows raised. "Time for another lesson, woman," he said. "Come. Hold him."

What? It was laughable that Louisa could hold Ulfarr anywhere—but oh, Ulfarr wasn't even slightly resisting as Killik shoved him up against the tree, that gleaming dagger still kissing at his throat. And Ulfarr's eyes flicked toward

Louisa too, warm and wicked and eager, and for an instant, there was his voice, from just a moment ago…

This has been a great help to me also, and brought me this same… healing.

So Louisa lurched forward, nodding, and when Killik waved his dagger at Ulfarr's arms, she willingly grasped them, and shoved them up over his head. Holding him there, holding all this quivering power beneath her fingers, while Killik swung the chain around the tree, and then yanked it tight against Ulfarr's bare, heaving chest. And as Louisa blinked at it, the belated understanding crashed all through her at once, because of course this chain—the one Ulfarr always wore for a belt—was meant for this, too.

"This one is far better suited for him, you ken," Killik coolly told her, as he grasped at the chain's locking mechanism, and yanked it tight against Ulfarr's sternum. "He has not escaped it yet."

Louisa shot a heated glance up at Ulfarr's face, at where his eyes already looked hazy, his tongue brushing his lips. "Yet," he drawled back at Killik. "Some day, pup."

It felt too affectionate to be a threat, and though Killik rolled his eyes, Louisa didn't miss that telltale flush creeping up his neck. "Ach, but who is trussed to a tree now?" he demanded, as he lightly touched his dagger to Ulfarr's bound chest. "And who is now going to dance and squeal for us, just as the captured prey he is?"

Ulfarr's eyelids lowered, his lips parted, his attention fully fixed on where Killik was slowly drawing his dagger's gleaming blade lower, and lower, and lower. Down over Ulfarr's navel, his hairy lower belly, and then—Louisa's breath choked—slipping slow and deliberate down into his still-tied *trousers*. And good gods, Killik couldn't even see what he was doing, what if he—

The trousers sagged downwards, falling slack and loose around Ulfarr's hips, because—oh. Killik had cut the string that had been tying them up. And now—now Louisa could see Ulfarr's huge swollen length, jutting up above the sagging fabric...

"Strip him, woman," Killik ordered, with a twitch of his dagger toward her. "Show me what I have caught, this morn."

Louisa's glance up at Ulfarr found him watching her, that warmth again shimmering in his eyes. Wanting this just as much as she did, and she nodded as her shaky hands reached, and obliged. Shoving the trousers downward, off Ulfarr's hips, so his swollen cock behind them could bob free, jutting out huge and obscene toward them.

Louisa swallowed hard, blinking at the sight, because— damn. It was impossible, it was gigantic, and it was—it was *healed*. The scars were still there, yes, marked thick and messy all over him—but they were all shiny and faded, with no visible redness, no blood. Leaving it to do this, to look like this, like a gods-damned tree-branch growing out of him, leaking its sweet sap from the tip.

"Ach, just thus," Killik murmured, husky, his eyes hooded on the sight. "Touch it for me, woman."

Louisa barely bit back her groan, but nodded again, met Ulfarr's hungry, waiting eyes. And then slipped her hand toward that huge jutting cock, gently trailing her fingers down the velvety-smooth length of it, felt it bob and quiver at her touch, oh.

"Good," Killik murmured, his eyes glinting, his dagger making that *keep-going* motion. "More, woman. Show it off for me."

Ulfarr shuddered at the order, his eyes fluttering—so Louisa drew in a shaky breath, and again... obeyed. Slowly circling her hand around that thick shaft, stroking it, sliding up. Feeling it swell even fuller, oh hell, pumping out a little spurt of white from the tip, as Ulfarr's chained body spasmed and groaned.

"Good," Killik said again, husky, still circling his dagger. "More. Give me a good show. Make my prey dance for me."

Louisa rolled her eyes at Killik, even as she gave a choked chuckle, and kept going. Stroking up and down Ulfarr's massive length, milking out more soft spurts of that white seed. And then bringing over her other hand, too, caressing those heavy hairy bollocks, showing them off for Killik, too. While against the tree, Ulfarr kept shivering and gasping, his hips now gently pumping into the steady strokes of her hands.

"More, woman," came Killik's implacable voice. "Speak to him, also. Tell him how pretty he is, with his fat Skai prick."

Louisa gulped and nodded, her gaze flicking between the sight at Ulfarr's groin, and his hungry, glittering eyes. "You're so—handsome, sweetheart," she breathed. "With your—your fat Skai prick. With how sweet and smooth and gorgeous it is, with all these impressive scars all over it. Showing how much of a warrior you are. How strong you are."

Ulfarr's groan was long and sustained, his eyes glinting on Louisa's face, so she kept stroking him, flaunting him, praising him. "Feels so good to touch," she murmured. "So hot and lovely and alive. Just like you, sweetheart, and I could never get tired of touching you, looking at you, being with you—"

But wait, wait, that was dangerous ground, dragging another low moan from Ulfarr's throat, and Louisa shot a helpless, apologetic glance at Killik, at his unreadable watching eyes. "Ach, Wolf, she cannot get enough Skai prick," Killik drawled, with just a faint edge on his voice. "You ought to have seen her last eve, when she begged and squealed and *spurted* upon my strong ploughing."

Louisa grimaced, darted an uncertain look up at Ulfarr's face—but oh, gods, his warm eyes just glanced eagerly between them, his shaft swelling even fuller in Louisa's hand.

"Ach, it was enough to only read her letter of this," he gasped back, between heavy breaths. "This must have been a stunning sight. And this must have felt so good for you also, pup. So hot and tight and wet, all around you."

Killik shrugged, though his eyes were hooded again, his finger drawing down the length of his dagger. "Not as wet as she is now, I ken," he replied coolly, "after I flooded her twice last eve. It shall take her *days* to dry up from me, I ken."

Louisa stared and sputtered at Killik, but he ignored her, and gave a purposeful wave of his dagger toward Ulfarr. "Mayhap you ought to test this, Wolf," he said. "Undress her for us, so we can judge."

And oh, Ulfarr's warm hand was already here, catching on Louisa's hip over her dress. Because Killik hadn't actually bound up Ulfarr's hands, he'd only bound his chest—and Ulfarr willingly drew Louisa closer, his heavy eyes searching hers. "I should be honoured, Louisa," he breathed. "But only should you wish."

But of course Louisa wished, and she rapidly nodded, her tongue brushing her lips. And she even pressed into his touch, into the shivery feeling of his big hands as they unfastened her belt, and then moved to the dress' front buttons. Undoing them one by one, and then drawing the dress apart, exposing her front to the air, to the bright morning light. And also exposing—she cringed as she glanced downwards—her new loincloth, too.

But Ulfarr only groaned again as he looked at it, his eyes fluttering, his hand spreading warm and possessive over her almost-bare hip. "She has again dressed in Skai garb for us, pup," he said, husky, as his other hand gently guided her around to face Killik. "Pretty, ach?"

Killik didn't reply, his lips pursing as his eyes flicked up and down Louisa's bared front. But he'd circled his dagger again, at Ulfarr this time, and oh, it meant Ulfarr's hand was already slipping downwards, sliding beneath the loincloth.

Touching and stroking so slowly, so softly, his warm finger-tips seeking into the wet heat of her crease, and then easing further, deeper between her thighs...

"Still wet, then?" asked Killik's dispassionate voice, his brows rising, and oh, Ulfarr's careful fingers kept obeying, slipping deeper, while Killik watched. The sounds slick and betraying, far too loud, and Louisa was already trembling, shaking all over, staggering back against Ulfarr's solid strength behind her.

"Ach, she is yet dripping with you, pup," came Ulfarr's heated murmur, his fingers now gently squelching as they slipped in and out of her. "But mayhap you ought to test this, also."

Wait, did he mean that—and was Killik even considering it, eyeing Louisa like that, with such glittering triumph in his eyes. "Ach, mayhap," he said. "Present her to me, then."

Ulfarr groaned and nodded, and turned Louisa around to face him again. And oh, he was even smiling at her again, so warm and approving, as one of his hands caressed her face, and the other one slid down to her hip. So he could—so he could draw up her loincloth, and then bend her upper body lower, guiding her hips back. Presenting her for Killik, oh gods, fully exposing her for him. And was Louisa really doing this, letting them do it, standing there trembling as she waited. As she could feel Killik sauntering closer, closer, until—

His touch. And it wasn't—fingers, this time. No, no, it was that hard jutting cock. Not testing, not nudging—just instantly finding its place, and carving sure and swift inside her. And Louisa's sharp cry scraped through the air, her entire body writhing upon it, around it—and behind her Killik laughed, smug and satisfied, as Ulfarr's big hands stroked her face. "Remember to breathe, Louisa," he murmured. "Draw up strength deep from the earth, and wield it to be soft and open, so you can welcome my lusty pup inside you."

That almost made it worse, swaying the earth beneath Louisa's feet, while Ulfarr glanced back toward Killik, with warm hungry approval in his eyes. "Was she thus last eve also, pup?" he asked, husky. "Quaking all over at your first thrust?"

Killik laughed again, the utter bastard, as he slowly drew out, breath by breath—and then plunged back inside, hard enough to make Louisa's teeth chatter. "Ach, just thus," he said, his voice far too cool. "Could scarce hold still enough to write your letter, you ken. But"—another draw out, a dizzying plunge in—"she is yet wetter now, too. Wet enough even for your prick, Wolf, I ken."

With that, he yanked himself out again, and gave a light slap to Louisa's arse. Leaving her empty and shaking again, her eyes wildly searching Ulfarr's face, catching on the blazing hunger in his eyes...

"Good, Louisa," Ulfarr breathed, as his hands reached for her, drew her back up toward him. And then—Louisa gasped—he hoisted her fully up off the ground, with her legs spread wide against his waist, oh gods.

"Good," he murmured again. "Open wide for me, and I shall grant you what you seek, ach?"

Oh, gods, yes, Louisa wanted that, needed that, needed the bizarre unreal truth of this massive orc—still bound by the chest to a damned tree—holding her up so easily against him, his glistening grey cock settling long and heavy against her bare belly. But wait, now Killik was behind her too, helping to shift her weight, so Ulfarr's huge swollen length could slip lower, its slick head moving down over her coarse hair, until it nudged up into her pulsing, wide-open heat beneath...

"Ach," Ulfarr groaned, his head tilting backwards against the tree, as his hands began guiding Louisa closer. Slowly, powerfully, opening her around him, impaling her whole upon him. Moving her as easily as if she was a doll, sliding her entire quivering body down onto his huge jutting length. And she could only gulp and clutch at him, cling to his broad solid shoulders, feel him opening her wider, and wider. Like he was slowly but surely skewering her on his tree branch, attaching her to him, stretching her to the edge of her strength, and it was too much, so much, his eyes blazing, his body bulging even fuller inside her—

"Remember to breathe, woman," came Killik's clipped voice, too close in her ear, because he was still behind her, his head peering over her shoulder, so he could blatantly watch this, watch Ulfarr spearing her whole upon him. "Cannot have you falling into a fainting spell, and thus missing my show. Most of all when you have such a good seat."

Louisa managed a growl and a sideways glare at Killik, but in return he only smirked at her, and even reached around her to lightly tweak her hard nipple. "Ach, do not spurn my good show, woman," he drawled. "You like the great beast I hunted and tamed for you. You like dancing upon him for me."

Louisa rolled her eyes this time, but she was breathing again, following that slow steady rise and fall of Killik's shoulders. "Oh, fuck you, Killik," she gasped, between her dragging breaths. "In case you haven't—noticed, Ulfarr is the one—who's doing all the—work here!"

Killik's brows snapped up, and his eyes flashed with disbelief, or maybe mockery. "You ken I do naught here, woman?" he demanded. "You wish to know what more I can do?"

Louisa spluttered another curse at him, and then darted a look at Ulfarr's flushed face. Because he'd stopped moving her, he was now just holding her half-impaled upon him, their bodies still not yet near enough to touch. And his eyes on hers were warm and indulgent, but maybe—she blinked—maybe a little stern, too.

"Killik always works far more than any of us see, Louisa," he murmured. "I should never forbid you two barking and playing together, but you shall not dishonour him thus before me."

A strange shiver ran up Louisa's back—had she truly displeased him?—and Ulfarr shifted her closer, so he could lean forward, and brush a soft kiss to her cheek. "Mayhap you should now wish to honour Killik instead, then," he said. "Shall you do this with me?"

Louisa fervently nodded, her hands still clinging to Ulfarr's shoulders, her body convulsing against his still-invading strength. And oh, the way he smiled at her, as he again shifted his grip, and began... guiding her upper body backwards. Tilting her back against Killik's solid chest behind her, but now Killik was moving back, too. And his own strong hands were grasping beneath Louisa's shoulders, drawing her out flat between them, as if she was lying on empty air, her head dangling back. And wait, there, now, hovering too close above her blinking eyes, was Killik's hard, dripping cock.

"Use her mouth, pup," came Ulfarr's low, heated order. "Share her with me. Show me how pretty she is, and how she feels, with two strong Skai pricks inside her."

Louisa's breath shuddered, her body trembling all over—but somehow, despite the position, she nodded. Saying, yes, yes, catching and holding Killik's wide eyes, and only vaguely following the way his tongue licked his lips, his cheeks flushed with unmistakable red...

But then he nodded too, and shifted his hands beneath her, repositioning her, gaining a better grip. So he could lean forward, and smoothly slide his hard wet cock straight into her open, gasping mouth.

It was a bizarre, awkward angle, with Louisa's head

tipped back like this, almost upside-down, as Killik's seeking flesh delved deeper, prodding toward her throat. While between her legs, Ulfarr's pole was sinking deeper too, throbbing and juddering as he drew her closer, closer. The movement pulling her away from Killik, sliding him out of her desperately sucking mouth—but then, oh, Ulfarr slid her back again. Back toward Killik, sinking him deeper into Louisa's throat, before gently drawing her forward onto him again.

"How is this, Louisa?" came Ulfarr's low question. "Is aught too much, or pain?"

Louisa somehow shook her head, even with Killik still half-inside her like that, and she could hear Ulfarr's soft purr of approval, his hands again drawing her closer. "Good," he murmured. "You are so pretty, thus, Louisa. So lovely, when you are so bared and open and ready for us. When you allow us to share you between us, and fill you with our strong Skai pricks."

His words were yet more craving, more fierce flashing hunger coiling in Louisa's belly, clamping her around his invading strength. And maybe around Killik's, too, sucking him tighter and deeper into her mouth, and oh, now Ulfarr was sliding her back onto Killik again, and even chuckling as Killik betrayed a low, broken groan. "Good, pup," Ulfarr breathed. "She is so tight, and so hot, and so sweet, ach?"

And wait, Killik was nodding, nodding as that flush kept creeping up his face, and a spurt of sweetness pulsed into Louisa's sucking mouth. But he was already guiding her deeper onto Ulfarr's huge jutting strength, their hips nearly touching now—and then Ulfarr slid her back toward Killik again. Moving her back and forth between them, settling into a slow steady rhythm, sharing her, taking turns with her, as Louisa's longing charged higher, hotter, dangerous and delirious. This shouldn't be so good, nothing should be so good, these two orcs blatantly using her in a forest, taking turns filling her, while one of them was still chained to a tree. Until Ulfarr's big hands finally drew her impaled body all the way against him, skin pressed to skin, his huge cock now fully buried inside her, stretching her wide open around him...

"You are so good, Louisa," Ulfarr gasped. "And you also, pup. Ach, this is such a great gift from Skai-kesh, my hungry bedmates, my fierce defenders—"

It was too much, too bright, everything, his body his voice his hands, his hunger and his longing and his gratitude— and suddenly the tension snapped, and shattered. Soaring into raw raging relief, thundering through Louisa again and again, and oh, now Killik and Ulfarr were both crying out too, as their shuddering bodies surged out into her. Ulfarr's packing them even tighter together, filling her with even more of his overpowering strength, while Killik's hands shook as he jammed himself deeper, and poured out straight down into Louisa's throat. And she didn't even need to swallow, just needed to sink into their staggering pleasure, to lose herself in the rapture and the relief, the brief shimmering perfection of this wondrous, hanging truth.

They were hers. *Hers.*

It was Killik who finally moved first, carefully shifting his softening length out of Louisa's mouth, before guiding her upright again. And then Ulfarr helped to lift her the rest of the way, releasing her from his cock with a thick squelch, and unleashing yet another unholy mess from between them.

But Killik betrayed a low moan at the sight, and Ulfarr's eyes were blatantly watching too, fluttering with undeniable hunger. "Ach," Ulfarr said, a low breathless rasp, as he slowly set Louisa back onto her unsteady feet. "Ach, Louisa. This was—you are—"

His wide shimmering eyes on hers looked wild, suddenly, almost alarmed, and as Louisa swayed and blinked up at him, the colour seemed to drain at once from his face, his hands skittering against her skin. "Are—are you well?" he croaked. "I have not—we have not—harmed you—have we?"

The urgency in his voice snapped through Louisa's own hitching, hazy thoughts, and she belatedly shook her head, clutched back at his broad sweaty shoulders. "Of—of course not, sweetheart," she gasped. "It was—perfect."

Ulfarr kept staring at her like that, the distress still deepening in his eyes, and thank the gods, here was Killik. Leaning in beside Louisa to pat reassuringly at Ulfarr's heaving chest, and flash a swift, stunning smile up at his pale face.

"You ken I was scenting her all this time, Wolf," Killik said firmly. "And I ken I have never scented her so happy, as she was amidst this. As when she was stuck upon our two strong Skai pricks, and squealing and dancing for us."

Louisa shot a sharp look toward Killik, elbowing at his side, but he only gave a cool smile back, his brows raised. "You should have only been happier if we had filled your third hole also," he said placidly. "Ought to have brought Wolf's *rassja*—or another hungry Skai or two, mayhap. I wonder how loud she shall squeal then, Wolf?"

Louisa attempted another glare at Killik, even as something clutched deep in her groin—and wait, Ulfarr's softened length had slightly spasmed against her, too. But his expression shifted again, his face a little less pale, his eyes flinty on Killik's face.

"Killik," he said reprovingly. "I wished to come here to thank Louisa, and honour her. Not to—to frighten her with talk of ruts."

But Killik rolled his eyes, and smirked at Louisa's hot-feeling face. "You ken this is frightened?" he drawled. "I ken she was more frightened by her breakfast this morn. Or mayhap by"—he flipped up the dagger he was still holding, pointing it toward a nearby tree—"that squirrel."

Louisa's mouth opened and closed, her eyes narrowing

on the chattering squirrel above them, while Killik laughed, and gave a light slap to her arse. As if he wasn't at all bothered by the thought of such a thing. As if he might even *want* it...

Louisa shot a helpless glance at Ulfarr, who—curse him—didn't look at all bothered, either. And that was another faint stirring of his softened length against her belly, his eyes glimmering with warmth, with... with hope.

"Now, enough hankering, you two," came Killik's curt voice, as he patted Ulfarr's sweaty chest, and reached to unfasten the chain's latch. "We have much work at the camp to do first."

Right. Louisa shook herself a little, gulped down a shaky breath, even as her eyes kept searching Killik's face. Much work to do... *first*. Because that wasn't... another challenge, was it? It wasn't him again saying, *Prove it. Show me.* Was it? Especially since after this, they would be down to three more nights... right?

But even so, Louisa drew herself tall, and smoothed out her dress. She could face this. She would.

"I'm ready," she said, with as much certainty as she could muster. "Let's get started."

A short time later, Louisa was standing with Killik and Ulfarr in the middle of the camp's clearing, and gazing up at the camouflaged shelters above them.

"What else, exactly, do you want to do to get it ready?" she asked. "It already seems so well appointed, don't you think?"

But Killik followed her eyes, and sharply shook his head. "We need to build a new *kofi*," he said, waving toward the little shelters. "One large enough for Simon and Maria and their sons. We also need to dig and build a latrine, and more ladders. And a garden, and a smokehouse—Thomas has been asking for these, and they should show us well ready to host more humans here, ach?"

Right. Louisa's eyes settled on where Thomas and his son Angus were crouched at the edge of the clearing, perhaps gathering herbs. While Flora and Galmr were both seated nearby braiding rope, and above them, multiple orcs were climbing up in a large oak tree, no doubt seeking a location for Simon and Maria's new *kofi*.

"And," Killik continued, as he waved irritably toward the

nearest tree, "Sune has told us he wishes to build a *kofi* of his own here, also! And Wolf has gone and *agreed* to this!"

Louisa's gaze snapped up, following Killik's hand—and yes, yes, there was Sune. Standing high on a new little platform above them, and giving Killik a cool, imperious glare.

Louisa's grin flashed across her face, because gods, Sune looked so much better—and he didn't have his crutches anymore, either. And when she swiftly signed a hello up toward him, he inclined his head, and signed a hello back. Followed by a brief, furtive *thank you.*

It tightened in Louisa's throat, prickled behind her eyes. And as she kept beaming up toward Sune, it occurred to her that if he really wanted to build a *kofi* of his own here at the camp, maybe—maybe he wanted to stay here, too. Maybe—forever.

Fix this, he had begged her, back in Ulfarr's dark little room. *Fix this.*

"Ach, I am glad to help our son build this *kofi* today," Ulfarr cut in, as he clasped firmly at Killik's shoulder. "And mayhap you and Louisa can fetch wood for us—if you are yet sure you wish to help, Louisa?"

His eyes were searching, uncertain on her face—but Louisa instantly nodded, without a moment's hesitation. Because—yes. Yes. She was facing this. Proving this.

So she willingly followed Killik out into the surrounding forest, and carefully listened to his instructions about what kinds and sizes of wood they needed. And soon they were tromping through the woods together, gathering fallen trees and logs and branches. Tying what they could into bundles, and hauling them into the camp for the orcs to use, and then heading back out again.

And while it was a dirty, sweaty job, working with Killik again turned out to be surprisingly enjoyable. Perhaps because he again pointed out tracks and nests and burrows to Louisa as they went, and guided her through any tricky terrain, and even helped her hunt a rabbit to eat for lunch. And perhaps also because he didn't balk at her various questions about the camp, or building the *kofis*, or even about Sune.

"Ach, Sune *can* speak aloud, if he wishes," Killik told her, when she tentatively asked. "But he does not oft wish to, and we have no wish to force this. Our kin ought to learn to sign instead, and Wolf and I have sought to uphold this. Both in our school, and throughout the mountain."

It was very generous of them, to Louisa's mind—but when she told Killik so, he only huffed a laugh, and shook his head. "Ach, you ken not how I have suffered for this," he said wryly. "That Rosa went and formed a *Society for Skai Signing Scholarship and Dissemination*, and has not ceased nattering me over it since! As if she has not yet granted me enough grief with her *Orc Mountain Educational Congress!*"

Louisa laughed, earning an aggravated roll of Killik's eyes toward her. But her thoughts were still caught on Sune, and on another question that had been vaguely nagging at her ever since Sune had first shown up at her door.

"Did Sune ever tell you," she began, careful, "why he ended up on Rikard's property in the first place? Was he looking for you and Ulfarr?"

Killik huffed a laugh, and shook his head. "No, he well knew where we went," he replied. "He came there to look for *you*. He wished to face the woman who will *steal Wolf away from us*, he said."

Louisa's breath caught, her eyes widening on Killik's face, because—Sune hadn't really thought that, had he? And why was Killik telling her this? Was he—was this another test, somehow? Another challenge?

"I hope you—clarified that for him, then," she said, a little too stiffly. "I did try to tell him myself, too. I know how much Ulfarr needs you, and loves you. Both of you."

Killik shot her a brief, searching look, and then jerked a

dismissive, too-casual shrug. And blinking back at him, Louisa was again suddenly, bizarrely reminded of Sune. And of the way Sune had looked, the way he'd answered, when she'd told him she knew Killik cared for him. *Maybe. I'm not sure.*

"Oh, right, I forgot, Ulfarr would never want *you*," Louisa drawled, in her best attempt at mimicking Killik's usual mocking voice. "He doesn't like you at *all*, Killik. That's why he's always watching you, and doting on you, and talking about you. Praising your hunger and your wisdom and your loyalty. Calling you his *fierce lusty pup*, the Skai's *finest weapons wielder*, with your *strong Skai seed*."

The derision was far too strong in her voice, ringing out between them. And in return, that might have been a quiver, rippling up Killik's lean body beside her—so Louisa huffed a low laugh, and elbowed him in the side. "Gods, didn't you hear your wolf just this morning," she added, "when he scolded me for dishonouring you? And had you punish me by holding me upside-down, and jamming yourself down my throat?"

That was definitely a quiver from Killik this time, and then a hoarse little laugh. "Ach, this was almost as he was... before," he replied, quiet. "As if he was... the Wolf of the Skai again. So calm and settled and easy, you near forget he has teeth—until he spins around and *slaughters* you."

Louisa's breath caught, even as a smile quirked at her mouth. "Just like his favourite pup, right?" she said lightly. "But I'm—glad to hear it, Killik. And"—her smile faded, her eyes intent on his face—"you know, he really is lucky to have you."

It came out sounding wistful, enough that Killik shot a narrow glance toward her. And though she braced herself for some kind of mockery, he only gave a low exhale, a jerky shrug of his shoulder. "Ach, the luck is all mine," he replied. "Wolf saved me, when I needed him most. Thus I shall never cease upholding him, not until he asks this of me. And mayhap"—a bitter little laugh—"mayhap not even then."

Louisa studied him for another long, silent moment, her head slowly tilting. Did Killik really still think Ulfarr would stop wanting that? Stop wanting *him*? Maybe that Ulfarr would finally heal, and move on with that new son, and leave Killik behind waiting and longing, like a lost little pup whose owner had forgotten him...

Louisa swallowed, opened her mouth—but Killik had stalked off up ahead, without looking back. And as she followed him back toward the camp, the longing and the determination settled deeper into her belly. She needed to do this. Fix this. For Killik, for Sune, for Ulfarr. For herself.

So she threw herself into the rest of the day's work with as much enthusiasm as she could muster. Helping Killik sort and stack all the wood they'd hauled, and then consulting with him and Thomas on the best place for a garden, and the latrine. And then she did some braiding with Flora and Galmr, during which she learned how to knot ropes for ladders and hammocks, and even managed to make a hammock for Sune's new *kofi*. And finally, she worked with Leikr and his little friends to clear rocks from the clearing, and add them to the firepit. Just doing whatever Killik said needed to be done, without question or complaint, until the sun hung low on the horizon.

But once Killik had climbed high into the oak tree with Elgr and Igull, finally setting the bones of the new *kofi* in place, Louisa found herself wiping her sweaty forehead, and blinking around at it all. Because yes, the camp already looked better, tidier, the clearing more open and welcoming. And Sune's *kofi* was almost finished, now, a cozy little bough-covered hut against the tree, with Louisa's new hammock hanging outside.

But. Even if they finished it all, the new *kofi* and the garden and the latrine, would it be... enough? Surely it would help, of course, but Simon was coming here to judge *Ulfarr*, not the state of his camp. Right?

Louisa twitched as Ulfarr himself slid down the rope from Sune's new *kofi*, his face and chest covered in a sheen of sweat. "Ach, Louisa," he said, as he settled his warm hand against her back. "You must be weary, for you have done so much for us today. I thank you, yet again."

He leaned over, pressed a kiss to her hair, and Louisa willingly sank against him, inhaled the sweaty-sweet scent of him. And drew up the question she didn't want to ask, but...

"What do you think Simon will really be... looking for, when he comes?" she ventured, with a wince. "What's most likely to sway his opinion of you? His... judgement?"

Ulfarr's body stiffened, and Louisa could hear the sudden rapid thud of his heartbeat, too loud against her ear. "When Simon first cast judgement upon me," he replied, halting, "he said I must earn his reward. I must work for our clan, and our kin, until I again gain his trust."

Right. And the camp was work, yes, it was helping the Skai, helping Ulfarr's kin... but surely Simon would want to see more than that. He would want to see... what? *A good show*, Killik had said. Ulfarr had to earn this, gain his trust...

But how? What else could they do? What could show such an intangible thing? What would be sure to be... enough?

"Wolf!" hissed a voice from above, and when Louisa glanced over, it was Ragni, furiously signing from his watch-tree, and waving toward the south. And in return, Ulfarr jerked around to look, frowning, while the rest of the camp went suddenly, curiously still. Except for the faint flashes of blades being drawn, and Louisa could see Killik slipping down from the oak tree, landing in a silent low crouch. Signing swiftly toward Ragni, who signed back into the forest, and then back at Killik. Who stared for an instant, and then let out—a groan?

"We're here to see Louisa," called a voice, a familiar voice, ringing high and clear through the trees. "Could you let her know we're here?"

Louisa startled, and then lurched forward, jogging across the clearing toward the voice. Toward where—wait—there was an entire group of orcs, climbing up out of the tunnel that led to the mountain. And at the front of them, beaming brightly toward Louisa, was—Rosa.

"We wanted to accept your invitation to come visit your new camp," Rosa announced. "And more importantly"—she drew herself up straighter—"we're here to help you save it."

44

Rosa had come to help save the camp.

That bizarre claim jangled through Louisa's muddled brain as she stammered her thanks to Rosa, and welcomed her fellow travellers. Which turned out to include not only Rosa's mate John-Ka and their sons, but also John-Ka's closest Ka-esh brothers—two handsome, vaguely familiar orcs named Tristan and Salvi. Who, Louisa belatedly recalled, she'd met back when she'd first helped Rosa—and who, apparently, were now also fathers to Rosa and John-Ka's sons, and had come to care for them, while Rosa and John-Ka helped... *save the camp.*

But Rosa didn't elaborate as she cheerfully greeted the rest of the camp, and then willingly accepted Ulfarr's offer to stay the night. And as Ulfarr guided Tristan and Salvi and the orclings off toward the brand-new *kofi*, Louisa took Rosa and John-Ka down into the underground common-room, with Killik close behind them.

"Er, so what do you mean?" Louisa finally asked, once she was seated with Rosa and John-Ka at one of the common-room's tables, while Killik hovered behind her with palpable annoyance. "Why do you think the camp needs saving?"

Rosa had been rummaging in a pack she'd brought, and she swept out a sheaf of paper, several quills, and a bottle of ink. "Two things," she said crisply, as she began preparing her quill. "First of all, back at the mountain, you said that horrid Lord Rikard threatened both you and the camp—and we've seen enough of these lords to know you *cannot* ignore that threat. And secondly..."

She angled a wary glance up behind Louisa, toward where Killik still looked supremely irritated, his lip curling, his arms crossed over his chest—but his brows had snapped up, too, his eyes glittering on Rosa's face. As if daring her to say the rest of it, and to Rosa's credit, she straightened in her chair, and drew in a breath.

"And secondly," she repeated, "I know Simon and Maria are coming here soon, and Simon will be evaluating your camp, and Ulfarr's leadership. And while I like and respect Simon, and I know he's a good Enforcer, I also think"—she took another breath—"he's far too close to the situation to be trusted to make a clear judgement on it. And while Skai leadership structures are a matter for another day, for now we're stuck with it, which means"—she jabbed her quill between Louisa and Killik—"if you want to redeem Ulfarr, you need to reach beyond Simon. You need to convince the rest of the Skai, too, and maybe even the rest of the clans. You need to make a plan, and make an *impression*."

Louisa had already nodded, amidst that memory of Killik saying, *We must put on a good show.* But when she glanced back toward him, he was still glowering at Rosa, and he had one of his daggers in hand, too. "We have already made a good plan," he snapped back. "We seek to show our camp as strong and safe, and Wolf as a good leader and host. And as for this fool lord, we are watching him each day, and guarding these lands. He shall not bring harm to any of our kin *again*."

He shot a brief, narrow glance toward Louisa, and it jolted sudden and odd in her chest. Killik had been—spying on Rikard? Guarding her land against him? Every day?

But across the table, Rosa scoffed, and shook her head. "It's not just Rikard you need to worry about, Killik," she countered. "This camp is only a short walk away from Dusbury, and do you realize"—she jabbed her quill toward him—"that's the nearest any orc settlement has been to a human town in at least a hundred years? And if Rikard can get an entire town of people worked into a frenzy about the trespassing orcs in their terrifying camp, *that's* what you need to worry about."

The truth of that alarming statement struck Louisa to stillness, because yes, that was absolutely something Rikard would do, wasn't it? Especially if he couldn't find another way to throw her—and the orcs—off the property?

And what if Rikard did succeed in whipping up the town against the camp? Would anyone notice or care if a rabid mob attacked the camp, or drove the orcs off Louisa's property? Would the orcs have any real recourse, beyond fighting back? An action that could surely lead straight into a war?

Louisa's uneasy glance back at Killik found his mouth pressed tight, his hand rigid on his dagger. But he wasn't replying this time, and Rosa drew in another bracing breath. "And," she continued, "I don't think your plans for impressing Simon and your clan are going to cut it, either. Your camp being strong and safe, and Ulfarr being a good leader—that's all the bare minimum, isn't it? You need to do something bigger. Something so spectacular, *no one* will question it."

Louisa's breath caught, and she hadn't even noticed she was clutching her own knife, her fingers clammy and tingling. Because it was too close to her own thoughts, wasn't it? Their current plan wasn't enough. They needed to put on a good show. Something spectacular.

"I agree with you, Rosa," she said, in a rush. "We need to do everything we can. Ulfarr is too important. This camp is too important."

Her voice sounded hoarse, pleading, and her glance up at Killik felt pleading, too. But he still wasn't speaking, still just frowning at her, and gripping his dagger. But maybe... maybe listening.

"Did you—have anything in mind?" Louisa asked Rosa, squaring her shoulders. "Any ideas or suggestions? Initiatives that have worked in similar situations before? Maybe"—she groped back through her memories—"some kind of expanded communications effort in Dusbury? Continuing the work you've been doing there, somehow?"

Rosa looked deeply gratified by this suggestion, but then her eyes again flicked up to Killik. "I think we need to hear from the Skai first," she said, slower. "Your clan has borne so much, maybe more than any of the other clans. So"—her head cocked sideways—"what's something you think the clan needs, Killik? If you could conjure up anything to help your clan, anything at all—what would it be?"

Killik blinked, as if this wasn't a question he'd ever before considered—and then he jerked a shrug, and gave an aimless wave of his dagger toward the room around them. "Just—a place such as this," he said, his voice cracking. "A place where we can rest, and heal, and welcome the weak and weary amongst us. A place with good tall trees to live in, and deep tunnels to hide in, where our sons can play, and learn, and grow—and mayhap meet humans nearby to be friends and mates with, also. A place where we can finally be Skai, and yet be... *safe.*"

His longing quivered through the air, clutching in Louisa's belly, and perhaps Rosa felt it too, her eyes large and bright, her tooth biting at her lip. "A place to be Skai," she repeated, hushed. "And to welcome the weary, and play, and grow. And meet humans..."

She was tapping her quill on the table, her expression now distant, thoughtful, focused. And then she choked an excited little yelp, and began writing. Her quill rapidly sweeping across the page, while Louisa exchanged a brief, bemused glance with Killik behind her. But then his narrow gaze flicked back to Rosa, and to where her mate John-Ka was smiling at her with fond approval, and even reaching over to tap his claw at something she'd written on the page.

"Yes, I agree," Rosa replied, with a quick, distracted smile toward him, before writing even faster. "The entire town. And the mountain. And all the other camps?"

John-Ka nodded, while Louisa's bemusement just kept rising, and finally she took a breath, cleared her throat. "Well?" she asked. "What are you suggesting, then?"

Rosa's sparkling eyes snapped up, her grin warm and eager. "You need an open house," she said firmly. "Or a camp-warming party. Or better yet"—she gave a triumphant flourish of her quill—"an official *Skai Summit for Rehabilitation, Reconciliation, and Rejuvenation. All ages welcome!*"

45

Louisa's mouth dropped open, as disbelief cracked through her whirling thoughts. An official *Skai Summit for Rehabilitation, Reconciliation, and Rejuvenation*? Really?

Her disbelieving gaze darted back up toward Killik, who looked just as stunned as she felt—but he quickly recovered, and jabbed his dagger toward Rosa. "No," he snapped. "No, you irksome Ka-esh. We shall not"—he took a breath—"call it this!"

Louisa jolted, gaping up at Killik's face, because he was quibbling over—the name. Not the idea altogether. Right?

"No Skai shall even be able to *speak* this," Killik continued, with another sharp jab of his dagger toward Rosa. "Let alone invite their kin to this *Summit for Rehabilitation, Reconciliation, and Rejuvenation!*"

There was an instant's startled silence, but then Rosa's mouth quirked, and she rolled her eyes. "Oh, fine," she snapped back. "What far superior name would *you* give it, then?"

Killik sniffed, and pursed his lips, and flipped his dagger in his fingers. "Just the Skai Summit, I ken," he muttered, under his breath. "Ought to be more than enough."

Rosa's delight lit up her face, and Louisa felt her own smile widening, too—but she still wasn't even fully following, damn it. "So you mean—we'll host an event here?" she asked carefully. "And... invite people to attend? While Simon and Maria are here?"

Rosa vigorously nodded, and she was already taking more notes, her quill streaking across the page. "Yes, exactly," she replied. "We invite as many Skai as we can think of, and we'll welcome orcs from all the clans, too. And"—another flourish from her quill—"we invite the town. We welcome them to come and tour an authentic orc camp, with tunnels and tree-houses and food and games and prizes!"

Louisa's brain was still lurching to catch up, though she was leaning forward in her chair, gripping at the table. "And we can help to prevent any fear-mongering from Rikard, too," she said slowly. "We give people a chance to see the camp for themselves."

Rosa nodded again, her eyes dancing on her page of notes. "And as you suggested, sister, it will be an *excellent* addition to our ongoing communications campaigns," she said firmly. "We've already done plenty of in-person outreach in town, along with all our flyers and publications—so this is a logical next step, isn't it? Inviting them to experience orc culture and an orc community firsthand, and to show them that it's not scary or intimidating. To prove to them that they can have fun here, and be *safe*."

Louisa's heart skipped, while Rosa frowned up at Killik, and tapped her quill at her chin. "And I think it would be good for the Skai, too," she added, quieter. "So much of your culture and history was lost in the war, and you ought to be supported in celebrating what you still have. Honouring it, and rebuilding it, and sharing it. With each other, and the other clans, and humans, too."

She sounded so earnest, so intent, and Louisa's glance back at Killik found him looking—thoughtful. Disarmed. Almost... hopeful.

"And you really think," Louisa ventured, "we can just... do that? Decide that? And make sure it all happens while Simon is here?"

She'd asked it to Killik, rather than Rosa, and she winced at the darkness again flickering through his eyes—but across the table, Rosa sniffed, and snatched over a new sheet of paper. "Of course we can," she said crisply. "Simon doesn't own your clan, does he? If anything, Ulfarr's history as a Skai leader goes back *far* further than his. And besides"—her mouth curved into a dark little smile—"what kind of leader would Simon be, to miss the Skai event of the decade? Or maybe even the century?"

Louisa's laugh choked in her throat, and she shot another amused glance up at Killik, who was finally smiling, too. "Ka-esh," he muttered, but it sounded almost indulgent. "No, he would not miss it, I ken."

Well, then. Louisa's hopefulness simmered in her chest, and her hand found Killik's, squeezing it tight. Feeling him squeeze back in return, even as his eyes flicked toward the door. Toward where Ulfarr had just come down, his head tilting as he strode toward them.

"Wolf ought to hear this, also," Killik said now, as he signed something toward Ulfarr, and then waved him into a chair. "Mayhap you could explain this again, Rosa?"

It was surprisingly polite, coming from Killik, and Ulfarr looked surprised, too—but he willingly sat, and glanced warily between them. While Rosa drew in a breath, straightened her notes, and then—to Louisa's ever-rising astonishment—launched into an in-depth presentation of the plan. Speaking with startling clarity and enthusiasm, and even creating impromptu charts and diagrams as she went.

By the end of it, Ulfarr looked thoroughly stunned,

gazing blankly at Rosa, and then at Louisa, and then at Killik, who had finally sunk himself into a chair. "And you wish for this, pup?" Ulfarr asked. "You should welcome this, for us?"

Killik's throat convulsed, but he twitched a brief, decisive nod. "Ach, Wolf," he said. "I would."

Ulfarr nodded too, and his gaze slid back toward Louisa. "And you, Louisa?" he asked, slower. "This Summit would be on your land. It would show you as an ally to orcs, far beyond all the rest you have yet done. It may worsen this strife from your neighbour, and make you more of a target for him. Or mayhap for other lords and powerful humans, also."

Right. Louisa grimaced, because he wasn't wrong about that—and he reached across the table, and grasped her hand in his. "You have already done so much for us, Louisa," he said. "For our kin, and for the camp, and for—for me. I do not wish to ask you to bear more risk or pain or fear on our behalf—or to draw this risk upon the kin you care for. This is your land, and your home, and you do not owe us this—or aught else. You do *not*."

Louisa swallowed, searching Ulfarr's eyes, feeling that gentle caress of his fingers on her hand. "So if you do not fully wish for this, Louisa," he continued, "I do not, either. Your welfare and your safety are of the utmost worth to us, and no matter what you choose upon this, we shall uphold you, with all our strength."

He glanced toward Killik, as if including him in that statement, too—and though Louisa couldn't quite read Killik's expression, he gave a curt nod. And then raised his brows toward her, as if saying, *So? What do you decide?*

And as Louisa blinked between them, it again felt like it had at the mountain, when she'd prayed to Skai-kesh. When that certainty, that peace, had settled itself upon her, and sunk deep into her bones. Ulfarr was considering her needs, and asking her permission, and accepting her choice. He was recognizing her ownership of her land, and her responsibilities toward her people. And he was offering to uphold her and her choices. To share his strength with her. To face this with her.

And Louisa—wanted to face this. She wanted to support the camp. She wanted to keep helping the people Lord Scall had harmed. She wanted to keep making amends. Seeking hope, and healing, and peace.

And maybe—she shot another look at Killik—she wanted to keep proving it, too. She wanted to stand tall with the Wolf of the Skai. And maybe—maybe with his favourite pup, too.

So she squeezed Ulfarr's hand, and drew in breath from the earth. Drew in that strength, that hope, that... peace. Hers.

"Yes," she said, without a trace of hesitation in her voice. "Let's do it."

46

They stayed up late into the night, intensively discussing their plans for the Skai Summit. First working through a draft schedule, and then priorities for safety and security, and finally, a list of possible activities, games, and events.

"What kinds of games and activities would you consider traditionally Skai?" Rosa asked Ulfarr and Killik, as her quill raced across what must have been her dozenth sheet of paper. "Something your fathers would have done, maybe? Or their fathers?"

Killik and Ulfarr exchanged a thoughtful look, and it was Ulfarr who spoke first. "Knife-throwing, and tracking, and sparring-matches, always," he said slowly. "Any Skai gathering ought to have a sparring tournament. But"—he grimaced—"we should not wish to frighten the humans with blood or wounds, either."

But Killik's mouth pursed, his head tilting. "Unless we could gain a healer for the Summit. A Skai healer, mayhap."

"Wait, there are Skai healers?" Rosa cut in, her voice sharp. "Who? Where?"

Killik shook his head, and twitched a wry half-smile.

"Only one," he said, "up in the north. Though we may regret inviting him, I ken."

But Rosa was already writing it down, and frowning irritably between them. "What else?" she demanded. "What other Skai secrets are you keeping from us?"

Ulfarr was still looking thoughtful, his fingers drumming on the table. "I have not seen rope-walking since I was an orcling," he said, with a wry glance toward Killik. "But I should like to see you try this, pup. And do you recall the *hirthskalds* who once ran in Sichfrith's pack?"

Killik cracked a bright, sudden laugh, his eyes glinting on Ulfarr's face. "Ach, and their wild tales," he replied. "And how they sought to best each other with their drums and *flyting*! They were as fierce as any warrior, I ken."

Ulfarr was grinning now too, and his hand dropped to grip Killik's knee under the table. "I should like to see you try this, also," he said. "You and Louisa together, mayhap."

Louisa's brows snapped up, and Killik angled a brief, lingering glance toward her, as though he might have been considering it—while Rosa frantically took notes, her mouth set thin. "I have *never heard of this before*," she said, sounding scandalized by this fact. "And you *will* do it, Killik. And then explain to me all about it!"

Killik rolled his eyes at her, but didn't actually argue, either. "We could also show forging, and rope braiding, and rope swinging," he added. "And what about honey hunting? I yet remember my father climbing to the treetops with a pole and a basket."

Rosa's breath caught, and she scribbled even faster. "Brilliant," she said breathlessly. "This is an excellent list, thank you. And"—she shot a piercing glance between Killik and Ulfarr—"you'll also tailor some of these activities for orclings and children, right? So you can both lead some classes during the Summit, too?"

Ulfarr blinked, while Killik's brow furrowed—and before

either of them could speak, Rosa frowned, and waved her quill between them. "Teaching is absolutely an extensive Skai skill, whether you realize it or not," she said flatly. "And the Summit is the perfect time to showcase that, and maybe also to start advertising for your school, too. Because you *are* going to start a school here, aren't you? A satellite for the mountain's school, perhaps?"

Wait. Killik and Ulfarr were going to start a school? *Here*? But when Louisa gaped between them, they weren't at all arguing this, just exchanging a long, meaningful look. "Ach, mayhap, if Louisa would welcome this," Ulfarr replied carefully, with a glance toward her. "The orclings here ought to have a school, so they do not fall behind. But we do not yet have a safe place we can devote to this."

He cast a rueful look across the room, to where a few telltale moans and slaps were emanating from the beds beyond the curtain. While Killik gave a disgruntled huff, and pointed his dagger toward Rosa. "We *wished* to dig more rooms and tunnels here for this," he snapped, "but the Ka-esh have left us to moulder at the bottom of their fool *list*!"

Rosa sniffed and kept writing, seemingly unconcerned. "I told you, I have no control over that list," she replied primly. "And you ought to have a better sense of your school's potential attendance before you start sourcing a venue anyway—especially since you might have human children wanting to attend, too! Now, I've added classes to our list, so"—she raised her brows between Killik and Ulfarr—"is there anything else you can think of to add? Or anyone else we ought to consult with?"

Ulfarr and Killik exchanged another glance, and finally Ulfarr took a breath, squared his shoulders. "I should yet wish to ask—Simon," he said slowly. "Not only upon these games, and the school—but whether he and Maria would welcome this Summit at all. I have vowed to honour and serve them, and I should never wish them to see this as a stand from me against them."

No one argued this, though neither Rosa nor Killik looked pleased about it, either. "I can write him a letter, I suppose," Rosa replied, without enthusiasm, as she pulled out a fresh sheet of paper. "Can you have it sent to him as soon as possible? We don't have much time to prepare all this."

Ulfarr nodded, while Killik huffed a sigh, and swiped the sheet of paper out from under Rosa's nose. "*We* shall write the letter," he said, as he plunked the paper in front of Louisa. "Make it as pretty as you can, woman."

Louisa blinked at him, as something simmered in her belly—Killik wanted her to write the letter, on their behalf? But yes, he was watching, waiting, his brows raised—so she nodded, and took Rosa's proffered quill. And then began writing, doing her damnedest to make the letter as clear, compelling, and respectful as she possibly could.

We truly feel this event would honour and celebrate Skai culture, she wrote, *while also helping to protect the camp, and build connections with the broader community. We want to offer Skai an opportunity to rest and play and learn together, while also meeting new friends and possible mates. And if you would welcome it*—she shot a furtive look at Killik, but wrote it anyway—*we would be delighted to host you as our guests of honour.*

But once the letter was done, both Rosa and Ulfarr praised it, and even Killik looked grimly satisfied. "Igull is on the mountain run tonight," he told Ulfarr, as he passed the sealed letter toward him. "Have him wait for Simon's reply, and bring it back tomorrow, ach?"

Ulfarr nodded, and clasped both Killik and Louisa's shoulders before striding out of the room. While Rosa began gathering up her papers, a satisfied smile on her mouth.

"Excellent work," she said. "Now, tomorrow we'll need to start preparing advertisements and invitations, and organizing security, and planning distribution and outreach. And also"—she narrowed her eyes at Killik—"this doesn't mean you can stop your plans for updating and preparing your camp, either. I'd also suggest you arrange a special place for Simon and Maria to stay when they visit, too. Something large enough for them and their sons."

Killik gave a deep, exasperated groan—as well he might, since Rosa and her family were now staying in the *kofi* they'd originally planned for Simon and Maria. "And also," Rosa continued, with relish, "we'll need to decorate! And some signage would be helpful, don't you think? And"—she wrinkled her nose at John-Ka, who was still watching her with fond approval—"I have a thought about digging those tunnels. None of us will like it, though."

On that ominous note, she swept up her papers, and sailed from the room, with John-Ka close behind her. Leaving Louisa and Killik alone at the table, looking at each other, while those gasps and grunts kept filtering from beyond the curtain. But it was late, and the room was otherwise empty, and Killik slowly stretched in his chair, his eyes glittering on Louisa's face, and then...

He leapt up, and grabbed her. Gripping her waist, hoisting her up bodily onto the table, so he could... so he could start *shoving up her skirts.*

"Killik!" Louisa hissed, darting a look toward the door, where anyone could walk in at any moment. "What the hell are you *doing!*"

She should have expected that derisive roll of Killik's eyes, the mocking scoff in his throat. "Climbing a tree," he replied. "Playing a lute. Churning butter."

Louisa's cursed mouth twitched, even as she sputtered an incoherent protest back toward him. While he just kept prodding her upper body back to lie on the table, so he could crowd himself between her legs, oh gods...

"I am finally gaining some relief," he snapped, as he snatched his dagger out of his hair, and flipped it in his fingers. "For thanks to *you*, I have borne naught but toil and pain all this eve! Ka-esh come to stay! Classes for *human* younglings! Another new *kofi*! A school! *Decorations*! And a *Skai Summit for Rehabilitation, Reconciliation, and Rejuvenation*!"

His voice was viciously sharp, but it wasn't at all matched by the bright, gleaming glint in his eyes. As if he... didn't really mind. He was only... barking at her. Seeking to play.

"You are such an ungrateful cockroach!" Louisa managed, between her already-gasping breaths. "We're just trying to help you! And help your camp! And—"

Her voice wrenched into a yelp, because Killik had snapped his dagger toward her mouth, and... thrust its blade between her *teeth*. Not sharp, not painful, only the blunt length of it pressing long against her mouth, just enough to stop her from speaking.

"I said, I wish for *relief*," Killik drawled, his eyes glittering, as his hand reached down to the front of her dress, and began yanking it open. "And peace, and *quiet*. Not a wild Skai harpy wailing yet more demands at me!"

Louisa sputtered and glared at him, gritted her teeth against that dagger—and she should have just spat it out, thrown it straight back at him, but she didn't. She didn't, and Killik kept smirking at her as he grasped that chain belt on her dress, and drew it out with a flourish.

"So you shall *behave* for once, woman," he drawled, as he swiped for her arm, and thrust it down to the table's hard wood above her head. "And you shall *learn*."

Oh, gods, he wasn't doing this, shoving her other arm up over her head alongside the first—and then wrapping that chain swiftly around her wrists. Binding them close together, and then deftly swinging the chain's other end down around the table leg, and—trapping her there. Trapping Louisa here, on this table, in this public room, with a dagger between her teeth, and with—she shot a chagrined glance downwards—her entire front now bared for his cool, glinting eyes. Except for that leather loincloth, hanging over where her legs were now spread around his hips...

But with an easy flick of Killik's hand, the loincloth flipped up, too. While his other hand yanked down his own trousers, revealing the sudden, shocking sight of his rigid leaking cock. Waiting, hovering, jutting straight out toward her...

"Better," Killik breathed, his eyes gleaming on the sight. "Now open wide, woman."

Oh, hell. And Louisa should have argued, or made some effort to extract herself—right? But instead, she was... nodding. Obeying. Opening her thighs wider, waiting, breaths gasping and heart pounding, as Killik leaned forward, lined them up, and then plunged himself fast and deep inside.

Louisa's moan rang through the room, her body convulsing and clamping against Killik's jabbing strength inside her—but he hadn't betrayed even a gasp, and was already drawing out again. And then snapping back inside, hard enough to make her teeth clack on the dagger, her breasts jiggling for his cool watching eyes.

"Even better," Killik drawled, as he drew out again, and sank back inside. "You are so much sweeter, woman, when you are stuck silent and shivering upon a strong Skai prick."

Louisa growled and glared at him, but still didn't spit out the dagger, and he smirked at her as he kept plunging, faster and harder, his bollocks slapping, the slick sounds rising between them. And Louisa's groans were rising too, thick with longing and craving and frustration, and curse him, Killik was enjoying this. He was doing this on purpose, making a damned show of her, his smug eyes sliding sideways, toward—

Ulfarr. Ulfarr, standing just inside the common-room's door, and staring at them. His lips parting as his eyes swept over Louisa's chained hands, her blocked mouth, her juddering jostling breasts, and Killik still pounding away between her legs.

"Come mark this, Wolf," Killik said, without even a catch in his voice, or a break in his rhythm. "She has finally stopped with the ceaseless demands, ach?"

Ulfarr's mouth twitched, and he strode over toward them, his hand adjusting the front of his trousers. "*Killik*," he said, as he came to stand behind him, his eyes still raking up and down Louisa's chained, jiggling body. "She may yet wish to speak."

His tone was admonishing, even disapproving, but it didn't at all reflect the hungry glitter in his eyes, the brush of his black tongue against his lips. While Killik rolled his eyes, and then reached and snatched the dagger from Louisa's mouth. "Ach, then, woman?" he demanded. "Aught to say?"

Louisa gulped for air, tugged at the chain, and glared up at Killik's face. "Such a tyrant," she gasped at him. "Such an arrogant, belligerent *degenerate*, so obsessed with your damned show—"

But Killik promptly shoved the blade back in place between her lips, and gave Ulfarr a smug, placid smile. "See?" he said. "Much better to shut her up, you ken."

Louisa growled back at him through the dagger, and Ulfarr's tongue again brushed his lips, his eager eyes flicking back and forth between them. As if he liked this, wanted more of this, and Killik's grin quirked higher as he searched Louisa's flushed face.

"And if she thinks this is *degenerate*, Wolf," he drawled, "I ken she needs another lesson, ach? And a better seat in my show."

Wait, wait, what did he mean, but he was slowly drawing out again, bobbing fully free of her with a slick squelch. And then he gripped both hands at Louisa's thighs, and shoved them upwards, backwards, toward her chest. So his glistening, dripping length could slide further down her slippery open crease, lower and lower, until...

Louisa choked, her body quaking all over, her eyes jolting wide—but Killik only raised his brows, and kept giving her that cool, challenging smile. Waiting for her to refuse this, perhaps, to spit out his dagger and demand he release her. To tell him she would never allow him to do such a thing, let alone where anyone might walk in and see it. And perhaps more importantly, where Ulfarr would see it...

But when Louisa darted a glance at Ulfarr, his eyes were still warm, glittering, approving. As if he wanted this, too—and he'd even shifted closer, so he could stroke his hand against her hot sweaty cheek. "Should you ever need it, Louisa," he murmured, "this is our sign to stop."

He'd raised his other hand, fingers outstretched, and flicked it sideways. A small movement, but an obvious one, and one that could still be used with bound wrists, too. And Ulfarr was telling Louisa this, because Ulfarr wanted this— and gods, yes, she wanted it too. Enough that she nodded at him, at Killik, and then made that circling motion with her hand, instead. Saying, *Keep going.*

Killik's grin curved higher, and yes, he was gently prodding into Louisa now, into that place where even Lord Scall had never once touched her. And it felt so foreign, so strange, Killik's hard tip seeking into her tight rim, and—oh—maybe even sinking a little inside. Because they were both so wet and slick already, and she could feel more of that thick fluid sputtering out of him, seeping its way inside her, oh...

"Careful, pup," murmured Ulfarr's low voice, making

Louisa's heart skip—and his glinting eyes were intently watching this, one hand again adjusting the bulge in his own trousers, as his other hand stroked Killik's back. "Be gentle, and *slow*. Grant her as much seed as you can, to ease the way."

Fuck. Even his voice twisted Louisa's hunger harder, surging it deeper into her belly. And perhaps Killik felt it too, because instead of making some snide comment in return, he only nodded, and shifted his grip on Louisa's thighs. So he could drop one hand down to his cock, and begin... pumping. Milking himself with firm, steady strokes, and Louisa could feel his gently invading tip shuddering against her, squeezing out more of that slickness inside her, so he could sink a little deeper, please, yes, *please*.

His eyes stayed intent on what he was doing, on his body slowly, slowly pressing into her, sinking deeper and deeper, opening her wider and wider. He was doing this, *Louisa* was doing this, craving this, needing this. She was bound and gasping and arching on a table, in public, as an orc coolly, casually fed himself into her most secret place, skewering her whole upon him, while a second orc watched, and *approved*.

"Breathe, Louisa," Ulfarr murmured, as his warm hand slid down, and curved against one of her heaving breasts. "Seek to be soft for my pup, and open."

Right, right, and somehow Louisa nodded, and obliged. Dragging in a deep, desperate breath, drawing up the strength of the table beneath her, willing her body to relax, to welcome this. To welcome Killik's hard intruding flesh, still pressing in breath by breath, pushing his way through her resistance, slower, and slower, deeper and deeper, until...

She arched and groaned as Killik's skin met hers, his hips jutted tight against her arse. Because he was inside her, he was all the way inside her, his cock straining and pulsing, his eyes hazy and hungry on her face. "Ach, thus, woman," he breathed. "And now, you need another strong Skai ploughing, I ken."

Louisa gasped through his dagger and glared at him, even as her body powerfully clamped against his invading strength—and she didn't miss Killik's low hiss through his teeth, his cock's long, sustained spasm inside her. While Ulfarr hissed too, his eyes angling narrow and flinty toward Killik's face. "I said, *gentle*, pup," Ulfarr ordered, as his own hand carefully stroked Louisa's peaked nipple. "And guide her through this with you, also. You shall *not* harm her."

Killik betrayed another hard shudder inside her, but again, he didn't argue, or protest. And instead, he even bowed his head toward Ulfarr, and swiftly signed something that might have been, *I understand, Wolf*, before meeting Louisa's eyes again.

"Keep breathing, woman," Killik said, low, as he slowly began sliding himself out again. "Follow my breaths. Draw up strength from my strong Skai prick inside you."

Oh, gods, he wanted Louisa to draw strength from *that*. And it was absurd, ridiculous, but somehow—somehow— she was doing it. Following Killik's breaths, feeling that power of him still inside her—and when she clamped tight, as if wanting to stop him from pulling out any further, he obliged, and waited. Waited, holding her gaze as he let her clutch him, feel him, pull that strength from him.

And when her bound hand jerked another sign at him—*keep going*—Killik obliged with that, too. Sliding slow and careful back into her, breath by breath, and then waiting there, buried all the way, while she shuddered and grasped against him, drew up his air and his strength, the truth of his body within her, filling her, making her his, oh.

Ulfarr was still watching it, the warm approval flashing in his eyes, as his hand kept stroking Louisa's jiggling breasts. All of it so strong, so painfully intimate, so close and raw it ached. Killik's breaths guiding, Ulfarr's hand caressing, as Killik's cock just kept on plundering, easing in and out, so slow and steady, and so thoroughly, desperately devastating. She needed this so much, craved him so much, please...

And did Killik know it, could he see it, just looking at her with those half-lidded eyes as he ground himself deeper, pressing, straining, gouging—but fuck, now he was groaning, stiffening, hissing hoarse and low. And suddenly she could feel his hot fluid flowing, flooding up into her, deeper and deeper, while he quaked and spasmed and crumpled inside her, oh gods, oh *gods*...

And for a breath, as Louisa gasped and shuddered and took it, there was an unthinkable, appalling urge to—to weep. To weep, and to spit out that dagger, so she could beg him to keep going, to give her more. And maybe even to ask if she'd proven it, if he would stay, he would forget the three nights. Or was it just two now, *no*...

But Killik's eyes had already dropped from hers, holding on the sight of their joined-together bodies. On where he was now prodding in and out a little, giving a probing little circle inside her, making her gasp and twitch with every slight movement.

"I ken you could now try a turn, Wolf," he said toward Ulfarr, smooth and almost casual. "She is soft and wet, and there is not a trace of pain in her scent."

Oh. Oh, sweet gods, he wouldn't, they wouldn't. But something flared in Ulfarr's eyes, something damnably like eagerness—and he reached up, and carefully plucked the dagger from Louisa's mouth. "Is this good for you also, Louisa?" he murmured, as he absently slid the dagger back into Killik's topknot. "Might you wish to try more?"

Louisa's groan choked out on its own, her head rapidly nodding. "Yes," she gulped. "Yes, Ulfarr, please."

The warmth and the approval flashed across Ulfarr's eyes, his hand gently caressing her face. And then he reached down, loosened his belt, and drew out his huge, dripping cock.

Damn. It looked even more massive than Louisa remembered, and he wanted to put it—*there.* And gods, wait, was this even physically possible? Surely it wasn't, not even with Killik still there inside her, and circling a little stronger, as if opening her up more, oh...

"Ach, she longs for this, Wolf," Killik drawled, his eyes glittering on her face. "Longs to prove she can handle the most powerful seat in my show."

Louisa groaned again, and valiantly attempted a glare up toward him. "And then it's your turn, you great snake," she managed, through her shaky breaths. "We'll finally get to see you impaled on your own damned dagger."

Killik's scoff was loud and instant, but there was no denying the sudden shudder of his cock inside her. While a low, husky groan rumbled from Ulfarr beside him, and oh, Ulfarr was stroking his own exposed length now, his hand sliding smooth and brazen, pumping out an ever-lengthening string of glossy white. And his eyes darting between Killik and Louisa looked hopeful, even reverent, as he leaned sideways, and drew in a long, deep breath against Killik's hair.

Killik rolled his eyes back toward him, but he didn't actually protest, and finally he began drawing out of Louisa, away. The feeling so strong, so strange, and she gasped as he slipped free with a soft wet sound. Leaving her empty, and—and *open.* So open, damn it, her body lax and slack and fully on display, with Killik's hot seed now seeping out from inside her...

Killik and Ulfarr were both looking, blatantly watching it, and oh, Killik even grasped a familiar hand to Ulfarr's straining shaft, drawing him closer toward Louisa, toward *there.* Until that dripping-wet head just gently brushed against her, and both Louisa and Ulfarr groaned at once, as

Killik coolly began stroking. Pumping out more of Ulfarr's seed onto her, into her, as Ulfarr settled a little closer, and Louisa felt the full dizzying breadth of his slick nudging cock, oh gods.

"You are sure, Louisa?" Ulfarr murmured, with a searching glance at her face. "You yet wish for this?"

Even the question stirred something, flaring it stark in Louisa's chest. He was again asking, making sure it was her choice—and she was facing this, she was speaking truth, she was proving this. Hers.

"Gods, yes," she gasped. "Please, Ulfarr. Please, give this to me."

But there was no judgement in Ulfarr's eyes, only relief, and hot hungry approval, and maybe another glimmer of that reverence. "I shall be honoured to grant you this, Louisa," he murmured, as he again reached up, and stroked her sweaty face. "And you shall again follow my pup's good guidance amidst this, ach? And speak or sign to us of any pain?"

Louisa's nod was again rapid, fervent, and oh, the way Ulfarr kept looking at her, as his huge hardness nudged closer, deeper. Not pushing, not demanding, just letting her feel him there, feel the warmth and the power of him, that hot fluid still steadily pulsing out from inside him...

"Breathe with me, woman," came Killik's low order, darting Louisa's eyes back toward him. "Draw up from Wolf's great strength within you."

Right, that again, and yes, yes, she would. Feel Ulfarr's strength, welcome him, draw from him, let him come a little closer, a little deeper...

"Good," Killik said, his eyes glinting as they flicked downwards, and then back up again. "More. *Breathe.* In, and out."

His shoulders purposefully rose and fell as he spoke, making it easy for Louisa to follow, and she was suddenly, frantically grateful to him, nodding as she followed, in, and out. And in, and out, again, and again, softening, opening, welcoming that prodding warmth, willing herself to let it in...

She moaned as it pressed a little harder, opening her wider, but Killik was still here, still holding her eyes, still breathing in and out. "Good," he said again. "He feels good, ach?"

Louisa jerked another nod, her eyes darting to Ulfarr's flushed, reverent face. Because yes, yes, he always felt so good, always—but somehow, doing this here like this together, while Killik watched, it was more than just pleasure. It was something even deeper, raw and rippling and... right. She was safe. She was alive. She was whole.

She was theirs, and they were hers.

And with another desperate, dragging breath, Louisa bore down, and... welcomed it. Welcomed the full, impossible girth of that gently prodding head, the slow inexorable stretch of it, opening her wider and wider around it. Until she was taut and straining, quivering and gasping at the shocking tightness of it, the whispering promise of pain—but oh, a cool touch of fingers to her cheek, tilting her head, drawing her eyes back to his face. Killik's face, Killik's glittering eyes, Killik's steady, deliberate breaths.

"More," he murmured. "Draw up the Wolf of the Skai's great strength. Make this yours."

Hers. And yes, this was hers, she wanted this, she needed this. And she would draw up that strength, drink up its stretch and its burn, its power and its safety. She would open more, welcome more, feel it fully spreading her, breaching her, ramming its way inside her, oh...

She arched and cried out at the truth of it, the utter unreality of it, because Ulfarr was—inside her. *Inside* her. And his eyes were blazing, his broad shoulders heaving, his huge invading flesh spasming, juddering even fuller. Quaking her whole body upon it, because oh, they were fully locked together, stuck together, trapped. Hers.

"Good," came Killik's low, heated purr, and oh, he was truly smiling at her, without even a whisper of mockery in his eyes. "Now keep breathing, and swallow him deeper, whilst I make you dance."

Louisa nodded again, swift and urgent, dragging in another breath—and yes, yes, Killik's clever fingers were now slipping downwards, sliding against her slick, open, spasming crease. Stroking it, oh gods, teasing it, while she bucked and cried out, her taut invaded body clamping on Ulfarr's stabbing strength, and then... softening. Opening. Taking more.

"Ach," Ulfarr groaned, his eyes rolling back, and oh, Killik's smirk only drew higher, his playing fingers delving a little deeper. Scattering out more impossible, overwhelming sensation, shivering Louisa all over, gripping her harder against Ulfarr, swallowing him deeper, oh...

"Ach, dance for us, woman," Killik breathed, heavy and hot, as his fingers kept taunting, playing, stroking. "Show us how hungry you are for my wolf's perfect Skai prick. Show us how you quake and squeal for him. How deeply you long for him, and his strong Skai seed."

It was too much, so much, consuming Louisa from the inside out, but she was still nodding, yes, yes, as her stretched, burning, overfilled body writhed and shouted, her arms straining against the chain. "Yes," she moaned, helpless, lost. "Yes, Wolf, yes, Killik, oh gods, *please.*"

It didn't make sense, nothing made sense, nothing but the power and the pleasure plundering her, consuming her, wrenching her inside out. And Killik's stroking hand, his sinking fingers, pressing even deeper, his low voice crooning, taunting, in her ear. "Keep begging, woman. Beg for my wolf's power, and his seed."

Yes, yes, Louisa's trapped body bucking and dragging for air, her eyes frenzied on Ulfarr's flushed, stunned-looking face. "Please," she gasped. "Please, Wolf, grant me your power, and your seed. I need it, I need this, I need *you.*"

And fuck, fuck, Ulfarr was staggering too, his groan rising to almost a roar—and then he was breaking, bellowing, as his strength inside her shuddered, and sprayed. Surging out its molten seed in burst after burst, flowing into where it already felt so full from Killik, but there was still more, pulsing and squeezing and filling, finding room, flooding her with both of them, hers, hers, hers...

And it was that certainty that finally wrenched Louisa to the edge, to the dazzling shimmering height—and then it all crashed down in furious flashing torrents. Clamping her against Killik and Ulfarr again and again and again, wrenching them tighter and tighter together, wringing out more of that hot sweet seed, drawing up their strength, making it her own. Hers.

The truth of it crackled and shimmered and swayed, spinning the room around them, and for a brief, beautiful moment, there was only peace. Only certainty, and contentment, and that same quiet, whispering rightness. *Hers.*

It was Killik who shifted first, his hand snatching away from her, while Ulfarr just stayed there, breathing hard, as his body slowly softened inside her. His eyes gone hazy and hooded, his lips parted, his cheeks deeply flushed. "I—I th-thank you, Louisa," he stammered, his voice rough. "You are—this was—"

Louisa swallowed and nodded, her smile quivering on her mouth. "So good," she whispered. "So fucking *good,* sweetheart."

Ulfarr's eyes fluttered as he nodded back, his groan rumbling low from his throat. "Ach," he rasped. "You are so—*right,* Louisa. So fierce, and so true. So—so *Skai.*"

So Skai. It sounded grateful, almost worshipful, hovering there between them—but then Ulfarr's eyes flared with unease, with panic, as they darted toward—toward Killik.

Toward where Killik's expression was carefully distant again, his hand flipping a dagger back out of his hair.

"Ach, she is Skai," he said, clipped. "You ken I would bring you a simpering Grisk? Or a bossy, nattering, vexing Ka-esh?"

He shot a baleful look toward the door, his mouth twisting with genuine, bitter distaste. Enough that Louisa suddenly seemed caught in it, blinking up at Killik's face. He'd complained about the Ka-esh so often, more than almost anything else...

And maybe it was the lingering contentment, or Ulfarr's half-hard strength still within her, or that still-whispering truth. *Hers.* But somehow, Louisa drew in a breath, met Killik's eyes, and finally just... asked. "What do you have against the Ka-esh, anyway? What did... what did they do to you?"

Because there had to be something, right? Killik could be petty, yes, and vindictive, and cold—but he always had a reason for what he did, too. And even if he was frowning, now, holding his gaze purposefully away from her, Louisa could still perhaps follow it, because so many of Killik's reasons seemed to have to do with...

Her eyes trailed back toward Ulfarr, to where his face looked more drawn than before, his swallow spasming in his throat. "I... near had a mate, once," he said, very quiet. "But she... left me. For a Ka-esh."

Oh. The sympathy stabbed through Louisa's chest, together with the swirling comprehension—and a stark, rising disbelief. "But—why?" she demanded. "How could she possibly have left *you*, sweetheart? What the hell was she thinking?"

Too late, she winced, and clamped her fool mouth shut. But damn it, she'd said it, and now Ulfarr was staring at her, his eyes flaring strange and intent. While beside him, Killik's lips pursed, and he gave a firm clap to Ulfarr's shoulder.

"Ach, just thus, woman," he said flatly. "And just as I have told him, again and again."

But Ulfarr grimaced, and shook his head. "The blame was not hers," he said. "I was oft... burdened, back then, and heartsick, and wrathful. And she did not wish to bear a rut to become my mate, also."

Right. The rut. The... sharing. And Louisa's still-rising sympathy caught, stuttered, because yes, that was still an appalling requirement to put on a woman, especially that possibility of bearing another orc's son...

But Killik's snort was sharp, scornful, and his dagger waved irritably at Ulfarr's chest. "You spoke not a single harsh word to that fool woman," he snapped. "You doted upon her, just as you doted upon your pack. And in this rut, you should have lavished her with pleasure, until she was screaming for more—and you should have made sure she bore your son, also!"

Louisa blinked blankly between them, because how could any orc have made sure of such a thing—but Killik had already followed the question, his gaze flicking toward her face. "There are ways," he said, clipped. "Ach, lest the orc in charge has weakened seed, as long as he goes first—and takes his time and care upon this—the son shall always be his."

Oh. The vision of Ulfarr taking time and care upon another woman, making sure to grant her his son, was coiling in Louisa's belly, burning tight in her throat, oh gods. And she was not going to weep over something so foolish, she was not...

"Well," she said, with a wavering smile at Ulfarr's still-haggard face. "She still would have been a very lucky woman, then. And"—she swallowed—"I'm sure she's missing you now, sweetheart. And your favourite pup, too."

For a long moment, Ulfarr blinked back toward her, looking blank, almost dazed. And then he slowly bent forward, closer over her, so he could—so he could inhale, his nostrils flaring as he drew in deep. As if he was seeking to prove this, to scent her truth in this...

And oh gods, maybe he thought Louisa was lying, and she pulled in another thick, unsteady breath. "I mean, not to say Killik still isn't an arrogant tyrant," she said, too quickly, "but he does put on a good show, don't you think?"

And curse her, what was she saying, why was she giving Killik this, again—and what was Killik thinking, what was that odd glint in his eyes, flicking from her, to Ulfarr, to her again...

"Ach, I had naught to do with that woman," Killik finally said, his voice flat. "She was Wolf's alone. And *she* would not allow him to touch any others, either. Most of all me."

Oh. Just like Louisa hadn't allowed Ulfarr to touch Killik either, at the start of all this. And then that woman had taken Ulfarr away from Killik, she'd hurt Killik, and then... then she'd turned around and hurt Ulfarr, too. She'd left Ulfarr, and left Killik to pick up the pieces.

"Well, clearly you're both better off, then," Louisa said, a little too sharp. "And to be fair to her, she's probably better off too, because you two probably never would have been able to stay away from each other. You'd have ended up sneaking around in some dark tunnels somewhere, chaining each other up, while she was stuck at home alone and pregnant!"

There was another instant of startled silence, Ulfarr's eyes still blinking with odd intensity on Louisa's face, while Killik huffed a wry chuckle. "Wrong, woman," he replied. "For Wolf does not chain *me* up, ach?"

Louisa laughed too, rolling her eyes at him. "Not yet, you mean," she said, as lightly as she could. "But now that I've kept my part of the bargain"—she gave a shaky nod down toward where she and Ulfarr were still locked together—"we now have a new show to look forward to. The one where *you're* stabbed on this huge dagger of his, and screaming for mercy."

She gave Killik her coolest, most complacent smile, as he scoffed and sputtered, jabbing his dagger toward her face. "You need to *prove* this first, woman," he snapped. "And I told you, a true Skai woman does not just swallow her orc's prick, and sit pretty upon it. She must welcome its rutting, and its good strong ploughing!"

Louisa scoffed back at him, because gods, he was enraging, he was changing the rules to suit him, like the slimy snake he was. And she should be saying all that, demanding Killik keep his part of the bargain, and instead she was only thinking of...

"But," she said, and was that a crack in her voice, "we only have—two nights left. Right?"

Yet more silence followed her voice, falling like a heavy crushing weight, and she couldn't at all follow that look in Killik's eyes, in Ulfarr's eyes. In how they were looking at each other, holding too long, too intent—until Ulfarr's eyes squeezed shut, his head jerking a curt nod.

And blinking up toward him, it occurred to Louisa—for perhaps the first time—that Ulfarr wouldn't defy Killik in this. And even if she had tried to concoct some plan to keep seeing Ulfarr after this, or to steal him away altogether—he wouldn't have done it. He cared about Killik too much, about his family, about Sune.

And maybe Louisa should have been hurt by that, or insulted—but instead it only wrenched the longing deeper. Ulfarr was such a good father. Such a good partner. And she was going to miss him so much, miss them so much, and she wasn't going to weep again, she wasn't—

"Ach, two more nights," Killik finally said, into the taut silence. "Two more nights to show us your mettle, woman. To prove how you dance, how you beg, how you *scream*."

It sounded hard, merciless, almost menacing—but

Killik's eyes were glinting, with a look Louisa knew all too well. And suddenly it caught, clutched, careened through her screeching thoughts.

Because it was—it was still the challenge. Wasn't it? She had two more nights to show him. To prove this.

"Fine, you absolute tyrant," Louisa said, breathless, as the hope pounded through her heart. "Two more nights."

47

That night, Louisa ended up collapsing with Killik and Ulfarr in one of the common-room's beds. Tucking her body close against Ulfarr's solid strength, while Killik sprawled over them both, his dagger still in hand.

But just as she'd been falling asleep, she jolted awake again, staring wide-eyed at Killik's bemused face. "My staff!" she exclaimed. "I completely forgot to tell them I'd be gone so long, and—"

"Naught to fret over, woman," Killik's husky voice cut in, as he gave a gentle tap of his dagger to her back. "I again sent Halthorr to them, and he shall stay, and take good care of them. He swore he would fix your stable roof, also."

Oh. Louisa's smile was swift and relieved, and she even leaned over Ulfarr, and pressed a brief, furtive kiss to Killik's cheek. "Thank you," she murmured. "That was so thoughtful of you. As always."

Killik rolled his eyes and settled back against Ulfarr again, but his warm hand was still on her back, his cool dagger-blade still nudging against her skin. And while it perhaps should have been unnerving, it was instead a cozy, fluttery feeling, easing her quiet and easy into sleep. Two more nights.

The next morning, Louisa joined Killik and Ulfarr for their daily prayers—which, it turned out, they usually did together, crouching beneath a huge oak tree just outside the camp, their hands over their hearts. And while praying to Skai-kesh still felt new to Louisa, and a bit unnatural, it was also a lovely, quiet way to greet the day, breathing in the damp morning air, as the orange sun filtered through the trees.

Afterwards, once Killik and Ulfarr had set to work with Sune on the next new *kofi*, Louisa and Rosa brought up a table to the clearing, and began writing out invitations to their lengthening list of Skai Summit guests. Which included not only anyone at Orc Mountain who wanted to attend, but also specific key leaders, like Jule and her captain mate, and the Skai's Right Hand Drafli and his family. The guest list also included leaders and members at the other Skai camps, and individual Skai living across the realm, Killik's healer among them. And at Rosa's urging, Louisa also personally wrote letters to some of her old friends and contacts in Dusbury, too. People she hadn't stayed in touch with, but who might—perhaps—still be willing to consider a visit.

After the letters, they turned to their plans for advertising the Summit. It turned out that Rosa's kin had hauled a large, heavy hand-press all the way here with them, along with a shocking quantity of ink—meaning that they could start printing and distributing signs and flyers without delay. However, that also meant agreeing on the flyers' messaging, which turned out to more fraught than expected. Especially with Killik—who was still ostensibly working above them on the new *kofi*—apparently also listening to every word, and frequently dropping down to peer disapprovingly over their shoulders.

"No," he snapped, upon seeing Rosa's latest preferred flyer—a drawing of a broadly smiling orc with a rope in his hand, and the headline *Come Swing, Spy, and Play with the Skai!* "No, you vexing Ka-esh. They shall think we either wish to plough them, or hunt them! Or both!"

"Well, it's probably true!" Rosa snapped back, but she crumpled up the draft, and tossed it toward him. "I don't see you coming up with anything better! You haven't even given the camp a *name* yet!"

Killik's mouth pursed, his eyes darting up toward where Ulfarr and Sune were still working on the *kofi* above, together with a few other orcs. "It ought to be the Wolf-Camp," he finally replied. "Even if Wolf cannot stay. And even if Simon does not allow this Summit at all."

Right. Simon. It had almost been easy to ignore that nagging question, while sitting here cheerfully working and chatting together, as the children ran and played around them. But that uncertainty was still hovering, looming over all of it, because yes, they were still waiting on Igull, and that letter they'd sent to Simon the night before. None of this was yet decided, Simon could still say no...

But then, shortly after noon, Igull jogged back into the camp, a broad grin lighting up his face. "The Skai Summit shall soon be upon us!" he announced, as he swiftly signed up toward Killik and Ulfarr in the tree. "With our Enforcer Simon and his kin as our guests of honour!"

A loud, relieved cheer rose through the clearing, and soon it seemed like the entire camp had gathered around their table, talking and asking questions at once. Prompting Killik and Ulfarr to call a camp-wide meeting, during which they presented the entire Summit plan, and began assigning volunteers for each project.

And as Louisa watched Ulfarr lead the meeting in his usual deep, decisive way, while Killik added frequent explanations and the occasional wry joke, it again felt... right, somehow. Right that Killik and Ulfarr should be working together, standing up there together, guiding and supporting their kin. Just the way the camp felt right. Just the way Louisa still felt right, being here. Being... Skai. *Hers.*

That certainty lingered throughout the rest of the evening, which included a delicious supper, courtesy of Thomas' excellent cooking—and then, at Ulfarr's suggestion, Killik and Louisa made a brief trip back to her house. Where they found Halthorr and Joan playing ball in the yard with the children, while Elise and Gladys cheered them on.

It was a promising sight, and once Louisa and Killik had joined in for a round, Louisa sat them all down, and told them about the Summit. And to her vague surprise, none of them seemed overly distressed by the news, even Elise—and Joan actually agreed to attend. Earning a bright, delighted grin from Halthorr, who eagerly promised to serve as her escort—and also, to stay and guard the house until the Summit, too.

Louisa fully expected Elise or Gladys to argue this plan, but Elise only looked away, brushing out her skirts, while Gladys gave a curt nod. And beside Louisa, Killik looked smugly satisfied, and signed something at Halthorr that might have been, *Nice work, brother.*

"Ach, then this is settled," Killik said firmly, out loud. "And Louisa shall come back to the camp, and stay another few nights with us."

What, she would? But Killik had already grasped Louisa's elbow, steering her away toward the camp in the deepening darkness. And perhaps she should have protested, but she only rolled her eyes, and called a cheerful goodbye to her staff over her shoulder. Because again, it felt like part of that promise. That challenge. Two more nights. *Prove this.*

"Wish for another lesson, woman?" Killik abruptly asked, once they'd reached a more open part of the path, where glimmers of moonlight filtered through the trees. "Mayhap you could seek to listen, and find me?"

There was no way Louisa was refusing, not now—and after a few instructions from Killik, soon they were playing an actual game of hide-and-seek together in the dark. With Louisa searching for Killik amidst the trees and the shadows, taking slow, quiet steps as she carefully watched and listened, and even sniffed for traces of his scent in the air.

It made for an eerie, unnerving game, creeping around the silvery forest in the darkness—but Louisa managed to catch Killik several times, and each time, he offered more pointers and guidance. Teaching her to create and follow a pattern as she walked, to keep her eye on the moon, to pay attention to the sounds of birds and insects, too.

By the end of it, Louisa felt hyper-aware of every noise and movement around her, her nerves taut and scraping, her heartbeat thudding in her ears. But she could almost taste Killik's approval in the air, in the brief pat of his hand against her back. "And now, we switch," he murmured. "You run ahead, whilst I cover my eyes and nose, and hunt *you*."

It was doomed to failure, of course, but Louisa gave it her best attempt, creeping as quickly and quietly as she could through the forest. Heading toward the camp, closer and closer, until she was almost, almost there—

When a pair of strong hands grabbed her, and pinned her hard to a tree.

It sent instant panic pounding through Louisa's chest, screeching in her skull—and even a few weeks ago, she would have flinched, flailed, fought to strike or run. But this time, she held herself tall and still, drawing in breath from the tree, from the earth beneath her feet. Staying, holding, listening and waiting, even when a cool, blunt-edged blade gently nudged against her throat. Killik's dagger.

"Caught you," Killik whispered, close and hot in her ear. "Now what shall you do?"

His voice coiled into her groin, flickered behind her eyes, and the forest felt shimmery and strange, impossibly alive in the dark. And it was ludicrous, unthinkable, Louisa should be fighting back, escaping, proving this, but all she wanted was...

She sank to her knees on the moss before him, fumbling for his trousers, yanking them downwards. And yes, Killik was already hard, he was ready, he wanted it too—and he even softly chuckled as he leaned forward and sank himself into her mouth, his blade still just touching cool and menacing at her throat.

"Good," he murmured. "And you remember the sign to stop if you need it, ach?"

Louisa fervently nodded, sucked him deeper—and that was a husky groan, another low, approving laugh. And then he was moving, sliding himself in and out, while Louisa sucked and licked and caressed him. Even as she kept listening, watching, noticing those faint breaks of his breath, the tremors in his thighs, the rising tightness in his bollocks. Urging him closer, closer, please—until he bucked and shot out into her mouth, swarming her with rich molten sweetness, as a smoky growl burned from his throat.

Afterwards, he only drew his blade away and yanked up his trousers, without so much as a thank you—but as they started walking again, his hand slipped down to pat against Louisa's arse. "When we see Wolf," he said, his voice deceptively light, "you go kiss him. On the mouth."

Kiss him, on the mouth. Louisa's breath caught, her head snapping toward him, because she and Ulfarr hadn't once kissed like that yet, had they? And was that—was that because Killik hadn't yet ordered it, and allowed it?

But he was allowing it now, and Louisa swallowed and nodded, her heartbeat again far too loud in her ears. And once they walked into the camp's familiar clearing, with the large fire still crackling in the midst of it, she strode over to where Ulfarr was still working with Igull, securing a ladder onto Simon and Maria's brand-new *kofi*.

"Louisa!" Ulfarr said, with genuine pleasure, as he released the ladder, and slipped a warm hand around her waist. "How was this—"

But his voice broke beneath Louisa's touch, her skittering hands drawing his face down toward her. And her lips, brushing light and careful against his, as his big body jolted to stillness, his breath exhaling sudden and harsh.

Louisa twitched backwards just as quickly, her cheeks already burning—oh, gods, what if he hadn't wanted that?—but Ulfarr's eyes were flashing in the firelight, and his hands drew her close again. And then one hand slid to her cheek, tilting her face up as he bent down, and fitted his mouth to hers.

It was so gentle, and yet so thoroughly overwhelming, just as he always was—and Louisa shuddered and groaned against him, softening, opening. Welcoming the press of his lips, the deep plunder of his hungry seeking tongue, the throbbing rumble of his groan as he tasted her—and surely tasted Killik on her, too. All of it so urgent, so thrilling, that she had to stop herself from clutching at him, climbing him, begging him, please...

And maybe he'd sensed that, gently drawing back from her, away. Though his eyes were still shimmering, his lips wet and full, his tongue slipping brief against them. "You taste," he murmured, "so good, Louisa."

A hard shiver rippled up Louisa's back, and she huffed a short, breathless laugh. "Well, it's all Killik, as I'm sure you know," she said, with a wry glance back at where he was smugly watching from across the clearing. "This was—a message from him, you could say."

Ulfarr laughed too, low and fond, his eyes glinting as they held on Killik's face. "Then mayhap you could grant Killik a message from me," he murmured. "And tell him I wish to see you both underground. Now."

Now. It flashed another shudder up Louisa's spine, another genuine grin across her mouth. And soon she indeed found herself underground in the bustling common-room, kneeling on all fours on one of the beds, and gasping and begging as Ulfarr again fed his huge bulk into her tightest, most tender place.

"Better," Killik purred at her, once Ulfarr was gently easing himself in and out of her, his bollocks lightly slapping with every thrust. "And better for you too, ach, Wolf? It pleases you, to plough this tight rump with your perfect Skai prick?"

Ulfarr replied with a choked, desperate howl, his hips bucking harder, and Killik laughed aloud as the molten liquid poured, flooding into Louisa, filling her from the bottom up. Her own pleasure so close, so close, teetering on the edge—and it only took one brief, careless grind of Killik's hand to hurl her into ecstasy, her body quaking all over as her cries rang through the room.

"Ach, you milk my wolf, woman," Killik crooned, raising his now-slick hand, caressing it at her cheek. "You swallow him whole, and suck his good seed deep into your rump. You honour the Wolf of the Skai in his camp, and in his home. His Wolf-Camp."

Louisa could only gasp and nod, dragging for air, while Ulfarr groaned behind her, his big hands running shaky down her sides. His longing almost strong enough to taste, so heavy with its hunger, its hope. The Wolf of the Skai, in his Wolf-Camp. His home.

It kept whispering in Louisa's thoughts, even once they'd cleaned up again, and sagged back into the bed together. Into a different bed than the night before, since Elgr was currently sprawled on the bed beside them, and grinding himself up into Thomas' sucking mouth.

"Have you ever thought about building a *kofi* of your own here, too, sweetheart?" Louisa asked, snuggling closer into Ulfarr's side. "In case you ever did want the privacy? Or just the same bed two nights in a row?"

Ulfarr slightly stiffened against her, his throat convulsing, even as unmistakable yearning flashed across his eyes. Suggesting that yes, he did want that, very much—but damn it, surely he was thinking again of Simon, and of that impending judgement. Of how he still might not be able to stay here at all.

"Ach, I have told him this, also," Killik cut in, with a firm pat to Ulfarr's chest. "There is a good spot across from Sune I have been eyeing for him. The Wolf of the Skai ought to have a place of his own, most of all when his clan comes to stay, ach?"

Ulfarr's breath heaved in and out, his eyes glimmering on Killik's face. Looking so eager, so damnably hopeful, and Louisa drew up a little, patting her hand beside Killik's on his chest. "And a place for your favourite pup, too," she said lightly. "You two would live there together, wouldn't you?"

She shot a brief, teasing look at Killik, because of course he would welcome that too—but wait. Killik's eyes had frozen, stilled, and Ulfarr stiffened again, too. Both of them now glancing at each other, and away again. As if... as if they didn't want to?

Louisa frowned between them, at where Killik now looked a little hunted, his shoulders hunching, his eyes darting darkly toward her. While Ulfarr was carefully studying Killik, drawing in a breath, and rubbing his hand at his mouth.

"Ach, I ken Killik should rather his own *kofi* also," he said, and though his voice was steady, it sounded a little flat. "One where he does not need to bear my snoring each night, I ken."

Louisa blinked, because Killik clearly didn't care about

Ulfarr's snoring whatsoever—but as she kept glancing between them, it occurred to her that Ulfarr knew that, and he was giving Killik an easy escape. And Killik's shoulders hunched even higher, his eyes now fixed on the wall beyond them, all his previous warmth vanished into a taut, careful distance.

But it didn't make sense, not with everything Louisa knew about them—and damn it, with everything Killik had come out and told her, too. *I shall never cease upholding him. He needs me.*

"Well, I'm sure Killik doesn't mind a bit of snoring," Louisa replied, with a dismissive wave of her hand. "And I'm sure he'd be happy to share with you, too. As long as *you* wanted it, Ulfarr."

She was surely pushing this too hard now, forcing it out between them, but suddenly she needed to know it, too. Needed to know why they kept looking at each other like that, Killik again like a wounded puppy, Ulfarr with dark, empty resignation in his eyes. And for an instant, Louisa was wrenched back to the Ulfarr she'd first met, the one who'd so often looked like this, so sad and lost and alone.

"Ach, it matters naught, woman," Killik cut in, clipped. "After all this, Wolf deserves a place of his own. A place to rest, and gain *peace*."

But when Louisa glanced at Ulfarr again, he didn't look peaceful. He still looked resigned, and weary, and sad. Even as he nodded, and twitched a wan smile toward Killik's frowning face. "And I wish you to have your freedom also, pup," he said. "And to do aught you might wish, without needing to think of me. You have already granted me enough, ach?"

Louisa kept frowning between them, digesting that. Ulfarr wanted to give Killik freedom, to do whatever he wished. And was that a reference to—to Killik's other bedmates? To the way Killik hadn't yet made any commitments of fidelity to Ulfarr, beyond their ten nights? Their nights which were now—Louisa winced—down to just one?

Or—was this just another excuse from Ulfarr? Another easy way out? But no, no, Killik's fears of him couldn't be... true. Could they? Ulfarr would never leave Killik, right? Not even for a son? No. No. He wouldn't.

But neither of them were speaking, now, and Killik only jerked a tight nod, his face still hard, unreadable. While Ulfarr briefly clasped Killik's shoulder, giving him a firm little shake, before drawing in breath, and closing his eyes. Shutting them out, Killik and Louisa both—and now Killik's narrow eyes caught on Louisa's, as his hand swiftly, surreptitiously signed toward her. *No. Stop. Leave it.*

Louisa blinked, but then nodded, and sank back down against Ulfarr. But she could still almost taste Killik's anger, along with Ulfarr's miserable resignation, twitching through his body against her. But they still weren't speaking, and gods, why couldn't they? Why couldn't they just talk about this, and work this out? Especially when they obviously cared for each other so much?

The question followed Louisa into sleep, nagging in her dreams—and it was still there when she awoke again, too. There in Ulfarr's tired, carefully distant eyes, and in the way Killik didn't look at either of them as he shoved out of bed. Stalking away from them, around the curtain, his hands in tight fists at his sides.

"No," came his voice, suddenly sharp and irritable from behind the curtain. "No, no, *no!* We shall not bear this Ka-esh here, digging our tunnels!"

Louisa and Ulfarr exchanged a brief, alarmed glance— and then they both scrambled out of bed at once, Ulfarr tying up his trousers, Louisa straightening her rumpled dress. And when they rushed around the curtain, they found Killik with his hair down, and both his daggers clutched in his hands. Facing off against Rosa, and—a new orc.

And this orc was—different. Different than any orc Louisa had yet met, with his long curved talons, his tall gaunt body, and his pale, chalky skin. And wait, what had first looked like cropped hair on his head actually seemed to be *tattoos*, written across his bare scalp in a tight, unreadable script. And the tattoos also ran down his jaw and neck, beneath his simple grey tunic, and—Louisa's eyes darted downwards—all the way to his pale, long-fingered hands, with those curved, deadly-looking black claws.

"Look, *you* wanted your tunnels dug," Rosa snapped at Killik, her arms folded over her slim chest. "And believe me, I'm not excited about this either—but Filak can dig excellent tunnels, as long as he has the right incentive!"

Killik glowered straight back at Rosa, and at this orc—Filak, apparently—who didn't seem even slightly interested in their argument. And instead, his deep black eyes were gazing toward—Louisa?

"Ach, and what is the *right incentive*?" Killik shot back at Rosa. "We hand him every jewel and metal he can sniff out, across all these lands?"

"Well, it's not like you're using them now!" Rosa countered, her voice rising. "They're just buried there doing nothing, and this is Louisa's land, so it's not even your decision to make! And also—"

She broke off there, because this Filak orc had taken a smooth step closer to Louisa, his eyes glittering intently on her face. And then he snapped up one of those pale clawed hands, and... signed toward her. Signed something—familiar. Something very similar to what Sune had asked her, back on that first day they'd met.

Are you mated? it meant. *To Killik and Ulfarr?*

Louisa blinked, and then shot a surreptitious glance between Killik and Ulfarr—but both of them had gone strangely, suddenly still, so she drew in breath, shook her head. "Er, no," she replied, with a wince. "We're just—friends."

But this Filak didn't show any sign of comprehension, just gazing like that toward her. So she attempted to sign it, too—the word *friend*, and then Killik and Ulfarr's names. And yes, perhaps it had worked, because Filak's mouth curved up, and he signed back something else. First gesturing between himself and Louisa, and then... then jabbing two of his clawed fingers into his closed fist, and thrusting them in and out. As if he meant—good gods, he surely didn't mean—

"No, Filak!" snapped Rosa's indignant voice from beside Louisa. "*Not* appropriate! And good gods, not in front of *them!*"

She furiously signed as she spoke, ending with a wild wave toward Killik and Ulfarr—who, Louisa now realized, were both looking downright murderous. Ulfarr's big body taut and coiled, his brow deeply furrowed, his eyes narrow and hard—while Killik's daggers were now both spinning in his hands, and he gave a sudden laugh, cool and brittle and dangerously light.

"Ach, Wolf, mark this fool Ka-esh, speaking thus before you, in *your* camp," Killik said, his voice easy, almost conversational. "I wonder what tongue he shall scream in, when my blades cut out all his fancy marks? Or how he shall dance as he feeds this earth with his blood?"

"Killik!" Rosa hissed, now sounding deeply scandalized. "He's going to dig your tunnels, so you can't murder him! Just tell him he can't touch Louisa, and offer him the gems! If Louisa's actually even willing to agree, that is, especially after your appalling behaviour!"

Killik snarled and bared his teeth toward Rosa, but now Ulfarr gripped at his arm, holding him still. "No, pup," he said, though his jaw still flexed in his cheek. "We need the tunnels. And"—his dark gaze flicked toward Louisa—"it is Louisa's land, and thus her choice to make. And *only* hers."

Louisa's brain still felt too sluggish, too scrambled, and she drew in a shaky breath. "So you mean," she began, "Filak can dig the tunnels for us—but he wants to keep whatever he finds in them?"

Rosa nodded, and cast a dark look toward him. "And I'll warn you, he won't follow directions, either," she said glumly. "He'll dig straight to wherever the best deposits are. But he seems to think there are some promising options here, and John-Ka says Filak's tunnels are always stable, and follow the natural grains of the stone. Maybe even better"—she winced, wrinkled her nose—"than our engineers can do."

Right. Well. And they did need the tunnels dug, and Louisa hadn't the least idea how to find ore deposits herself, did she? And also, tunnels that followed the grain of the stone sounded... right, somehow. Right in just the same way the camp was right, tucked carefully into the trees, respecting the nature around it.

"Well, let's do it, then," Louisa said, as firmly as she could. "What does he need to get started?"

Rosa winced again, but signed the question to Filak, who gave a slow, sharp-toothed smile, and began pointing out various orcs around the room. Elgr, and Igull, and Ragni and Kori and Fasti, and Ulfarr and Killik too—every Skai currently in sight.

Killik cursed under his breath, and shoved his daggers toward Ulfarr beside him. "No, you will not have all of them," he spat at Filak, signing along with furious gestures from his hands. "You can have *three*. And Wolf will choose them. And no seeking to plough any of them, either, and taint them with your foul Ka-esh scent, or else I will *gut* you!"

With that, he snatched his daggers back from Ulfarr, and stalked off toward the door—and then whirled back around again, and sharply waved toward Louisa. "Come, woman," he snapped. "We shall take Sune and mark your borders, whilst Wolf handles this."

Louisa shot a searching glance toward Ulfarr, and Rosa, too—but Rosa looked deeply relieved, and Ulfarr even gave a curt nod, and an approving pat to Louisa's back. So she nodded too, and after a brief squeeze to Ulfarr's arm, she ran to follow Killik outside for the border-marking project.

It was one of the many Skai Summit preparation tasks on their list, to ensure that no guests accidentally wandered onto Rikard's land. And while it should have been an enjoyable way to spend a morning, tromping through the forest with Killik and Sune, tying strips of cloth to stakes and trees, Louisa could still feel Killik's anger, and his frustration. Perhaps not only about Filak and his tunnel-digging, but perhaps about the night before, too. About how Ulfarr hadn't wanted to live with him.

But Louisa couldn't dare bring it up again, not with Sune here listening—so she spent most of the time talking with Sune instead. Asking how he was enjoying his new *kofi*, and what kinds of activities he liked to do with his friends, and whether he'd like to try riding her horses again. And when he showed genuine interest at that, Louisa told him he was welcome at her stable whenever he pleased, and only to make sure he checked in with Joan first.

That flashed a smile across Sune's face, and he shot a hopeful glance toward Killik—who nodded, and signed back. His expression slightly softening, for perhaps the first time that morning—so Louisa then asked him if he'd ever ridden a horse, either. Which apparently he had, but then he'd tried standing on its back to reach a tree, and had knocked himself out on a branch, and knocked off a dozen apples, besides.

It was a ridiculous tale, perhaps told mostly for Sune's amusement—but by the end of it, both Killik and Sune were laughing, and cheerfully signing at one another. And as

Louisa watched them, and did her best to keep up, there was again that whispering sense of... rightness. Of... hope. They could face this. They could do this. They could get through this Summit, and Killik and Ulfarr would work this out, and...

And then Killik whirled around and away from them, shoving Sune behind him, and whipping both his daggers from his hair. His gaze fixed narrow and intent on the west, on the line of forest across that small clearing, and...

It was Rikard.

48

Rikard was here. Again. Interrupting yet another lovely moment with his vermin self, this time seated astride a cantering horse that was far too large for him.

"Louisa!" he called as he dismounted, and tied the horse to a nearby tree. "What the hell is *this*?"

This. He'd thrust a hand into his pocket, and it came out clutching—oh. A rumpled, familiar-looking sheet of paper, with large block letters, and a clever drawing of a tree house.

EXPERIENCE A DAY IN AN ORC CAMP! it proclaimed. *Bring your friends and family for games, activities, workshops, snacks, stories, and prizes. Plus, explore tunnels and tree-houses, cheer in an orc tournament, and climb high for honey! Fun for all ages!*

It was the flyer they'd begun printing and distributing the day before, with the text they'd all finally agreed upon. And at Rosa's suggestion, Louisa had reluctantly agreed to have one delivered to Rikard, with a personal written invitation for him to attend. In foolish hopes that perhaps it was a kind neighbourly gesture, or at least a fair warning, if nothing else.

But predictably, Rikard only looked enraged, his eyes goggling, his hand furiously waving the flyer in midair. "Answer me, Louisa!" he demanded. "What the hell is this?!"

Louisa's irritation was already far too close, and she couldn't stop her heavy sigh, or the roll of her eyes. "What the hell do you think it is, Rikard?" she shot back. "A biscuit? A boat? A barn?"

Behind her, both Killik and Sune snickered, and Rikard rounded toward them, his mouth contorting. "How dare you," he hissed. "How *dare* you do something like this, Louisa! Most of all with *them!*"

He waved aggressively at Sune and Killik, who were both glaring back toward him, even as Sune edged further behind the safety of Killik's taut, armed body. And Louisa felt her own hand clutching for her knife, gripping it tight, while a low growl scraped from her throat. "It's none of your business who I spend time with, Rikard. Just like it isn't your business if I decide to hold an event on *my* property!"

But more fury flashed through Rikard's beady eyes, and he jabbed his finger toward her, and then toward the now-marked property line running between them. "It is my business," he snarled, "because those orcs are a hazard to my safety, and my property, and my *life*. I've warned you multiple times, and if you don't cancel this travesty of an *event* at once"—he gave another wild wave of the flyer—"I will be forced to take drastic action, Louisa!"

Louisa opened her mouth, about to protest that there was nothing he could legally do, *nothing*—but suddenly she seemed caught, trapped, in that look in his eyes. In how he looked gleeful, triumphant, invincible. Just like how Lord Scall had looked when he'd made his threats, and...

"I know how to *ruin* you, Louisa," Rikard growled. "I can destroy you. Not just your ridiculous *event*, but your *life!*"

A sharp chill wrenched up Louisa's spine, and though she barked a loud scoff, it was too weak, too late. "You will not," she countered. "I have every right to be here, to hold an event here, and—"

But at that, there was a touch, faint but purposeful, at her shoulder. Claws. Killik's claws. And when Louisa darted a sharp look toward him, he swiftly signed back, the exact same thing he'd said in bed the night before. *No. Leave it.*

It took an instant for Louisa to follow that—*Killik* was telling her to leave it?—but then her shoulders sagged, her hand rubbing at her eyes. He was right, damn it. Rikard was trying to goad her, and there was no point in losing her temper with him, or offering up information he could later use against her. She needed to escape him, forget him, Lord Scall was dead...

She drew in a shaky breath and spun around, walking away as fast as she could, with Killik and Sune already in step beside her. But no matter how fast she walked, Rikard's words kept echoing, ringing in her ears. *Drastic action. I know how to ruin you...*

"You *will* cancel this, Louisa," called Rikard's voice behind her, shrill and vicious. "And get rid of the orcs. Or get ready to say your farewells, forever!"

Farewells. Forever. Only a short time away, only one night left, *I know how to ruin you, forever...*

Killik's hand was firm on Louisa's elbow now, marching her away, away. "Breathe, woman," he murmured. "Draw up the earth. In, and out."

Louisa desperately fought to obey, but her hands were trembling, and something had clamped around her chest, squeezing her breaths fast and shallow. *Farewell. Forever.* Jolting up the dark, bitter terror, in a way she hadn't felt in days, or weeks, perhaps since they'd started all this—and no, no, even the light was flickering, her ears ringing, her feet staggering beneath her. And she barely heard Killik saying something to Sune about returning to the camp, and...

"*Breathe*, woman," Killik said again, deeper than before,

as his hands gripped her shoulders, his eyes glinting, commanding on hers. "Look at me, and follow my breaths. Naught shall harm you. You are safe."

Safe. It scraped into Louisa's thoughts, sliced through the mayhem juddering in her chest—and she fought to focus on Killik's face, his eyes, his breaths. "You are safe," he said again, as he breathed in, and out. "You are safe, Louisa. This fool bleating man shall *never* harm you."

It sank a little deeper, catching, quivering, and Louisa dragged in a breath, though it still trembled and faltered in her chest. *I know how to ruin you. I know.*

"But what if," she choked, "what if he can. What if he— what if he—"

But Killik gave her shoulders a gentle shake, something flashing hard in his eyes. "He cannot," he said, deeper now. "We will not allow this. I told you, we are watching this man, and guarding you. You are safe, Louisa."

Right. Right. It sliced a little sharper, drew the breath deeper, and Louisa desperately searched Killik's steely eyes. "But what about—the camp," she gulped. "And the house, and my staff, and the children? You don't understand, Killik, if something happens to me"—she gulped for air—"Rikard gets everything. My house, my land, my staff, the camp. *Everything.*"

It surged more sharp, genuine terror up her back, flashing it white behind her eyes, and she gripped back at Killik's arms, her nails digging into his skin. "I can't change it," she said, her voice rising. "I tried. I don't have a husband or a son, or any male relatives closer than Rikard. And you realize he can do anything, and get away with it, and it's just like Lord Scall, he always does whatever he wants, and no one *cares!*"

Her wild eyes were searching Killik's face, pleading with him to see, to understand. And that was something strange in his eyes, in that crease on his brow—but he drew in another deep breath, as his strong hands stroked up and down her arms. "Ach, I ken," he said, low. "But now Lord Scall is dead."

Lord Scall was dead. But yes, yes, he was, wasn't he? And Killik wouldn't lie about that, Killik knew that, Killik could be trusted. And maybe that meant he really could help her, he could—and somehow, Louisa nodded, rapid and relieved, and then sank toward him, into the safety of his strong arms, the gentle scrape of his claws stroking her back. Lord Scall was dead. *Dead.*

"And now we are with you," Killik added, even quieter. "We shall face this, together. And you ken"—a slow exhale against her hair—"you can speak truth to us, ach? Aught you might wish. And no matter what this is, we shall yet stand beside you, and keep you safe."

It flared a sharp shudder up Louisa's back, and a sudden, helpless longing. Gods, she wanted to tell him, wanted to just babble it all out into the warmth of his chest—but she couldn't. Couldn't. It was too risky, *drastic action, destroy you,* Lord Scall was dead...

But Killik didn't press it, or ask again. Instead, he just kept standing there, holding Louisa, stroking her, breathing in and out. Until finally, at some point, her awareness crept back in again—and with it, the realization that she was standing in the middle of the woods, clinging helplessly to Killik, and sniffling against his chest. Because apparently— she flinched backwards—she'd gone and had a full-on nervous collapse, and dragged him straight into the midst of it.

"Gods, I'm sorry," she croaked, rubbing both hands at her hot face. "I shouldn't have—I didn't mean to—damn it. I think I should go home, and—"

She flapped a hand in the direction of her house, and lurched a step toward it—but wait. Killik again. And that wasn't concern in his eyes now, or confusion, but instead a cool, taunting challenge. "You shall not," he said, clipped, "for Wolf shall wish to hear of this at once, and we shall work together to further bolster our Summit's safety. And, I ken I ought to start giving you lessons on *flyting*, if we truly seek to do this together at the Summit. And"—a faint twist on his mouth—"we ought to help Wolf start his new *kofi*, also."

Oh. Really? Killik still wanted to build Ulfarr's *kofi*? And give Louisa more lessons, too? But wait, he was trying to distract her, he was helping her, being kind to her. And it shouldn't have prickled like this behind her eyes, or—curse her—sent her staggering back toward him, her arms clutching around his waist.

"Thank you, Killik," she whispered, into his chest. "Again."

Killik scoffed, but again stroked at her back with surprising gentleness until she drew away again. And he didn't even look annoyed as he waved her after him through the trees, and then began pointing out animal tracks and scents. As if this was just another lesson, and that was all.

But it helped, too, slowing Louisa's thoughts, calming her breaths. And by the time they entered the camp again, Rikard's threats felt somewhat fainter, though they still kept whispering, nagging at the back of her brain. *I know how to ruin you. Cancel it. Get rid of the orcs. Say your farewells, forever.*

But Killik kept to his word, and first escorted Louisa back down into the common-room, to where Ulfarr and Rosa were both supervising as Filak and his little crew—Elgr, Igull, and Ragni—struck at the common-room wall with pickaxes. And once Killik had shared the news about Rikard's threat, Rosa launched into a gratifying tirade about belligerent narrow-minded lords, while Ulfarr drew Louisa close, and stroked her with big steady hands. "Naught to fear, Louisa," he murmured, again and again. "We shall keep you safe, and keep all our kin safe, also."

It was more relief, more shimmering comfort in Louisa's chest, and she willingly joined them for another meeting to discuss and strengthen the Summit's plans for security. Which led to more letters, written specifically to some of the best spies and fighters in Orc Mountain, asking them to serve as guards and scouts for the event.

Afterwards, Killik ordered Ulfarr to go start gathering wood for his new *kofi*—a demand that Ulfarr didn't argue, despite the intent way he searched Killik's face. And next, as promised, Killik took Louisa back outside for a lesson in the lost Skai tradition of *flyting*. Which was apparently a kind of competitive storytelling, in which partners took turns snapping out verses, against a backing rhythm—often just foot-stomps, but apparently sometimes weapon-strikes, too. And when Killik noticed Sune watching them from his *kofi* above, he waved him down, and then handed over one of his daggers, so Sune could use it to clash against his own dagger, making a sharp, metallic beat.

"Ach, just thus," Killik told Sune, with an approving grin. "And then verses are spoken to this. There were some verses all the *hirthskalds* knew, but they would oft make up their own as they went, and weave taunts and jibes within them. And at the end, the sharpest speaker would win. Just like a sparring-match, mayhap."

His eyes sparkled as he spoke, and beside him, Sune looked genuinely intrigued, too. And at Louisa's request for a demonstration, Killik waved at Sune to begin the rhythm— and then, once Sune's beat was ringing through the air, Killik drew in a deep breath, and began to speak.

And while the words were foreign, deep and tangled in his throat, his voice was swift and smooth, and striking steadily along with the rhythm. As if it was a drum of its own, sweeping and swaggering to the beat, turning it into some-thing between a chant and a story and a song. And the longer Louisa listened, the sharper Killik's voice seemed to swing around her, catching her into its convulsive thrum. Like he was flying, or fighting, and whipping them up with him, dragging them into his thrall.

When he finished, Louisa could only stare at him, her mouth slack, her heart thumping oddly in her chest. While beside her, Sune was chuckling, and signing something about the bloody lord's skull—because right, he'd have understood the words, and of course they'd been about defeating some kind of enemy. And Killik's grin looked almost soft as he signed back, a faint flush creeping up his neck—and then he glanced sideways, toward... oh. His audience. Kori and Fasti, both grinning. Galmr, looking stunned, with his knobbly hand over his heart. And Ulfarr, with a wide, wavering smile, and something shining in his eyes.

"Ach, listen to you, pup," he said, his voice catching. "It has been thirty summers since I have heard *flyting* thus, I ken."

Beside him, Galmr fervently nodded, and signed for Killik and Sune to continue. And after another grin that looked almost boyish, Killik did it again. But this time, he translated part of the verse into common-tongue, and then kept returning to it, almost like a theme. Like... a lesson.

I fear you not, feeder of wolves. I scorn you and slay you and sup from your skull.

And as he spoke it again, his voice so fierce and fluid and deadly, he signed at—Louisa. Saying, *Speak this with me.*

Louisa nearly choked, but belatedly made her best attempt. Her voice faltering at first, but then settling smoother, steadier. Until she could say it in perfect time with Killik, and then, the next time, he didn't say it at all. Just letting her voice carry it, before coming back in with the next line. As if it really was a duel, or maybe a dance—and then the next time, Killik altered the line. *I stab you and storm you and stomp on your skull.*

So on the next breath, Louisa attempted to alter it, too—*I smash you and slash you and shatter your skull.*

Killik's grin was swift and stunning, his hand signing, *Keep going.* So Louisa kept going, throwing it back and forth with him, even as it became harder and harder, and then truly ridiculous. And by the end of it, she was laughing too much to continue, and Killik thrust both hands up into the air, and proclaimed his victory, while their audience clapped and cheered.

But Louisa still couldn't seem to stop smiling, and the warm, juddery thrill of it seemed to keep pulsing, echoing through her chest. And the memory of Rikard and his threats suddenly seemed very far away, beneath the strength and the certainty of Killik's voice, Killik's verse. *I fear you not, feeder of wolves.*

And maybe he'd chosen that on purpose, and maybe it had—again—been an attempt to help her, and comfort her. And suddenly Louisa couldn't seem to look at him, couldn't bear the longing in her belly, wringing deeper with every breath. Gods, she wanted this. She wanted it so damned much it ached. She wanted the camp, and she wanted this, her house and her people, her home. Hers.

It was again enough to drive her through the rest of the day, working and helping as much as she could. Organizing more flyers for delivery, digging in Thomas' new garden, helping to build the new smokehouse, and finally, late in the afternoon, climbing up to see Ulfarr's new *kofi*. Which he'd begun to build in exactly the place Killik had wanted, high in an oak tree at the heart of the camp. It was a respectable distance from Sune's *kofi* across the clearing, enough that they could both still have privacy—but close enough that they could call and sign to one another as needed, too.

Ulfarr's *kofi* was also far larger than Sune's, and Louisa gasped aloud when she first followed Killik up into it. Its floor was made of fresh-planed pine, and it wrapped almost all the way around the oak tree's big, rough-barked trunk. Ulfarr had already built two walls, too—all made of slim, tightly wedged trunks and branches, lined up vertically along the platform's edges, as if they were yet more trees, growing up out of the floor. Many of the trunks even still branched out above, creating an intricate, tangled skeleton roof, its wood criss-crossed against the tree's branches and leaves above, letting in dappled sunlight against the pale pine floor.

"This is incredible," Louisa said, breathless, with an awed smile toward Ulfarr. "How did you build so much so quickly?"

"Ach, I have had good help," Ulfarr replied, with a fond smile toward where Sune was kneeling and fitting a new branch into the wall. "And with a little more, my kin, mayhap we could finish it this eve."

My kin. It had surely been a slip of the tongue—surely? But Ulfarr was still smiling at Sune, so Louisa nodded and plucked a branch from the stack on the floor, and went over to kneel beside him. Watching how he stood his branch on the platform, and bound it to its neighbour with tightly knotted twine. *Now you place yours*, he signed at her, *whilst I find another.*

Louisa obliged as well as she could, and it soon made for a steady, easy rhythm, alternating back and forth between them. And it was only once she'd placed four more branches that she realized Killik and Ulfarr were both still standing there watching, Ulfarr with an approving little smile, Killik with a strange flicker in his eyes. But upon meeting Louisa's gaze, he glanced away, and squared his shoulders. "I shall go fetch more wood for you, then," he said. "And some furs, also."

So Louisa kept working, moving steadily down the wall, until she and Sune ran out of wood, and needed to wait for more from Killik. While Ulfarr climbed around on the outside of the *kofi*, fortifying and fastening it together with nails and steel wire, and weaving the roof's branches tighter together. And by sundown, they'd fully enclosed the platform, and Killik had indeed scrounged up a few large furs, and spread them out on the pine floor.

"This shall make you a good *kofi*, Wolf," Killik said, sweeping his gaze over their work. "All you need now is a tarp for when it rains, and a bed, and a chest or two for your goods."

Ulfarr was blinking around at his new *kofi* too, and suddenly his eyes looked very bright, his mouth twisting. "Ach, I ken," he said. "I—I thank you for your help, my kin. Skai-kesh has so greatly blessed me."

My kin, again. And though he surely still hadn't meant to include Louisa in that, her throat still felt tight, her eyes warm and weepy on his face. "You deserve it, sweetheart," she told him. "I hope you'll be very happy here."

Ulfarr smiled back at her, slow and wavering—and in a surge of movement, his big arms swept around her, and Killik and Sune, too. Drawing them all into his chest, and squeezing them almost painfully tight. "I am sure I shall," he said thickly. "Now, join me for supper, ach?"

The succulent smell of roasting poultry was wafting up from below—more of Thomas' delicious cooking—and Louisa again joined the Skai in a hearty supper around the roaring fire. While also cheerfully chatting with all her new friends, and learning all the day's news. Including how they'd now printed and distributed over a thousand flyers, and how the new latrines were finished, and how Filak and his team had apparently dug all the way beneath the clearing, and thereby unearthed an excellent deposit of amethyst.

Afterwards, once they'd said goodnight to Sune, Ulfarr silently led Louisa back to his new *kofi*, with Killik close behind. And once they'd all climbed up into it, Killik turned toward her, and squared his shoulders.

"We have reached the last of our ten nights, woman," he said, his eyes shifting oddly on hers. "So tonight, mayhap I shall allow you to choose your lesson. What should you wish for, from us?"

Right. Their last night. The truth of it thudding in Louisa's chest, tightening painfully in her throat. Damn it, how had they gotten here already? And was Killik really— offering her this? Letting her choose what she wanted from them?

They were both watching her, now, Ulfarr with wary uncertainty in his eyes, Killik with a tense, tight-jawed stubbornness. As if he really had meant that, but gods, what did she want? What would she wish she'd done, if this truly was their last night, forever? What would she wish she'd learned? Face this, prove this, Skai, hers...

"Thank you, Killik," she finally whispered, her hand over her heart. "And for my last lesson, I just want to see—you. Both of you, in your own show. Together."

49

She wanted to see both of them. In their own show.

It surely wasn't what either of them had expected, and Killik's eyes briefly met Ulfarr's, as something Louisa couldn't read passed between them. And then Ulfarr swallowed, squared his shoulders, drew in a breath.

"But—we wish for *your* pleasure, Louisa," he said, low. "And it grants you naught, to only witness *ours*."

But Louisa's determination was only sinking deeper—yes, yes, this was what she wanted—and she shrugged, and twitched a shy-feeling smile back toward him. "Oh, I think it will grant me plenty," she replied, as lightly as she could. "But if you're really that concerned"—she felt her face heating—"is that *rassja* of yours still around?"

And gods, what was she saying, was she really suggesting this? But yes, she was—and though Ulfarr only stared at her, Killik's mouth quirked into a wry little smile, and he turned and strode toward the *kofi*'s door. To where he'd apparently stashed his pack, and after a moment's fishing inside it, he indeed produced the *rassja*, and held it up toward them.

Louisa huffed a shaky laugh, and gave a brief squeeze to

Ulfarr's hand. "See, sweetheart?" she murmured. "I'm all set. Ready to sit back, and enjoy your show."

Ulfarr's expression was still searching, uneasy, but Killik shrugged, and angled a conspiratorial glance at Ulfarr's shifting eyes. "Ach, well enough," he said, with a shrug. "Undress, then, Wolf. On the fur."

Oh. He was agreeing to this, they were really doing this—and Louisa watched with intent, greedy eyes as Ulfarr slowly stripped off his clothes, and sank down onto the fur. His gaze still darting warily between Killik and Louisa, while Killik snatched for the chain from Ulfarr's discarded belt, and thrust it into Louisa's hand. "You shall yet help, woman," he ordered. "Bind his wrists for me. Carefully."

Louisa swallowed and nodded, and knelt beside Ulfarr on the fur. Drinking in the sight of him, his big powerful body, his scarred spasming cock, as he obligingly sank onto his back for her, and raised both arms over his head. Allowing her to circle the heavy chain around his wrists, winding it just the way Killik had taught her.

"I bet you won't escape this one, sweetheart," she murmured, as she double-checked his wrists, made sure it wasn't too tight. "Feel all right?"

Ulfarr jerked a nod, his eyes glimmering strange on hers, while Killik kicked off his own trousers, and then sank to his knees on the fur on Ulfarr's other side. And with a swift, graceful movement, he bent low over Ulfarr's groin, grasped his scarred, spasming cock in hand, and...

And sucked it deep into his throat.

Louisa gasped together with Ulfarr, her eyes frozen on the sight, because there was no way Killik was doing this. Smug, arrogant, angry Killik, sucking Ulfarr's huge cock almost all the way into his mouth, his lips stretched wide and tight around it. Taking it so deep he was struggling to breathe, his swallows loud and laboured—but he just kept doing it, as his fluttering eyes flicked to Ulfarr's face, and held there. Wanting Ulfarr to see him doing this, offering this.

And yes, Ulfarr was watching it with stunned, transfixed eyes, holding on the sight of Killik now slowly, deliberately sliding up again. Revealing that huge, scarred, slick shaft again, easing bit by bit out of Killik's stretched sucking mouth. Until Killik's lips released it with an obscene-sounding pop, so he could swirl around it with his long black tongue. Brazenly licking it, lavishing it, seeking deep into its dripping cleft, while it spasmed and sputtered in return, squeezing out generous spurts of that thick white seed onto Killik's lips and tongue. Kissing him in return, feeding him, marking him with his scent...

And then Killik sank back down again. So sudden and sharp that Ulfarr howled, his body kicking and thrashing, his big arms straining against the chain. His eyes held rapt and glittering on the sight, on the truth of his favourite pup swallowing him whole, burying him full and deep into his throat.

And perhaps Killik was just putting on a show, or maybe this was even another test for Louisa, another challenge. But as Killik kept going, gouging Ulfarr again and again into his throat, Louisa could only keep staring, while the ache and the craving burned hard and hot in her belly. Caught in the intensity of this, the reckless ardour of it, the way it felt almost like... like adoration, like worship. Like Killik would single-handedly, single-mindedly suck out his wolf's soul, and beg him for more.

And Ulfarr needed it just as much, his body shuddering all over, his eyes wild and frenzied, his breath escaping in deep, shaky groans. As his arms yanked harder against the chain, as if he wanted to stop Killik, to take Killik, to offer up anything and everything Killik ever wanted...

"Are you—all right, sweetheart?" Louisa gasped at Ulfarr, without at all meaning to. "Still good?"

Ulfarr's nod was instant, fervent, though his body kept spasming, his eyes almost pleading on Louisa's face. As if he'd liked her talking, he wanted her talking, and after a brief, searching glance at Killik's glinting eyes—he didn't look disapproving, did he?—Louisa drew in a shaky breath, and caressed a hand down Ulfarr's sweaty chest.

"Then breathe, sweetheart," she said, through her own too-dry throat. "In, and out."

Ulfarr choked and nodded, and dragged in his next breath with her—and then exhaled with her, too. And yes, yes, it was already soothing him, settling him, bringing more awareness back to his frantic eyes, so Louisa kept going. Shifting down to lie against his side, breathing with him, stroking his chest, and even pressing a brief kiss to his sweaty cheek.

"Good, sweetheart," she murmured. "So good. You're so handsome when you're having your cock sucked, aren't you?"

And oh, the way Ulfarr moaned at that, his nostrils flaring—and Killik might have groaned too, burying that huge heft deeper into his throat. Enough that Louisa drew in more breath, drew up from the fur beneath her, and pressed another lingering kiss to Ulfarr's hot cheek. "So good, sweetheart," she said again, husky. "So strong and powerful, when you're filling up your favourite pup's throat like this. Making him *choke* on you."

Ulfarr groaned as his hips reflexively bucked up, his fervid eyes glimmering on Killik's face. On where Killik was looking dazed, too, even gagging a little as Ulfarr gouged deeper into his throat. And a bizarre, brazen part of Louisa slid her hand downward, and caressed it against Killik's silken hair, now slightly slipping from his topknot.

"And your pup is so good too, isn't he?" she whispered toward Ulfarr, and when he fervently nodded, she pressed another lingering kiss to his cheek. "Then why don't you tell him so? Use your tongue when he's using his, remember?"

She half-expected Ulfarr to balk, or refuse—but he only jerked a nod, and bucked up harder into Killik's mouth. "A-ach," he gasped. "So—so good, pup. So tight. So sweet."

Killik's moan was low but unmistakable, his glittering eyes holding raw and needy to Ulfarr's face. Wanting more, yes, and Ulfarr surely caught that, gulping in more breath. "So good, pup. Always so good, with your clever mouth, your hot tight throat. And your pretty form, and your swiftness and ease, and your sharp words and quick smile. You are—I am—"

Killik's breath choked, his eyes snapped very wide, and Ulfarr heaved for air, hauled it in as if he was drowning—and then his body quaked all over, his voice a roaring bellow, his hips thrusting up hard into Killik's mouth. And oh, Louisa could see his thick shaft pulsing as he poured out into Killik, as Killik braced himself, and took it. Sucking Ulfarr even harder, drawing down deep desperate gulps of him, as his eyes fluttered closed, his groans hot and harsh and helpless.

Finally Ulfarr sagged heavily back against the fur, his shaft visibly softening in Killik's mouth. And only then did Killik carefully draw off him, leaving him slack and shiny, with long, new reddened scrapes that must have been from Killik's teeth.

But if it hurt, Ulfarr showed no sign of it, only blinking at Killik with hazy, awestruck eyes. "So good, pup," he whispered. "Always so, so good to me."

Killik's eyes briefly dropped, his face flushing—but then Louisa could see him squaring his shoulders, drawing in that strength through his breath. And without warning, he roughly pushed Ulfarr onto his side facing Louisa, and then sank down onto the fur behind him. Now shoving up one of Ulfarr's legs, so he could lurch closer behind him, line himself up, and...

Ulfarr arched and stiffened, his eyes rolling back, his

breaths heaving through his chest. While Killik huffed a low, shaky laugh, curving his arm against Ulfarr's front, pulling him tighter—and oh, that was the sound of skin slapping skin, in time with Killik's steady bucking hips. Making Ulfarr shudder and gasp again, his big body taut and straining, his eyes catching, brief and urgent, on Louisa's face.

It almost felt panicked again, like Ulfarr was sure she would judge him, with Killik now pumping rhythmically behind him, and doing... this. Ploughing him, filling him, owning him, while he quivered and gasped and... took it. Gave it. Offered it. And there was something in that, something deep and powerful, especially when Killik's hand groped behind them on the fur, and then thrust something toward Louisa's face. The *rassja*.

"Thought you wished for this, woman," he hissed, his voice hitching with his thrusts. "Strip to your loincloth, and use it. Let him see it."

Louisa could only shiver and nod, her hunger now wheeling and swerving, almost too powerful to bear—and with shaky hands, she yanked off the dress and shift she'd still been wearing, and tossed them aside. And then she sank onto the fur facing Ulfarr again, raising her leg to mirror his, and settled the *rassja*'s cool head against her slick heat, just where she craved it most...

And on Killik's next hard thrust, she sank the *rassja* inside, fast and smooth and deep. Gasping as it opened her, invaded her, filled her and owned her, just as Killik was doing to Ulfarr.

And oh, gods, Ulfarr was watching it, his expression twisting at the sight of it, because—Louisa's eyes darted downwards—oh. He himself was soft again, slack again. Even as he kept arching, kept groaning, kept offering them his beautiful body, and his stunning, aching pleasure.

"So good, sweetheart," Louisa gulped, holding the *rassja*

in place with one hand, as her other hand stroked his sweaty cheek. "So handsome, and so strong, and so—so generous. Giving us such gifts. Letting us enjoy you like this."

Ulfarr's breath choked, his eyes glimmering on her face, so Louisa kept stroking, shuddering at the feel of his solid stone circling against her, grinding in with the steady slaps of Killik's hips. "So generous," she said again, between her dragging breaths. "Letting us have the Wolf of the Skai, all to ourselves. Giving yourself over to us, offering up your gorgeous body to us, showing us how lovely and kind you are. How you won't ever, ever harm us."

Ulfarr choked again, juddering to sudden stillness all over, as his eyes snapped wider on hers. And wait, now even Killik had faltered behind him, shoving up so he could blink down at Ulfarr's face. At where Ulfarr's mouth was quivering, oh gods, almost as if he might—weep. As if—as if Louisa had just stumbled on something... new.

How you won't ever, ever harm us, she'd said.

And that—meant something to Ulfarr. Something important. And as Louisa blinked at his shimmering eyes, his trembling mouth, even the chain binding his wrists, the awareness of it seeped into her, quiet and certain and sad. The chain wasn't just about Ulfarr wanting to be desired, the way she'd thought. It wasn't just about him finding relief apart from his guilt.

It was also about... his fear. His fear that he would harm the people he cared for. His fear, perhaps, that he was still... a monster.

And maybe—maybe being chained like this was a way to shut that fear away. To... escape it, and forget it. To prove that even for a moment, he was weak, he was harmless, he was... safe.

I had no intent, cannot bear to bring more shame, more harm, more blood and wrath and death...

Louisa's throat spasmed, and she fervently stroked at him, held his glimmering eyes with hers. "You won't ever, ever harm us," she whispered. "You won't. Because you're such a good, strong, generous Wolf. You're so devoted to your kin, and so committed to caring for them. You're such a good father, and such a good partner to Killik, too. You are."

Ulfarr rapidly shook his head, his eyes urgent and pleading on hers. Saying he wasn't, he wasn't—and in a shaky flare of movement, Louisa fumbled up for his bound wrists, and yanked at the chain. But her fingers were too weak, too useless, and yes, that was Killik's hand, slipping steady against hers, snapping apart the latch. Releasing Ulfarr's hands, so Louisa could draw one down, and... kiss it. Kiss his palm, his fingers, his sharp, drawn-in claws, trailing her tongue slow and deliberate against them.

"You won't ever, ever harm us, Wolf," she whispered, holding his raw, watching eyes. "You won't. We know you. We *trust* you."

Ulfarr attempted to shake his head again, but oh, that was Killik leaning in closer behind him, kissing with sharp teeth at his straining neck. "Ach, we trust you, Wolf," he said. "Have always, always trusted you."

Ulfarr shuddered all over, his eyes still disbelieving on Louisa's face. On where she was still kissing his claws, one by one, and then—in another shaky movement—shoving his hand down between her thighs. Down to where the *rassja* had almost fully slipped out of her, and she pushed it into his fingers, and guided it back toward her again. And yes, yes, its hard stone nudge was already so careful, so gentle, opening her up slow and smooth, sinking its way inside.

"See?" she breathed, her eyes fluttering at the feel of it, the truth of it—and she even raised her trembling hand again, slipped a slick finger into Ulfarr's mouth. Watched his eyes shift as he sucked it, as he carefully tongued it, kept it away from his teeth—and when she attempted to move it, to maybe cut her skin on one of his sharp fangs, he drew the finger deeper into his throat, trapping it in place. Because he wouldn't let her hurt herself, he wouldn't give her pain, he wouldn't. And she needed to help him face that, just as he'd helped her face so much, too.

"You won't hurt us, Ulfarr of Clan Skai," she breathed, promised, to his shifting, watching eyes. "You won't. Ever."

That was another attempt at shaking his head, even as Louisa felt something... stirring, against her hip. He was stirring, that slack bulge at his groin already swelling again, thickening and lengthening—and oh, that was Killik's hand, slipping around to stroke at it, to pump it fuller, to squeeze out that slippery white seed. And then stroking the seed up and down, too, coating Ulfarr with it, making him shiny and slick and dripping, so he could...

Oh. Ohhh. Yes. And Louisa met Killik's eyes, felt the silent understanding flick between them—and then she twisted herself around, onto her side. Facing away from Ulfarr, her back to his heaving chest, her arse facing his groin. Facing that wet, hard length in Killik's hand, already plumbing its smooth rounded head into Louisa's crease, seeking her tight resisting ring, ordering her to open for its ploughing...

But then—Ulfarr. Ulfarr's hand, catching Killik's, yanking it away. Because Ulfarr wouldn't let Killik hurt her, either, and he was already easing himself backwards, away from her, no—and Louisa frantically clutched at him, at his hand, drawing it around her. Pressing it against the *rassja* still filling her in front, as she ground herself back against that slick dangerous head prodding in behind.

"Please, Ulfarr," she gasped. "Please, grant me your strong Skai ploughing. On both your perfect Skai cocks."

Ulfarr's moan was hot and ragged, his hand spasming against her thigh, but she could still feel his resistance, the strength of his concern. "But this shall be—too much," he choked. "I do not wish to—hurt you, Louisa."

But now it was Louisa shaking her head, brazenly pushing herself back further, willing herself to soften, to open. "You won't," she whispered. "I trust you, Wolf. I want this from you, and I trust you to give it to me. *Now*."

He groaned again, low and desperate, as his slick prodding flesh gave a sustained spasm against her—but oh, gods, yes, that was it. His warm, alive cock shifting, gently pressing, opening her, sinking its way into her, as Louisa gasped and writhed and nodded, and shoved back more. Needing more, more, even with that massive fullness still jammed in front, too. It was so full, so tight, so utterly, impossibly overwhelming, swallowing all her awareness, all her senses. Coiling it down to all his sheer staggering power plunging into her, filling her, anchoring her on its slow stabbing strength.

"More," she gasped. "All the way. Please. *Now*."

Ulfarr groaned again, his hand shuddering against her front, against where he was just holding that *rassja* inside her. But he didn't move any faster, didn't listen to her command, just kept slowly sinking, his face now buried deep into her neck, his breath dragging deep. As if he was... scenting her, scenting for pain, keeping her safe.

It was so much, too much, everywhere, everything, and Louisa was fully babbling now, begging him, pleading for more, faster, harder. But he still didn't listen, only easing in so slow, so careful, until his hips finally pressed against her, his huge cock shuddering deep inside. Both of his cocks buried deep inside, oh gods, both of them consuming her, breaking her, flashing her full of something reckless and rampant, more, more, more—

"Plough me," she gasped. "Please, Ulfarr, please, Wolf, *please*."

She only vaguely heard Killik's laugh behind them, husky and approving. "Ach, mark that sweet begging, Wolf," he said. "I ken she can bear it. And I wish to witness both your pricks ploughing her. Making her scream for you."

Ulfarr groaned again, and oh, yes, please, he was slightly drawing back, out of her, away—but his press back inside was still so slow, so gentle. Taking his time, taking such care with her, even as Killik hissed behind him, and that slapping of hips sharpened again, rising up loud and sloppy between them. "Harder, Wolf," Killik ordered. "Fuck her."

But Ulfarr didn't listen, didn't obey. Just kept up that slow, deliberate pace, now sliding so sweetly in and out, and keeping her full in front, while Louisa writhed and moaned and begged upon it. Sinking deeper into the sheer sensation of it, the stark sweeping power of it, the certainty of it. Ulfarr was filling her, fucking her, making her his in every way possible, and he was doing it his way. Even as he opened her so wide, consumed her, he was keeping her safe. He was the Wolf, he was utterly in control, she could trust him, she was safe, she was whole—

The bliss blared and burst without warning, flashing white wheeling chaos behind Louisa's eyes, tearing from her mouth in a shrill, desperate shout. Her entire body thrilling and thrashing on the power of the stone and flesh inside her, so hard there was no control, no consciousness, just reckless crashing ecstasy. And yes, yes, now Ulfarr was shouting too, his voice a shaky roar into Louisa's throat, his body surging out deep inside her, flooding her with streams of molten heat. While Killik's hiss felt like a fizzing scraping burn, breaking into a low strangled moan behind them, and then the rapid, rhythmic gulps of his swallows.

Louisa couldn't follow, not even when Ulfarr carefully slid the *rassja* out of her, and then drew her closer back against his sweaty, heaving chest. His softened body still nudged inside her, but suddenly Louisa couldn't bear to lose it—and when she shoved back a little harder, needing, unthinking, Ulfarr only tucked her tighter, pressing a soft, sweet kiss against the side of her hot neck.

"Good, Louisa," he murmured. "This was so good. So sweet."

Louisa shuddered all over, pressed back further against him, because while the words sounded vaguely familiar—like something she'd once said to him, maybe—they felt so bare and new, quivering low and powerful in her belly. "It was—all you," she whispered. "You giving us this, Wolf. Keeping us safe."

Ulfarr slightly stilled behind her, but didn't immediately reply—and Louisa twisted a little sideways, enough to see his face. To drink up the flush in his cheeks, the glint in his eyes, the convulsive swallow in his throat. And—and the way Killik's mouth was buried deep in his neck, sucking, drinking, surely enough to be painful.

But Ulfarr's hand had only slipped up and back, sinking into Killik's messy hair, as his eyes kept holding, glimmering, on Louisa's face. As if wanting to hear her say it again. As if... as if he might almost, *almost* believe it.

And that—that had been the entire damned point, hadn't it? And Louisa fought through her cloudy thoughts, fought to hold her hazy eyes on his intent watching face. "You did this, Ulfarr of Clan Skai," she breathed. "You gave us this pleasure, this—this power. And you made this—safe. You showed us, again, how much we can trust you."

It glimmered again in Ulfarr's watching eyes, because it was true, it was. And he had to smell it, he had to feel it, he had to know. "I trust you, Ulfarr of Clan Skai," Louisa whispered. "You, and your favourite pup, too. You're such a good Wolf, such a good Skai, and I'm so, so lucky to have had these ten nights with you."

The truth of it shuddered through her, prickled and pooled behind her eyes, and even streaked down her cheeks. Foolish, foolish, but there was no judgement in Ulfarr's eyes, as his gentle hand slid up, wiped at her wet cheek. "The blessing is all mine, Louisa of Clan Skai," he murmured back. "I thank you, for the great gift of this time with you. You have brought me such kindness. Such... peace."

Louisa rapidly nodded, as more water streaked down her cheeks. And oh, gods, she was weeping, because maybe she couldn't bear to say goodbye after all, not yet. Not after this, not when they were still so close, and she wasn't going to beg them, she wasn't...

But then behind Ulfarr, Killik—sighed. Groaned. Rolled his eyes. And then reached around Ulfarr, and jabbed Louisa with his claw. "Ach, enough weeping, woman," he said, though his voice sounded husky, too. "You have done well, these past nights. And I ken"—he raised a brow toward her—"mayhap I could grant you a few more. If—*if*—you keep behaving for me."

Louisa froze, jerked up, stared at Killik's face, at the wry little smile on his red-streaked mouth. "And I mean *behave*, you vexing harpy," he added. "And I shall not grant you the rest of your coin until we are done, either."

But gods, Louisa couldn't even bear the thought of coin right now, because this meant—this meant she'd proven it. Hadn't she? And now, Killik was giving her another chance. Another challenge. Beyond the ten nights, beyond the contract, into something... new.

And Ulfarr knew it too, twisting around to smile at Killik, drawing his head down for a slow, succulent kiss. His tongue twining, surely tasting himself on Killik's mouth, as a low, contented groan rumbled through his chest.

"Thank you, pup," Ulfarr said, so soft. "And you shall now stay here with me, ach? Both of you."

Stay, both of you. And surely he only meant the night, surely—but Louisa's breath still caught, and her eyes again met Killik's, the awareness crackling between them. Ulfarr wanted them to stay. Both of them.

"Good," Ulfarr murmured now, with another brief kiss to Killik's lips, before he turned to face Louisa again. Gathering her close into his arms, his strength, his peace. "Now sleep, my pups."

Sleep. His pups. His. *Hers.* And with a breath and a shudder, Louisa curled up closer against his warm steady safety, and slept.

50

When morning came, the whole world felt... changed. Felt bright, and shimmering, and new.

Maybe it was just waking up in a tree, with the cheerful birdsong all around, and the dappled sunlight peeking through the entwined branches of the *kofi*'s roof. Or maybe it was Ulfarr's soft steady snores, and the relaxed contentment on his sleeping face.

Or maybe it was Killik. Lying sprawled and sleepy on Ulfarr's other shoulder, squinting a bleary eye over at Louisa—and then shoving up onto his hands and knees, and prowling over Ulfarr toward her. Flicking at Ulfarr's cheek on the way by, enough to stir him awake, and then turning his attention back to Louisa, rolling her onto her belly, settling his lean warm body over her. And then—Louisa gasped—his slick prodding head slipped into her crease, and found the place Ulfarr had filled the night before. It was still supple and soft, almost as if waiting for this, welcoming this—and in a smooth, single stroke, Killik sank himself deep inside.

Louisa moaned and writhed at the sudden shock of it, but there was no thought of protesting, not in the trees and the sunlight and the birdsong. And not with Ulfarr now lying on his side watching, his head propped on his hand, an approving smile curving on his mouth. "Gentle, pup," he murmured, husky. "She may yet be tender from last eve."

But Killik only snorted, and even gave a light slap to Louisa's bare arse. "She is yet wide open and dripping wet from you, Wolf," he said coolly. "I ken she can scarce feel this, ach, woman?"

Louisa could still most certainly feel it, and she shot a disdainful look over her shoulder toward Killik, even as she shuddered and groaned. And oh, that was Ulfarr's hand on her cheek, Ulfarr's soft, searching gaze on her face. Still making sure she was safe, even now, and she twitched a smile at him, between her sharp, shaky gasps.

"Your pup is a—a tyrant, Wolf," she breathed, as Killik picked up speed, his bollocks slapping against her skin. "An infuriating, unfeeling tyrant—who can't let anyone else— run his show—for one damned day!"

But Ulfarr only smiled back at her, so fond and approving, while Killik gave her arse another stinging slap, followed by a snap of teeth near her ear. "Ach, just thus," he purred. "You are learning, woman. Now be good, and suck your fresh Skai seed deep, where it belongs."

Oh, hell, he was already grinding, gouging, his claws pricking into her shoulders—and that was yet more flooding heat, pooling in fast and deep. Filling her, yet again, and it should not have felt that good, that... *right*. And Ulfarr should not be leaning over to kiss Killik like that as he poured out, slow and filthy with tangling tongue—and then drawing away and guiding up Louisa's face, so he could kiss her, too. Sending more shivery rightness up her spine, especially when Killik sagged heavy against her back, and then yawned, and gave a slow, luxurious stretch. "Better," he murmured. "Now behave, woman, and mayhap I shall grant you more."

More. It caught Louisa's breath, because again, it really did mean—the ten nights were over. And she was still here, still in their bed. As if she truly was proving this, and had almost—almost—earned it.

Louisa's grin was swift and genuine, the warmth simmering in her belly—and once they'd all washed and dressed, she eagerly joined Killik and Ulfarr in another busy morning at the camp. First prayers and breakfast, and then more Summit preparations with Rosa, and then another session of *flyting* with Sune and Killik, and now with Kori and Fasti, too. And next, Louisa and Killik worked more on the *kofi* with Ulfarr, helping him build a large bed out of supple, springy boughs, covered with multiple thick furs.

The bed was big enough for two—or even three—people, but Killik still kept referring to it as Ulfarr's, so Louisa followed suit, too. And while she still wanted to push that further, to demand why in the name of Skai-kesh Killik couldn't just move in, she couldn't bear to break the lightness that kept sparkling between them. Making it easy to talk and laugh and sign with them, and then, beneath the early afternoon sunlight, to join Killik in helping Ulfarr christen his new bed. This time just making Ulfarr lie back between them on the furs, so they could both take turns touching and tasting him, spoiling him, adoring him.

But this, too, felt easy, and warm, and bright. Like Killik's thoughts, Killik's desires, were crackling into Louisa's very thoughts, and together they kept deepening that new awareness from the night before. Ulfarr was afraid of hurting them, of failing them—and that meant they needed to prove him wrong. They needed to praise him, to call him strong and safe, to show him how deeply they trusted him. And as part of that, neither of them even looked at the chain, still hanging on Ulfarr's trousers—and it was even better to have Ulfarr's big hands caressing them, guiding them, skittering into their hair, stroking their hot cheeks.

"Ach, my pups," he gasped afterwards, once they were all sprawled on the new bed together. "What have I done to deserve this?"

Louisa and Killik exchanged a brief, satisfied look, as a hot thrill hurtled up Louisa's spine. *My pups*, he'd said again, to both of them, and Louisa impulsively kissed his cheek, and gave a gentle, audacious pat to his soft, saliva-streaked prick. "You're just—*you*, sweetheart," she said, a little helpless. "How can we not adore you?"

Killik's flickering eyes again met Louisa's, looking almost pleased, almost... approving. And even as they climbed back down to the camp, she could still feel the thrill of it, the rightness of it. Killik was pleased with her. She was proving this to him. She was.

That certainty kept shimmering for the rest of the day, even when Louisa accompanied Rosa on a trip to town, where they hand-delivered more invitations to the Summit. A venture that Louisa only reluctantly agreed to, at Rosa's repeated urging—but she soon discovered, to her genuine surprise, that she almost enjoyed seeing her old friends and acquaintances again. That it didn't seem to carry the same tinge of loss and loneliness it once had, back when she'd been trapped with Lord Scall, or crushed beneath his debts. Lord Scall was dead.

Of course, Rikard's name still frequently came up in their conversations, especially since he'd apparently already begun spreading word in town of the trespassing orcs. But Louisa and Rosa countered his claims as firmly as they could, and reminded the townspeople of all the good the orcs had done throughout the province these past few years. And by the end of the afternoon, they'd gained multiple expressions of interest in the Summit, and at least a few tentative promises to attend.

Louisa was still smiling when they returned to camp again, and didn't even pretend to argue when Killik ordered her down into the common-room to write more letters. These ones turned out to be updates to the various Skai leaders on the Summit's final schedule—which now included a few days only for the Skai, along with the public Open House. And as Louisa wrote out letter after letter, adding in all the bits of diplomatic flattery Killik was entirely incapable of, he didn't once complain, and afterwards he even bent down to nibble lightly at her neck.

"Good, woman," he murmured. "Just as pretty as a Ka-esh, but without any of the torment."

It was a true compliment, and Louisa nearly floated through the rest of the evening, which culminated in another glorious session together in Ulfarr's bed. And though they again didn't use the chain, it was still Killik in charge, snapping heated orders as Ulfarr's big body moved and groaned over Louisa—so afterwards, once they were all sprawled and sated together, Louisa waggled her brows toward Killik, and even gave a light pat to his cheek.

"And maybe next time, it'll finally be your turn for some strong Skai ploughing," she told him. "You can't think I've forgotten our deal, have you?"

Killik sputtered and scoffed, though an unmistakable flush was creeping up his neck, his eyes darting narrow toward Ulfarr. "There was no *deal*," he snapped. "This was only your wishful thinking, woman!"

Louisa pouted back, but didn't miss how Ulfarr was looking away now, too. Not even hinting that he might want such a thing from Killik, even though Louisa knew—she *knew*—he did. And Killik had glanced away too, his mouth tight and thin, as if this was again something they couldn't talk about, or couldn't do. Just like they couldn't live together in this *kofi*, either. But—why? Why the hell couldn't they? What the hell was stopping them?

But when morning came, with yet more dappled sun and birdsong, it was so easy to shove the questions away, and embrace another day of busy, intriguing work. Prayers, and a delightful hunting trip with Killik and Sune, followed by a surprisingly enjoyable sparring lesson, during which Killik snapped out orders and praise from the sidelines, while Louisa and Sune faced off against each other with fur-wrapped wooden daggers. Circling and attacking again and again, until they were both sweaty and grinning at each other.

Afterwards, they practiced more *flyting* together, first with Kori and Fasti, and then with Igull and Polly and Elgr, too. Working through all the verses Killik could remember, and then trying out a few of their own, too. Preparing for what had somehow become an actual performance, written in black and white on Rosa's draft schedule.

The Summit was now less than a week away, and it had begun to feel more momentous—and perhaps more intimi-dating—with every passing day. And as much as Louisa fought to forget, those threats of Rikard's kept hovering over it all, too. *I know how to ruin you. Cancel it. Get rid of the orcs. Or say your farewells, forever...*

But—no. No. They'd already expanded the Summit's security, scheduling guards and patrols throughout, and Louisa couldn't bear even the thought of cancelling it, not now. She needed to see this Summit through. She needed to keep helping Ulfarr, and seeking amends, and finding peace. And she often found herself repeating that first *flyting* verse she'd learned, one they often returned to in their practice, too. *I fear you not, feeder of wolves. I fear you not.*

So as the next few days passed, full of plans and meetings and hunting and *flyting*, Louisa did her damnedest to keep hoping. To keep praying. To keep trying. And keep enjoying this time with all these lovely new friends, with Rosa, with Sune, with Killik and Ulfarr.

And while Killik and Ulfarr didn't again return to any serious discussions—either the *kofi*, or to that still-hanging question of Ulfarr ploughing Killik—Killik didn't bring up the ten nights, or the payment, either. And instead, they just kept spending every night together in Ulfarr's bed, playing together, enjoying each other. Sometimes with the chains, but often without—and some nights, if Ulfarr's body wasn't in agreement, without his hard prick, either. But Louisa and Killik took care to still lavish and praise him, to welcome his hands and his mouth and his *rassja*, and to remind him that he was desired, he was trustworthy, he was safe.

And every morning, waking up in the sky amidst the birdsong, Ulfarr seemed... better. Easier. His smiles coming swifter and brighter, his hands relaxed and hungry against them. And he commanded Louisa and Killik more, now, too—not only in the bedroom, but also outside it. Never in a way that felt overbearing or demanding, but in a way that felt natural and familiar upon him. As if he was long used to being in charge, and directing the busy world around him, while also accommodating his kin's needs, and considering their advice.

"Pup, I wish you to stay with me today, so we can welcome our kin together," he told Killik, on the morning their Summit guests were due to start arriving. "I shall have much need of your sharp wits and wise guidance. And Louisa, I wish you by our side also, but first you ought to again visit your sisters, ach?"

Over the past week, Louisa had indeed continued making regular trips back to her house, meeting with her staff, and working out plans for the Summit. It had taken some careful discussions, and much reassurance from Halthorr and Joan, but Elise and Gladys had even agreed to open the house to host any families with children who wanted to sleep indoors, so the camp's common-room could instead serve as a dedicated place for Skai to eat and gather together.

"Of course, sweetheart," Louisa said now, leaning up to

press a kiss to Ulfarr's cheek. "I'll take Sune again too, if you don't mind."

But Ulfarr always endorsed Louisa spending time with Sune, and his grin was broad and grateful, his hand patting her arse. "Ach, Sune shall welcome this, most of all if you again offer up your horses," he replied. "Thank you, my sweet Louisa."

Louisa flushed and waved it away, while Killik snatched up his nearby pack, and shoved it into her hands. It always seemed to have a full waterskin inside, as well as a good quantity of Sune's favourite dried meat, and fruit for her to eat, too. And Louisa foolishly smiled at Killik as she slung the pack on her back, and then lurched up to press a furtive kiss to his hard cheek, too.

The trip to her house now seemed far shorter than it once had, especially with an excited Sune to sign with along the way. And once she'd helped Sune saddle Max, Louisa headed for the house, where she found her staff all in the kitchen with Halthorr, and discussing their hosting plans for the Summit. Which seemed to be progressing well, apart, perhaps, from Elise's ongoing anxiety about the situation.

"Look, I'm willing to go along with the rest of you on this," Elise said, frowning down at the dough she was kneading. "But you can't blame me for being concerned about having a dozen strange orcs in the house, for some *summit* that has nothing to do with us!"

Louisa winced and opened her mouth, but Halthorr had already stepped closer toward Elise, his hand over his heart. "I swear to you, my lady, my kin should never harm you," he told her. "And some of these orcs are my close brothers, and they all have mates of their own, also."

Elise shot him a dark look, but it had none of the fear she'd once held toward him—and Halthorr offered her a kind, encouraging smile, and came a careful step closer. "I should yet be honoured to do all I can to ease your distress upon this, my lady. Mayhap I could sleep outside your door, should you welcome this."

It was perhaps a sign of how many nights Halthorr had now spent here, sleeping in odd locations around the house, because Elise still didn't look slightly alarmed, and instead aimed another sharp glare toward him. "Oh, really?" she asked, in icy tones, as she hurled her dough onto the counter. "But what about Joan? You wouldn't want to leave *her* at risk too, would you?"

A hunted look crossed Halthorr's eyes, and he glanced uneasily toward Joan, who was watching all this in silence, her arms folded over her chest. "N-no, my lady," Halthorr replied, too quickly. "Mayhap you—you two could bed together, so I could guard you both at once?"

The hopefulness was almost comical on his face, while Elise and Joan exchanged a furtive, speaking look, and then frowned away from one another. Leaving Halthorr to blink helplessly between them, his shoulders sagging, and finally Louisa took pity on him, and cleared her throat. "I think that's an excellent idea," she said firmly. "And with the children's room attached to Elise's, it makes the most sense for them, too."

She didn't wait for them to argue further, just ducked out the door again, smiling to herself as she headed toward the stable. Where she found Sune riding Max in a swift, fluid canter around the paddock, and Louisa's smile drew higher as she watched him sweep past. He was a natural rider, with an easy affinity with the horses, and it had been a genuine pleasure seeing his rapid progress, and the true joy he'd seemed to find in it.

Looking good, Louisa signed at him, when he came around again. *Max likes you.*

Sune's face ducked, but he furtively signed back on his next swing past, saying, *Thank you.* And then, *Do we have to leave already?*

"Well, our guests are arriving, and I promised Wolf I'd come back to help," Louisa replied. "But I also promised we'd set up some horseback rides, so why don't we take them back together?"

Sune's grin flashed wide and stunning across his face, and he eagerly nodded. And soon they were companionably riding south together, as that warmth again shimmered in Louisa's belly. Ulfarr wanted her by his side. He wanted her to meet his kin. He was working so hard to earn Simon's approval, to regain his place amongst his kin—and he wanted her to be part of it with him, and with Killik. His pups.

They were so close. They were so, so close to making this work. To redeeming Ulfarr, and making this his home. Gaining that peace.

Louisa drew in a deep, contented breath, drawing up strength from May beneath her—when she caught sight of Sune signing at her. The movements quick and furtive, almost as if he didn't want to ask.

Now that you live at the camp, he said, *will you now wed Ulfarr, and grant him a son?*

Louisa nearly choked, her hands spasming on May's reins, as the warmth caught, curdled into something cold and still. Would she wed Ulfarr, and grant him a son.

It was as though time had swallowed her up, somehow, and spat her out weeks ago, when she'd first taken Sune on horseback, and he'd asked her this same question. Because—because the answer hadn't actually changed since then. Had it? Despite all her time with Killik and Ulfarr at the camp, there had still been no agreements, no commitments between them. Any night could still be the last, and Killik only had to choose it, and say it, for it to be the end. Forever.

Get rid of the orcs, shouted Rikard's voice, deep in her skull. *I can ruin you. Get ready to say your farewells...*

"Um," Louisa began, with a grimace. "No. We're still just"—she swallowed—"friends."

But Sune frowned straight back at her, and then gave an exaggerated roll of his eyes. *I can scent you*, he signed. *You are not only friends.*

Right. Louisa swallowed again, drew in the breath from May beneath her. "Look, it's just—I've already been married, and it was an absolute disaster, and I already have people I need to care for, and..."

Her voice trailed off, because she probably deserved that incredulous look in Sune's eyes—and she sighed, squeezed her eyes shut. "We just—haven't made any commitments," she finally said. "I'm not sure we're all... ready for that yet. Or if we ever will be."

She hoped it wasn't too much, or betraying Killik and Ulfarr somehow, but Sune's expression cleared, his hand again signing toward her. *But you love them. And they love you.*

What? Louisa nearly laughed, but stopped it just in time, biting her lip—but Sune was frowning again, and nodding. *Wolf loves you*, he signed. *Killik, also.*

Louisa's thoughts were swimming, her heart erratically pounding, because—no. Ulfarr, maybe—but not Killik. Of course not. No. They'd learned how to get along, how to find pleasure together—but it still wasn't *that*. Right? Killik hadn't even wanted her at all, he'd only done this for Ulfarr...

So you shall now stay, Sune signed at her, his mouth tight. *You shall wed them, and grant them sons.*

There was no reply to that, no words in Louisa's churning brain, but perhaps Sune didn't expect an answer, frowning darkly forward over Max's head. Almost as if... as if again, *he* still didn't want that. He didn't like the prospect of Louisa marrying Killik and Ulfarr, and having their sons. Did he?

Sune wished to face the woman who will steal Wolf away from us...

But no. Louisa would never have sons. Theirs, or

anyone's. And she hauled in a deep breath, let it out, as a distant whine rattled in her chest. Because after all this time, she still hadn't brought up that one crucial point with Sune—or with Killik and Ulfarr, either. She'd never spoken it to anyone, not once, not ever, not after Scall had died. It was too risky, too dangerous, she needed to escape, forget, run, run...

But Sune was still frowning like that, his jaw set tight as he glared straight ahead. And gods, he deserved to know, didn't he? They all did, especially Ulfarr—because what if he still wanted more sons, too? And Louisa needed to face it, needed to try, *I fear you not, I fear you not...*

"Sune, you really don't—" she began, between her gasping breaths. "It's not—I can't—"

But before she could continue, Sune straightened in the saddle, his nostrils flaring—and then he bent low, and kicked into a gallop. Heading toward the camp with obvious urgency, and Louisa raced to catch up, her heartbeat thundering, jolting between alarm and relief. She'd escaped it for now, but now—

Now there were people. Multiple new people. The first of their guests, beginning to arrive for the Summit. And Sune had already leapt off Max's back, so he could sprint straight toward two of the guests—his friends Timo and Cecily, both broadly grinning as they hauled him into a tight, excited hug.

Oh. Louisa's driving heartbeat slowed as she watched, and a small smile pulled at her mouth. And then she startled all over as Killik materialized beside her, and grasped May's bridle. "This was a good surprise for him, ach?" he said, with a nod toward Sune and his friends, and then beyond them, too. "It has gone well, so far."

Right. Louisa fought to follow Killik's eyes, to focus on the moment, on the camp. On this. On all the new adults milling around behind Sune and his friends, cheerfully conversing with Ulfarr and their campmates. There was

Argarr, the Skai smith, and Kitty with her two mates, and Geva, the director of Orc Mountain's school, together with a big, handsome orc, and an adorable, bright-eyed orcling.

And as Louisa's gaze settled on Ulfarr speaking to them, smiling as he welcomed them and introduced his camp-mates, she felt her breath exhaling, her heartbeat slowing further. Because Ulfarr looked—at home. In charge. Confident, and caring, and capable, just as a leader should be. Just as a Wolf should be.

Killik was watching too, his swallow bobbing in his throat, and for a breath, there was an almost overpowering urge to draw him close, to squeeze him tight. To say, *Even if this doesn't work, even if Simon doesn't forgive Ulfarr, even if he's never fully restored to his kin—you still did it, Killik. You've helped him. You saved him.*

But if it was done, finished, then where did that leave Louisa? *I can ruin you. Prove this. Say your farewells. You shall wed them, and grant them sons. I have no wish for you. The woman who will steal Wolf away from us...*

"Come, woman," Killik's low voice said, as he passed May's reins into a nearby Ragni's hand. "Prove this to me."

Prove this. It was enough to shove the rest of it away, for now, at least—and Louisa nodded and stumbled over toward the group, smoothing out her slim black dress. She would face this. Prove this.

Ulfarr's eyes brightened as Louisa stepped in beside him, and his hand slipped around her back, drawing her closer, while his other hand reached for Killik, too. Wanting them both here beside him, flanking him, supporting him.

So Louisa drew in breath, and poured her full focus into it. Helping Ulfarr greet and welcome their guests, asking after their journeys and their children, waving them toward where Thomas had assembled a stunning buffet on all the camp's tables. She also helped sort out who would be staying at her house, and then guided them over to Ragni, who had agreed to escort them there—and who, together with Sune, had also begun offering the horseback rides around the clearing, much to the orclings' delight.

It was intriguing to meet some of the other Skai leaders, too, and to match their faces to all the letters Louisa had written. Tarr from the western camp was a big, burly fellow with a mashed nose and a broad grin, and Airik from the south was lean and watchful, speaking in fluent signs to Killik and Ulfarr. While Rurik, the Skai healer Killik had mentioned, was tall and startlingly handsome, with a cool smile that didn't at all touch his pale, glittering eyes.

"Another bored noblewoman, then?" he asked Killik, with a jerk of his head toward Louisa. "Of all the women in the realm you could have hunted for your *elskan*?"

Louisa blinked, while beside her, Killik's eyes blazed with sudden, surprising ferocity, his hand clamping against her side. "Ach, and you ken you could do better," he drawled, "than a fierce, hungry, handsome woman with good lands, much Skai skill, and the ear of the most powerful orcs and women amongst us!"

Rurik's mouth pursed, his eyes running up and down Louisa's body, while Killik's mouth widened into a chilly, vicious smile. "And what woman have you found for your own *elskan*?" he added. "Or do you even yet have one? Ach, there is a northern Ka-esh here who you may wish to scent, I ken."

A look of genuine alarm flashed across this Rurik's eyes, and he spun around and stalked off, his claws jutting from his fingers. Leaving Louisa to angle an uneasy glance toward Killik, who rolled his eyes, and gave her arm a reassuring little pat. "Rurik's favourite pet is a pretty little orc at the mountain who Filak has been ploughing for many moons now," he said lightly. "What curse has Skai-kesh cast upon me, that I am *gladdened* by a Ka-esh stealing a Skai's mate."

Louisa laughed, but her heart was oddly skipping—not

only at Killik telling her this, gossiping with her like this, but also at what he'd said about her. *A fierce, hungry, handsome woman, with much Skai skill...*

But Killik was already looking away, grinning at where the Skai's Right Hand Drafli had arrived with his mates and son—and behind Drafli was a beaming Jule, with her own mate and sons in tow. "Louisa!" Jule exclaimed, rushing over to pull Louisa into a tight hug. "Oh, it's so good to see you again! And so brilliant of you to organize this Summit, too."

Louisa smiled as she waved it away, but she'd again caught Killik's eyes, and found them glinting with something almost like pride. As if he really had meant what he'd said about her being a fierce, hungry, worthy woman. A woman who was pleasing him, proving this to him...

So Louisa again focused on speaking, smiling, standing by Ulfarr's side, being a good host to their guests. And it still all seemed to be going even better than they could have hoped—at least, until Ulfarr stiffened beside Louisa, his eyes snapped toward the trees.

Toward where—Louisa stilled, too—Simon and Maria had arrived.

51

The judges of Ulfarr's fate were here.

They both looked distinctly uneasy, Maria clutching their younger son close, while Simon gazed straight ahead, his hand clasped to their older son's shoulder. And for a breath, the rest of the activity around them seemed to go still, the voices quieting to hushed whispers, every eye intent on the sight.

Beside Louisa, Ulfarr still hadn't moved—he had that blank, distant look in his eyes—but after a glance toward Killik, Louisa joined him in guiding Ulfarr forward to meet Simon and Maria. "It's so good to see you again!" Louisa told them, smiling as brightly as she could. "We're so glad you came, and we've even built a new *kofi* for you! Are any of you hungry? Or would your sons like a horseback ride, perhaps?"

Their older son—Bjorn—visibly brightened at this suggestion, especially when Sune strode up beside Louisa, and signed swiftly toward him. *You will like this, little brother,* he said. *Come, I will show you. Should your father allow this.*

Bjorn shot a beseeching glance up at Simon, whose expression had softened, and he nodded as he waved Bjorn forward. And thankfully, the voices and activity had begun rising around them again, too—but when Louisa glanced upwards, Ulfarr still hadn't spoken, still just standing there with that empty blankness in his eyes. So Louisa again stroked at his stiff back, and even gave a brief, surreptitious squeeze to his arse. He could do this, he could face this, he could....

"It is—an honour, my brother and sister," Ulfarr finally said, rushed and hoarse, as he put his fist to his heart, and bowed low toward first Simon, and then Maria. "A true blessing from Skai-kesh, to host the Enforcer and his fierce mate and sons as our guests of honour at this Skai Summit. We shall welcome your strength here, and your good guidance toward us all."

It still sounded stiff, perhaps rehearsed, but he'd said it, and he'd even thrust out his hand toward Simon. Holding it there, despite the faint tremor in it, twitching his fingers. Waiting, waiting, until...

Simon—nodded. Nodded, and clasped his own hand to Ulfarr's wrist. And then he even stepped close, brief but purposeful, and thumped his big fist against Ulfarr's back.

"We are glad for this Summit, and for your hosting it here, brother," Simon replied, in his deep, steady voice. "We have long needed a meeting such as this, bringing us together, and honouring our clan. It was wise of you to see this, and offer this."

As he spoke, he cast a narrow, knowing look at Killik, who was wearing a placid, innocent smile. "Ach, and Ulfarr has long wished for this also," Killik replied blandly. "Most of all for our mates and sons who need this care from us."

He'd jerked his head behind them, toward where most of Ulfarr's former packmates were lingering close by—Ragni and Kori and Fasti, Leikr and his friends, Polly and Igull, Annie and her son, even Thomas and Elgr and Angus. And when Simon followed Killik's gaze, he exhaled, and gave a curt nod. As if... he was agreeing to this. Supporting Ulfarr, in this.

It was something, maybe it was everything, and Ulfarr slightly sagged beside Louisa, a tentative but genuine smile on his mouth. "Thank you, brother," he said, bowing his head, his hand over his heart. "And you also, sister. Now"— he squared his shoulders, and glanced behind them—"have you yet met Hrafn's young son? Or Igull's?"

There was nothing like adorable babies to settle some tension, and Louisa eagerly joined Simon and Maria in cooing over them, and then laughed when Maria began teasing Simon about having another son of their own, too. "I'm more than ready for it," she told Louisa, with a wry grin. "It's Simon who can't handle the thought of it, right, love?"

Simon's glance toward Maria looked equal parts fond and alarmed, and he reached to take their heavy-looking toddler from her arms. "You ken we shall make another hungry, hearty son who shall never let you sleep, my Maria," he replied. "I only wish you to be well, and *safe*."

It was such a Skai thing to say—like something Ulfarr himself would say—and Louisa exchanged another knowing grin with Maria before waving her toward the camp. "Can I give you a tour?" she asked. "And we can give your hungry son some of Thomas' delicious cooking, maybe?"

Maria willingly agreed, and soon Louisa was escorting her around the camp, while Simon stayed behind with Killik and Ulfarr and Drafli. They were already deep in discussion, and that seemed promising, too, settling the determination deeper in Louisa's belly. She was doing this. Facing this. Proving this.

The rest of the afternoon passed in a whirl of activity— welcoming and settling their guests, confirming numbers for supper, and then meeting with multiple orcs and women to finalize preparations for the next day's public Open House. A project that still felt impossibly massive, but they'd been preparing for weeks now, and Louisa was determined to do her best, and carry it off as well as possible. To do whatever she could to help, and to face this. *I fear you not.*

"We thank you for all your work upon this, Louisa," Ulfarr regretfully told her after the meeting, as he stroked a hand against her back. "I ken this was not at all what you wished for, when you first began sharing your lands with us."

Louisa smiled and waved it away, but Killik's sidelong glance was a little too knowing, his hand giving a gentle slap to her arse. "Ach, and thus tonight, you shall rest, and forget all this," he said. "And only enjoy a good Skai frolic with us."

Louisa certainly wasn't about to argue, especially when it turned out that a *good Skai frolic* included not only a delicious feast around the roaring fire, but also drums and dancing, and an adults-only party in the common-room. And once Killik had signed a good-night to Sune—and ordered him and his friends to behave—he grasped Louisa and Ulfarr, and drew them down into the midst of the party.

It was already busy inside, with multiple guests drinking and eating and chatting together, and one of the drummers was beating out a steady, sensual rhythm from a corner. And Louisa caught a glimpse of movement and bare skin in one of the beds behind the curtain, along with the distinctive sound of a low, hungry groan.

But Killik didn't lead them toward the beds, or the curtain. Instead, he took them straight toward the blazing, crackling fireplace, and shoved Ulfarr down onto his back on the large fur before it. And then—in full view of the room—Killik knelt over him, and began unfastening his trousers.

Louisa froze—Killik wasn't truly doing this, here, now, in the middle of a party?—but his narrow look toward her said that yes, yes, he was. "Our kin know not to allow the younglings down here," he said, under his breath. "And you can do as you wish, but I wish to honour the Wolf of the Skai before his clan, on the night he has gained so much before them."

Oh. So Killik thought today had gone well too, then. As if maybe, maybe, this was working, and Ulfarr was proving this. Serving and honouring his kin, showing himself worthy of Simon's approval, and earning his place as a good leader, and a strong Skai.

And Ulfarr wasn't protesting, only blinking at Killik with such longing and gratefulness shining in his eyes. Wanting this, too, or maybe needing it, because yes, he deserved it. He'd worked and prayed and fought so hard for it, and now it was so close, almost here, near enough to touch.

And suddenly it seemed—right, somehow, that Killik should strip off Ulfarr's clothes, and then his own, too. Right, that he should lie down long and languid beside Ulfarr on the fur, kissing slow and soft at his neck, while his hand lazily stroked up Ulfarr's bare belly. Honouring him, showing him as strong and capable and desirable, in the camp that meant so much to him. In the place Ulfarr longed to keep as his home.

And Louisa longed for that too, needed that too, far stronger than the curious eyes glancing toward them—and in a shaky movement, she sank down to Ulfarr's other side, and touched a hand to his warm, silken skin. Stroking him with Killik, kissing him with Killik, tasting the salty sweetness of him, feeling the hungry shudders of his big body beneath them.

Killik had kissed his way up Ulfarr's cheek to his mouth, plundering it with his teeth and his long twining tongue— and when he drew away, he nudged Ulfarr's face toward Louisa. So she could kiss him too, softer and sweeter, but still kindling the hunger hot in her belly. He tasted so good, he looked so good, he was the Wolf of the Skai, showing his strength, regaining his place amongst his kin—and in this moment at least, he was theirs. *Theirs.*

And Killik knew it too, his hand now stroking possessively up and down Ulfarr's slowly swelling cock, while Louisa fondled and caressed at his bulging bollocks. Their hands brushing, their mouths still taking turns kissing him, their gasps deepening into groans. And Killik's bare groin was rhythmically rocking against the side of Ulfarr's hip, his long leg hooked around his thigh, and Louisa was beginning to feel distinctly irritated by her dress, how it felt clammy and constricting in the crackling warmth from the fire. And when she awkwardly tugged at it, Killik's steady hand was there, guiding it up her leg, higher and higher. His eyes glinting on hers in a silent question, and then casting a brief, meaningful glance around the ever-filling room—but Louisa was doing this now. Facing this, proving this, *I fear you not...*

Killik helped her tug the dress and shift off over her head, leaving her clad only in her boots and loincloth. And though the air prickled on her bare skin, firing a furious shudder up her back, she drew up strength from the fur, from Ulfarr's strong body against her, the hazy awe in his blinking, watching eyes. And then—oh, please—that was Killik's hand on her face, drawing her across Ulfarr toward him, so he could press a brief, scraping kiss to her mouth, too.

Louisa moaned, hoarse and breathless—and beneath them, Ulfarr moaned too, vibrating all through his big warm body. And with another purposeful nudge from Killik, she and Killik bent down to kiss Ulfarr's mouth together, sloppy and hungry. Tasting him, sharing him, honouring him, and oh, those were hands, Ulfarr's hands, guiding Louisa up closer upon his solid body, settling her over that leaking ridge on his belly, oh.

It felt so good, grinding so thick and hard just where Louisa most craved it, bare skin to bare slippery skin. And she was distantly grateful for her still-present loincloth, both concealing the worst of this, and offering such warm indecent wonders beneath it. Ulfarr's slick pulsing shaft, sliding long and fat and ridged against her hot crease, opening it wider and wider. And she only had to shift a little, meet where Killik's steady hand was already between them, guiding that hard cock up, notching its slick head into place...

"Fuck," Louisa gasped, arching up upon it, against the sweet perfect press of it. Showing off far too much, giving the whole room a damned good show—but yes, she was doing this, proving this. She was taking Ulfarr's huge, shuddering heft inside her, and she was doing it without any of their usual preparation, without any of Killik's slick seed easing the way. And she was watching that look on Ulfarr's flushed face as she did it, the awe and the frenzy glimmering in his eyes, as his trembling hands caressed her, drew her closer. Drew them ever deeper together, his body sinking into hers breath by breath, please, please...

"So good," he whispered, his voice cracking, his eyes flashing. "So good, sweet Louisa. So kind, so brave, so perfect. *Mine.*"

His. A sharp, shaky thrill wrenched up Louisa's body, clamping her tighter upon him—and Ulfarr bucked up to meet it, his eyes rolling back. "Mine," he repeated, harder now. "My woman. My good, fierce Skai woman. Ach?"

It was as though he'd plunged himself into her throat, too, yanking out her truth, because Louisa was choking, nodding, holding his shimmering eyes. "Yes," she gasped. "Yes, Wolf. Yours."

She sank down the rest of the way as she said it, full of the strength and the bulk and the ache, the truth of him twitching and spasming inside her. But Ulfarr's eyes were steady, now, satisfied, and he nodded, brought up his hand to caress her face.

"Good," he murmured. "Now show me. Fuck me. Honour me."

Damn. It shot like a streak to Louisa's groin, stabbing her

certain and deep, sparking out with wild, convulsive need. The need to oblige him, to honour him, to offer him this, to prove this. And her nod was rapid and desperate, her gaze tearing away toward Killik, because he was—

Watching. Staring. Still.

Louisa's thoughts skipped, stumbled backwards, because—oh. *Mine*, Ulfarr had said. *Mine. Show me. Fuck me.*

With no... no Killik.

And Killik had heard that, watched that, caught that— and it had meant something to him, something Louisa couldn't at all read in his eyes. Was it shock, was it fury, was it... *hurt.*

But wait, yes, Ulfarr had caught it too, his eyes following Louisa's, his hand slipping up to skitter against Killik's cheek. "And she is yours also, pup," he breathed. "Do this with us, ach?"

Killik's breath shuddered out, but he nodded, quick and furtive, his eyes dropping. And then, without a word, he shifted around behind Louisa, his warm familiar body settling against her, sliding up the back of her loincloth, and prodding... *there.*

Louisa's eyes snapped wide, her breath caught in her throat—was he really going to do this, did he really even want this, did they need to talk about this? But oh, Killik was still jabbing, seeking, and now Ulfarr's hand was here again, his eyes were here again, searching her, safe.

"You are sure you wish for this with us?" he asked her, quiet, darting a purposeful glance around at the room. "Both of us? Here?"

Louisa hauled in a breath, fought to consider the question, as her gaze followed his around the room. Which had continued to fill up with guests and revellers, most of them caught in their own drinks and discussions and laughter— but some of them were watching, too. Including the Skai smith Argarr, wearing an appreciative smile, and Filak, lurking in the opening of his new tunnel, his eyes glinting in the firelight. And also the healer Rurik, sprawled on a bench with his arms crossed, his pale eyes balefully flicking toward Filak, and then back toward Louisa on the fur. As if he was... assessing her. Judging.

Louisa's face heated, her gaze darting away, and finding... Rosa. Rosa, giving an encouraging little grin over her shoulder, and then settling down over John-Ka, who'd been reading at one of the tables. And who was now marking his place in his book, so he could slide his clawed hands up Rosa's short skirt, scraping red lines into her pale skin, while she arched and gasped upon him.

And wait, they weren't the only ones in a similar state, either—Jule's mate Grimarr had her backed against a wall, while the Right Hand Drafli was fondling both his mates at once. And over there, even Simon was sitting bared on a bench, hazily watching an also-bared Maria as she slid down onto his thick, glossy, Ulfarr-sized heft.

And it was that, perhaps, that finally set Louisa nodding, her eyes finding Ulfarr again, her hands clutching to his shoulders. Yes. Yes, she wanted this, wanted to prove this, to feel this. To feel Ulfarr's solid strength filling her, anchoring her, as Killik kept guiding himself in behind. Using his hand to pump out more slickness, to help ease the way, but it was already so tight, so full, oh gods—because despite everything they'd done, they still hadn't done it like this. Not all together like this, two hard male bodies on either side of her, seeking to share her, to sink into her at once...

"More," Louisa gasped, and even with the stretch and the pain she needed this, needed it so much it felt alive, like a shouting scrabbling clamour inside her. She needed them, more of them, needed to honour them, prove it to them, face this, fix this...

"Breathe," Killik hissed behind her, with no tenderness in his voice, or in his strong hands drawing her wider apart.

Showing the whole room this, now, his hard length stabbing into her, sinking deeper, bit by bit. While Ulfarr stayed embedded deeper below, swelling and spasming, waiting for Killik to find his seat, to prod deeper and deeper, breathe, relax, breathe...

Louisa jolted all over as Killik finally sank to the hilt, skin pressed tight to skin, his breath skating shaky across her back. Oh, hell, he was in, they were both inside her at once, shuddering and squeezing out their slick seed, stretching her wide open. And anyone could see this, everyone could see this, Louisa's body hot and quivering and impaled upon two hard, hungry Skai pricks.

And then—then—movement. Killik's embedded strength lifting her up on Ulfarr's thick length, and then guiding her down again. And then Ulfarr holding her there, gouged deep upon him, while Killik slowly slid out, until he'd bobbed free of her. His slick heft lightly slapping her skin, streaking her even wetter, before slowly, steadily sinking back inside. Putting on a show, damn him, more brazen and obscene than anything else he'd ever done, with all these people watching—and Louisa could only shudder and spasm upon it, and beg and wait for more.

"More, *please*," she gasped, earning a smattering of low, approving laughter from behind her, but it didn't matter, nothing mattered, but the strong Skai orcs taking turns with her, sliding themselves in and out of her, swifter and smoother with every breath. While Louisa clung to Ulfarr and welcomed it, wanted it, needed more and more of it, all of it, closer, please...

She shouted as the ecstasy careened and crashed, wrenching through her again and again. Stabbing her with wave after wave of raw, rampant relief, crushing it against all that hot flesh buried inside her—and then Killik stiffened, stuttered, while Ulfarr arched and groaned, yanked her down tight and deep. And then they were both shaking too, falling with her into the abyss, their bodies pulsing and pouring her full of them, flooding her inside and out. So much, so much, everything, everything, she'd done it, she'd honoured them, she'd proven it. She had.

The truth of it sagged her heavy down onto Ulfarr, into the strength of his warm waiting arms, curling around her back. Already caressing her, comforting her, as he kissed her damp hair, and a low, contented growl rumbled through his chest.

"So good, Louisa," he breathed, so soft. "*Mine.*"

It shuddered Louisa all over, struck at something solid and deep and true. And she couldn't stop clinging to him, breathing in the sweet safe scent of his neck, dragging in his strength and his truth. As she felt him relaxing further and further beneath her, his breaths gone slower and deeper, until they escaped in a heavy, rumbling snore. Asleep.

Louisa's eyes had fluttered closed too, her own awareness shimmering away into peace, into this sweet perfect safety— until a movement jarred against her, within her. Killik, finally slipping out and away from her—but now, where he'd been, there was something soft, a rag, tucking in close. And then warmth, heavy and velvety, drawing over her. A fur.

But—wait. Wait, now Killik was shifting sideways, he was swiping for his trousers, he was—he was *leaving*? And just in time, Louisa's hand snapped out, clutched tight against his wrist, against his strangely clammy skin.

"Wait," she breathed, forcing her hazy eyes to focus, to find Killik's kneeling body in the dimming firelight. "Where—where are you going?"

There was a beat of stillness, filled by the distant babble of voices and groans, the low pulsing drum. Until finally Killik sighed, and shrugged, and ran a hand against his messy hair.

"To build a wagon," he replied, a little flat. "Or poke a wasps' nest. Or write some pretty Ka-esh letters, mayhap."

What? Louisa's flinch was too obvious, too betraying—and that was hurt, coiling sudden and dull in her chest. He... he didn't want to tell her. He'd just done that with her, with Ulfarr—and now he wanted to leave. And he didn't want her to know why...

And—wait. This was ringing at something, something familiar, something crucially important. Enough that Louisa clutched Killik's wrist tighter, frantically searched his unreadable eyes.

"Just—don't go off with someone else," she croaked. "Please, Killik. *Don't.*"

Killik's shoulders rose and fell, his eyes shifting away, almost as if—as if that was exactly what he'd been about to do, gods curse him. He'd worked so hard to help Ulfarr, he'd honoured him before his kin, he'd gotten him a woman, and the camp. He'd perhaps done everything he'd set out to do, and now—

Now all he had to do was slide the dagger deep, right where it would hurt most, and then walk away.

"Don't do it, Killik," Louisa breathed, begged. "Don't, for the love of Skai-kesh. Ulfarr still needs you. He *loves* you."

But that was pain, flaring brief but unmistakable in Killik's eyes, as he shot a glance down at Ulfarr's relaxed, softly snoring face. "Ach, does he?" he asked, far too steady, too calm. "And when has he ever spoken this? Or shown me this? When has he ever told *me* to fuck him, and honour him? Or called me *his*?"

Louisa's mouth opened and closed, and she drew in an unsteady breath. "He praises you all the time, Killik!" she countered. "He calls you quick and clever and loyal, his fierce lusty pup, with your sharp words and your strong prick and—"

But Killik's hand snapped up, signing, *No, leave it*, even as he barked a thin, hoarse laugh. "Any worthy Skai speaks praise thus to his bedmates," he replied, clipped. "Most of all ones he wishes to keep. But it is not the same"—he jabbed a wavering claw toward her—"as how he speaks to a true mate. To one he wishes to claim as *his*, for always."

Louisa's throat spasmed, her eyes darting back down to Ulfarr's sleeping face. Because of course he wanted to claim Killik as his for always, right? Surely he did, Louisa was certain of it. Because the way he looked at Killik, the way he touched him, the way he spoke of him, the way he'd been so upset about Killik's other bedmates. Ulfarr did love Killik, he did, but...

But why—why hadn't he ever said those things? Done those things? And now Louisa's thoughts were flicking back to how Ulfarr hadn't wanted to share his *kofi* with Killik— and how he'd kept avoiding the topic of fucking Killik, too. And then, how Killik had told her he would never stop upholding Ulfarr, even if Ulfarr didn't want it anymore...

And surely Killik had caught Louisa's confusion, because he laughed, low and almost easy. "Now you follow, ach?" he said, again with that unnatural lightness in his voice. "I am... useful. Always at hand. A good friend, a lusty bedmate, a good loyal pup, forever underfoot. But I am not"—he drew in a guttering breath—"not *thus*. Not... *wanted*."

He'd given another sharp jab toward Louisa, still wrapped safe and warm in Ulfarr's strong arms. Because— because he was saying Ulfarr wanted *her*, not him. But it didn't make sense, Ulfarr did want him, he did—

"He does want you, Killik," Louisa gasped, because it had to be true, it had to be. "He loves you. I *know* he does."

But Killik only shrugged and laughed again, his eyes unnervingly empty on her face. "Ach, do you?" he drawled. "After these few short nights? When Wolf has had *twenty whole summers* to say this, or do aught about this?"

Louisa couldn't find her voice, her eyes again searching Ulfarr's relaxed, sleeping face. Curse it, why hadn't he done anything? *He was happiest with a woman. He has always longed for a woman. Sune wished to face the woman who will steal Wolf away from us...*

"Then just—ask him, Killik," Louisa said, pleaded. "Just—give it one more night. Give him a chance to explain, before you run off and do something you'd regret. It's been a long day, and we have a big day tomorrow, and I'm sure we're all tired, and..."

But Killik was already looking away, she was already losing him, of course she was. Twenty *years*, and Ulfarr had never said anything, but now he had gone and said all these things to her. And Ulfarr couldn't even speak for himself now, he couldn't try to make Killik stay, but...

But Louisa could. She could prove this. Face this. Fix this.

"And I—I need you, Killik," she whispered. "I—I can't bear the thought of you going off with someone else. Not now, not after all this. *Please*."

Killik's eyes snapped back toward her, his brow deeply furrowing, but he was listening, yes, yes—and Louisa drew in breath, strength, truth. "I need you here," she choked. "With me. With us. Most of all with this Summit tomorrow, I don't know how you expect me to deal with everything involved in it, when I know—when I know you've *left!*"

Her voice had risen too high, too shrill, her eyes pleading on his face. "I would—I would make you mine," she breathed. "If you'd allow it, Killik. I'd give you everything I could, tell you anything you ever wanted to hear. Because I... I love you."

The words cracked in her voice, prickled behind her eyes—because they were probably shameful, surely pathetic, and most certainly... truth.

She loved Killik. She'd loved him for so damned long. Maybe since that first night he'd shown up in her bedroom, and told her of the sad, wounded kin-brother he'd do anything to save.

And gods, the way he was staring at her. Like she'd

shouted at him, thrown something at him, slapped him across the face. "No, woman," he finally replied, his voice wooden, his hand flipping his dagger out of his hair, jabbing it at Ulfarr's sleeping face. "You love him. *Him!*"

And yes, yes, that was true too, and Louisa jerked a nod, gripped her hand tighter at Killik's arm. "Yes," she whispered. "Him, and you. *You*, Killik."

He was shaking his head, his eyes too wide on her face, but Louisa had to keep saying it, keep trying, proving this, showing him. "I know we haven't always gotten along," she rasped. "I still think you're rude and obnoxious and infuriating, and the most enraging tyrant in the realm. But"—she flapped her hand at him, fought to find the words—"you're also... brilliant. Loyal. Funny. Generous. You see so much, you know so much, you do so much. You're a spectacular teacher, you're a devoted father, and you're an absolute fiend in bed. I will never, *ever* get over you, Killik."

It was more raw, humiliating truth, hurled out between them, smacking Killik across the face. And not even his dagger could defend him, or hide that sharp flinch raking up his back—

And wait. Wait, that was more hurt, there in his eyes. More... pain. As if Louisa truly had wounded him with this, somehow struck her own dagger deep, without even knowing how, or why. No, no, no...

"I must—go," Killik finally said, too fast, too shaky on his breath. "I shall—see you come morn."

And that was his hand, coming to his chest, saying, *Sorry, sorry, forgive me—*

And then he leapt to his feet, and left.

52

Louisa slept badly that night, despite the solid safety of Ulfarr's body beneath her, and the warmth of the fur and the fire.

Killik had gone. Killik thought Ulfarr didn't care. Killik had maybe—maybe—spent the night with someone else.

It all wrenched and churned in Louisa's belly, dark and angry and hopelessly jealous. It had been so close, so good and right between them, and now Killik had to run off and ruin everything, again.

But the longer Louisa lay there, trying and failing to sleep, the stronger the suspicion grew. Twisting into a single sharp, devastating question, shouting again and again through her thoughts...

Had Killik *planned* to do this? Had he planned... to *leave*?

Because—the way he'd looked. The way he'd spoken. It had all felt so... resigned. So... finished, as if it had all gone according to his plan. His plan to heal Ulfarr, to find him a woman, to help him regain his place, and build a home. To offer the ultimate gift, the ultimate sacrifice, to the orc he'd always loved so much, the orc he didn't believe loved him the same in return...

And afterwards, once it was done, Killik would sink that dagger deep, and walk away. Knowing he'd done all he could, and given his best possible farewell.

The woman who will steal Wolf away from us.

Louisa squeezed her eyes shut, fought to steady her shaky breaths, but the questions just kept shouting louder, harder. Alongside all those memories of Killik's reluctance, Killik's anger, Killik's other bedmates, Killik saying no, Killik walking away again and again. As if he'd been fighting this, fighting his decision on this, losing his patience and his temper—but then always, always coming back. Guiding Louisa and Ulfarr. Directing them. Helping them. Making sure it worked, making sure they fell in love. Making sure Louisa... stayed.

But now—what was Killik planning next? Had he meant to move away? To leave the camp? To leave *Sune*, and make a life somewhere else, maybe at the mountain, or another camp? But no, no, he wouldn't... or would he?

Louisa desperately wanted to go find him, to hunt him down and demand answers, demand his truth—but no. No. Gods only knew where he'd gone, and she couldn't risk alerting the entire clan to some major conflict between them, not now. Not with Ulfarr's fate still in question, and the camp's fate still in question, with the Summit's public Open House in the morning...

But it made for an awful night's sleep, full of misery and fury and frustration. And when Ulfarr finally stirred awake beneath Louisa, what felt like an eternity later, he must have instantly caught it on her face, or maybe in her scent.

"Is aught amiss, Louisa?" he asked, his bleary eyes sharpening on hers. "Where is—where is Killik?"

The alarm was already there, too close in his raspy voice, and at least Louisa didn't need to lie, not entirely. "I—I'm not sure," she replied. "Maybe just out for a walk. Or hunting?"

But Ulfarr was fully frowning now, his eyes darting between Louisa and the door, and he groped for her dress, and passed it toward her. "We shall find him," he said grimly. "Come."

Louisa nodded, and once she'd cleaned up and dressed, she quietly followed Ulfarr toward the door, past the huddles of their sleeping, snoring guests. And though Ulfarr held his gaze straight ahead, she could feel the urgency radiating from him, twitching all through his big body. Because— because he couldn't bear Killik leaving, either. He loved Killik, he did. And if Killik had gone off and spent the night with someone else, Louisa truly was going to murder him.

Outside, it was very early morning, the sun just rising through the trees, the camp just beginning to stir. Several guests were climbing out of tents and shelters, and a yawning Thomas was already cooking by the fire, raising a hand in greeting toward them. And there was a bleary-eyed but pleased-looking Ragni, returning from his overnight shift on guard duty with several bulky orcs from the mountain, and Kori and Fasti were stretching together in one of the hanging hammocks, their limbs and hair askew.

And blinking toward it, toward this cozy, lovely camp in the rising sunlight, there was suddenly only longing, so deep and heavy Louisa swayed on her feet. Gods, she wanted this. She wanted all of this. She wanted to stay here. She wanted to fix this, and make this work. She wanted Ulfarr, and she wanted...

"Killik!" she exclaimed, with shaky, staggering relief, as his lean, bare-chested body swung down from the trees above. He was still here, he hadn't left, thank the gods...

But wait. He hadn't come from Ulfarr's *kofi*, so that meant he'd slept... somewhere else. And who had he slept with, had he still ruined everything—

Beside Louisa, Ulfarr had stiffened all over, his eyes narrow and surprisingly flinty on where Killik was striding toward them. But Killik's face was carefully smooth, expressionless, what had he done, what had he decided...

"Where were you, Killik?" Ulfarr demanded, his voice harsh enough to make Louisa blink. "Why did you leave us?"

Killik blinked too, and flicked a brief, almost imperceptible glance toward Louisa's face. "I stayed the night with Sune," he said, too lightly. "Thought one of us ought to make sure he stayed out of trouble."

Oh. Louisa's relief shuddered through her breath, dropped her stiff shoulders—but damn it, Killik could still be lying, he could still have found another bedmate first... right? And perhaps Ulfarr thought the same, because he lurched toward Killik, and thrust his face down into his neck. So he could... smell him. So he could make sure he was telling the truth.

But yes, yes, Ulfarr's breath exhaled with obvious relief, his hand clapping firm against Killik's shoulder. While Killik's eyes stayed carefully unreadable, even as he gave Ulfarr's back a brisk pat in return.

"Good morn to you also, Wolf," he said. "Now, we ought to make ourselves ready for this Summit, ach? Sune says Cecily has set out fancy clothes for us, and we have much left to prepare, do we not?"

Right. The official Open House was set to begin at noon, with their full slate of games, classes, and activities. And while they'd set much of it up already, there were still multiple crucial items on their list for the morning. So Louisa drew in breath, and made herself nod, even as her eyes kept searching Killik's face. While beside her, Ulfarr nodded too, and then turned toward—oh. Sune.

Louisa hadn't even seen Sune standing there, but he'd clearly been watching, his narrow eyes flicking from Ulfarr, to Killik, to Louisa, and back again. *What is amiss?* he signed. *Why do you all scent thus?*

There was an instant's awkward silence, in which Ulfarr rubbed at his nose, and Louisa shot another searching glance toward Killik. Who sighed, and then squared his shoulders, and met Sune's eyes. "I only failed to tell them I was staying with you last eve," he replied, his voice carefully light. "But now they know, and we three shall speak more together later, ach? After this Open House is done."

Sune's expression relaxed again, and Ulfarr's stiff body softened, too. And something leapt, bright and hopeful in Louisa's belly, because even if Killik had walked out like that last night, maybe—maybe he'd actually listened to her, after all. Maybe he'd just needed time and space to think about it. And if he really wanted to talk more about it later, maybe—maybe he was finally going to be honest with Ulfarr, too.

Which meant—they could still fix this. They could. They *would*.

"That sounds good," Louisa said firmly, with a wavering, hopeful smile toward Killik's face. "Thank you, Killik."

He nodded back, though his eyes didn't quite meet hers. And as Louisa blinked toward him, suddenly there was the awareness, the weight, of all those heavy, deeply betraying things she'd told him the night before. *I love you. I need you. I will never, ever get over you.*

It flushed hot in her face, dropped her eyes to the mossy earth at her feet, while Killik cleared his throat. "We ought to eat, and set to work," he said. "This day carries great weight, and has the power to alter much for us."

Right. Yes. It was a critically important day, and it was vital that they carry it off. And Louisa sank into the firm strength of Ulfarr's hand on her shoulder, guiding her closer, together with Killik and Sune. And once they were all clustered together in a ring, Ulfarr said a heartfelt prayer to Skaikesh, asking for his blessing, and his guidance, and his safety.

And though he didn't speak it, Louisa could again feel Ulfarr's longing, his desperate hope. His need to earn this, to show this, to gain his clan's forgiveness. To gain this as his home.

And when they drew apart again, there was only determination, low and powerful in Louisa's belly. They would do this. They would gain this, together. As a clan, and maybe even as... a family.

And yes, it was there in Killik's eyes too, and in Sune's. They were Skai. They were family. They were home.

"Then let's go," Louisa said, making the sign for victory. "And put on a damn good show."

53

The first-ever Skai Summit Open House was a wild, chaotic success.

They'd finished setting up right on schedule, and Louisa had felt almost nauseous as they'd waited for their official launch at noon. What if no one came? What if only a few people came? What if Louisa's old friends all came and mocked her and left?

But as they'd waited, Rosa had remained unfailingly optimistic, pointing out that one could always rely on people to be nosy—and that even if no one else came, there were still dozens of orcs and women and children already here to enjoy the day's activities. But even all the Skai milling about had seemed nervous too, quietly murmuring to each other, and glancing repeatedly toward the road.

But then Ragni had called down from his watch-tree, and soon the first group of guests had come around the corner— a family who Louisa had invited, who'd once lived on her street in Dusbury. And she had almost tripped as she'd stumbled over toward them, shaking their hands, and welcoming them to the camp.

They'd seemed shy and wary at first, but unmistakably curious, too, just as Rosa had promised. And as soon as Louisa had sent them off with Jule for their first guided tour, another group showed up, and then another. And then a long steady stream of them, men and women and children too, all blinking up at the camp with wide, awestruck eyes.

Louisa stayed on welcoming duty throughout, enthusiastically greeting anyone she recognized by name, and handing out the activity schedule and map Rosa had printed. And soon the camp was full of chattering voices and shouting children, and Louisa's heart skipped every time she turned to look.

Because it truly did look—wonderful. The camp was decorated with hundreds of paper lanterns and streamers, cheerfully waving and spinning in the branches above, and ropes and ladders also hung from every tree, inviting guests to climb and swing and explore. They'd also set up multiple snack and drink tables, along with signage and gathering points for their planned schedule of activities.

And along with the ongoing rotation of guided tours, many activities were well underway, too. Killik was leading the honey-hunting expeditions—the "honey" all dangling copper coins, tucked amidst the trees—while Ulfarr had begun knife-throwing lessons, showing their attendees how to throw at a huge wooden target, which had multiple funny creatures stamped upon it. Argarr had also set up a makeshift forge in the clearing, teaching guests how to make nails, and Thomas and Elgr were leading children and orclings in a treasure hunt, with clues and prizes hidden throughout the forest.

There were multiple activities set up down in the common-room, too, and during a break in the guest arrivals, Louisa ducked down to look. Filak now had three separate tunnels to explore, all winding off in opposite directions, and apparently—in some bizarre stroke of generosity—he'd even decided to allow each visiting child to mine a small piece of amethyst. While out in the common-room itself, Igull and Polly presided over a dice tournament at the tables, and by the fire, Flora and Galmr were demonstrating how to braid rope. And at yet another table, Rosa and Geva sat beside a large sign that proclaimed, *Eager to educate your children in an enriching cross-cultural environment? Sign up for updates on the Wolf-Camp's new school!*

"This is unbelievable, Lou," came a familiar voice behind her, and when Louisa whipped around, it was Joan, a wry grin on her face. And with her were Elise and Gladys and the children, too, all of them looking cautious but curious, while Halthorr beamed proudly behind them.

"Oh, I'm so glad you came!" Louisa exclaimed, lurching forward for a round of quick hugs. "Would you like to try mining some amethyst? Or braiding some rope?"

Both Stefan and Ame shyly nodded, and then traipsed off with Halthorr toward the rope-braiding. While Elise's wary eyes had caught on Rosa and Geva's table, as if she might actually be interested—so Louisa cheerfully waved her over and introduced her, while her heartbeat thumped oddly in her chest.

Gods, she wanted this so much. And they were so close. So close.

She drew down a deep breath as she headed back up to the clearing again, just in time for Killik's rope-walking lesson. A small crowd had gathered around where they'd tied a long, sturdy rope between two trees—not high enough to be truly dangerous, but still high enough that Louisa's breath caught at the sight of Killik easing himself out onto it. He was dressed in a crisp white tunic, and a pair of slim black trousers—all courtesy of Cecily—and he looked impossibly elegant as he held to the tree behind him, and felt the rope beneath his feet. His soft leather boots seeking, settling—and then he carefully released the tree behind him, and stepped forward.

A few whistles and cheers broke out around them, but Killik's eyes stayed focused straight ahead, and Louisa could see him drawing in breath, grounding himself into the rope. And then taking step after careful step, his arms outstretched, his lean body taut, the muscles shifting beneath his lovely clothes.

And watching him, Louisa's heart skipped in her chest, the longing pooling deep in her belly. Gods, he was stunning, he was one of the most beautiful things she'd ever seen in her life—and then his hand carefully reached up to his hair, and plucked out one of his daggers. Hurling it in a single smooth stroke toward the tree-trunk ahead of him, where it sank deep with a thud. And in another swift movement, he threw his second dagger to join it, as his hair fell long and black and shining over his shoulders.

The sight of it skittered Louisa's longing even deeper, and she exhaled at the feel of Ulfarr settling behind her, his warm hand curving around her waist. And when she glanced up at his face, his eyes were fixed on Killik, glimmering with yearning and pride. "He is magnificent, is he not?" he murmured. "My fierce, perfect pup."

Louisa swallowed and nodded, and sank a little closer against him. "He is," she murmured back. "And I think—I think he'd love to hear that from you, sweetheart. If you'd be willing to tell him."

Ulfarr's chest hollowed, his gaze catching strange on hers—but then he nodded, short and curt. And it was enough to settle Louisa's shoulders, sinking her even heavier against him. Ulfarr loved Killik, and Killik loved him. And they would finally talk about this, and sort it out. They would.

She joined the crowd's loud, raucous cheers as Killik

reached the tree-trunk—where he made a show of yanking out his daggers, and then spinning around, and hurling them both into the opposite tree instead. Whipping up more delighted cheers around them, Ulfarr's perhaps booming loudest of all.

Afterwards, Killik helped multiple orclings and children give rope-walking a try, striding along on the ground beside them as they lurched and wobbled on the rope. One of the orclings was Simon and Maria's older son Bjorn, and as he walked, clutching tight at Killik's shoulder, Louisa's gaze kept darting sideways to Simon and Maria, who were both standing nearby, watching with fond smiles on their faces. They'd both seemed to enjoy the Open House so far, and they'd often been surrounded by friends and well-wishers— and Louisa had even overheard one elderly Skai congratulating Simon on such an excellent Skai event.

It all settled Louisa's hope even deeper, because damn it, this *was* an excellent event. They'd brought the Skai together, they'd introduced the camp to the community, they'd brought humans and orcs just a little closer together. And while some of the human guests had kept their distance, preferring to watch rather than participate, Louisa could still see how it helped. Showing them orcs who weren't warriors or enemies, but instead teachers, and athletes, and crafters, and engineers.

However, the sparring tournament was yet to come—and at a meaningful sign from Rosa, Louisa nudged Ulfarr over toward the pair of fighting rings they'd set up, just outside the clearing. The tournament's other Skai participants were already assembling, and at a loud whistle from Igull, their human guests began to filter over, too.

"Next, we welcome you to our Skai Summit Sparring Tournament," Ulfarr announced in his deep steady voice, once the crowd had gathered. "Skai sparring is not meant to harm or wound, but only to test our speed and strength, and grant us joy with our kin. But to make sure of this"—he waved toward a bored-looking Rurik, standing at the edge of the ring—"our medic will stand by, and offer his help whenever this is needed."

Thankfully, no one seemed to question any of this, and next Ulfarr called forward four Skai—including Killik, now stripped to the waist—for their first pair of matches. And once Ulfarr had introduced each Skai by name, they paired off and bowed to each other, clasping their hands tight. And then, at another whistle from Igull, they faced off in the rings, and attacked.

The human audience gasped, the tension and alarm rippling through the air—but once the sparring orcs had settled into a rhythm, punching and kicking and ducking and twisting, the tension seemed to skitter into curiosity, or even excitement. Because while it was clear that each orc wanted to win, it was also obvious that this was only a contest, only a game. And Louisa's mouth drew up at the sight of Killik leaping and whirling and kicking, his movements exaggerated and flamboyant, perhaps intended less for combat effectiveness, and more to entertain the audience. To put on a good show.

"He's good, right?" came a familiar voice, and when Louisa twisted to look, it was Maria, with a wry grin on her mouth. "One of my absolute favourites to watch. Go, Killik!"

Louisa blinked, but then grinned back, and loudly hollered Killik's name, too. Earning a brief glance from him over toward her, and even a swift sign from his hand—*watch this*—as he swung a sweeping kick to his opponent's head.

Louisa laughed and cheered together with Maria, while more warmth and hope bubbled in her chest. They were doing this. They were really, really doing this. And it truly was lovely to talk and laugh with Maria, and cheer Killik on together, until he finally did gain the win, tackling his opponent to the ground with an impressive flourish.

"Our first winner," Ulfarr announced afterwards, grasping Killik's hand, and raising it high. "Killik, of Clan Skai!"

Louisa cheered as loudly as she could, while Maria whistled and stomped beside her. And as the rest of the tournament progressed, Maria offered helpful explanations and commentary, too—about different orcs' backgrounds and fighting styles, and which ones she favoured to win. Of course, Simon was her favourite, and he soon proved to be a truly outstanding fighter—but when Ulfarr finally entered his own first round, Maria praised his speed and technique, too. And then she even cheered along with Louisa as Ulfarr easily won his match, flashing a rueful smile through the crowd toward them.

After that, Louisa was fully caught up in the excitement, cheering for match after match, as the pool of winners grew smaller and smaller. Both Killik and Ulfarr proved to be fierce contestants, and Killik finally only lost to the lean Right Hand Drafli, who also turned out to be a stunningly vicious fighter. While Ulfarr won every single one of his matches, wielding his size and weight to his full advantage— at least, until he found himself facing none other than—Simon.

There was an instant's hushed silence all around them, and beside Louisa, Maria had gone silent and still—but then Ulfarr gave a low bow toward Simon, his hand in a fist on his sweaty, heaving chest. "I should be glad to forfeit, brother," came Ulfarr's voice, decisive and carrying. "Our Enforcer deserves this honour, as our clan's faithful leader, and our Summit's favoured guest."

There was another moment's stillness—but then Simon reached out, and firmly clapped his hand to Ulfarr's shoulder. "Ach, come and fight, brother," he replied. "I ken we shall show our guests a good fair match."

Ulfarr's astonishment flashed across his eyes, stilled his

sweaty body—but then he smiled, slow and grateful, as he bowed low again. And when Igull gave the starting whistle, Ulfarr lunged forward with shocking speed, and blocked Simon's surging attack with a sharp swing of his forearm.

Beside Louisa, both Killik and Maria shouted at once—Killik had come over to join them, too—and Louisa's hands clapped over her mouth, her eyes frozen on the match. On Ulfarr and Simon punching and ducking and swinging and swerving, their big bodies moving almost too fast to follow, their heavy grunts ringing through the clear-ing. And despite her racing heartbeat, Louisa could appre-ciate just how well matched they were, with their similar height and weight, and their similar style of fighting, too. Enough that at one point, they both threw and blocked the exact same punch at once, a development that drew a genuine-sounding laugh from Simon, and a grin from Ulfarr, too. Almost as if—as if they truly were enjoying this.

"Watch his right, Wolf!" Killik shouted beside Louisa, prompting Ulfarr to duck just in time, while Maria signed at Killik with what looked like a curse, and shouted Simon's name even louder. Her voice carrying over the stomps and claps and cheers, enough that Simon glanced toward her, squared his shoulders, and then lunged forward again. And though Ulfarr twisted sideways, Simon just caught his arm— and suddenly it was over, Simon crashing Ulfarr to the earth and twisting his arm behind him, while Ulfarr shook his head, and signed his defeat.

Killik loudly groaned, glowering viciously toward Maria, but Maria was grinning and hollering, and Louisa couldn't stop smiling, either. It had been a fair, well-met match, and Simon had agreed to face Ulfarr, and treat him as an equal. Which suddenly seemed far more important than who had won or not, especially with this crowd of cheering, chattering Skai all around them. Witnessing Ulfarr's defeat, yes—but also how Simon smiled as he reached down, and drew Ulfarr back up to his feet.

"Well met, brother," Simon's loud voice called, over the hubbub all around. "A good match."

Ulfarr's grin was broad and delighted, and perhaps a little weepy, too. Enough that Killik abruptly stalked back over to the ring, where he called out Simon as the winner, and then announced the final match of the tournament, between Simon and Drafli.

It turned out to be another spectacular fight, drawing gasps and shouts from the crowd. But after a quick word to Maria, Louisa went over to join Killik—and now Sune and his friends, too—in offering Ulfarr their enthusiastic congratulations on such a well-fought match.

Ulfarr's eyes were still unusually bright, his nose betraying an unmistakable sniff, but he gratefully smiled and thanked them all, and then drew Killik and Louisa and Sune tightly into his arms. "I thank you, my kin," he choked. "You are all so, so good to me."

My kin again. It shimmered yet more warmth and hope into Louisa's belly, and she squeezed him tight until his breaths felt steady again. And then they all cheered together for Simon and Drafli's match, until Simon finally tackled Drafli to the earth, and shouted his victory.

Once Simon and Drafli had both risen to their feet again, Drafli wryly shaking his head, Ulfarr went and proudly announced Simon as their winner, to almost dizzying applause. And when Simon grinned over at Maria, she leapt up and rushed toward him, and laughed as he swept her into his arms. Both of them seeming so happy, at ease, even with Ulfarr standing there beaming back toward them, and then carefully placing a braided rope crown onto Simon's head.

It felt so right, so strong, a juddering ache in Louisa's chest—and then Ulfarr raised his hands, and called for the final event of the day. "Skai of ages past oft honoured *hirthskalds*, who battled each other with words, rather than blades," he said, his voice carrying over the crowd. "Now I welcome my kin to bring this back amongst us, so we can all share in this gift."

Louisa's heart hammered as she walked with the rest of their group into the ring, where they all knelt together in a large circle. With Killik and Sune to Louisa's right, and beside them were Ragni and Kori and Fasti, and Thomas and Angus and Elgr, and Igull and Polly. Orcs and humans coming together, kneeling and waiting together, as Sune began the beat, his daggers striking sharp and bright. And then more beats joined into it, deepening and syncopating it, until it echoed through the clearing, and rang through the trees above.

Beside Louisa, Killik drew in breath, drew up strength from the earth—and then he spoke. This one a new verse, one they'd created together just for this, fully in common-tongue. "Hail, my kin. Hale you be. Hie to the hall of the wolf, and hold high our home to the skies."

Killik's voice thudded against the drums, striking like a drum of its own, and then he glanced at Louisa—and with a silent prayer to Skai-kesh, she spoke her own part of the verse. "Hail, my kin. Happy you be. Answer the call of the wolf, and howl our hymn to the sky."

Her heart was pounding, but she'd said it, she'd done it—and then Polly spoke beside her, adding her own variation. Sweeping around the circle, each speaker speaking their own truth, making the verse their own, deepening and strength-ening it. Until they'd almost circled around again, Fasti, then Kori, and then Ragni. And next would have been Sune, but they always skipped him, and—

And then Sune—signed at Killik. Took a breath. And when Ragni finished his turn, Killik gripped Sune's hand, as Sune squared his shoulders, and... spoke.

"Hail, my kin," he said, his voice raspy, but audible. "Hale you be. Howl your thanks to our wolf, who holds you safe in his home."

It was the first time Louisa had ever heard Sune speak, and there were multiple other gasps around them, too—but beside her, Killik had already repeated Sune's verse, and after a swift sign toward the circle, they all repeated it together. *Howl your thanks to our wolf, who holds you safe in his home.*

Sune's eyes had flicked over to Ulfarr, who was at the front of the crowd, his hand over his heart. And there was water streaking down his cheeks, his hand thumping his chest, and then signing Sune's name. *I love you too, Sune.*

It choked in Louisa's throat, enough that she nearly missed her next line—but she somehow managed it, and the verse swung around again. And though Sune skipped it this time, there was a small smile on his mouth, his beats ringing a little louder than before.

When the verse finished, there was a breath of hovering stillness—and then one clap, and another. Until the entire audience was cheering and whistling, and at the front of the crowd, Simon was clapping too, and stomping his feet. And several older Skai were full-on weeping, and beside Simon, even Drafli looked rather stunned, and drew his mates closer against his side.

Louisa's own eyes were still prickling, and when she met Killik's eyes, they looked unusually bright, too—but then he drew in breath, and signed at them to continue. So they launched into the next verse, now in the orcs' tongue, and then the next. And finally, they finished with that very first verse they'd learned, the one that still pulsed so often through Louisa's thoughts. *I fear you not, feeder of wolves.*

When they finished, the entire camp echoed with shouts and stomps, and Louisa felt hot and fluttery as their group all smiled and signed back *thank you*, their hands flat over their hearts. And she scarcely heard Ulfarr's final thank-you and farewell to their guests, though she could almost feel his own emotion, his own simmering happiness. His hope.

They'd done this. They'd held the Summit, they'd honoured their clan, they'd welcomed their community. They'd put on a magnificent show. And amidst it all, Ulfarr had shown himself a humble, capable, hardworking leader, worthy of respect and redemption.

And as Louisa watched Ulfarr standing beside the road, saying farewell to their guests, and handing out paper lanterns and streamers as souvenirs, there was again that... rightness. That certainty. Because even if Simon still didn't see it, even if he didn't offer Ulfarr his forgiveness, Ulfarr had still done it. He'd still gained it. He'd still faced his past, faced his fears, and stood tall as the Wolf of the Skai.

And when Louisa glanced at Killik beside her, she knew he could see it, too, his eyes blinking, his tooth biting his lip. He'd helped Ulfarr. He'd gained all he'd planned, all he'd set out to do.

He didn't resist when Louisa found his clammy hand, squeezing it tight. And they stood in silence together, watching, and perhaps praying, as Simon strode over toward Ulfarr, and clapped him firmly on the shoulder. And then Simon spoke something to Ulfarr, something that had them both glancing over their shoulders, toward—Louisa and Killik.

Louisa twitched, and she could see something shifting in Ulfarr's eyes, quivering on his mouth—and then he gave a low, jerky bow toward Simon, his hand over his heart. To which Simon smiled back, and again clapped Ulfarr's shoulder, and then... then waved him forward. Toward Louisa and Killik.

Louisa watched Ulfarr as he came, her throat tightening, because he was—smiling. Smiling at them, wider and brighter than she'd perhaps ever seen it, and his eyes were still so bright, his mouth quivering. As if whatever Simon had told him, it had been important, crucially important, almost as if... as if...

"What did Simon tell you?" Killik demanded, as soon as Ulfarr was within reach. "*What*, Wolf?"

Ulfarr's breath shuddered out, and he grasped both Killik and Louisa by the shoulders, steering them away. Away from the clearing, from their kin, from their chattering lingering guests. Deeper west into the forest, where they soon found Airik and another orc from the mountain, still armed and on patrol along Rikard's border. But after a quick sign from Killik, they nodded, and headed back toward the camp. Leaving Louisa and Killik and Ulfarr alone here, so Ulfarr could draw in breath, and say...

"Simon—praised the Summit," Ulfarr finally said, his voice choked. "He praised our work, and our cleverness, and our wisdom. And he praised my clever hardworking kin, and he said—he said—"

They'd halted in the trees, and Ulfarr's breath was heaving now, his hand rubbing at his eyes. "He said," he gulped, "he wished to speak more later, but for now, he has—released me from my vow. My vow not to marry, or take a mate."

Louisa's heart skipped, her hands spasming at her sides. Because yes, Ulfarr had sworn not to take a mate, not until he'd proven himself to Simon. And now—now—

Now Killik was staring at Ulfarr, his throat bobbing—and then he signed something toward him, too swift for Louisa to catch. But Ulfarr was nodding, exhaling, his hand over his heart, his head bowing low toward Killik, and then...

Then he turned to Louisa. Clasped her hand in his. And...

And sank to one knee before her.

"Louisa," he said, his eyes shimmering on hers, his low voice barely audible over the screeching thud of her heart-beat. "You have been such a blessing, and such a joy. You have been so kind, so brave, so hungry, and so true. I have never longed for a woman the way I long for you, and I—"

He broke off there, heaving for breath, drawing her hand to his mouth. Kissing it so gently, so sweetly, so warm and hopeful and reverent, oh gods, oh gods...

"My sweet Louisa," he whispered, holding her eyes. "Will you marry me?"

54

M arry him. Marry him. *Marry him.*

Something swayed and swooped in Louisa's chest, while a sudden shrill whine blared through her skull. Ulfarr wanted to marry her. To *marry* her?!

She couldn't stop gaping at him, at where he was still kneeling before her, looking at her like that, with such soft, reverent hope glimmering in his eyes. While Louisa's brain just kept spinning, shouting louder and louder. He wanted to *marry* her.

"But—why?" she finally asked, numb, into the sudden, waiting silence. "Why—marriage? You've spoken so often of—of mates, so I thought—"

And oh, gods, what had she thought? What had she hoped? That Ulfarr would ask her to be his mate, perhaps, her and Killik both—and no, no, she hadn't once thought of marriage. Of going through with another wedding, risking another disaster like Lord Scall. Lord Scall was dead...

"Ach, matehood is most oft the orc way of this," cut in Killik's voice, snapping Louisa's blinking eyes toward him. "But many orcs choose to wed their human mates, also. And if you and Wolf wed"—his eyes glittered, strange and intent—"this will better help you. Better keep you safe."

It would? Louisa kept staring at Killik, uncomprehending, and he nodded back, his mouth set. "If you have a husband," he said, "then by your human laws, *he* shall be seen as the owner of this land, not you. And thus, any attacks against you would then be turned toward him. You should never need to fear this Rikard again, or face his threats or strikes against you. *Ever.*"

Louisa's heartbeat skipped—he didn't want her to face Rikard, to fear Rikard? And Killik nodded again, his eyes grim and glinting on her face. "This man has been hunting you for many days now," he said, quieter. "Seeking to bring you harm. And we should far rather he seek to hunt Wolf instead, ach?"

Louisa swallowed, and darted a look at Ulfarr—who firmly nodded as he rose to his feet again, his hand still clasping hers. As if he truly wanted this. Wanted to take on this risk for her. Wanted to *marry* her. But gods, why hadn't they told her this, was Rikard truly hunting her, they wanted her to escape Rikard, to forget...

"And also," Killik continued, snapping her gaze back to his face, "if you and Wolf wed, you then have surety for your sisters and their younglings. You have no more need to fear what might befall them, or their home, if aught ever befalls *you.* For you ken we should care for them, always, on your behalf."

Oh. Oh, gods. So it was also about the—the inheritance. The property. The house. About how by marrying her, Ulfarr would replace Rikard as Louisa's heir. And how that would make sure Louisa's kin were taken care of, if anything ever happened to her.

And wait. Surely—Louisa rapidly searched Killik's eyes— surely it was about the camp, too. About ensuring the camp could stay here, on her lands, no matter what. Ensuring Killik and Ulfarr's own kin were cared for, too.

And while a distant part of Louisa's brain could see the logic of all this—and could even appreciate the neat, obvious solution in it—the rest of her was still stuck, staggering, shrieking. They wanted to get married. They wanted her to offer up her land and her safety and her *life*, after she'd sworn never to put herself at such risk again, after all the hell Lord Scall had put her through. But no, no, Lord Scall was dead...

"And—you *want* that?" Louisa croaked, toward Ulfarr's flushed, watching face. "You really want to—get married? To *me*?"

Because yes, yes, that was a rising whispering hope, wasn't it? Maybe Ulfarr didn't really want it, maybe this was just Killik pushing him into it, maybe—

But Ulfarr's eyes just kept shimmering like that on hers, and he brought her hand to his mouth, gave it a soft, gentle kiss. "I should be most honoured, Louisa," he whispered, hoarse. "And I should swear to honour you in return, and uphold your wishes, for always. And the payment we have been gathering for you shall yet be only yours, however you wish for this."

The payment they'd been gathering? Wait, did they not even have it yet? And it all just kept catching, spasming in Louisa's gut, swift and dark and painful, because that was just what Lord Scall had done too, wasn't it? Just what he'd promised? Marry him, and he would care for her, honour her, support her. But it had all been a lie, it had been for the dowry, for the coin he'd so desperately needed from her father, for the fool war he kept fighting, for the orcs he wanted to kill. For the sons he expected her to give him...

Louisa twitched, jolted, bit her lip, hard. No. *No.* Lord Scall was dead. *Dead.*

But the terror was still there, jostling and churning far

too close, and her wild eyes searched, and found... Killik. Killik, still standing here watching this, now with his fists and jaw clenched tight. His eyes shifting, his head slowly tilting as he studied her...

"But what," Louisa somehow gasped, and yes, this was something solid, something else she could cling to, please. "But what about—Killik?"

There was more ringing, dangling silence, and now Ulfarr's eyes darted to Killik, too. Looking him up and down, as his brow slowly furrowed, and his head tilted, too. "Killik wishes for this, also," Ulfarr said, though his voice wavered. "Ach, Killik?"

Killik's nod was too smooth, too quick, his smile too cool and practiced on his mouth. "Ach, I do," he said lightly. "I have always wished to see you settled and happy with a good woman, Wolf. And now I have granted you this, to all our gain."

Granted you this, to all our gain. So easy, so generous and dismissive, and dredging up such sharp, painful bitterness in Louisa's gut. *Granted you this*, he'd said. *You.* Meaning... Ulfarr. Not... not himself.

And Killik even had the audacity to reach toward Louisa, to gently caress his hand against her cheek. To make her look at him, so he could smile at her, and sway her, and say...

"Breathe, woman," he murmured. "You have naught to fear from this. You and Wolf shall find much joy and peace together, and you shall be good, strong leaders to our camp, and good parents to our son. I have oft tested you these past weeks, and you have proven yourself to me as a strong, fierce, faithful, worthy woman, ach?"

I have oft tested you. You have proven yourself to me. It swerved and juddered in Louisa's chest, snapped her to staggering stillness. Because—because yes, she should be rejoicing that she'd finally proven it, she'd shown him, she'd gained his approval, his permission...

But Killik was still talking about *them*. About Louisa and Ulfarr, apart, separate from him. Right? And he'd even fucking brought Sune into it, and that truth jolted deeper, harsher. Did Killik really think he could just hand Sune over to Louisa, did he really still think—was he really still planning to—to—

"And," Killik continued, so soft, he was still talking, still touching her, damn him, *damn* him. "And mayhap soon, you and Wolf shall welcome a son of your own, also."

A son of their own. Louisa startled, stared, but Killik just kept talking, kept smiling. "A good, strong Skai son," he said, lower. "A son of Wolf's own blood, and yours. A son who shall know only safety, and *peace*."

A son. A son. *A son.*

And it was that, finally, that sliced through all the wailing mayhem clamouring in Louisa's skull. And escaped in a shrill, grating laugh, echoing cold and empty through the trees. A son, a son, a son...

"No," she hissed, at Killik's lying, *lying* face. "No. I can't."

55

She couldn't.

It came out like a curse, spat stark and decisive and furious into Killik's face. And yes, yes, she'd wanted to see him twitch like that, to see the confusion flicker in his eyes, because he was such a lying tyrant *snake* and she was saying no, no, *no.*

She waited while Killik fought to find his composure again, drawing up his breath from the earth. And even putting on that look in his eyes again, that soft tolerant warmth, as if he wanted to comfort her, as if he fucking *cared.*

"Breathe, Louisa," he murmured, with another light, infuriating pat to her face. "You are a strong, hearty, capable woman, and there is naught you cannot—"

But Louisa laughed again, or maybe it was a sob, or a roar, as she slapped his hand away from her. "No, Killik," she snarled. "I can't. I tried, and I tried, and I tried, and—"

She had to haul for her own breath, drag it up from the earth, fight to see through her blinking clouding eyes. She could say it. She could finally admit it. She could speak truth, face it, fucking face it, *I fear you not, I fear you not...*

"I can't," she choked. "I can't have sons. I can't have—children. At all. Ever."

There. There, she'd said it, she'd faced it, but curse her, she was shaking, she was weeping, the water escaping hot and miserable from her eyes. "I tried," she gasped, toward the ground. "I tried so hard. I wanted children—so much."

There was only silence, ringing sudden and empty all around them, and Louisa gulped for more air, more truth, face it, face it. "I had—four miscarriages," she croaked. "One of them at—six months. I almost—I almost *died*."

The pure panic of that day, of how she'd screamed in agony in the latrine as Gladys had hovered and wept, still blazed with too much horror to bear—and she whipped her head back and forth, dragged her shaky hands down her face. "Afterwards, once we finally got the physician"—another too-loud laugh—"it turned out it was—it was all because of the infection Scall gave me. The infection that almost killed me. It killed all my children, too."

She was fully sobbing now, and twitched all over at the feel of a touch, tentative on her back—but oh, it was Ulfarr, just Ulfarr, and she lurched toward him, buried her face in his solid chest. And then shuddered and wept as he stroked her, so gentle and careful, his heartbeat racing beneath her hot, wet cheek.

"I am so sorry to hear this, Louisa," he whispered, into her hair. "This must have brought you such grief. Such fear."

It seemed to only make her sob harder, weeping as she perhaps hadn't wept in years. She'd kept it shoved down for so damned long, keeping it deep and secret and forgotten, because it could never be fixed, not ever. Lord Scall was dead, and that had been the only answer, the only victory, and...

"You did not... scent this upon her, Killik?" came Ulfarr's voice, quiet and perhaps almost accusing. "Would there not have been... some trace?"

Louisa flinched, because—wait. Ulfarr meant—he meant

he'd wanted to know about this. Because he thought this was important. Damn it, *damn* it—

With a flailing flap of her hands, Louisa shoved away from him, staggered away from that warm, steady strength. "There were—complications," she rasped, wiping shaky at her eyes. "From the stillbirth. I had to have my womb—removed. It was apparently a miracle I survived, and the fever that almost killed me at least killed Scall's infection too, so maybe—maybe it affected how it scented—"

She was babbling, spitting it out too fast and too urgent. And why was she even saying this, giving them this, throwing out all her pain and grief before them—

But then her swollen, bleary eyes found Killik again, found his stunned, staring face. And yes, yes, that was why she was saying this. She couldn't bear for Killik to claim that yes, he had long ago smelled the truth of all this upon her, and he hadn't thought to mention it to Ulfarr, because it hadn't fucking mattered.

Because—it did matter. It did. It was there on both their faces, shouting at Louisa, scraping like sharp claws up her spine. Ulfarr looking so pale, so haggard and sad, while Killik's watching eyes flashed between shock, and disbelief, and finally, rage.

"Why," he hissed, very low, "did you not tell us of this, woman?"

Louisa's quivering mouth opened, the truth hovering so close, so dangerous, so deadly. *I've never told anyone, ever, because it gave me—because then I had—because then they might suspect—*

But no, no, no, and she quaked all over, dragged desperately for air, for truth. For other truth, for some part of it she could say, please—

"I didn't—I didn't think it mattered!" she finally stammered, her voice shrill and painful in her ears. "You told me Ulfarr couldn't father children, and then you told me *you* didn't want to, either! So I thought it was fine, I thought it was good! I suppose I thought it was even—providence, somehow, a gift from the gods! But then..."

But then—then Ulfarr had been healed. Maybe enough to have sons, after all. And gods, what had Killik said, back when he'd told her about that? *Should Wolf wish for this, I should welcome this for him. We shall not need to think of it for some time yet...*

And again, Killik had made it sound like it hadn't mattered. Like it made no difference to him, or to Ulfarr. But now, gazing at Killik's furious face, his tight twisting mouth, more bitter, miserable comprehension flashed across Louisa's thoughts, hard enough to sway her on her feet.

Mayhap soon, you and Wolf shall welcome a son of your own. A good, strong Skai son, of Wolf's own blood...

"You *wanted* Ulfarr to have a son," Louisa breathed at Killik, over the horrified drumbeat in her ears. "It was part of your fucking *plan.*"

For an instant, there was only silence, pulsing out between them, while Killik's mouth twisted even tighter. Saying—yes. Yes, that had been his plan. Of course it had been, it had been so, so obvious, how hadn't Louisa fucking seen it? Killik seeking her out, setting her up with Ulfarr, teaching them how to please and care for each other...

Killik hadn't only wanted to give Ulfarr a woman for ten nights. He'd wanted to give him a whole new family. A whole new son.

The woman who will steal Wolf away from us.

"You slimy, lying *snake*," Louisa growled, and suddenly she could scarcely breathe through the pounding, plunging fury. "Was anything you told me the truth? Did the ten nights mean anything at all? Or"—she gulped for breath—"was it all about testing me, and getting me attached, and giving Ulfarr a new son? Giving him a new *family*, to replace the one he already has?!"

Ulfarr startled, staring toward Killik, while Killik's mouth opened and closed, his mouth oddly twitching. "No, woman," he snapped, though his voice wavered. "I should never seek to replace Sune. I only..."

His eyes darted to Ulfarr, to where Ulfarr was still looking at him like that, with such shock and confusion in his eyes. And finally Killik grimaced, shrugged, let out a shaky breath.

"I only wish for—your happiness, Wolf," he rasped. "And I know—a son is what you have always longed for most, beyond all else. A son of your own blood. So you can grant him all the safety and peace that was stolen from you."

It sounded—it sounded like a direct quote, his voice even deepening, as if to mimic Ulfarr's. And—yes, yes, Ulfarr recognized it, his body flinching, because oh gods, he'd said that? He'd told Killik that? He wanted a son of his blood, more than anything—*anything*—else?

But Ulfarr wasn't—denying it. Wasn't protesting it. Was still just staring at Killik, with that stunned bewilderment in his eyes.

"Did you," he finally said, his voice a low croak, "did *you* wish for this also, Killik? For a woman, and a son?"

Killik's throat convulsed, his face now unnaturally pale, and he darted a brief, furtive look toward—Louisa. And she only distantly heard her own laugh, scraping horrible and miserable out of her blocked throat.

"Don't lie to him, Killik," she snarled. "You did it all for him. *Only* him. And once it was done, you were going to fuck off and *leave* us, forever!"

But no, damn it, no, she shouldn't have said that, not now, maybe not ever—because Ulfarr's mouth made a strange, strangled noise, and he staggered on his feet. His eyes shot wide and wounded on Killik's face, as though Killik had struck him, or stabbed both his daggers deep into his gut.

"No," Ulfarr rasped, as if he was forcing out the word.

"No. Killik would not leave thus. Not—not forever. He has always stood beside me, as my strongest, fiercest friend. My dearest, most faithful pup. He would not do this to me. He would not do this to Sune."

But he was speaking faster, now, as if he was trying to convince himself, trying to convince them. Trying to make Killik counter it, but Killik wasn't fighting it, he wasn't—and his shoulders slowly dropped, as his head dropped, too.

"But I have never been—enough for you, Wolf," he said, so weary, so defeated. "I will never be enough. So ach, I thought"—a slow, heavy sigh—"I sought to grant you someone... better."

Someone better. Louisa's throat spasmed, and Killik gave a sharp wave toward her, his head still bowed low. "And I did this, ach?" he continued. "Louisa is kind and strong and fierce and hungry. She has offered her help and work and fealty to our camp and our kin, and treated you with care. She has also been good to Sune, and shall make a good parent to him—a better parent than I have been, ach?"

What? The words kicked through Louisa's belly, because Killik didn't really believe that, he couldn't—but he jerked a shrug, rubbed at his nose. "And mayhap," he said, a little faster now, "mayhap if you take Louisa to Efterar or Rurik, she can yet be healed, also. And then you can have this new son you long for, Wolf, and this—this happiness. This peace."

This happiness. This peace. Oh, gods, what was Killik saying? Ulfarr would never be happy without him, without their little family, no, no—

And no, that was a choked sniff from Ulfarr, his palm rubbing hard at his eye. "But—Killik," he whispered, hoarse, almost pleading. "I—I need *you*. We need you. All of us."

He'd given a shaky wave at Louisa, including her in that—but somehow that pulled Killik straighter again, drawing in his breath, his strength. Putting that cool, nonchalant look back in his eyes, as if he almost, *almost* didn't care.

"No, do you?" he said, in a voice much like his usual drawl. "If this was truth, Wolf, I ken you should have found a way to speak this, or show me this, these past twenty summers. But no, you have not, for all this time. And thus, I ken you only wish"—he flipped out his dagger, jabbed it at Ulfarr's face—"for a helpmeet. A vassal. A sharp sword by your side, and a hard prick in your bed. And you can find all this elsewhere, without me. Most of all now that you shall also have a woman, a *wife*, the true Skai mate and son you have always longed for!"

His voice grated through the air, scraping pain through Louisa's ears, and deep into her belly. And Ulfarr looked so struck, so shocked and stunned and wounded, just the way he'd used to look back at the start of this. And Louisa couldn't bear it anymore, it was too much, too much, no, no, no—

"No," she whispered, thin and strained in her throat— but it was enough that they both snapped to look at her. Ulfarr still so wan and haggard, Killik with that grim determination, and with something like... like jealousy, or even rage. Because damn Killik, no matter what he said now, he would forever hate Louisa after this. He would never get over Ulfarr, he would never be able to stay away from him. And she had to face this, speak truth, *I fear you not...*

"No," Louisa said again, steadier this time. "*No*, both of you. I already told you, I can't have children. And even if by some miracle I could"—she drew in breath, drew up strength, truth, *truth*—"I'm not interested. Not anymore."

Killik twitched, and Ulfarr's head tilted, his brow furrowing—and somehow Louisa found more air, more truth. "I'm—past it," she said thickly. "I've moved on. I've found— other priorities. Other people to care for."

But yes, yes, that felt right, that felt true—so Louisa

gulped in more air, more strength from the earth. "And even if I could be healed somehow," she went on, "I have no interest in being pregnant again. I don't want to go through more miscarriages, let alone childbirth and nursing and sleepless nights. I've fought my way out of my past, I've finally made my own life, and I—I want to live out the rest of it on my own terms."

It was a strange, shaky relief to finally face it, to speak it, to see it for the truth it was—but it was truth. It was. And perhaps Louisa hadn't even known it, or faced it, until this moment.

"And furthermore," she said, on another deep, bracing inhale, as she turned to fully face Ulfarr. "I'm so very sorry, sweetheart, because I do love you so much, and I desperately want you to be happy and well, too. But"—more air, more courage, please—"I don't want to be married again, either. Not to you, and not—to anyone. Ever."

Ulfarr didn't move or speak, beyond a convulsive swallow in his throat, and Louisa had to force down the air now, drag up the strength. "After Lord Scall," she said, laboured now, "I swore—I swore I would never give a man that kind of power over me again. And it's not that I don't trust you, sweetheart, or even that I don't want to be bound to you—and of course I want to make sure my sisters and the camp are taken care of. And I appreciate you wanting to protect me against Rikard, too, but..."

She flailed her shaky hand at the forest around them, at the camp, her house, herself. "But if I marry you," she gasped, "I'd still be handing you the ultimate power over my property, my freedom, my *life*. And I just"—she squared her shoulders—"I'm just not willing to do that again. I'm sorry."

It seemed to hang there, ringing bare and unfinished between them, but Louisa needed to finish this, needed to face it, to speak truth. "And also," she made herself continue, "I have no desire whatsoever to come between you two, or to break up your family. You're so damned *lucky* to have a son, and such a lovely one at that. And I will not"—her voice deepened, more certain now—"I will not be part of any ridiculous scheme that involves parting Sune from one of his fathers—or Skai-kesh forbid, trying to *replace* them! He deserves better from us, and from you. From both of you!"

She'd belatedly remembered her knife, still strapped at her side like always, and she gripped it tight, drew up more breath, more truth. "And as part of that," she added, even harder, "you two need to sort out your relationship, too. You need to actually have the difficult conversations you've clearly been putting off for *years*. You need to be honest with each other about how you feel, and what you need. And if you can't work it out"—she yanked out her knife, and jabbed it between them—"then you need to separate like rational adults, and find a way to still be competent co-parents. Without any of this childish scheming and sneaking about, or this martyring yourself for someone else's hypothetical happiness! Or, this foolish pretending as though you're not desperately obsessed with each other, after twenty damned years of it!"

Killik and Ulfarr exchanged a brief, furtive look, and then both glanced away again. But a trace of colour had returned to both their faces, and their bodies had eased a little closer together, too. And it was enough to settle Louisa's stiff shoulders, her exhale coming out heavy and relieved.

They did still care. They could still face this, and fix this. They could put Sune first, and work it out, and keep their family. And maybe—she swallowed—maybe they could even find a way to be happy together, after all. They could find... peace.

"I'm—very sorry to disappoint you," she said, tight in her throat. "But perhaps—perhaps once you work it out, you can go find another woman, together. Another way to possibly have another son. And of course I'll still keep allowing the camp, and supporting it, for as long as I can."

There was a beat of silence, a spasm of Killik's hand on his dagger. "You do not," he said, very low, "think this is *over*, woman."

But Louisa took another shaky breath, let it out. "Actually, yes, I do," she replied. "I only signed up for ten nights of this, and while I've had a lovely time"—she attempted a smile toward Ulfarr—"our ten nights were over long ago. I wish you both all the best, and I—I thank you both for all your kindness toward me. It truly did help me, and I'm so grateful."

Both Killik and Ulfarr blinked at her, and Ulfarr made to step forward, to clasp her hand—but Louisa backed away, too quickly, before she could lose it, before she broke down weeping...

"And now, I could really use a walk," she said, as lightly as she could. "Good luck, and goodbye."

56

Louisa walked without looking, without purpose. Just letting her feet follow her old familiar path through her lands, up and down hills, over logs and rocks and roots.

She'd done the right thing. She'd done what was best for Sune. She'd done what was best for Killik and Ulfarr. She'd done what was best—she drew in a shaky breath—for herself.

Because yes, she could admit, she still loved Ulfarr. She still even loved Killik, even if that snake didn't deserve it, even if he didn't care about her. Even if it had all been a lie, all this time.

And—another breath, an angry swipe of her hand at her prickling eyes—she still loved Sune, too. It had been such a privilege getting to know him, spending all that time with him. Helping him build, teaching him to ride, sparring with him, learning *flyting* beside him. He was such a good, clever, hardworking boy, and Killik and Ulfarr really were so lucky to have him, and she would miss him so damned much.

But it still settled Louisa's certainty deeper, tight in her set jaw, her clenched fists. She'd done the right thing. She wouldn't have been able to live with herself, knowing she'd broken up their family. She couldn't have borne the prospect of being Killik's—*replacement*, in Ulfarr and Sune's lives. Killik's ultimate sacrifice, on the altar of Ulfarr's happiness.

And worst of all, she couldn't have borne the truth about Ulfarr wanting that son. Even if she'd wanted it too, she still couldn't have borne that weight, that constant pressure to produce an outcome that was fully beyond her control. It would have felt like Lord Scall all over again, like a failure forever hovering over her, demeaning her, grinding her down into hopeless, helpless misery.

No. She wouldn't. She'd borne it once, and never again. Lord Scall was dead. *Dead.*

But then—Louisa jolted. Froze in the middle of the path. Because there, standing before her in the late afternoon sun, was—

Lord Scall.

Big, frowning, hulking. With his hunched shoulders, his beady little eyes, his wild dark hair. Even his favourite gem-encrusted longsword, dangling at his side...

The forest flickered and whirled, slid sharp and sideways, as a shrill distant howl echoed through Louisa's skull. Lord Scall was... here. Lord Scall was... *alive*?!

"There you are," he snarled, deep and menacing. "Finally free of your orcs, are you?"

Louisa stumbled, staggered backwards, rubbed her trembling hand at her frantically blinking eyes. No. No. Lord Scall was dead. Dead...

"They haven't let you walk alone in *weeks*," his deep voice continued, his dark eyes glittering with strange, gleeful relish. "Ever since they took you off to that cursed camp!"

The camp. The *camp*. And wait, *wait*, Lord Scall couldn't know about the camp, Lord Scall was dead, dead, dead. She'd seen the blood, she'd seen the life fading from those beady little eyes, and...

It was Rikard. Fucking *Rikard.*

The relief shot through Louisa's quaking body in a furious careening crash, squeezing her eyes shut, swaying her on her feet. It was Rikard. Only Rikard.

"What the hell do you want," she said, in a faint, wavering voice that didn't sound at all like hers. "This is *my* property, Rikard."

But at that, Rikard—laughed. Laughed, loud and uproarious, as he lurched a step closer toward her. "No, Louisa," he shot back. "This property ought to be mine. Most of all now that you've thoroughly defiled it with those thieving, bloodthirsty beasts, and marched half the town through it today! You've turned my uncle's prized lands into a mockery! A freak show!"

A freak show. It brought up a bizarre, sudden vision of Killik, and somehow Louisa gripped her knife, found her breath again. "This property is mine, Rikard," she replied, a little steadier. "It is *mine*, by law, and I'll decide what I do with it! And right now"—she drew in another shaky breath—"you're trespassing, and I want you to go the hell away! *Now!*"

But her heart was hammering, now, her thoughts flashing back to what Killik had told her, only moments ago. *This man has been hunting you for many days now. Seeking to bring you harm.* And Killik had sent the patrol away too, leaving her alone here, no...

Louisa's throat convulsed, and before her, Rikard only laughed again, and came a jerky step closer. So close Louisa could see the spittle on his lips, the whites around his eyes...

"You can't control me, Louisa," Rikard said, in a light, sing-song voice. "And I warned you again and again about those foul orcs. I warned you what would happen next, if you didn't send them away."

Louisa twitched, her breath stopped in her throat, and Rikard kept coming closer, closer. Forcing her to stumble sideways, backwards, away from his wild eyes, his smile, his hot, ale-tainted breath. Smelling so much like Scall had, too, raising the bile in her throat, no, no, run, escape, forget...

"Because I *know*, Louisa," Rikard crooned at her. "I *know* what you did."

Louisa staggered backwards again, shaking her head, no. Rikard was manic, he was a weak, vile vermin, he didn't know, he couldn't...

"You're imagining things, Rikard," Louisa said, though her voice was trembling. "I have no conception what you're talking about!"

But Rikard just kept pushing her backwards, off the path, further and further toward the trees. And too late, Louisa shot a desperate glance around her, at the near-impenetrable wall of brush to the left, and the deep swampy bog to the right. The same bog Killik had led her through, and it wasn't safe to walk into, Rikard had trapped her here, damn it, *damn* it—

"Oh, you know exactly what I'm talking about," Rikard drawled, as he drew Scall's longsword from his belt. "Don't you, Louisa? Especially"—he gave a wide wave at the forest around them—"especially *here*."

Here. Louisa's heart skipped, her breaths now rapid and shallow, her eyes again darting at the brush, the bog—and then, curse it, at Killik's white property marker, fluttering before her in the brush. Because no, no, they'd crossed onto Rikard's land now—and this was the only swampy, impassable section he had left. But it was still far too familiar, a place Louisa knew far too well, and...

The fear trickled up Louisa's spine, numb and clammy and cold, and she dragged for air, jolted another step backwards. Her hand gripping tighter at her knife, her eyes sweeping over the brush, the ground, the bog, that long gleaming sword in Rikard's hand. At the way he was holding it out, much too far to the front, leaving his side exposed...

"I know you did it," Rikard hissed, frenzied, triumphant. "I know you did it here. And now, you're finally going to face justice for your crimes!"

Louisa's terror jolted higher, but she forced herself to hold still, to keep watching, keep waiting. Keep breathing, draw up the earth, remember all Killik's lessons, wait, quiet, listen, breathe...

"You murdered my uncle, Louisa," came Rikard's voice, deep and terrible. "You killed Lord Scall!"

It thudded through Louisa like a drum, like a scream, like a quiet ringing certainty. Like all her deepest, darkest secrets finally lain bare, hurled out into the open. Face this, face this, truth, truth...

Truth. *I fear you not.*

"Yes," Louisa whispered, as she clutched her knife close to her chest. "I did. And now"—her mouth pulled into something like a smile—"now I'm going to kill *you.*"

And with one last, desperate breath, she lunged, and struck her knife for his throat.

57

Louisa would have done it.

Her charge was strong, her aim true. Her knife-blade driving straight toward where she wanted it, into the soft meaty flesh of Rikard's pale, sweaty throat.

Because if Rikard knew—if Rikard told—then it would be the end of everything. Her property. Her home. Her sisters' home. Her camp. Her orcs. Her life.

No. She wouldn't allow it. Not after all she'd borne. She would face it, and fix it. She was Skai. *I fear you not.*

And as she lunged for Rikard's throat, her blade even— scraped. Broke the skin. Drew out a sharp, tantalizing line of that sweet red blood. So close Louisa could taste it, she almost, almost had it—

When her ankle—caught. Jolted. Yanked. And dragged her back and downwards, face-first onto the rocky earth, as sharp, blinding pain flashed through her torso, her arms, her knees, her ankle. What the fuck, what the hell, what why how no no *NO*—

Rikard's laugh was loud, lurid, blistering in Louisa's ringing ears. And then—she crumpled, cried out—something slammed into her side, something hard and powerful and shockingly painful. And when her frantic, fluttering eyes finally found the cause of it, it was... Rikard's boot. Rikard had fucking *kicked* her.

"Now that's better, isn't it, Louisa?" Rikard's grating voice asked, between heavy breaths. "That's just where you belong, you vicious murderous *hag*. On the ground, caught in my trap, kneeling at my *feet*."

Caught in his trap. Oh, gods *crush* this vile little cockroach, of course it was one of his damned traps. This bastard had cornered her into one, pushed her straight into it. And curse Louisa, why hadn't she even *considered* that, she needed to get up, call for help, run—

She scrabbled to shove herself up, to lunge for freedom, or even for her knife—but more pain crashed against her side, and wrenched sharp around her ankle. While another loud laugh clanged through her ears, cold and mocking and triumphant.

"Don't even bother, Louisa," Rikard hissed, and when she struggled to look up again, he was crouching before her, and dangling her knife, her *knife*—in front of her face. "Can't you see how the gods are on my side in this? I've been lining this border with fresh traps for weeks, and at this point, anyone would have sufficed—but now I've captured the greatest prize of all. The prey I've been hunting all this time. *You*."

No, no, this wasn't happening, no—but Rikard coldly smiled at her, and even nicked her knife-point painfully at her hot cheek. "And you could have so easily avoided this, Louisa," he continued. "I gave you multiple chances to remove the orcs from my rightful property. I even offered you my hand in *marriage*. But you refused, so now I'm removing *you* from my property instead!"

He was removing—her. Fuck this bastard swine, he'd set her up, and now he was going to murder her. And he'd known the truth about Scall, all this time, and he'd still offered to *marry* her...

But it didn't make sense, none of it made sense, the panic screeching through Louisa's skull, rattling her leg against the pain clamping it tight. Against where it felt cold now, numb, sticky, just like her arms and her hands and her torso, and her twitchy glance downwards found her lovely Skai dress ripped and torn, exposing multiple deep, bloody gashes cut into her skin beneath.

Oh gods, what was she supposed to do, there was no way to face this or fix this or even fucking move. Rikard was going to destroy her and he was going to take everything, the camp, her land, her house, her sisters, the children, no, no, no...

"No," she gasped, with a foolish, *foolish* swipe for her knife in his hand. "*No*."

But Rikard only laughed again, yanking the knife away, screeching more panic through Louisa's trembling, bleeding body. Because he was—he was enjoying this, the utter bastard. He wanted to drag it out, and watch her bleed, and make her suffer. He hated her that much, maybe even more than he hated the orcs, and...

Wait. The orcs. The *orcs*. And most of all Killik. Killik, holding Louisa's eyes, speaking with such fierce truth in his voice. *We are guarding you. I must keep you safe. This fool bleating man shall never harm you. Lord Scall is dead...*

Killik had sworn to guard her. To help her. And even now, even after everything Killik had said and done, Louisa still... believed him. She did.

And somehow, somehow, she found her breath again. Drew it up from the solid earth beneath her, sank it into the pain, into the blood and the cold and the fear.

Lord Scall was dead. But she wasn't dead, not yet. She could still try. She could face this. She could face Rikard, find a way to delay him, to distract him, to keep him from—she startled, dropped her eyes—from noticing that faint rustle in the trees above...

"But—how, then?" Louisa asked, not fighting the

weakness in her voice now, the bitter twist on her mouth. "How did you know I killed Lord Scall?"

Rikard laughed again, but a little lighter this time, or even gleeful. Because yes, yes, he'd wanted her to ask. He wanted to lord his superiority over her. He was too confident in his power, his invulnerability, just like Lord Scall had been...

"I'll admit it was cleverly done, on your part," Rikard replied, with a too-casual shrug. "We all knew Scall liked his late-night rides around his land, even when he'd had too much to drink. But I still knew my uncle, Louisa, and"— Rikard's chest puffed out—"he still knew his own land. He would *never* have ridden his horse this way, let alone fallen off and split his head open. Unless someone else did it. Unless *you* did it!"

Rikard jabbed his thick finger toward the place where Scall had died, now perhaps only a dozen paces away. Flaring the memory of it sharp and vivid behind Louisa's eyes, just as clear as if it had been yesterday.

She'd arranged for a rich meal. She'd purchased multiple bottles of Scall's favourite vintage, and kept his glass full. And once he'd been staggering drunk, she'd slipped in a few capfuls of pure distilled spirits, too, and lightly suggested he take his usual evening ride out on his lands. And then she'd gone to bed, and crept out the window, and met him just there, on the path. And it had been so, so easy to call out to him, to draw him off his horse, to bring him confused and raging toward her...

And then to smash the huge, sharpened rock onto his head. To hear his shocked, affronted screech—but then she'd knocked him down, and swung the rock again, and again. Aiming for the same place, deepening that gaping wound, until Scall's screams had faded into rattling gasps, his blood bubbling warm into the earth.

And then, finally, silence.

It had never been something Louisa had imagined

herself doing, something she'd ever thought herself capable of. But she'd been so helpless, so desperate, so lost, and by then it had been the only choice. The only option left.

Because not only had Scall risked Louisa's own life with that infection, and killed all her children—but he'd blithely kept on doing it to other women, too. To his mistresses. To the women who worked in the establishments he frequented. And just the week prior, Louisa had not only heard about one of Scall's mistresses' deaths—but she'd also found Joan weeping in a corner of the stable, with Scall's familiar handprints still marked into her wrists.

But no one else had noticed. No one else had cared. And finally, death had become the only answer. The only path forward. The only way a cruel, all-powerful lord like Scall would ever face justice.

Luckily, there had been no inquiry around Scall's death—his head wounds had been consistent with a bad fall, and his predilection for drunken late-night rides had been broadly known. But even so, Louisa had nearly had a nervous collapse at the funeral, and afterwards she'd had nightmares for weeks, echoing again and again with the sounds of Scall's screams, the scent of his blood.

And ever since, the guilt and fear had been a quiet, constant weight, haunting her, dragging her into darkness. Enough that she'd never again spoken of her griefs, her losses, and most of all, her inability to have children. Because it all gave her a very clear motive, an excellent reason to have killed her philandering, disease-spreading lord husband. And she couldn't risk it, couldn't face it, she'd just wanted to run, to forget it, to escape it, forever...

At least, until Killik. Until Ulfarr. Until their kindness, and their generosity, and their amends. Their redemption. Their peace. *I fear you not.*

And now—even now, lying here broken and helpless in this cursed trap, Louisa finally didn't regret what she'd done.

She didn't fear it. By killing Lord Scall, she'd saved Joan, and gods knew how many other women, too. She'd faced it, and fixed it, and helped the people who'd needed her most.

And now, with the camp, she was making her own amends, too. Seeking her own redemption. Helping the people her husband had harmed. Wielding his death and his land for good. For peace.

And she wouldn't give up yet. She wouldn't. She was strong, she was alive, she was whole. She was Skai. *I fear you not.*

"So why, Rikard," Louisa began, because she had to keep thinking, keep him talking, please. "Why did you offer to marry me, if you knew—if you *knew* I killed your uncle, all this time?"

And yes, yes, that had been the right question, bringing another smug, superior smile to Rikard's mouth. "I was giving you a *chance*, Louisa," he said coolly. "I knew my uncle was a raging drunk, and I knew he had that horrid pox, too. I knew he was ill, and not—himself, by the end. And you getting rid of him worked quite well for me—or so I thought. Until I found out you'd somehow gotten him to split off this piece of land, and leave it to *you*!"

And perhaps Louisa was already delirious with the cold and the blood loss, because she couldn't hide the grim smile, pulling across her lips. Because yes, yes, she'd done that, too. She'd dug deep into the old property records, and discovered that one piece of the property had been added later, and therefore could be separated from the original legal requirements of the entail. And while it had been a very tricky business, she'd again used Scall's frequent drunkenness to her advantage, along with—she could admit—his mental confusion from his ever-deepening illness, too. And the day they'd had the final meeting with the lawyer, Scall had thought it had been routine paperwork, rather than him signing a piece of his prized property away.

Of course, it had still been the worst part of the property, and it hadn't dealt with the debts or the mortgages—and the money Louisa had siphoned from Scall's accounts before his death had vanished very, very quickly. But it was still legally her land, and it had still given her the space and the freedom she'd desperately longed for. She'd earned this land, and she'd damn well deserved it.

"So what was your plan, then?" Louisa made herself ask, her eyes fighting to focus on Rikard's still-smiling face. "With the marriage proposal? You would get the land back, and then wait until I let my guard down, and kill me in return?"

Rikard's smile thinned—he'd clearly expected to shock Louisa with that revelation, too—and he gave an attempt at a magnanimous shrug. "Maybe," he said, clipped. "But if you had shown yourself an adequate, adoring, appropriately grateful wife, and quickly granted me a proper heir, then *maybe* I would have let you live. But instead"—he laughed, hard and mocking—"you've repeatedly shown yourself as the greedy, ungrateful, *frigid* old hag you are! No wonder my poor uncle was fucking half the town, and drinking himself to death!"

Louisa's breath hissed through her clenched teeth, but no, no, she wasn't rising to his rubbish, not now. And she had to keep breathing, keep trying, anything…

"And how do you plan to cover up *this*?" she asked, with a wincing glance down at her caught ankle, her torn dress, her bloody, aching body. "My death, in your trap, on *your* land?"

But Rikard only laughed, and gave a careless wave of his hand. "Oh, Louisa," he drawled, smug and infuriating. "No one is even going to *think* of blaming me! *You* were the one who invited half the town here, to witness all those vicious orcs squatting and brawling with each other on *your* property! And I've already established that they keep trespassing on my property, haven't I? It'll be obvious that *they* killed you. *They'll* be the killers here! Again!"

Oh, gods curse this utter swine, and the way he kept laughing, kept touching her knife, like he had every right to it. "I even have an orc-forged knife right here," he said, his tone light, conversational. "It'll be a nice little gift to leave on your mutilated body, won't it?"

Louisa's growl burned from her throat, her hands scrabbling, every instinct shouting, screaming, run, attack, *run*. But she was still caught, still trapped, even as Rikard snapped out a hand, clutched a fistful of her hair...

"And then," he continued, "I'll publicly avenge my dear neighbour's untimely death. I'll call for justice, and ensure those trespassing, violent orcs carry all the blame. I will personally end that entire peace-treaty, Louisa, and then I will destroy those orcs, and finally get my land back!"

No. No. He couldn't. But damn it, yes, yes, he would. He was a lord, just like Scall. He was invincible, he would do whatever he wanted, and he would never face justice, never...

Rikard laughed again as he grasped Louisa's hair tighter, yanking her head upwards, exposing her throat, to her own damned knife. And though she wrenched and writhed and shoved at him, she was too cold and weak, he was too strong, she was going to die—

"Goodbye, Louisa," he drawled, as he jerked her hair back harder, and raised her knife. "I hope you enjoy this."

Louisa choked, swallowed, hauled in one last, sweet breath. Braced for the pain, the agony, the end, she'd failed, she'd failed—

When something—crackled. Shifted. Dropped. Streaking down from the tree above, and landing in a cool, easy crouch.

"Oh, she shall enjoy this, fool man," crooned Killik's voice, as his daggers flashed sharp and bright. "She shall."

58

For an instant, the world stopped. Time stopped. And there was only Killik, Killik smiling that cool, glittering smile, as he plucked Louisa's knife from Rikard's slack hand, and placed it firmly back into her own numb, trembling fingers.

"You said *orcs* shall be the killers?" Killik continued, still smiling, even as Rikard roared, and lunged toward him. "I ken for once you were right, fool man."

He leapt backwards as he spoke, easily avoiding Rikard's attack, not betraying even a hitch in his breath. "Ach, and I warned you," Killik purred, as he leapt back again. "I told you what should come next, if you harmed this woman."

Rikard was on his feet, now, breathing hard, and he shot a dark, assessing glance back toward Louisa, his hand slightly raising his sword. As if he was about to spin and run for her after all, swing that shining blade straight down onto her neck—

But then he jolted, his eyes snapped wide, fixed on something beside Louisa—and wait, it was... *Ulfarr*. Ulfarr, *here*. Crouched huge and hulking beside her, and where had he even come from, and he—

He looked furious. Malevolent. Deadly. With his glinting flashing eyes, his furrowed brow, his bared white teeth. And he had a massive, gleaming scimitar gripped in his big hand, while his other hand gently settled against Louisa's heaving back, stroked slow and careful against it.

"No," he growled at Rikard, deep and dangerous in his throat. "No. You shall never touch our woman *again*."

Rikard's mouth contorted, his body skittering backwards, away. "How dare you orcs threaten me," he gasped. "You can't do *anything* to me. Everyone will instantly know who did it! The camp of killer orcs next door!"

But Ulfarr's dark expression didn't waver, and Killik laughed again, tinkling and amused. "Ach, but as you said, fool man, we are on *your* land," he said. "With your own fool traps, scattered all about, where anyone might step."

Rikard shot a furtive glance at the ground around them, and shook his head. "I know my land," he snarled, even as he took a step backwards. "I know where my traps are, and I—ahhhhh!"

He reared up, wildly kicking with his leg, because— there. One of the sharp steel traps, now clamped tight and vicious around his ankle.

But it hadn't been there before, Rikard had even stepped in that same spot before—right? But somehow, the chain attached to the trap had been hidden beneath the leaves, snaking away toward... toward Killik. Who was gripping the end of the chain in his hand, and giving it a brief, experimental yank.

Rikard flailed and staggered, and then crashed down to his knees on the earth. "How *dare* you, you foul brute," he spat, between heavy gasps. "I am a—lord of this realm—and you will release me—at *once*!"

But Killik only laughed again, tipping his head back, his eyes narrowed to glittering slits. "How does it feel, fool man?"

he asked. "Mayhap you now regret doing this to *my* woman? And to *my* son?"

Louisa could see Rikard fighting to collect himself, to push through the pain—and then he shoved up to his feet, raised his sword, and lunged. Staggering straight toward Killik, closer, closer, too close, as Louisa's heart leapt and screamed. Rikard was going to attack Killik, and kill him, no, no, *no*—

When Killik—stepped aside. So calm, so fluid and graceful. And he'd somehow swung up the chain, twisting it around Rikard's other leg, so Rikard tripped, and then crashed headfirst into the earth.

Killik's laugh was light and merry, his dagger spinning in his hand. "Last chance, fool man," he purred. "Shall you now be wise enough to beg for my mercy, and swear never to touch or threaten my kin again?"

Rikard snarled and staggered upwards again, glaring at Killik with wild eyes. "You won't get away with this, orc," he gasped. "You kill me here, in the exact same place where my uncle died, on the same day when you had hundreds of orcs crawling all over the property? You'll still take the fall for this. You'll still take down your precious treaty, and launch a *war*!"

He was slowly advancing toward Killik again, his trapped foot dragging, his hand gripping at his sword—because he was trying to distract Killik, damn it, so he could rush in, and use that sword to kill him. While Killik just kept standing there, now thoughtfully tapping his dagger against his chin, and even glancing back at Ulfarr.

"Ach, what do you ken, Wolf?" Killik asked, his tone easy, conversational. "Mayhap he is not wrong upon this. Mayhap it would be safer for him to die alone in his bed. Mayhap next week?"

And oh, the way Ulfarr was smiling back at Killik, his teeth sharp and white, as the sheer malevolence kept glittering in his eyes. "Ach, this sounds best, pup," he replied. "So do not mark him up too much, I ken."

Killik huffed a heavy, resigned sigh, and then finally glanced back at Rikard. At where Rikard had still been staggering closer, sweeping up that huge sword, aiming it straight at Killik's neck. No, no, he couldn't, no—

But even as Louisa yelped, her hand outstretched, Killik's dagger flashed. Flipped. Flew. Flew straight toward... Rikard's *face*.

Rikard screamed and staggered backwards, his hand frantically clutching at—at his *eye*. And Killik laughed as he spun his second dagger, even gave it a long, leisurely lick with his curling black tongue—and then hurled it at Rikard, too, deep into his—his *belly*.

Rikard bent double, and his shriek rang through the air, shrill with panic and pain. And then he staggered, and tilted, and spun, and then—then—

Thud.

Louisa flinched, cringed, her eyes wrenched shut—but the sound seemed to keep reverberating, singing again and again around them. *Thud.*

Rikard was... dead?

And then—a laugh. Killik's laugh, bright and gleeful, carrying through the air. Catching strange in Louisa's breath, snapping her eyes up—to where Killik was clutching at his shaking waist, the mirth so blithe and amused in his sparkling eyes.

"You hear him squeal, Wolf?" he said toward Ulfarr, between chuckles. "And how he danced! Ach, I have been dreaming of that for *weeks*."

Something odd was twitching on Louisa's mouth, jostling in her chest, and she shot a blinking, helpless look at Ulfarr. Perhaps expecting him to admonish Killik, to correct him...

But oh gods, Ulfarr was smiling, too. His grin broad and stunning, despite that danger still glinting sharp in his eyes.

"Good work, pup," he said, deep and decisive. "And these look to be good clean wounds, also."

Killik beamed proudly back toward him, looking for an instant almost like a hunting-dog who'd just gained a kill for its approving owner. An owner whose smile only went fonder as Killik laughed again, his shoulders shaking with sheer, delighted glee.

And as Louisa watched, blinking, that jostling in her chest finally shuddered up, burst up out her throat—and somehow she was laughing, too. Shrill, sharp, helpless, shaking her all over, so convulsive she couldn't stop. And oh gods, what must they think of her, it wasn't funny, it wasn't, Lord Rikard was *dead*—

Or was he? And when Louisa shot a wincing, searching glance up at Ulfarr, he was smiling back at her too, so warm and indulgent—but his other hand was signing swiftly toward the trees. "Rurik, come and do all you can to cover this, and grant this man a few more days' life," he said. "But come see Louisa, first."

Wait. Rurik? *Rurik* was here? But yes, there he was, striding coolly out from behind a tree, and coming over to kneel beside Louisa. Touching his hand beside Ulfarr's on her back, and then sliding it downwards, over her hip, her thigh, her knee, her ankle.

"Naught that ought to last," he told Ulfarr, clipped. "But get this trap off her, and tend the wound, and I shall look again after."

Ulfarr nodded and signed a swift *thank-you* toward him, but Rurik was already turning and walking away. Toward where Killik was now kneeling over Rikard's fallen form, and carefully drawing out his daggers. Spattering fresh blood all over him, and over Rikard, too.

"This is yet a mess, brother," Rurik snapped at Killik, settling his hand over Rikard's slack, unseeing face. "Did you need to puncture his *eye*?"

"Ach, I did," came Killik's cool reply. "You ought to be glad I did not stab the other one to match."

Rurik gave an irritated huff, but his brow was furrowed in concentration, both his hands pressed over Rikard's face. As if—wait. Was Rurik—*healing* him?

Louisa shot a wide-eyed, questioning glance toward Ulfarr, but he'd now shifted down beside her, his gaze focused and intent on her ankle. On that damned horrible trap, still cutting through the leather of her boot, sinking painfully into her skin.

"Igull and Elgr," Ulfarr called over his shoulder, his voice deep and decisive, even as his eyes stayed fixed on the trap. "You two seek for any scents of blood, and cover this as best you can. Ragni and Kori and Fasti, you cover the tracks, most of all the ones from Louisa's land. Halthorr, you stand watch, and scent for any men. And Sune, you come help me with this."

Louisa twitched, twisted around, stared—because wait, they were all here, too. All of Ulfarr's faithful former pack, fanning out into the trees, following his orders. Igull and Elgr were already pacing around them, scenting for the blood, and Ragni and Kori and Fasti were jogging back toward Louisa's land, as Halthorr headed toward Rikard's. While Sune slipped from behind a nearby tree, and strode over to Ulfarr and Louisa. His hands signing at Ulfarr as he knelt, and then together they gripped the trap on Louisa's ankle, and yanked it open.

The relief was sudden and staggering, shuddering through Louisa's aching body. And she twitched again at the feel of Ulfarr tearing her boot further open, and then—the warm, shocking sensation of his mouth. Gently kissing and licking the ragged wound the trap had left behind, as his soft eyes met Louisa's. "You shall be well again soon," he murmured. "This shall help you heal, ach?"

It would? But Ulfarr's eyes were still so steady, so certain, even as his hand signed something else toward Sune. Something about cleaning the trap, and… setting it again?

But yes, yes, of course, that made sense. They wanted to leave the scene just how they'd found it. And then… and then…

A distant, jangling hope was whispering in Louisa's belly, even as her thoughts kept streaming with questions, with uncertainty, with the wondering wheeling disbelief. They couldn't truly get away with this… could they? Whatever the hell it was?

"So what," she gasped, between her shallow breaths, "what are you planning here, exactly?"

Ulfarr's glance toward her was warm, and he gave another gentle kiss to her stinging ankle. "As Killik said," he murmured, "it would not be wisest to kill this man here, so close to your lands, and so close to where his uncle died, also. So instead"—he nodded toward Killik and Rurik—"we shall heal his outward wounds, and take him home to his bed, and wait for him to meet his death there."

Louisa blinked at him—they could really do that?—and Ulfarr nodded, gave her ankle another careful kiss. "Rurik is a clever healer, ach?" he said. "I ken this man shall not wake again, but it shall look as though he died in his sleep. Heart trouble, mayhap."

Louisa's breath caught, her eyes darting back to Rikard's sprawled, unconscious body. "But—how will you even get him back home? He has staff, right? And men? Guards?"

But Ulfarr's mouth quirked up, his head shaking. "I ken one of Filak's new tunnels now near reaches his house, and that shall be a great help," he replied. "And as for his guards, I ken they are yet patrolling the rest of his border, and keeping watch for you. They have been doing this each night for many days now, and oft crossing onto your lands seeking you, also."

Right. Just as Killik had said, too. And Louisa stared at

Ulfarr for a long, unseeing moment, as her thoughts whirled and churned. Rikard had been stalking her, and trying to *murder* her, and Killik and Ulfarr had *known*, and...

"But why didn't you tell me before?" she demanded, and curse it, that was too much hurt in her voice, in her eyes. "If you knew that, all this time?"

Ulfarr winced and exhaled, angling a brief glance back toward Killik. "I wished to tell you," he replied, slow. "But..."

A bitter laugh escaped Louisa's mouth, because he didn't even need to say it, did he? "Let me guess, Killik didn't want to tell me?" she asked, too sharp. "Because I needed to keep trying to impress him first? I needed to prove I was good enough to know such things? Worthy enough?"

Ulfarr blinked at her, his brow slowly furrowing, but Louisa couldn't stop now, it was all too much, too strong, too painful. "But I wasn't," she breathed, pleaded, at Ulfarr's eyes. "I wasn't good enough for him. I've never been good enough for him, no matter what I did. So he *lied* to me, again and again and again, and then he decided to *leave*!"

Her voice scraped out around them, betraying her to all the orcs still moving around them, and she belatedly winced, shook her head. No, no, this wasn't important, she didn't need to bring this up now, and...

But Ulfarr just kept looking at her like that, his forehead furrowed, the bewilderment shimmering in his eyes. "Ach, no, Louisa," he said, as he carefully grasped her scraped hand, and brought it to his mouth. Kissing there, too, gently trailing his tongue against the raw, stinging skin. "Killik wished to leave due to *my* failings, not yours. And I ken you have greatly pleased him, with all you have done. I have never seen him care for a woman, or hunger for her, as he has with you."

What? No. That was ridiculous, Killik didn't care about her, Killik had tried to *leave*—but Ulfarr's eyes looked very certain, now, his lips still softly kissing at her stinging palm. "And Killik only did not tell you all we knew of this Rikard's plans," he continued, "because he had sworn this vow to guard you, and protect you. And he knew how deeply this man distressed you, and he did not wish to bring you more fear and worry and pain. Most of all before this Summit, and all that came with it."

Louisa swallowed, shook her head, as Ulfarr's mouth just kept kissing, now moving up her wrist, to the raw skin on her forearm. "Killik swore to me he would tell you after the Summit," he said. "But we lost sight and scent of this Rikard for long enough that he found you. And this was again our failing, Louisa, and *only* ours. Not yours."

Louisa shook her head again, but Ulfarr's mouth kept kissing, licking, tending. "None of this was your failing, Louisa. You have shown yourself so kind, and so brave, and so true. You have granted us so much help, and so much strength, and so much joy. So much"—he swallowed, gave her a sad little smile—"so much peace, sweet Louisa."

So much peace. It caught in Louisa's throat, in her chest, because despite all this mess, they'd still given her so much peace, too. Both Ulfarr and Killik had, with their safety and their certainty and their pleasure, with the lessons and the camp and all of it, all of it. And Louisa had tried so hard, done so much, hoped so much, but...

"But," she gulped, on a shaky breath. "But it wasn't enough for *you*, either. You really wanted a son, all that time. More than anything else."

Ulfarr's eyes briefly closed, and that was genuine pain, tightening on his mouth. "Ach," he said, heavy. "I will not deny that I have wished for a son. It has always seemed to me the... the height of what a strong, worthy Skai ought to gain. A son of Skai blood to care for, to fight beside, to carry my name beyond me."

Louisa's eyes dropped, the ache twisting in her belly,

because yes, of course, she could understand that. She'd perhaps felt the same way, for so long, until...

"But these past moons," Ulfarr added, "and mayhap these past summers also, I have come to see... other ways. I have seen all I have gained, without this. I have seen this camp. I have seen my teaching at the school. I have seen the son I have already gained. The son who has been such a great, great gift from Skai-kesh."

His eyes had flicked toward the east, where Sune's dark head was scarcely visible, bent over where he was still resetting the trap. "When we three fought, back there on the path," Ulfarr continued, quieter, "Sune... overheard this. I did not scent him there, and I ken Killik was too distressed to scent him, also. But after you left, when Sune showed himself, he was weeping, and he said—he said—"

Ulfarr's breaths sounded ragged now, his eyes glimmering as they held on Sune's bowed head. "He said he has always known he would never be as good or as worthy as a blood-son," he whispered. "But he begged us not to send him away, even once we gained a new son. A *better* son. And ach, I could not—I cannot—"

A streak of water escaped Ulfarr's eye, and he shook his head, flexed his jaw tight. "I cannot bear that he even *thought* this," he croaked. "I thought he knew how much we care for him. There is naught in this realm that could take him from me, for he is my son. He is Killik's son. He shall always, *always* be our son."

His voice was fierce, utterly certain, as his hand slipped to his heart, closed tightly against it. "So I vowed this to him, before Skai-kesh," he continued. "I told him I had no wish for a new son. No need for a new son. And this... this was truth."

His voice shifted again, softened, his blood-streaked hand wiping at his wet face. "This was truth," he repeated, as something like relief shimmered in his eyes. "I have spent so many of my days caring for the orclings of my pack, and fearing for them, and teaching them, and seeking to keep them safe. I ken I have raised many, many sons, ach? And now"—his breath exhaled, slow—"they raise... *me.* They stand and fight beside me. They bring me such honour, and such joy. And when I am gone, they shall carry my name beyond me. They shall speak of the good I have brought this clan, and not the grief, or the pain."

Louisa swallowed, glancing at all the diligently working Skai around them. Igull and Elgr, Ragni and Kori and Fasti, Halthorr, Sune. "And now, they begin to have their own sons, too," Ulfarr said, with unmistakable awe in his voice. "And I wish to—to be part of this. I wish to... savour this. I wish to cherish this time with them, and most of all, with Sune. I wish to welcome all I have, and be thankful for these gifts, without always seeking out more. Most of all if gaining more might bring... less. Less of what I most long for, in the end."

His eyes caught, lingered on where Killik was now standing up again, stretching both arms over his head. His lean, blood-streaked body looking so powerful, so dangerous, so... content.

"I long to be a good father to Sune, and to my brothers," Ulfarr continued, low. "But I also long for *you*, Louisa. I long for you, and for Killik. I long for what we have built between us, these past weeks. I care not what we name this, and I have no need to make you a wife—but I yet wish for this joy, and this comfort, and this peace. This... family."

This family. It rung low and true in Louisa's belly, so stark and raw with longing, and she followed Ulfarr's eyes back toward Killik, who was now striding toward them with swift, steady steps. He had blood smeared not only over his hands, but also his chest, his face, even his mouth—but Ulfarr's expression was still so warm, so fond. His hand swiftly signing, *Good, Killik. Thank you.*

Killik waved it away, his intent gaze now darting between

Ulfarr and Louisa, and Ulfarr drew in a slow, heavy breath. "I have just been speaking to Louisa," he said, "of all we spoke of with Sune. Of how we have no need of a new son, or a wife. And how we yet long for her, and wish her to stay with us."

Killik twitched, but then he went unnaturally still, and his eyes on Louisa looked hunted, almost afraid. "But," he began, with a wince. "I ken you should yet be happier, Wolf, if you—"

Louisa's stomach plunged, because Killik was again saying no, no, no. And before he could speak any further, she choked a swallow, made herself nod. Made herself face this. Speak truth.

"I have no desire to—to push Killik into something he doesn't want," she told Ulfarr, too quickly. "And he doesn't want—me. He only did all this with me for—for *you*, sweetheart."

She even tried to smile at Ulfarr, but found to her surprise that he was—frowning. Frowning between her and Killik, his mouth hard, his eyes flashing with... disapproval. With stark, genuine anger.

"No," he hissed. "No. I have had enough of this, from both of you. I shall bear no more foolishness, and no more falsehoods. And today, I shall finally have"—his voice deepened, decisive, dangerous—"your truth. *Now*."

59

Ulfarr would have their truth. Now.

Louisa froze, blinked at him, and then at Killik, who looked just as startled as she felt. And for an instant, as their eyes held, it was almost as though that old familiar crackle of understanding passed between them, speaking their confusion aloud. *Is this Wolf? Is he actually angry with us? What does he want?*

But now Ulfarr loudly cleared his throat, raising his hand. Instantly calling the attention of all the Skai around them, all of them pausing their work to look, even Sune. "I thank you for your good work, brothers," Ulfarr said, his voice clear and carrying. "I now need a spell alone with my—with Killik and Louisa. Igull and Elgr, I shall be grateful if you yet stand guard for us. And Sune"—his eyes flicked over toward where Sune was intently studying them—"if you and your friends should go ready a bath and fresh clothes for Louisa at her house, we should all be most thankful."

Louisa exchanged another brief, uncertain glance with Killik, but through the trees, Sune nodded, as a small smile spread across his mouth. *Ach, Pa,* he signed back. *You can depend upon me.*

It was the first time Louisa had seen him use the sign *Pa*—his fist briefly touching his forehead—and Ulfarr smiled back too, slow and almost painfully fond. *Thank you, son*, he signed back. *We love you.*

Sune ducked his head, and then spun around and left, his back very straight. And when Louisa met Killik's eyes again, they looked oddly bright, his mouth pressed thin. As if Sune calling Ulfarr *Pa* had meant something to him, too.

"Now," Ulfarr said, as his eyes shifted back to Louisa, and then Killik. "My scenting is not what it once was, but I can yet scent the truth of this. Thus"—he waved Killik closer—"you shall now help me tend Louisa's wounds, pup. You shall show her your fealty and your care. And whilst you do this, you shall speak. You shall tell Louisa your *truth*."

A curious little shiver swept up Louisa's spine, and Killik twitched too, his gaze darting between Ulfarr and Louisa. Looking uncertain, resistant, maybe even afraid...

"Do this, Killik," came Ulfarr's voice, heavy with decision, with command. "Speak your truth to her. *Now*."

Killik twitched again, shot Ulfarr a glance that was almost pleading—but Ulfarr just frowned back at him, waiting. Until Killik finally jerked a nod, and then dropped to his knees beside Louisa on the ground. The movement unusually stilted, awkward, and he didn't meet her eyes as he snatched for her still-bloody hand, and brought it to his mouth.

"A-ach," he said, hoarse, followed by a brief, furtive lick against Louisa's palm. "I—I wished—for this, woman. With—you."

He shot another brief, helpless glance toward Ulfarr, but Ulfarr kept frowning back, even as he lifted Louisa's other hand, and began kissing it, too. "From the start?" he demanded. "Or only after you came to know her better? Tell us the tale, Killik."

Killik's hot breath shuddered out against Louisa's skin,

and that was another brief, shaky touch of his tongue. "I had no—no wish for this, at the start," he replied, hoarse. "Humans are so oft fickle, and foolish, and *selfish*. They spew their falsehoods, they make vows they do not keep, they condemn our ways, they call down shame and judgement and death upon us. Why would I wish for any of this?"

Ulfarr nodded, his eyes still held to Killik's face. Waiting as Killik drew in a shaky inhale, his tongue again trailing against Louisa's skin. "But I yet knew how much *you* wished for a woman, Wolf," he croaked. "So ach, I let you believe I wished for it someday also, so I might better learn what you longed for. And then"—he shuddered out an exhale—"I went hunting."

Ulfarr kept waiting, watching, while Killik drew in another slow, ragged breath, and pressed another kiss to Louisa's skin. "I watched dozens of women, over many moons," he continued. "But I could not bear any of them, and most of all, I could not bear the thought of them with *you*, Wolf. I was sure I had failed, until"—his eyes darted to Louisa's face—"I heard Rosa and Jule speaking of this Louisa who had helped them. And they said Simon had met her, also—so I went to him, and asked his counsel. And he did not know I was asking for you, and he said—he said she would make me a good, worthy Skai mate, and he would be glad to uphold this."

Louisa's hand trembled against Killik's mouth, but he kept kissing, kept speaking. "So I watched her for many, many days," he said, faster now. "I watched her hunt, and work, and care for her kin. She was brave, and true, and did not whine or falter, or blame her hardships on others. But I yet wished to test her, and be sure she was worthy of you—so I carved the *rassja*, and told her to use this, and prove this to me. I was sure she would fight this, or flee from this, but instead, she... welcomed this. She welcomed my pleasure, and my command."

Louisa's memories flicked backwards to that first night, to that stain across the front of Killik's trousers. And perhaps he recalled it too, betraying another hard little quiver, his kiss now skating up her wrist, to the torn skin of her forearm. "This... surprised me," he whispered. "And... pleased me. But I wished her for *you*, Wolf, so I sought to forget this, and grant her to you, and drive her away from me—but I could not stay away. I could not stop longing for this, could not keep to my own aims, and—"

He was breathing hard, now, as if every word was a struggle, and he raised his head to glare at Ulfarr, his teeth bared. "And *you* kept pushing this," he rasped. "You kept drawing me into this, binding me into this. Telling me to speak to her, to comfort her, to walk her home, to take her hunting. Sending me off to plough her, alone, and then come tell you the tale!"

Louisa blinked—had sweet, guileless Ulfarr really done all that?—but his smile toward Killik was slow, deliberate, and surprisingly wicked. "I only granted you what you wished for, pup," he murmured. "I did not see you fighting me, ach?"

Killik gave an exaggerated roll of his eyes, and jabbed his claw at Ulfarr's face. "I was seeking to help *you*, you great brute," he snapped. "I wished to please you, and bring you joy, and *peace!*"

But at that, Ulfarr's expression sobered, and his hand reached to spread against Killik's back. "And you did, pup," he said, quiet. "Both of you. You have brought me such peace, and such hope, and such healing. And ach, I loved how you scented together, I loved how you played and laughed and worked together, and found such joy together. And the longer we did this, the more I hoped—I prayed—that you would both forget these ten nights, and come to welcome this, also. For you are so much alike, ach? So fierce and lusty and kind and true."

Killik's eyes darted toward Louisa, and then away again. But an unmistakable flush was creeping up his neck, and he abruptly bent down again, pressing his mouth to the scrapes on her forearm. As if still hiding from this, perhaps, resisting this, not wanting to speak this...

When Ulfarr's big hand grasped the back of Killik's neck, and yanked him up. Making him look at him, and at Louisa, and even giving him a gentle little shake. "Did I say you were done, pup?" he hissed, his eyes glittering. "I need you to keep speaking. I need you to show Louisa what I can scent upon you. I need you to stand beside me, and show her how much we care for her. I need you to prove this to me, Killik. *Now.*"

Prove this. Now. It rang all through Louisa's body, resonating hard and deep—while Killik shuddered, spasmed, his eyes blown wide on Ulfarr's face. And when Ulfarr released him, Killik jerked a nod, and then—then scrabbled for Louisa's skirts. Shoving them up, spreading her legs apart, his body skittering down in between, so he could...

So he could kneel before her, and bury his face between her thighs.

Louisa gasped, stared, trembled all over—but oh, oh, Killik was doing this. His mouth latched between her legs, his tongue plunging deep. Kissing her, lavishing her, licking her from the inside out. And he'd never, never done this before, not once, and Louisa couldn't stop shaking, staring, shivering at the sight of it, the feel of it, the truth of it. Killik's hard mouth, his demanding tongue, his sharp teeth, all working with such desperate determination upon her, feasting upon her, firing her full of heat and hunger and raw, breathless need.

He was... proving this.

And his frantic, fluttering eyes even held on hers as he did it, as if begging her to see, to understand. To see the truth in this, even if he couldn't yet speak it. He wanted this, he wanted her, even though he'd lied to her, he'd made those awful plans, he'd tried to walk away…

"Better, pup," came Ulfarr's low voice, his hand again curving around the back of Killik's neck. "But she yet cannot scent you, ach? I told you to speak."

A hard shudder wrenched through Killik's entire body, even into his tongue still thrusting inside Louisa, sparking out bliss all around it—but he didn't pull away, and his eyes glimmering on hers looked almost pleading. Almost… in pain, somehow, because he couldn't speak it, he couldn't, because…

You only wish for a helpmeet. A vassal. A sharp sword by your side, and a hard prick in your bed…

"Wolf," Louisa began, before she'd even caught it. Snapping Ulfarr's gaze to hers, his head tilting, his brow furrowing. Listening. And she had to think, damn it, think through the rampaging pleasure of Killik's feasting mouth, his seeking gorging tongue, please…

I am… useful. Always at hand. But I am not… wanted. When has he ever spoken this? Or shown me this?

"Look, I think," she told Ulfarr, between heavy breaths. "I think—Killik needs to know your truth first. He needs you to tell him. To show him."

Ulfarr's eyes caught, flickered, and then dropped to Killik's kneeling form. And then held there, glimmering with something like grief, like worry, like… fear.

And maybe it was the pleasure, reeling Louisa's certainty close. Or maybe it was the memory of that epiphany she and Killik had stumbled upon, that night with the chain in the *kofi*. The night they'd finally seen Ulfarr's fear, and taken that chain off, and told him they'd trusted him.

"You won't hurt him, sweetheart," Louisa said, quiet but steady. "He's not your small, weak, innocent pup anymore. You don't need to protect him, or keep him safe from you."

Ulfarr's eyes darted back to hers, looking for an instant

almost as pleading as Killik's—and Louisa took a ragged breath, held his gaze. "You don't, Wolf," she insisted. "If anything, Killik has protected *you.* He's stood beside you for twenty damned years. He's dragged you from the darkness again and again. He's given you hope, and purpose, and peace. He's given you a home, and a *family.*"

Killik's mouth between her legs faltered, his eyes now strange and still on her face, and she drew up his strength, his truth. "Killik is a strong, capable, *brilliant* Skai," she said. "And whatever your truth is, he can handle it. He deserves it."

Ulfarr blinked down at Killik's still-kneeling form, and his broad shoulders rose and fell, heaving with his breaths. His hand rubbing at his mouth, as that fear kept glimmering, shimmering in his eyes. While Louisa kept waiting, her heart skipping, her shaky fingers finding Killik's silken hair, feeling the way he was faintly trembling beneath her touch...

"Show us, sweetheart," she whispered, searching Ulfarr's face. "We want to know. Please."

Ulfarr's eyes squeezed shut, his breath filling his chest... and then—a nod. A shudder. A jerk of his hand to the chain of his belt. Drawing it out, off, away from his trousers, so he could...

So he could lunge forward, and swing it around Killik's *neck.*

60

Louisa startled and stared, her mouth fallen open, her heartbeat pummelling in her chest.

Ulfarr was... chaining Killik. Trapping him. Circling that thick, strong steel around his neck, and drawing it close.

And Killik looked—stunned. Incredulous. His mouth slack, his eyes blank, his hand snapping up to feel the truth of that chain. Not pulled tight, not enough to break the skin, but still solid, powerful, dangerous.

"You yet wish for this?" came Ulfarr's voice, sounding resigned, shaky, hungry. "Both of you?"

But Louisa's eyes had caught to Killik's, the silent awareness flying and flashing between them—and they both nodded at once, rapid, desperate. Needing this, whatever the hell this was, while Ulfarr drew in another ragged breath, and...

He *snapped*. His huge body snatching for Killik, yanking him hard beneath him, shoving him face-down into the earth. Keeping one hand gripped to that chain, while the other reached for Killik's trousers, dragged them down with a sharp ripping sound—because his powerful thighs had already spread Killik's knees wide apart, pinning him to the earth, oh gods. So Ulfarr could mount up over Killik's prone body, looming massive and deadly and vicious, with his scarred, swollen, pendulous cock prodding downwards, his full bollocks swaying behind them.

"Then open wide, pup," he growled, hot and dark in Killik's ear, as he gave a firm tug on the chain. "And beg your wolf to fuck you, and *own* you."

The sheer disbelieving shock again flashed across Killik's eyes, but it was instantly chased by hunger, by a wild pleading craving. "Ach, yes, Wolf," Killik gasped. "Fuck me. Own me."

Ulfarr's growl went deeper, harder, and his huge hanging shaft prodded downwards, even as he shook his head. "More," he hissed, with a hard, ringing slap of his big hand to Killik's bared arse. "Beg me. Use your sharp clever mouth for me."

Killik shivered and nodded, hauled in a deep breath. "Fuck me, Wolf," he choked. "Use me. Fill me. Grant me that perfect Skai prick, and your strong Skai seed. Teach me how this feels, how it scents, let me milk this from you, and taste this great gift. Please, Wolf. *Please.*"

It was unlike anything Louisa had ever heard Killik say, unlike anything she'd ever seen on his face. That frenzied, abject yearning, that fierce urgent need, without even a twinge of his usual coolness or sarcasm or pride. And oh, Ulfarr knew it too, his eyes fluttering as he shoved Killik's legs wider apart, as his dripping, pulsing head bobbed for its place, searching, settling, prodding...

And then it... plunged. Punched sharp and deep, in one single, devastating stroke.

Killik flailed and shouted, his head arching up, his eyes rolling back—but Ulfarr only grunted, and yanked the chain down again. Shoving Killik's still-bloody face into the earth, as his other hand spread wide against his back, holding him tight and firm. So he could watch his own huge length slowly sliding out of Killik, slick and glossy with his seed—and then he drove it back in, even harder than before.

Killik juddered, moaned, but that was still only pleasure in his eyes, all over his flushed face. Wanting this, needing this, maybe waiting for this for twenty damned years. The Wolf of the Skai overpowering him, holding him down, mounting him, and ploughing him with all his strength. Making him his.

"You are *mine*, Killik of Clan Skai," Ulfarr snarled, with a snap of his teeth toward Killik's pointed ear. "You have *always* been mine. And henceforth, you shall never touch another *again*, without my leave."

Killik's nod was instant, fervent, but it wasn't enough, Ulfarr's hand yanking on the chain, his steady plunges driving harder into Killik's trembling body beneath him. "Never, Killik," Ulfarr hissed. "And when I wish you in my bed, you shall *be* there. You shall *stay* there. You shall not speak false to me. You shall not keep plots or secrets from me. And"—another loud, ringing slap at Killik's red arse—"you shall never again plan to leave me! You are *mine!*"

Killik wrenched all over, his moan breaking into a cry— but he nodded again, jerking his neck hard against the chain. "A-ach," he gasped. "Ach, Wolf. Yours."

Ulfarr's grunt was low and satisfied, but he still nipped sharply at Killik's ear this time, his hips driving in that same furious rhythm. "And," he continued, "you shall honour this good woman you have hunted us. You shall treat her as the rare Skai prize she is. And when I ask you to tend her, and speak truth to her, you shall do this. You shall stop play-acting as though you care naught for her, when you have just gutted this man for her, and would do it again in a breath!"

Killik's wild eyes flicked toward Louisa, but he nodded

again, and moaned into Ulfarr's furious onslaught. "Ach," he choked. "I will, Wolf. I shall."

Ulfarr grunted again, and shoved Killik down harder, jerking the chain sideways. Baring more of Killik's exposed neck for his hard, greedy eyes, and oh, Killik's head was even tilting further away, as if offering it, wanting it. As Ulfarr's growling mouth drew closer, his breath sharply inhaling, his plunges gone slower, harder, gouging in with deep, ruthless purpose—

"Suck your wolf's good seed deep," he hissed, into Killik's ear. "And beg me to drink you, my sweet pup."

Killik's voice was babbling now, begging in words Louisa couldn't understand, his hips shoving up, his eyes furiously fluttering—and then Ulfarr thrust his head into Killik's exposed neck, his jaw clamping down tight. As his hips plunged in one last time, ramming Killik into the earth—

Killik's roar tore through the air, his body kicking and writhing, his eyes squeezed shut. As Ulfarr kept grinding hard against him, pouring himself out into him, his throat rapidly, rhythmically swallowing. Taking from Killik, and giving to Killik, giving and giving and giving—until Killik finally sagged heavy and defeated beneath it, his body sprawled and slack against the earth.

Only then did Ulfarr twitch backwards, drawing his reddened mouth away from Killik's neck. His eyes blinking down toward it, hazy and dazed at first—but then wider and wider, as his breath caught, and his shoulders stilled. And as he stared, his face went paler and paler, his head shaking, his hand dropping the chain to the earth with a clatter.

As if—he was shaken. Shocked. Appalled at the sight of Killik lying beneath him, his trousers torn and ragged, his body covered with mud and dried blood.

Killik had half-turned to look at Ulfarr too, his mouth opening and closing, and then—quivering. As if he was about to start weeping, oh gods, but as Louisa blinked at him, she knew he wasn't hurt, or in pain. No, no, it was just the relief, and the pleasure, and the sheer aching joy in it. The... peace.

But perhaps Ulfarr couldn't see that right now, or scent it, not with the mud and the chain, the shock and the horror slowly etching into his sweaty, haggard face. And Killik couldn't say it, either—couldn't just say *I loved that, I love you, thank you—*

And gods, this was just what had gotten them into this mess in the first place, wasn't it? And before she'd even caught it, Louisa shifted her own muddy, bloody body down beside them, and patted her hand at Killik's hot, flushed face.

"Yes, you ought to weep," she told him, as lightly as she could. "After finally gaining your wolf's strong ploughing, after so many years. Even better than you've always dreamt, wasn't it?"

Killik's fluttering eyes slid toward her, but yes, that was relief, warming those eyes, wavering on his mouth. So Louisa let her smile draw higher, into something smug and satisfied, as she gave another pat to his cheek. "It was even better than *I* dreamt, too," she said. "Seeing you stuck and stabbed on our wolf's good seat, and screaming for mercy. My favourite part of this show so far."

Killik scoffed and rolled his eyes, and even jabbed a wavering claw toward her face. "Still not your show, you greedy harpy," he replied, between heavy breaths. "It is *mine*. You dance for *me!*"

But his expression was warm, even grateful, he was just meeting her, just playing. And Louisa rolled her eyes back at him, and gave a purposeful, sweeping wave down at where Ulfarr's big body was still pinning Killik to the earth, his softening cock still jutted halfway into Killik's crease. And yes, yes, Ulfarr's expression had softened again too, his eyes slowly clearing, and flicking almost hungrily between Killik and Louisa's faces.

"You keep telling yourself that, you wily weasel," Louisa drawled at Killik, with another pat at his sweaty cheek. "Pretend as though we all didn't just see you begging, and whimpering, and squealing, just like a sweet, helpless, adorable little puppy—"

But she was cut off by Killik's sharp, thrilling growl, his body kicking up with astonishing speed, and landing over hers. And oh, now his legs were shoving hers apart, his own hard cock seeking up between—and then sinking deep inside her, while she choked and moaned upon it.

But oh, it felt so good, so perfect, most of all with Ulfarr now settling shaky and heavy onto his side next to them, his hand skittering against Killik's back. "Gentle, pup," he said, hoarse. "She is yet wounded, you ken. And mayhap— mayhap *you* are wounded now, also."

His voice cracked, his eyes still too hazy and bright, but Killik only rolled his eyes back, and then leaned toward Ulfarr, and pressed a brief, biting kiss to his mouth. "I ken I have never felt so good in all my life, Wolf," he murmured. "I... I thank you."

His gaze briefly dropped, his face flushing, and Ulfarr blinked hard, his body shifting closer, so he could inhale deep at Killik's neck. "I thank you also, my sweet pup," he whispered. "And"—his eyes flicked toward Louisa—"and you, sweet Louisa. You spoke such truth upon us, upon this, for I ken I have—I have—"

Both Louisa and Killik turned to look at Ulfarr, waiting, and Killik leaned in for another brief kiss to his mouth, even as his shaft quivered and pulsed inside Louisa, and her invaded heat clutched back. Both of them still wanting this together, yes, but both of them needing this from Ulfarr, too. Needing to help him face this.

"I have loved you so deeply, Killik," Ulfarr rasped, on a slow, heavy exhale. "For so long. For all these summers I have known you. And ach, I have thus so greatly feared—harming you, also. Drawing you into my weakness, and my darkness, and my grief, and my—evil. When I had vowed with all my strength to care for you, and keep you safe."

His eyes glimmered on Killik's face, his truth heavy in his voice, and he drew in a deep breath. "I have not—trusted myself with you," he continued. "I have not trusted I could keep you safe, most of all if I forever bound you to me, in the ways I most longed for. And thus, I have pushed you away, and hidden my own truth, for so long. Even as I have wished for yours. Even as I have raged with envy every time I have seen or scented you with another."

Killik's expression flickered as he watched, as something like comprehension—or even relief—flashed across his eyes. While Ulfarr dragged in another slow, shaky breath, shuddering all through his big, sweaty body. "And in this, just now, pup, I should not—I ought not—I yet had—no right. I lost my bearings, lost my control, ought not have commanded you, and pushed you, and—"

He was speaking so quickly, stumbling over the words, the distress again rising in his eyes. But oh, that was another lingering kiss from Killik to his mouth, a caress of his hand to Ulfarr's sweaty cheek.

"Ach, I follow now, Wolf," he murmured. "But I have always wished for this from you. And I should be most glad if you should yet grant it to me."

It felt so simple, so soft, even gentle, in a way Louisa couldn't ever recall seeing from Killik before. Offering Ulfarr his forgiveness, his truth, his hope, with such openness, such quiet, ready ease. With such... love.

And Ulfarr seemed struck by it too, his throat convulsing, his hand skittering down Killik's back. His eyes shining with reverence, with hunger, with raw, radiant adoration. "Ach, then," he whispered. "I shall, pup."

It shot a swift, stunning smile across Killik's face, swelling him fuller inside Louisa, too—and he drew Ulfarr close again, kissing him so sweet and so hungry, even as his hips against Louisa finally started circling, grinding himself slow inside her. Feeling so foreign, so strange and soft and new, because he'd never done it like this before—and he'd certainly never tugged Ulfarr up behind him, and flashed him such a taunting, tender smile.

"Again, Wolf," he murmured. "But more gentle this time, mayhap."

Ulfarr's exhale was half-laugh, half-moan, but he wasted no time in shifting up behind Killik again, and—Louisa could feel Killik startle—easing back inside him. Indeed moving slow and careful, now, his movements gently rocking Killik into Louisa, while Killik gazed down at her with hooded, fluttering eyes. But not speaking, just looking, breathing, as his body kept filling her, meeting her, shuddering deep within her...

But then his head dropped, his face bent into her neck, his pointed ear lightly tickling at her cheek. "You ken I love you," he whispered, so quiet, into her ear. "Ach?"

Louisa twitched, and exhaled a breath that felt like relief, like wonder. "I... hoped you might," she whispered back. "I... wanted you to. So much."

Killik's laugh was low, choked, his hot breath huffing against her skin. "How could I not?" he murmured. "My strong, fierce, hungry harpy, fighting with me, playing with me, hunting with me, even *flyting* with me. Seeking my help and my wisdom, and seeking to help me, also. Showing such kindness to my wolf and my son and my kin. Even bearing the Ka-esh for me, and writing all these pretty letters, to spare me such pain."

Louisa huffed a shaky laugh, but her hands had circled up around him, slipping into his sweaty, straggly hair. While his mouth gave a soft, gentle nip at her neck, his body still grinding slow and sweet between her legs. "And all this pleasure, also," he said. "Sucking me, tasting me, screeching upon me. Tending and taunting Wolf with me. Ach, even writing that curst letter to Wolf of me. Speaking of how I thronged within you, and granted you such great and wondrous gifts."

Louisa shivered all over at even the memory of it, and wait, that was a low chuckle from Ulfarr behind Killik, as he gently drew one of the daggers from Killik's loosening hair, and then set it carefully onto Louisa's collarbone, where Killik could still see it. "Ach, this letter," he said, with a twitch of a smile down at Louisa's face. "I caught him reading it, with his prick in his hand. Twice."

Killik shot a sharp, betrayed look up over his shoulder, but Ulfarr just smiled back at him, so fond, and pulled out the other dagger, too, and set it onto Louisa with the first. Releasing Killik's hair in a dark silken curtain, falling around Louisa's face, and she could just make out Ulfarr nuzzling against Killik's head, inhaling slow and deep. "This pleased you, pup," he murmured. "It has always pleased you, to be thanked, and to be honoured. To be... seen, for all you do, and all the great gifts you grant to us."

Killik made a face, but he didn't argue, and his glance back toward Louisa looked almost embarrassed. But no, no, he couldn't be, and Louisa held his eyes, drew in his strength. "So many gifts, Killik," she whispered, beneath the shifting fall of his hair. "So many things I didn't even realize. Not just the food, and the help on the property, but all those lessons, all those explanations, even when you thought—when you thought you were teaching me to *replace* you. Not to mention Rikard, and how you guarded me from him, and defended me, and—and *killed* him. Or—almost killed him."

It still sounded hushed on her voice, not quite real, but Rikard's immobile body was still just over there, only a few paces away. While she was so alive, so whole and warm and safe, with Killik twitching her such a wry, satisfied little smile. "Ach, I have been plotting to murder him for weeks," he said lightly. "Since that first day he dared to touch what was *mine*."

Since that first day. And that day... that had been way back at the beginning, hadn't it? After that first good night with Ulfarr in her bed? After she and Killik had fought, and Killik had threatened her and stormed out, and now...

Killik glanced away again, wincing, but didn't argue it, either. As if he really had considered Louisa *his* for that long, for all that time. And the truth of it flipped in her belly, tightened against his hard body still filling her, rocking so slow and steady and safe.

"Thank you, Killik," she murmured. "It was so good of you."

And yes, yes, he did like that, the warmth deepening on his cheeks, sparkling in his eyes. And when Louisa drew him down for a kiss, he willingly met it, his mouth so soft, so sweet, his tongue tangling slick and languid against hers.

"And you really didn't mind," Louisa whispered, once he'd drawn back again, "about Lord Scall, either?"

Killik blinked at her, looking briefly bewildered—and then his expression cleared, and he laughed, bright and almost merry. "Ach, no," he said. "I scented his death upon you from the start. We well knew the measure of this man, and this only raised you in my eyes, ach? Made me see you as a better woman for my wolf."

Wait. Wait, wait, wait. Killik had—known? He'd known she'd killed Lord Scall, all that time? And oh gods, had Ulfarr known, too?

But Louisa's glance up toward Ulfarr said that yes, yes, he had—and Louisa had kept it from them, that entire time. And damn it, they'd both even hinted at it, hadn't they? They'd both given her opportunities to tell them, to be honest with them. *You can speak truth to us, ach? And no matter what this is, we shall yet stand beside you, and keep you safe...*

"I'm sorry," Louisa croaked, blinking back and forth

between them. "I'm so sorry I didn't tell you. I was so—so afraid of it, for so long, and I just wanted to—forget. To keep it buried forever, where it might be—safe."

But there was no judgement in their watching eyes, only patience, or even sympathy. Though Killik's head tilted, his brows raising, as if he was... waiting. Wanting to hear the rest.

"Living with Lord Scall was like being trapped in a night-mare," Louisa made herself say, her voice catching. "I had to watch everything I said, everything I wore, everything I did. And if I angered him, or gods forbid, lost my temper in return"—she gulped for breath—"he would do whatever the hell he wanted with me. Shout at me, throw things at me, pressure me into his bed, lock me in the cellar. I even went into debt to buy a townhouse in Dusbury, all on my own, just to escape him—but I hated being trapped there too, with no forest or horses or fresh air, and nothing productive to do with my time. But it was enough to get by, to keep up appear-ances, and there was nothing I could do against him, and—and—"

She was breathing too hard, but Killik was still above her, still inside her, his hair still shielding her face—and above him, Ulfarr was still here, too. She could speak this. She was safe.

"And then I found out about Scall's infection," she whis-pered. "The reason I kept having those miscarriages. And he didn't just do it to me—he was infecting other women, too. Killing them, just as carelessly as he killed the orcs he kept warring against. And then he started turning his attention toward Joan, and I just—I just couldn't bear it anymore. I had to do something. Had to—try."

Her voice broke, but above her, Killik nodded, and pressed a soft, quiet kiss to her mouth. "You did well, Louisa," he murmured. "You did all you could to care for your kin, and keep them safe. This is what any good Skai would do, ach? This was the hand of Skai-kesh upon you, I ken."

The hand of Skai-kesh. It was just what Ulfarr had told her, too, back on their very first night together—and despite her prickling eyes, her too-tight throat, Louisa felt her breath exhaling, her body sinking heavier into the earth. Into relief, into safety, into... peace.

Lord Scall was dead, and she was alive. She was whole.

"But this was yet a heavy burden for you to bear, most of all alone," Killik added, his eyes shifting on Louisa's face. "I ken I ought to have sought deeper for your truth, and taken more care with you. Ought not to have pushed you so much, or fought you, as I did. Most of all"—he sighed—"upon *this*."

This. He meant his hips grinding against her, his hard body still buried inside her, and Louisa swallowed, shook her head. "But you were so patient, too," she said thickly. "You helped me so much. Both of you."

Killik's head tilted again, listening, and Louisa drew in a deep, shaky breath. "You gave me all those lessons," she whispered. "You guided me, and encouraged me, and made this—safe. You showed me an entirely different side of it, and gave me joy, and safety, and peace. And now"—her voice cracked—"I truly love doing this with you. Both of you."

She darted a glance up at Ulfarr, who was softly smiling toward her, his hand stroking warm against her hair. While Killik's mouth quirked up, and relief—or even approval— glimmered in his watching eyes. "Ach, I did scent this upon you," he said lightly. "You could not hide your longing for strong Skai prick, ach?"

Louisa smiled and rolled her eyes back toward him, but then felt the smile fading, twisting into a grimace. "I did hide," she whispered, "the son part, though."

Killik's mouth pursed, his breath slowly exhaling. "Ach, you did," he replied, quiet. "But mayhap this was also the hand of Skai-kesh, and a great gift toward us. For I would not have chosen you in my hunt, had I known."

He wouldn't have chosen her. A convulsive shiver rippled up Louisa's back, her eyes briefly closing—but wait, that was another kiss from Killik, firm on her mouth. "A great gift," he repeated. "For with another woman, with a new son, I ken—I ken I would yet have left, ach?"

Right. Because Killik hadn't wanted the woman to begin with, he hadn't wanted another son—and above him, Ulfarr gave a low growl, a sharp nip at his ear. Enough that Killik winced, and sighed, and twisted up to meet Ulfarr's eyes.

"I could not have left Sune, ever," he said, harder. "And mayhap I could not have stayed away from you forever either, Wolf. But I should not have cared for this woman, or shared your bed with her, or wished to make her our—"

He broke off there, but Ulfarr's eyes cleared, and he nuzzled at Killik's hair again, drawing in a deep, relieved breath. "Our mate," Ulfarr finished firmly. "You wish for this also, ach, pup? For the three of us?"

Louisa's heart skipped, her eyes widening, as a shivery thrill flashed up her spine. Ulfarr still wanted to make them mates? All three of them, together?

But above her, Killik hesitated, his eyes carefully searching hers. "But mayhap *you* do not wish for this, Louisa," he said. "You did not wish to be a wife, ach? And whilst matehood bears no legal standing amongst humans thus, it is yet much the same."

Right. Louisa inhaled as she considered that, turning it over in her thoughts. But there was no judgement in Killik's watching eyes, no impatience, no command. As if Louisa truly could... choose. Could choose to say yes, or no. Or perhaps...

"Could I just... think about it, for a while?" she finally asked. "Is there any... rush?"

Killik's gaze again angled up toward Ulfarr, but Ulfarr

shook his head, and gave a soft smile toward her. "We shall be glad to wait as long as you need, Louisa," he murmured. "And we shall be here whenever you are ready—or even if you are never ready at all. You have granted us so much, and we should be most honoured to grant you whatever best pleases you."

Louisa sagged heavy against the earth, sinking into the truth of it, the relief of it. In both Killik and Ulfarr giving her the choice in this, recognizing her autonomy, respecting her needs. Making it clear that this truly wasn't about the land, or the camp, or their kin. They cared about her. *Hers.*

"Thank you, sweetheart," she whispered, with a slow smile back at Ulfarr's watching face. "And you know, if you'd really like to please me, maybe you could..."

She shot a meaningful glance toward Killik, but oh, Ulfarr was already nodding, the comprehension glinting warm in his eyes. "Ach," he murmured, as he pressed another kiss against Killik's hair. "I shall yet take a mate tonight."

There was a jolt of stillness, and then Killik's eyes snapped wide, his head whipping around to stare up at Ulfarr's face. But Ulfarr only smiled back at him, fond and wicked, as his hand gently loosened the chain still around Killik's neck. "I have waited long enough," he said. "And tonight, Killik, I shall finally make you *mine.*"

Killik's gasp was hoarse and disbelieving, his eyes fluttering, while Ulfarr only kept smiling at him, and then kissed his way down to the fresh red teeth-marks he'd left on Killik's neck. "I shall need to rut you, you ken," Ulfarr breathed, hot, and oh, he was grinding into Killik again, shifting him purposefully against Louisa. "Before all our clan."

Killik groaned and shuddered all over, his head tilting away to welcome more of Ulfarr's kiss, his seeking mouth. As if—as if he didn't mind the prospect of this rut whatsoever. As if he would... welcome it.

But even the thought of it choked in Louisa's breath, and flashed sudden and cold all down her form. "But—doesn't the rut mean you'd still *share* him?" she demanded at Ulfarr. "With—*other partners*? After all this?"

And curse her, that was distinct disapproval in her voice, or even jealousy. Enough that Killik and Ulfarr exchanged another brief, speaking glance, Ulfarr's eyes narrowing, while distinct redness crept up Killik's cheeks.

"No, I shall not share him in this," Ulfarr said, flat and decisive, as his eyes met Louisa's again. "But we spoke of how Simon altered this rut, ach? Apart from the hunt, it is yet how we claim a mate—but now all parties must freely choose who else is part of this. And should you wish, Louisa, in claiming Killik, I should welcome only... you."

Oh. Only her. The relief shuddered through Louisa's breath, and she quivered a small, grateful smile back toward him. "Then I'd be honoured, sweetheart," she murmured. "Of course. We can put on a good show together, don't you think? Make your adorable puppy spurt and scream for us."

Killik loudly snorted, but Louisa and Ulfarr ignored it, and grinned at each other. And already Ulfarr was grinding against Killik again, his face seeking hungry against his throat, while Killik gasped and shuddered, and swelled fuller inside Louisa. Sparking and stoking her own hunger, and she clutched back against him, sank her hands into his beautiful silken hair. And then drew his head down for a deep, dragging kiss, because she could do that now, she could—and oh, he even moaned into it, his tongue plunging deep, his teeth scraping against her lips.

It was perfect, perfect, their bodies all locked together, rocking together with such sweet, staggering bliss. Wringing them higher, closer, tighter, Ulfarr's slow, heavy thrusts juddering Killik into Louisa, all over Louisa, his claws skittering at her face, tilting it to the side. So he could scrape those sharp teeth over her bare, exposed neck, in a silent, tantalizing threat—but Louisa didn't care, she didn't, and she might have even drawn him down harder, please…

She arched and gasped as the pain flashed deep—and oh, oh, at Killik's very first gulp, his cock inside her shuddered, and sprayed. Streaming her full of slick molten heat, even as his hard, rhythmic swallows rang through her ears. Drinking her, even as she drank him, clutched to him, gasping beneath his strength and his seed and his teeth— and fuck, her own pleasure seized, surged, crashed. Milking at Killik again and again, swallowing more and more and more, firing her full of fizzing, flaring ecstasy. While behind Killik, Ulfarr was shouting too, his weight pinning them both to the earth, as his own hard swallows gulped against Killik's arched throat.

The world seemed to blink away beneath the strength of it, leaving only the pleasure, the warmth, the relief. The truth of Louisa held so certain, so sheltered, beneath her fierce powerful orcs. She was safe. She was whole. She was… Skai.

But no, no, perhaps not entirely, not officially, not yet. And for an instant, there was the reckless, overwhelming urge to just say, *Yes, yes, make me your mate, please*—

But then Killik drew himself up, away from her throat. And when Louisa's hazy eyes found his face, it was streaked with red, his long black tongue licking slow and decadent against his stained lips. While behind him, Ulfarr licked at his own red lips, and then frowned down at the broken, throbbing skin of Louisa's neck.

"Killik," he said, his husky voice almost, almost disapproving. "That is a mating-bite."

Killik's brows rose, his eyes leisurely sliding down to hold on Louisa's neck. "No, is it?" he drawled. "I thought it was a bee-sting. Or a new Ka-esh tattoo, mayhap."

Ulfarr's expression wavered, clearly caught between amusement and rebuke—and somehow, curse her, Louisa smiled up toward them both, too fond, too grateful. Her hands even drawing Killik's face down again, so she could find his mouth, taste herself on his lips.

"Tyrant," she murmured, and then kissed him again. "You and your damned show."

But Killik was smiling against her lips, huffing a laugh into her mouth. "Ready yourself, harpy," he whispered back. "For it has only just begun."

61

When Louisa finally stood to her feet again, she found herself covered in mud and twigs and blood, and sore and sticky all over.

Killik and Ulfarr didn't look much better—gods, Killik looked like he'd just crawled through a battlefield—but neither of them seemed concerned. If anything, Killik looked decidedly pleased with himself, and even shot a satisfied grin toward—Rurik?

Louisa had fully forgotten about Rurik, but yes, he was still here, leaning impatiently against a tree, with his arms crossed over his chest. "Finally," he snapped, as he strode toward them, and then knelt to touch a hand at Louisa's bloody ankle. "Is this wound yet pain, woman?"

Louisa blinked downwards—gods, she'd nearly forgotten about her wounds, too. "It does seem much better," she replied, with genuine relief. "It just stings a bit, maybe."

Rurik nodded, and his hand carefully shifted against it, as something prickled beneath Louisa's skin. Dragging up another question, one that had been vaguely nagging at the back of her thoughts. "So your healing really is... magic?" she asked him, careful. "Like Efterar's, at the mountain? Is that—something Skai can usually do?"

Rurik shrugged, and shifted his hand again on her ankle. "No," he said, without looking up. "But one of my fathers was Ash-Kai, and his seed granted me some of his skill, before I was birthed. I am not near as gifted as Efterar, but"—he rose to his feet, gave a smug smile—"I have my eye on an Ash-Kai in the north who may rival him, with time."

It seemed like such a Skai thing to say, suddenly, and Louisa couldn't help smiling back at him, even as she gave an experimental roll of her ankle. "Well, I wish you luck," she replied. "And thank you."

Rurik nodded, and then glanced toward Rikard's unconscious, still-sprawled body. Which now showed no signs of actual wounds, beyond his torn, bloody clothes—but Louisa could still make out his breath, faintly rising and falling in his chest. "I have also healed this man's wounds, as best I could," Rurik said. "Even the eye, as long as no one looks too closely at this. And I have thickened the veins around his heart, to match those of a long-held illness. He ought to live yet three or four more days, but no more than a week."

It seemed like such a cold, calculated death, suddenly, and Louisa winced as she glanced at Rikard's pale, familiar face. "And he won't wake up again?" she asked, tentative. "Or be in pain?"

Beside her, Killik scoffed, and muttered something about Rikard planning to mutilate her with her own knife—but Rurik shook his head. "His brain shall not again awaken," he said firmly. "But I shall help carry him off to his bed, to make sure of this. I shall need four of your packmates as bearers, I ken."

Ulfarr readily nodded, and signed toward Igull, Elgr, Halthorr, and Ragni, all of whom had re-emerged through the trees. And after a brief discussion of how they would cover the deception—cleaning off Rikard's blood, dressing him in nightclothes, placing him in bed—they quickly built a makeshift stretcher from nearby deadwood, and heaved Rikard's unconscious bulk onto it.

"We again thank you, brother," Ulfarr said toward Rurik, once the four orcs had lifted the stretcher between them. "Your help has been a great gift from Skai-kesh toward us."

But Rurik only waved it away, and gave Killik and Ulfarr a cool, assessing look. "You can thank me by sending help to build my own camp, when I am ready," he replied. "And by inviting me to join your rut upon your woman, also."

What? Louisa's mouth dropped open, but Rurik only spun around, and waved for the orcs to carry Rikard away. Leaving Louisa to dart a disbelieving look between Killik and Ulfarr, who were both looking... *thoughtful.* As though they were actually *considering* this bizarre demand of Rurik's?

"Ach, you could do worse, woman," Killik said, with a sly grin toward her. "I hear healers make for clever bedmates, ach?"

Louisa spluttered at him, her face flooding with heat, her eyes helplessly darting toward where Rurik and the orcs had already disappeared through the trees. "You really would both be fine with that?" she demanded, too sharp. "I thought—I thought you said you didn't *want* to do the sharing anymore!"

Ulfarr's brow had been slowly furrowing, but at that last bit, it abruptly cleared again. "No, I should not wish to share either of you, as I have borne with Killik," he replied. "But it would not be... the same, in a rut thus, together."

Louisa blinked blankly toward Ulfarr—what did he mean, it wasn't the same? And she should be offended by that, right? Appalled that he would want to *share* her, with orcs like Rurik?!

But wait, now Killik stepped between them, his hand stroking up and down Louisa's back. "Wolf means," he said, with a sharp look toward Ulfarr, "the scents are not the same, when it is done thus. In a rut, if Wolf leads this, all else shall yet scent of him and serve him, ach? Not only you, but any other orcs he grants you, also. It would speak of Wolf's standing amongst his kin, that he can wield such power, and share such a gift."

Louisa shot an uncertain glance toward Ulfarr, who was nodding gratefully at Killik, and then sliding his hand around her waist, too. "But there is yet no need for this, Louisa," he said, with a gentle kiss to her hair. "None at all."

But when Louisa drew away to study him, he did look... flushed. Interested. His breaths drawing in deep, his eyes warm and bright on hers. And wait, were his trousers bulging? Again?

"Really?" she demanded, staring at him, and then darting a helpless look at Killik, too. "And *you* actually would want this rut, too?!"

Killik shrugged, though his eyes on hers were thoughtful, considering. "Ach, if you both wished for this, I would," he said, with a shrug. "Ruts have long been a deep Skai rite, and we do not oft fuss over scents, as some other clans do. And I ken"—his eyes glinted with distinct satisfaction—"it should not be a hardship to flaunt and command our lusty Skai woman before all our clan. To bring them all to their knees for her, and then watch her spurt and squeal upon the biggest, most perfect prick of them all, ach?"

He shot a saucy glance toward Ulfarr, who betrayed a low gasp, his hand adjusting his tented trousers. While something heated low and strange in Louisa's belly, too—and she belatedly shook her head, drew up breath, and strength. Truth. Skai.

"But," she managed, though her voice was hoarse. "I wouldn't want to share—*you*. Either of you."

She braced for their answer, for maybe their mockery, for even the end of this, after all—but Ulfarr's hand just kept stroking her back, while Killik laughed, and rolled his eyes.

"No, you ken?" he drawled. "We would have never guessed this, woman."

Louisa glared at him, even as a skittering relief fluttered through her belly. "I mean it, Killik," she insisted. "It wouldn't be—fair. I wouldn't be able to handle it. I would just be—too jealous. And if that's what you both really want, then maybe you should still find someone else, someone who—"

But her voice broke there, because Ulfarr's strong arms dragged her close, wrapping her tight against his solid chest. "Ach, no, Louisa," he breathed. "None of this. I yet have no wish to bed any others, beyond Killik, and *you*."

Oh. Louisa sagged against him, her breath heaving out, and that was again the feel of Killik's arm too, circling around her and Ulfarr both. "You shall *not* now leave us, woman," Killik said, clipped. "And again, this is not the same, for I can scent you. I can scent every orc you touch. I can scent whether you bear true longing for him, or not. You *cannot* hide this from me. But when you cannot scent this..."

His voice faded, and when Louisa twitched to look at him, he was studying Ulfarr, with a strange new stillness on his face. "When you cannot fully scent this," he repeated, slower, "you cannot... know. You can only see me ploughing and touching and kissing another. You can only seek to trust the words I speak to you, and hope them to be truth. But if I speak no words, then..."

He grimaced, his eyes briefly closing, his hand sliding up to spread against Ulfarr's face. "I am sorry, Wolf," he murmured. "This was not... fair, to you."

Ulfarr swallowed, his eyes shifting, but Louisa could feel his hand spasming against her, his former hardness rapidly softening in his trousers. Suggesting that not being able to smell Killik's truth truly had made this more difficult for him—or perhaps even made him believe that Killik didn't care about him at all.

"But wouldn't it feel the same... with me?" Louisa finally

asked, into the silence. "Wouldn't that also upset you, sweetheart?"

Ulfarr grimaced, and his glance toward Killik was almost pleading—to which Killik huffed a laugh, and leaned over to nip at Louisa's neck. "You cannot think Wolf would ever allow you to run off and find pleasure without him, as I did?" he said flatly. "No. He should only grant this whilst you are gasping in his arms, and leaking his fresh seed. And whilst I am there to scent you, and make sure you behave for us."

Louisa's breath exhaled in a rush, her gaze again finding Ulfarr—and yes, he was nodding, the relief flickering in his eyes. "Ach, just thus," he said, soft. "But again, there is no need for this, should you not wish. You have already granted us such great joy, Louisa. More than I could ever have dreamt."

Louisa smiled back at him, slow and wavering, while Killik scoffed, and gently slapped her arse. "Well, dream more, Wolf," he said lightly. "She shall come around, I ken."

Louisa shot a glare at him, but he only grinned back, and patted her cheek. "Think upon it," he said. "Now, are we done here? I should be most glad to wash off this man's stench."

He waved toward the blood still spattered across his face and chest, and Louisa choked a laugh as she glanced down at her tattered dress, too. She was a filthy mess, yes, but she was safe. She was whole. She was Skai.

And even if it wasn't fully official yet, it still felt... right. True. In the way Killik and Ulfarr fell into step on either side of her as they turned toward the road, Ulfarr's hand spreading on her back. Walking together, breathing together, as more contented warmth shimmered up Louisa's spine. She still had Killik and Ulfarr. She still had her sisters and the children. She still had her home, her property, the camp. And she still had—herself. Her health. Her life.

But gods, it had still been so close. Only a few more

moments, and she would have been lying there dead, and everything she'd built would have been lost forever. And gods only knew what fool lord would inherit Rikard's lands after his death, and she still had all those debts, and...

Wait. The debts. And there was still something to that, something they hadn't yet addressed...

"You mentioned, back there," Louisa abruptly said, with a sideways glance at Ulfarr, "that you were... *gathering* that payment we agreed on. Didn't you?"

Her voice came out steady, not judging or angry, but just... asking. Just wanting to hear the truth, to finally set it all out between them. Because that payment was something else she hadn't wanted to face, wasn't it? Something she'd wanted to escape, and forget.

But perhaps Ulfarr had wanted to escape it too, his mouth twisting, while on her other side, Killik gave a gentle slap to her arse. "Ach, we are yet gathering it," he replied. "And you shall yet have it, woman. It has only taken longer than we meant."

Louisa studied him for a long moment, searching for the truth in that, seeking to find the right question. Because perhaps she'd realized, over these past weeks, that Killik and Ulfarr weren't wealthy. They didn't have that much extra coin lying around. And neither did their campmates, or even their clan, and...

"You're borrowing it, then?" she asked, her voice careful. "From where?"

Killik shrugged, and gave a vague wave ahead toward the camp, toward their mountain. "From many places," he replied. "But naught that shall bring us harm, or lead to your land being lost. So there is no need to fret over it, ach?"

Louisa watched him for another long, hitching breath, as her stomach flipped in her gut. They were—taking her debts upon themselves. And they weren't even trying to take that part of their agreement back, even now that they'd settled the rest of it between them. They'd made a vow to pay her debts, and they were keeping it.

"Well," Louisa said, through her choked throat. "I've decided I want to break that vow. We didn't keep to the ten nights, and I don't want the rest of your coin, either."

There was more silence, from Killik and Ulfarr both, and they exchanged a meaningful glance, as Ulfarr's hand caressed against her back. "But—we yet wish to help you, Louisa," Ulfarr said, low. "We wish to uphold your wishes. And you wish to keep your home, and guard your kin, ach? You wish to have control over *your property, your freedom, and your life.*"

Right. It was a direct quote of what Louisa had told him earlier, and she drew in breath, searched for truth. "I do still want all that," she replied slowly. "But maybe—maybe we can face it together, and find another way. Like we did with the Summit. Your last payment was enough to keep the property safe for at least a while longer, and in terms of the inheritance issue..."

Her feet suddenly tripped, faltered, her gaze blank and unseeing on the darkening horizon. While both Killik and Ulfarr snapped to stillness too, Ulfarr's hand tense on her back, Killik's circling tight around her wrist.

"What?" Killik demanded. "What is amiss?"

Louisa huffed a half-laugh, and shook her head. "I just..." she began, and her heart was pattering faster, her breaths heaving short and shallow. "I was just thinking"—she darted a look between them—"marriage isn't the only option, right? Maybe we could consider—another family connection, instead?"

Both Ulfarr and Killik were just watching her now, waiting, and Louisa found the earth beneath her feet, drew it in deep. Drew in strength, truth, Skai...

"What if," she said, as the hope caught, held, shimmered. "What if I adopted Sune?"

62

What if she adopted Sune.

Louisa flinched at even the sound of it, the shocking presumptuousness of it. The utter arrogance, to think she could just waltz in and adopt Killik and Ulfarr's son, but—but—

"I don't mean to say Sune would need to—honour it," she said, too quickly. "Or see me as his mother, or any kind of authority over him. And I wouldn't at all want him to feel obligated, or coerced, or anything like that! I just"—she had to pull in a breath—"I still have no interest in getting married again, or having another baby, but I still want to protect my land, and I feel I could trust Sune to honour my wishes, and I've still always wanted a—"

She cringed, shook her head, snapped her mouth shut, far too late. No, no, it wasn't about that, and gods, the way Killik and Ulfarr were both looking at her now, Ulfarr's eyes blank and unseeing, Killik's glittering with something she couldn't at all read. And gods, she was making a mess of this, she sounded like some kind of son-stealing creep, and...

"I mean," she gasped, "we'd still need to talk to lawyers, make sure it could work. But if we can make Sune legally my son, he would also be—my heir. Because under the terms of the treaty, he's just the same as a human now, right? And that way, if anything ever happens to me, or if any more murderous lords show up"—she hauled in another shaky breath—"I'd still protect my sisters, and my property, and the camp, without any need for marriage whatsoever. Right? And maybe Sune would feel more settled that way, too, because he could be sure he always has a place here, with his family. With—our family. All of us."

Ulfarr was still staring at Louisa, his body utterly still, but Killik's eyes were flashing, not with anger, or judgement. But with—with approval. With appreciation.

And then Killik lurched toward her, yanked her close, and laughed. Laughed with bright, genuine joy, the sound carrying through the trees. "You should wish for this?" he breathed, hot into her ear. "Truth, Louisa?"

He pulled back to look at her, searching her eyes, his nostrils flaring—but Louisa could only beam back toward him, her eyes prickling. "Yes," she said, steady and certain. "Truth, Killik."

She meant it, meant it with all her breath, all her soul. And Killik's smile was smaller now, softer, his claws tickling gentle at her cheek. "Good," he murmured. "We shall go speak to Sune at once. And Rosa, also."

He truly had to be pleased, if he wanted to speak to Rosa, and Louisa grinned back at him, and nodded. And then glanced toward Ulfarr, too, wanting to include him in this— but he was still just staring at them. Still with that stunned, distant blankness in his eyes.

But it wasn't the look he'd worn so often before, with all that uncertainty and loss. No, no, it was just surprise, and delight—and in a lurch of movement, he swept Louisa into his arms, too. Rocking her back and forth, squeezing so hard it hurt.

"I am so honoured," he whispered, "that you would wish to make our son your own, also."

Louisa clutched him back as tightly as she could, her eyes blinking hard. "But only if he even wants it, that is," she said. "Could you talk to him together, and make sure you hear his honest response, and give him time to consider it? And the freedom to refuse, without any constraints whatsoever?"

Her sideways glance at Killik found him nodding, his hand gently gripping at her shoulder. "We shall," he replied. "We have no wish to push him into this, either. We wish him to know how much we care for him, just as he is."

Ulfarr's breath exhaled, and he nodded too, while Killik gave a wry roll of his eyes toward Louisa. "And ach, I shall tell Sune this," he said. "I shall keep telling him this, and showing him this, until he is sure of it."

It settled more warmth in Louisa's chest, bright and steady and safe, because when Killik made a commitment, he wouldn't waver. He would see it through. He would stay, and keep being a good father to Sune. He would.

The rest of the trip to Louisa's house passed with surprising speed, and it turned out that Sune was impatiently waiting in the lane to greet them, his narrow eyes darting between Killik and Louisa. Or rather, between their necks, which were both bearing fresh sets of teeth-marks.

Did you claim them, Pa? Sune signed at Ulfarr. *Are they now yours, for good?*

Ulfarr angled a brief, searching glance toward Louisa, because no, she hadn't committed to that *mate* point yet. But blinking at him, and then at Sune, and then at Killik, there was more steady certainty, circling in her chest. Whatever they decided to call it, she was still committed to them, and to this. She was.

Her nod was brief, but decisive, and Killik gave a satisfied nod back before waving Sune over toward them. "Ach, Wolf did this, son," he said, as he yanked Sune tightly into his arms. "Finally. You shall now never be rid of me."

Sune squeezed Killik back with surprising intensity, his face buried into his shoulder—and then he lurched to embrace Ulfarr, too. And the look on Ulfarr's face as he held his son was so reverent, so utterly adoring, it ached in Louisa's belly. They belonged together. A family.

She had to wipe at her wet eyes with her tattered sleeve, and when she blinked up again, she found—Cecily. Who'd just come from the house with Timo, but now she halted in place, one hand gripping Timo's arm, the other clapping over her mouth.

"You Skai!" she exclaimed, her voice shrill. "What the *hell* did you all do?!"

Louisa startled, glancing uncertainly around them—but wait, Cecily was looking at her dress. Her lovely, well-suited Skai dress, which was now torn, stained, and bloody—and thanks to Rikard's trap, one of her beautiful leather boots was ruined, too. And while Ulfarr's trousers might still be salvageable, they were still covered in dirt, while Killik's new trousers were hanging from his hips in thick, muddy, bloody ribbons.

"Ach, just a bit of hunting," Killik told Cecily, with a not-so-nice smile. "Mayhap some playing, also."

Cecily snorted, and shot an aggrieved glare toward Sune, and then toward Timo beside her. "Honestly, Timo!" she wailed. "Why do I even *bother* trying to make them presentable?"

Timo seemed in full agreement, regretfully nodding and wrinkling his nose. "Ach, but it could have been worse, Cecy," he said, with a reassuring pat to her shoulder. "I ken they waited until *after* the Summit to start killing, at least."

Cecily sighed and nodded, and then threw up her hands as she spun toward the house. "We've drawn you a hot bath, sister," she called, over her shoulder. "But those two louts can fend for themselves."

Louisa laughed despite herself, and called a genuine thank-you after her. And then, after a brief glance at Killik and Ulfarr—Ulfarr's arm still heavy around Sune's shoulder—she gestured toward the house, too. "I'll go wash up, then," she said, "and meet you three later?"

Killik met her eyes, gave a brief nod—which meant he would use the time to talk to Sune, as he'd promised. And Louisa was still smiling as she headed for the kitchen, the warmth and the hopefulness again bubbling in her chest. No matter what happened, they would face this together. They were a family.

The kitchen door was latched when she pulled on it, but with a familiar jiggle of one of its rusted nails, she shoved it open. That latch was something else she should mention to Killik, perhaps Argarr could make them a new one, and...

She halted halfway through the door, her breath caught, her heartbeat suddenly screaming in her ears. Because someone was quaking and whimpering against the counter in the dim light, and it was—*Elise*. Elise, dishevelled and trembling all over, while a distraught-looking Joan tried to comfort her, and something—something moved. Beneath Elise's skirts. Something *alive*.

Louisa's knife was in her hand in an instant, her breaths slow and steady, her feet moving silently on the stone floor. Feeling the earth, breathing it in, circling for the attack...

She was almost, almost there when Joan caught sight of her, her dark eyes snapped wide—and then Joan yelped, and frantically flailed her hands between them. "Lou!" she gasped. "No! It's not what it looks like! It's just—just—"

Louisa's heart skipped a beat, her body jolted still, as she stared at Joan's face, and then back at Elise. Who, upon closer inspection, was biting her lip, her cheeks becomingly flushed, her full breasts almost spilling out of her bodice.

And her eyes were more dazed than afraid, though they sharpened into horrified alarm as they stared at Louisa, and then snapped down toward the...

Toward the *orc*, now shifting out from beneath her skirts. Toward... Halthorr?!

"Ach, greetings, my lady," Halthorr said to Louisa, sounding only slightly breathless as he rose to his feet, and gave a brief bow toward her. "Forgive me, for I did not scent you there. Have Wolf and Killik returned, also?"

Louisa mutely nodded—Halthorr had been up Elise's *skirts*—and he even gave a swift, hungry lick at his lips as he nodded back. "Ought to go meet them, I ken," he said, too lightly, before flashing a grin at Elise's shocked face. "Mayhap we can finish this later, my lovelies?"

With that, he leaned in, and pressed a sweet, chaste kiss to Elise's reddened cheek, even as his other hand gave a greedy grasp to Joan's arse through her trousers. And then he turned and sauntered out the kitchen door, leaving all of them silent and staring after him.

"Um," Joan finally said, into the silence. "Sorry, Lou. Shouldn't have—"

But Louisa waved it away with a flap of her hand, and suddenly she was beaming at them, smiling so hard it hurt. "He's a lovely orc," she said firmly. "I do hope you enjoy yourselves."

Joan and Elise exchanged a brief, astonished look, Elise's eyes still very wide—but then Joan squared her shoulders, and slid her hand around Elise's waist. "We will," she said, hoarse. "So... you don't mind him staying over, then? With us?"

Louisa shook her head, and felt her smile softening. "Of course not," she replied. "This is your home, too. I consider you both"—she drew in a breath—"my sisters. My family. I want you to be happy here, and keep making your lives here with me. And you, Gladys, too."

She'd just caught sight of Gladys hovering outside the opposite door, perhaps avoiding the scene, or monitoring it, or both. And though Gladys' face was flushed, too, she gave them all a prim smile as she strode into the room, smoothing out her skirts. "I knew that one had his eye on you, too," she told Elise, with a sniff. "You two had best make sure he works hard for his dinner."

Elise gave a choked, gasping giggle, while Joan snorted, and rolled her eyes. Looking so suddenly, endearingly Skai that Louisa wanted to hug her, but instead she grinned between them, and stroked contentedly at the knife still in her hand. Her home. Her family.

She was still smiling to herself as she headed upstairs, and settled into the hot, luxurious bath that was waiting for her in her bedroom. And it did feel so lovely to clean off all the blood and dirt, and to wash her lingering wounds, too. But most of them had already begun to heal over, and Louisa sent a silent thanks to Skai-kesh for Rurik, and for all Killik and Ulfarr's care, too. Both of them there for her, helping her, when she'd most needed them. As they'd so often done, all this time.

And yes, even now, that was a faint noise at the window, the sash sliding up. And Louisa smiled as she stood and stepped out of the bath, and strode over to meet Killik at the window. Not caring if she was naked and dripping wet, or if he was only slightly less bloody than before, and trailing mud on her floor. Because it only mattered that her tall beautiful orc was here, looking her up and down with cool perusal, and then willingly bending down to meet her brief, hungry kiss.

"There you are, handsome," Louisa murmured, against his lips. "How did it all go?"

She drew back to study him, her heart pulsing faster in her chest, because what had Sune thought about the adoption idea? What had they decided?

Killik shot a wry grin back toward her, and gave a gentle slap to her bare arse. "Ach, well," he said, with a shrug. "I spoke to Rosa, and she squealed and hopped up and down, and then ran off—which I ken must be Ka-esh for pleasure, ach? As for Sune..."

He let it hang there between them, and Louisa gripped at his arms, rapidly searched his eyes. "Tell me, Killik," she demanded. "What did he say? Was he willing to consider it?"

Killik's brows rose, because damn him, he was dragging this out, taunting her, enjoying this. "Ach, he pondered this," he replied blandly. "And he asked good questions. And then..."

Louisa groaned, clutched tighter at him, gave him an impatient little shake. "Then what," she insisted. "Tell me, you infuriating *termite.*"

But oh, the way Killik's eyes flashed, the smile wicked on his mouth. "You wish to meet my termites, woman?" he drawled at her. "Wish to have them move in, and start making a mess?"

Louisa's groan was loud and disgusted, but Killik only kept grinning as he gripped her hips with strong hands, and walked her backwards to the desk. And then spun her around, bent her down over it, and—she gasped—kicked her legs apart. Exposing her bare crease to the room, to him, to that familiar wonderful hardness, just prodding against her...

"This seems a good place to release my swarm," he purred. "Ready yourself to be overrun, woman."

Louisa scoffed, glared back at him—but then he slammed inside, slicing deep in a single staggering stroke. And then again and again and again, already caught in his sharp furious rhythm, while Louisa shouted and scrabbled beneath him. Cursing him, and blessing him, and begging him, while he merrily laughed, and slapped her arse. And then he reached over her toward the desk, and snapped a quill into her hand.

He didn't even need to say it, and Louisa quivered beneath his onslaught as she yanked over a sheet of paper, and began to write, with a shaky hand. Addressing the letter to her sweet beloved Wolf, telling him of his lusty powerful pup, bending her over the desk, and mounting her with such vigour and zeal and ease. How she could only whimper and tremble and beg beneath his strength, and plead for more of his gifts and his favour.

You have chosen the realm's fiercest, most generous orc as your mate, she wrote. *Not only does he stroke and tease and inflame me, but he has promised to swarm me, and overrun me. To fill me with his abundance, and pour out his blessings upon me—*

She broke off there, her hand skittering on the page, as Killik yanked her hips tight, and ground deep—and yes, yes, there it was, the hot teeming spurts of his seed, as his hand slipped around her, circling hard and perfect, until her own release sparked and flashed, caressing him, milking him, more, more, more...

Until I am again thronged with him, she wrote. *I am consumed with him, lost with him, found with him. He is the most wondrous gift I have ever known, and I shall always, always cherish him, and the stunning, greathearted Wolf who shares him with me.*

She let the quill clatter aside, her body sinking down onto the desk. And into the shivery whispering fear that maybe it was still too much, maybe Killik would still laugh, or mock her, or...

Or carefully slide her hair away from her neck. Settle his sharp teeth to her skin. And then sink them deep, as his low, rumbling moan vibrated into her, weaving into her lifeblood, into her heart.

Afterwards he kissed the broken skin, cleaned it with surprising care, and it distantly occurred to Louisa that it was on the other side than last time, perhaps making another mark, staking another claim. Adding his scars to the others she carried, but these ones speaking only of pleasure, of safety. She was whole. Skai. Home.

"Sune said he should be most glad of this," Killik finally murmured, close into Louisa's ear. "He said you are a kind and worthy woman, and you have done Wolf and I much good. And"—his voice lowered—"he said he knows if you are part of this, I shall stay. Because you shall demand this of me, whilst Wolf shall give me whatever I please, even if this is leaving him."

He huffed a laugh, though it sounded almost sad. "I did not follow how much Sune saw of my plan," he added, quieter. "Or how well he knows me, mayhap. And you ken"—another low, hollow laugh—"he caught *himself* in that curst trap, ach? He *wished* to draw you into this. He *wished* to bring you to the mountain, and keep you there. He wished for your help for Wolf, and for us. For all of us."

Louisa's breath stilled, her eyes staring unseeing at the desk, because—of *course*. Of course Sune had done it on purpose. He was such a clever, agile, watchful boy, and of course he wouldn't have trespassed by accident, let alone gotten caught in one of Rikard's fool traps. And even the way he'd pushed her to take him to the mountain, when he'd known Killik and Ulfarr wouldn't be there...

And the way he'd done it, even when he'd thought Louisa would try to replace him. When he'd thought she would give Ulfarr a new son. *A better son*, he'd said.

Louisa's eyes were prickling, and she swallowed hard, drew in a ragged breath. "Gods, he's so much like you, Killik," she whispered. "I hope you thanked him. And told him how clever he is, and how much you love and appreciate him. And how you would never leave him, or replace him, either."

She could hear Killik's swallow too, could feel his heavy exhale on her ear. "Ach, I sought to," he replied, low. "I could already hear your shrill harpy voice raging at me, if I did not. Calling me a weasel, or a leech, or a *termite*."

Louisa elbowed sharply up into his ribs, even as a shaky laugh escaped her mouth. And Killik gave a gentle nip at her ear, a slap at her hip, before yanking himself out of her, and swiping her letter off the desk.

"Wolf shall enjoy this," he said lightly, as he rolled it up, and gave a smug smile toward his mess now spilling down Louisa's thighs. "And you shall enjoy cleaning my droppings."

Louisa gagged and made a face at him, to which he only grinned back, and gave another slap to her hip. "Meet you downstairs," he said. "Wish to hear what Rosa has to say next."

And with that astonishing statement still ringing through the air, he spun around and strode toward the window. Not even looking back as he slipped out of it, but Louisa couldn't stop smiling after him, wiping at her damnably wet cheeks. Sune wanted her help. Sune wanted her to stay. Sune wanted her to... *adopt* him.

It still felt too impossible, too surreal, but once Louisa bathed—again—and then dressed and headed downstairs, she found Sune waiting for her on the landing, with Timo and Cecily flanked behind him. And at the sight of Louisa, Sune squared his shoulders, and drew in a breath.

You were kind to say you wished to adopt me, he signed at her. *But I hope you did not feel pushed to this, or bound to this. And you must not feel you need to care for me.*

Louisa stared at him for a blank, hanging instant, as more wetness stung behind her eyes. "But of course I care for you, Sune," she croaked at him, and she signed along with it, too. "It's been such a pleasure getting to know you, and spending time with you. And I don't want you to feel obligated to care for me, either, but no matter what"—she wiped at her wet eyes—"it really would be such an honour. To keep getting to spend this time with you."

Sune's shoulders heavily sagged, his eyes glittering with

relief, and beside him, Timo grinned, and clasped his arm. While Cecily glanced between Sune and Louisa, and then cleared her throat. "And you'll let Sune come around whenever he wants?" she asked. "And keep using your horses?"

It sounded like a challenge, like some kind of test—but Louisa only nodded, and gave a fond smile toward Sune's face. "Of course," she said, over the catch in her throat. "Whatever he likes. Just no more trespassing on murderous neighbours' property, though, *please*."

Sune twitched a small smile at that, while Cecily firmly nodded, and gave him an imperious glare. "Oh, he knows," she said flatly. "*Right*, Sune?"

Sune's glance back toward Cecily was both taunting and unrepentant, and soon the three of them were loudly bickering, and clattering down the stairs together. While Louisa grinned and followed after them, the warmth again shimmering in her chest. Home. Skai. A son.

Ulfarr was waiting for her at the bottom of the stairs, looking still rumpled, but far less muddy than before. And his eyes lit up at the sight of her, his hand reaching out to clasp hers, bringing it to his mouth. And then he bent his head into her shoulder, into exactly where Killik had just bitten her, and gave a deep inhale against it, followed by a soft, lingering kiss. Knowing exactly what Killik had done upstairs, and... liking it. Wanting it.

"I hope my lusty pup pleased you, Louisa," he said softly, his eyes shining, once he'd drawn away. "Now, Rosa has called us together in your drawing room, should you come?"

Louisa nodded, and after an impulsive kiss to his cheek, she accompanied him into the drawing room. Where a flushed-looking Rosa was indeed waiting, together with John-Ka, and Jule and Grimarr and Drafli, and Sune and Timo and Cecily, and Killik.

"Oh, good, we're all here!" Rosa said brightly, as Louisa and Ulfarr walked in. "I know it's been a busy day, but time is of the essence. We heard of your adoption plan, and not only is it brilliant, but"—she beamed at Louisa, and then at Sune—"it might offer us a significant advantage, too. And some excellent property."

Louisa wasn't at all following, even when Rosa gave a hopeful, wheedling smile toward her. "Your neighbour's property," she said meaningfully. "Your neighbour. Your *relative*. Who's going to be dead soon. Without an heir."

Without an heir. Louisa's brain was still dragging, struggling to catch up, and she grimaced, shook her head. "I can't inherit Rikard's property, if that's what you're suggesting," she said. "It was difficult enough to gain just this piece of it. Legally, with the entail, it can only go to the closest male relative."

But Rosa was still beaming, and rapidly nodding. "Yes, exactly," she said, with a purposeful glance toward... *Sune.* "The closest male *relative*."

The closest male relative. Sune. And Louisa stared at him, at his equally confused eyes, as her heart skipped in her chest. Would Rikard's closest male relative now be... *Sune*? Would *Sune* inherit Rikard's property?

"But," she said, breathless. "I haven't even adopted Sune yet! They'll see the dates, and they'll suspect, and—"

But her heart was still thundering, her eyes pleading on Rosa's face, because gods, yes, she wanted that property. She wanted Sune to have that property. She didn't want another horrid lord waltzing in, breathing down her neck, threatening her kin and her camp...

But Rosa just kept smiling, and whipped a sheaf of papers up off the table. "You're all Skai, Louisa," she said firmly. "Surely you can manage a little forgery? Dating these a month ago, perhaps, and then slipping them into your lawyer's office? Killik told me you visited him a few weeks ago, with some paperwork you wanted him to review?"

Louisa stared at the papers, her mouth opening and

closing, because—yes. Yes, she had done that, hadn't she? And of course Killik had been spying on her then too, of course he'd known all that, and this couldn't possibly... work. Could it?

"It's certainly worth trying," Jule cut in, with a determined glint in her eyes. "Those lords have used adoption in the past to their own benefit, so why can't we do the same? And I'll be honest, we'd be very happy to gain access to Rikard's property, and keep it out of those lords' hands. It's a good location, a good defensive position, if we ever needed it."

Beside her, Grimarr nodded, his eyes settling heavy on Louisa's face. "And it shall also be a great gain to us," he said, "to keep building this camp here, and welcoming humans to it, and deepening these bonds between us. With not only these clever Summits, or other events thus—but with this school you are planning, also."

Right. The school. More warmth bubbled in Louisa's belly, and she smiled back, and squeezed Ulfarr's hand. "Of course," she replied. "It's been such a pleasure, and we'd love to do more. To keep offering our kin a place to rest, and heal, and learn and grow, and be safe."

Ulfarr's hand drew hers closer, while Killik stroked up her back, his eyes soft and approving on her face. "Ach," he said, quiet. "Just thus."

Louisa fervently nodded, her eyes prickling, and soon she was seated across from Rosa at the nearest table, reading contracts and signing papers, while Killik peered over her shoulder. Watching as Louisa swore to care for Sune, to treat him as her own, to appoint him as her lawful son and heir.

She couldn't help a reflexive sniff as Sune signed the papers too, and then flashed her a careful, stunning smile. And once it was all settled, Killik gave an approving pat to Louisa's cheek, and snatched the envelope into his hand.

"I shall take this to your lawyer myself, and place it with

your file," he said. "And then we shall meet back at the camp, and have a grand Skai revel in honour of all these gains, ach?"

A grand Skai revel. It still didn't feel real, but beside Louisa Ulfarr smiled and nodded, and signed his thanks toward Killik. While Rosa nodded too, beaming back and forth between them. "It's been a very productive project," she said, with satisfaction. "Thank you for letting me be part of it."

But now Louisa's eyes were prickling again, and she shook her head. "No, thank *you*, Rosa," she replied, her voice hitching. "You didn't need to do any of this, and you've just been so, so generous. It was so good of you, and it's meant so much to us. All of us. Thank you."

Rosa dismissed it with a careless flap of her hand, though her eyes looked bright, too. "It's truly my pleasure, sister," she said. "Back when we first met, you were so kind to me, and helped me so much, when I needed it most. You didn't blame me, or judge me, or ask for anything in return, and I just"— she lurched toward Louisa, squeezed her tight—"I just wanted to return the favour. Thank you, sister."

Oh gods, now Louisa was full-on weeping, the water streaking down her face, and she squeezed Rosa back, and gulped into her shoulder. "I hope you'll keep coming by," she said, between sniffles. "I've really loved working with you."

Rosa was sniffling too, but when she backed away she was beaming again, and giving a decisive nod. "Of course," she said. "We also need to keep protecting you from Filak, don't we? And besides"—she drew herself taller—"you'll need help setting up your new school! We ought to establish a new committee at once, don't you think? How about the *Wolf-Camp Wilderness and Wellness Educational Colloquium*?"

Killik barked a loud, exasperated groan, as Louisa and Ulfarr exchanged an uneasy glance—but then Rosa merrily laughed, and swatted Killik's arm with her papers. "It really is too easy," she said cheerfully. "But whatever you decide to call it, I'm your secretary. I'll send you word of the first meeting."

With that, she spun and flounced off with John-Ka toward the door. Leaving Killik to stare after them with mingled disbelief and outrage, and maybe—maybe—just a twinge of amusement, too. But just to be sure, Louisa yanked out her knife, and pointed it toward his chest. "You *will* be nice to her, Killik," she said flatly. "And you will be *grateful*."

Killik scowled and spluttered, whipping out his own dagger to point back at her. "I shall not be grateful for a title such as this!" he shot back. "You ken any Skai alive shall wish to be part of a *Wolf-Camp Wilderness and Wellness Educational Colloquium*?"

Louisa scoffed back at him, while Ulfarr gave a low, rolling chuckle, and then hauled them both into his arms. Not even seeming to notice their blades both scraping into his chest, but instead kissing both their foreheads, and then squeezing them even tighter against him.

"Ach, my fierce pups," he murmured, so husky, so fond. "Skai-kesh has so greatly blessed me, with you."

And blinking at Killik, at his own flushed, squashed face, Louisa could only nod, and smile, and breathe in deep. Breathe in Killik, and Ulfarr, and the truth of Skai-kesh's blessing upon them. Teeming and thronging with so much life, and so much hope.

She was Skai, and she was home.

63

That night, in front of the camp's roaring bonfire, Ulfarr and Louisa laid Killik out between them, and put on a show.

Louisa hadn't expected a rut to have ceremonial aspects, but Killik and Ulfarr had both followed its traditions with surprising care. Ulfarr had first formally asked Sune and his former pack to stand guard out in the forest, and once they'd fanned out into the trees, the rest of the clan circled the clearing to bear witness. With Simon, Maria, and Drafli all among them, and Ulfarr had then bowed low toward them, and asked their blessing.

Thankfully, they'd all given it—Simon had even praised Ulfarr's choice in a mate—and then Ulfarr had called Killik forward. And when Killik had slipped out of the trees, Louisa had gasped aloud at the sight of him, with his tall, scrubbed-clean body, the long, shining fall of his black hair, and—the *clothes*. The ever-present trousers had vanished, replaced only by a leather loincloth, and there was a large silvery fur tied around his shoulders, making him look surprisingly bulky, powerful, dangerous.

Ulfarr had startled at the sight too, and he'd looked

almost shy as he'd taken Killik's hand, and kissed it. And then he'd asked Louisa to come forward, too, and join him in holding this rut upon Killik, and claiming him as his lifelong bonded mate.

Louisa had willingly complied, striding forward to meet them, dressed in only her own loincloth, too. And at Ulfarr's sign, she'd carefully taken off Killik's fur, smiling at his flushed face, his bright glinting eyes. And then she'd knelt, and spread the fur out onto the packed earth before the fire, while Ulfarr drew Killik close, pressed a soft, reverent kiss to his mouth, and...

He attacked. Tackling Killik bodily down to the fur, pinning him onto his back, kicking his legs wide apart. And with a fierce, jolting thrust, Ulfarr buried himself deep inside, his hips powerfully plunging, his hand clamped tightly to Killik's straining neck.

For a breath, Louisa only stood and stared, her mouth dry, the shock sparking through her chest—but Ulfarr's face was already buried in Killik's throat, inhaling, making sure he was safe. And when Ulfarr sharply signed toward Louisa—*tend him for me*—she rapidly nodded, and dropped down beside them. Her gaze sweeping over Killik, his stunned face, his flushed ears, the wild light in his eyes...

"Look at you, pup," she breathed into Killik's ear, as she stretched long against him, and caressed her hand against his gasping, trembling chest. "You're so good, aren't you? So handsome. So brave, when you're opened up wide, and taking your big wolf's strong ploughing."

Killik's eyes glimmered, flicking hungry to Ulfarr's face, and Louisa shifted closer beside him on the fur, slipping her hand further down to stroke at his half-hard cock. "So gorgeous, love," she murmured. "And you'll be even more stunning when you're full of your wolf's strong Skai seed, won't you?"

Killik jerked a nod, brief but urgent, his wide eyes still

fixed to Ulfarr's driving body above him. While his mouth opened and closed, as if he wanted to speak, but couldn't— and Louisa kissed his cheek, stroked up and down his hardening shaft. "Can you sign it, sweetheart?" she murmured. "Tell our wolf your truth?"

Killik gasped and shuddered, his body wrenching beneath every slam of Ulfarr's hips, but then he raised his hand and signed, shaky but clear. *Yes, Wolf. Fuck me. Rut me. Harder.*

Ulfarr's growl was almost a roar, and after another sharp inhale against Killik's neck, he obeyed. Clamping his hand tighter around Killik's throat, shoving him down into the fur, his thrusts powerful enough to chatter Killik's teeth. But Killik kept signing it, kept begging for more, while Louisa kept caressing him, praising him. Feeling how he quivered and responded to her touch, his cock now rigid and leaking beneath her stroking fingers, his eyes fluttering, his back arching up—

He cried out as he came, spilling all over Louisa's fingers, spraying across his bare sweaty chest, his neck, even his chin. And at the sight of it, Ulfarr gave one last, ramming thrust, his groan ragged and deep—and then he poured out, too. His entire body shuddering, his head tilted back, the howl tearing out of his throat.

But instead of waiting, or stopping, Ulfarr yanked out of Killik again, and then grasped for his waist. Flipping Killik forward onto his hands and knees, so he was now facing Ulfarr's softened, dripping cock. And after another sharp inhale against Killik's head, Ulfarr caught a large handful of his loose hair, and dragged Killik's sweaty face forward. "Make me hard again, pup," he hissed, "and suck me down your throat."

Killik groaned and nodded, and instantly sucked Ulfarr's slack bulge into his mouth, while Ulfarr buried his fingers deeper into Killik's hair. Holding Killik in place like this, kneeling low before him, and it belatedly occurred to Louisa that he was showing Killik off, too. Showing off where he'd opened Killik wide, where the hot seed was already escaping from inside him, streaking down his thighs.

And despite Killik's fervent efforts on Ulfarr's groin, the sounds wet and sloppy and slurping, Louisa could see him still trembling, the flush now bright red on his ears and cheeks. Wanting this, no question—especially with Ulfarr regularly scenting for it like this—but perhaps also not used to being the one exposed, on his knees, on display...

And Louisa wasn't doing this, she wasn't, stroking her way down Killik's shivering back, trailing kisses against his sweaty skin. Until she was kissing at his opened, leaking crease, letting her tongue slip between, lower, lower. Until she could taste that spurt of Ulfarr's sweet seed, dribbling hot onto her lips...

Killik's shudders were more like quakes now, his body wrenching between Louisa's mouth, and Ulfarr's groin. Or rather, Ulfarr's slick, fully hard cock, now gliding swift and strong between his sucking lips, sinking deep into his throat. Hard enough that those were tears, streaking down Killik's cheeks, but his shaky hand was still signing, saying, *Yes, harder, more. Give it to me, feed me, flood me full of you...*

Ulfarr howled again as he poured out, bearing down into Killik's throat. Holding himself there for a long, sustained moment before yanking out again, his softened bulge bobbing before Killik's eyes, as a long string of shiny saliva dangled down toward the fur.

"Good, pup," Ulfarr said, rough, after another deep inhale against Killik's mussed hair. "But you have not yet thanked me."

Killik's eyes fluttered, his moan thick in his throat, but he nodded, and leaned forward to gently kiss at the tip of Ulfarr's slack, dripping cock. "Thank you, Wolf," he said, hoarse. "For granting me leave to suck you, and drink your strong Skai seed."

Ulfarr grunted and nodded, his hand caressing Killik's flushed face, patting his cheek. And then he guided Killik down onto his back on the fur, and gently nudged Louisa on top. "A reward, pup," he murmured, as he settled down beside Killik, and nipped at his ear. "Our woman's sweet womb upon you."

Killik shivered and gratefully nodded, his eyes hazy and hungry on Louisa's face—and they moaned together as she settled his hard cock against her, and sank down upon it. Feeling the fierce carving strength of him, even now, and grinding slow and deep, watching his lashes flutter, his breaths deepening—and then, once his eyes looked focused again, she rode him faster, harder. Taking him swift and strong, just the way he liked most, even if it flooded heat to her own cheeks, her heart pounding, her bare breasts jiggling. But Killik liked that, he was watching that, only snapping his dazed eyes away when Ulfarr kissed him, their tongues tangling, teeth scraping, leaving red streaks in their wake.

Killik shouted as he arched up, emptying deep into Louisa in pulse after shuddering pulse—but then Ulfarr shot a narrow, wicked look toward her, and then back toward Killik's mouth. And then his big hands reached for her, drawing her upwards, so she was—

Straddling Killik's *face.*

"Drink deep, pup," Ulfarr ordered, as he guided Louisa down harder onto Killik's hot, trembling mouth. "Swallow all the good Skai seed I give you."

Killik groaned and nodded, plunging his tongue up into Louisa's pulsing heat, his throat rapidly gulping, swallowing. While she shouted and shook over him, the shock and the pleasure wrenching her from the inside out—and only then did she catch one of the watching orcs' eyes. Because gods, they were all still watching this, watching her pour Killik's seed back into his desperately sucking mouth, while Ulfarr shifted back down between Killik's sprawled thighs, spread them wide, and rammed himself deep.

It sounded slick and sloppy this time, shuddering Killik's tongue, choking in his throat—and at that, Louisa eased off him, searched his wild, hazy eyes. And then she kissed him, again and again, tasting herself all over him, before kissing down his seed-streaked belly, and swallowing his leaking cock deep into her throat.

He shouted and writhed and kicked, but Ulfarr held him still, as his other hand sank into Louisa's hair. Guiding her up and down, fast and hard, milking Killik, coaxing him closer and closer—but when Killik began arching, begging, Ulfarr pulled Louisa off, holding Killik's cock straight up, so they could all see it spraying, firing high into the air, and then splattering down all over his belly, his chest, Louisa's face.

The sight of it made Ulfarr groan, and he yanked himself out of Killik—and with a sharp pump of his hand, he was spraying out, too. Covering Killik's already-spattered chest with him, coating him in thick, heavy ropes of white.

Louisa could only touch it, shiver down to kiss it, to lick her way up Killik's slick heaving chest, to find his trembling mouth. "So beautiful, love," she gasped. "So hungry, so strong, so perfect."

He clutched back toward her, as if almost desperate for her, for the praise, even as he signed at Ulfarr again, *Don't stop, don't stop, please.* But now Ulfarr was bending down too, again breathing in deep against Killik's neck—and then turning him onto his side, and settling down behind. So he could keep going, yes, sinking back inside Killik, making Killik writhe and jolt upon him—but softer this time, gentler. Enough that Killik and Louisa could find each other again too, Killik's jabbing length just holding inside her, pressing there, as if drawing up strength from this, from her.

So Louisa kept caressing him, praising him, stroking his face and his body and his hair. Not caring how messy or sticky it was, because he was hers, he was theirs, theirs, *theirs*—and Ulfarr was gasping again, his sharp teeth seeking against Killik's sweaty straining neck. And when he bit down, Killik bucked and moaned, wrenching himself hard and desperate into Louisa as he surged out again—and this time, Louisa's own relief finally crashed and charged, thundering through her, breaking her apart beneath its furious flying ecstasy.

When the world flickered back in again, Louisa found Killik still curled up tight against her, his eyes closed, his swollen mouth softly sucking at her breast. And for a breath, she could only blink down at him, stroking his sweaty, messy hair, as her heart skipped, and her swallow caught in her throat. "So good, love," she whispered, hoarse. "Such a good, brave pup, aren't you? So strong, and so stunning. So sweet."

That sound from Killik might have been a whimper, his mouth sucking a little harder, and now Ulfarr was caressing Killik too, kissing softly up his reddened, still-dripping neck. "Ach," he murmured. "You have so greatly honoured me, pup. I thank you, for granting me such power, and such fealty. Such... kindness."

Louisa fervently nodded, kissing at Killik's hair, because yes, yes, this had again been kindness, too. Killik publicly prostrating himself, exposing himself, for Ulfarr's gain. When he surely could have asked for it the other way around, and put Ulfarr on his knees instead—and Louisa knew Ulfarr would have done it, if Killik had asked.

But this way—this way, Killik had given Ulfarr yet another gift, another sign of his loyalty, and his love. He'd offered this, and in it, he'd upheld Ulfarr, and shown him as strong and virile and commanding—and perhaps caring, too. He'd shown Ulfarr as a worthy, powerful Skai, deserving of forgiveness. Deserving to be fully part of the clan again.

And when Ulfarr slowly, regretfully pulled away from Killik, and heaved up to his feet, Louisa could almost feel that power hovering around him, flickering in his eyes. Even radiating through his big, bared, sweaty body, his bulky muscles and silver-streaked hair, his soft, scarred, still-dripping cock at his groin. He was the Wolf of the Skai, and he was standing exposed and vulnerable before his kin, and seeking their regard. Their favour. Their... forgiveness.

And Louisa could see the Skai glancing at each other, and most of all glancing toward... Simon. Simon, who had murmured something to Maria beside him, and then stepped forward, his fist over his heart. "I see your gain, Skai," he called out, his words ringing heavy through the trees around him. "You have my blessing."

Ulfarr's shoulders heavily sagged, and he bowed his head toward Simon, his fist also clenched tightly over his heart. But before he could look up again, another Skai spoke it, and then another. And then all of them, their voices rising into the firelit darkness. *I see your gain. I see your gain.*

And Louisa could see how strongly Ulfarr felt it, how each voice seemed to draw him straighter and taller, his fist thumping against his heart. And then he tilted his head back to the sky, squeezing his eyes shut, his mouth moving in a silent, fervent prayer, as water streaked down his cheeks.

Louisa felt her own hand skittering to her thundering heart, and beside her, Killik had shoved himself up to his knees, his fingers trembling as they closed tight, too. As if all of them were caught in a hushed, reverent prayer, begging Skai-kesh for forgiveness, for comfort, for strength. For a path to amends. For peace.

The prayer only ended when Simon stepped forward, and strode across the clearing toward them. His expression hard, inscrutable, and Louisa could feel Killik stiffening beside her, his breath stopped in his chest. As if Simon might... he might...

Grasp Ulfarr's hand in his, and raise it to the sky.

"Three summers past, our brother Ulfarr raised his strength against us, and brought fear, strife, and harm to our clan," Simon said, steady and clear. "But since then, he has borne his punishment without protest, and sought to serve his kin, and earn our trust, and regain his place amongst us."

Ulfarr's chest was heaving, his eyes still squeezed shut, and Simon gave his hand a firm shake in the air. "He has taught our sons our ways," Simon continued. "He has built this camp to guard and house his kin. He has stood against men who seek to harm us. He has called and hosted this Skai Summit, to bring our clan together, and build our bond with this town. And tonight, he has gained the hand of Killik, one of our swiftest, most faithful scouts, and"—Simon's eyes flicked to Louisa—"he has gained the fealty of this good Skai woman, also. A woman who has sworn to share her good lands with us, and grant us her help and wisdom and her strength."

Oh. Louisa's stomach flipped, her hand groping for Killik's, squeezing it tight. And he squeezed back, his body still held utterly still, his eyes frozen on Simon's face.

"Thus, tonight, I wish to honour Ulfarr, and his faithfulness," Simon called, louder now. "I wish to call an end to his punishment, and return him fully amongst us. I wish to call him the leader of this camp. And should he wish for it"—a brief, knowing smile, pulling at Simon's mouth—"I wish to again call him the Wolf of the Skai."

Oh, gods. Louisa felt Killik swaying beside her, his hand spasming, trembling, against his chest. While Ulfarr—Ulfarr stared at Simon, his eyes wide and disbelieving, as more water streaked down his cheeks. And with a sudden jerk of movement, they were caught in a tight embrace, Simon's big hand clapping against Ulfarr's back. While around them, the watching Skai broke into a round of stomps and cheers, with more than a few wolf-howls amongst them.

"I have missed you, brother," Louisa could just make out Simon telling Ulfarr, over the hollering voices, as he drew back again. "It shall be good to have your strength by our side again."

Ulfarr was still weeping, shaking his head, but he was smiling, too. "You are a better orc than I, brother," he said, his voice choked. "For now that I have also known the truth of having my woman stolen away"—his warm wet eyes flicked down toward Louisa—"I ken I could not find a way to forgive this."

Louisa gave a wobbly-feeling smile back toward him, even as she cast a worried glance at Simon—but he was nodding over toward the trees, toward where Maria was looking a little weepy, too. "Ach, but like you, I have a strong, wise Skai woman," Simon said firmly. "One who is glad to be tested, and willing to face her fears, and her truth. One who is quick to seek amends and forgiveness, and to offer these in return."

It felt so familiar, so... right, just like that softness on Ulfarr's face, the gratitude in his eyes. The way he bowed low toward Maria, and signed, *Thank you, sister. You honour me.*

Maria waved it away, but her smile had gone even warmer, flicking brief but knowing toward Louisa's face. And on another day, when Louisa wasn't still mostly naked, and covered with sticky slickness, she might have rushed over, and hugged her—but instead she signed her fervent thanks toward Maria too, her hand over her heart. And then, *You've been so generous. I'd love to stay in touch.*

Maria grinned and nodded back, and signed her agreement. And then her gaze flicked back to Simon, and she signed something else, swift and surprisingly obscene. *Now come here, you big gorgeous Enforcer, and fuck me full of your strong Skai seed.*

At this, Simon gave a deep, satisfied grunt, and instantly strode off toward her, tugging at the front of his tented trousers. While Louisa huffed a short, shaky laugh, glancing toward Killik beside her—but wait, he was still swaying on his knees, his eyes stunned and glassy, his face sweaty and pale.

"Wolf," Louisa said, low, darting his eyes toward her— and at her meaningful nod toward Killik, Ulfarr flinched, and then lurched down to his knees beside him.

"Ach, pup," he breathed, the alarm flaring bright in his eyes. "Are you ill? In pain? Did I hurt you, is aught amiss with you—"

His voice was rising, his hands skittering against Killik's face, tilting it up toward him. While Killik gave a twitchy smile, a roll of his eyes that felt more halfhearted than usual. "Naught is amiss, Wolf," he said, his voice a rasp. "It has only been—a long day. I scarce slept last eve, and then we had this Summit to hold, and Sune to comfort, and our woman to save, and this fool man to kill, and these plots to untangle, and this lawyer's office to break into. And now—"

He snapped his mouth shut, wincing, and then shoved himself up to his feet, slightly staggering as he drew in breath. "And now you have gained Simon's forgiveness," he said, with obvious effort, "and regained your place amongst us. I am—so glad for you, Wolf. And so proud. And so honoured to call you my—my—"

His breath shuddered, his sharp tooth biting his lip—and before him, Ulfarr gulped a soft little sob, and lurched forward. Sweeping Killik entirely up off his feet, and cradling him tightly in his arms. "My mate," Ulfarr croaked, burying his face in Killik's hair. "My fierce, faithful mate, who always, always gives so much, and asks for naught in return. Now come home, pup, and let us care for you."

Come home. Killik blinked at that, looking just as bewildered as Louisa felt—but Ulfarr nudged Louisa over toward his *kofi*, and then he carried Killik toward it, too. Even keeping hold of Killik as he climbed up the ladder, and then he took him inside, and set him gently on the soft, fur-covered bed.

Killik sank down with a shaky, heavy exhale, while Ulfarr turned to light a lamp that Louisa didn't recall seeing before. And now, in the lamp's warm glow, she could see the cozy, familiar *kofi*, but with—new things. With more soft furs and pillows on the bed, and a small washstand in the corner, and two new wooden chests. And on the walls were new hooks, and—wait. Were those Killik's daggers? And Killik's sword? And Killik's clothes and boots? And Louisa's clothes, too?

Killik blinked blearily around at it all, his eyes particularly squinting toward the daggers. "Left those with Sune," he said. "Told me he would guard them with his life, but…"

Ulfarr gave a low, husky laugh, and settled down onto the bed beside Killik, waving for Louisa to join them, too. "Sune and his packmates helped me ready our *kofi* for you," he murmured. "And now I shall guard your daggers, pup, just as I shall guard you. For you are my mate, Killik of Clan Skai. And henceforth, you shall stay here with me. With"—his eyes flicked toward Louisa—"with us."

With us. It fluttered warm and alive in Louisa's belly, and she smiled at Ulfarr as she nodded, and stroked her hand up Killik's sticky, sweaty chest. And then, after a glance toward the new washbasin, she went over to collect a cloth, and began carefully washing Killik, wiping the blood and seed away.

Ulfarr was still kissing him, too, tending the fresh bite-marks on his neck, and then tipping Killik's lax body onto his side, and slipping slowly, purposefully downward behind him. His mouth caressing, licking, slurping, until Killik gave a telltale shudder, his reddened cock again helplessly straining against Louisa's thigh.

So Louisa slipped down too, and then gently took that bobbing length into her mouth, stroking and soothing until Killik bucked and released, a low moan gasping from his throat. And once she'd swallowed it all, she carefully kissed up him again, while Ulfarr did the same behind him. Tending to him, adoring him together, until Killik finally let out a breathless little sigh, and then a faint, telltale snore.

Louisa couldn't recall ever seeing Killik fully asleep like this before, and she met Ulfarr's eyes, found him looking just as fond as she felt. "Ach, my fierce mate has borne much this day," Ulfarr murmured, as he pressed a kiss to Killik's sweaty temple. "Too much of it from me, I ken."

He sounded truly regretful, even worried, his eyes glimmering on Killik's sleeping face. But Louisa reached over to squeeze his shoulder, and shook her head. "He wanted it, Wolf," she said. "He wanted it so, so much. And I know"— she gave him a gentle little shake—"he wanted it just like that. With you showing your entire clan how much you needed him. How you would do *anything* to have him, and make him yours."

Ulfarr swallowed, audible in his throat, and let out a low breath, his eyes heavy on Killik's face. "Ach, I wished to show this also," he replied, quiet. "He deserved this from me, after I failed him for so long."

Louisa shook her head, but now it was Ulfarr clasping her arm, stroking up and down. "I did fail him," he said thickly. "And it was—you, Louisa, who showed us both such kindness, and helped us through this. And even you, today"—his eyes glimmered on her face—"who said you wished to wait, and think upon this, before becoming my mate. And thus, you granted Killik this rut from me tonight, only for his own."

Louisa would have waved it away, but Ulfarr's eyes were too steady, too searching. And finally she shrugged, twitched him a wry little smile. "I'll get my own," she said lightly. "When I'm ready."

Ulfarr's smile drew up, the warmth so strong, so tender in his eyes. "Ach, you shall," he murmured back. "You shall have all I can grant you. For you have granted so much to me, and to Killik, and to Sune. So much kindness, so many gifts, such great... hope. You have—saved us, Louisa."

Louisa shook her head, but she couldn't seem to speak now, through the quiver in her throat. While Ulfarr just kept smiling at her, and then leaned forward, and pressed a soft, sweet kiss to her mouth. "I love you, Louisa," he whispered. "And you shall be my mate. *Our* mate. And this shall be our home, together. Our family. Ach?"

And Louisa could only smile, and nod, and choke out a shaky laughing sob, as the warmth unfurled and flared through her chest. Shimmering her full of life, and hope, and peace. She was safe. She was whole. She was Skai.

"Yes, sweetheart," she whispered back. "Ours."

EPILOGUE

These days, Louisa barely recognized her own house.

She drank up the sight of it as she strode up toward the kitchen door, eyeing the fresh paint, the new shutters, the large open field for playing games, and the expanded, well-tended garden. It all made the house look like a cheery, welcoming place, a place to learn and play and grow, and that was reinforced by the new sign out front, printed in large, familiar block letters.

THE WOLF-CAMP WILDERNESS SCHOOL, it announced. *A Caring, Contemporary Cross-Cultural Educational Experience!*

Of course, Killik had thrown a tantrum over the subtitle, but he'd gotten his way with the school's actual name, at least. And as the president of the Wolf-Camp School *Rath*—or Council—Killik had continued to get his way with the school's curriculum, too. Ensuring it taught not only the usual subjects like languages, history, and mathematics, but also multiple Skai-focused subjects, like hunting, tracking, climbing, knife-throwing, and rope-braiding. They'd also added a variety of other practical pursuits, too—horseback riding, gardening, swimming, shelter building, and even tunnel digging, with regular guest appearances from Filak and his lovely new mate.

But Louisa's favourite classes of all were the ones that studied and shared the forgotten parts of Skai culture. She'd continued working with Rosa and Ulfarr to unearth more Skai history, often with the help of Skai elders scattered across the realm—and so far, they'd discovered Skai drumming, a Skai ball game, and even a near-forgotten board game of secrets and strategy. And of course, they'd continued with *flyting*, too, and these days it was common to see the school's students *flyting* together for fun, laughing and challenging and teasing one another.

But now—Louisa gave a warning knock on the kitchen door, and then eased it open—their two dozen students were all gone for the day, and it ought to be only the teachers left. And she'd already seen Kori and Fasti playing ball outside with the cheerfully squealing trio of Leikr and Stefan and Ame, so that meant...

"Joan?" Louisa called, as she strode through the ground floor—first the three schoolrooms, then the art room, and then the shrine, with its new carving of Skai-kesh. "Halthorr? Elise?"

But yes, there, a voice, in the new library—but even as Louisa pushed the door open, she faltered, and wrinkled her nose. Because yes, that scent was far too clear, and now—

Now the truth of it was here, before Louisa's bemused, blinking eyes. Halthorr sprawled naked on the floor in the library, with Joan's lean brown body—dressed only in a loincloth—straddled over his bucking hips. While Elise's plump pale form was spread over Halthorr's face, and her own face was caught in Joan's hand, their kisses hungry and fervent, as Halthorr jerked and moaned and slurped beneath them.

Louisa briefly considered leaving, but she was already here, and gods knew she'd caught these three in similar states multiple times before. The only slight obstacle was still Elise, who now—predictably—gasped and cringed at the sight of Louisa at the door, clapping a hand over her full breasts. While Joan fondly rolled her eyes at her bashful mate, and then raised her brows toward Louisa, even as she kept grinding against Halthorr's bucking hips.

"I just wanted to let you know," Louisa told Joan, "that Sune is taking May to the mountain soon. He's planning to stay there with his friends for a few days, so if you could make sure he has everything May needs, I'd be grateful."

Joan nodded, and gave Louisa a too-knowing grin, without even slightly breaking her rhythm. "Getting him out of the camp for the night, are you?" she asked. "Don't want him to stumble on something he shouldn't?"

Louisa rolled her eyes back at Joan, even as her face heated. "My son is far too clever to stumble on something he shouldn't," she said archly. "But—yes. It's just—"

She couldn't even speak it, suddenly, and Joan gave a wry laugh, and shook her head. "We'll be wishing you luck, Lou," she replied. "And we'll see you in a few days, I expect."

Louisa swallowed and flashed a rueful smile back, but her face still felt hot as she waved goodbye, and headed toward the door again. Because tonight, after almost a year together—tonight, Louisa would finally become Ulfarr's mate. In a large, public Skai rut, before all their clan.

And yes, the prospect still felt deeply daunting, but it simmered low and hot in her belly, too. She'd taken her time thinking about it, learning about it, even experimenting a little with it. One night, Ulfarr had allowed a handsome visiting Skai to lie with them in bed, watching and stroking his own prick, and another night, he'd allowed another Skai to kiss Louisa's breasts and her neck. And on another, vividly memorable night, when Louisa had been riding Killik on a bench, Ulfarr had allowed a watching orc to kneel before them, and lavish the rest of her invaded crease with his slick hungry tongue.

And while it had felt surreal, and salacious, and still a little dangerous, it had also made it undeniably clear to Louisa that it *was* different, like this. It wasn't her going off alone and finding pleasure elsewhere, the way Killik had for all those years. No, this was Ulfarr guiding this, commanding this, approving of this. It was the Wolf of the Skai, flaunting and caring for his prized woman, and generously sharing her as he pleased.

And, Louisa had begun to realize, it was the Wolf of the Skai showing off his fierce, lusty pups, too. Showing her and Killik together, as a matched set. How they fought each other, and faced each other, and fucked each other, often with their gleaming blades in hand, or between their teeth. Putting on a show, perhaps, for each other, for anyone who wanted to see. And most of all for their wolf, who watched them with such wicked indulgent fondness, and so often goaded them on, commanded more.

"You shall not speak to my mate thus, Louisa," he'd ordered one night a few months before, when a sparring lesson from Killik had turned into a mess of insults and dagger-waving. "Silence her, pup. Teach your wilful mate how to behave."

Killik had already shoved Louisa down to her knees before him, his hand yanking open his trousers—but at that, they'd both halted, and stared at Ulfarr. Louisa with shock juddering through her chest—had he just called her Killik's *mate*?—and Killik with wry resignation in his eyes, or maybe even guilt. And when Louisa had aimed her disbelieving look up toward him, he'd only shrugged, though a slight flush had crept up his cheek.

"I hunted you, all those moons ago," he'd murmured.

"Then marked you, with my seed and teeth. Thus for us, it has long been done, but I ken you did not wish to—"

But Louisa had growled at him, and then lurched forward, and sucked his bobbing cock deep into her mouth. And when Killik had tilted his head back, looking supremely satisfied, she'd bitten him as hard as she dared, earning a sharp yelp in return. And then a firm slap at her cheek, too, and then she'd slapped him back, and then they'd been at it again, rolling on the floor and hissing and snapping at each other, until Ulfarr had ordered them to stop, and make love to each other. And afterwards, once Killik had asked if she'd really wanted it, he'd whispered the vows of matehood in her ear, cradling her face in his hand, kissing so softly at her throat.

It had felt right, so right, and whenever Ulfarr had flaunted them together after, that had felt right, too. She and Killik were mated, perhaps they had always been, and of course their wolf could show them off together, and command them however he pleased.

But it still left Ulfarr and Louisa without a vow, without that same kind of promise. And Louisa had felt herself wanting it, craving it, until finally one night she'd just asked him, when they were all curled up together in their *kofi*. "Would you still mate me too, Wolf?" she'd asked, searching his eyes. "With the rut?"

Ulfarr's breath had choked, his eyes snapped wide—and then he'd clutched her close, squeezing her tightly to his chest. "Ach, Louisa," he'd croaked. "I should be most—most honoured."

It had led to a glorious session of lovemaking, with Louisa gasping and writhing on Ulfarr's hungry tongue, while Killik had plunged in behind—but afterwards, as they'd sprawled sated together on the fur, Ulfarr's eyes had gone watchful, careful on hers. "And how would it best please you to do this rut, Louisa?" he'd asked. "With only

Killik and me, mayhap? Or with... more? Whatever you wish."

But Louisa hadn't missed that hungry shudder of his softened bulge against her thigh, and she'd smiled fondly toward him, leaned up to kiss his cheek. "I'd be fine with more, sweetheart," she'd murmured. "As long as you both are, too."

She'd meant it, because along with their experimenting, she'd also gradually told Killik and Ulfarr more and more about Lord Scall, too. About various memories that still lingered, or ways all those years of marriage had impacted her. And in return, Killik and Ulfarr had listened, and comforted her, and murmured their own harrowing tales into the darkness. Facing the past with her, rather than seeking to escape, or forget.

But it had somehow weakened the old memories even further, sapping them of their power. And these days, intimacy had lost any connection whatsoever to Lord Scall, and had been fully consumed by this. By the stunning Skai orcs in her bed, in her heart.

"You are certain, Louisa?" Ulfarr had asked next, his eyes rapidly searching hers. "You would welcome other Skai, in this rut? How many? And only touching you, or tasting you, or..."

He'd left that question hanging, but Louisa had smiled at him again, and twitched a shrug. "Whatever you think is best, sweetheart," she'd replied. "And however many you prefer, too."

Ulfarr had betrayed a full-body shudder at that, his eyes wide and disbelieving on her face, while Killik had bent his head into her neck, and inhaled. Making sure she meant it, making sure it was truth.

"And who should you wish to have in your rut, woman?" Killik had asked, with an edge of challenge in his voice. "And when?"

He'd again been testing her, still smelling for the truth of it, and Louisa had shrugged again, and held her gaze to Ulfarr's. "We can do it whenever you like," she'd told him. "And you can choose who you'd like to have as part of it, sweetheart. Whoever you think would be best."

Ulfarr's body had spasmed again, his breath exhaling harsh, because yes, she'd known he'd wanted that, too. He'd wanted that right, that power, and maybe even that leverage. Not only over her, but over whatever orcs he allowed to touch her. And Louisa had known that he would already have a mental list, a breakdown of Skai he'd wanted to court, or bring closer to him and the camp—and that the rut would offer a powerful incentive. A bond.

And maybe that had been wrong, or drawing too much on the darker ways of the Skai, and of the old packs—but at some point, Louisa had found that she hadn't much cared. Over the past year, Ulfarr had gradually become the clan's most respected resource and advocate for Skai history and traditions, and if anyone should plan and lead a rut in the old Skai ways, it should be him. It should be the Wolf of the Skai.

After that night, Louisa had often heard Ulfarr and Killik discussing options, but she'd tried to ignore it, and to trust that they would make the best choices for them, and for her. And then she'd even written the letters of invitation, as she always did, with Killik reading over her shoulder.

And now—now, it was the night. And Louisa sought to breathe in deep from the earth as she strode back to the camp, moving swiftly and silently along the path—until she happened upon an unsuspecting pheasant. So she made a quick, clean kill with her knife, and then dressed it on a nearby rock before carrying it back into the camp.

Thomas roundly thanked her for the meat, and then let her know a new letter had come in for her from the lawyer. So Louisa gratefully took the distraction, and headed down into the common-room. Where she poured her full focus into evaluating this latest update against Rosa's extensive notes, and then writing out a detailed response. Doing her damnedest to make her case, and reclaim Rikard's land for her son.

It had turned into a complicated legal battle over the past year, after Rikard's death in bed from his so-called sudden illness. A distant cousin of Rikard's on his maternal side had materialized to claim the land and the title, but his claim was far weaker than Louisa and Sune's—partly due to the fact that one of the realm's northern lords, Lord Nash of Albajar, had recently used adoption to cut out his own firstborn son from inheriting his own entailed property. Meaning that there was a well-established legal precedent in place, and one that the realm's ruling Council wasn't eager to revoke.

And while the matter wasn't yet settled, it was settled enough that the orcs had been hunting on Rikard's land for months now, and tending its herds and valuable crops. And thereby bringing in enough coin that Louisa had finally paid the last of Lord Scall's mortgages, and gained her property for her own. Forever.

And together with her kin and her friends—and especially Rosa—Louisa was confident they would gain the rest of it, too. They would keep working together to face this, and to build the biggest, safest, most prosperous Skai camp in all the realm.

But first, she had to get through tonight. The rut.

"Finished?" came a husky voice from behind her, along with a telltale nip at her neck—and Louisa smiled at Killik over her shoulder, and handed up her letter for him to review. And though he read it without comment, she could see in his smug little smile that he approved, and he even signed at Ragni and his new mate across the room to come fetch it, and deliver it at once.

"I scent fresh blood upon you," Killik murmured afterwards, with another nip at her neck. "Pheasant?"

Louisa nodded, tilting her head away to welcome more of his kiss, more of that sweet scrape of his teeth. "Good," he said. "Now come. Wolf wished me to tend you and ready you for tonight."

He had? Louisa's brows shot up, but she didn't argue as Killik led her toward one of the common-room's multiple tunnels, the one heading east. The one where they'd carved out a second room of their own, not far from the common-room, so they had a private place for meetings or lovemaking as needed. And now their room had a steaming washtub in the middle of it, along with a full bottle of oil, a large basket of fruit and dried meat, and several fresh towels and furs.

It was surely Ulfarr's doing, but Killik would have implemented it all, and Louisa kissed him and thanked him before lowering herself into the hot water. And instead of Killik leaving, as he usually would have—he was never one to lounge around relaxing—he settled behind her, and stroked his claws through her hair. As if he really did want to ready her, and prepare her for this.

It was a lovely, shimmering feeling, especially when he began washing her all over, and then carefully dried her off, too. And next he spread her out on the bed, and rubbed oil all over her heated body, his capable hands smoothing steady and firm. Until Louisa felt languid and drowsy and decadent with it, but Killik kept going, bending down to kiss softly at her neck, her ear.

"Rest, my sweet mate," his voice murmured, very far away. "For you shall need it, ach?"

And despite the flare of alarm at that thought, Louisa somehow did sleep, sprawled relaxed and boneless on the fur. And when she awoke again, it was to the feel of Killik patting her cheek, the scent of him strong in the air.

"Ready, woman?" he asked, his eyes glittering on hers. "Your wolf and his chosen band are ready for you."

Louisa's heart thudded, but she nodded, and allowed

Killik to draw her to her feet. And when he passed over her loincloth, she pulled it on, and then stood still as he swung a glossy grey fur over her shoulders. Tying it, and then spreading out her loose hair over it, and standing back to look, his eyes sweeping up and down.

"Good," he murmured, with a gentle pat to her cheek. "You look just as a Skai mate should. Now breathe, and come, and stand before your kin."

Breathe. Come. So Louisa clasped Killik's hand, and then drew down deep breaths as he led her down the tunnel again. Not to their main open common-room, but to the new one they'd dug, far deeper beneath the earth. This one much darker and cozier, with nooks and crannies cut into the walls, and fur-covered benches and platforms scattered throughout, many with conveniently placed drainage grates beneath. And lined along the walls, there were a variety of chains and shackles, and *rassjas*, and even dull knives and daggers. All meant not for harm, but for pleasure.

The room was called a *dýflissa*, and was in fact based on a similar Ka-esh room at Orc Mountain—and when Louisa had first taken Killik there, and suggested they build a *dýflissa* at the camp, he hadn't even pretended to argue. And then he'd willingly sat through all Rosa's lectures about safety, and agreed to her recommendation around only allowing entry after reading her extensive informative publication, and swearing a vow to adhere to its rules.

But once it had been done, the *dýflissa* had given them a whole new place to play together, and it had had the surprising side effect of bringing multiple curious Ka-esh to come visit, too. A development that had done wonders for inter-clan relations, because any irritation a Skai might have felt toward a pretty, chattering, scholarly Ka-esh was rapidly forgotten, once said pretty Ka-esh was gagged and bound and squealing beneath his daggers and his cock.

But tonight—Louisa's steps faltered at the door—tonight,

there were only Skai in the *dýflissa*. And in the dim torch-light, she could scarcely even make out their faces—but it felt like there were dozens of them, all waiting and prowling and hungry, watching for their prey. Almost like... a pack.

But Louisa knew Ulfarr's old pack would be standing guard outside—they'd even passed a few on the way here—and that many of the Skai would have come to bear witness, rather than participate. But it still sent a strange, shuddering thrill up her back, especially once she recognized some of their faces. Rurik, the healer. Argarr, the smith. Tarr, from the eastern camp. Airik, from the south.

And there at the front of the room, clad only in a loin-cloth, was Simon, with a heavily pregnant Maria on his lap. And Maria even smiled and waved toward Louisa at the door, and Louisa managed a smile back, despite the thunder now pounding through her chest, her ears. She was doing this, facing this. She wanted this. And she wanted—

Him. Her huge, hulking, dangerous wolf, standing in the middle of the room. Wearing a fur and a loincloth too, with his silver-streaked hair falling over his shoulders, his claws extended sharp from his fingertips. Looking, for a breath, like a true wolf, a predator, capable of causing great pain and grief and darkness.

But even so, the sight of him settled Louisa's shoulders, drew her breath in deep. She wanted him. She trusted him. He wouldn't hurt her, no matter what. He wouldn't.

So she held her head high, held her eyes on his dear familiar face, as she strode across the room toward him, with Killik silently prowling beside her. And when she reached her wolf, she waited as he gently took her hand, and brought it to his mouth. Kissing it, so soft, before turning her around, and raising her hand high into the air.

"One summer past, my faithful mate Killik hunted this woman for us," Ulfarr said, his voice deep and carrying. "He knew her to be a shrewd, strong, steady woman, and hoped she would grant us pleasure, and peace."

There was silence around the room, waiting, and Ulfarr reached to clasp Killik's hand, too, drawing him close to his other side. "As always, my clever pup showed great wisdom in this," Ulfarr continued. "For not only has Louisa granted us pleasure and peace, but she has granted us great hope, and great strength, and great joy. She has upheld us, and stood tall beside us, and freely shared her goods and her home with us. She has brought schooling to our sons, new mates to our brothers, and kindness to us all. She is a wise, worthy, wondrous woman, and tonight"—he drew in a breath, and bowed low toward Simon—"with your blessing, my kin, I wish you to join me in claiming her as our own, and as my bonded lifelong mate."

There was another moment's silence, quivering through the air—and then Simon rose to his feet, his hand over his heart. "You have my blessing, Wolf," he called back. "May Skai-kesh bring you great blessing, also."

There were multiple nods, and murmurs of agreement around the room, and then more voices, too. *You have my blessing. You have my blessing.*

It shivered up Louisa's spine, sparkling behind her eyes, and she trembled when Killik came to stand before her, his fingers carefully unfastening her fur, and spreading it on the large stone platform behind them. Baring her upper body for the entire room, even as he held his glittering eyes on hers, with a look she knew all too well. *Show me. Prove this.*

Louisa drew in a breath, gave a shaky nod—yes, yes, please—and in a jolting flash of movement, Killik swept forward, and tackled her onto her back on the fur-covered platform. His swift strong hands already grasping her wrists, pinning them above her head, and binding them together with Ulfarr's thick steel chain. As his knees swiftly kicked hers apart, his hard cock seeking, finding its place—and then he plunged deep in a sharp single stroke.

Louisa arched, cried out, but oh, yes, it was so good, he was always so good, so swift and strong and hungry. Her fierce, gorgeous mate, ploughing her hard and fast before all these watching Skai. Showing them something, proving something of his own. She was Killik's, because he'd found her first, and claimed her first. And she would always be his first, maybe even before Ulfarr.

But Ulfarr liked it that way too, wanted it that way—and he'd even settled his big body down beside them to watch, as he so often did. Stroking Killik's back with one hand, as his other hand gently caressed Louisa's face, and brought her mouth to his. "You are so stunning, my sweet Louisa," he murmured, between kisses. "It is such a great honour to claim you thus tonight. And if ever you wish to stop, or return to only us, you shall sign this, or speak this, ach?"

Louisa nodded and kissed him back, her hunger already blooming, her body arching beneath Killik's onslaught. "I will," she gasped. "But until then, I—I trust you, Wolf."

She drew back to hold his eyes, to make sure he understood it—she was giving him permission to run this, to command this, to do whatever the hell he wanted with this. He was the Wolf of the Skai, he was leading a rut upon her, and he was damned well going to do it properly.

But yes, yes, he understood, the warmth and the gratitude again glimmering in her eyes. "I thank you, Louisa," he murmured, with another soft, almost painfully tender kiss. "You honour me. And you ken I have granted our rutmates leave to touch you and taste you, and share your womb. But naught else beyond this, ach?"

Louisa nodded, because yes, they'd talked about this, and agreed on this—but then Killik's hand clutched around her neck, his body arching up, his hard cock gouging deep inside her. And he groaned as he poured out, flooding her with his hot slick seed, its distinctive rich scent rising through the air.

Louisa shuddered and gasped and inhaled, dragging in that heady scent deep. While above her, Killik twitched a fond smile toward her, and gave an approving little pat to her cheek, and then—

He yanked backwards, pulling himself out of her in a sharp, sudden movement. Showing off the mess he'd just made of her, streaming out from between her parted thighs. Showing how she belonged to him, how she was his to plough and fill first, before all others.

But oh, now Ulfarr was shifting on top instead. His big body so heavy, so familiar, so safe, his thick, leaking cock gently prodding into Killik's mess. And as always, he pressed inside her slowly, carefully, giving her time to adjust to him, to welcome him. And when he finally sank bollocks-deep, his pulsing shaft fully sheathed inside Louisa's tight heat, there were a few appreciative murmurs around the room, and even a low whistle.

Ulfarr took his time taking her, too, sinking in smooth and steady, while Killik sprawled long and languid beside her, kissing at her neck, pinching her nipples to tight, aching peaks. And once she was gasping and arching, her shaky hand signing for more, Ulfarr carefully drew back onto his knees, pulling her along with him. So her lower body was now propped up in his lap, her upper body fully on display on the fur. So they could all see Killik touching her, playing with her, showing them what was on offer...

"You may now come, my chosen rutmates, and lie with us," Ulfarr's low voice said, ringing like a dark, hazy bell through the room. "And you may take turns touching our woman, also, and letting her learn you. *Gently*."

Oh. Oh, gods, they were doing this, they were starting this. And yes, yes, a group of orcs were breaking from the rest of the room, and silently striding forward. Almost all of them dressed in loincloths, too, and Louisa's breath quickened as she scanned their faces. Yes, there was Rurik, and Argarr, and Tarr, and Airik. And a few other Skai she'd met over the past year—Dvergr, Vaeni, Hjalt—and then three more she'd never even seen before. One who must have been near seventy years old, one who might have been twenty-five, and one who was so scarred, Louisa couldn't even tell the original colour of his skin.

Her heart had begun pounding again—that meant there were twelve orcs total, including Killik and Ulfarr, *twelve*, and they were really doing this—but Ulfarr's hands stroking her were still steady, strong, safe. And Killik's hand had begun stroking now, too, his teeth gently nibbling at her ear.

"Breathe, Louisa," he murmured, into her ear. "You are my mate. You have borne my hard ploughing all this past year, and my wolf's perfect prick, also. And thus, I *know* you shall easily bear a band of Skai in your bed—and you shall enjoy this. Ach?"

Louisa gulped for air, followed his steady breaths, and nodded. Because yes, she could do this, yes, she wanted this, yes, she could face this. And she could even face the orc who settled nearest to her on the bed—Tarr, the burly camp leader from the west. His gaze warm and genial on hers, his soft rounded belly gently brushing her hip. "So pretty," he murmured, with an appreciative glance up and down her impaled, gasping body. "May I touch you, beautiful?"

Killik was still breathing in and out beside her, his breaths slow and steady enough that Louisa could easily follow—and somehow, somehow, she nodded at Tarr. Saying—yes. And then watched, with a dazed juddering disbelief, as Killik cupped her quivering breast, and guided it toward Tarr's big waiting hand. As if it was... a gift. An offering.

Tarr's first gentle touch to her peaked nipple felt like a jolt, wrenching all through her—but that look in his eyes was only awe, or even reverence. And his glance toward Killik was grateful as he touched her again, more certain this time. But still soft, careful, and now another orc—the lean southern leader Airik—had knelt beside him, and signed the request to touch her, too. And when Louisa agreed, his touch on her belly was more confident, his hand warm, his claws very gently scraping. Scattering Louisa full of more hunger, more pleasure, most of all with Ulfarr's strength still gently grinding within her, and Killik still lying by her side, lazily stroking her. Showing them how to touch her, and then murmuring it aloud to them, too. Giving them—a lesson.

"Gentle with her nipples," he told Tarr. "No claws there, or"—his hand slid down, brazenly stroked around where Ulfarr's thick shaft was still plunged inside her—"or here. But she likes them otherwise, ach, woman? And tongues, also."

And wait, that was a hint, his eyes dancing on hers—but Tarr was already bending closer, stroking her nipple with his slick black tongue. While Airik's claws gently scraped lower, down the inside of Louisa's thigh. All of it flickering and fluttering with pleasure, firing it through her trembling body, and on her next deep breath with Killik, she glanced around at the rest of them, and signed, *Yes. More.*

And then—yes—there were more. More hands, more claws, more slick hungry tongues. Too much to even follow, to break apart, but Killik and Ulfarr were both here, both guiding this, directing this. Ulfarr even signing for Tarr to move aside, so another orc could lie beside her and have a turn, and then another. Rotating through all of them, so Killik could give them lessons, could touch her with them, could murmur softly into her ear.

"This is Asbrandr," he breathed, as the twenty-odd-year-old tentatively carefully caressed her breast, his face bright red. "He has never before touched a woman, ach? Same as

Stigr, and Saxar. This is a great gift from Wolf toward them, and one they shall return with their fealty."

Stigr was the older orc, and Saxar the scarred one, and the awareness made it easier for Louisa to lean into their tentative touch, to gasp with their pleasure. To watch that awe shimmering across their eyes, shivering through their bodies, straining beneath their loincloths. But none of them had gone any further than touching and kissing, just stroking her tingling skin with hands and hungry tongues.

At least, until Rurik settled down across from Killik, and gave him a sly, sharp-toothed smile. "Saving me for last, ach?" he said coolly. "You ken she shall care naught for the others, after me."

There were a few low growls from around them, and Killik glared darkly toward Rurik, too—but he didn't stop Rurik's long-fingered hand from spreading wide against Louisa's belly, and then sliding smoothly downwards. Making straight for her crease, for where Ulfarr was still stretching her wide open around him, and then—

Louisa shouted as the pleasure sparked and flared, flashing deep—*within* her. Within her, oh hell, beneath her very skin, as if her nerves were on fire, shouting and blazing and gasping for more. As if it was—magic.

And oh, Ulfarr had even picked up his pace, his own eyes fluttering, while Rurik huffed a satisfied laugh, and leisurely stroked his hand lower. Convulsing Louisa tighter around Ulfarr, oh gods, his fingers' touch so brazen and obscene, curving up against Ulfarr's straining shaft, too. Enough that Killik growled at Rurik, baring all his teeth, and glanced sharply toward the door. Clearly saying, *If you keep touching him, you leave.*

Rurik rolled his eyes back at Killik, but accordingly slid his hand back to Louisa again. Stroking her, tingling that shimmering pleasure beneath her skin, whipping the sheer sensation higher, hotter, closer, oh—until Louisa's relief thundered through her, raging and roaring, clamping her against Ulfarr again and again. Enough that he gasped, arched, plunged himself deep—and then poured out in sharp, shuddering surges, as his howl echoed through the room.

It left Louisa shivery and shaky all over, but Killik kissed her, whispered praises into her ear, while his hand reached down to where Ulfarr was slowly sliding out of her. Feeling Ulfarr's mess, even lingering his fingers into it—and then stroking it up Louisa's belly, painting it onto her nipples, slipping his wet fingers into her mouth. "Good, woman," he murmured. "Now, I ken Rurik ought to clean up his mess, ach?"

He shot a saucy glance at Rurik, his brows raised—and oh, gods, Rurik wasn't even arguing. He only glanced dispassionately down toward where Killik and Ulfarr's combined seed was now streaming from between Louisa's legs, and then he shrugged, and shifted downwards. As if he was going to—he was going to—

Louisa shouted again at the first touch of Rurik's tongue, firing out more impossible sparkling sensation beneath it. Licking her, tasting her, caressing her. And Rurik was doing this, *Rurik*—and Killik even reached down a hand, and shoved Rurik's dark head in closer, while vindictive satisfaction flashed through his eyes. "Better," Killik snapped. "Taste good, clever healer?"

Rurik replied with an obscene sign from his hand, so Killik just shoved his licking face in deeper, and returned to kissing Louisa's neck. "Near as bad as a Ka-esh," he muttered. "Enjoy it whilst you can, woman, for *never again*."

Louisa shuddered a laugh, maybe a groan, because it did feel good, impossibly, unthinkably good, most of all with Tarr now lying on her other side again, caressing and kissing her, his tongue so hot and sweet. His thick cock now grinding against her thigh, streaking wetness against her skin, while the pleasure between her legs kept coiling, skittering, rising. Rurik's brilliant sparkling tongue thrusting deeper, his throat rapidly gulping, swallowing, fuck, *fuck*—

The pleasure again wrenched through Louisa's body, wringing her out with astonishing power, blazing her hot and bright all over. So strong she very nearly wept with it, but Killik was still here beside her, kissing her, and her wildly fluttering eyes had found Ulfarr, too. Ulfarr, who'd had his hand on Rurik's shoulder all that time, and was now drawing him away, and… smiling at him. Smiling that sharp, wicked wolf smile of his, as he gave Rurik an approving little shake.

"Good, Rurik," he said, his voice firm. "I thank you, for granting our woman such joy, and readying her for our rutmates."

But wait, wait, was that what Rurik had done? Preparing Louisa for the rest? But he only shrugged and nodded, wiping at his wet face, and giving Louisa a not-so-nice smile. "It is good practice," he replied. "I shall have my own woman crawling after me begging, I ken."

Killik loudly scoffed, and irritably waved him away—and then signed for Tarr to take his place. But Louisa's awareness had begun flickering back in again, and Tarr… wasn't kneeling, like Rurik had. No, no, he was instead shifting aside his loincloth, and revealing his bulky, jutting, liberally leaking cock. One not quite as large as Ulfarr's, but close, and Ulfarr was even watching—approving—as Tarr stroked it fuller, slicking it with his wetness…

"Are you ready for your next ploughing, woman?" Killik murmured, hot in her ear. "You ken you can open wide for him?"

Louisa drew in a deep breath with him, and blinked down at Tarr, at his worshipful eyes and round belly, his slick thick cock. And Ulfarr's hand on his shoulder, Ulfarr's eyes now searching her face, too. Because yes, Ulfarr had chosen this for her, chosen Tarr as her first after them, and Louisa trusted him, she did.

"Yes," she gasped, before she'd even caught it. "Yes, please."

Tarr's groan was husky and low, his hand signing a shaky thank-you toward her. And as he leaned forward toward Louisa, lining himself up, Killik even drew her thigh higher, opening her wider. Watching with intent, glittering eyes as Tarr's leaking crown settled against her own leaking, quivering body, and slowly pressed in.

Louisa moaned, dragged for air, clutched back against Tarr's thick warm shaft—and yes, yes, it felt different. It felt foreign and salacious and—strange. New. To have another orc, another body, inside her, filling her, finding pleasure with her. Because yes, yes, that was unquestionably pleasure on Tarr's flushed face, fluttering his eyes, spasming his cock inside her…

But as Louisa wildly glanced between Killik and Ulfarr, both of them watching this with hooded eyes, it didn't feel— wrong. No, not wrong, because it was still both of them, allowing this, offering her this. Them giving her this experience, this connection, this power over their kin.

And it *was* power, Louisa realized, as Tarr gasped and moaned, his belly shuddering, his head tilted back. It was Ulfarr and Killik's power, yes—but it was also her own. Binding this strong, influential Skai leader closer to her, to them, and thus gaining his scent, his protection, his allegiance. And if Louisa ever needed his help, he would offer it, without hesitation.

So she gasped for him, clutched at his fat Skai cock, even praised him and begged for him, when she felt him getting close. And when he bucked, and spurted out into her in sharp, irregular torrents, she welcomed the great gift of his Skai seed, swarming into her, marking her, fusing that bond between them.

"Thank you, handsome," she murmured afterwards, and that might have been tears, glittering in Tarr's eyes—but he fervently nodded, and signed his own thanks back toward her with shaky hands. And when he drew away, releasing yet another surge of hot fluid between Louisa's thighs, that was only pride in Ulfarr's eyes, in his big hand slowly caressing Louisa's trembling thigh. And Killik looked smug, even chipper, as he gave a sharp little nip at her ear.

"Good show, woman," he purred. "He shall be dreaming of my mate for *years*, after this."

The satisfaction was almost vicious in his eyes, in his wicked gleeful smile, and he curtly waved the next orc forward—Airik, from the south. And while Airik was far harder to read than Rurik or Tarr, and didn't speak a single word toward Louisa, his cock was eager and hungry, delving into her dripping, open body with swift, willing ease. Filling her with lean, solid Skai strength, and then plunging, pumping in and out with firm slaps of his hips.

"Gentle, Airik," Ulfarr chided him, earning a wry scoff from Airik, and then a purposeful glance down at the sticky mess spurting out all around him—but after another sharp look from Ulfarr, Airik sighed and nodded, and slowed his thrusts. But oh, now Killik's hand was slipping downwards, straight into the mess, and Louisa gasped as he slipped one finger inside her, and then another. Filling her together with Airik, oh hell, while Airik moaned and shuddered, his thrusts slowing, deepening.

"I ken he only needs a little help," Killik murmured lightly, as his fingers stroked and tickled inside her. "No wonder, for I ken I should not wish to plough a womb after Wolf and Tarr, either."

Louisa made a face at Killik, but he only grinned back at her, and kept stroking. "Now beg for him, woman," he whispered. "Make him forever dream of my mate, also."

So Louisa did, gasping and begging Airik for his strong

Skai seed. And yes, yes, he liked that, his growl rumbling low as he emptied himself in a smooth steady stream, his head arched back, his eyes closed.

Afterwards, Louisa thanked him too, and then smiled at Ulfarr's next choice—Argarr, the smith. Whose veined, tapered cock was already seeking, finding its place, and then plunging deep with a loud, obscene-sounding squelch. "Ach, to feel that again," he breathed, as he held himself deep, let both him and Louisa feel it. "A hot, hungry Skai womb, full to bursting with my clanmates' strong Skai seed, and seeking to milk out mine. There is naught else like it, I ken."

Beside him, Ulfarr gave a brief, knowing nod—as if he *agreed* with this?—and again smiled at Louisa, and caressed approvingly at her thigh. Watching as Argarr just kept circling inside her, his groans deepening—until he flooded out too, with what seemed to be a shocking quantity of seed. Enough that when he drew away, Killik even shoved up to look, watching with smug satisfaction as it spewed from inside Louisa's quivering, overfull body.

But Ulfarr didn't clean it up, though he did bend down, and inhale slow and deep. And then he drew over the next orc—Asbrandr, his face still deeply flushed, his slim cock ruddy and leaking. And then, together with Killik, Ulfarr proceeded to give Asbrandr another comprehensive lesson, and then watched approvingly as he carefully slid in and out of her, his eyes stunned and awed on the sight.

Next was the older orc Stigr, who needed some help from Rurik to finish, but afterwards fervently thanked Louisa, and told her how beautiful she was. And next was the hulking, heavily scarred Saxar, whose prick wasn't much to look upon, either, with its strange curve and veins and heavy scarring—but it felt wondrous inside, thick and ridged and alive, and Louisa gladly told him so, and begged him for more.

And throughout it all, the pleasure kept rocking and writhing, whipping up tighter and closer, and she didn't care anymore how she looked, now pouring out that constant stream of Skai seed, or how it sounded, slick and slippery and squelching. Only how it felt, with the orcs who had already had their turns still touching her, caressing her, while the remaining orcs gave her their bodies, their praise, their gasps, their seed. Feeling more and more like power with every breath, like vivid wild life, sparkling beneath her skin, between her trembling thighs. They were marking her together, making her theirs, making her Skai in a way she hadn't at all understood, until this moment.

And when she gasped and begged upon Hjalt—the last orc, who had water streaking freely down his face—she could almost understand about the son, too. If she'd been able to bear a child from this, it would have felt like—all of theirs. As though they'd made it together, knitted it together inside her, with the sweet messy blend of their seed. And when the son was born, they all would have welcomed him, cared for him, treated him as their own.

Louisa nearly wept as she thanked Hjalt, too, and told him how lovely he was, how good he felt. And when he drew out, it was a teeming flooding mess, spattering all over him, and onto Ulfarr behind him, too.

But Ulfarr just clapped Hjalt on the shoulder, and thanked him for his care and his good seed. And then, once Hjalt had collapsed down onto the platform, Ulfarr stepped closer between Louisa's legs, his eyes glinting on the mess between them. And he even spread her thighs wider, gently tilted them up, so he could look his fill—and then he slid his hand down, too. Stroking against her soft, spewing, wide-open heat, and then sinking three fingers slow and easy inside.

"Ach, we have well ploughed and planted her, my lusty rutmates," he murmured, as he slipped his fingers in and out, squelching in the mess. "I have never before witnessed her opened so wide, or pouring forth such rich bounty."

There were a few appreciative murmurs, a few of the orcs shifting around to look. One of them—Argarr—even bending down to lap against it, his tongue tingling against Louisa's swollen skin, and Ulfarr indulgently watched, and then slipped his slick hand further down her open, messy crease. Nudging carefully against where it was still tight, resisting, despite all the hot fluid pouring down over it.

"Come, pup, and open this," Ulfarr murmured. "Make your mate ready for your wolf's strong ploughing."

Both Louisa and Killik groaned at once, and Louisa willingly turned onto her side for Killik, fought to breathe and open for him. But they both knew this so well, now—it was so often part of their show, their dance—and they both groaned again as Killik sank inside, into the place that was still untouched by the others, still only theirs.

And once he was in, locked tight and deep, he grasped her, and rolled onto his back. Rolling Louisa up with him, so she was again looking at Ulfarr, splayed and exposed for Ulfarr, waiting for Ulfarr—but now already gasping upon the strength of Killik inside her. And Ulfarr was watching that, too, watching that hot seed flow down onto Killik with hooded, approving eyes. His slick, dripping-wet hand now stroking his own jutting cock, which looked thicker than Louisa had ever seen it, oozing out a steady stream of white toward the floor.

"Tend her, my rutmates, and honour her," Ulfarr ordered, husky. "Whilst I stopper all your good Skai seed, and plough it deeper inside her, ach?"

There were multiple gasps and groans around them, and then more warm caressing hands, more hot sliding tongues. Shivering and skittering all over Louisa, and strongest of all was Rurik's hand, slipping downwards, sparkling sheer sensation in its wake. But then it all splintered, scattered, as Ulfarr finally put his huge, leaking, pulsing head to Louisa's streaming, wide-opened crease, holding, opening. Watching her swollen, tender body clutching and kissing against him, coating him with more of his rutmates' Skai seed, tempting him inside...

One more breath, one shudder against her—and then Ulfarr plunged deep, in a single shattering stroke. Hard enough that Louisa screamed, the sound ringing through the room—but there was no pain, no sharp scent of blood. Only the raw raging intensity of it, of being jammed so impossibly, tenuously full. Full of not only Killik, but all that seed, and Ulfarr's own huge demanding cock. A cock that had never taken her like that before, and Ulfarr held her eyes as he drew out, almost all the way—

And then he rammed back in. And then again, and again, pounding into Louisa, ploughing all that rich blended seed deeper inside. Mounting her, rutting her, claiming her with all his strength and will, while all his rutmates urged them on. And Louisa was begging, weeping, pleading for more, for everything, for all he could possibly give her, signing it and speaking it and needing it. They were so close, almost there, almost mates, please, please, please—

The rush struck like a blow, like a great towering wave, like a fuelling raging inferno. Burning and charging and trampling, flattening all the world in its wake. Blasting out sheer seizing ecstasy, unlike anything Louisa had ever known, ever tasted—and it just kept wheeling, reeling, in the strength of her wolf, the strength of his fiercest pup, the strength of his rut-pack. All of it pouring out onto her, into her, the scents and the heat and the bliss, the power, the honour, the safety.

She was Skai. Skai. *Skai.*

She couldn't have said when it finished, or whose hands were touching her, or whose seed had spattered all over her quivering, sticky body. Because there was only the Wolf of the Skai, here, still locked and mounted upon her, cradling her face in his trembling hands. Kissing her again and again, not only on her mouth, but her nose, her eyelids, her forehead, her cheeks. Kissing with such sweet, aching tenderness, as warm salty liquid dropped onto her cheeks, her lips.

"My mate," Ulfarr whispered, hoarse, raw, disbelieving. "My mate. *Mine.*"

Louisa nodded, brief but fervent, and oh, the chain had released around her wrists, freeing her tingling hands. And she finally fluttered them downwards, touched all that warm, powerful, sweaty skin above her. The Wolf of the Skai. Her mate.

"Mine," she repeated, her voice a croak, as she clutched him closer—and then her hand scrabbled downwards, found Killik's own hand too, laced her fingers tightly with his. "Mine."

Ulfarr nodded and kissed her again, again, again—down her cheek now, to her jaw, her throat. His sharp teeth seeking, finally finding their place, after so long—and when they bit down, sudden and deep, Louisa didn't feel even a flicker of pain. Only more of that shaky, aching pleasure, that relief, that safety. Her mate. Hers.

And when Ulfarr finally drew away again, his mouth smeared with red, his eyes glittering wild on her face, she could only caress him, try to smile at him, to sign at him, through the water streaking down her own cheeks.

I love you, Wolf. I love you. Mine.

Ulfarr's eyes shifted, shone, and he signed it back, his hands just as shaky as hers. *I love you, Louisa. You are mine, Louisa.*

Her name was a downwards dagger-strike, a mirror image to Killik's, and though they'd settled on it months and months ago, Louisa still shivered whenever she saw Ulfarr sign both of their names like this, both his hands striking at once. But this time, it was together with that—*Mine. Mine, Louisa-Killik. Mine, Killik-Louisa. Mine.*

Louisa signed it back, and then pulled up Killik's other

hand, too. All of them now saying it, swearing it together, and somehow it was a vow of its own, shimmering out pure and new between them. She was theirs, and they were hers. Mates. Skai.

"I see you, my brave mate," Ulfarr whispered now, soft, holding her eyes. "I pledge you my sword, and my favour, and my fealty. I shall keep you *safe*, so long as I am able, and so long as you shall wish."

The vow caught Louisa's breath, shot deep into her chest, and now she was full-on weeping, and nodding, and trying to sign it back at him. And oh, the tenderness in his eyes, the pride, as he nodded, and then gave her one more slow, worshipful kiss.

And then, finally, he drew backwards, out of her, away. Revealing Louisa's sprawled, sated, seed-spattered body, ploughed wide open by her new mate, and again pouring out his riches. All the bounty, all the great gifts he had given her, all his powerful rut-pack still crouched around her.

The Wolf of the Skai had claimed a mate.

"I see your gain, Skai," called a voice, Simon's voice. "You have my blessing."

The rest of the Skai's voices rose around it, speaking aloud their assent, their favour. *I see your gain. I see your gain.*

And again, still lost in the hazy spinning wonder, Louisa could see it, too. Could see it, and feel it, like a soft tangible thing, glowing in her chest. With this rut, Ulfarr had gained a mate, yes—but he'd also gained, perhaps, a second pack, a shadow pack, to run alongside his first. A group of Skai who would support him, and guard him, and uphold him—and who would offer the same to his mate. To... *their* mate.

But no, that wasn't right, not quite—and when Louisa shifted to look at Killik, he was already meeting her, shifting too. Releasing yet more slick seed from inside her as he settled beside her on the fur, his face again buried in her neck. "What is it?" he murmured. "Any pain?"

Louisa shook her head, drew in a breath with him. "So what am I now," she whispered, "to them?"

She glanced at all the orcs still around them, and comprehension flashed across Killik's eyes. "Ach, they are all yet your rutmates," he murmured. "They are each bound to help you, and guard you, until they swear vows to a mate of their own. And should your mates meet death, any unmated orcs amongst them would come to you and offer to mate you, instead."

Oh. Of course. So it was also a way to protect the woman, to guard her even beyond death. And suddenly it felt almost—generous. Almost noble, to share a mate like this, and to ensure she and her children were cared for, no matter what befell them. And amidst that endless war, death would have come for the Skai so often—and the danger for their human mates would have been so great, too.

But even now, even without that, it was still a gift. Still a pack, a band, strengthening Louisa, supporting her. And as she blinked at the orcs surrounding her, she could suddenly appreciate Ulfarr's care in choosing them, and in gaining such a breadth of them. Powerful orcs, and common orcs. Known orcs, and unknown orcs. Orcs at multiple camps, orcs at the mountain. Fighters and healers and craftsmen, young and old and scarred and hale. Making sure Louisa had many, many options, spread across the Skai and across the realm.

Ulfarr had still been standing before the platform, his head bowed toward the watching Skai, his hand over his heart. Praying to Skai-kesh, Louisa knew, and she offered up a brief, heartfelt prayer of her own. She was so, so blessed. So grateful.

She only distantly noticed Killik gesturing for Rurik to look her over, or the brief touch of Rurik's hand stroking against her, firm and efficient this time. Because her eyes were only on her mate, her wolf. Waiting for him to turn back toward her, to drink up the sight of what he'd done to her, marked and claimed and safe amidst the pack he'd chosen for her.

"I thank you for your great fealty tonight, my rutmates," Ulfarr told them, his hand over his heart. "Now you may kiss her farewell, until next time."

Until next time. It shot a shivery little thrill up Louisa's back, her eyes darting toward Killik—but he hadn't even blinked, and his eyes looked almost indulgent on Hjalt as he leaned in, and gave a soft, reverent kiss to Louisa's cheek. And then Vaeni, and Dvergr, and Saxar, working their way backwards, one by one. Until Tarr was kissing her reverently on the mouth, his tongue brushing hers, his hand cupping her sweaty cheek.

"I hope to see you again soon, beautiful," he murmured. "You have brought me such joy this night."

Beside Louisa, Killik scoffed and rolled his eyes, and then he drew her in for a kiss, too. His teeth sharp and scraping, in a way none of the others had dared to do, and Louisa moaned beneath it, clutching back toward him, while a few indulgent laughs rose around them.

And then it was Ulfarr again, her mate, her *mate*, kissing her with his usual deep, steady thoroughness. Making her his, his, his, and then slipping his strong arms beneath her, lifting her up close into his warm, safe chest. And after one more thank-you to their rutmates, he strode from the room, with Louisa in his arms, and Killik striding beside him.

She inhaled Ulfarr's sweet, beloved scent as he carried her down the tunnel to their room, and then settled her carefully on the fur-covered bed. Not seeming to care about the mess she was making on the fur, and when Louisa grimaced and glanced downwards, Killik was already here, settling back in his familiar place beside her, patting her cheek.

"No bathing until the morn," he said lightly. "Need to let the seed settle, and sink inside you."

Louisa blinked vaguely back toward him—why did they

need to do that?—and now here was Ulfarr, her strong, gorgeous new mate, sinking down onto her other side, inhaling deep against her hair. "This will deepen the bonds between you and your new rutmates," he murmured, "and make it easier for them to track and scent you, should we ever need this. And mayhap, if Skai-kesh has blessed us, their seed shall grant you traces of their strength, also."

Traces of their strength? Louisa still wasn't following, but Ulfarr gathered her a little closer, pressed a kiss against her hair. "All your rutmates bore great gifts, ach?" he said. "Tarr is mayhap the strongest orc amongst the Skai, and Argarr our best smith, and Hjalt our best scenter. And Stigr and Saxar are both fearsome warriors, and Rurik—"

"Ach, do not even speak of Rurik, Wolf," Killik cut in, his voice sharp. "He did not even grant her his seed! Cannot bear the thought of another Skai healer to rival him, I ken."

Wait, were they implying—did they think all those orcs' gifts would now—filter into Louisa, somehow? And some-how—become *hers*?

"Ach, but Rurik yet gave us much else, I ken," Ulfarr said, his voice mild. "And his skill in pleasure greatly pleased you, ach, my sweet mate?"

Louisa couldn't quite seem to meet Ulfarr's eyes now, though a convulsive shiver rippled up her back. And when she curled closer into him, his warm arms circled around her, his mouth gently kissing at her hair. So lovely, so perfect, but that question still kept nagging, scraping at Louisa's thoughts.

"You don't really think," she murmured, "orc seed is strong enough to transfer an orc's—skills? And strength?"

But when she drew back to look at Ulfarr, his nod was immediate, his eyes on hers astonishingly sincere. While Killik scoffed, or maybe laughed, and flicked his sharp claw at her cheek. "Ach, no, woman," he drawled. "Have you not seen yourself hunt, these past moons? Or climb? Or spar? Or have you not heard how oft you speak of scents? Ach, how just last week"—he jabbed his claw at her—"you told me *you* could scent the Ka-esh stench, also!"

Louisa wrinkled her nose and grimaced, because it wasn't a *stench*, exactly—just a sharp flavour that the Ka-esh all seemed to share. And while orcs from all five clans seemed to carry a distinct clan scent, the Ka-esh somehow seemed the strongest, and Louisa could now understand—far more than before—how it could be particularly irksome, when combined with chattering and condescension and correction, too.

"Ka-esh smell just fine," Louisa said loyally, to which Killik loudly snorted, and even Ulfarr chuckled, too. But Louisa's thoughts were still caught on this, spinning on this, because—they couldn't possibly be right. Could they?

"And if you should wish to bed any of your rutmates again," Killik continued, with a shrug, "their gifts may yet grow stronger upon you, also."

What? There was again far too much to untangle in that statement, and Louisa's mouth opened and closed, as her traitorous thoughts flicked back to Tarr, kissing her with such gentleness. *I hope to see you again soon, beautiful.* And how Ulfarr had said, *You may kiss her farewell, until next time...*

"But," she began, her eyes darting back to Ulfarr's watching face. "You wouldn't still—*want* that, now that the rut is over. Would you?"

And no, no, of course he wouldn't, not after how he'd struggled with Killik's other bedmates for all those years—but damn it, Louisa knew that look in Ulfarr's eyes. That longing. That... *hunger.*

"I wish for naught you do not wish for, my sweet mate," Ulfarr murmured, with another soft kiss to her hair. "And your rutmates shall always offer you their fealty, whether or not they share your bed again."

But Louisa frowned up at him again, searching his too-familiar eyes. "But you—wouldn't care?" she demanded, and then glared at Killik, too. "Or you?"

But Killik briefly met Ulfarr's eyes, and then shrugged, shook his head. "I should care if you ran off and did this without us," he replied, "just as Wolf cared when I did this, ach? But should we bring your rutmates into our bed now and then, I shall gladly make them dance in my show, until they are begging and weeping for my mate. Except"—he frowned, jabbed his finger between Louisa and Ulfarr—"no Rurik! I am *done* with Rurik!"

Ulfarr nodded, smiling fondly toward Killik, as if this was already decided. While Louisa could only seem to keep gaping between them, the disbelief pounding through her skull. And perhaps they'd both scented it, Killik bending down to nip at her neck, while Ulfarr gathered her back against him, close into his strong safe chest.

"Ach, Louisa," he murmured. "You must ken—you are yet our mate. Only our mate, for always. I have claimed you, I have led a rut upon you, I have sworn the vows of matehood to you. I have made you mine. *Ours*. And there is naught in the realm that shall alter this, or weaken the depth of my love for you. My fealty, and my care."

Louisa nodded, but then drew back, needing to see his eyes. His warm, glimmering eyes, so soft and intent on hers. "And when I offered these orcs to you, in this rut," he continued, slower, "I... showed you my care. I showed myself a good mate. I showed myself a wise, strong, generous Skai, who offers great pleasure to his mate, and grants her many strong Skai to guard her and help her and keep her safe. Many strong Skai to rely upon, whenever she might need this. For she is the mate of the Wolf of the Skai, and she deserves this right. This power."

Right. And yes, yes, Louisa could admit, she understood that. She'd seen that in all their plans for the rut, and then all throughout it, too. Ulfarr had seen the rut not only as a tradition, a way of gaining pleasure—but as a way to show himself a good partner. A worthy, powerful Skai mate. The Wolf of the Skai.

"And in this," Ulfarr added, "I also offered gifts to my kin. I offered fealty to the strongest and wisest amongst us. I offered comfort to orcs who needed this. I offered guidance to orcs who have never before touched a woman, so they may seek their own mates, and carry less fear upon this. I ken"—he hesitated, his eyes flicking brief to Killik's—"I showed myself what I always wished my father to be, ach? A wise, watchful Wolf of the Skai, with great reach and power, who wields his power for not his own gain, but for all his clan."

Louisa swallowed and nodded, because Ulfarr still so rarely mentioned his father, let alone admitting he wanted to be like him, even in some small way. But she could see the truth in his eyes, could maybe even scent it upon him. So strong, so decisive, so passionate about his people and camp and his clan. Just as the Wolf of the Skai should be.

And blinking toward him, it occurred to Louisa that it was such a bizarre, stunning difference from just over a year ago. From when Ulfarr had been so quiet, so uncertain, so resigned.

I fear for my wolf's life, Killik had told her. *I fear that one day, he shall awaken, and find he can no more bear the shame.*

And now—now their wolf was here, warm and powerful and alive. Speaking so earnestly of his longing and his truth and his care. Following through on his repentance with his amends, and his peace. *Hers.*

"Well, then, sweetheart," Louisa said, her voice thick in her throat. "I'd be happy to try it, if you like. Of course."

Ulfarr's grin was broad and delighted, while Killik rolled his eyes, and gently scraped his claws at Louisa's neck. "Ach, it did not even take you a day, woman," he drawled. "I ken you only wish Tarr and Stigr to call you *beautiful* again."

Louisa twisted to scoff at him, elbowing him in the gut.

"Well, when have *you* ever called me beautiful?" she demanded. "It's always a shrill vicious harpy, or—"

But Killik clapped his hand over her mouth, his eyes glittering on her face. "I called you comely this first day we met," he shot back. "And this was after you called me a *rude entitled trespasser!*"

Louisa uselessly tried to shove at his hand, and then snapped up her own hand, and signed in front of his face. *You are a rude entitled trespasser, Killik of Clan Skai, and you ought to be—*

But now Ulfarr's hands were here, clasping at both of theirs, drawing them downwards. "Peace, my quarrelsome pups," he said, though his smile was so approving, so fond. "I wish to give Louisa a mating-gift."

He did? Louisa and Killik both jerked to look at once, because yes, Ulfarr was reaching behind him, and pulling up something wrapped in cloth. And he looked almost shy as he gently placed it in Louisa's hand, his eyes searching her face.

"I hope these will please you, my beautiful mate," he murmured. "And I hope they shall please you also, Killik."

Louisa's hand trembled as she carefully unfolded the cloth, and found—daggers. A new, gleaming, matched pair of daggers, exactly like—Louisa's eyes snapped toward his hair—exactly like Killik's.

"I gave Killik his blades soon after he first joined my pack," Ulfarr said, soft. "And they have helped to keep him safe for me ever since, even when I have otherwise failed him. And tonight"—he gave a wavering smile—"I wish to offer you this safety also, Louisa."

Louisa's eyes were prickling, blinking hard at the daggers, and she couldn't hide her helpless sniffle, her weepy little smile. Gods, it was so good of Ulfarr, so generous, as he always, always was—and she hurled herself closer toward him, squeezed him as tightly as she could. "Thank you, sweetheart," she choked. "They're so perfect. Just like you. And just like your perfect pup, too."

Ulfarr squeezed her back, his breaths shaky in his throat. While behind them Killik gave a low chuckle, and reached over to swipe the daggers out of Louisa's hand. "Ach, they are just the same, Wolf," he said, after a few experimental spins in his fingers. "Argarr knows his work, if not his ploughing. Now"—another satisfied spin of the dagger—"I shall need to teach you to wield them well, woman, and put on a good show."

But he sounded smugly pleased at the prospect, and he'd even reached for Louisa's sweaty, sticky hair, and began binding it up. Doing it just the same way he always did his own, and it felt so right, so good. So... Skai. Just the way her clothes did, just the way the camp did, the hunting, the *flyting*, the school—maybe even the rut, too. *I fear you not.*

So Louisa breathed in deep, and nodded, and turned to smile up at her first fierce mate. Earning one of his rare, genuine smiles in return, his hand lightly patting her cheek. "Better," he murmured, his eyes lingering on her hair. "Shows you even more ours than before, ach?"

Even more theirs. It seemed a rather ludicrous statement, suddenly, considering how Louisa had just gone to bed with ten other orcs—but as always, Killik's too-quick eyes caught that, and he shifted himself up in the bed, settled his body long on top of hers. "You wear our blades and our chain," he murmured. "You live in our *kofi*, and sleep in our bed, and carry our vows, and raise our son. And even as you leak all this"—his hard cock was already jabbing, sinking deep into it, as Louisa arched and gasped—"you yet reek of Wolf and me, far stronger than the rest. This only shouts of our power over them, and"—his head bent down, his teeth nipping at her throat—"our power over *you*. For you are *ours* now, woman, both of ours, for all the rest of your days."

Louisa nodded and clung to him, wrapped her arms and

legs around him, just needing his certainty, his strength. She was theirs, they were hers, and now Ulfarr was shifting up behind Killik, and finding his place, too. All three of them here, healed, together, Skai.

And as the pleasure flashed and surged, danced them high into the light and the flame, there was only more rightness, more certainty. All of Louisa's deepest longings, all her amends, her forgiveness, here beneath her hands, safe in her bed, quiet in her heart. Finally, finally, at peace.

"Yes, Killik," she whispered. "For always."

BONUS EPILOGUE

It was the night of Sune's coming-of-age revel, and Louisa felt like the proudest mother in the realm.

"We are honoured to raise you amongst us this night, my son," Ulfarr announced, his deep voice carrying through the camp's firelit clearing. "You have shown yourself a strong, wise, and watchful Skai. An orc who well guards his lands, cares for his kin, and upholds our clan's ways."

Before Ulfarr, Sune was standing tall and still, looking as calm and collected as ever, though Louisa didn't miss the faint flush in his cheeks, the brief bob in his throat. Or the flicker in his dark eyes as three orcs stepped forward from the crowd of watching Skai—Halthorr, Igull, and Killik.

"And thus, my son, we wish to grant you the three great gifts of the Skai," Ulfarr continued. "The gifts of shelter, and strength, and safety."

He nodded toward Halthorr, who beamed fondly at Sune as he slung a large, shining new fur over his shoulders, and tied it tight. And next was Igull, stepping around behind Sune, and holding aloft an ancient-looking wooden cup for all to see—and then he carefully poured it out over Sune's head. And it wasn't water or oil, Louisa knew, but fresh wolf-blood, streaking bright red down Sune's face. Marking him, claiming him with a scent that would never fade.

And once Sune had tasted the blood, licked it red across his lips, Killik stepped forward, and raised up something bright and silver—a gleaming, brand-new sword. A Skai scimitar of Sune's own, made by Argarr in the Skai forge just for him, meant to keep him safe for all his days.

Sune's eyes stilled on the sight of the sword, his mouth slightly quivering, but his hands were steady as he took the blade from Killik, and carefully slid it through his belt. And then, with a sudden lurch, he and Killik were clasped tightly together, Killik slapping one hand at Sune's back, and rustling the other in his bloody hair.

"You have been such a gift from Skai-kesh, son," Louisa could just hear Killik saying, his voice a rasp. "I am so honoured. So proud."

Sune buried his face deeper into Killik's shoulder, while behind them, Ulfarr smiled with almost painful fondness, and raised both his hands to the sky. "Our brother Sune, of Clan Skai," he called out. "We welcome him as a full Skai amongst us, and grant him our favour, our honour, and our blessing!"

He followed it with a loud, bellowing howl, his head thrown back—and in answer, the rest of the gathered Skai howled, too, together with a chorus of claps and cheers. The clamour ringing wild around them, and Louisa added her own howl to it, her hands clapping, her feet stomping, as water escaped her eyes, and streaked down her cheeks. Her son. Her *son*.

She'd already been at the front of the crowd, and she was the first to rush forward to congratulate Sune, hurling her arms tightly around him. "Look at you, son," she said, yanking back to smile at his beloved, blood-streaked face. "All grown up. Such a good, faithful Skai. Granting us so many gifts."

Gods, she was weeping again, and Sune's eyes looked bright, too, even as his head twitched back and forth. *Ach, it is naught, Mammi,* he signed. *You are too good to me.*

But Louisa signed sharply back toward him, still smiling and weeping. *Such a good son. So proud of you.*

It wasn't even the slightest exaggeration, because over the past five years, Sune had truly shown himself a clever, thoughtful, hardworking Skai. He had finally gained full ownership of Rikard's lands two years before, and he'd taken his responsibilities as a landowner very seriously—learning all he could about herds and fields, hiring and managing staff, and renting out rooms in the huge manor to Skai who needed them. And rather than spending all his considerable new income on himself, he'd invested the bulk of it back into the property, the camp, and the school. Using it to support his Skai kin, just as a good Skai should.

Of course, he'd also heavily relied on help from Louisa and Killik and Ulfarr, and there had been multiple challenges and learning experiences along the way—including several serious threats from humans. But Sune had faced it all with his typical quiet composure, and whenever he needed time to think, he would take out his beautiful new mare Mjoll, and make his usual circuit over his property. And Louisa would never tire of seeing him canter past, his lean body relaxed and easy on Mjoll's back, his hair whipping out of his topknot.

Louisa still often rode out with him, too, whether making the rounds, doing work on the property, or travelling to the mountain. A trip they all made on a regular basis these days, sometimes for trade or meetings, but often just visiting with their friends and kin, too. Sune always became particularly restless whenever he'd gone too long without seeing Timo and Cecily—and even now, he was smiling as he glanced beyond Louisa, toward where they were both impatiently hovering, and beaming back toward him.

"Congratulations, Sune," Cecily gulped, lurching forward into his chest, while Timo slipped a hand behind Sune's head, and pressed a brief, biting kiss to his bloody mouth. And Sune's eyes fluttered as he kissed Timo back, and then sank into his strong, caressing arms.

Louisa fondly smiled toward the three of them—she adored Timo and Cecily, and they were both so good for Sune, too. Timo supporting him with his steady Grisk loyalty, and Cecily with her laughter, hard work, and excellent Ash-Kai taste. She always kept Sune beautifully dressed, and whenever he inevitably destroyed his clothes—usually in some typical Skai activity—Cecily would only roll her eyes, and pull out some new ones from her ever-growing stash.

"I've learned to accept it," she'd told Louisa, a year or two before. "Especially since he's given me a budget. This way, I can always keep him in style, too."

She'd said it with a satisfied smirk toward Sune, who had loudly scoffed from beneath the new silk tunic Cecily had been urging him to try on. But when Cecily had then gone and begun smoothing it down over his slim chest, Sune had only stood and watched her, with a dark, hungry glint in his eyes.

It was rather the same look he was wearing now, as his mouth settled deeper into Timo's bulky shoulder. And when Louisa glanced up, her gaze caught on Killik, who was standing behind them, and giving a longsuffering roll of his eyes toward her.

"We shall now never be rid of them," he muttered to Louisa, once he'd come over and tickled his claws at her back. "My strong Skai son, mated to a simpering Grisk, and a bossy, scheming Ash-Kai."

Luckily, no one else seemed to hear this—more Skai had come over to greet Sune, offering enthusiastic praise and best wishes—and Louisa elbowed Killik in the side, and rolled her eyes back toward him. "They aren't mated yet," she said lightly. "And you never know, maybe he'll still find a lovely Ka-esh, too."

Killik's snort was harsh and incredulous, his claws slipping up to scrape sharp at Louisa's neck. "Hush, you curst harpy," he hissed back. "Do not give him ideas!"

But they both knew Killik's ire toward the Ka-esh was mostly—mostly—just teasing these days, and Louisa couldn't see Sune looking for another partner, either. He'd been devoted to Timo and Cecily for years now, and he'd willingly put up with Cecily's overprotective Ash-Kai family, who'd made no secret of their strong aversion to Cecily gaining a pair of orc mates anytime soon, let alone bearing their sons.

"*You* hush, you overbearing tyrant," Louisa murmured back, even as she leaned into that glorious scrape of Killik's claws on her neck. "And if you behave, maybe you'll even get a Skai grandson out of this."

Killik huffed, but his eyes on Sune looked almost speculative, or even hopeful. And while he would probably never admit it, Louisa knew Killik did want that grandson. He was still so good with children, and still such a devoted father to Sune, too—and Louisa had loved seeing their relationship shift and deepen as Sune had grown older. The two of them becoming not just father and son, but true fierce friends, with similar outlooks and opinions, and many interests in common. And Louisa knew that part of Killik's complaining about Timo and Cecily was just his fear that he would lose Sune—not just from the clan, but from the camp, too, or even from his life.

Killik's eyes were still studying Sune, but now Louisa could catch a telltale flicker of darkness in them, hinting at sadness, or even loss. A look Louisa had caught on him too often these past few months, and she swallowed hard as she slipped her arm around Killik's waist, and squeezed him tight. Wanting to reassure him that Sune would never leave the camp, would never leave their lives for good…

But at the same time, Sune hadn't often spoken of his future plans, either. Plans that most certainly included Cecily and Timo, who both made their homes at the mountain with their own clans and families. And while the mountain wasn't a great distance away, it would still feel so different to have Sune gone, forever—and as Louisa blinked back up at Killik, she could almost taste that loss on him, that dark empty ache. And he was such a good father, such a fierce and generous mate, he deserved all the best things, all he ever wanted. And Louisa wished—she wanted—

"Ach, there is the proud father!" came a familiar voice, as a firm hand clapped to Killik's shoulder. "And the proud mother, too!"

It was a cheerful older Skai named Sigtryggr, with his own mates and adult son in tow, and Louisa surreptitiously wiped her eyes as she smiled back, and managed a thank-you. And beside her, Killik was grinning too, his eyes warm and easy on Sigtryggr's face, his claws again tickling at Louisa's back.

It was enough that she could find the breath again, and soon she was talking and laughing too, and greeting their many enthusiastic guests. The camp was a popular destination for the Skai these days, and it seemed like the entire clan had come out to celebrate—including not only all Ulfarr's former packmates and their families, but also Simon and Maria and their sons, Rurik and his mates, and even a few of Louisa's rutmates, too. Vaeni, and Saxar, and Asbrandr, and Tarr.

It was always lovely seeing them, and Louisa willingly embraced them all, and even met Tarr's familiar, gentle kiss. They'd all continued to share her bed on occasion, offering her their bodies and their strong Skai seed, while Killik and Ulfarr watched and commanded and approved—and last time, Tarr had brought a handsome young friend to join them, too. But it was always subject to Ulfarr's approval, and Louisa always took care to honour his wishes, and defer to his judgement. Understanding, now, on a fundamental level, how much power the sharing gave Ulfarr—and how part of that, for him, was also the ability to say no. The right to keep his woman only for himself and his beloved pup, whenever he wished.

And on a night like tonight, Louisa knew, with Sune and his friends nearby, and so many guests, Ulfarr wasn't likely to be in a sharing mood. And when he strode over toward them, his eyes rather flinty on Tarr's face, Louisa willingly sank into her wolf's embrace, and stroked her greedy hands over his solid familiar chest. Feeling him relax beneath her, his own hand curving possessively over her arse, as he gave a warm, rather wolflike smile toward Tarr, and asked after his camp kin.

Tarr wryly smiled back, and soon they were embroiled in a deep discussion about camp governance, and the latest news and Skai politics from the mountain. A subject that Ulfarr knew very well these days, as his role of the Wolf of the Skai had continued to expand. Not only serving as a resource for Skai history and culture, and an advocate for Skai education—but also helping to codify Skai governance and practices. Serving to support and protect Skai orcs and women of all ages and backgrounds, offering clear guidelines and laws, and standardizing processes for correction and reconciliation.

Much of it was work Ulfarr had done together with Simon, and over the past few years, they had even developed a deep, genuine friendship. Built not only on their shared love for the Skai clan, but on their similar natures, too—they were both big, stubborn, decisive leaders and fighters, with good intentions, kind hearts, and an unflinching devotion to their kin. To the point where Ulfarr now often went to Simon for guidance and support, and not a moon went by without Simon and Maria bringing their family to visit the camp, too.

And there were Simon and Maria now, striding over to join them—and Ulfarr grinned at Simon, clapping him on the shoulder, while Louisa dragged Maria in for a tight embrace. "It's such a lovely party, sister, as always," Maria told her, once they'd pulled apart again. "You must be so proud."

Maria had shot a smile over toward where Sune was still surrounded by well-wishers, and Louisa rapidly nodded, as that strange, bittersweet longing again caught in her throat. "Gods, so proud," she said, her voice hitching. "It's almost enough to make me wish I'd—"

She bit it off just in time, but couldn't help the brief, traitorous glance down at her waist. And damn it, what was she saying, what was she even thinking—and she rapidly shook her head, attempted a smile toward Maria's face. "Forget I said that," she added, too quickly. "It's nothing. I've just been feeling a little—off, lately, is all."

Maria blinked back toward Louisa, her hand clutching at her dagger. "How so?" she asked, far sharper than before. "What's wrong? You're not ill, are you?"

Louisa grimaced and waved it away, shaking her head. "No, nothing like that!" she replied. "I'm fine, really."

But Maria had that telltale stubborn glint in her eyes, and after a swift sign toward Simon and Ulfarr—*we'll be back*— she grasped Louisa's arm, and tugged her a short distance off into the trees. Where she whirled around to face Louisa, frowning, and made that too-familiar spinning motion with her dagger. Saying, *Keep going. Or else.*

Louisa gave a shaky laugh, and ran a hand against her hair, feeling the reassuring steel of her own daggers. "Well, I suppose I—I've just had some trouble sleeping lately," she said, with a sigh. "And overheating, and the like. Killik even dragged me off to Efterar, and Rurik and Hakon, too"—she waved toward the clearing, toward Rurik's burly Ash-Kai healer mate—"but they all said it's perfectly normal, it's my body deciding it's time for me to—"

And good gods, why couldn't she even say it, and she shook her head, took a deep breath. "It's just—time for me to move past having children," she added, hoarse. "Forever. Which I couldn't even do anyway! And which I don't *want* to do! So I have no idea why I even care! It's just..."

She shot another wet-eyed glance toward the clearing, toward where Killik now had his arm hooked around Sune's shoulder, both of them grinning at how Halthorr's two small sons were climbing on his shoulders at once. And Louisa could almost scent Maria's comprehension, and then her sudden, heartfelt sympathy.

"Have you talked to Gwyn about it, too?" Maria asked, nodding toward where the mountain's midwife was chatting by the fire with a group of Skai and her mate Joarr. "I'll go fetch her now."

Louisa opened her mouth to protest, but like the typical Skai Maria was, she'd already spun and strode off toward Gwyn, her dagger still clutched tight. And after a few quick signs from Maria, Gwyn nodded, and followed her back to Louisa in the trees.

Louisa had come to consider Gwyn a good friend these past years—she was calm and capable, and excellent at her chosen profession. And despite Louisa's erratically pounding heartbeat, it was almost a relief to pour out the whole foolish tale to Gwyn, and see the easy, open understanding in her warm eyes.

"It's perfectly normal to feel that way, sister," Gwyn said firmly. "Especially when your body is changing in ways that don't feel familiar to you. But it will settle and feel more comfortable in time, I promise. And I always tell women it's a gift from the goddess toward us. A blessing."

Louisa wasn't following, now, but perhaps Gwyn had

caught that, because she gave Louisa an encouraging smile, and reached to squeeze her hand. "It's a gift of freedom," she continued. "Women can finally be free from the burden of monthly cycles, and the risks and difficulties of childbirth. We can focus on our own lives, our own goals, and our own communities. We can live our lives on our own terms."

Right. It felt familiar, it felt like Louisa's own words, her own priorities, her own damned decisions—and curse it, how had she ever forgotten that? But Gwyn gave her another understanding smile, another firm squeeze at her hand. "It's also completely normal to have fluctuating thoughts and emotions around it, too," she said. "Just be patient with your-self, and give yourself plenty of time to rest—and extra time and lubrication in the bedroom if you need it, too. I also always recommend keeping busy and active, and staying connected to the people you care about. Because if you choose it, your freedom can be a great gift to them, too."

A gift to them, too. Louisa took a deep breath, and her gaze flicked back to Killik and Sune in the clearing. To where Killik was now frowning straight through the trees toward her, and his hand snapped up, signing over Sune's head. *What is amiss?* it demanded. *Come here, now.*

Louisa huffed a wry laugh, and then put her hand to her heart, and fervently thanked Gwyn—and Maria, too. And then she obeyed Killik's summons, though she jabbed him in the side when she got there, and earned a stinging slap on the arse in return.

"Behave, harpy," Killik snapped, even as he bent his head, and inhaled deep at her neck. "And what is amiss? Why do you scent thus?"

Louisa briefly considering dissembling, but lying to Killik was always a fool's errand, and she exhaled, and shot an uneasy glance at the party all around them. "Could we talk later?" she asked. "It's nothing urgent, I promise."

Killik's eyes sharply narrowed on hers, his mouth

pursing, but he twitched a brief nod. Trusting her, as he always did, and Louisa leaned into his side, and inhaled his rich, familiar scent. He was such a good mate, such a fierce and faithful friend, and she wasn't going to weep again, not now—

She was rescued by the sudden appearance of a beaming, pregnant Rosa, with a sheaf of papers in her hand. "You can't keep avoiding me, Killik," Rosa said, cheerfully thrusting her papers toward him. "You promised to proofread the *Skai Signing Guide*, and it's almost ready to print! Do you want me to switch the title back to the *Comprehensive Compendium of Skai Signs and Signals*?"

Killik loudly groaned, but his eyes were tolerant, and Rosa's eyes were twinkling, too. The two of them had continued their friendly antagonism over Rosa's projects— and particularly Rosa's titles—but Louisa now knew how much Killik appreciated being involved, too. He still felt very strongly about teaching and sharing Skai culture, and as the Wolf of the Skai's mate—with his keen eye for details—he was perhaps the best Skai in the clan to help guide any Skai-focused written publications. And Louisa well knew that if Rosa hadn't asked him to proofread her signing manual, he would have stomped around complaining about ignorant Ka-esh for weeks on end.

So Louisa smiled fondly between them, and after a brief kiss to Killik's cheek, she left them to it, and turned her focus back to the party. Chatting first with Jule, and then Sigtryggr's lovely mate Lydia, and then Drafli and his mates and sons, too. And finally she made her way over to Sune again, who had somehow ended up in the midst of a group of noisy talking Ash-Kai—many of them Cecily's family members—and who was now wearing a distinctly hunted look on his blood-streaked face.

"Could I borrow you for a moment, son?" Louisa loudly asked him, once she'd eased her way through the group. "I just need to fetch something, and could use an escort in the dark."

It was a blatant lie, of course—Louisa's night vision was actually much improved these days—but Sune shot her a grateful look, and willingly extracted himself from the Ash-Kai, and accompanied her toward the forest. And once they were striding through the trees together, she could hear his exhale, slow and heavy with relief.

"Thank you, *mammi*," he murmured, his voice low and musical. "You ken I love Cecy, but those Ash-Kai—*ach*."

Louisa chuckled, and shot a rueful, appreciative glance toward him. He still didn't often speak out loud, preferring mostly to sign, especially around larger groups of people— but it always felt like a privilege when he did choose to speak aloud. A gift, saved for those he cared for most, and Louisa was truly honoured to be counted among them.

"They never stop speaking," Sune continued, with a not-quite-amused sigh. "Kesst would not stop giving me hints about the costly jewels I ought to give Cecy, upon her own coming-of-age party—amidst also saying she shall take no mates until she is thirty summers old!"

Louisa laughed again, because gods, Sune sounded like Killik sometimes, and she knew Killik was also particularly irked by Kesst, Cecily's beloved and highly fashionable Ash-Kai uncle. But Louisa also knew that this had been an ongoing theme with Cecily's family, and she searched Sune's profile in the dark, and gave a gentle knock of her shoulder against his. "But Cecily will make up her own mind, right?" she asked. "I know how much she cares about you, son."

Sune inhaled and exhaled, biting at his lip. "Ach," he replied, quiet. "But of late, she has also kept asking me when I shall... move to the mountain. For good."

Oh. Louisa's steps faltered, her breath held in her throat, as her heart thundered in her chest. Because this was the question, the one they'd all expected and dreaded—and of course they needed to support Sune in whatever he chose. And Louisa shouldn't be envisioning how wrong it would be with Sune gone, his *kofi* quiet and empty, his lands left for his kin to look after in his absence. And suddenly she was on the verge of weeping again, and she swallowed hard, drew in a deep breath from the earth.

"And have you decided, then?" she asked, as steadily as she could. "When you'll be going?"

But at that, Sune halted in place, and shot a careful, searching look toward her. "No," he said, his voice low, but decisive. "I have thought much upon this these past moons, but—no. I shall not leave here."

What? Louisa startled, and blinked toward him, uncomprehending. "But," she began, "I know how much you care about Cecily, and how you want…"

Her voice trailed off, into genuine confusion, but Sune shook his head, and gave a rather Killik-like jab of his claw toward her. "This is my home, *mammi*," he replied flatly. "These are my lands, and my responsibilities, and you and Skai-kesh have granted them to me to care for. My kin are here, my *kofi* is here, and there is a good school here for my sons, when I have them. And I wish my sons to grow up here, free beneath the open sky, as I have these past five summers. For this land shall one day be theirs, and they shall need to well care for it, also."

Oh. The water was again prickling behind Louisa's eyes, her lip damnably quivering. Of course Sune would be thinking about his kin, and his land. He was such a good and faithful son, and did he really want to stay, and have sons, more than one son, was he really *planning* for this—

"But what about," Louisa said, her voice scraping against her tight throat. "But what about Cecily?"

But Sune sighed, and twitched a shrug. "She is yet here, I ken," he said, with a rueful half-smile over his shoulder, back toward the camp. "And Timo has long ago sworn he shall not leave me. So mayhap she shall come to terms upon this, or mayhap Timo and I shall need to seek our sons elsewhere."

His mouth betrayed a pained little twist, but his eyes still looked utterly calm, certain on Louisa's face. And blinking back toward him, Louisa was again so starkly reminded of Killik, and his fierce commitment to those he cared for. To how hard he'd worked to save Ulfarr, and find him a woman. A son.

"I'm sure you'll work it out, son," Louisa told him, her voice wavering—and before she'd even caught it, she lurched toward him, and squeezed him tight. "And you know Cecily would be an absolute fool to leave you. She wouldn't *dare*."

Sune huffed a shaky laugh into Louisa's shoulder, and squeezed her back. "Ach, I hope thus, *mammi*," he murmured, hoarse. "She should at least regret not gaining these fool jewels I am now bound to buy her, you ken."

Louisa laughed as she drew back again, and shot a weepy smile up toward his face. He was such a good Skai, so damned generous, and she was so, so proud of him. So blessed. Her son.

She startled at the sound of movement in the nearby trees, but then gave another watery smile, because she'd already caught a tinge of the scent, too. Of Killik, now striding out toward them, his eyes glinting on Sune's face.

Sune rolled his eyes back toward Killik, but didn't protest the blatant eavesdropping, as he otherwise might have done. And instead, he even reached an arm for Killik, and yanked him close. Neither of them speaking, but perhaps they didn't need to, Killik's shaky fist thumping like that at Sune's back again and again.

"Ought to go tell your heart-father, son," Killik finally told Sune, his voice thick, as he drew back again. "He shall be most glad, I ken."

Sune twitched a nod, and with a brief farewell sign to Louisa, he spun and strode away, his back very straight. And

Louisa's eyes kept leaking as she watched him go, her heartbeat skipping in her chest. He would stay. He would stay, and care for the camp, and the land. He would grant it to his sons. His *sons*.

She twitched at the feel of Killik's hand on her back, but then hurled herself against him, her face buried in his chest. Feeling his strong steady safety, but also his own relief, shuddering out sweet in his breath. Because yes, he'd wanted Sune to stay too, they'd all wanted it so much—and it still felt wrong to be this relieved about it, especially when it might still cost Sune his own happiness.

"Do you think Cecily will leave him, over this?" Louisa murmured, into Killik's chest—and she was deeply gratified by his loud snort, the spasm of his claws against her back.

"Ach, no," he snapped. "You ought to scent her when she looks at him. I ken this was all some fool Ash-Kai scheme, seeking to call him to heel, ach? She shall learn not to test our son, I ken."

The vicious satisfaction rang through his voice, and Louisa drew back to grin fondly toward him. Though her face was still wet, her eyes still damnably prickling, and Killik's head cocked, his hand flicking at her wet cheek. "Just as you ought to know not to test me, woman," he said, cooler now. "Now, what is it you have been moping about all eve, and hiding from me? Tell me."

The command rang through his voice, and Louisa swallowed and exhaled, searched for truth. She trusted Killik, she could face this, she could...

"I've still just—been struggling a bit with these— changes, lately," she said, with a flailing wave of her shaky hand toward her torso. "And Gwyn and Maria were very lovely, Gwyn says it's normal to feel conflicted about it, but I can't help but wonder—"

She broke off there, breathing hard, and she couldn't meet Killik's eyes now, could only blink at his hard chest. "I guess I've wondered," she whispered, "if—if *you* might not regret it. Not having another son. *Ever.*"

There was an instant's silence, ringing out between them, and Louisa hauled for air, for courage. "And if you did," she choked, "You, or Wolf—you know I would... I would support you, Killik. Stand beside you. Even if you wanted to—to find another woman, or bring her into our—our bed. Skai-kesh knows you've shared me countless times, and I should be able to—to—"

Gods curse her, she couldn't even finish, the sobs lurking too close and dangerous in her throat. She shouldn't care, she shouldn't, but even the thought of Killik granting his seed and his son to another woman was so breathtakingly painful, stabbing deep in her gut. She might be able to bear sharing him in bed, maybe, but the son, it was—it was—

The silence kept ringing between them, louder and louder, as a strange sharpness twined through Killik's scent—and when Louisa finally glanced up, found his eyes, he looked... incredulous. Appalled. His mouth dropped open, his hand looking almost shaky as it snatched one of his daggers out of his hair, and—

And jammed it hard against Louisa's throat.

"What rotten dreck have you been drinking, woman?" he demanded. "In what realm do you ken I would trade *you*, for a *son*?!"

His voice was sharp, suddenly furious, his teeth bared toward her. "How long have you thought this? And why have you thought this? Did anyone *tell* you to think this?!"

His eyes glittered as they darted back in the direction of the camp, and Louisa made a strange choking sound, and flapped her hand toward him. "No one told me!" she countered. "And I just—I've just seen how you've been a little—down, lately, about Sune! And with me now never being able to have sons, I—"

She sounded too shrill, too desperate, her hand now

waving again at her belly—and Killik stared at her for a long instant, before loudly scoffing in her face. "You could *never* have sons, woman!" he hissed at her, as he drew his dagger back from her throat, so he could point it at her eyes. "And this pleased me! This has always pleased me! Just as *you* have always pleased me, just as you are! Ach"—he grimaced, shook his head—"you are just as if I handed a fool Ka-esh *list* to Skai-kesh, written with all I wish for in a woman—and he has then dropped you here alive before me! You ken I care if you can now *again* not have sons? This is a *gift*, woman! My one and only relief from the endless orcling *scourge!*"

Louisa blinked at him, her mouth slightly wavering, while Killik gave a wild, furious flare of his dagger. "I should be a fool to throw this away, for some other fool woman," he snarled. "And do not play-act with me that you should share me or Wolf with her, when we both know you should only be dreaming of gutting her in her sleep! I should never be able to turn my back on you *again!*"

Louisa blinked again, but her hand had somehow found the safety of her own knife-hilt at her side, her fingers circling reflexively against it—and Killik's too-aware eyes had followed the movement, as another loud scoff rang from his throat. "And ach, this is just as it ought to be, for you are Skai," he snapped. "And Skai do not well bear others stealing their mates. You ken I should sit back and twiddle my daggers whilst some other orc moves into your bed, and your life?! This is not at all the same as allowing them to grant you pleasure with us, when we choose! For part of this is saying no, and lording this over them as they thirst after my mate! Not *keeping* them, or having *sons* with them!"

Right. Right, and Louisa knew that, she did—but it was still a strange, shaky relief to hear Killik say it, to see that blazing fury in his eyes. "And as for Sune," he continued, "I was only *down* about this because I feared he should leave his home, for a silly Ash-Kai human who wishes to trap him at her whim in that mountain, like a pretty Skai prize in her hoard! And you ken we could not push or command him upon this, for he needed to see this for himself—but you ken he would have been happy thus? Away from the sun, his horses, his duties, his *home*? He should have come to hate her for it, and by then he should have had a son to bind him there, also! You ken I wish for this cruel fate for my good Skai son?"

Louisa stared at him, her mouth opening and closing, because—of course. Of course Killik had known that, all that time, and he—he—

"Then—why didn't you tell me?" she demanded at him. "Why didn't you just fucking *say* that was what you were worried about?!"

She couldn't quite hide the hurt in her voice, and Killik betrayed a faint grimace, his gaze flicking beyond her. "I knew you feared Sune leaving, also," he said, quieter. "And knew you also have felt... *down*, thus. Did not wish to add to this."

Oh. Louisa swallowed, attempted a glower toward him—but that was true concern in his eyes flickering back toward her. "And *you* did not tell *me*," he snapped, "how you have begun to take leave of your senses! Thinking I wish for another son! I am now *forty summers old*, woman!"

Louisa scoffed back toward him, and gave an unsteady wave back toward the camp. "Well, you've made it very clear you want that Skai grandson!" she shot back. "You can pretend you don't all you want, Killik, but I *know*!"

Killik made a face, but his jab of his dagger toward her felt half-hearted. "Ach, so there is *one* orcling in the realm I might wish for," he said, his voice flat. "But *only* because it is Sune's! And I ken how much you and Wolf wish for this, too! And just as Sune said, if he has sons here, then they shall stay here, and carry on our good work. They shall keep granting this good home to our Skai kin, and offering them safety, and *peace.*"

Right. Louisa exhaled and nodded, because yes, yes, she wanted that too. She wanted to protect the Skai living here now, but also the Skai to come. From the lords, the threats, the inevitable challenges that they would continue to face.

But she couldn't seem to meet Killik's eyes, suddenly, blinking at his chest. "Well, you still could have told me!" she finally said, jabbing a finger toward him. "Instead of making me think—"

But yes, please, Killik's dagger was here again, nudging cold and demanding at her throat. "I made you think naught!" he hissed. "I have told you a hundred times I have no wish for a son! It is *you* who is too stubborn a Skai to hear me, and learn my lesson!"

Louisa hauled in breath, and raised her eyes to meet his—and suddenly she was lunging at Killik, and he was lunging back, clutching her tight. And in a sharp whirl of movement, he thrust her down onto her back on the earth, holding her there while she kicked furiously up toward him. But he was too heavy, too fast, too damned strong, and with another powerful lurch, he leapt up to straddle her chest, pinning both her arms to the earth over her head.

"Wild harpy," he hissed, baring his teeth. "You shall listen to me, and you shall *learn!*"

With that, he yanked down his trousers, releasing his familiar grey cock before Louisa's blinking eyes. And of course he was already hard, bobbing and leaking, swelling larger with every breath—but still giving her room to say no, to refuse. But she wouldn't, she needed this, needed him so much, yes, *please*—

And Killik knew it. He saw it, scented it, the way he always did—and with another furious flash of movement, he shoved up onto all fours over her, and plunged that hard cock straight down into her mouth.

Louisa kicked and flailed and shouted at him, but her mouth was full, and he was already bearing down further, prodding toward her throat. "Better," he breathed. "Suck it, harpy."

Louisa growled back, but Killik only gouged deeper. "Do you not hear me?" he demanded, with a light slap of his hand to her hot cheek. "Suck me, and learn!"

Louisa glared back up at him, pulled in air through her nose—and then bit down on that invading flesh, as hard as she could. Instantly tasting the rich salt of his blood beneath her teeth, oh gods—but Killik barely betrayed a hiss, and even drew out a little to look at it. And then, as Louisa gasped for breath, he dropped his hand, and dragged his own sharp claw the rest of the way up his shaft. Drawing a far thicker line of blooming red, before plunging back into her throat, flooding her mouth with the taste of it, *oh*.

"Now no more," he hissed. "Obey me!"

And yes, yes, between that rich fresh salt of that cut, and the sweet succulent seed pooling from his tip, Louisa could only shiver, groan, and obey. Drinking down deep, desperate draughts of him, and then sucking as hard as she could, drawing out more. Because it tasted so damned good, so sweet and salty and luscious and perfect, all Killik's essence pouring into her at once. Feeding her, filling her, flooding her with his strength.

Above her, Killik gave a low grunt of satisfaction, and shifted his body a little closer, his hips now pumping up and down. Fucking himself down into Louisa's mouth, into her frantically sucking throat, as he pinned both her hands tighter to the earth. "Better," he breathed. "Now hear me, woman. I have no wish for another son. I wish for *you*!"

Louisa attempted a nod, sucking harder, and Killik plunged faster, deeper, enough to make her gag. "I wish for you," he repeated. "Ach?"

Louisa nodded again, dragging down that hot salty-sweetness, taking all he would give her, please—but that was another slap of his hand to her cheek, a deeper gouge into her throat. "Wish to taste this in your scent," he snapped. "Wish you to believe me!"

But Louisa couldn't think, couldn't even fight it, could only try to swallow, to show him, to prove this. But maybe she couldn't, maybe this wasn't enough either, please, please—

When in a sudden jolt, Killik stopped. Halted, his breaths heaving, his head snapping sideways. Toward—oh. Ulfarr. Standing amidst the trees, and blinking toward where Louisa was sprawled on her back on the muddy ground, with Killik on his hands and knees over her face, his cock jammed into her mouth.

"Ach, my pups," Ulfarr said, as he swiftly strode toward them, and knelt down to inhale first at Killik's neck, and then at Louisa's messy hair, already falling from its daggers. "What is this? Why do you scent thus?"

There was an instant's silence, broken only by Louisa's quiet little swallows, from where Killik was still half-buried in her mouth—and with a firm pull of Ulfarr's hand, Killik drew back, away. Exposing his red-streaked cock to Ulfarr's watching eyes, with that red line still cut down the length of it—but Ulfarr only blinked at it for an instant, and then bent down again, this time to inhale deeply at Louisa's throat.

"Ach, you may yet plough her, pup," he ordered Killik now. "But *gently*. And as you do this, you shall speak truth to me, and to each other. Both of you."

Killik made a face, and perhaps Louisa did, too—but there was no fighting their wolf, most of all when he had that hard, glittering look in his eyes, that tightness in his jaw. Saying, very clearly, that if they didn't obey him, he would gladly chain them together until they did.

It was something he'd only done a few times, but even the thought of it sent a furious shudder through Louisa's body, her hands reflexively skittering against Killik's shoulders. Because yes, he was obeying too, his lean body shifting down to lie over hers, his knees now shoving hers apart. So his hard, slick cock could nudge up between her legs, and find its place—

And then he sank inside, slow and steady and smooth. Gently, just as Ulfarr had commanded, and Louisa again shuddered all over, her arms tightening around him. Needing him, oh gods, needing this so much—and needing the safety of their wolf, now lying beside them, stroking his hand at Killik's back.

"Did you not hear me, my pups?" he demanded, glancing between them with raised brows. "I said, speak."

Louisa and Killik exchanged a brief, wincing look, and finally Louisa took a breath, forced out the words. "I—I've just been feeling a bit out of sorts lately, about my body—changing," she gulped. "And I noticed Killik was feeling... off, about Sune. Sad. So I started to think—to wonder—if maybe he might have—changed his mind, about sons, now that the option is gone forever. So"—she dragged in a bracing breath—"I told him if he ever wanted to, or—or *you* did, sweetheart, you could still find another woman, and have another son, and I would support it, support *you*, no matter what, and—"

And oh gods, she was about to start weeping again, her voice cracking—but wait. Ulfarr was growling, low and harsh, not toward her, but... toward Killik?

"And you wished to teach our woman a *lesson* over this?" Ulfarr thundered at Killik, as his big hand snapped up, and clutched at the back of Killik's neck. "Our sweet mate, who has been ill, and grieving over Sune, also? After she offered to grant you a *son*, at great cost to herself?"

Killik's mouth opened and closed, his eyes wide and almost panicked as they darted between Louisa and Ulfarr. "She wished for this from me, also!" he said, high-pitched. "And I sought to tell her the truth, and she would not believe me! She kept scenting *thus*! So I wished to show her, instead! To prove this!"

He flailed his hand toward her, and Ulfarr followed it, searching Louisa's eyes, and again leaning in to inhale against her neck. "Ach, now I follow, pup," he said, low. "Then try this again. But yet be gentle this time, as you plough her. With kisses, and soft touches."

Killik grimaced at Ulfarr, but Ulfarr bared his teeth back—and finally Killik sighed, and met Louisa's eyes. And then settled down a little lower over her, as his strength gently rocked between her legs, and one of his hands came up to skitter at her face. Making her look at him, at his strange shimmering eyes, as he bent down, and pressed a brief, trembly kiss to her mouth.

"I wish for you, woman," he choked, thick in his throat. "Not for a son. For *you*."

Louisa's eyes were stinging, and she nodded, kissed him back. Wanting to believe it, so much, because she loved him so much, she so desperately wanted him to be happy, and...

"Again, pup," Ulfarr said firmly. "Speak her name this time."

Killik squeezed his eyes shut, but nodded, and took a shaky breath. "I wish for you, Louisa," he whispered, as he kept rocking into her, stroking at her face. "For my own fierce Skai mate. Could not bear to lose you, over a son."

Louisa swallowed hard, shook her head, even as she clutched tighter against him. Needing him closer, needing him here, everywhere, please...

Ulfarr had signed something to Killik this time, and Killik exhaled, kissed her again. "Could not bear to lose you," he repeated, his voice cracking. "Ach, cannot even bear you feeling as you have, scenting all this unhappiness upon you, this—this *fear*. I thought this was fear of losing Sune, so I did not wish to make this worse, but—"

His breath shuddered out, his body clutching hers closer

beneath him, his lips trembling against hers. "But now to know this was fear of *me*," he croaked. "Fear of me wishing for a son! As if I would ever, *ever* choose this, over you!"

His voice scraped against her skin, his pain and disbelief almost palpable in his scent. And beside them, Ulfarr had shifted closer, one big hand caressing against Killik's neck, the other now cradling Louisa's cheek. "Now you, Louisa," he murmured, soft. "Speak truth to my sweet pup, ach?"

Truth. Louisa quivered, nodded, held Killik's glimmering eyes. Truth, face this, truth...

"I think maybe—maybe the thought of losing Sune," she gulped, "just made me wonder what—else I could lose. I just—I love you so much, you've just been so, so good to me, such a perfect mate, so fierce and loyal and generous and hardworking, and I—I so desperately want you to be happy. I need you to have everything you've ever wanted, Killik, *everything*. Even if I can't give it to you."

The words shuddered through her hands, her voice, her body all around him, and she scarcely heard Ulfarr's soft command for Killik to kiss her. But she felt it, tasted Killik's trembling lips, breathed in the sharp fervent need in his scent. His need to show her, to make her believe it, to teach her this lesson...

"But I do have all I want, Louisa," Killik whispered back. "I have this. I have you, and Wolf, and Sune, and our camp, our kin, our home. There is naught more I need, but for you to know this, also. For you to... trust me. To grant me this gift."

To trust him. A gift. Oh, gods. And suddenly Louisa was fully weeping again, clinging to him with all her strength, dragging him down, burying her face in his shoulder. Because she did trust him, she did, and maybe—maybe this was all her not trusting... herself. Losing sight of her own truth, her own priorities, amidst all these changes.

"I do trust you," she whispered, into his warm, rich-scented neck. "Always, Killik."

She could feel him sagging against her, his breath exhaling, his neck arching into her mouth. Into her mouth kissing his skin, tasting that sweet truth of him, scenting all that rich lush blood pulsing just beneath...

And oh, that was Ulfarr's hand, slipping beneath her head, drawing it closer. Guiding her deeper into Killik's neck, her lips parting, her teeth gently scraping. And Killik's mouth hissed in return, his cock shuddering inside her, the sharp craving firing through his scent...

"Then suck me," he breathed. "Drink me, and learn."

Drink him. Louisa inhaled, ragged and harsh, but then settled her mouth closer, just where it felt best—and then she bit down, hard. Hard enough to feel that skin break, and give her—

Oh. *Oh.* Rich, salty, warm and thick and alive, filling her mouth, swarming into her throat. And all she could do was drink, suddenly, swallow as hard and fast as she could, while Killik gasped and groaned above her, and spasmed even fuller inside her. Wanting this, wanting this from her, trusting her to do it, just as she trusted him...

She couldn't have said when Ulfarr mounted Killik, filling and driving him from behind, but she could feel Killik's body shuddering beneath it, his own thrusts deepening inside her. But he didn't draw his neck away from her mouth, didn't stop pouring his lifeblood into Louisa's greedy gulping throat. And it didn't make sense, it was bizarre and foreign and unthinkable, but it still felt so—so right. Her fierce fearless mate offering all his strength to her, showing her she could trust him. Proving this to her.

And when Killik stiffened and arched, pouring out his strong Skai seed out between Louisa's legs, it all flashed up, whirled into truth, trust, her mate, her home—and then it crashed and blazed, rushing out in charge after charge of wild, shattering bliss. Flooding her with heat and life and power, with freedom, with peace. Peace.

When the world finally flickered into place again, Louisa felt strange and shivery all over, her tongue thick, the air scenting almost drugged with sweetness. And scenting of Killik, somehow, not just in him, here above her, but in... *her*. Within her, perhaps deeper than ever before.

"Ach, that is better," came Ulfarr's low murmur. "Good, my pups. Both of you."

Louisa could scarcely focus on Ulfarr's eyes, on his own slowly smiling mouth above her, now also streaked with red. "Now you must tend your mating-bite, Louisa," he said softly. "Gently, until you can feel it healing."

Her mating-bite? But Ulfarr didn't wait to explain, only bent his own head to the other side of Killik's neck, where— oh. He had bitten him, too. And where he was now kissing it, licking it, tending it with his usual thoroughness and care.

So in the shimmering daze, Louisa bent up again, and obeyed. Kissing and licking at Killik's broken neck, again and again, while his breaths shuddered out slow and harsh. And when the taste of that rich saltiness finally seemed to fade from his skin, she drew back again, licking her lips, sagging heavy to the earth.

And only then did she catch Killik's eyes. Killik's warm, hazy eyes, flickering on hers with such... approval. Such awe. As he bent down again, met her lips, slid his tongue into her mouth. Tasting himself on her, oh, and Louisa willingly opened for it, arched into it, please.

"Ach," he murmured when he drew away, his eyes glittering on hers. "Much better, I ken."

Louisa shivered beneath him, and kissed him again, again. It was much better, it was all much better, the scent and the taste and *him*, inside her, all around her. And their safe powerful wolf crouching above them both, guarding and guiding them, showing them the way.

"Thank you, Wolf," Killik breathed now, flashing one of his genuine, stunning smiles over his shoulder. "Good lesson."

Ulfarr's chuckle was low and fond, and he inhaled deep at Killik's hair. "Ach, I ken you had the right idea, pup," he murmured back. "Most of all with this extra feeding. We shall only need to tend our sweet mate more closely throughout this, I ken, and offer her much good Skai strength."

Louisa shivered again, her eyes warm and grateful on Ulfarr's face, and he smiled back, caressing his hand at her cheek. "And we must also remind her that we are hers, and we have all we need," he said firmly. "The hand of Skai-kesh has been upon us, and granted us so many gifts."

So many gifts. Louisa fervently nodded, blinking between them both, as her thoughts flicked back to Ulfarr's voice as he'd spoken over Sune at the party, to those three great gifts of the Skai. Shelter, strength, and safety.

And Louisa had them all here, now, beneath her hands, in her life, in her home—and now she even had this new gift of freedom, too. This renewed focus on her own life, her own goals, her own priorities. Living out the rest of her days on her own terms.

And perhaps best of all, now her son was staying, too. Forever. And Louisa's smile suddenly spread across her face, the warmth simmering in her belly. Skai. Hers. Home.

"Thank you both," she told Killik and Ulfarr, squeezing them both tight. "So much."

They both squeezed her back, and when they drew away, Ulfarr looked a little weepy, too—but Killik only grinned, and flicked his claw at her cheek. "And now that we have all ruined our fancy clothes for the day," he said lightly, with a glance down at Louisa's muddy dress, "we shall go back to our party, and prance happily about. And thus cause great distress to all those uppity Ash-Kai, ach?"

He sounded so viciously pleased with himself, and Louisa could only laugh, bright and merry, her eyes shimmering warm on her dear mate's face. And on her wolf's face too, on where he was grinning between his pups. Wanting them to play.

So Louisa laughed again, and licked at her bloody lips. "Ach, then," she said. "Let's go cause some pain."

❧

THE END

❧

THANKS FOR READING!

Thank you so much for joining me for this epic adventure among the Skai! It's been such an honour to share this story with you.

For even more Killik and Ulfarr, they show up throughout my Orc Sworn series! You can learn more about Ulfarr's villainous past in *The Duchess and the Orc*, and Killik and Ulfarr start their teaching adventures in *The Governess and the Orc*. And as a special bonus for my generous Patreon supporters, I've recently written an entire bonus backstory novella, all from Ulfarr's point of view! It explores Ulfarr's dark history with the Skai, how Killik forever earned Ulfarr's fealty, and how Ulfarr felt about finally taking Killik and Louisa as his mates. It's available for supporters at all levels on my author Patreon.

Of course, we'll also keep seeing Killik and Ulfarr in the future... along with many Orc Sworn friends. I am especially excited to return to the Ka-esh with Filak's story... stay tuned for more! (And keep reading for a brand-new teaser!)

Plus, on my website you can also find my mailing list, which has all kinds of free bonus content for you—including artwork from this book, and a free Orc Sworn story. I'd love to stay in touch with you!

Thank you again for joining me on this adventure! Your support means so much to me, and I wish all Skai-kesh's greatest blessings upon you. Hugs!

ACKNOWLEDGMENTS

The Widow and the Orcs was an intense, all-consuming book to write, and I am just so grateful to all the generous readers and friends who supported me along the way!

First, I need to thank my incredible Patreon supporters—your kindness and enthusiasm has been such a gift, and it's been an absolute privilege to partner with you on this journey. Skai-kesh has truly blessed me!

I'm also deeply thankful to all the early readers and consultants who shared their perspectives on this book: Amy F., Amy G., Anne-Marie, Ari, Cookie, Erin, Judi Szabo, Karen Meeus, Lauren Mauchley, Lou M., Mary Lynne Nielsen, MK, Serena, Stacy, Twilla Love, Þórey H., and authors Elizabeth Stephens, Jo Henny Wolf, Jordyn Alexander, Kahaula, and V.C. Lancaster. I'm especially grateful to Goddess Ruby Dixon for all her insights and support, and to author Lillian Lark for being a constant source of wisdom and friendship amidst the Skai-induced chaos! And my deepest gratitude to author Eris Adderly/Octavia Hyde for again serving as this book's editor, and sharing her utterly brilliant brain with me.

As I've written this Skai book, I've been especially inspired by my Skai sisters who have been so generous with their fierceness and fealty: Amy, our faithful and unflappable Discord Skaibrarian; Erin, artist extraordinaire and fearless leader of the Skai Mafia PR team; and Stacy, who along with Amy and EJ has continued to create the fabulous Tales from the Orc Den podcast. (Which I highly recommend!)

I'm also eternally grateful to my Bautul Enforcer

Marykate, for the constant help and guidance; to Morning Dove, for being such a generous and hilarious Grisk sister; to Coco for all the amazing character designs and illustrations; to Vio and Clay for the lovely Discord greetings; to my fantastic audio publishers at Podium for making my audiobooks possible; to Katie at Romantically Inclined Reviews for all the laughs and support; and to all the creators and commissioners who have shared their stunning Orc Sworn artwork with us. (Special thanks to Anna K., Elaine Ho, Elizabeth, Serene Yoshiko, and Skemz!)

And finally, as always, my deepest gratitude to my own fierce Skai mate, who offers me such unflinching care, and grants me such peace. You ken I love you, my Wolf.

CODA

Filak followed the scent with his eyes closed, and his claws trailing against the jagged stone wall. Seeking, scenting, closer, closer...

He had been searching for so many moons now. So many empty, glaring moons, away from his kin, away from his home. Praying, fasting, calling, etching his pleas onto his skin.

He would find it. He would.

And mayhap—his nostrils flared—mayhap he would find it there. In that odd cavern up ahead. That strange... emptiness. Something carved, something hidden, something he had never scented here before.

Filak's feet strode faster, his claws drawing harder against the stone, as awe thudded into his heartbeat. He had not scented this here before, for there had not been someone in it before. Someone marking it, tainting it, painting it with their sweet scent...

Filak halted before the cavern's narrow opening, and stared into the room before him. Yes. Yes. This was something. And the scent... the scent was...

Her.

A woman.

Here.

She whirled around to stare at him, her human eyes wide in her shocked little face. And Filak stared back toward her, as fierce, gleeful triumph shot through his marks, his prick, his heart.

He had finally found it. And he had finally found *her*.

He spread his hand wider against the stone beside him, feeling the veins and weight of it, digging his claws deep. Seeking, seeking, speaking a silent plea...

And with his firm shove at the stone, the tunnel fell behind him, crashing into rubble and dust. Trapping him here, in this cavern, for as long as he wished. For as long as he needed.

The woman's scream rang through the air, sweet and lovely, and Filak smiled, with mayhap the first true joy he had known in many, many moons.

She had guided him here. She had granted him this, after so long. And now, tonight...

Tonight, she would be his.

～

Filak's book is next!
To learn more, visit finleyfenn.com/filak.

THE DUCHESS AND THE ORC

He's a massive, mocking, murderous monster. And there's only one thing he wants from her...

In a world of recently warring orcs and men, Maria is desperate for escape. She's trapped in an opulent prison, tainted by rumours of madness, and wed to a cold, vindictive duke who hungers only for war.

But with no family, no funds, and no hope, there's nowhere left to run—except for the one place even a duke can't reach. The place where women almost always meet their doom...

Orc Mountain.

It's a grim, deadly fortress, filled with fierce, bloodthirsty beasts—**and the first orc Maria meets is the most terrifying of them all.** A huge, hostile, hideous brute, hardened by hatred and war, who instantly accuses her of foul trickery, and threatens her with death—

But this orc also wants something. Something that kindles deep in his gleaming black eyes, in his rough, rugged scent, in the velvet heat of his voice. Something that just might grant Maria his safety... but only if she grants him *everything* in return.

Her defeat.

Her dignity.

Her devotion...

And surely, a duchess wouldn't dare make such a shameful deal with the devil—or would she? Especially when surrender might spark yet more war... **or bring the mighty Orc Mountain to its knees?**

ALSO BY FINLEY FENN

THE LADY AND THE ORC

He's the most feared monster in the realm. And she's what he needs to win his war...

In a world of warring orcs and men, Lady Norr is condemned to a childless marriage, a cruel lord husband, and a life of genteel poverty—until the day her home is ransacked by a horde. And leading the charge is their hulking, deadly orc captain: the infamous Grimarr.

And Grimarr has a wicked plan for Lady Norr, and for ending this war once and for all. She's going to become his captive—and the perfect snare for Lord Norr.

There's no possible escape, and soon Lady Norr is dragged off toward Orc Mountain in the powerful arms of her greatest enemy. A ruthless, commanding warlord, with a velvet voice and mouthwatering scent, who awakens every forbidden hunger she never knew she had...

But Grimarr refuses to accept half measures—in war, or in pleasure. And before he'll conquer Lady Norr's deepest, darkest desires, she needs to surrender *everything*.

Her allegiance.

Her wedding-ring.

Her future...

And with her husband's forces giving chase, Lady Norr can't afford to play such a dangerous game—or can she? **Even if this deadly orc's plans might be the only way to save them all?**

ALSO BY FINLEY FENN

THE LIBRARIAN AND THE ORC

He's a fierce, ferocious, death-dealing beast. And he's reading a book in her library...

In a world of recently warring orcs and men, Rosa Rolfe leads a quiet, scholarly life as an impoverished librarian—until the day she finds an *orc*. In her library. Reading a *book*.

He's rude, aggressive, and deeply terrifying, with his huge muscled form, sharp black claws, and cold, dismissive commands. But he doesn't *seem* truly dangerous... at least, until night falls. **And he makes Rosa a shocking, scandalous offer...**

Her books, for her surrender.

Her ecstasy.

Her enlightenment...

Rosa's no fool, and she knows she can't possibly risk her precious library for this brazen, belligerent orc. Even if ·he *is* surprisingly well-read. Even if he smells like sweet, heated honey. Even if he makes Rosa's heart race with fear, and ignites all her deepest, darkest cravings at once...

But surrender demands a dangerous, devastating price. A bond that can't easily be broken. And a breakneck journey to the fearsome, forbidding Orc Mountain, where a curious, clever librarian might be just what's needed to stop another war...

ABOUT THE AUTHOR

Finley Fenn is "the queen of dark orc romance" (Virgo Reader), and her ongoing Orc Sworn series has been praised as "sexy, romantic, angsty, and captivating ... utter brilliance" (Romantically Inclined Reviews).

When she's not obsessing over her stories, Finley loves reading, drooling over delicious orc artwork, and spending time with her incredible readers on Patreon, Discord, and Facebook. She lives in Canada with her beloved family, including her very own grumpy, gorgeous orc husband.

For free bonus stories and epilogues, special offers, and exclusive Orc Sworn artwork, sign up at www.finleyfenn.com.